THE LOEB CLASSICAL LIBRARY

FOUNDED BY JAMES LOEB

EDITED BY

G. P. GOOLD

HOMER

I

LCL 104

HOMER

THE ODYSSEY

BOOKS 1–12

WITH AN ENGLISH TRANSLATION BY

A. T. MURRAY

REVISED BY

GEORGE E. DIMOCK

HARVARD UNIVERSITY PRESS
CAMBRIDGE, MASSACHUSETTS
LONDON, ENGLAND
1995

First published 1919
Second edition 1995

Library of Congress Cataloging-in-Publication Data

Homer.
[Odyssey. English & Greek]
The Odyssey / Homer : with an English translation by A.T. Murray :
revised by George E. Dimock.
p.   cm. — (Loeb classical library : L104–L105)
Includes bibliographical references (p.) and index.
ISBN 0–674–99561–9 (v. 1) — ISBN 0–674–99562–7 (v. 2)
1. Epic poetry, Greek—Translations into English.   2. Odysseus
(Greek mythology)—Poetry.   I. Murray, A. T. (Augustus Taber),
1866–1940.   II. Dimock, George.   III. Series.
PA4025.A5M74   1995   93–37392
883′.01—dc20   CIP

Typeset by Chiron, Inc, Cambridge, Massachusetts.
Printed in Great Britain by St Edmundsbury Press Ltd,
Bury St Edmunds, Suffolk, on acid-free paper.
Bound by Hunter & Foulis Ltd, Edinburgh, Scotland.

PREFACE

Augustus Taber Murray (1866–1940), Professor of
Greek at Stanford University for forty years from 1892,
produced his Loeb edition of the *Odyssey* in 1919; the
Iliad followed a few years later. No more faithful transla-
tion of Homer was ever made, and its elegance matched
its fidelity. Homer's formulaic epithets, phrases, and
sentences were consistently rendered, and his artificial
amalgam of dialects and archaic vocabulary were, as was
perfectly acceptable in those days, reflected in archaic
English.

Translation today, however, has to satisfy different
expectations. Yet it seemed unlikely that a new translation
would surpass or even match the fidelity and readability of
Murray's work, these being the qualities most valued in the
Loeb series. Accordingly it has been decided to revise
Murray's translation in such a way as to preserve its excel-
lences while bringing all that sounds unnatural into line
with today's canons of English. The Loeb Classical Library
is deeply grateful to the distinguished Homerist Professor
Emeritus George E. Dimock of Smith College for under-
taking this delicate task and for performing it so well.

G.P.G.

In preparing this second edition of the Loeb *Odyssey*, I
have altered Murray's Greek text in only six places: 7.74

vii

PREFACE

(οἷσί for ᾖσί), 9.483 (line retained), 10.456 (line retained), 16.161 (πως for πω), 20.383 (ἄλφοι for ἄλφοιν), and 23.48 (line retained).

Footnotes refer to book and line of the Greek regardless of whether the note concerns primarily the Greek or the English text. I have distinguished Murray's footnotes from my own by appending the initials M. and D.

I have rendered the Greek adjective φίλος as "staunch" rather than "dear" wherever loyalty to the family or other group seemed more prominent than personal affection. In a few other cases, where it modifies parts of the body or "native land," etc., I have rendered it as "own."

G.E.D.

THE ODYSSEY

INTRODUCTION

There was a rich tradition of epic poetry in early Greece. We know of epics dealing with legends of the royal house of Thebes, with the voyage of the Argo, with the deeds of Heracles and of Theseus, with the events surrounding the Greek expedition against Troy, and with many other myths and legends of the Heroic Age. Apart from brief quotations and later paraphrases or allusions all but two of them have perished. The two that have survived, the *Iliad* and the *Odyssey*, were from earliest times attributed to the same poet, Homer, and appear to have been valued above all others for their quality and authority. Both dealt with the Trojan War, the *Iliad* centering on an incident in the final year of the Greek siege of Troy, the *Odyssey* recounting the long return home of one of the commanders after the victory.

Even in antiquity a few thought, as many do today, that the *Odyssey* was not composed by the same poet as the *Iliad*, but no one doubted that each was the work of a single poet. An era of scepticism, however, began at the end of the eighteenth century. Following the suggestions of F. A. Wolf and others, scholars argued that both epics had been woven or patched together from shorter poems composed at different times by various poets. This view, which dominated most critical discussion for more than a cen-

tury, seemed to explain the inconsistencies and repetitions found in the epics and to confront the fact that writing was not known in the Dark Ages. There was speculation about the very existence of Homer and what contribution a bard of that name might have made to the epics in their present form. These problems came to be known as "the Homeric question." In antiquity the term *chorizontes*, "separators," was given to those who ascribed the two epics each to a different poet; now it could be applied to those who believed that for each epic there was multiple authorship and not a single unifying origin.

A revolutionary change of view followed upon the investigations of Milman Parry, who in the 1920s and 1930s showed that the method of composition of the epics resembled the practice of illiterate bards. They should therefore not be judged by the criteria of written literature. So it is possible again, and now with more sophisticated theoretical and comparative evidence, to visualize a single bard as the author of a whole epic. Whether the same poet produced the *Iliad* and the *Odyssey* remains a disputed question. Separate authorship for the *Odyssey* has by no means been proved, however, and until it is we would do well to follow the practice of the centuries and think of a single poet named Homer as the author of both epics.

Study of the narrative poetry of illiterate cultures has made it clear that the *Iliad* and the *Odyssey*, traditionally 15,693 and 12,110 lines long respectively, are examples of "oral poetry." Professional singers like Phemius and Demodocus in the *Odyssey* learn by listening to their predecessors' performances a version of their own native language which obeys not only that language's grammatical rules, but also the metrical or other formal rules of the

poetic medium. In this poetic language the singer can think, and while doing so produce no unmetrical utterance. Hence the oft-repeated metrical phrases or "formulas," each designed to dovetail with the next, which students of oral poetry have so intensively investigated.

At *Iliad* 2.484–93 Homer names the source both of the singer's poetic language and of its content:

> Tell me now, you Muses, who have your homes on
>   Olympus—
> for you are goddesses, and are present, and know
>   everything,
> while we hear only the rumor of things and know
>   nothing—
> who were the leaders of the Greeks, and who the
>   commanders;
> the multitude I shall not speak of, nor name them
>   over,
> not even if I had ten tongues and ten mouths
>   besides,
> a voice that did not break, and the heart within me
>   were bronze;
> only the muses of Olympus, daughters of Zeus who
>   wears the aegis,
> could mention by name every man who came under
>   Ilium's walls.
> I then shall tell who commanded fleets and the
>   numbers of their ships.

From these words we can conclude that whatever occurs to the singer's mind and sensibility in the muses' metrical language as he begins his song is for him the guaranteed truth of divine eyewitnesses. This "Catalogue of Ships,"

3

which from our point of view we can explain only as a feat of memorization of traditional material, is ostensibly for the poet and his audience the voice of Truth itself.

Since he thought of himself as the mouthpiece of Truth, it would not be surprising if the poet sought and found in his consultation of the muse or muses larger unities than could be communicated in an evening's performance. Hence the many thousands of lines of the *Iliad* and of the *Odyssey*; hence also the eventual division of the poems into 24 "books," each book exhibiting a certain unity and each identified by a letter of the Greek alphabet.

Mention of the Greek alphabet brings us at once to Homer's first manuscripts. His orally composed words, in order to survive, had immediately to be subjected to the writing process, whether by autograph or dictation. The possibility that Homer's poetry was orally transmitted from bard to bard until it was finally written down seems excluded by the fact that oral poets never repeat themselves at any length word for word, whatever they may claim to the contrary.[1] If by "Homer" we mean the author of the *Iliad* and the *Odyssey*, Homer himself produced the first manuscripts of the texts we read today.

In his *Homer, Hesiod, and the Hymns* (Cambridge, 1982), Richard Janko suggests that the *Iliad* was composed about 750 B.C. and the *Odyssey* about 735. The sixth-century Homeric Hymn to Delian Apollo and the scholiast on Pindar *Nemeans* 2.1 on the Homeridae provide attractive evidence that Homer founded a clan or guild on the

[1] Adam Parry, ed., *The Making of Homeric Verse: The Collected Papers of Milman Parry*, Clarendon Press, Oxford, 1971, p. 336.

island of Chios which possessed written texts and contin-
ued to foster their honored ancestor's reputation after his
death. To the degree that we accept this we can think of
Homer as the eighth-century B.C. Ionian Greek who first
brought literacy to Greece and, in a sense, to the world.

The oldest manuscripts of the *Odyssey* are of the tenth
century, and they provide a remarkably stable and con-
sistent text. The earliest surviving papyri (3rd century B.C.)
and quotations of Homer in classical authors show, how-
ever, that at an earlier stage there were many differences
from the text we now possess. The standardization was
undoubtedly due to the labors of scholars at the library of
Alexandria in the third and second centuries B.C., especially
of the successive heads, Zenodotus, Aristophanes of
Byzantium, and Aristarchus, who compared different ver-
sions and commented on the text. Many of their observa-
tions are preserved in the scholia, the annotations which
appear in the margins of some manuscripts, including their
rejection of lines and passages for linguistic, factual, or
ethical reasons. There are reports also of a much earlier
attempt to collect and standardize the Homeric epics
for recitation at Athens at the time of Pisistratus in the
sixth century B.C. Study and interpretation of the poems
continued throughout antiquity and is often reflected in
the scholia.

BIBLIOGRAPHY

This bibliography includes basic texts, commentaries, and works of reference together with a brief selection of studies and interpretations in English which represent a variety of approaches to the Homeric poems. Works that deal solely or principally with the *Iliad* have been excluded.

Critical texts

T. W. Allen (ed.): *Homeri Opera* (OCT), vols III^2 (*Od.* 1–12) and IV^2 (*Od.* 13–24), Oxford 1917 and 1919.

P. von der Mühll (ed.): *Homeri Odyssea*^{3} (Teubner), Stuttgart 1984.

Wilhelm Dindorf, *Scholia Graeca in Homeri Odysseam*, Oxford 1885.

Editions and commentaries

W. W. Merry and J. Riddell: *Homer's Odyssey: Books I–XII*, Oxford 1886.

D. B. Monro: *Homer's Odyssey: Books XIII–XXIV*, Oxford 1901 (with a copious and valuable appendix).

W. B. Stanford: *The Odyssey of Homer*^{2}, 2 volumes (1–12

and 13–24), London 1959 and 1958, repr. with addenda 1971.

Alfred Heubeck, Stephanie West, and J. B. Hainsworth: *A Commentary on Homer's Odyssey*, vol. I (Introduction and Books 1–8), Oxford 1988.

Alfred Heubeck and Arie Hoekstra: *A Commentary on Homer's Odyssey*, vol. II (Introduction and Books 9–16), Oxford 1989.

Joseph Russo, Manual Fernández-Galiano, and Alfred Heubeck: *A Commentary on Homer's Odyssey*, vol. III (Introduction and Books 17–24), Oxford 1992.

(The preceding three volumes constitute an English version of the six-volume Italian edition sponsored by the Fondazione Lorenzo Valla 1981–1986, which included a critical text and an Italian translation by G. Aurelio Privitera.)

R. B. Rutherford: *Homer: Odyssey Books XIX and XX*, Cambridge 1992.

Recent translations

(1) Verse

Robert Fitzgerald, *Homer: The Odyssey*, New York 1961 (with commentary: Ralph Hexter, *A Guide to the Odyssey*, New York 1993).

Richmond Lattimore, *The Odyssey of Homer*, New York 1965.

Albert Cook, *Homer: The Odyssey*, New York 1967, repr. 1993 (with a selection of essays).

Allen Mandelbaum, *The Odyssey of Homer*, Berkeley and Los Angeles 1990.

BIBLIOGRAPHY

(2) Prose

T. E. Lawrence, *The Odyssey of Homer* [by T. E. Shaw], Oxford and New York 1932, repr. 1991.

W. H. D. Rouse, *The Story of Odysseus*, London and New York 1937, repr. (as *The Odyssey*) 1949.

E. V. Rieu, *Homer: The Odyssey*, Harmondsworth and New York 1945, revised 1991.

Walter Shewring, *Homer: The Odyssey*, Oxford 1980.

R. D. Dawe, *The Odyssey: Translation and Analysis*, Lewes, Sussex 1993 (with provocative commentary).

Reference

Albin Lesky, "Homeros," *RE* Supplementband XI 687–846 (also published separately), Stuttgart 1968.

P. von der Mühll, "Odyssee," *RE* Supplementband VII 696–768, Stuttgart 1940.

Rudolf Pfeiffer, *History of Classical Scholarship from the Beginnings to the End of the Hellenistic Age*, Oxford 1968.

Odette Touchefeu-Meynier, *Thèmes odysséens dans l'art antique*, Paris 1968.

A. J. B. Wace and F. H. Stubbings, edd., *A Companion to Homer*, London 1962 (including essays by J. A. Davison on the transmission of the poems and by L. R. Palmer on the language).

Bibliographical articles in *Classical World*: F. M. Combellack, 49 (1955–56) 17–55; J. P. Holoka, 66 (1972–3) 257–293, 73 (1979–80), 83 (1989–90) 393–461, and 84 (1990–91) 89–156; M. E. Clark, 79 (1985–86) 379–394.

BIBLIOGRAPHY

Linguistic

Pierre Chantraine, *Grammaire homérique*, 2 volumes, Paris 1948, 1953.

R. J. Cunliffe, *A Lexicon of the Homeric Dialect*, London 1924.

Henry Dunbar, *A Complete Concordance to the Odyssey of Homer*, completely revised and enlarged by Benedetto Marzullo, Hildesheim 1971.

D. B. Monro, *A Grammar of the Homeric Dialect*[2], Oxford 1891, repr. 1992.

G. P. Shipp, *Studies in the Language of Homer*[2], Cambridge 1972.

Bruno Snell (ed.), *Lexikon des frühgriechischen Epos*, Göttingen 1955–.

General works on Homer

Howard Clarke, *Homer's Readers: A Historical Introduction to the Iliad and the Odyssey*, Newark, Del. 1981.

J. B. Hainsworth, *Homer* (*Greece and Rome* New Surveys in the Classics No. 3), Oxford 1969.

G. S. Kirk, *The Songs of Homer*, Cambridge 1962.

Albert B. Lord, *The Singer of Tales*, Cambridge, Mass. 1960.

H. O. Lorimer, *Homer and the Monuments*, London 1950.

J. V. Luce, *Homer and the Heroic Age*, London 1975.

Gregory Nagy, *The Best of the Achaeans: Concepts of the Hero in Archaic Greek Poetry*, Baltimore 1979.

Gregory Nagy, *Pindar's Homer: The Lyric Possession of an Epic Past*, Baltimore 1990.

BIBLIOGRAPHY

Adam Parry, ed., *The Making of Homeric Verse: The Collected Papers of Milman Parry*, Oxford 1971.

William G. Thalmann, *Conventions of Form and Thought in Early Greek Epic Poetry*, Baltimore 1984.

T. B. L. Webster, *From Mycenae to Homer*, London 1958.

F. A. Wolf, *Prolegomena to Homer [1795]*, translated with introduction and notes by A. Grafton, G. W. Most, and J. E. G. Zetzel, Princeton 1985.

Studies on the Odyssey

Norman Austin, *Archery at the Dark of the Moon*, Berkeley and Los Angeles 1975.

G. E. Dimock, *The Unity of the Odyssey*, Amherst, Mass. 1989.

B. Fenik, *Studies in the Odyssey, Hermes* Einzelschrift 30, Wiesbaden 1974.

M. I. Finley, *The World of Odysseus*[2], London and New York 1978.

Denys L. Page, *The Homeric Odyssey*, Oxford 1955.

Denys L. Page, *Folktales in Homer's Odyssey*, Cambridge, Mass. 1973.

W. B. Stanford, *The Ulysses Theme: A Study in the Adaptability of a Traditional Hero*[2], Oxford 1963.

M. H. A. L. H. van der Valk, *Textual Criticism of the Odyssey*, Leiden 1949.

W. J. Woodhouse, *The Composition of Homer's Odyssey*, Oxford 1930, repr. 1969.

BOOKS 1–12

A

Ἄνδρα μοι ἔννεπε, Μοῦσα, πολύτροπον, ὃς μάλα πολλὰ
πλάγχθη, ἐπεὶ Τροίης ἱερὸν πτολίεθρον ἔπερσεν·
πολλῶν δ' ἀνθρώπων ἴδεν ἄστεα καὶ νόον[1] ἔγνω,
πολλὰ δ' ὅ γ' ἐν πόντῳ πάθεν ἄλγεα ὃν κατὰ θυμόν,
5 ἀρνύμενος ἥν τε ψυχὴν καὶ νόστον ἑταίρων.
ἀλλ' οὐδ' ὣς ἑτάρους ἐρρύσατο, ἱέμενός περ·
αὐτῶν γὰρ σφετέρῃσιν ἀτασθαλίῃσιν ὄλοντο,
νήπιοι, οἳ κατὰ βοῦς Ὑπερίονος Ἠελίοιο
ἤσθιον· αὐτὰρ ὁ τοῖσιν ἀφείλετο νόστιμον ἦμαρ.
10 τῶν ἁμόθεν γε, θεά, θύγατερ Διός, εἰπὲ καὶ ἡμῖν.
ἔνθ' ἄλλοι μὲν πάντες, ὅσοι φύγον αἰπὺν ὄλεθρον,
οἴκοι ἔσαν, πόλεμόν τε πεφευγότες ἠδὲ θάλασσαν·
τὸν δ' οἶον νόστου κεχρημένον ἠδὲ γυναικὸς
νύμφη πότνι' ἔρυκε Καλυψὼ δῖα θεάων
15 ἐν σπέσσι γλαφυροῖσι, λιλαιομένη πόσιν εἶναι.
ἀλλ' ὅτε δὴ ἔτος ἦλθε περιπλομένων ἐνιαυτῶν,
τῷ οἱ ἐπεκλώσαντο θεοὶ οἶκόνδε νέεσθαι
εἰς Ἰθάκην, οὐδ' ἔνθα πεφυγμένος ἦεν ἀέθλων
καὶ μετὰ οἷσι φίλοισι. θεοὶ δ' ἐλέαιρον ἅπαντες
20 νόσφι Ποσειδάωνος· ὁ δ' ἀσπερχὲς μενέαινεν
ἀντιθέῳ Ὀδυσῆϊ πάρος ἣν γαῖαν ἱκέσθαι.

[1] νόον: νόμον Zenodotus

12

BOOK 1

Tell me, Muse, of the man of many devices, driven far astray after he had sacked the sacred citadel of Troy. Many were the men whose cities he saw and whose minds he learned, and many the woes he suffered in his heart upon the sea, seeking to win his own life and the return of his comrades. Yet even so he did not save his comrades, for all his desire, for through their own blind folly they perished—fools, who devoured the cattle of Helios Hyperion; whereupon he took from them the day of their returning. Of these things, goddess, daughter of Zeus, beginning where you will, tell us in our turn.

Now all the rest, as many as had escaped sheer destruction, were at home, safe from both war and sea; but that man alone, filled with longing for his return and and for his wife, did the queenly nymph Calypso, that beautiful goddess, keep prisoner in her hollow caves, yearning that he should be her husband. But when, as the seasons revolved, the year came in which the gods had ordained that he should return home to Ithaca, not even then was he free from toils and among his own people. And all the gods pitied him except Poseidon; he continued to rage unceasingly against godlike Odysseus until at length he reached his own land.

ἀλλ' ὁ μὲν Αἰθίοπας μετεκίαθε τηλόθ' ἐόντας,
Αἰθίοπας τοὶ διχθὰ δεδαίαται, ἔσχατοι ἀνδρῶν,
οἱ μὲν δυσομένου Ὑπερίονος οἱ δ' ἀνιόντος,
25 ἀντιόων ταύρων τε καὶ ἀρνειῶν ἑκατόμβης.
ἔνθ' ὅ γ' ἐτέρπετο δαιτὶ παρήμενος· οἱ δὲ δὴ ἄλλοι
Ζηνὸς ἐνὶ μεγάροισιν Ὀλυμπίου ἀθρόοι ἦσαν.
τοῖσι δὲ μύθων ἦρχε πατὴρ ἀνδρῶν τε θεῶν τε·
μνήσατο γὰρ κατὰ θυμὸν ἀμύμονος Αἰγίσθοιο,
30 τόν ῥ' Ἀγαμεμνονίδης τηλεκλυτὸς ἔκταν' Ὀρέστης·
τοῦ ὅ γ' ἐπιμνησθεὶς ἔπε' ἀθανάτοισι μετηύδα·
  "ὢ πόποι, οἷον δή νυ θεοὺς βροτοὶ αἰτιόωνται·
ἐξ ἡμέων γάρ φασι κάκ' ἔμμεναι, οἱ δὲ καὶ αὐτοὶ
σφῇσιν ἀτασθαλίῃσιν ὑπὲρ μόρον ἄλγε' ἔχουσιν,
35 ὡς καὶ νῦν Αἴγισθος ὑπὲρ μόρον Ἀτρεΐδαο
γῆμ' ἄλοχον μνηστήν, τὸν δ' ἔκτανε νοστήσαντα,
εἰδὼς αἰπὺν ὄλεθρον, ἐπεὶ πρό οἱ εἴπομεν ἡμεῖς,
Ἑρμείαν πέμψαντες, ἐΰσκοπον ἀργεϊφόντην,
μήτ' αὐτὸν κτείνειν μήτε μνάασθαι ἄκοιτιν·
40 ἐκ γὰρ Ὀρέσταο τίσις ἔσσεται Ἀτρεΐδαο,
ὁππότ' ἂν ἡβήσῃ τε καὶ ἧς ἱμείρεται[1] αἴης.
ὣς ἔφαθ' Ἑρμείας, ἀλλ' οὐ φρένας Αἰγίσθοιο
πεῖθ' ἀγαθὰ φρονέων· νῦν δ' ἀθρόα πάντ' ἀπέτισεν."

[1] ἱμείρεται: ἐπιβήσεται

But now Poseidon had gone among the far-off
Ethiopians—the Ethiopians who dwell divided in two, the
farthermost of men, some where Hyperion sets and some
where he rises—there to receive a hecatomb of bulls and
rams, and there he was taking his joy, sitting at the feast;
but the other gods were gathered together in the halls of
Olympian Zeus. Among them the father of gods and men
was the first to speak, for in his heart he thought of
flawless[a] Aegisthus, whom far-famed Orestes, Agamem-
non's son, had slain. Thinking of him he spoke among the
immortals, and said:

"It's astonishing how ready mortals are to blame the
gods. It is from us, they say, that evils come, but they even
by themselves, through their own blind folly, have sorrows
beyond that which is ordained. Just as now Aegisthus,
beyond that which was ordained, took to himself the wed-
ded wife of the son of Atreus, and slew him on his return,
though well he knew of sheer destruction, seeing that we
told him before, sending Hermes, the keen-sighted
Argeïphontes,[b] that he should neither slay the man nor
woo his wife; for from Orestes shall come vengeance for
the son of Atreus when once he has come to manhood and
longs for his own land. So Hermes spoke, but for all his
good intent he did not prevail upon the heart of Aegisthus;
and now he has paid the full price for it all."

[a] Used to the formulaic style as we are not, Homer's audience
was more able than we to separate the generic description from the
particular event. "The loud-barking dogs fawned and did not bark"
(16.4f). D.

[b] Epithet of Hermes of uncertain meaning. The poet probably
interpreted it as "slayer of Argus" (Io's watchdog). D.

τὸν δ' ἠμείβετ' ἔπειτα θεά, γλαυκῶπις Ἀθήνη·
45 "ὦ πάτερ ἡμέτερε Κρονίδη, ὕπατε κρειόντων,
καὶ λίην κεῖνός γε ἐοικότι κεῖται ὀλέθρῳ·
ὡς ἀπόλοιτο καὶ ἄλλος, ὅτις τοιαῦτά γε ῥέζοι·
ἀλλά μοι ἀμφ' Ὀδυσῆι δαΐφρονι δαίεται ἦτορ,
δυσμόρῳ, ὃς δὴ δηθὰ φίλων ἄπο πήματα πάσχει
50 νήσῳ ἐν ἀμφιρύτῃ, ὅθι τ' ὀμφαλός ἐστι θαλάσσης.
νῆσος δενδρήεσσα, θεὰ δ' ἐν δώματα ναίει,
Ἄτλαντος θυγάτηρ ὀλοόφρονος, ὅς τε θαλάσσης
πάσης βένθεα οἶδεν, ἔχει δέ τε κίονας αὐτὸς
μακράς, αἳ γαῖάν τε καὶ οὐρανὸν ἀμφὶς ἔχουσιν.
55 τοῦ θυγάτηρ δύστηνον ὀδυρόμενον κατερύκει,
αἰεὶ δὲ μαλακοῖσι καὶ αἱμυλίοισι λόγοισιν
θέλγει, ὅπως Ἰθάκης ἐπιλήσεται· αὐτὰρ Ὀδυσσεύς,
ἱέμενος καὶ καπνὸν ἀποθρῴσκοντα νοῆσαι
ἧς γαίης, θανέειν ἱμείρεται. οὐδέ νυ σοί περ
60 ἐντρέπεται φίλον ἦτορ, Ὀλύμπιε. οὔ νύ τ' Ὀδυσσεὺς
Ἀργείων παρὰ νηυσὶ χαρίζετο ἱερὰ ῥέζων
Τροίῃ ἐν εὐρείῃ; τί νύ οἱ τόσον ὠδύσαο, Ζεῦ;"
    τὴν δ' ἀπαμειβόμενος προσέφη νεφεληγερέτα Ζεύς·
"τέκνον ἐμόν, ποῖόν σε ἔπος φύγεν ἕρκος ὀδόντων.
65 πῶς ἂν ἔπειτ' Ὀδυσῆος ἐγὼ θείοιο λαθοίμην,
ὃς περὶ μὲν νόον ἐστὶ βροτῶν, περὶ δ' ἱρὰ θεοῖσιν
ἀθανάτοισιν ἔδωκε, τοὶ οὐρανὸν εὐρὺν ἔχουσιν;
ἀλλὰ Ποσειδάων γαιήοχος ἀσκελὲς αἰεὶ
Κύκλωπος κεχόλωται, ὃν ὀφθαλμοῦ ἀλάωσεν,
70 ἀντίθεον Πολύφημον, ὅου κράτος ἐστὶ μέγιστον
πᾶσιν Κυκλώπεσσι· Θόωσα δέ μιν τέκε νύμφη,

16

BOOK 1

Then the goddess, flashing-eyed Athene, answered him: "Father of us all, son of Cronos, high above all lords, clearly that man lies low in a destruction that is his due; so, too, let any other also be destroyed who does such deeds. But my heart is torn for wise Odysseus, ill-fated man, who far from his friends has long been suffering woes in a sea-girt isle, where is the navel of the sea. It is a wooded isle, and on it dwells a goddess, daughter of Atlas of baneful mind, who knows the depths of every sea, and himself holds the tall pillars which keep earth and heaven apart. His daughter it is that keeps back that unfortunate, sorrowing man; and continually with soft and wheedling words she beguiles him that he may forget Ithaca. But Odysseus, in his longing to see were it but the smoke leaping up from his own land, yearns to die. Yet your heart does not regard it, Olympian. Did not Odysseus beside the ships of the Argives win your favor by his sacrifices in the broad land of Troy? Why then did you will him such pain, O Zeus?"[a]

Then Zeus, the cloud-gatherer, answered her and said: "My child, what a word has escaped the barrier of your teeth? How should I, then, forget godlike Odysseus, who is beyond all mortals in wisdom, and beyond all has paid sacrifice to the immortal gods, who hold broad heaven? No, it is Poseidon, the earth-bearer, who is constantly filled with stubborn wrath because of the Cyclops, whose eye Odysseus blinded—namely the godlike Polyphemus, whose strength is greatest among all the Cyclopes; and the

---

[a] In the Greek (1.62) there is a play upon the verb ὀδύσσασθαι "to will pain to" and the name Ὀδυσεύς, the latter suggesting the meaning "man of pain." The pun is repeated at 5.340, 423; 16.145–47; 19.275, 407–9. D.

Φόρκυνος θυγάτηρ ἁλὸς ἀτρυγέτοιο μέδοντος,
ἐν σπέσσι γλαφυροῖσι Ποσειδάωνι μιγεῖσα.
ἐκ τοῦ δὴ Ὀδυσῆα Ποσειδάων ἐνοσίχθων
75 οὔ τι κατακτείνει, πλάζει δ' ἀπὸ πατρίδος αἴης.
ἀλλ' ἄγεθ', ἡμεῖς οἵδε περιφραζώμεθα πάντες
νόστον, ὅπως ἔλθῃσι· Ποσειδάων δὲ μεθήσει
ὃν χόλον· οὐ μὲν γάρ τι δυνήσεται ἀντία πάντων
ἀθανάτων ἀέκητι θεῶν ἐριδαινέμεν οἶος."
80   τὸν δ' ἠμείβετ' ἔπειτα θεά, γλαυκῶπις Ἀθήνη·
"ὦ πάτερ ἡμέτερε Κρονίδη, ὕπατε κρειόντων,
εἰ μὲν δὴ νῦν τοῦτο φίλον μακάρεσσι θεοῖσιν,
νοστῆσαι Ὀδυσῆα πολύφρονα[1] ὅνδε δόμονδε,
Ἑρμείαν μὲν ἔπειτα διάκτορον ἀργεϊφόντην
85 νῆσον ἐς Ὠγυγίην ὀτρύνομεν, ὄφρα τάχιστα
νύμφῃ ἐϋπλοκάμῳ εἴπῃ νημερτέα βουλήν,
νόστον Ὀδυσσῆος ταλασίφρονος, ὥς κε νέηται·
αὐτὰρ ἐγὼν Ἰθάκηνδ' ἐσελεύσομαι, ὄφρα οἱ υἱὸν
μᾶλλον ἐποτρύνω καί οἱ μένος ἐν φρεσὶ θείω,
90 εἰς ἀγορὴν καλέσαντα κάρη κομόωντας Ἀχαιοὺς
πᾶσι μνηστήρεσσιν ἀπειπέμεν, οἵ τέ οἱ αἰεὶ
μῆλ' ἀδινὰ σφάζουσι καὶ εἰλίποδας ἕλικας βοῦς.
πέμψω δ' ἐς Σπάρτην[2] τε καὶ ἐς Πύλον ἠμαθόεντα
νόστον πευσόμενον πατρὸς φίλου, ἤν που ἀκούσῃ,
95 ἠδ' ἵνα μιν κλέος ἐσθλὸν ἐν ἀνθρώποισιν ἔχῃσιν."
        ὣς εἰποῦσ' ὑπὸ ποσσὶν ἐδήσατο καλὰ πέδιλα,
ἀμβρόσια χρύσεια, τά μιν φέρον ἠμὲν ἐφ' ὑγρὴν[3]
ἠδ' ἐπ' ἀπείρονα γαῖαν ἅμα πνοιῇς ἀνέμοιο·

----

[1] πολύφρονα: δαΐφρονα

18

nymph Thoösa bore him, daughter of Phorcys who rules
over the barren sea; for in the hollow caves she lay with
Poseidon. From that time forth Poseidon, the earth-
shaker, does not indeed slay Odysseus, but beats him off
from his native land. But come, let us who are here all give
thought to his return, how he may come home; and
Poseidon will let go his anger, for he will in no way be able,
against all the immortal gods and in their despite, to con-
tend alone."

Then the goddess, flashing-eyed Athene, answered
him: "Father of us all, son of Cronos, high above all lords, if
indeed this is now well-pleasing to the blessed gods, that
the wise Odysseus should return to his own home, let us
send forth Hermes, the guide, Argeïphontes, to the isle
Ogygia, that with all speed he may declare to the fair-
tressed nymph our fixed resolve, namely the return of
steadfast Odysseus, that he may come home. But, as for
me, I will go to Ithaca, that I may the more arouse his son,
and set courage in his heart to call to an assembly the
long-haired Achaeans, and speak his word to all the suitors,
who continue to slay his thronging sheep and his spiral-
horned shambling cattle. And I will guide him to Sparta
and to sandy Pylos, to seek tidings of the return of his
staunch father, if perchance he may hear of it, that good
report among men may be his."

So she spoke, and bound beneath her feet her beautiful
sandals, immortal, golden, which were wont to bear her
both over the waters of the sea and over the boundless land
swift as the blasts of the wind. And she took her stout

---

[2] Σπάρτην: Κρήτην Zenodotus; cf. 285.
[3] Aristarchus rejected lines 97–101.

εἵλετο δ' ἄλκιμον ἔγχος, ἀκαχμένον ὀξέι χαλκῷ,
100 βριθὺ μέγα στιβαρόν, τῷ δάμνησι στίχας ἀνδρῶν
ἡρώων, τοῖσίν τε κοτέσσεται ὀβριμοπάτρη.
βῆ δὲ κατ' Οὐλύμποιο καρήνων ἀίξασα,
στῆ δ' Ἰθάκης ἐνὶ δήμῳ ἐπὶ προθύροις Ὀδυσῆος,
οὐδοῦ ἐπ' αὐλείου· παλάμῃ δ' ἔχε χάλκεον ἔγχος,
105 εἰδομένη ξείνῳ, Ταφίων ἡγήτορι Μέντῃ.
εὗρε δ' ἄρα μνηστῆρας ἀγήνορας. οἱ μὲν ἔπειτα
πεσσοῖσι προπάροιθε θυράων θυμὸν ἔτερπον
ἥμενοι ἐν ῥινοῖσι βοῶν, οὓς ἔκτανον αὐτοί·
κήρυκες δ' αὐτοῖσι καὶ ὀτρηροὶ θεράποντες
110 οἱ μὲν οἶνον ἔμισγον ἐνὶ κρητῆρσι καὶ ὕδωρ,
οἱ δ' αὖτε σπόγγοισι πολυτρήτοισι τραπέζας
νίζον καὶ πρότιθεν, τοὶ δὲ κρέα πολλὰ δατεῦντο.
    τὴν δὲ πολὺ πρῶτος ἴδε Τηλέμαχος θεοειδής,
ἧστο γὰρ ἐν μνηστῆρσι φίλον τετιημένος ἦτορ,
115 ὀσσόμενος πατέρ' ἐσθλὸν ἐνὶ φρεσίν, εἴ ποθεν ἐλθὼν
μνηστήρων τῶν μὲν σκέδασιν κατὰ δώματα θείη,
τιμὴν δ' αὐτὸς ἔχοι καὶ δώμασιν[1] οἷσιν ἀνάσσοι.
τὰ φρονέων, μνηστῆρσι μεθήμενος, εἴσιδ' Ἀθήνην.
βῆ δ' ἰθὺς προθύροιο, νεμεσσήθη δ' ἐνὶ θυμῷ
120 ξεῖνον δηθὰ θύρῃσιν ἐφεστάμεν· ἐγγύθι δὲ στὰς
χεῖρ' ἕλε δεξιτερὴν καὶ ἐδέξατο χάλκεον ἔγχος,
καί μιν φωνήσας ἔπεα πτερόεντα προσηύδα·
    "χαῖρε, ξεῖνε, παρ' ἄμμι φιλήσεαι· αὐτὰρ ἔπειτα
δείπνου πασσάμενος μυθήσεαι ὅττεό σε χρή."

[1] δώμασιν: κτήμασιν

spear, tipped with sharp bronze, heavy and huge and strong, with which she vanquishes the ranks of men, of heroes, with whom she is angry, she, the daughter of the mighty sire. Then she went darting down from the heights of Olympus, and took her stand in the land of Ithaca at the outer gate of Odysseus, on the threshold of the court. In her hand she held the spear of bronze, and she was in the likeness of a stranger, Mentes, the leader of the Taphians. There she found the proud suitors. They were taking their pleasure at checkers in front of the doors, sitting on the hides of oxen which they themselves had slain; and of the heralds[a] and busy squires, some were mixing wine and water for them in bowls, others again were washing the tables with porous sponges and setting them out, while still others were portioning out meats in abundance.

The godlike Telemachus was far the first to see her, for he was sitting among the suitors, troubled at heart, seeing in thought his noble father, should he perchance come from somewhere and make a scattering of the suitors in the palace, and himself win honor and rule over his own house. As he thought of these things, sitting among the suitors, he beheld Athene, and he went straight to the outer door; for in his heart he counted it shame that a stranger should stand long at the gates. So, drawing near, he clasped her right hand, and took from her the spear of bronze; and he spoke, and addressed her with winged words:

"Hail, stranger; in our house you shall find entertainment, and then, when you have tasted food, you shall tell what you have need of."

[a] It has seemed better to render the word κῆρυξ uniformly by "herald," although the meanings range from "herald" in battle scenes to "page" or "henchman" in scenes portraying life in the palace. M.

21

125   ὣς εἰπὼν ἡγεῖθ', ἡ δ' ἕσπετο Παλλὰς Ἀθήνη.
οἱ δ' ὅτε δή ῥ' ἔντοσθεν ἔσαν δόμου ὑψηλοῖο,
ἔγχος μέν ῥ' ἔστησε φέρων πρὸς κίονα μακρὴν
δουροδόκης ἔντοσθεν ἐυξόου, ἔνθα περ ἄλλα
ἔγχε' Ὀδυσσῆος ταλασίφρονος ἵστατο πολλά,

130   αὐτὴν δ' ἐς θρόνον εἷσεν ἄγων, ὑπὸ λῖτα πετάσσας,
καλὸν δαιδάλεον· ὑπὸ δὲ θρῆνυς ποσὶν ἦεν.
πὰρ δ' αὐτὸς κλισμὸν θέτο ποικίλον, ἔκτοθεν ἄλλων
μνηστήρων, μὴ ξεῖνος ἀνιηθεὶς ὀρυμαγδῷ
δείπνῳ ἁδήσειεν, ὑπερφιάλοισι μετελθών,

135   ἠδ' ἵνα μιν περὶ πατρὸς ἀποιχομένοιο ἔροιτο.
χέρνιβα δ' ἀμφίπολος προχόῳ ἐπέχευε φέρουσα
καλῇ χρυσείῃ, ὑπὲρ ἀργυρέοιο λέβητος,
νίψασθαι· παρὰ δὲ ξεστὴν ἐτάνυσσε τράπεζαν.
σῖτον δ' αἰδοίη ταμίη παρέθηκε φέρουσα,

140   εἴδατα πόλλ' ἐπιθεῖσα, χαριζομένη παρεόντων·
δαιτρὸς δὲ κρειῶν πίνακας παρέθηκεν ἀείρας
παντοίων, παρὰ δέ σφι τίθει χρύσεια κύπελλα·
κῆρυξ δ' αὐτοῖσιν θάμ' ἐπῴχετο οἰνοχοεύων.
ἐς δ' ἦλθον μνηστῆρες ἀγήνορες. οἱ μὲν ἔπειτα

145   ἑξείης ἕζοντο κατὰ κλισμούς τε θρόνους τε,
τοῖσι δὲ κήρυκες μὲν ὕδωρ ἐπὶ χεῖρας ἔχευαν,
σῖτον δὲ δμῳαὶ παρενήνεον ἐν κανέοισιν,
κοῦροι δὲ κρητῆρας ἐπεστέψαντο ποτοῖο.
οἱ δ' ἐπ' ὀνείαθ' ἑτοῖμα προκείμενα χεῖρας ἴαλλον.

150   αὐτὰρ ἐπεὶ πόσιος καὶ ἐδητύος ἐξ ἔρον ἕντο
μνηστῆρες, τοῖσιν μὲν ἐνὶ φρεσὶν ἄλλα μεμήλει,
μολπή τ' ὀρχηστύς τε· τὰ γὰρ τ' ἀναθήματα δαιτός·

22

So saying, he led the way, and Pallas Athene followed. And when they were within the lofty house, he carried the spear and set it against a tall pillar in a polished spear-rack, where were set many spears besides, to wit, those of stead-fast Odysseus. Athene herself he led and seated on a chair, spreading on it a linen cloth—a beautiful chair, richly wrought, and below was a footstool for the feet. Beside it he placed for himself an inlaid seat, apart from the others, the suitors, lest the stranger, vexed by their din, should loathe the meal, seeing that he was in the company of arro-gant men; and also that he might ask him about his father that was gone. Then a handmaid brought water for the hands in a beautiful pitcher of gold, and poured it over a silver basin for them to wash, and beside them drew up a polished table. And the grave housekeeper brought and set before them bread, and with it dainties in abundance, giving freely of her store. And a carver lifted up and placed before them platters of all sorts of meats, and set by them golden goblets, while a herald continually walked to and fro pouring them wine.

Then in came the proud suitors, and thereafter sat down in rows on chairs and high seats. Heralds poured water over their hands, and maidservants heaped by them bread in baskets, and youths filled the bowls brimful of drink; and they put out their hands to the good cheer lying ready before them. Now after the suitors had put away the desire for food and drink, their hearts turned to other things, to song and to dance; for these things are the crown

κῆρυξ δ' ἐν χερσὶν κίθαριν περικαλλέα θῆκεν
Φημίῳ, ὅς ῥ' ἤειδε παρὰ μνηστῆρσιν ἀνάγκῃ.
155 ἦ τοι ὁ φορμίζων ἀνεβάλλετο καλὸν ἀείδειν.
αὐτὰρ Τηλέμαχος προσέφη γλαυκῶπιν Ἀθήνην,
ἄγχι σχὼν κεφαλήν, ἵνα μὴ πευθοίαθ' οἱ ἄλλοι·
"ξεῖνε φίλ', ἦ καί μοι νεμεσήσεαι ὅττι κεν εἴπω;
τούτοισιν μὲν ταῦτα μέλει, κίθαρις καὶ ἀοιδή,
160 ῥεῖ', ἐπεὶ ἀλλότριον βίοτον νήποινον ἔδουσιν,
ἀνέρος, οὗ δή που λεύκ' ὀστέα πύθεται ὄμβρῳ
κείμεν' ἐπ' ἠπείρου, ἢ εἰν ἁλὶ κῦμα κυλίνδει.
εἰ κεῖνόν γ' Ἰθάκηνδε ἰδοίατο νοστήσαντα,
πάντες κ' ἀρησαίατ' ἐλαφρότεροι πόδας εἶναι
165 ἢ ἀφνειότεροι χρυσοῖό τε ἐσθῆτός τε.
νῦν δ' ὁ μὲν ὣς ἀπόλωλε κακὸν μόρον, οὐδέ τις ἡμῖν
θαλπωρή,[1] εἴ πέρ τις ἐπιχθονίων ἀνθρώπων
φῆσιν ἐλεύσεσθαι· τοῦ δ' ὤλετο νόστιμον ἦμαρ.
ἀλλ' ἄγε μοι τόδε εἰπὲ καὶ ἀτρεκέως κατάλεξον·
170 τίς πόθεν εἰς ἀνδρῶν; πόθι τοι πόλις ἠδὲ τοκῆες;
ὁπποίης τ' ἐπὶ νηὸς ἀφίκεο· πῶς δέ σε ναῦται
ἤγαγον εἰς Ἰθάκην; τίνες ἔμμεναι εὐχετόωντο;
οὐ μὲν γάρ τί σε πεζὸν ὀίομαι ἐνθάδ' ἱκέσθαι.
καί μοι τοῦτ' ἀγόρευσον ἐτήτυμον, ὄφρ' ἐὺ εἰδῶ,
175 ἠὲ νέον μεθέπεις ἦ καὶ πατρώιός ἐσσι
ξεῖνος, ἐπεὶ πολλοὶ ἴσαν ἀνέρες ἡμέτερον δῶ
ἄλλοι, ἐπεὶ καὶ κεῖνος ἐπίστροφος ἦν ἀνθρώπων."
τὸν δ' αὖτε προσέειπε θεά, γλαυκῶπις Ἀθήνη·
"τοιγὰρ ἐγώ τοι ταῦτα μάλ' ἀτρεκέως ἀγορεύσω.

---

[1] θαλπωρή: ἐλπωρή

of a feast. And a herald put the beautiful lyre in the hands of Phemius, who sang among the suitors under compulsion; and he struck the chords in prelude[a] to his sweet lay.

But Telemachus spoke to flashing-eyed Athene, holding his head close, that the others might not hear: "Dear stranger, will you be angry with me for the word that I shall say? These men are busied with things like these, the lyre and song, without misgiving, seeing that without atonement they devour the livelihood of another, of a man whose white bones, it may be, rot in the rain as they lie upon the mainland, or the waves roll them in the sea. Were they to see him returned to Ithaca, they would all pray to be swifter of foot, rather than richer in gold and in raiment. But now he has thus perished by an evil doom, nor for us is there any comfort, no, not though any one of men upon the earth should say that he will come; gone is the day of his returning. But come, tell me this, and declare it truly. Who are you among men, and from where? Where is your city and where your parents? On what sort of ship did you come, and how did sailors bring you to Ithaca? Who did they declare themselves to be? For I do not suppose you came here on foot. And tell me this also truly, that I may be certain of it, whether this is your first visit here, or whether you are indeed a friend of my father's house. For many were the men who came to our house as guests, since he, too, had traveled much among men."

Then the goddess, flashing-eyed Athene, answered him: "Therefore I will frankly tell you all. I declare that I

---

[a] Or ἀνεβάλλετο may be used of the voice: "so he struck the chords and lifted up his voice in sweet song." M.

180 Μέντης 'Αγχιάλοιο δαΐφρονος εὔχομαι εἶναι
υἱός, ἀτὰρ Ταφίοισι φιληρέτμοισιν ἀνάσσω.
νῦν δ' ὧδε ξὺν νηὶ κατήλυθον ἠδ' ἑτάροισιν
πλέων ἐπὶ οἴνοπα πόντον ἐπ' ἀλλοθρόους ἀνθρώπους,
ἐς Τεμέσην μετὰ χαλκόν, ἄγω δ' αἴθωνα σίδηρον.
185 νηῦς δέ μοι ἥδ' ἕστηκεν ἐπ' ἀγροῦ νόσφι πόληος,
ἐν λιμένι Ῥείθρῳ ὑπὸ Νηΐῳ ὑλήεντι.
ξεῖνοι δ' ἀλλήλων πατρώιοι εὐχόμεθ' εἶναι
ἐξ ἀρχῆς, εἴ πέρ τε γέροντ' εἴρηαι ἐπελθὼν
Λαέρτην ἥρωα, τὸν οὐκέτι φασὶ πόλινδε
190 ἔρχεσθ', ἀλλ' ἀπάνευθεν ἐπ' ἀγροῦ πήματα πάσχειν
γρηὶ σὺν ἀμφιπόλῳ, ἥ οἱ βρῶσίν τε πόσιν τε
παρτιθεῖ, εὖτ' ἄν μιν κάματος κατὰ γυῖα λάβῃσιν
ἑρπύζοντ' ἀνὰ γουνὸν ἀλωῆς οἰνοπέδοιο.
νῦν δ' ἦλθον· δὴ γάρ μιν ἔφαντ' ἐπιδήμιον εἶναι,
195 σὸν πατέρ'· ἀλλά νυ τόν γε θεοὶ βλάπτουσι κελεύθου.
οὐ γάρ πω τέθνηκεν ἐπὶ χθονὶ δῖος 'Οδυσσεύς,
ἀλλ' ἔτι που ζωὸς κατερύκεται εὐρέι πόντῳ
νήσῳ ἐν ἀμφιρύτῃ, χαλεποὶ δέ μιν ἄνδρες ἔχουσιν
ἄγριοι, οἵ που κεῖνον ἐρυκανόωσ' ἀέκοντα.
200 αὐτὰρ νῦν τοι ἐγὼ μαντεύσομαι, ὡς ἐνὶ θυμῷ
ἀθάνατοι βάλλουσι καὶ ὡς τελέεσθαι ὀίω,
οὔτε τι μάντις ἐὼν οὔτ' οἰωνῶν σάφα εἰδώς.
οὔ τοι ἔτι δηρόν γε φίλης ἀπὸ πατρίδος αἴης
ἔσσεται, οὐδ' εἴ πέρ τε σιδήρεα δέσματ' ἔχῃσιν·
205 φράσσεται ὥς κε νέηται, ἐπεὶ πολυμήχανός ἐστιν.
ἀλλ' ἄγε μοι τόδε εἰπὲ καὶ ἀτρεκέως κατάλεξον,

am Mentes, the son of wise Anchialus, and I am lord over the oar-loving Taphians. And now I have put in here as you see, with ship and crew, while sailing over the wine-dark sea to men of strange speech, on my way to Temese for copper; and I bear with me shining iron. My ship lies yonder beside the fields away from the city, in the harbor of Rheithron, under woody Neion. Friends of one another do we declare ourselves to be, just as our fathers were, friends from of old. You may, if you will, go and ask the old hero Laertes, who, they say, comes no longer to the city, but afar in the fields suffers woes attended by an aged woman as his handmaid, who sets before him food and drink, after weariness has laid hold of his limbs, as he creeps along the slope of his vineyard plot. And now I have come, for indeed men said that he, your father, was among his people, but it seems the gods are thwarting his return. For not yet has noble Odysseus perished on the earth, but still, I suppose, he lives and is held prisoner on the broad sea in a seagirt isle, and cruel men keep him, a savage folk, that constrain him perhaps against his will. Indeed, I will now prophesy to you, as the immortals put it in my heart, and as I think it shall be brought to pass, though I am no soothsayer, nor one versed in the signs of birds. Not much longer shall he be absent from his own native land, no, not though bonds of iron hold him. He will contrive a way to return, for he is a man of many devices. But come, tell me this and declare it truly, whether indeed, tall as you are,

εἰ δὴ ἐξ αὐτοῖο τόσος πάϊς εἰς Ὀδυσῆος.
αἰνῶς μὲν κεφαλήν τε καὶ ὄμματα καλὰ ἔοικας
κείνῳ, ἐπεὶ θαμὰ τοῖον ἐμισγόμεθ' ἀλλήλοισιν,
210 πρίν γε τὸν ἐς Τροίην ἀναβήμεναι, ἔνθα περ ἄλλοι
Ἀργείων οἱ ἄριστοι ἔβαν κοίλης ἐνὶ νηυσίν·
ἐκ τοῦ δ' οὔτ' Ὀδυσῆα ἐγὼν ἴδον οὔτ' ἔμ' ἐκεῖνος."
        τὴν δ' αὖ Τηλέμαχος πεπνυμένος ἀντίον ηὔδα·
"τοιγὰρ ἐγώ τοι, ξεῖνε, μάλ' ἀτρεκέως ἀγορεύσω.
215 μήτηρ μέν τέ μέ φησι τοῦ ἔμμεναι, αὐτὰρ ἐγώ γε
οὐκ οἶδ'· οὐ γάρ πώ τις ἑὸν γόνον αὐτὸς ἀνέγνω.
ὡς δὴ ἐγώ γ' ὄφελον μάκαρός νύ τευ ἔμμεναι υἱὸς
ἀνέρος, ὃν κτεάτεσσιν ἑοῖς ἔπι γῆρας ἔτετμε.
νῦν δ' ὃς ἀποτμότατος γένετο θνητῶν ἀνθρώπων,
220 τοῦ μ' ἔκ φασι γενέσθαι, ἐπεὶ σύ με τοῦτ' ἐρεείνεις."
        τὸν δ' αὖτε προσέειπε θεά, γλαυκῶπις Ἀθήνη·
"οὐ μέν τοι γενεήν γε θεοὶ νώνυμνον ὀπίσσω
θῆκαν, ἐπεὶ σέ γε τοῖον ἐγείνατο Πηνελόπεια.
ἀλλ' ἄγε μοι τόδε εἰπὲ καὶ ἀτρεκέως κατάλεξον·
225 τίς δαίς, τίς δὲ ὅμιλος ὅδ' ἔπλετο; τίπτε δέ σε χρεώ;
εἰλαπίνη ἠὲ γάμος; ἐπεὶ οὐκ ἔρανος τάδε γ' ἐστίν·
ὥς τέ μοι ὑβρίζοντες ὑπερφιάλως δοκέουσι
δαίνυσθαι κατὰ δῶμα. νεμεσσήσαιτό κεν ἀνὴρ
αἴσχεα πόλλ' ὁρόων, ὅς τις πινυτός γε μετέλθοι."
230 τὴν δ' αὖ Τηλέμαχος πεπνυμένος ἀντίον ηὔδα·
"ξεῖν', ἐπεὶ ἄρ δὴ ταῦτά μ' ἀνείρεαι ἠδὲ μεταλλᾷς,
μέλλεν μέν ποτε οἶκος ὅδ' ἀφνειὸς καὶ ἀμύμων
ἔμμεναι, ὄφρ' ἔτι κεῖνος ἀνὴρ ἐπιδήμιος ἦεν·
νῦν δ' ἑτέρως ἐβόλοντο θεοὶ κακὰ μητιόωντες,

you are the son of Odysseus himself. Wondrously like his are your head and beautiful eyes; for many were the times we consorted with one another before he embarked for the land of Troy, whither others, too, the bravest of the Argives, went in their hollow ships. But since that day neither have I seen Odysseus, nor he me."

Then wise Telemachus answered her: "Therefore, stranger, will I frankly tell you all. My mother says that I am his child; but I do not know this, for never yet did any man know his parentage of his own knowledge. Ah, would that I had been the son of some fortunate man, whom old age took among his own possessions. But now, since you ask me about this, they say that I was begotten by him who was the most ill-fated of mortal men."

Then the goddess, flashing-eyed Athene, answered him: "Surely, then, no nameless lineage have the gods appointed for you in time to come, seeing that Penelope bore you such as you are. But come, tell me this and declare it truly. What feast, what throng is this? What need have you of it? Is it a drinking bout, or a wedding feast? For this plainly is no meal to which each brings his portion, with such outrage and arrogance do they seem to me to be feasting in your halls. Angered would a man be at seeing all these shameful acts, any man of sense who should come among them."

Then wise Telemachus answered her: "Stranger, since indeed you ask and question me about this, our house once bade fair to be rich and irreproachable, so long as that man was still among his people. But now the gods have willed otherwise in their evil devising, seeing that they have

235 οἳ κεῖνον μὲν ἄιστον ἐποίησαν περὶ πάντων
  ἀνθρώπων, ἐπεὶ οὔ κε θανόντι περ ὧδ' ἀκαχοίμην,
  εἰ μετὰ οἷς ἑτάροισι δάμη Τρώων ἐνὶ δήμῳ,
  ἠὲ φίλων ἐν χερσίν, ἐπεὶ πόλεμον τολύπευσεν.
  τῷ κέν οἱ τύμβον μὲν ἐποίησαν Παναχαιοί,
240 ἠδέ κε καὶ ᾧ παιδὶ μέγα κλέος ἦρατ' ὀπίσσω.
  νῦν δέ μιν ἀκλειῶς ἅρπυιαι ἀνηρείψαντο·
  οἴχετ' ἄιστος ἄπυστος, ἐμοὶ δ' ὀδύνας τε γόους τε
  κάλλιπεν. οὐδέ τι κεῖνον ὀδυρόμενος στεναχίζω
  οἶον, ἐπεί νύ μοι ἄλλα θεοὶ κακὰ κήδε' ἔτευξαν.
245 ὅσσοι γὰρ νήσοισιν ἐπικρατέουσιν ἄριστοι,
  Δουλιχίῳ τε Σάμῃ τε καὶ ὑλήεντι Ζακύνθῳ,
  ἠδ' ὅσσοι κραναὴν Ἰθάκην κάτα κοιρανέουσιν,
  τόσσοι μητέρ' ἐμὴν μνῶνται, τρύχουσι δὲ οἶκον.
  ἡ δ' οὔτ' ἀρνεῖται στυγερὸν γάμον οὔτε τελευτὴν
250 ποιῆσαι δύναται· τοὶ δὲ φθινύθουσιν ἔδοντες
  οἶκον ἐμόν· τάχα δή με διαρραίσουσι καὶ αὐτόν."
    τὸν δ' ἐπαλαστήσασα προσηύδα Παλλὰς Ἀθήνη·
  "ὦ πόποι, ἦ δὴ πολλὸν ἀποιχομένου Ὀδυσῆος
  δεύῃ, ὅ κε μνηστῆρσιν ἀναιδέσι χεῖρας ἐφείη.
255 εἰ γὰρ νῦν ἐλθὼν δόμου ἐν πρώτῃσι θύρῃσι
  σταίη, ἔχων πήληκα καὶ ἀσπίδα καὶ δύο δοῦρε,
  τοῖος ἐὼν οἷόν μιν ἐγὼ τὰ πρῶτ' ἐνόησα
  οἴκῳ ἐν ἡμετέρῳ πίνοντά τε τερπόμενόν τε,
  ἐξ Ἐφύρης ἀνιόντα παρ' Ἴλου Μερμερίδαο —
260 ᾤχετο γὰρ καὶ κεῖσε θοῆς ἐπὶ νηὸς Ὀδυσσεὺς
  φάρμακον ἀνδροφόνον διζήμενος, ὄφρα οἱ εἴη
  ἰοὺς χρίεσθαι χαλκήρεας· ἀλλ' ὁ μὲν οὔ οἱ

caused him to pass from sight as they have no other man. For I should not so grieve for his death, if he had been slain among his comrades in the land of the Trojans, or had died in the arms of his friends, when he had wound up the skein of war. Then would the whole host of the Achaeans have made him a tomb, and for his son, too, he would have won great glory in days to come. But as it is, the Harpies have swept him away and left no tidings: he is gone out of sight, out of hearing, and for me he has left anguish and weeping; nor do I by any chance mourn and groan for him only, seeing that the gods have brought upon me other painful troubles. For all the princes who hold sway over the islands—Dulichium and Same and wooded Zacynthus— and those who lord it over rocky Ithaca, all these woo my mother and lay waste my house. And she neither refuses the hateful marriage, nor is she able to settle the matter; but they with feasting consume my property: before long they will bring me, too, to ruin."

Then, stirred to anger, Pallas Athene spoke to him: "Ah, me! You have indeed bitter need of Odysseus who is gone, that he might lay his hands upon the shameless suitors. Would that he might come now and take his stand at the outer gate of the house, with helmet and shield and two spears, such a man as he was when I first saw him in our house drinking and making merry, on his way back from Ephyre, from the house of Ilus, son of Mermerus. For thither, too, went Odysseus in his swift ship in search of a deadly drug, that he might have it to smear his bronze-tipped arrows with; yet Ilus did not give it to him, for he

δῶκεν, ἐπεί ῥα θεοὺς νεμεσίζετο αἰὲν ἐόντας,
ἀλλὰ πατήρ οἱ δῶκεν ἐμός· φιλέεσκε γὰρ αἰνῶς —
265 τοῖος ἐὼν μνηστῆρσιν ὁμιλήσειεν Ὀδυσσεύς·
πάντες κ' ὠκύμοροί τε γενοίατο πικρόγαμοί τε.
ἀλλ' ἦ τοι μὲν ταῦτα θεῶν ἐν γούνασι κεῖται,
ἤ κεν νοστήσας ἀποτίσεται, ἦε καὶ οὐκί,
οἷσιν ἐνὶ μεγάροισι· σὲ δὲ φράζεσθαι ἄνωγα,
270 ὅππως κε μνηστῆρας ἀπώσεαι ἐκ μεγάροιο.
εἰ δ' ἄγε νῦν ξυνίει καὶ ἐμῶν ἐμπάζεο μύθων·
αὔριον εἰς ἀγορὴν καλέσας ἥρωας Ἀχαιοὺς
μῦθον πέφραδε πᾶσι, θεοὶ δ' ἐπὶ μάρτυροι ἔστων.
μνηστῆρας μὲν ἐπὶ σφέτερα σκίδνασθαι ἄνωχθι,
275 μητέρα δ', εἴ οἱ θυμὸς ἐφορμᾶται γαμέεσθαι,
ἂψ ἴτω ἐς μέγαρον πατρὸς μέγα δυναμένοιο·
οἱ δὲ γάμον τεύξουσι καὶ ἀρτυνέουσιν ἔεδνα
πολλὰ μάλ', ὅσσα ἔοικε φίλης ἐπὶ παιδὸς ἕπεσθαι.[1]
σοὶ δ' αὐτῷ πυκινῶς ὑποθήσομαι, αἴ κε πίθηαι·
280 νῆ' ἄρσας ἐρέτῃσιν ἐείκοσιν, ἥ τις ἀρίστη,
ἔρχεο πευσόμενος πατρὸς δὴν οἰχομένοιο,
ἤν τίς τοι εἴπῃσι βροτῶν, ἢ ὄσσαν ἀκούσῃς
ἐκ Διός, ἥ τε μάλιστα φέρει κλέος ἀνθρώποισι.
πρῶτα μὲν ἐς Πύλον ἐλθὲ καὶ εἴρεο Νέστορα δῖον,
285 κεῖθεν δὲ Σπάρτηνδε παρὰ ξανθὸν Μενέλαον·[2]
ὃς γὰρ δεύτατος ἦλθεν Ἀχαιῶν χαλκοχιτώνων.
εἰ μέν κεν πατρὸς βίοτον καὶ νόστον ἀκούσῃς,

---

[1] Line 278, rejected by Rhianus, is bracketed by many editors;
cf. 2.197.

32

stood in awe of the gods that are forever; but my father gave it, for he was terribly fond of him. Would, I say, that in such strength Odysseus might come among the suitors; then should they all meet with a swift death and a bitter marriage. Yet this lies on the knees of the gods to be sure, whether he shall return and wreak vengeance in his halls, or whether he shall not; but for yourself, I urge you take thought how you may drive out the suitors from the hall. Come now, give ear, and hearken to my words. Tomorrow call to an assembly the Achaean heroes, and speak your word to all, and let the gods be your witnesses. As for the suitors, tell them to scatter, each to his own; and for your mother, if her heart bids her marry, let her go back to the hall of her powerful father, and there they will prepare a wedding feast, and make ready the gifts in their abundance, all that should go with a well-loved daughter. And to yourself I will give wise counsel, if you will listen. Man with twenty rowers the best ship you have, and go to seek tidings of your father, who has been long gone, in case any mortal may tell you, or you may hear a rumor from Zeus, which oftenest brings tidings to men. First go to Pylos and question noble Nestor, and from there to Sparta to fair-haired Menelaus; for he was the last of the brazen-shirted Achaeans to reach home. If you hear that your father is alive and coming home, then surely, though you are much

---

² κεῖθεν δὲ Σπάρτηνδε κ.τ.λ.: κεῖθεν δ' ἐς Κρήτην τε παρ' Ἰδο-
μενῆα ἄνακτα, "and thence to Crete to the lord Idomeneus,"
Zenodotus.

ἦ τ' ἂν τρυχόμενός περ ἔτι τλαίης ἐνιαυτόν·
εἰ δέ κε τεθνηῶτος ἀκούσῃς μηδ' ἔτ' ἐόντος,
290 νοστήσας δὴ ἔπειτα φίλην ἐς πατρίδα γαῖαν
σῆμά τέ οἱ χεῦαι καὶ ἐπὶ κτέρεα κτερεΐξαι
πολλὰ μάλ', ὅσσα ἔοικε, καὶ ἀνέρι μητέρα δοῦναι.
αὐτὰρ ἐπὴν δὴ ταῦτα τελευτήσῃς τε καὶ ἔρξῃς,
φράζεσθαι δὴ ἔπειτα κατὰ φρένα καὶ κατὰ θυμὸν
295 ὅππως κε μνηστῆρας ἐνὶ μεγάροισι τεοῖσι
κτείνῃς ἠὲ δόλῳ ἢ ἀμφαδόν· οὐδέ τί σε χρὴ
νηπιάας ὀχέειν, ἐπεὶ οὐκέτι τηλίκος ἐσσι.
ἦ οὐκ ἀίεις οἷον κλέος ἔλλαβε δῖος Ὀρέστης
πάντας ἐπ' ἀνθρώπους, ἐπεὶ ἔκτανε πατροφονῆα,
300 Αἴγισθον δολόμητιν, ὅ οἱ πατέρα κλυτὸν ἔκτα;
καὶ σύ, φίλος, μάλα γάρ σ' ὁρόω καλόν τε μέγαν τε,
ἄλκιμος ἔσσ', ἵνα τίς σε καὶ ὀψιγόνων ἐὺ εἴπῃ.
αὐτὰρ ἐγὼν ἐπὶ νῆα θοὴν κατελεύσομαι ἤδη
ἠδ' ἐτάρους, οἵ πού με μάλ' ἀσχαλόωσι μένοντες·
305 σοὶ δ' αὐτῷ μελέτω, καὶ ἐμῶν ἐμπάζεο μύθων."
    τὴν δ' αὖ Τηλέμαχος πεπνυμένος ἀντίον ηὔδα·
"ξεῖν', ἦ τοι μὲν ταῦτα φίλα φρονέων ἀγορεύεις,
ὥς τε πατὴρ ᾧ παιδί, καὶ οὔ ποτε λήσομαι αὐτῶν.
ἀλλ' ἄγε νῦν ἐπίμεινον, ἐπειγόμενός περ ὁδοῖο,
310 ὄφρα λοεσσάμενός τε τεταρπόμενός τε φίλον κῆρ,
δῶρον ἔχων ἐπὶ νῆα κίῃς, χαίρων ἐνὶ θυμῷ,
τιμῆεν, μάλα καλόν, ὅ τοι κειμήλιον ἔσται
ἐξ ἐμεῦ, οἷα φίλοι ξεῖνοι ξείνοισι διδοῦσι."
    τὸν δ' ἠμείβετ' ἔπειτα θεά, γλαυκῶπις Ἀθήνη·
315 "μή μ' ἔτι νῦν κατέρυκε, λιλαιόμενόν περ ὁδοῖο.

afflicted, you could endure for another year. But if you hear that he is dead and gone, then return to your own native land and heap up a mound for him, and over it pay funeral rites, sumptuous ones as is due, and give your mother to a husband. Then when you have done all this and brought it to an end, thereafter take thought in mind and heart how you may slay the suitors in your halls whether by guile or openly; for it does not beseem you to practice childish ways, since you are no longer of such an age. Or have you not heard what fame the noble Orestes won among all mankind when he slew his father's murderer, the guileful Aegisthus, because he slew his glorious father? You too, my friend, for I see that you are comely and tall, be valiant, that many a one of men yet to be born may praise you. But now I will go down to my swift ship and my comrades, who, I doubt not, are chafing much at waiting for me. For yourself, give heed and have regard to my words."

Then wise Telemachus answered her: "Stranger, in truth you speak these things considerately, as a father to his son, and never will I forget them. But come now, tarry, eager though you are to be gone, in order that when you have bathed and satisfied your heart to the full, you may go to your ship glad in spirit, and bearing a gift costly and very beautiful, which shall be to you an heirloom from me, such a gift as dear friends give to friends."

Then the goddess, flashing-eyed Athene, answered him: "Keep me now no longer, when I am eager to be

δῶρον δ' ὅττι κέ μοι δοῦναι φίλον ἦτορ ἀνώγῃ,
αὖτις ἀνερχομένῳ δόμεναι οἰκόνδε φέρεσθαι,
καὶ μάλα καλὸν ἑλών· σοὶ δ' ἄξιον ἔσται ἀμοιβῆς."

　　　ἡ μὲν ἄρ' ὣς εἰποῦσ' ἀπέβη γλαυκῶπις Ἀθήνη,
320　ὄρνις δ' ὣς ἀνόπαια διέπτατο· τῷ δ' ἐνὶ θυμῷ
θῆκε μένος καὶ θάρσος, ὑπέμνησέν τέ ἑ πατρὸς
μᾶλλον ἔτ' ἢ τὸ πάροιθεν. ὁ δὲ φρεσὶν ᾗσι νοήσας
θάμβησεν κατὰ θυμόν· ὀίσατο γὰρ θεὸν εἶναι.
αὐτίκα δὲ μνηστῆρας ἐπῴχετο ἰσόθεος φώς.

325　　τοῖσι δ' ἀοιδὸς ἄειδε περικλυτός, οἱ δὲ σιωπῇ
ἧατ' ἀκούοντες· ὁ δ' Ἀχαιῶν νόστον ἄειδε
λυγρόν, ὃν ἐκ Τροίης ἐπετείλατο Παλλὰς Ἀθήνη.
τοῦ δ' ὑπερωιόθεν φρεσὶ σύνθετο θέσπιν ἀοιδὴν
κούρη Ἰκαρίοιο, περίφρων Πηνελόπεια·
330　κλίμακα δ' ὑψηλὴν κατεβήσετο οἷο δόμοιο,
οὐκ οἴη, ἅμα τῇ γε καὶ ἀμφίπολοι δύ' ἕποντο.
ἡ δ' ὅτε δὴ μνηστῆρας ἀφίκετο δῖα γυναικῶν,
στῆ ῥα παρὰ σταθμὸν τέγεος πύκα ποιητοῖο,
ἄντα παρειάων σχομένη λιπαρὰ κρήδεμνα·
335　ἀμφίπολος δ' ἄρα οἱ κεδνὴ ἑκάτερθε παρέστη.
δακρύσασα δ' ἔπειτα προσηύδα θεῖον ἀοιδόν·

　　　"Φήμιε, πολλὰ γὰρ ἄλλα βροτῶν θελκτήρια οἶδας,
ἔργ' ἀνδρῶν τε θεῶν τε, τά τε κλείουσιν ἀοιδοί·
τῶν ἕν γέ σφιν ἄειδε παρήμενος, οἱ δὲ σιωπῇ
340　οἶνον πινόντων· ταύτης δ' ἀποπαύε' ἀοιδῆς
λυγρῆς, ἥ τέ μοι αἰεὶ ἐνὶ στήθεσσι φίλον κῆρ
τείρει, ἐπεί με μάλιστα καθίκετο πένθος ἄλαστον.
τοίην γὰρ κεφαλὴν ποθέω μεμνημένη αἰεί,

gone, and whatever gift your heart bids you give me, give it when I come back, to bear to my home, choosing a very beautiful one; it shall bring you its worth in return."

So spoke the goddess, flashing-eyed Athene, and departed, flying upward like a bird; and in his heart she put strength and courage, and made him think of his father even more than before. And in his mind he marked what had happened and marveled, for he suspected that she was a god; and at once he went among the suitors, a godlike man.

For them the famous minstrel was singing, and they sat in silence, listening; and he sang of the return of the Achaeans—the woeful return from Troy which Pallas Athene laid upon them. And from her upper chamber the daughter of Icarius, wise Penelope, heard his wonderful song, and she went down the high stairway from her chamber, not alone, for two handmaids attended her. Now when the fair lady had come to the suitors, she stood by the doorpost of the well-built hall, holding before her face her shining veil; and a faithful handmaid stood on either side of her. Then, as the tears filled her eyes, she spoke to the divine minstrel:

"Phemius, many other things you know to charm mortals, deeds of men and gods which minstrels make famous. Sing them one of these, as you sit here, and let them drink their wine in silence. But cease from this woeful song which always harrows the heart in my breast, for upon me above all women has come a sorrow not to be forgotten. So dear a face do I always remember with longing, my

ἀνδρός, τοῦ κλέος εὐρὺ καθ᾽ Ἑλλάδα καὶ μέσον
Ἄργος."[1]

345   τὴν δ᾽ αὖ Τηλέμαχος πεπνυμένος ἀντίον ηὔδα·
"μῆτερ ἐμή, τί τ᾽ ἄρα φθονέεις ἐρίηρον ἀοιδὸν
τέρπειν ὅππῃ οἱ νόος ὄρνυται; οὔ νύ τ᾽ ἀοιδοὶ
αἴτιοι, ἀλλά ποθι Ζεὺς αἴτιος, ὅς τε δίδωσιν
ἀνδράσιν ἀλφηστῇσιν, ὅπως ἐθέλῃσιν, ἑκάστῳ.
350 τούτῳ δ᾽ οὐ νέμεσις Δαναῶν κακὸν οἶτον ἀείδειν·
τὴν γὰρ ἀοιδὴν μᾶλλον ἐπικλείουσ᾽ ἄνθρωποι,
ἥ τις ἀκουόντεσσι νεωτάτη ἀμφιπέληται.
σοὶ δ᾽ ἐπιτολμάτω κραδίη καὶ θυμὸς ἀκούειν·
οὐ γὰρ Ὀδυσσεὺς οἶος ἀπώλεσε νόστιμον ἦμαρ
355 ἐν Τροίῃ, πολλοὶ δὲ καὶ ἄλλοι φῶτες ὄλοντο.
ἀλλ᾽ εἰς οἶκον ἰοῦσα τὰ σ᾽ αὐτῆς ἔργα κόμιζε,[2]
ἱστόν τ᾽ ἠλακάτην τε, καὶ ἀμφιπόλοισι κέλευε
ἔργον ἐποίχεσθαι· μῦθος δ᾽ ἄνδρεσσι μελήσει
πᾶσι, μάλιστα δ᾽ ἐμοί· τοῦ γὰρ κράτος ἔστ᾽ ἐνὶ οἴκῳ."
360   ἡ μὲν θαμβήσασα πάλιν οἰκόνδε βεβήκει·
παιδὸς γὰρ μῦθον πεπνυμένον ἔνθετο θυμῷ.
ἐς δ᾽ ὑπερῷ᾽ ἀναβᾶσα σὺν ἀμφιπόλοισι γυναιξὶ
κλαῖεν ἔπειτ᾽ Ὀδυσῆα φίλον πόσιν, ὄφρα οἱ ὕπνον
ἡδὺν ἐπὶ βλεφάροισι βάλε γλαυκῶπις Ἀθήνη.
365   μνηστῆρες δ᾽ ὁμάδησαν ἀνὰ μέγαρα σκιόεντα,
πάντες δ᾽ ἠρήσαντο παραὶ λεχέεσσι κλιθῆναι.
τοῖσι δὲ Τηλέμαχος πεπνυμένος ἤρχετο μύθων·
   "μητρὸς ἐμῆς μνηστῆρες ὑπέρβιον ὕβριν ἔχοντες,
νῦν μὲν δαινύμενοι τερπώμεθα, μηδὲ βοητὺς
370 ἔστω, ἐπεὶ τόδε καλὸν ἀκουέμεν ἐστὶν ἀοιδοῦ

38

husband's, whose fame is wide through Hellas and mid-Argos."

Then wise Telemachus answered her: "My mother, why do you begrudge the good minstrel to give pleasure in whatever way his heart is moved? It is not minstrels that are to blame, but Zeus, I suppose, is to blame, who gives to bread-eating men, to each one as he will. With this man no one can be angry if he sings the evil doom of the Danaans; for men praise that song the most that comes the newest to their ears. For yourself, let your heart and soul endure to listen; for not only Odysseus lost in Troy the day of his return, but many others likewise perished. Now go to your chamber, and busy yourself with your own tasks, the loom and the distaff, and bid your handmaids be about their tasks; but speech shall be men's care, for all, but most of all for me; since mine is the authority in this house."

She then, seized with wonder, went back to her chamber, for she laid to her heart the wise saying of her son. Up to her upper chamber she went with her handmaids, and then wept for Odysseus, her dear husband, until grey-eyed Athene cast sweet sleep upon her eyelids.

But the suitors broke into uproar throughout the shadowy halls, and all prayed, each that he might lie in bed with her. And among them wise Telemachus was the first to speak:

"Suitors of my mother, arrogant in your insolence, for the present let us make merry with feasting, but let there be no brawling, for this is a pleasant thing, to listen to a

---

[1] Line 344 was rejected by Aristarchus; cf. 4.726, 816, 15.80.

[2] Lines 356–59, rejected by Aristarchus, are bracketed by many editors.

τοιοῦδ' οἷος ὅδ' ἐστί, θεοῖς ἐναλίγκιος αὐδήν.
ἠῶθεν δ' ἀγορήνδε καθεζώμεσθα κιόντες
πάντες, ἵν' ὑμῖν μῦθον ἀπηλεγέως ἀποείπω,
ἐξιέναι μεγάρων· ἄλλας δ' ἀλεγύνετε δαῖτας,
375 ὑμὰ κτήματ' ἔδοντες, ἀμειβόμενοι κατὰ οἴκους.
εἰ δ' ὑμῖν δοκέει τόδε λωίτερον καὶ ἄμεινον
ἔμμεναι, ἀνδρὸς ἑνὸς βίοτον νήποινον ὀλέσθαι,
κείρετ'· ἐγὼ δὲ θεοὺς ἐπιβώσομαι αἰὲν ἐόντας,
αἴ κέ ποθι Ζεὺς δῷσι παλίντιτα ἔργα γενέσθαι·
380 νήποινοί κεν ἔπειτα δόμων ἔντοσθεν ὄλοισθε."
    ὣς ἔφαθ', οἱ δ' ἄρα πάντες ὀδὰξ ἐν χείλεσι φύντες
Τηλέμαχον θαύμαζον, ὃ θαρσαλέως ἀγόρευεν.
    τὸν δ' αὖτ' Ἀντίνοος προσέφη, Εὐπείθεος υἱός·
"Τηλέμαχ', ἦ μάλα δή σε διδάσκουσιν θεοὶ αὐτοὶ
385 ὑψαγόρην τ' ἔμεναι καὶ θαρσαλέως ἀγορεύειν·
μὴ σέ γ' ἐν ἀμφιάλῳ Ἰθάκῃ βασιλῆα Κρονίων
ποιήσειεν, ὅ τοι γενεῇ πατρώιόν ἐστιν."
    τὸν δ' αὖ Τηλέμαχος πεπνυμένος ἀντίον ηὔδα·
"Ἀντίνο', ἦ καί μοι νεμεσήσεαι[1] ὅττι κεν εἴπω;
390 καὶ κεν τοῦτ' ἐθέλοιμι Διός γε διδόντος ἀρέσθαι.
ἦ φὴς τοῦτο κάκιστον ἐν ἀνθρώποισι τετύχθαι;
οὐ μὲν γάρ τι κακὸν βασιλευέμεν· αἶψά τέ οἱ δῶ
ἀφνειὸν πέλεται καὶ τιμηέστερος αὐτός.
ἀλλ' ἦ τοι βασιλῆες Ἀχαιῶν εἰσὶ καὶ ἄλλοι
395 πολλοὶ ἐν ἀμφιάλῳ Ἰθάκῃ, νέοι ἠδὲ παλαιοί,
τῶν κέν τις τόδ' ἔχῃσιν, ἐπεὶ θάνε δῖος Ὀδυσσεύς·
αὐτὰρ ἐγὼν οἴκοιο ἄναξ ἔσομ' ἡμετέροιο
καὶ δμώων, οὕς μοι ληίσσατο δῖος Ὀδυσσεύς."

minstrel such as this man is, like to the gods in voice. But in the morning let us go to the assembly and take our seats, one and all, that I may declare my word to you outright that you depart from these halls. Prepare yourselves other feasts, eating your own stores and moving from house to house. But if this seems in your eyes to be a better and more profitable thing, that one man's livelihood should be ruined without atonement, waste on. But I will call upon the gods that are forever, in hopes Zeus may grant that deeds of requital occur. Without atonement, then, would you perish within my halls."

So he spoke, and they all bit their lips and marveled at Telemachus, because he spoke boldly.

Then Antinous, son of Eupeithes, answered him: "Telemachus, surely the gods themselves are teaching you a lofty style, and to speak with boldness. May the son of Cronos never make you king in seagirt Ithaca, which thing is by birth your heritage."

Then wise Telemachus answered him: "Antinous, will you be angry with me for the word that I shall say?[1] Even this should I be glad to accept from the hand of Zeus. Do you truly think that this is the worst fate among men? No, it is no bad thing to be a king. Straightway one's house grows rich and oneself is held in greater honor. However, there are other kings of the Achaeans in plenty in seagirt Ithaca, both young and old. One of these, it may chance, will have this honor, since noble Odysseus is dead. But I will be lord of our own house and of the slaves that noble Odysseus plundered for me."

---

[1] ἦ καί μοι νεμεσήσεαι: εἴ πέρ μοι καὶ ἀγάσσεαι, "even though you be angry"

τὸν δ' αὖτ' Εὐρύμαχος Πολύβου πάϊς ἀντίον ηὔδα·
400 "Τηλέμαχ', ἦ τοι ταῦτα θεῶν ἐν γούνασι κεῖται,
ὅς τις ἐν ἀμφιάλῳ Ἰθάκῃ βασιλεύσει Ἀχαιῶν·
κτήματα δ' αὐτὸς ἔχοις καὶ δώμασιν οἷσιν ἀνάσσοις.
μὴ γὰρ ὅ γ' ἔλθοι ἀνὴρ ὅς τίς σ' ἀέκοντα βίηφιν
κτήματ' ἀπορραίσει, Ἰθάκης ἔτι ναιετοώσης.
405 ἀλλ' ἐθέλω σε, φέριστε, περὶ ξείνοιο ἐρέσθαι,
ὁππόθεν οὗτος ἀνήρ, ποίης δ' ἐξ εὔχεται εἶναι
γαίης, ποῦ δέ νύ οἱ γενεὴ καὶ πατρὶς ἄρουρα.
ἠέ τιν' ἀγγελίην πατρὸς φέρει ἐρχομένοιο,
ἦ ἑὸν αὐτοῦ χρεῖος ἐελδόμενος τόδ' ἱκάνει;
410 οἷον ἀναΐξας ἄφαρ οἴχεται, οὐδ' ὑπέμεινε
γνώμεναι· οὐ μὲν γάρ τι κακῷ εἰς ὦπα ἐῴκει."
τὸν δ' αὖ Τηλέμαχος πεπνυμένος ἀντίον ηὔδα·
"Εὐρύμαχ', ἦ τοι νόστος ἀπώλετο πατρὸς ἐμοῖο·
οὔτ' οὖν ἀγγελίῃ ἔτι πείθομαι, εἴ ποθεν ἔλθοι,
415 οὔτε θεοπροπίης ἐμπάζομαι, ἥν τινα μήτηρ
ἐς μέγαρον καλέσασα θεοπρόπον ἐξερέηται.
ξεῖνος δ' οὗτος ἐμὸς πατρώϊος ἐκ Τάφου ἐστίν,
Μέντης δ' Ἀγχιάλοιο δαΐφρονος εὔχεται εἶναι
υἱός, ἀτὰρ Ταφίοισι φιληρέτμοισιν ἀνάσσει."
420 ὣς φάτο Τηλέμαχος, φρεσὶ δ' ἀθανάτην θεὸν ἔγνω.
οἱ δ' εἰς ὀρχηστύν τε καὶ ἱμερόεσσαν ἀοιδὴν
τρεψάμενοι τέρποντο, μένον δ' ἐπὶ ἕσπερον ἐλθεῖν.
τοῖσι δὲ τερπομένοισι μέλας ἐπὶ ἕσπερος ἦλθε·
δὴ τότε κακκείοντες ἔβαν οἰκόνδε ἕκαστος.
425 Τηλέμαχος δ', ὅθι οἱ θάλαμος περικαλλέος αὐλῆς
ὑψηλὸς δέδμητο περισκέπτῳ ἐνὶ χώρῳ,

Then Eurymachus, son of Polybus, answered him: "Telemachus, this matter surely lies on the knees of the gods, who of the Achaeans shall be king in seagirt Ithaca; but as for your possessions, keep them yourself, and be lord in your own house. Never may that man come who by violence and against your will shall wrest your possessions from you, while men yet live in Ithaca. But I am moved, good sir, to ask you about the stranger, where this man comes from. Of what land does he declare himself to be? Where are his kinsmen and his native fields? Does he bring some tidings of your father's coming, or did he come here to further some matter of his own? How he started up and was instantly gone! Nor did he wait to be known; and yet he seemed no base man in looks."

Then wise Telemachus answered him: "Eurymachus, surely my father's homecoming is lost and gone. No longer do I put trust in tidings, from wherever they may come, or pay attention to any prophecy which my mother perchance may learn from a seer, when she has called him to the hall. But this stranger is a friend of my father's house from Taphos. He declares that he is Mentes, son of wise Anchialus, and he is lord over the oar-loving Taphians."

So spoke Telemachus, but in his heart he knew the immortal goddess.

Now the suitors turned to the dance and to heart-stirring song, and made merry, and waited till evening should come; and as they made merry dark evening came upon them. Then they went, each man to his house, to take their rest. But Telemachus, where his chamber was built in the beautiful court, high, in a place with a sur-

ἔνθ' ἔβη εἰς εὐνὴν πολλὰ φρεσὶ μερμηρίζων.
τῷ δ' ἄρ' ἅμ' αἰθομένας δαΐδας φέρε κεδνὰ ἰδυῖα
Εὐρύκλει', Ὦπος θυγάτηρ Πεισηνορίδαο,
430   τήν ποτε Λαέρτης πρίατο κτεάτεσσιν ἑοῖσιν
πρωθήβην ἔτ' ἐοῦσαν, ἐεικοσάβοια δ' ἔδωκεν,
ἶσα δέ μιν κεδνῇ ἀλόχῳ τίεν ἐν μεγάροισιν,
εὐνῇ δ' οὔ ποτ' ἔμικτο, χόλον δ' ἀλέεινε γυναικός·
ἥ οἱ ἅμ' αἰθομένας δαΐδας φέρε, καί ἑ μάλιστα
435   δμῳάων φιλέεσκε, καὶ ἔτρεφε τυτθὸν ἐόντα.
ὤιξεν δὲ θύρας θαλάμου πύκα ποιητοῖο,
ἕζετο δ' ἐν λέκτρῳ, μαλακὸν δ' ἔκδυνε χιτῶνα·
καὶ τὸν μὲν γραίης πυκιμηδέος ἔμβαλε χερσίν.
ἡ μὲν τὸν πτύξασα καὶ ἀσκήσασα χιτῶνα,
440   πασσάλῳ ἀγκρεμάσασα παρὰ τρητοῖσι λέχεσσι
βῆ ῥ' ἴμεν ἐκ θαλάμοιο, θύρην δ' ἐπέρυσσε κορώνῃ
ἀργυρέῃ, ἐπὶ δὲ κληῖδ' ἐτάνυσσεν ἱμάντι.
ἔνθ' ὅ γε παννύχιος, κεκαλυμμένος οἰὸς ἀώτῳ,
βούλευε φρεσὶν ᾗσιν ὁδὸν τὴν πέφραδ' Ἀθήνη.

rounding view, there he went to his bed, pondering many things in his mind; and with him, bearing blazing torches, went true-hearted Eurycleia, daughter of Ops, son of Peisenor. Her long ago Laertes had bought with his wealth, when she was in her first youth, and gave for her the price of twenty oxen; and he honored her even as he honored his faithful wife in his halls, but he never lay with her in love, for he avoided the wrath of his wife. She it was who bore for Telemachus the blazing torches; for she of all the handmaids loved him most, and had nursed him when he was a child. He opened the doors of the well-built chamber, sat down on the bed, and took off his soft tunic and laid it in the wise old woman's hands. And she folded and smoothed the tunic and hung it on a peg beside the corded bedstead, and then went forth from the chamber, drawing the door to by its silver handle, and driving the bolt home with the thong. So there, the night through, wrapped in a fleece of wool, he pondered in his mind the journey that Athene had shown him.

B

Ἦμος δ' ἠριγένεια φάνη ῥοδοδάκτυλος Ἠώς,
ὤρνυτ' ἄρ' ἐξ εὐνῆφιν Ὀδυσσῆος φίλος υἱὸς
εἵματα ἑσσάμενος, περὶ δὲ ξίφος ὀξὺ θέτ' ὤμῳ,
ποσσὶ δ' ὑπὸ λιπαροῖσιν ἐδήσατο καλὰ πέδιλα,
5   βῆ δ' ἴμεν ἐκ θαλάμοιο θεῷ ἐναλίγκιος ἄντην.
αἶψα δὲ κηρύκεσσι λιγυφθόγγοισι κέλευσε
κηρύσσειν ἀγορήνδε κάρη κομόωντας Ἀχαιούς.
οἱ μὲν ἐκήρυσσον, τοὶ δ' ἠγείροντο μάλ' ὦκα.
αὐτὰρ ἐπεί ῥ' ἤγερθεν ὁμηγερέες τ' ἐγένοντο,
10 βῆ ῥ' ἴμεν εἰς ἀγορήν, παλάμῃ δ' ἔχε χάλκεον ἔγχος,
οὐκ οἶος, ἅμα τῷ γε δύω κύνες[1] ἀργοὶ ἕποντο.
θεσπεσίην δ' ἄρα τῷ γε χάριν κατέχευεν Ἀθήνη.
τὸν δ' ἄρα πάντες λαοὶ ἐπερχόμενον θηεῦντο·
ἕζετο δ' ἐν πατρὸς θώκῳ, εἶξαν δὲ γέροντες.
15 τοῖσι δ' ἔπειθ' ἥρως Αἰγύπτιος ἦρχ' ἀγορεύειν,
ὃς δὴ γήραϊ κυφὸς ἔην καὶ μυρία ᾔδη.
καὶ γὰρ τοῦ φίλος υἱὸς ἅμ' ἀντιθέῳ Ὀδυσῆι
Ἴλιον εἰς εὔπωλον ἔβη κοίλῃς ἐνὶ νηυσίν,
Ἄντιφος αἰχμητής· τὸν δ' ἄγριος ἔκτανε Κύκλωψ
20 ἐν σπῆι γλαφυρῷ, πύματον δ' ὡπλίσσατο δόρπον.

---

[1] δύω κύνες: κύνες πόδας

46

BOOK 2

As soon as early Dawn appeared, the rosy-fingered, up from his bed rose the staunch son of Odysseus and put on his clothing. About his shoulder he slung his sharp sword, and beneath his shining feet bound his fair sandals, and went forth from his chamber like a god to look upon. At once he bade the clear-voiced heralds to summon to the assembly the long-haired Achaeans. And the heralds made the summons, and the Achaeans assembled quickly. Now when they were assembled and met together, Telemachus went his way, holding in his hand a spear of bronze—not alone, for along with him two swift dogs followed; and wondrous was the grace that Athene shed upon him, and all the people marveled at him as he came. He sat down in his father's seat, and the elders gave place.

Then among them the hero Aegyptius was the first to speak, a man bowed with age and wise with wisdom untold. Now he spoke, because his dear son, the spearman Antiphus, had gone in the hollow ships to Ilium, famed for its horses, in the company of godlike Odysseus. But him the savage Cyclops had slain in his hollow cave, and made of him his latest meal. Three others there were; one,

τρεῖς δέ οἱ ἄλλοι ἔσαν, καὶ ὁ μὲν μνηστῆρσιν ὁμίλει,
Εὐρύνομος, δύο δ' αἰὲν¹ ἔχον πατρώϊα ἔργα.
ἀλλ' οὐδ' ὣς τοῦ λῆθετ' ὀδυρόμενος καὶ ἀχεύων.
τοῦ ὅ γε δάκρυ χέων ἀγορήσατο καὶ μετέειπε·

25   "κέκλυτε δὴ νῦν μευ, Ἰθακήσιοι, ὅττι κεν εἴπω·
οὔτε ποθ' ἡμετέρη ἀγορὴ γένετ' οὔτε θόωκος
ἐξ οὗ Ὀδυσσεὺς δῖος ἔβη κοίλῃς ἐνὶ νηυσί.
νῦν δὲ τίς ὧδ' ἤγειρε; τίνα χρειὼ τόσον ἵκει
ἠὲ νέων ἀνδρῶν ἢ οἳ προγενέστεροί εἰσιν;

30   ἠέ τιν' ἀγγελίην στρατοῦ ἔκλυεν ἐρχομένοιο,
ἥν χ' ἡμῖν σάφα εἴποι, ὅτε πρότερός γε πύθοιτο;
ἦέ τι δήμιον ἄλλο πιφαύσκεται ἠδ' ἀγορεύει;
ἐσθλός μοι δοκεῖ εἶναι, ὀνήμενος. εἴθε οἱ αὐτῷ
Ζεὺς ἀγαθὸν τελέσειεν, ὅτι φρεσὶν ᾗσι μενοινᾷ."

35   ὣς φάτο, χαῖρε δὲ φήμῃ Ὀδυσσῆος φίλος υἱός,
οὐδ' ἄρ' ἔτι δὴν ἧστο, μενοίνησεν δ' ἀγορεύειν,
στῆ δὲ μέσῃ ἀγορῇ· σκῆπτρον δέ οἱ ἔμβαλε χειρὶ
κῆρυξ Πεισήνωρ πεπνυμένα μήδεα εἰδώς.
πρῶτον ἔπειτα γέροντα καθαπτόμενος προσέειπεν·

40   "ὦ γέρον, οὐχ ἑκὰς οὗτος ἀνήρ, τάχα δ' εἴσεαι αὐτός,
ὃς λαὸν ἤγειρα· μάλιστα δέ μ' ἄλγος ἱκάνει.
οὔτε τιν' ἀγγελίην στρατοῦ ἔκλυον ἐρχομένοιο,
ἥν χ' ὑμῖν σάφα εἴπω, ὅτε πρότερός γε πυθοίμην,
οὔτε τι δήμιον ἄλλο πιφαύσκομαι οὐδ' ἀγορεύω,

45   ἀλλ' ἐμὸν αὐτοῦ χρεῖος, ὅ μοι κακὰ ἔμπεσεν οἴκῳ
δοιά· τὸ μὲν πατέρ' ἐσθλὸν ἀπώλεσα, ὅς ποτ' ἐν ὑμῖν

¹ δύο δ' αἰὲν: δύο δ' ἄλλοι

Eurynomus, consorted with the suitors, and two continued to keep their father's farm. Yet even so, he could not forget that other, mourning and sorrowing; and weeping for him he addressed the assembly, and spoke among them:

"Hearken now to me, men of Ithaca, to the word that I shall say. Never have we held assembly or session since the day when noble Odysseus departed in the hollow ships. And now who has called us together? On whom has such need come either among the young men or among those who are older? Has he heard some tidings of the army's return, of which he might give us a sure report, having been the first to learn of it? Or is there some other public matter on which he is to speak and address us? A good man he seems in my eyes, a blessed man. May Zeus fulfill for him some good, whatsoever he desires in his heart."

So he spoke, and the staunch son of Odysseus rejoiced at the word of omen; nor did he thereafter remain seated, but was eager to speak. So he took his stand in the midst of the assembly, and the staff was placed in his hands by the herald Peisenor, wise in counsel. Then he spoke, addressing first the old man:

"Old man, not far off, as you shall soon learn yourself, is that man who has called the host together—even I; for on me above all others has sorrow come. I have neither heard any tidings of the army's return, of which I might give you a sure report, having been the first to learn of it, nor is there any other public matter on which I am to speak and address you. No, it is my own need, seeing that evil has fallen upon my house in a double form. First, I have lost my noble father who was once king among you here, and was

49

τοίσδεσσιν βασίλευε, πατὴρ δ' ὡς ἤπιος ἦεν ·
νῦν δ' αὖ καὶ πολὺ μεῖζον, ὃ δὴ τάχα οἶκον ἅπαντα
πάγχυ διαρραίσει, βίοτον δ' ἀπὸ πάμπαν ὀλέσσει.

50 μητέρι μοι μνηστῆρες ἐπέχραον οὐκ ἐθελούσῃ,
τῶν ἀνδρῶν φίλοι υἷες, οἳ ἐνθάδε γ' εἰσὶν ἄριστοι,
οἳ πατρὸς μὲν ἐς οἶκον ἀπερρίγασι νέεσθαι
Ἰκαρίου, ὥς κ' αὐτὸς ἐεδνώσαιτο θύγατρα,
δοίη δ' ᾧ κ' ἐθέλοι καί οἱ κεχαρισμένος ἔλθοι ·

55 οἱ δ' εἰς ἡμέτερον πωλεύμενοι ἤματα πάντα,
βοῦς ἱερεύοντες καὶ ὄις καὶ πίονας αἶγας
εἰλαπινάζουσιν πίνουσί τε αἴθοπα οἶνον
μαψιδίως · τὰ δὲ πολλὰ κατάνεται. οὐ γὰρ ἔπ' ἀνήρ,
οἷος Ὀδυσσεὺς ἔσκεν, ἀρὴν ἀπὸ οἴκου ἀμῦναι.

60 ἡμεῖς δ' οὔ νύ τι τοῖοι ἀμυνέμεν · ἦ καὶ ἔπειτα
λευγαλέοι τ' ἐσόμεσθα καὶ οὐ δεδαηκότες ἀλκήν.
ἦ τ' ἂν ἀμυναίμην, εἴ μοι δύναμίς γε παρείη.
οὐ γὰρ ἔτ' ἀνσχετὰ ἔργα τετεύχαται, οὐδ' ἔτι καλῶς
οἶκος ἐμὸς διόλωλε. νεμεσσήθητε καὶ αὐτοί,

65 ἄλλους τ' αἰδέσθητε περικτίονας ἀνθρώπους,
οἳ περιναιετάουσι · θεῶν δ' ὑποδείσατε μῆνιν,
μή τι μεταστρέψωσιν ἀγασσάμενοι κακὰ ἔργα.
λίσσομαι ἠμὲν Ζηνὸς Ὀλυμπίου ἠδὲ Θέμιστος,
ἥ τ' ἀνδρῶν ἀγορὰς ἠμὲν λύει ἠδὲ καθίζει ·

70 σχέσθε, φίλοι, καί μ' οἶον ἐάσατε πένθεϊ λυγρῷ
τείρεσθ', εἰ μή πού τι πατὴρ ἐμὸς ἐσθλὸς Ὀδυσσεὺς
δυσμενέων κάκ' ἔρεξεν ἐϋκνήμιδας Ἀχαιούς,
τῶν μ' ἀποτινύμενοι κακὰ ῥέζετε δυσμενέοντες,
τούτους ὀτρύνοντες. ἐμοὶ δέ κε κέρδιον εἴη

50

gentle as a father; and now there has come a far greater
evil, which will presently altogether destroy my house and
ruin all my livelihood. Upon my mother suitors have
fastened against her will, own sons of those men who are
here the noblest. They shrink from going to the house of
her father, Icarius, that he may himself see to his
daughter's bride-gifts, and give her to whom he will, that is,
to him who meets his favor; instead, thronging our house
day after day they slay our oxen and sheep and fat goats,
and keep revel, and drink the sparkling wine recklessly; the
larger part of our substance is already gone. For there is
no man here, such as Odysseus was, to ward off ruin from
the house. We ourselves in no way have the strength for it:
in the event we would only prove how feeble we are and
how ignorant of battle. Yet truly I would defend myself, if I
had but the power; for now deeds past all enduring have
been done, and my house has been destroyed beyond all
show of fairness. Be ashamed yourselves, and feel shame
before your neighbors who dwell round about, and fear the
wrath of the gods, lest it happen that they turn against you
in anger at evil deeds. I pray you by Olympian Zeus and by
Themis who dissolves and gathers the assemblies of men,
stop this, my fellow Ithacans, and leave me alone to pine in
bitter grief—unless indeed my father, noble Odysseus, in
his hostility did evil to the well-greaved Achaeans, in requi-
tal whereof you do me evil in your hostility, urging these
suitors on. For me it would be better that you should your-

75　ὑμέας ἐσθέμεναι κειμήλιά τε πρόβασίν τε.
　　εἴ χ᾽ ὑμεῖς γε φάγοιτε, τάχ᾽ ἄν ποτε καὶ τίσις εἴη·
　　τόφρα γὰρ ἂν κατὰ ἄστυ ποτιπτυσσοίμεθα μύθῳ
　　χρήματ᾽ ἀπαιτίζοντες, ἕως κ᾽ ἀπὸ πάντα δοθείη·
　　νῦν δέ μοι ἀπρήκτους ὀδύνας ἐμβάλλετε θυμῷ."
80　　　ὣς φάτο χωόμενος, ποτὶ δὲ σκῆπτρον βάλε γαίῃ
　　δάκρυ᾽ ἀναπρήσας· οἶκτος δ᾽ ἕλε λαὸν ἅπαντα.
　　ἔνθ᾽ ἄλλοι μὲν πάντες ἀκὴν ἔσαν, οὐδέ τις ἔτλη
　　Τηλέμαχον μύθοισιν ἀμείψασθαι χαλεποῖσιν·
　　Ἀντίνοος δέ μιν οἶος ἀμειβόμενος προσέειπε·
85　　　"Τηλέμαχ᾽ ὑψαγόρη, μένος ἄσχετε, ποῖον ἔειπες
　　ἡμέας αἰσχύνων· ἐθέλοις δέ κε μῶμον ἀνάψαι.
　　σοὶ δ᾽ οὔ τι μνηστῆρες Ἀχαιῶν αἴτιοί εἰσιν,
　　ἀλλὰ φίλη μήτηρ, ἥ τοι πέρι κέρδεα οἶδεν.
　　ἤδη γὰρ τρίτον ἐστὶν ἔτος, τάχα δ᾽ εἶσι τέταρτον,
90　　ἐξ οὗ ἀτέμβει θυμὸν ἐνὶ στήθεσσιν Ἀχαιῶν.
　　πάντας μέν ῥ᾽ ἔλπει καὶ ὑπίσχεται ἀνδρὶ ἑκάστῳ
　　ἀγγελίας προϊεῖσα, νόος δέ οἱ ἄλλα μενοινᾷ.
　　ἡ δὲ δόλον τόνδ᾽ ἄλλον ἐνὶ φρεσὶ μερμήριξε·
　　στησαμένη μέγαν ἱστὸν ἐνὶ μεγάροισιν ὕφαινε,
95　　λεπτὸν καὶ περίμετρον· ἄφαρ δ᾽ ἡμῖν μετέειπε·
　　　"'κοῦροι ἐμοὶ μνηστῆρες, ἐπεὶ θάνε δῖος Ὀδυσσεύς,
　　μίμνετ᾽ ἐπειγόμενοι τὸν ἐμὸν γάμον, εἰς ὅ κε φᾶρος
　　ἐκτελέσω, μή μοι μεταμώνια νήματ᾽ ὄληται,
　　Λαέρτῃ ἥρωι ταφήιον, εἰς ὅτε κέν μιν
100　μοῖρ᾽ ὀλοὴ καθέλῃσι τανηλεγέος θανάτοιο,
　　μή τίς μοι κατὰ δῆμον Ἀχαιιάδων νεμεσήσῃ.
　　αἴ κεν ἄτερ σπείρου κεῖται πολλὰ κτεατίσσας.'

selves eat up my treasures and my flocks. If you were to
devour them, some day there might be recompense; we
should go up and down the city pressing our suit and asking
back our goods, until all was given back. But now past cure
are the woes you put upon my heart."

Thus he spoke in wrath, and dashed the staff down
upon the ground, bursting into tears; and pity seized all the
people. Then all the others kept silent, and no man had
the heart to answer Telemachus with angry words. Anti-
nous alone answered him, and said:

"Telemachus, lofty orator, dauntless of spirit, what a
thing you have said, putting us to shame; you would like to
fasten the blame upon us! But it is not the Achaean suitors
who are in any way at fault; it is your own mother, who is
clever above all women. For it is now the third year, and
the fourth will soon pass, since she has been cheating the
hearts of the Achaeans in their breasts. To all she offers
hopes, and has promises for each man, sending them
messages, but her mind is set on other things. And she
contrived in her heart this guileful thing also: she set up in
her halls a great web, and fell to weaving—fine of thread
was the web and very wide; and at once she spoke among
us:

"'Young men, my suitors, since noble Odysseus is dead,
be patient, though eager for my marriage, until I finish this
robe—I would not have my spinning come to naught—a
shroud for the hero Laertes, against the time when the
cruel fate of pitiless death shall strike him down; for fear
any of the Achaean women in the land should cast blame
upon me, if he were to lie without a shroud who had won
great possessions.'

"ὣς ἔφαθ', ἡμῖν δ' αὖτ' ἐπεπείθετο θυμὸς ἀγήνωρ.
ἔνθα καὶ ἠματίη μὲν ὑφαίνεσκεν μέγαν ἱστόν,
105   νύκτας δ' ἀλλύεσκεν, ἐπεὶ δαΐδας παραθεῖτο.
ὣς τρίετες μὲν ἔληθε δόλῳ καὶ ἔπειθεν Ἀχαιούς·
ἀλλ' ὅτε τέτρατον ἦλθεν ἔτος καὶ ἐπήλυθον ὧραι,
καὶ τότε δή τις ἔειπε γυναικῶν, ἣ σάφα ᾔδη,
καὶ τήν γ' ἀλλύουσαν ἐφεύρομεν ἀγλαὸν ἱστόν.
110   ὣς τὸ μὲν ἐξετέλεσσε καὶ οὐκ ἐθέλουσ' ὑπ' ἀνάγκης·
σοὶ δ' ὧδε μνηστῆρες ὑποκρίνονται, ἵν' εἰδῇς
αὐτὸς σῷ θυμῷ, εἰδῶσι δὲ πάντες Ἀχαιοί·
μητέρα σὴν ἀπόπεμψον, ἄνωχθι δέ μιν γαμέεσθαι
τῷ ὅτεῴ τε πατὴρ κέλεται καὶ ἀνδάνει αὐτῇ.
115   εἰ δ' ἔτ' ἀνιήσει γε πολὺν χρόνον υἷας Ἀχαιῶν,
τὰ φρονέουσ' ἀνὰ θυμόν, ὅ οἱ πέρι δῶκεν Ἀθήνη
ἔργα τ' ἐπίστασθαι περικαλλέα καὶ φρένας ἐσθλὰς
κέρδεά θ', οἷ' οὔ πώ τιν' ἀκούομεν οὐδὲ παλαιῶν,
τάων αἳ πάρος ἦσαν ἐυπλοκαμῖδες Ἀχαιαί,
120   Τυρώ τ' Ἀλκμήνη τε ἐυστέφανός τε Μυκήνη·
τάων οὔ τις ὁμοῖα νοήματα Πηνελοπείῃ
ᾔδη· ἀτὰρ μὲν τοῦτό γ' ἐναίσιμον οὐκ ἐνόησε.
τόφρα γὰρ οὖν βίοτόν τε τεὸν καὶ κτήματ' ἔδονται,
ὄφρα κε κείνη τοῦτον ἔχῃ νόον, ὅν τινά οἱ νῦν
125   ἐν στήθεσσι τιθεῖσι θεοί. μέγα μὲν κλέος αὐτῇ
ποιεῖτ', αὐτὰρ σοί γε ποθὴν πολέος βιότοιο.
ἡμεῖς δ' οὔτ' ἐπὶ ἔργα πάρος γ' ἴμεν οὔτε πῃ ἄλλῃ,
πρίν γ' αὐτὴν γήμασθαι Ἀχαιῶν ᾧ κ' ἐθέλῃσι."
    τὸν δ' αὖ Τηλέμαχος πεπνυμένος ἀντίον ηὔδα·
130   "Ἀντίνο', οὔ πως ἔστι δόμων ἀέκουσαν ἀπῶσαι

"So she spoke, and our proud hearts consented. Then day by day she would weave at the great web, but by night would unravel it, having had torches placed beside her. Thus for three years she by her craft kept the Achaeans from knowing, and beguiled them; but when the fourth year came as the seasons rolled on, then it was that one of her women, who knew all, told us, and we caught her unraveling the splendid web. So she finished it against her will, perforce. And here is the suitors' answer to you, that you yourself may know it in your heart, and that all the Achaeans may know: send away your mother, and command her to wed whomever her father bids and whoever is pleasing to her. But if she shall contiue for long to vex the sons of the Achaeans, possessing in her mind those advantages with which Athene has endowed her above other women, knowledge of beautiful handiwork, and good sense, and cleverness, such as we have never yet heard that any of the women of old knew, those fair-tressed Achaean women who lived long ago, Tyro and Alcmene and Mycene of the fair crown—of whom not one was like Penelope in shrewd device; yet this at least she devised improperly. For so long shall men devour your livelihood and your possessions, as long, that is, as she shall keep the counsel which the gods now put in her heart. Great fame she wins for herself, but for you regret for your abundant substance. As for us, we will go neither to our lands nor elsewhere, until she marries that one of the Achaeans whom she will."

Then wise Telemachus answered him and said: "Antinous, in no way can I thrust out of the house against her

ἥ μ' ἔτεχ', ἥ μ' ἔθρεψε· πατὴρ δ' ἐμὸς ἄλλοθι γαίης,
ζώει ὅ γ' ἦ τέθνηκε· κακὸν δέ με πόλλ' ἀποτίνειν
Ἰκαρίῳ, αἴ κ' αὐτὸς ἑκὼν ἀπὸ μητέρα πέμψω.
ἐκ γὰρ τοῦ πατρὸς κακὰ πείσομαι, ἄλλα δὲ δαίμων
135 δώσει, ἐπεὶ μήτηρ στυγερὰς ἀρήσετ' ἐρινῦς
οἴκου ἀπερχομένη· νέμεσις δέ μοι ἐξ ἀνθρώπων
ἔσσεται· ὣς οὐ τοῦτον ἐγώ ποτε μῦθον ἐνίψω.
ὑμέτερος δ' εἰ μὲν θυμὸς νεμεσίζεται αὐτῶν,
ἔξιτέ μοι μεγάρων, ἄλλας δ' ἀλεγύνετε δαῖτας
140 ὑμὰ κτήματ' ἔδοντες ἀμειβόμενοι κατὰ οἴκους.
εἰ δ' ὑμῖν δοκέει τόδε λωίτερον καὶ ἄμεινον
ἔμμεναι, ἀνδρὸς ἑνὸς βίοτον νήποινον ὀλέσθαι,
κείρετ'· ἐγὼ δὲ θεοὺς ἐπιβώσομαι αἰὲν ἐόντας,
αἴ κέ ποθι Ζεὺς δῷσι παλίντιτα ἔργα γενέσθαι.
145 νήποινοί κεν ἔπειτα δόμων ἔντοσθεν ὄλοισθε."
    ὣς φάτο Τηλέμαχος, τῷ δ' αἰετὼ εὐρύοπα Ζεὺς
ὑψόθεν ἐκ κορυφῆς ὄρεος προέηκε πέτεσθαι.
τὼ δ' ἕως μέν ῥ' ἐπέτοντο μετὰ πνοιῇς ἀνέμοιο
πλησίω ἀλλήλοισι τιταινομένω πτερύγεσσιν·
150 ἀλλ' ὅτε δὴ μέσσην ἀγορὴν πολύφημον ἱκέσθην,
ἔνθ' ἐπιδινηθέντε τιναξάσθην πτερὰ πυκνά,
ἐς δ' ἰδέτην πάντων κεφαλάς, ὄσσοντο δ' ὄλεθρον·
δρυψαμένω δ' ὀνύχεσσι παρειὰς ἀμφί τε δειρὰς
δεξιὼ ἤιξαν διά τ' οἰκία καὶ πόλιν αὐτῶν·
155 θάμβησαν δ' ὄρνιθας, ἐπεὶ ἴδον ὀφθαλμοῖσιν·
ὥρμηναν δ' ἀνὰ θυμὸν ἅ περ τελέεσθαι ἔμελλον.
τοῖσι δὲ καὶ μετέειπε γέρων ἥρως Ἁλιθέρσης
Μαστορίδης· ὁ γὰρ οἶος ὁμηλικίην ἐκέκαστο

will the mother that bore me and reared me; and, as for my father, he is in some other land, whether he is alive or dead. It would be unfair for me to pay back a great price to Icarius, as I must, if of my own will I send my mother away. For from her father's hand shall I suffer evil, and heaven will send other ills besides, for my mother as she leaves the house will invoke the dread Furies; and I shall have blame, too, from men. Therefore will I never speak this word. And for you, if your own conscience is offended at these things, leave my halls and prepare yourselves other feasts, eating your own stores and moving from house to house. But if this seems in your eyes to be a better and more profitable thing, that one man's livelihood should be ruined without atonement, waste on. But I will call upon the gods that are forever, in hopes Zeus may grant that deeds of requital take place. Without atonement then would you perish within my halls."

So spoke Telemachus, and in answer far-seeing Zeus sent forth two eagles, flying from on high, from a mountain peak. For a time they flew in the stream of the wind side by side with wings outspread; but when they reached the middle of the many-voiced assembly, then they wheeled about, flapping their wings rapidly, and down on the heads of all they looked, and death was in their glance. Then they tore with their talons one another's cheeks and necks on either side, and darted away to the right across the houses and the city of those who stood there. The people were seized with wonder at the birds when their eyes beheld them, and pondered in their hearts what was to come to pass. Then among them spoke the old hero Halitherses, son of Mastor, for he surpassed all men of his day in knowl-

ὄρνιθας γνῶναι καὶ ἐναίσιμα μυθήσασθαι·

160 ὅ σφιν ἐὺ φρονέων ἀγορήσατο καὶ μετέειπε·

"κέκλυτε δὴ νῦν μευ, Ἰθακήσιοι, ὅττι κεν εἴπω·
μνηστῆρσιν δὲ μάλιστα πιφαυσκόμενος τάδε εἴρω·
τοῖσιν γὰρ μέγα πῆμα κυλίνδεται· οὐ γὰρ Ὀδυσσεὺς
δὴν ἀπάνευθε φίλων ὧν ἔσσεται, ἀλλά που ἤδη

165 ἐγγὺς ἐὼν τοῖσδεσσι φόνον καὶ κῆρα φυτεύει
πάντεσσιν· πολέσιν δὲ καὶ ἄλλοισιν κακὸν ἔσται,
οἳ νεμόμεσθ' Ἰθάκην ἐυδείελον. ἀλλὰ πολὺ πρὶν
φραζώμεσθ', ὥς κεν καταπαύσομεν· οἱ δὲ καὶ αὐτοὶ
παυέσθων· καὶ γάρ σφιν ἄφαρ τόδε λώιόν ἐστιν.

170 οὐ γὰρ ἀπείρητος μαντεύομαι, ἀλλ' ἐὺ εἰδώς·
καὶ γὰρ κείνῳ φημὶ τελευτηθῆναι ἅπαντα,
ὥς οἱ ἐμυθεόμην, ὅτε Ἴλιον εἰσανέβαινον
Ἀργεῖοι, μετὰ δέ σφιν ἔβη πολύμητις Ὀδυσσεύς.
φῆν κακὰ πολλὰ παθόντ', ὀλέσαντ' ἄπο πάντας
ἑταίρους,

175 ἄγνωστον πάντεσσιν ἐεικοστῷ ἐνιαυτῷ
οἴκαδ' ἐλεύσεσθαι· τὰ δὲ δὴ νῦν πάντα τελεῖται."

τὸν δ' αὖτ' Εὐρύμαχος Πολύβου πάις ἀντίον ηὔδα·
"ὦ γέρον, εἰ δ' ἄγε νῦν μαντεύεο σοῖσι τέκεσσιν
οἴκαδ' ἰών, μή πού τι κακὸν πάσχωσιν ὀπίσσω·

180 ταῦτα δ' ἐγὼ σέο πολλὸν ἀμείνων μαντεύεσθαι.
ὄρνιθες δέ τε πολλοὶ ὑπ' αὐγὰς ἠελίοιο
φοιτῶσ', οὐδέ τε πάντες ἐναίσιμοι· αὐτὰρ Ὀδυσσεὺς
ὤλετο τῆλ', ὡς καὶ σὺ καταφθίσθαι σὺν ἐκείνῳ
ὤφελες. οὐκ ἂν τόσσα θεοπροπέων ἀγόρευες,

185 οὐδέ κε Τηλέμαχον κεχολωμένον ὧδ' ἀνιείης,

edge of birds and in uttering words of fate. He with good intent addressed their assembly and spoke among them:

"Hearken now to me, men of Ithaca, to the word that I shall say; and to the suitors especially do I declare and announce these things, since on them a great woe is rolling. For Odysseus shall not long be away from his friends, but even now, I doubt not, he is near, and is sowing slaughter and death for these men, one and all. Yes, and to many others of us also who dwell in clear-seen Ithaca will he be an evil. But long before that let us take thought how we may make an end of this—or rather let them of themselves make an end, for this is without doubt their better course. Not as one untried do I prophesy, but with sure knowledge. I declare that for that man all things are fulfilled just as I told him when the Argives embarked for Ilium and he went with them, resourceful Odysseus. I said that after suffering many ills and losing all his comrades he would come home in the twentieth year unknown to all; now all this is being brought to pass."

Then Eurymachus, son of Polybus, answered him and said: "Old man, up now, go home and prophesy to your children, for fear in days to come they suffer ill. In this matter I am better far at prophesying than you. Many birds there are that pass to and fro under the rays of the sun, and not all are fateful. As for Odysseus, he has perished far away, as you also should have perished with him. Then you would not have so much to say in your reading of signs, or be urging Telemachus on in his anger, looking for

σῷ οἴκῳ δῶρον ποτιδέγμενος, αἴ κε πόρῃσιν.
ἀλλ' ἔκ τοι ἐρέω, τὸ δὲ καὶ τετελεσμένον ἔσται·
αἴ κε νεώτερον ἄνδρα παλαιά τε πολλά τε εἰδὼς
παρφάμενος ἐπέεσσιν ἐποτρύνῃς χαλεπαίνειν,
190 αὐτῷ μέν οἱ πρῶτον ἀνιηρέστερον ἔσται,
πρῆξαι δ' ἔμπης οὔ τι δυνήσεται εἵνεκα τῶνδε·[1]
σοὶ δέ, γέρον, θωὴν ἐπιθήσομεν, ἥν κ' ἐνὶ θυμῷ
τίνων ἀσχάλλῃς· χαλεπὸν δέ τοι ἔσσεται ἄλγος.
Τηλεμάχῳ δ' ἐν πᾶσιν ἐγὼν ὑποθήσομαι αὐτός·
195 μητέρα ἥν ἐς πατρὸς ἀνωγέτω ἀπονέεσθαι·
οἱ δὲ γάμον τεύξουσι καὶ ἀρτυνέουσιν ἔεδνα
πολλὰ μάλ', ὅσσα ἔοικε φίλης ἐπὶ παιδὸς ἕπεσθαι.
οὐ γὰρ πρὶν παύσεσθαι ὀίομαι υἷας Ἀχαιῶν
μνηστύος ἀργαλέης, ἐπεὶ οὔ τινα δείδιμεν ἔμπης,
200 οὔτ' οὖν Τηλέμαχον μάλα περ πολύμυθον ἐόντα,
οὔτε θεοπροπίης ἐμπαζόμεθ', ἥν σύ, γεραιέ,
μυθέαι ἀκράαντον, ἀπεχθάνεαι δ' ἔτι μᾶλλον.
χρήματα δ' αὖτε κακῶς βεβρώσεται, οὐδέ ποτ' ἶσα
ἔσσεται, ὄφρα κεν ἥ γε διατρίβῃσιν Ἀχαιοὺς
205 ὃν γάμον· ἡμεῖς δ' αὖ ποτιδέγμενοι ἤματα πάντα
εἵνεκα τῆς ἀρετῆς ἐριδαίνομεν, οὐδὲ μετ' ἄλλας
ἐρχόμεθ', ἃς ἐπιεικὲς ὀπυιέμεν ἐστὶν ἑκάστῳ."
τὸν δ' αὖ Τηλέμαχος πεπνυμένος ἀντίον ηὔδα·
"Εὐρύμαχ' ἠδὲ καὶ ἄλλοι, ὅσοι μνηστῆρες ἀγαυοί,
210 ταῦτα μὲν οὐχ ὑμέας ἔτι λίσσομαι οὐδ' ἀγορεύω·
ἤδη γὰρ τὰ ἴσασι θεοὶ καὶ πάντες Ἀχαιοί.

---

[1] Line 191 is omitted in most MSS. Some of those which retain
it have οἶος ἀπ' ἄλλων instead of εἵνεκα τῶνδε.

a gift for your household, in hopes that he will provide it. But I will speak out to you, and this word shall be brought to pass. If you, wise in the wisdom of the old, shall beguile with your talk a younger man, and set him on to be angry, for him in the first place it shall be the more grievous, and secondly he will in no case be able to do anything because of these men here, while on you, old man, will we lay a fine which it will grieve your soul to pay, and bitter shall be your sorrow. And to Telemachus I myself, here among all, will offer this counsel. Let him bid his mother to go back to the house of her father, and they will prepare a wedding feast and make ready the gifts in their abundance, all that should go with a well-loved daughter. For before that, I think, the sons of the Achaeans will not cease from their grievous wooing, since in any case we fear no man—no, not Telemachus for all his many words—nor do we pay attention to any soothsaying which you, old man, may declare; it will fail of fulfillment, and you will be hated the more. Furthermore, his possessions shall be evilly devoured, nor shall requital ever be made, so long as she shall put off the Achaeans in the matter of her marriage. We on our part waiting here day after day continue our rivalry for that excellence of hers, and do not go after other women, whom each one might fitly wed."

Then wise Telemachus answered him: "Eurymachus and all you other lordly suitors, in this matter I entreat you no longer, nor speak of it, for now the gods know it, and all

ἀλλ' ἄγε μοι δότε νῆα θοὴν καὶ εἴκοσ' ἑταίρους,
οἵ κέ μοι ἔνθα καὶ ἔνθα διαπρήσσωσι κέλευθον.
εἶμι γὰρ ἐς Σπάρτην[1] τε καὶ ἐς Πύλον ἠμαθόεντα
215 νόστον πευσόμενος πατρὸς δὴν οἰχομένοιο,
ἤν τίς μοι εἴπῃσι βροτῶν ἢ ὄσσαν ἀκούσω
ἐκ Διός, ἥ τε μάλιστα φέρει κλέος ἀνθρώποισιν·
εἰ μέν κεν πατρὸς βίοτον καὶ νόστον ἀκούσω,
ἦ τ' ἄν, τρυχόμενός περ, ἔτι τλαίην ἐνιαυτόν·
220 εἰ δέ κε τεθνηῶτος ἀκούσω μηδ' ἔτ' ἐόντος,
νοστήσας δὴ ἔπειτα φίλην ἐς πατρίδα γαῖαν
σῆμά τέ οἱ χεύω καὶ ἐπὶ κτέρεα κτερεΐξω
πολλὰ μάλ', ὅσσα ἔοικε, καὶ ἀνέρι μητέρα δώσω."
  ἦ τοι ὅ γ' ὣς εἰπὼν κατ' ἄρ' ἕζετο, τοῖσι δ' ἀνέστη
225 Μέντωρ, ὅς ῥ' Ὀδυσῆος ἀμύμονος ἦεν ἑταῖρος,
καὶ οἱ ἰὼν ἐν νηυσὶν ἐπέτρεπεν οἶκον ἅπαντα,
πείθεσθαί τε γέροντι καὶ ἔμπεδα πάντα φυλάσσειν·
ὅ σφιν ἐὺ φρονέων ἀγορήσατο καὶ μετέειπεν·
  "κέκλυτε δὴ νῦν μευ, Ἰθακήσιοι, ὅττι κεν εἴπω·
230 μή τις ἔτι πρόφρων ἀγανὸς καὶ ἤπιος ἔστω
σκηπτοῦχος βασιλεύς, μηδὲ φρεσὶν αἴσιμα εἰδώς,
ἀλλ' αἰεὶ χαλεπός τ' εἴη καὶ αἴσυλα ῥέζοι·
ὡς οὔ τις μέμνηται Ὀδυσσῆος θείοιο
λαῶν οἷσιν ἄνασσε, πατὴρ δ' ὣς ἤπιος ἦεν.
235 ἀλλ' ἦ τοι μνηστῆρας ἀγήνορας οὔ τι μεγαίρω
ἔρδειν ἔργα βίαια κακορραφίῃσι νόοιο·
σφὰς γὰρ παρθέμενοι κεφαλὰς κατέδουσι βιαίως
οἶκον Ὀδυσσῆος, τὸν δ' οὐκέτι φασὶ νέεσθαι.
νῦν δ' ἄλλῳ δήμῳ νεμεσίζομαι, οἷον ἅπαντες

the Achaeans. But come, give me a swift ship and twenty comrades who will accomplish my journey for me as I go here and there. For I shall go to Sparta and to sandy Pylos to seek tidings of the return of my father who has been long gone, in case any mortal man may tell me, or I may hear a rumor from Zeus, which oftenest brings tidings to men. If I hear that my father is alive and coming home, in that case, though I am much afflicted, I could endure for yet a year. But if I hear that he is dead and gone, then I will return to my dear native land and heap up a mound for him, and over it pay funeral rites in abundance, as is due, and give my mother to a husband."

So saying he sat down, and among them rose Mentor, who was a comrade of flawless Odysseus. To him, on departing with his ships, Odysseus had given charge of all his house, that it should obey the old man and that he should keep all things safe. He with good intent addressed their assembly and spoke among them:

"Hearken now to me, men of Ithaca, to the word that I shall say. Never henceforth let sceptered king of his own good will be kind and gentle, nor let him heed due measure in his heart, but let him always be harsh and do injustice, seeing that no one remembers divine Odysseus of the people whose lord he was; yet gentle was he as a father. But truly I begrudge not the proud suitors that they do deeds of violence in the evil contrivings of their minds, for it is at the hazard of their own lives that they violently devour the house of Odysseus, who, they say, will no more return. Rather, it is with the rest of the people that I am

---

[1] Σπάρτην: Κρήτην Zenodotus; cf. 1.93

240 ἦσθ' ἄνεῳ, ἀτὰρ οὔ τι καθαπτόμενοι ἐπέεσσι
παύρους μνηστῆρας καταπαύετε[1] πολλοὶ ἐόντες."

τὸν δ' Εὐηνορίδης Λειώκριτος ἀντίον ηὔδα·
"Μέντορ ἀταρτηρέ, φρένας ἠλεέ, ποῖον ἔειπες
ἡμέας ὀτρύνων καταπαυέμεν. ἀργαλέον δὲ
245 ἀνδράσι καὶ πλεόνεσσι μαχήσασθαι περὶ δαιτί.
εἰ περ γάρ κ' Ὀδυσεὺς Ἰθακήσιος αὐτὸς ἐπελθὼν
δαινυμένους κατὰ δῶμα ἑὸν μνηστῆρας ἀγαυοὺς
ἐξελάσαι μεγάροιο μενοινήσει' ἐνὶ θυμῷ,
οὔ κέν οἱ κεχάροιτο γυνή, μάλα περ χατέουσα,
250 ἐλθόντ', ἀλλά κεν αὐτοῦ ἀεικέα πότμον ἐπίσποι,
εἰ πλεόνεσσι μάχοιτο·[2] σὺ δ' οὐ κατὰ μοῖραν ἔειπες.
ἀλλ' ἄγε, λαοὶ μὲν σκίδνασθ' ἐπὶ ἔργα ἕκαστος,
τούτῳ δ' ὀτρυνέει Μέντωρ ὁδὸν ἠδ' Ἁλιθέρσης,
οἵ τέ οἱ ἐξ ἀρχῆς πατρώιοί εἰσιν ἑταῖροι.
255 ἀλλ' ὀίω, καὶ δηθὰ καθήμενος ἀγγελιάων
πεύσεται εἰν Ἰθάκῃ, τελέει δ' ὁδὸν οὔ ποτε ταύτην."

ὣς ἄρ' ἐφώνησεν, λῦσεν δ' ἀγορὴν αἰψηρήν.
οἱ μὲν ἄρ' ἐσκίδναντο ἑὰ πρὸς δώμαθ' ἕκαστος,
μνηστῆρες δ' ἐς δώματ' ἴσαν θείου Ὀδυσῆος.

260 Τηλέμαχος δ' ἀπάνευθε κιὼν ἐπὶ θῖνα θαλάσσης,
χεῖρας νιψάμενος πολιῆς ἁλὸς εὔχετ' Ἀθήνῃ·
"κλῦθί μευ, ὃ χθιζὸς θεὸς ἤλυθες ἡμέτερον δῶ
καί μ' ἐν νηὶ κέλευσας ἐπ' ἠεροειδέα πόντον
νόστον πευσόμενον πατρὸς δὴν οἰχομένοιο

---

[1] καταπαύετε Rhianus: κατερύκετε
[2] πλεόνεσσι μάχοιτο: πλέονές οἱ ἕποιντο the scholia (Aristarchus?)

64

indignant, that you all sit thus in silence, and utter no word
of rebuke to make the suitors cease, though you are many
and they but few."

Then Leiocritus, son of Euenor, answered him: "Men-
tor, you mischief-maker, you wanderer in your wits, what
have you said, bidding men make us cease? It is a hard
thing even for a majority to fight about a dinner. For even
if Odysseus of Ithaca himself were to come, eager at heart
to drive out from his hall the lordly suitors who are feasting
in his house, then would his wife have no joy at his coming,
much though she longed for him, but on the spot he would
meet a shameful death, if he fought with men that outnum-
bered him.[a] Your words miss the mark. But come now, you
people, scatter, each one to his own lands. As for this fel-
low, Mentor and Halitherses will speed his journey, for
they are friends of his father's house from of old. But I
think that he will long sit listening to rumors here in Ithaca;
he will never accomplish this journey."

So he spoke, and broke up the assembly, brief as it was.
They then scattered, each one to his own house; and the
suitors went to the house of divine Odysseus.

But Telemachus went apart to the shore of the sea, and
having washed his hands in the gray seawater, prayed to
Athene: "Hear me, you who came yesterday as a god to our
house, and bade me go in a ship over the misty deep to
seek tidings of the return of my father, who has long been

[a] Leiocritus appears to be making two points: first, that even
though the suitors' opponents are in the majority they will have to
fight to oust the suitors; and, second, that the question who is to
have Penelope is not one to be decided by superior numbers. If it
were, the claim of Odysseus himself, should he return, could be
ignored. D.

265 ἔρχεσθαι· τὰ δὲ πάντα διατρίβουσιν Ἀχαιοί,
μνηστῆρες δὲ μάλιστα κακῶς ὑπερηνορέοντες."
ὣς ἔφατ' εὐχόμενος, σχεδόθεν δέ οἱ ἦλθεν Ἀθήνη,
Μέντορι εἰδομένη ἠμὲν δέμας ἠδὲ καὶ αὐδήν,
καί μιν φωνήσασ' ἔπεα πτερόεντα προσηύδα·
270 "Τηλέμαχ', οὐδ' ὄπιθεν κακὸς ἔσσεαι οὐδ' ἀνοήμων,
εἰ δή τοι σοῦ πατρὸς ἐνέστακται μένος ἠύ,
οἷος κεῖνος ἔην τελέσαι ἔργον τε ἔπος τε·
οὔ τοι ἔπειθ' ἁλίη ὁδὸς ἔσσεται οὐδ' ἀτέλεστος.
εἰ δ' οὐ κείνου γ' ἐσσὶ γόνος καὶ Πηνελοπείης,
275 οὐ σέ γ' ἔπειτα ἔολπα τελευτήσειν, ἃ μενοινᾷς.
παῦροι γάρ τοι παῖδες ὁμοῖοι πατρὶ πέλονται,
οἱ πλέονες κακίους, παῦροι δέ τε πατρὸς ἀρείους.
ἀλλ' ἐπεὶ οὐδ' ὄπιθεν κακὸς ἔσσεαι οὐδ' ἀνοήμων,
οὐδέ σε πάγχυ γε μῆτις Ὀδυσσῆος προλέλοιπεν,
280 ἐλπωρή τοι ἔπειτα τελευτῆσαι τάδε ἔργα.
τῶ νῦν μνηστήρων μὲν ἔα βουλήν τε νόον τε
ἀφραδέων, ἐπεὶ οὔ τι νοήμονες οὐδὲ δίκαιοι·
οὐδέ τι ἴσασιν θάνατον καὶ κῆρα μέλαιναν,
ὃς δή σφι σχεδόν ἐστιν, ἐπ' ἤματι πάντας ὀλέσθαι.
285 σοὶ δ' ὁδὸς οὐκέτι δηρὸν ἀπέσσεται ἣν σὺ μενοινᾷς·
τοῖος γάρ τοι ἑταῖρος ἐγὼ πατρώιός εἰμι,
ὅς τοι νῆα θοὴν στελέω καὶ ἅμ' ἕψομαι αὐτός.
ἀλλὰ σὺ μὲν πρὸς δώματ' ἰὼν μνηστήρσιν ὁμίλει,
ὅπλισσόν τ' ἤια καὶ ἄγγεσιν ἄρσον ἅπαντα,
290 οἶνον ἐν ἀμφιφορεῦσι, καὶ ἄλφιτα, μυελὸν ἀνδρῶν,
δέρμασιν ἐν πυκινοῖσιν· ἐγὼ δ' ἀνὰ δῆμον ἑταίρους
αἶψ' ἐθελοντῆρας συλλέξομαι. εἰσὶ δὲ νῆες

gone. All this the Achaeans hinder, but the suitors most of
all in their evil insolence."

So he spoke in prayer, and Athene drew near to him in
the likeness of Mentor, both in form and in voice; and she
spoke, and addressed him with winged words:

"Telemachus, hereafter too you shall not be a base man,
or a witless one, if indeed your father's good courage has
been instilled in you, such a man was he to fulfill both deed
and word. So then shall this journey of yours be neither
vain nor unfulfilled. But if you are not the son of him and
of Penelope, then I have no hope that you will accomplish
your desire. Few sons indeed are like their fathers; most
are worse, and those better than their fathers are few. But
since hereafter too you shall not be a base man, or witless,
nor has the wisdom of Odysseus wholly failed you, there is
good hope that you will accomplish this task. Now there-
fore put from your mind the suitors' plans and inten-
tions—fools, for they are in no way either prudent or just,
nor are they at all aware of death and black fate, which in
truth is near at hand for them, to die all on one day. But
for yourself, the journey on which your heart is set shall not
be long delayed, so true a friend of your father's house am
I, who will equip for you a swift ship, and myself go with
you. But go now to the house and join the company of the
suitors; make ready stores, and stow them all in vessels—
wine in jars, and barley meal, the marrow of men, in stout
skins; meanwhile I, going through the town, will quickly
gather a crew of volunteers. And ships there are in abun-

πολλαὶ ἐν ἀμφιάλῳ Ἰθάκῃ, νέαι ἠδὲ παλαιαί·
τάων μέν τοι ἐγὼν ἐπιόψομαι ἥ τις ἀρίστη,
295   ὦκα δ' ἐφοπλίσσαντες ἐνήσομεν εὐρέι πόντῳ."
    ὣς φάτ' Ἀθηναίη κούρη Διός· οὐδ' ἄρ' ἔτι δὴν
Τηλέμαχος παρέμιμνεν, ἐπεὶ θεοῦ ἔκλυεν αὐδήν.
βῆ δ' ἰέναι πρὸς δῶμα, φίλον τετιημένος ἦτορ,
εὗρε δ' ἄρα μνηστῆρας ἀγήνορας ἐν μεγάροισιν,
300   αἶγας ἀνιεμένους σιάλους θ' εὕοντας ἐν αὐλῇ.
Ἀντίνοος δ' ἰθὺς γελάσας κίε Τηλεμάχοιο,
ἔν τ' ἄρα οἱ φῦ χειρί, ἔπος τ' ἔφατ' ἔκ τ' ὀνόμαζε·
    "Τηλέμαχ' ὑψαγόρη, μένος ἄσχετε, μή τί τοι ἄλλο
ἐν στήθεσσι κακὸν μελέτω ἔργον τε ἔπος τε,
305   ἀλλά μοι[1] ἐσθιέμεν καὶ πινέμεν, ὡς τὸ πάρος περ.
ταῦτα δέ τοι μάλα πάντα τελευτήσουσιν Ἀχαιοί,
νῆα καὶ ἐξαίτους ἐρέτας, ἵνα θᾶσσον ἵκηαι
ἐς Πύλον ἠγαθέην μετ' ἀγαυοῦ πατρὸς ἀκουήν."
    τὸν δ' αὖ Τηλέμαχος πεπνυμένος ἀντίον ηὔδα·
310   "Ἀντίνο', οὔ πως ἔστιν ὑπερφιάλοισι μεθ' ὑμῖν
δαίνυσθαί τ' ἀκέοντα[2] καὶ εὐφραίνεσθαι ἔκηλον.
ἦ οὐχ ἅλις ὡς τὸ πάροιθεν ἐκείρετε πολλὰ καὶ ἐσθλὰ
κτήματ' ἐμά, μνηστῆρες, ἐγὼ δ' ἔτι νήπιος ἦα;
νῦν δ' ὅτε δὴ μέγας εἰμὶ καὶ ἄλλων μῦθον ἀκούων
315   πυνθάνομαι, καὶ δή μοι ἀέξεται ἔνδοθι θυμός,
πειρήσω, ὥς κ' ὕμμι κακὰς ἐπὶ κῆρας ἰήλω,
ἠὲ Πύλονδ' ἐλθών, ἢ αὐτοῦ τῷδ' ἐνὶ δήμῳ.
εἶμι μέν, οὐδ' ἁλίη ὁδὸς ἔσσεται ἣν ἀγορεύω,

____

[1] μοι: μάλ'
[2] ἀκέοντα: ἀέκοντα Rhianus

68

dance in seagirt Ithaca, both new and old; of these will I choose out for you the one that is best, and quickly will we make her ready and launch her on the broad deep."

So spoke Athene, daughter of Zeus, nor did Telemachus tarry long after he had heard the voice of the goddess, but went his way to the house, his heart troubled within him. He found there the proud suitors in the halls, flaying goats and singeing swine in the court. And Antinous with a laugh came straight to Telemachus, and clasped his hand, and spoke, and addressed[a] him:

"Telemachus, lofty orator, dauntless in courage, let no longer any evil deed or word be in your heart. No, I urge you, eat and drink just as before. All these things the Achaeans will surely provide for you—the ship and chosen oarsmen—that with speed you may go to sacred Pylos to seek for tidings of your lordly father."

Then wise Telemachus answered him: "Antinous, in no way is it possible for me in your arrogant company to enjoy the feasting quietly and to make merry with an easy mind. Is it not enough, you suitors, that in time past you wasted many fine possessions of mine, while I was still a child? But now that I am grown, and gain knowledge by hearing the words of others, and my spirit indeed swells within me, I will try how I may fasten upon you fates of evil death, either going to Pylos or here in this land. For go I will, nor shall the journey be in vain of which I speak, though I

---

[a] The verb ὀνομάζω is most commonly, as here, followed by the name of the person addressed, or by something equivalent to it. In a number of passages, however, the word is freely used, and it has seemed best to adapt a rendering which suits all, or nearly all, cases. M.

ἔμπορος· οὐ γὰρ νηὸς ἐπήβολος οὐδ' ἐρετάων

320 γίγνομαι· ὥς νύ που ὔμμιν ἐείσατο κέρδιον εἶναι."

ἦ ῥα, καὶ ἐκ χειρὸς χεῖρα σπάσατ' Ἀντινόοιο

ῥεῖα· μνηστῆρες δὲ δόμον κάτα δαῖτα πένοντο.[1]

οἱ δ' ἐπελώβευον καὶ ἐκερτόμεον ἐπέεσσιν.

ὧδε δέ τις εἴπεσκε νέων ὑπερηνορεόντων·

325 "ἦ μάλα Τηλέμαχος φόνον ἡμῖν μερμηρίζει.

ἤ τινας ἐκ Πύλου ἄξει ἀμύντορας ἠμαθόεντος

ἢ ὅ γε καὶ Σπάρτηθεν, ἐπεί νύ περ ἵεται αἰνῶς·

ἠὲ καὶ εἰς Ἐφύρην ἐθέλει, πίειραν ἄρουραν,

ἐλθεῖν, ὄφρ' ἔνθεν θυμοφθόρα φάρμακ' ἐνείκῃ,

330 ἐν δὲ βάλῃ κρητῆρι καὶ ἡμέας πάντας ὀλέσσῃ."

ἄλλος δ' αὖτ' εἴπεσκε νέων ὑπερηνορεόντων·

"τίς δ' οἶδ', εἴ κε καὶ αὐτὸς ἰὼν κοίλης ἐπὶ νηὸς

τῆλε φίλων ἀπόληται ἀλώμενος ὥς περ Ὀδυσσεύς;

οὕτω κεν καὶ μᾶλλον ὀφέλλειεν πόνον ἄμμιν·

335 κτήματα γάρ κεν πάντα δασαίμεθα, οἰκία δ' αὖτε

τούτου μητέρι δοῖμεν ἔχειν ἠδ' ὅς τις ὀπυίοι."

ὣς φάν, ὁ δ' ὑψόροφον θάλαμον κατεβήσετο πατρὸς

εὐρύν, ὅθι νητὸς χρυσὸς καὶ χαλκὸς ἔκειτο

ἐσθής τ' ἐν χηλοῖσιν ἅλις τ' εὐῶδες ἔλαιον·

340 ἐν δὲ πίθοι οἴνοιο παλαιοῦ ἡδυπότοιο

ἕστασαν, ἄκρητον θεῖον ποτὸν ἐντὸς ἔχοντες,

ἑξείης ποτὶ τοῖχον ἀρηρότες, εἴ ποτ' Ὀδυσσεὺς

οἴκαδε νοστήσειε καὶ ἄλγεα πολλὰ μογήσας.

κλησταὶ δ' ἔπεσαν σανίδες πυκινῶς ἀραρυῖαι,

345 δικλίδες· ἐν δὲ γυνὴ ταμίη νύκτας τε καὶ ἦμαρ

ἔσχ', ἣ πάντ' ἐφύλασσε νόου πολυϊδρείῃσιν,

voyage in another's ship, since I may not be master of ship or oarsmen. That way, I suppose, seemed more to your profit."

He spoke, and drew his hand from the hand of Antinous easily, and the suitors were busy with the feast throughout the hall. They mocked and jeered at him in their talk; and thus would one of the proud youths speak:

"Telemachus is planning our murder for certain. He will bring men to aid him from sandy Pylos or even from Sparta, so terribly is he set upon it. Or he means to go to Ephyre, that rich land, to bring from thence deadly drugs, that he may cast them in the wine bowl and destroy us all."

And again another of the proud youths would say: "Who knows but he himself as he goes on the hollow ship may perish wandering far from his friends, even as Odysseus did? So would he cause us yet more labor; for we should have to divide all his possessions, and his house we should give to his mother to possess, and to him who should wed her."

So they spoke, but Telemachus went down to the high-roofed treasure chamber of his father, a wide room where gold and bronze lay piled, and clothes in chests, and stores of fragrant oil. There, too, stood great jars of wine, old and sweet, holding within them an unmixed divine drink, and ranged in order along the wall, if ever Odysseus should return home even after many grievous toils. Shut were the double doors, close-fitted; and there both night and day a stewardess remained, who guarded it all in wisdom of

---

[1] Line 322 was rejected by Aristophanes and Aristarchus.

Εὐρύκλει᾽, Ὦπος θυγάτηρ Πεισηνορίδαο.
τὴν τότε Τηλέμαχος προσέφη θαλαμόνδε καλέσσας ·
"μαῖ᾽, ἄγε δή μοι οἶνον ἐν ἀμφιφορεῦσιν ἄφυσσον
350 ἡδύν, ὅτις μετὰ τὸν λαρώτατος ὃν σὺ φυλάσσεις
κεῖνον ὀιομένη τὸν κάμμορον, εἴ ποθεν ἔλθοι
διογενὴς Ὀδυσεὺς θάνατον καὶ κῆρας ἀλύξας.
δώδεκα δ᾽ ἔμπλησον καὶ πώμασιν ἄρσον ἅπαντας.
ἐν δέ μοι ἄλφιτα χεῦον ἐυρραφέεσσι δοροῖσιν ·
355 εἴκοσι δ᾽ ἔστω μέτρα μυληφάτου ἀλφίτου ἀκτῆς.
αὐτὴ δ᾽ οἴη ἴσθι · τὰ δ᾽ ἀθρόα πάντα τετύχθω ·
ἑσπέριος γὰρ ἐγὼν αἱρήσομαι, ὁππότε κεν δὴ
μήτηρ εἰς ὑπερῷ᾽ ἀναβῇ κοίτου τε μέδηται.
εἶμι γὰρ ἐς Σπάρτην τε καὶ ἐς Πύλον ἠμαθόεντα
360 νόστον πευσόμενος πατρὸς φίλου, ἤν που ἀκούσω."
ὣς φάτο, κώκυσεν δὲ φίλη τροφὸς Εὐρύκλεια,
καί ῥ᾽ ὀλοφυρομένη ἔπεα πτερόεντα προσηύδα ·
"τίπτε δέ τοι, φίλε τέκνον, ἐνὶ φρεσὶ τοῦτο νόημα
ἔπλετο; πῇ δ᾽ ἐθέλεις ἰέναι πολλὴν ἐπὶ γαῖαν
365 μοῦνος ἐὼν ἀγαπητός; ὁ δ᾽ ὤλετο τηλόθι πάτρης
διογενὴς Ὀδυσεὺς ἀλλογνώτῳ ἐνὶ δήμῳ.
οἱ δέ τοι αὐτίκ᾽ ἰόντι κακὰ φράσσονται ὀπίσσω,
ὥς κε δόλῳ φθίῃς, τάδε δ᾽ αὐτοὶ πάντα δάσονται.
ἀλλὰ μέν᾽ αὖθ᾽ ἐπὶ σοῖσι καθήμενος · οὐδέ τί σε χρὴ
370 πόντον ἐπ᾽ ἀτρύγετον κακὰ πάσχειν οὐδ᾽ ἀλάλησθαι."
τὴν δ᾽ αὖ Τηλέμαχος πεπνυμένος ἀντίον ηὔδα ·
"θάρσει, μαῖ᾽, ἐπεὶ οὔ τοι ἄνευ θεοῦ ἥδε γε βουλή.
ἀλλ᾽ ὄμοσον μὴ μητρὶ φίλῃ τάδε μυθήσασθαι,
πρίν γ᾽ ὅτ᾽ ἂν ἑνδεκάτη τε δυωδεκάτη τε γένηται,

mind, Eurycleia, daughter of Ops, son of Peisenor. To her now Telemachus, when he had called her to the treasure chamber, spoke, and said:

"Nurse, draw me off wine in jars, sweet wine which is the choicest next to that which you save expecting that ill-fated one, if by chance Zeus-born Odysseus may come I know not whence, having escaped from death and the fates. Fill twelve jars and fit them all with covers, and pour me barley meal into well-sewn skins, and let there be twenty measures of ground barley meal. But keep knowledge of this to yourself, and have all these things brought together; for at evening I will fetch them, when my mother goes to her upper chamber on her way to bed. For I am going to Sparta and sandy Pylos to seek tidings of the return of my staunch father, in case I may hear any."

So he spoke, and the staunch nurse, Eurycleia, uttered a shrill cry, and lamenting spoke to him winged words: "Ah, dear child, how has this thought come into your mind? Whither do you intend to go over the wide earth, you who are an only son and well-beloved? But he has perished far from his country, the Zeus-born Odysseus, in a strange land; and these men, so soon as you are gone, will devise evil for you hereafter, that you may perish by guile, and themselves divide all these possessions. No, stay here in charge of what is yours; you have no need to suffer ills on the barren sea and go wandering."

Then wise Telemachus answered her: "Take heart, nurse, for not without divine sanction is this plan. But swear to tell nothing of this to my mother until the eleventh or twelfth day shall come, or until she shall herself

375 ἢ αὐτὴν ποθέσαι καὶ ἀφορμηθέντος ἀκοῦσαι,
ὡς ἂν μὴ κλαίουσα κατὰ χρόα καλὸν ἰάπτῃ."
ὣς ἄρ' ἔφη, γρῆυς δὲ θεῶν μέγαν ὅρκον ἀπώμνυ.
αὐτὰρ ἐπεί ῥ' ὄμοσέν τε τελεύτησέν τε τὸν ὅρκον,
αὐτίκ' ἔπειτά οἱ οἶνον ἐν ἀμφιφορεῦσιν ἄφυσσεν,
380 ἐν δέ οἱ ἄλφιτα χεῦεν ἐϋρραφέεσσι δοροῖσι.
Τηλέμαχος δ' ἐς δώματ' ἰὼν μνηστῆρσιν ὁμίλει.
ἔνθ' αὖτ' ἄλλ' ἐνόησε θεά, γλαυκῶπις Ἀθήνη.
Τηλεμάχῳ ἐϊκυῖα κατὰ πτόλιν ᾤχετο πάντῃ,
καί ῥα ἑκάστῳ φωτὶ παρισταμένη φάτο μῦθον,
385 ἑσπερίους δ' ἐπὶ νῆα θοὴν ἀγέρεσθαι ἀνώγει.
ἡ δ' αὖτε Φρονίοιο Νοήμονα φαίδιμον υἱὸν
ᾔτεε νῆα θοήν· ὁ δέ οἱ πρόφρων ὑπέδεκτο.
δύσετό τ' ἠέλιος σκιόωντό τε πᾶσαι ἀγυιαί,
καὶ τότε νῆα θοὴν ἅλαδ' εἴρυσε, πάντα δ' ἐν αὐτῇ
390 ὅπλ' ἐτίθει, τά τε νῆες ἐΰσσελμοι φορέουσι.
στῆσε δ' ἐπ' ἐσχατιῇ λιμένος, περὶ δ' ἐσθλοὶ ἑταῖροι
ἀθρόοι ἠγερέθοντο· θεὰ δ' ὤτρυνεν ἕκαστον.
ἔνθ' αὖτ' ἄλλ' ἐνόησε θεά, γλαυκῶπις Ἀθήνη.
βῆ ῥ' ἰέναι πρὸς δώματ' Ὀδυσσῆος θείοιο·
395 ἔνθα μνηστήρεσσιν ἐπὶ γλυκὺν ὕπνον ἔχευε,
πλάζε δὲ πίνοντας, χειρῶν δ' ἔκβαλλε κύπελλα.
οἱ δ' εὕδειν ὤρνυντο κατὰ πτόλιν, οὐδ' ἄρ' ἔτι δὴν
ἥατ', ἐπεί σφισιν ὕπνος ἐπὶ βλεφάροισιν ἔπιπτεν.
αὐτὰρ Τηλέμαχον προσέφη γλαυκῶπις Ἀθήνη
400 ἐκπροκαλεσσαμένη μεγάρων ἐῢ ναιεταόντων,
Μέντορι εἰδομένη ἠμὲν δέμας ἠδὲ καὶ αὐδήν·
"Τηλέμαχ', ἤδη μέν τοι ἐϋκνήμιδες ἑταῖροι

miss me and hear that I am gone, that she may not mar her fair flesh with weeping."

So he spoke, and the old woman swore a great oath by the gods to say nothing. But when she had sworn and made an end of the oath, at once she drew for him wine in jars, and poured barley meal into well-sewn skins; and Telemachus went to the hall and joined the company of the suitors.

Then the goddess, flashing-eyed Athene, had another thought. In the likeness of Telemachus she went everywhere throughout the city, and to each of the men she drew near and spoke her word, bidding them gather at evening beside the swift ship. Then, of Noemon, the glorious son of Phronius, she asked a swift ship, and he promised it to her with a ready heart.

Now the sun set and all the ways grew dark. Then she drew the swift ship to the sea and put in it all the gear that well-benched ships carry. And she moored it at the mouth of the harbor, and round about it the noble company was gathered together, and the goddess heartened each man.

Then the goddess, flashing-eyed Athene, had another thought. She went her way to the house of divine Odysseus, and there shed sweet sleep upon the suitors, and made their minds wander as they drank, and from their hands she knocked the cups. They rose to go to their rest throughout the city, and not for long remained seated, for sleep was falling upon their eyelids. But to Telemachus spoke flashing-eyed Athene, calling him forth before the stately hall, having likened herself to Mentor both in form and in voice:

"Telemachus, already your well-greaved comrades sit at

ἥατ' ἐπήρετμοι τὴν σὴν ποτιδέγμενοι ὁρμήν·
ἀλλ' ἴομεν, μὴ δηθὰ διατρίβωμεν ὁδοῖο."

405 ὣς ἄρα φωνήσασ' ἡγήσατο Παλλὰς Ἀθήνη
καρπαλίμως· ὁ δ' ἔπειτα μετ' ἴχνια βαῖνε θεοῖο.
αὐτὰρ ἐπεί ῥ' ἐπὶ νῆα κατήλυθον ἠδὲ θάλασσαν,
εὗρον ἔπειτ' ἐπὶ θινὶ κάρη κομόωντας ἑταίρους.
τοῖσι δὲ καὶ μετέειφ' ἱερὴ ἲς Τηλεμάχοιο·

410 "δεῦτε, φίλοι, ἤια φερώμεθα· πάντα γὰρ ἤδη
ἁθρό' ἐνὶ μεγάρῳ. μήτηρ δ' ἐμὴ οὔ τι πέπυσται,
οὐδ' ἄλλαι δμωαί, μία δ' οἴη μῦθον ἄκουσεν."
ὣς ἄρα φωνήσας ἡγήσατο, τοὶ δ' ἅμ' ἕποντο.
οἱ δ' ἄρα πάντα φέροντες ἐυσσέλμῳ ἐπὶ νηὶ

415 κάτθεσαν, ὡς ἐκέλευσεν Ὀδυσσῆος φίλος υἱός.
ἂν δ' ἄρα Τηλέμαχος νηὸς βαῖν', ἦρχε δ' Ἀθήνη,
νηὶ δ' ἐνὶ πρυμνῇ κατ' ἄρ' ἕζετο· ἄγχι δ' ἄρ' αὐτῆς
ἕζετο Τηλέμαχος. τοὶ δὲ πρυμνήσι' ἔλυσαν,
ἂν δὲ καὶ αὐτοὶ βάντες ἐπὶ κληῖσι καθῖζον.

420 τοῖσιν δ' ἴκμενον οὖρον ἵει γλαυκῶπις Ἀθήνη,
ἀκραῆ Ζέφυρον, κελάδοντ' ἐπὶ οἴνοπα πόντον.
Τηλέμαχος δ' ἑτάροισιν ἐποτρύνας ἐκέλευσεν
ὅπλων ἅπτεσθαι· τοὶ δ' ὀτρύνοντος ἄκουσαν.

---

[a] It is hard to determine with exactness to what extent the original meaning "strong" survives in the uses of ἱερός. It may be that in ἱερὴ ἲς (2.409, etc.) and ἱερὸν μένος (7.167, etc.) we should see a reference to the sanctity attaching to the royal station. M.

Subsequent scholarship has tended to confirm the justice of Murray's observation, particularly the suggestion that the phrases

the oar and await your setting out. Come, let us go, that we may not long delay the journey."

So saying, Pallas Athene led the way quickly, and he followed in the footsteps of the goddess. And now, when they had come down to the ship and to the sea, they found on shore their long-haired comrades, and the sacred strength[a] of Telemachus spoke among them:

"Come, friends, let us fetch the stores, for all are now gathered together in the hall. My mother knows nothing of this, nor the handmaids either: one only heard my word."

Thus saying, he led the way, and they went along with him. so they brought and stowed everything in the well-benched ship, as the staunch son of Odysseus ordered. Then on board the ship stepped Telemachus, and Athene went before him and sat down in the stern of the ship, and near her sat Telemachus, while the men loosed the stern cables and themselves stepped on board, and sat down upon the benches. And flashing-eyed Athene sent them a favorable wind, a strong-blowing West Wind that sang over the wine-dark sea. And Telemachus called to his men, and told them to lay hold of the tackling, and they hearkened to

have a connection with royal station. They may in fact have originated in Mycenean court titles. In the *Odyssey* they are used almost exclusively of Telemachus (7 times) and of Alcinous, king of the Phaeacians (7 times), in the latter case often, I suspect, with a certain irony. The one case which is used of someone other than Telemachus or Alcinous is ἱερὸν μένος ᾿Αντινόοιο at 18.34, where the suitor Antinous is assuming command most obnoxiously in Odysseus' house in Odysseus' presence. The similarity of the names Alcinous and Antinous may also have something to do with the case. D.

ἱστὸν δ' εἰλάτινον κοίλης ἔντοσθε μεσόδμης
425 στῆσαν ἀείραντες, κατὰ δὲ προτόνοισιν ἔδησαν,
ἕλκον δ' ἱστία λευκὰ ἐυστρέπτοισι βοεῦσιν.
ἔπρησεν δ' ἄνεμος μέσον ἱστίον, ἀμφὶ δὲ κῦμα
στείρῃ πορφύρεον μεγάλ' ἴαχε νηὸς ἰούσης·
ἡ δ' ἔθεεν κατὰ κῦμα διαπρήσσουσα κέλευθον.
430 δησάμενοι δ' ἄρα ὅπλα θοὴν ἀνὰ νῆα μέλαιναν
στήσαντο κρητῆρας ἐπιστεφέας οἴνοιο,
λεῖβον δ' ἀθανάτοισι θεοῖς αἰειγενέτῃσιν,
ἐκ πάντων δὲ μάλιστα Διὸς γλαυκώπιδι κούρῃ.
παννυχίη μέν ῥ' ἥ γε καὶ ἠῶ πεῖρε κέλευθον.

his call. The mast of fir they raised and set in the hollow socket, and made it fast with forestays, and hauled up the white sail with twisted thongs of oxhide. So the wind filled the belly of the sail, and the dark wave sang loudly about the stem of the ship as she went, and she sped over the wave accomplishing her way. Then, when they had made the tackling fast in the swift black ship, they set forth bowls brimful of wine, and poured libations to the immortal gods that are forever, and chiefest of all to the flashing-eyed daughter of Zeus. So all night long and through the dawn the ship cleft her way.

Γ

Ἥλιος δ' ἀνόρουσε, λιπὼν περικαλλέα λίμνην,
οὐρανὸν ἐς πολύχαλκον, ἵν' ἀθανάτοισι φαείνοι
καὶ θνητοῖσι βροτοῖσιν ἐπὶ ζείδωρον ἄρουραν·
οἱ δὲ Πύλον, Νηλῆος ἐυκτίμενον πτολίεθρον,
5   ἷξον· τοὶ δ' ἐπὶ θινὶ θαλάσσης ἱερὰ ῥέζον,
ταύρους παμμέλανας, ἐνοσίχθονι κυανοχαίτῃ.
ἐννέα δ' ἕδραι ἔσαν, πεντακόσιοι δ' ἐν ἑκάστῃ
ἥατο καὶ προύχοντο ἑκάστοθι ἐννέα ταύρους.
εὖθ' οἱ σπλάγχνα πάσαντο, θεῷ δ' ἐπὶ μηρί' ἔκαιον,
10   οἱ δ' ἰθὺς κατάγοντο ἰδ' ἱστία νηὸς ἐίσης
στεῖλαν ἀείραντες, τὴν δ' ὥρμισαν, ἐκ δ' ἔβαν αὐτοί·
ἐκ δ' ἄρα Τηλέμαχος νηὸς βαῖν', ἦρχε δ' Ἀθήνη.
τὸν προτέρη προσέειπε θεά, γλαυκῶπις Ἀθήνη·
"Τηλέμαχ', οὐ μέν σε χρὴ ἔτ' αἰδοῦς, οὐδ' ἠβαιόν·
15   τοὔνεκα γὰρ καὶ πόντον ἐπέπλως, ὄφρα πύθηαι
πατρός, ὅπου κύθε γαῖα καὶ ὅν τινα πότμον ἐπέσπεν.
ἀλλ' ἄγε νῦν ἰθὺς κίε Νέστορος ἱπποδάμοιο·
εἴδομεν ἥν τινα μῆτιν ἐνὶ στήθεσσι κέκευθε.
λίσσεσθαι δέ μιν αὐτός, ὅπως νημερτέα εἴπῃ·
20   ψεῦδος δ' οὐκ ἐρέει· μάλα γὰρ πεπνυμένος ἐστί."
τὴν δ' αὖ Τηλέμαχος πεπνυμένος ἀντίον ηὔδα·
"Μέντορ, πῶς τ' ἄρ' ἴω; πῶς τ' ἄρ προσπτύξομαι αὐτόν;

BOOK 3

And now the sun, leaving the beauteous water surface, sprang up into the brazen heaven to give light to the immortals and to mortal men on the earth, the giver of grain; and they came to Pylos, the well-ordered citadel of Neleus. Here the townsfolk on the shore of the sea were offering sacrifice of black bulls to the dark-haired Earth-shaker. Nine companies there were, and five hundred men sat in each, and in each they held nine bulls ready for sacrifice. Now when they had tasted the inner parts and were burning the thigh pieces to the god, the others put straight in to the shore, and hauled up and furled the sail of the shapely ship, and moored her, and themselves stepped forth. Forth too from the ship stepped Telemachus, and Athene led the way. And the goddess, flashing-eyed Athene, spoke first to him and said:

"Telemachus, no longer need you feel shame, no, not a whit. For to this end have you sailed over the sea, to seek tidings of your father—where the earth covered him, and what fate he met. But come now, go straight to Nestor, tamer of horses; let us learn what counsel he keeps hid in his breast. Beseech him yourself that he may tell you the very truth. A lie will he not utter, for he is wise indeed."

Then wise Telemachus answered her: "Mentor, how shall I go, and how shall I greet him? I am as yet all

οὐδέ τί πω μύθοισι πεπείρημαι πυκινοῖσιν·
αἰδὼς δ' αὖ νέον ἄνδρα γεραίτερον ἐξερέεσθαι."

25   τὸν δ' αὖτε προσέειπε θεά, γλαυκῶπις Ἀθήνη·
"Τηλέμαχ', ἄλλα μὲν αὐτὸς ἐνὶ φρεσὶ σῇσι νοήσεις,
ἄλλα δὲ καὶ δαίμων ὑποθήσεται· οὐ γὰρ ὀίω
οὔ σε θεῶν ἀέκητι γενέσθαι τε τραφέμεν τε."

        ὣς ἄρα φωνήσασ' ἡγήσατο Παλλὰς Ἀθήνη
30   καρπαλίμως· ὁ δ' ἔπειτα μετ' ἴχνια βαῖνε θεοῖο.
ἷξον δ' ἐς Πυλίων ἀνδρῶν ἄγυρίν τε καὶ ἕδρας,
ἔνθ' ἄρα Νέστωρ ἧστο σὺν υἱάσιν, ἀμφὶ δ' ἑταῖροι
δαῖτ' ἐντυνόμενοι κρέα τ' ὤπτων ἄλλα τ' ἔπειρον.
οἱ δ' ὡς οὖν ξείνους ἴδον, ἀθρόοι ἦλθον ἅπαντες,
35   χερσίν τ' ἠσπάζοντο καὶ ἑδριάασθαι ἄνωγον.
πρῶτος Νεστορίδης Πεισίστρατος ἐγγύθεν ἐλθὼν
ἀμφοτέρων ἕλε χεῖρα καὶ ἵδρυσεν παρὰ δαιτὶ
κώεσιν ἐν μαλακοῖσιν ἐπὶ ψαμάθοις ἁλίῃσιν
πάρ τε κασιγνήτῳ Θρασυμήδεϊ καὶ πατέρι ᾧ·
40   δῶκε δ' ἄρα σπλάγχνων μοίρας, ἐν δ' οἶνον ἔχευεν
χρυσείῳ δέπαϊ· δειδισκόμενος δὲ προσηύδα
Παλλάδ' Ἀθηναίην κούρην Διὸς αἰγιόχοιο·

        "εὔχεο νῦν, ὦ ξεῖνε, Ποσειδάωνι ἄνακτι·
τοῦ γὰρ καὶ δαίτης ἠντήσατε δεῦρο μολόντες.
45   αὐτὰρ ἐπὴν σπείσῃς τε καὶ εὔξεαι, ἧ θέμις ἐστί,
δὸς καὶ τούτῳ ἔπειτα δέπας μελιηδέος οἴνου
σπεῖσαι, ἐπεὶ καὶ τοῦτον ὀίομαι ἀθανάτοισιν
εὔχεσθαι· πάντες δὲ θεῶν χατέουσ' ἄνθρωποι.
ἀλλὰ νεώτερός ἐστιν, ὁμηλικίη δ' ἐμοὶ αὐτῷ·
50   τούνεκα σοὶ προτέρῳ δώσω χρύσειον ἄλεισον."

unversed in subtle speech, and moreover a young man has shame to question an elder."

Then the goddess, flashing-eyed Athene, answered him: "Telemachus, some things you yourself will devise in your breast, and other things heaven too will prompt you. For I do not think you were born and reared without the favor of the gods."

So spoke Pallas Athene, and led the way quickly; whereupon he followed in the footsteps of the goddess; and they came to the gathering and the companies of the men of Pylos. There Nestor sat with his sons, and round about them his people making ready the feast were roasting some of the meat and putting other pieces on spits. But when they saw the strangers they all came thronging about them, and clasped their hands in welcome, and bade them sit down. First Nestor's son Peisistratus came near and took both by the hand, and made them sit down at the feast on soft fleeces upon the sand of the sea, beside his brother Thrasymedes and his father. Thereupon he gave them servings of the inner parts and poured wine in a golden cup, and pledging her, he spoke to Pallas Athene, daughter of Zeus who bears the aegis:

"Pray now, stranger, to the lord Poseidon, for his is the feast whereon you have chanced in coming here. And when you have poured libations and have prayed, as is fitting, then give your friend also the cup of honey-sweet wine that he may pour, since he too, I doubt not, prays to the immortals; for all men have need of the gods. But he is the younger, of like age with myself, and so to you first will I give the golden cup."

ὣς εἰπὼν ἐν χειρὶ τίθει δέπας ἡδέος οἴνου·
χαῖρε δ' Ἀθηναίη πεπνυμένῳ ἀνδρὶ δικαίῳ,
οὕνεκα οἷ προτέρῃ δῶκε χρύσειον ἄλεισον·
αὐτίκα δ' εὔχετο πολλὰ Ποσειδάωνι ἄνακτι·

55   "κλῦθι, Ποσείδαον γαιήοχε, μηδὲ μεγήρῃς
ἡμῖν εὐχομένοισι τελευτῆσαι τάδε ἔργα.
Νέστορι μὲν πρώτιστα καὶ υἱάσι κῦδος ὄπαζε,
αὐτὰρ ἔπειτ' ἄλλοισι δίδου χαρίεσσαν ἀμοιβὴν
σύμπασιν Πυλίοισιν ἀγακλειτῆς ἑκατόμβης.

60   δὸς δ' ἔτι Τηλέμαχον καὶ ἐμὲ πρήξαντα νέεσθαι,
οὕνεκα δεῦρ' ἱκόμεσθα θοῇ σὺν νηὶ μελαίνῃ."
ὣς ἄρ' ἔπειτ' ἠρᾶτο καὶ αὐτὴ πάντα τελεύτα.
δῶκε δὲ Τηλεμάχῳ καλὸν δέπας ἀμφικύπελλον·
ὣς δ' αὔτως ἠρᾶτο Ὀδυσσῆος φίλος υἱός.

65   οἱ δ' ἐπεὶ ὤπτησαν κρέ' ὑπέρτερα καὶ ἐρύσαντο,
μοίρας δασσάμενοι δαίνυντ' ἐρικυδέα δαῖτα.
αὐτὰρ ἐπεὶ πόσιος καὶ ἐδητύος ἐξ ἔρον ἕντο,
τοῖς ἄρα μύθων ἦρχε Γερήνιος ἱππότα Νέστωρ·
"νῦν δὴ κάλλιόν ἐστι μεταλλῆσαι καὶ ἐρέσθαι

70   ξείνους, οἵ τινές εἰσιν, ἐπεὶ τάρπησαν ἐδωδῆς.
ὦ ξεῖνοι, τίνες ἐστέ; πόθεν πλεῖθ' ὑγρὰ κέλευθα;
ἤ τι κατὰ πρῆξιν ἦ μαψιδίως ἀλάλησθε
οἷά τε λῃστῆρες ὑπεὶρ ἅλα, τοί τ' ἀλόωνται
ψυχὰς παρθέμενοι κακὸν ἀλλοδαποῖσι φέροντες;"

75   τὸν δ' αὖ Τηλέμαχος πεπνυμένος ἀντίον ηὔδα
θαρσήσας· αὐτὴ γὰρ ἐνὶ φρεσὶ θάρσος Ἀθήνη
θῆχ', ἵνα μιν περὶ πατρὸς ἀποιχομένοιο ἔροιτο

So he spoke, and placed in her hand the cup of sweet wine; and Pallas Athene rejoiced at the man's wisdom and decorum, in that to her first he gave the golden cup; and at once she prayed earnestly to the lord Poseidon:

"Hear me, Poseidon, Earth-bearer, and do not begrudge in answer to our prayer to fulfill these requests. To Nestor, first of all, and to his sons vouchsafe renown, and then to the rest grant gracious requital for this glorious hecatomb, to all the men of Pylos. Grant furthermore that Telemachus and I return home having accomplished that for which we came here with our swift black ship."

Thus she prayed and was herself fulfilling it all. Then she gave Telemachus the handsome two-handled cup, and in like manner the staunch son of Odysseus prayed. Then when they had roasted the outer flesh and drawn it off the spits, they divided the portions and partook of the glorious feast. But when they had put from them the desire of food and drink, the horseman, Nestor of Gerenia, spoke first among them:

"Now truly it is seemlier to ask and enquire of the strangers who they are, since now they have had their joy of food. Strangers, who are you? Whence do you sail over the watery ways? Is it on some business, or do you wander at random over the sea, as pirates do, who wander hazarding their lives and bringing evil to men of other lands?"

Then wise Telemachus took courage, and made answer, for Athene herself put courage in his heart, so that he

ἠδ' ἵνα μιν κλέος ἐσθλὸν ἐν ἀνθρώποισιν ἔχῃσιν·[1]
"ὦ Νέστορ Νηληιάδη, μέγα κῦδος Ἀχαιῶν,
80   εἴρεαι ὁππόθεν εἰμέν· ἐγὼ δέ κέ τοι καταλέξω.
ἡμεῖς ἐξ Ἰθάκης ὑπονηίου εἰλήλουθμεν·
πρῆξις δ' ἥδ' ἰδίη, οὐ δήμιος, ἣν ἀγορεύω.
πατρὸς ἐμοῦ κλέος εὐρὺ μετέρχομαι, ἤν που ἀκούσω,
δίου Ὀδυσσῆος ταλασίφρονος, ὅν ποτέ φασι
85   σὺν σοὶ μαρνάμενον Τρώων πόλιν ἐξαλαπάξαι.
ἄλλους μὲν γὰρ πάντας, ὅσοι Τρωσὶν πολέμιζον,
πευθόμεθ', ἧχι ἕκαστος ἀπώλετο λυγρῷ ὀλέθρῳ,
κείνου δ' αὖ καὶ ὄλεθρον ἀπευθέα θῆκε Κρονίων.
οὐ γάρ τις δύναται σάφα εἰπέμεν ὁππόθ' ὄλωλεν,
90   εἴθ' ὅ γ' ἐπ' ἠπείρου δάμη ἀνδράσι δυσμενέεσσιν,
εἴτε καὶ ἐν πελάγει μετὰ κύμασιν Ἀμφιτρίτης.
τούνεκα νῦν τὰ σὰ γούναθ' ἱκάνομαι, αἴ κ' ἐθέλῃσθα
κείνου λυγρὸν ὄλεθρον ἐνισπεῖν, εἴ που ὄπωπας
ὀφθαλμοῖσι τεοῖσιν ἢ ἄλλου μῦθον ἄκουσας
95   πλαζομένου· πέρι γάρ μιν ὀιζυρὸν τέκε μήτηρ.
μηδέ τί μ' αἰδόμενος μειλίσσεο μηδ' ἐλεαίρων,
ἀλλ' εὖ μοι κατάλεξον ὅπως ἤντησας ὀπωπῆς.
λίσσομαι, εἴ ποτέ τοί τι πατὴρ ἐμός, ἐσθλὸς Ὀδυσσεύς,
ἢ ἔπος ἠέ τι ἔργον ὑποστὰς ἐξετέλεσσε
100   δήμῳ ἔνι Τρώων, ὅθι πάσχετε πήματ' Ἀχαιοί,
τῶν νῦν μοι μνῆσαι, καί μοι νημερτὲς ἐνίσπες."
    τὸν δ' ἠμείβετ' ἔπειτα Γερήνιος ἱππότα Νέστωρ·
"ὦ φίλ', ἐπεί μ' ἔμνησας ὀιζύος, ἣν ἐν ἐκείνῳ
δήμῳ ἀνέτλημεν μένος ἄσχετοι υἷες Ἀχαιῶν,

might ask about his father who was gone, and so that good report might be his among men:

"Nestor, son of Neleus, great glory of the Achaeans, you ask whence we are, and I will tell you. We have come from Ithaca that is below Neion; but this business whereof I speak is my own and does not concern the people. I come for far-flung report of my father, in case I may hear it, report of noble, steadfast Odysseus, who once, men say, fought by your side and sacked the city of the Trojans. For of all the others who warred with the Trojans, we have heard where each man died a woeful death, but of him the son of Cronos has made even the death to be past learning; for no man can tell surely where he has died—whether he was overcome by foes on the mainland, or on the deep among the waves of Amphitrite. Therefore I have now come to your knees, if perchance you will be willing to tell me of his woeful death, whether you saw it, it may be, with your own eyes, or heard the report of some other wanderer; for beyond all men did his mother bear him to sorrow. And do not out of consideration or pity for me speak soothing words, but tell me truly what evidence you came upon. I beseech you, if ever my father, noble Odysseus, promised you any word or deed and fulfilled it in the land of the Trojans, where you Achaeans suffered woes, be mindful of it now, I pray you, and tell me the unerring truth."

Then the horseman, Nestor of Gerenia, answered him: "My friend, since you have recalled to my mind the sorrow which we endured in that land, we sons of the Achaeans,

---

[1] Line 78 (= 1.95) is omitted in the best MSS.

105 ἠμὲν ὅσα ξὺν νηυσίν ἐπ' ἠεροειδέα πόντον
πλαζόμενοι κατὰ ληΐδ', ὅπῃ ἄρξειεν Ἀχιλλεύς,
ἠδ' ὅσα καὶ περὶ ἄστυ μέγα Πριάμοιο ἄνακτος
μαρνάμεθ'· ἔνθα δ' ἔπειτα κατέκταθεν ὅσσοι ἄριστοι.
ἔνθα μὲν Αἴας κεῖται ἀρήιος, ἔνθα δ' Ἀχιλλεύς,
110 ἔνθα δὲ Πάτροκλος, θεόφιν μήστωρ ἀτάλαντος,
ἔνθα δ' ἐμὸς φίλος υἱός, ἅμα κρατερὸς καὶ ἀμύμων,
Ἀντίλοχος, πέρι μὲν θείειν ταχὺς ἠδὲ μαχητής·
ἄλλα τε πόλλ' ἐπὶ τοῖς πάθομεν κακά· τίς κεν ἐκεῖνα
πάντα γε μυθήσαιτο καταθνητῶν ἀνθρώπων;
115 οὐδ' εἰ πεντάετές γε καὶ ἑξάετες παραμίμνων
ἐξερέοις ὅσα κεῖθι πάθον κακὰ δῖοι Ἀχαιοί·
πρίν κεν ἀνιηθεὶς σὴν πατρίδα γαῖαν ἵκοιο.
εἰνάετες γάρ σφιν κακὰ ῥάπτομεν ἀμφιέποντες
παντοίοισι δόλοισι, μόγις δ' ἐτέλεσσε Κρονίων.
120 ἔνθ' οὔ τίς ποτε μῆτιν ὁμοιωθήμεναι ἄντην
ἤθελ', ἐπεὶ μάλα πολλὸν ἐνίκα δῖος Ὀδυσσεὺς
παντοίοισι δόλοισι, πατὴρ τεός, εἰ ἐτεόν γε
κείνου ἔκγονός ἐσσι· σέβας μ' ἔχει εἰσορόωντα.
ἦ τοι γὰρ μῦθοί γε ἐοικότες, οὐδέ κε φαίης
125 ἄνδρα νεώτερον ὧδε ἐοικότα μυθήσασθαι.
ἔνθ' ἦ τοι ἧος μὲν ἐγὼ καὶ δῖος Ὀδυσσεὺς
οὔτε ποτ' εἰν ἀγορῇ δίχ' ἐβάζομεν οὔτ' ἐνὶ βουλῇ,
ἀλλ' ἕνα θυμὸν ἔχοντε νόῳ καὶ ἐπίφρονι βουλῇ
φραζόμεθ' Ἀργείοισιν ὅπως ὄχ' ἄριστα γένοιτο.
130 αὐτὰρ ἐπεὶ Πριάμοιο πόλιν διεπέρσαμεν αἰπήν,
βῆμεν δ' ἐν νήεσσι, θεὸς δ' ἐκέδασσεν Ἀχαιούς,[1]
καὶ τότε δὴ Ζεὺς λυγρὸν ἐνὶ φρεσὶ μήδετο νόστον

dauntless in courage—all that we endured on ship board, as we roamed after booty over the misty deep wherever Achilles led and all our fightings around the great city of king Priam; in a word, there all our best were slain. There lies Aias, dear to Ares, there Achilles, there Patroclus, the peer of the gods in council; and there my own dear son, strong alike and flawless, Antilochus, preeminent in speed of foot and as a warrior. And many other ills we suffered besides these; who of mortal men could tell them all? No, even if for five years' space or six years' space you were to abide here, and ask of all the woes which the noble Achaeans endured there, you would grow weary before the end and get yourself back to your native land. For nine years' space were we busied plotting their ruin with all sorts of wiles; and hardly did the son of Cronos bring it to pass. There no man ventured to vie with him in counsel, since noble Odysseus far excelled in all sorts of wiles—your father, if indeed you are his son. Amazement holds me as I look on you, for your speech could not be more like his; nor would one think that a younger man would speak so reasonably. Now all the time that we were there noble Odysseus and I never spoke at variance either in the assembly or in the council, but being of one mind advised the Argives with wisdom and shrewd counsel how all might be for the best. But when we had sacked the lofty city of Priam, and had gone away in our ships, and a god had scattered the Achaeans, then, even then, Zeus planned in his heart a

---

[1] Line 131, though found in the MSS, is out of harmony with what follows. It may have been interpolated from 13.317, where it is in place.

Ἀργείοις, ἐπεὶ οὔ τι νοήμονες οὐδὲ δίκαιοι
πάντες ἔσαν· τῶ σφεων πολέες κακὸν οἶτον ἐπέσπον
135 μήνιος ἐξ ὀλοῆς γλαυκώπιδος ὀβριμοπάτρης.
ἥ τ' ἔριν Ἀτρεΐδῃσι μετ' ἀμφοτέροισιν ἔθηκε.
τὼ δὲ καλεσσαμένω ἀγορὴν ἐς πάντας Ἀχαιούς,
μάψ, ἀτὰρ οὐ κατὰ κόσμον, ἐς ἠέλιον καταδύντα,
οἱ δ' ἦλθον οἴνῳ βεβαρηότες υἷες Ἀχαιῶν,
140 μῦθον μυθείσθην, τοῦ εἵνεκα λαὸν ἄγειραν.
ἔνθ' ἤ τοι Μενέλαος ἀνώγει πάντας Ἀχαιοὺς
νόστου μιμνήσκεσθαι ἐπ' εὐρέα νῶτα θαλάσσης,
οὐδ' Ἀγαμέμνονι πάμπαν ἑήνδανε· βούλετο γάρ ρα
λαὸν ἐρυκακέειν ῥέξαι θ' ἱερὰς ἑκατόμβας,
145 ὡς τὸν Ἀθηναίης δεινὸν χόλον ἐξακέσαιτο,
νήπιος, οὐδὲ τὸ ἤδη, ὃ οὐ πείσεσθαι ἔμελλεν·
οὐ γάρ τ' αἶψα θεῶν τρέπεται νόος αἰὲν ἐόντων.
ὣς τὼ μὲν χαλεποῖσιν ἀμειβομένα ἐπέεσσιν
ἔστασαν· οἱ δ' ἀνόρουσαν ἐϋκνήμιδες Ἀχαιοὶ
150 ἠχῇ θεσπεσίῃ, δίχα δέ σφισιν ἥνδανε βουλή.
νύκτα μὲν ἀέσαμεν χαλεπὰ φρεσὶν ὁρμαίνοντες
ἀλλήλοις· ἐπὶ γὰρ Ζεὺς ἤρτυε πῆμα κακοῖο·
ἠῶθεν δ' οἱ μὲν νέας ἕλκομεν εἰς ἅλα δῖαν
κτήματά τ' ἐντιθέμεσθα βαθυζώνους τε γυναῖκας.
155 ἡμίσεες δ' ἄρα λαοὶ ἐρητύοντο μένοντες
αὖθι παρ' Ἀτρεΐδῃ Ἀγαμέμνονι, ποιμένι λαῶν·
ἡμίσεες δ' ἀναβάντες ἐλαύνομεν· αἱ δὲ μάλ' ὦκα
ἔπλεον, ἐστόρεσεν δὲ θεὸς μεγακήτεα πόντον.
ἐς Τένεδον δ' ἐλθόντες ἐρέξαμεν ἱρὰ θεοῖν,
160 οἴκαδε ἱέμενοι· Ζεὺς δ' οὔ πω μήδετο νόστον,

woeful return for the Argives, since by no means were all prudent or just. Therefore many of them met an evil fate through the terrible wrath of the flashing-eyed goddess, the daughter of the mighty sire, for she caused strife between the two sons of Atreus. Now these two called to an assembly all the Achaeans, recklessly and in no due order, at sunset—and they came heavy with wine, the sons of the Achaeans—and they said their say, and told why they had gathered the host together. Then it was that Menelaus bade all the Achaeans think of their return over the broad back of the sea, but by no means did he please Agamemnon, for he wished to hold back the host and to offer holy hecatombs, that he might appease the dread wrath of Athene—fool! Little did he know that she was not to hearken; for the mind of the gods that are forever is not turned in a moment. So these two stood bandying harsh words; but the well-greaved Achaeans sprang up with a huge din, and twofold plans found favor with them. That night we rested, each side pondering hard thoughts against the other, for Zeus was bringing upon us an evil doom, but in the morning some of us launched our ships upon the bright sea, and put on board our goods and the women in their deep-bosomed garments. Half, indeed, of the host held back and remained there with Agamemnon, son of Atreus, shepherd of the host, but half of us embarked and rowed away; and swiftly the ships sailed, for a god made smooth the monster-harboring sea. When we came to Tenedos, we offered sacrifice to the gods, being eager to reach our homes; but Zeus did not yet purpose our return,

σχέτλιος, ὅς ῥ' ἔριν ὦρσε κακὴν ἔπι δεύτερον αὖτις.
οἱ μὲν ἀποστρέψαντες ἔβαν νέας ἀμφιελίσσας
ἀμφ' Ὀδυσῆα ἄνακτα δαΐφρονα, ποικιλομήτην,
αὖτις ἐπ' Ἀτρεΐδῃ Ἀγαμέμνονι ἦρα φέροντες·
165   αὐτὰρ ἐγὼ σὺν νηυσὶν ἀολλέσιν, αἵ μοι ἕποντο,
φεῦγον, ἐπεὶ γίγνωσκον, ὃ δὴ κακὰ μήδετο δαίμων.
φεῦγε δὲ Τυδέος υἱὸς ἀρήιος, ὦρσε δ' ἑταίρους.
ὀψὲ δὲ δὴ μετὰ νῶι κίε ξανθὸς Μενέλαος,
ἐν Λέσβῳ δ' ἔκιχεν δολιχὸν πλόον ὁρμαίνοντας,
170   ἢ καθύπερθε Χίοιο νεοίμεθα παιπαλοέσσης,
νήσου ἔπι Ψυρίης, αὐτὴν ἐπ' ἀριστέρ' ἔχοντες,
ἦ ὑπένερθε Χίοιο, παρ' ἠνεμόεντα Μίμαντα.
ᾐτέομεν δὲ θεὸν φῆναι τέρας· αὐτὰρ ὅ γ' ἡμῖν
δεῖξε, καὶ ἠνώγει πέλαγος μέσον εἰς Εὔβοιαν
175   τέμνειν, ὄφρα τάχιστα ὑπὲκ κακότητα φύγοιμεν.
ὦρτο δ' ἐπὶ λιγὺς οὖρος ἀήμεναι· αἱ δὲ μάλ' ὦκα
ἰχθυόεντα κέλευθα διέδραμον, ἐς δὲ Γεραιστὸν
ἐννύχιαι κατάγοντο· Ποσειδάωνι δὲ ταύρων
πόλλ' ἐπὶ μῆρ' ἔθεμεν, πέλαγος μέγα μετρήσαντες.
180   τέτρατον ἦμαρ ἔην, ὅτ' ἐν Ἄργεϊ νῆας ἐΐσας
Τυδεΐδεω ἕταροι Διομήδεος ἱπποδάμοιο
ἵστασαν· αὐτὰρ ἐγώ γε Πύλονδ' ἔχον, οὐδέ ποτ' ἔσβη
οὖρος, ἐπεὶ δὴ πρῶτα θεὸς προέηκεν ἀῆναι.
    "ὣς ἦλθον, φίλε τέκνον, ἀπευθής, οὐδέ τι οἶδα
185   κείνων, οἵ τ' ἐσάωθεν Ἀχαιῶν οἵ τ' ἀπόλοντο.
ὅσσα δ' ἐνὶ μεγάροισι καθήμενος ἡμετέροισι
πεύθομαι, ἣ θέμις ἐστί, δαήσεαι, οὐδέ σε κεύσω.
εὖ μὲν Μυρμιδόνας φάσ' ἐλθέμεν ἐγχεσιμώρους,

stubborn god, who roused evil strife again a second time. Then some turned back their curved ships and departed, following the lord Odysseus, the wise and crafty-minded, once more showing favor to Agamemnon, son of Atreus; but I with the full company of ships that followed me fled on, for I knew that the god was devising evil. And the dear to Ares son of Tydeus fled and urged on his men; and late upon our track came fair-haired Menelaus, and overtook us in Lesbos, as we were debating the long voyage, whether we should sail to seaward of rugged Chios, toward the isle of Psyria, keeping Chios itself upon our left, or to landward of Chios past windy Mimas. So we asked the god to show us a sign, and he showed it us, and bade us cleave through the midst of the sea to Euboea, that we might the soonest escape from misery. And a shrill wind sprang up to blow, and the ships ran swiftly over the fish-filled ways, and at night put in to Geraestus. There on the altar of Poseidon, we laid many thighs of bulls thankful to have traversed the great sea. It was the fourth day when in Argos the company of Diomedes, son of Tydeus, tamer of horses, stayed their shapely ships; but I held on toward Pylos, and the wind was not once quenched from the time when the god first sent it forth to blow.

"Thus I came, dear child, without tidings, nor know I anything of those others, who of the Achaeans were saved, and who were lost. But what tidings I have heard as I abide in our halls you shall hear, as is right, nor will I hide it from you. Safely, they say, came the Myrmidons that rage with

οὓς ἄγ’ Ἀχιλλῆος μεγαθύμου φαίδιμος υἱός,
190 εὖ δὲ Φιλοκτήτην, Ποιάντιον ἀγλαὸν υἱόν.
πάντας δ’ Ἰδομενεὺς Κρήτην εἰσήγαγ’ ἑταίρους,
οἳ φύγον ἐκ πολέμου, πόντος δέ οἱ οὔ τιν’ ἀπηύρα.
Ἀτρείδην δὲ καὶ αὐτοὶ ἀκούετε, νόσφιν ἐόντες,
ὥς τ’ ἦλθ’, ὥς τ’ Αἴγισθος ἐμήσατο λυγρὸν ὄλεθρον.
195 ἀλλ’ ἦ τοι κεῖνος μὲν ἐπισμυγερῶς ἀπέτισεν·
ὡς ἀγαθὸν καὶ παῖδα καταφθιμένοιο λιπέσθαι
ἀνδρός, ἐπεὶ καὶ κεῖνος ἐτίσατο πατροφονῆα,
Αἴγισθον δολόμητιν, ὅ οἱ πατέρα κλυτὸν ἔκτα.
καὶ σὺ φίλος, μάλα γάρ σ’ ὁρόω καλόν τε μέγαν τε,
200 ἄλκιμος ἔσσ’, ἵνα τίς σε καὶ ὀψιγόνων ἐὺ εἴπῃ.”[1]
    τὸν δ’ αὖ Τηλέμαχος πεπνυμένος ἀντίον ηὔδα·
“ὦ Νέστορ Νηληιάδη, μέγα κῦδος Ἀχαιῶν,
καὶ λίην κεῖνος μὲν ἐτίσατο, καί οἱ Ἀχαιοὶ
οἴσουσι κλέος εὐρὺ καὶ ἐσσομένοισι πυθέσθαι·[2]
205 αἲ γὰρ ἐμοὶ τοσσήνδε θεοὶ δύναμιν περιθεῖεν,
τίσασθαι μνηστῆρας ὑπερβασίης ἀλεγεινῆς,
οἵ τέ μοι ὑβρίζοντες ἀτάσθαλα μηχανόωνται.
ἀλλ’ οὔ μοι τοιοῦτον ἐπέκλωσαν θεοὶ ὄλβον,
πατρί τ’ ἐμῷ καὶ ἐμοί· νῦν δὲ χρὴ τετλάμεν ἔμπης.”
210   τὸν δ’ ἠμείβετ’ ἔπειτα Γερήνιος ἱππότα Νέστωρ·
“ὦ φίλ’, ἐπεὶ δὴ ταῦτά μ’ ἀνέμνησας καὶ ἔειπες,
φασὶ μνηστῆρας σῆς μητέρος εἵνεκα πολλοὺς
ἐν μεγάροις ἀέκητι σέθεν κακὰ μηχανάασθαι·
εἰπέ μοι, ἠὲ ἑκὼν ὑποδάμνασαι, ἦ σέ γε λαοὶ

---

[1] Lines 199f (= 1.301f) were rejected by Aristophanes and
Aristarchus.

the spear, whom the famous son of great-hearted Achilles
led; and safely Philoctetes, the glorious son of Poias. All his
company, too, did Idomeneus bring to Crete, all who
escaped the war, and the sea robbed him of none. But of
the son of Atreus you have yourselves heard, far off though
you are, how he came, and how Aegisthus devised for him a
woeful doom. Yet truly he paid the reckoning for it in ter-
rible fashion, so good a thing it is that a son be left behind a
man at his death, since that son took vengeance on his
father's slayer, the guileful Aegisthus, because he slew his
glorious father. You, too, friend, for I see you are a hand-
some man and tall, be valiant, that many a one among men
yet to be born may praise you."

Then wise Telemachus answered him: "Nestor, son of
Neleus, great glory of the Achaeans, truly indeed did that
son take vengeance, and the Achaeans shall spread his
fame abroad, that men who are yet to be may hear of it. O
that the gods should clothe me with such strength, that I
might take vengeance on the suitors for their grievous
transgression, who in wantonness devise mischief against
me. But no such happiness have the gods spun for me, for
me or for my father; and now I must simply endure."

Then the horseman, Nestor of Gerenia, answered him:
"Friend, since you have called this to my mind and spoken
of it, they say that many suitors for the hand of your mother
devise evils in your halls in your despite. Tell me, are you
willingly thus oppressed, or do the people throughout the

---

² πυθέσθαι: ἀοιδήν

215   ἐχθαίρουσ' ἀνὰ δῆμον, ἐπισπόμενοι θεοῦ ὀμφῇ.
       τίς δ' οἶδ' εἴ κέ ποτέ σφι βίας ἀποτίσεται ἐλθών,
       ἢ ὅ γε μοῦνος ἐὼν ἢ καὶ σύμπαντες Ἀχαιοί;
       εἰ γάρ σ' ὡς ἐθέλοι φιλέειν γλαυκῶπις Ἀθήνη,
       ὡς τότ' Ὀδυσσῆος περικήδετο κυδαλίμοιο
220   δήμῳ ἔνι Τρώων, ὅθι πάσχομεν ἄλγε' Ἀχαιοί —
       οὐ γάρ πω ἴδον ὧδε θεοὺς ἀναφανδὰ φιλεῦντας,
       ὡς κείνῳ ἀναφανδὰ παρίστατο Παλλὰς Ἀθήνη —
       εἴ σ' οὕτως ἐθέλοι φιλέειν κήδοιτό τε θυμῷ,
       τῶ κέν τις κείνων γε καὶ ἐκλελάθοιτο γάμοιο."
225   τὸν δ' αὖ Τηλέμαχος πεπνυμένος ἀντίον ηὔδα·
       "ὦ γέρον, οὔ πω τοῦτο ἔπος τελέεσθαι ὀίω·
       λίην γὰρ μέγα εἶπες· ἄγη μ' ἔχει. οὐκ ἂν ἐμοί γε
       ἐλπομένῳ τὰ γένοιτ', οὐδ' εἰ θεοὶ ὧς ἐθέλοιεν."
           τὸν δ' αὖτε προσέειπε θεά, γλαυκῶπις Ἀθήνη·
230   "Τηλέμαχε, ποῖόν σε ἔπος φύγεν ἕρκος ὀδόντων.
       ῥεῖα θεός γ' ἐθέλων καὶ τηλόθεν ἄνδρα σαώσαι.
       βουλοίμην δ' ἂν ἐγώ γε καὶ ἄλγεα πολλὰ μογήσας
       οἴκαδέ τ' ἐλθέμεναι καὶ νόστιμον ἦμαρ ἰδέσθαι,
       ἢ ἐλθὼν ἀπολέσθαι ἐφέστιος, ὡς Ἀγαμέμνων
235   ὤλεθ' ὑπ' Αἰγίσθοιο δόλῳ καὶ ἧς ἀλόχοιο.
       ἀλλ' ἦ τοι θάνατον μὲν ὁμοίιον οὐδὲ θεοί περ
       καὶ φίλῳ ἀνδρὶ δύνανται ἀλαλκέμεν, ὁππότε κεν δὴ
       μοῖρ' ὀλοὴ καθέλῃσι τανηλεγέος θανάτοιο."
           τὴν δ' αὖ Τηλέμαχος πεπνυμένος ἀντίον ηὔδα·
240   "Μέντορ, μηκέτι ταῦτα λεγώμεθα κηδόμενοί περ·
       κείνῳ δ' οὐκέτι νόστος ἐτήτυμος, ἀλλά οἱ ἤδη
       φράσσαντ' ἀθάνατοι θάνατον καὶ κῆρα μέλαιναν.

land hate you, following the voice of a god? Who knows but Odysseus may some day come and take vengeance on them for their violent deeds—he alone, it may be, or even all the host of the Achaeans? Ah, would that flashing-eyed Athene might choose to love you even as then she cared exceedingly for glorious Odysseus in the land of the Trojans, where we Achaeans suffered woes. For never yet have I seen the gods so manifestly showing love, as Pallas Athene did to him, standing manifest by his side. If she would be pleased to love you in such fashion and would care for you at heart, then might one or another of them utterly forget marriage."

Then wise Telemachus answered him: "Old man, I do not think that this word will ever be brought to pass. Too great is what you are saying; amazement holds me. No hope have I that this will come to pass, no, not though the gods should so will it."

Then the goddess, flashing-eyed Athene, spoke to him, and said: "Telemachus, what a word has escaped the barrier of your teeth! Easily might a god who willed it bring a man safe home, even from afar. And for myself, I had rather endure many grievous toils before I reached home and saw the day of my returning, than after my return be slain at my hearth, as Agamemnon was slain by the guile of Aegisthus and of his own wife. But clearly death that is common to all not even the gods themselves can ward off even from a man they love, whenever the fell fate of pitiless death strikes him down."

Then wise Telemachus answered her: "Mentor, no longer let us tell of these things for all our grief. For him no return is any longer possible; rather, before now the immortals have devised for him death and black fate. But

97

νῦν δ' ἐθέλω ἔπος ἄλλο μεταλλῆσαι καὶ ἐρέσθαι
Νέστορ', ἐπεὶ περὶ οἶδε δίκας ἠδὲ φρόνιν ἄλλων·
245 τρὶς γὰρ δή μίν φασιν ἀνάξασθαι γένε' ἀνδρῶν·
ὥς τέ μοι ἀθάνατος ἰνδάλλεται εἰσοράασθαι.
ὦ Νέστορ Νηληϊάδη, σὺ δ' ἀληθὲς ἐνίσπες·
πῶς ἔθαν' Ἀτρεΐδης εὐρὺ κρείων Ἀγαμέμνων;
ποῦ Μενέλαος ἔην; τίνα δ' αὐτῷ μήσατ' ὄλεθρον
250 Αἴγισθος δολόμητις, ἐπεὶ κτάνε πολλὸν ἀρείω;
ἦ οὐκ Ἄργεος ἦεν Ἀχαικοῦ, ἀλλά πη ἄλλη
πλάζετ' ἐπ' ἀνθρώπους, ὁ δὲ θαρσήσας κατέπεφνε;"
    τὸν δ' ἠμείβετ' ἔπειτα Γερήνιος ἱππότα Νέστωρ·
"τοιγὰρ ἐγώ τοι, τέκνον, ἀληθέα πάντ' ἀγορεύσω.
255 ἦ τοι μὲν τάδε καὐτὸς ὀίεαι, ὥς κεν ἐτύχθη,[1]
εἰ ζωόν γ' Αἴγισθον ἐνὶ μεγάροισιν ἔτετμεν
Ἀτρεΐδης Τροίηθεν ἰών, ξανθὸς Μενέλαος·
τῷ κέ οἱ οὐδὲ θανόντι χυτὴν ἐπὶ γαῖαν ἔχευαν,
ἀλλ' ἄρα τόν γε κύνες τε καὶ οἰωνοὶ κατέδαψαν
260 κείμενον ἐν πεδίῳ ἑκὰς ἄστεος,[2] οὐδέ κέ τίς μιν
κλαῦσεν Ἀχαιάδων· μάλα γὰρ μέγα μήσατο ἔργον.
ἡμεῖς μὲν γὰρ κεῖθι πολέας τελέοντες ἀέθλους
ἥμεθ'· ὁ δ' εὔκηλος μυχῷ Ἄργεος ἱπποβότοιο
πόλλ' Ἀγαμεμνονέην ἄλοχον θέλγεσκ' ἐπέεσσιν.
265 ἡ δ' ἦ τοι τὸ πρὶν μὲν ἀναίνετο ἔργον ἀεικὲς
δῖα Κλυταιμνήστρη· φρεσὶ γὰρ κέχρητ' ἀγαθῇσι·
πὰρ δ' ἄρ' ἔην καὶ ἀοιδὸς ἀνήρ, ᾧ πόλλ' ἐπέτελλεν
Ἀτρεΐδης Τροίηνδε κιὼν ἔρυσθαι ἄκοιτιν.

[1] ὥς κεν ἐτύχθη: ὥς περ ἐτύχθη, followed by a colon
[2] ἄστεος: Ἄργεος

now I would make inquiry and ask Nestor regarding another matter, since beyond all others he knows judgments and wisdom; for three times, men say, has he been king for a generation of men, and like an immortal he seems to me to look upon. Nestor, son of Neleus, tell me truly: how was the son of Atreus, wide-ruling Agamemnon, slain? Where was Menelaus? What death did guileful Aegisthus plan for the king, since he slew a man mightier far than himself? Was Menelaus not in Achaean Argos, but wandering elsewhere among men, so that Aegisthus took heart and did the murderous deed?"

Then the horseman, Nestor of Gerenia, answered him: "Since you ask, my child, I will tell you all the truth. You yourself have guessed how this matter would have fallen out, if the son Atreus, fair-haired Menelaus, on his return from Troy had found Aegisthus in his halls alive. Then for him not even in death would they have piled the up-piled earth, but the dogs and birds would have torn him as he lay on the plain far from the city, nor would any of the Achaean women have bewailed him; for monstrous was the deed he devised. We on our part stayed there in Troy fulfilling our many toils; but he, at ease in a nook of horse-pasturing Argos, kept seeking to beguile with words the wife of Agamemnon. Now at first she put from her the unseemly deed, the noble Clytemnestra, for she had an understanding heart; and with her was furthermore a minstrel whom the son of Atreus strictly ordered, when he set forth for the land of Troy, to guard his wife. But when at

ἀλλ' ὅτε δή μιν μοῖρα θεῶν ἐπέδησε δαμῆναι,
270 δὴ τότε τὸν μὲν ἀοιδὸν ἄγων ἐς νῆσον ἐρήμην
κάλλιπεν οἰωνοῖσιν ἕλωρ καὶ κύρμα γενέσθαι,
τὴν δ' ἐθέλων ἐθέλουσαν ἀνήγαγεν ὅνδε δόμονδε.
πολλὰ δὲ μηρί' ἔκηε θεῶν ἱεροῖς ἐπὶ βωμοῖς,
πολλὰ δ' ἀγάλματ' ἀνῆψεν, ὑφάσματά τε χρυσόν τε,
275 ἐκτελέσας μέγα ἔργον, ὃ οὔ ποτε ἔλπετο θυμῷ.

    "ἡμεῖς μὲν γὰρ ἅμα πλέομεν Τροίηθεν ἰόντες,
Ἀτρεΐδης καὶ ἐγώ, φίλα εἰδότες ἀλλήλοισιν·
ἀλλ' ὅτε Σούνιον ἱρὸν ἀφικόμεθ', ἄκρον Ἀθηνέων,
ἔνθα κυβερνήτην Μενελάου Φοῖβος Ἀπόλλων
280 οἷς ἀγανοῖς βελέεσσιν ἐποιχόμενος κατέπεφνε,
πηδάλιον μετὰ χερσὶ θεούσης νηὸς ἔχοντα,
Φρόντιν Ὀνητορίδην, ὃς ἐκαίνυτο φῦλ' ἀνθρώπων
νῆα κυβερνῆσαι, ὁπότε σπέρχοιεν ἄελλαι.
ὣς ὁ μὲν ἔνθα κατέσχετ', ἐπειγόμενός περ ὁδοῖο,
285 ὄφρ' ἔταρον θάπτοι καὶ ἐπὶ κτέρεα κτερίσειεν.
ἀλλ' ὅτε δὴ καὶ κεῖνος ἰὼν ἐπὶ οἴνοπα πόντον
ἐν νηυσὶ γλαφυρῇσι Μαλειάων ὄρος αἰπὺ

---

a So far as Greek grammar is concerned, the pronoun may
denote Agamemnon, Clytemnestra, the minstrel, or Aegisthus, but
it seems most natural for it to refer to Aegisthus, the grammatical
subject of the sentence in which it occurs and the logical subject of
the entire paragraph, in which Aegisthus is alluded to twelve
further times. It is Aegisthus' self-destructive decision to have
Clytemnestra at any cost which most interests the poet of the
Odyssey (1.29–43). Nestor here is doing what Zeus accuses mor-
tals in general of doing, blaming the gods for what is in fact a
mortal's own fault (ibid.). D.

length the doom of the gods bound him[a] that he should be overcome, then indeed Aegisthus took the minstrel to a desert isle and left him to be the prey and treasure trove of birds; and her, willing as he was willing, he led to his own house. And many thigh pieces he burned upon the holy altars of the gods, and many offerings he hung up, woven stuffs and gold, when he accomplished the monstrous deed his heart never hoped to achieve.[b]

"For we were sailing together on our way from Troy, the son of Atreus and I, in all friendship; but when we came to holy Sunium, the cape of Athens, there Phoebus Apollo assailed with his gentle[c] shafts and slew the helmsman of Menelaus, as he held in his hands the steering oar of the speeding ship—Phrontis, son of Onetor, who excelled the tribes of men in piloting a ship when the storm winds blew strong. So Menelaus tarried there though eager for his journey, so that he might bury his comrade and over him pay funeral rites. But when he in his turn, as he passed over the wine-dark sea in the hollow ships, reached in swift course the steep height of Malea, then

---

[b] "Monstrous deed," μέγα ἔργον, 3.275; cf. 3.261, μάλα γὰρ μέγα μήσατο ἔργον, "for monstrous was the deed he devised." "His heart never hoped to achieve"; cf. 1.37 "though well he knew of sheer destruction." Aegisthus is sacrificing in gratitude for his success in murdering Agamemnon, not in winning Clytemnestra. Nestor passes over the murder so lightly here because he realizes that he himself is in part responsible for Menelaus' failure either to protect his brother at the time of the crime or to avenge him afterwards. That Menelaus' absence is in Nestor's mind at this point is indicated by the otherwise inexplicable γὰρ ('for') which introduces the immediately succeeding paragraph explaining that absence. D.

[c] A gentle, painless death was thought to be due to Apollo's shafts. M.

101

ἷξε θέων, τότε δὴ στυγερὴν ὁδὸν εὐρύοπα Ζεὺς
ἐφράσατο, λιγέων δ' ἀνέμων ἐπ' ἀυτμένα χεῦε,

290   κύματά τε τροφέοντο[1] πελώρια, ἶσα ὄρεσσιν.
ἔνθα διατμήξας τὰς μὲν Κρήτῃ ἐπέλασσεν,
ἧχι Κύδωνες ἔναιον Ἰαρδάνου ἀμφὶ ῥέεθρα.
ἔστι δέ τις λισσὴ αἰπεῖά τε εἰς ἅλα πέτρη
ἐσχατιῇ Γόρτυνος ἐν ἠεροειδέι πόντῳ·

295   ἔνθα Νότος μέγα κῦμα ποτὶ σκαιὸν ῥίον ὠθεῖ,
ἐς Φαιστόν, μικρὸς δὲ λίθος μέγα κῦμ' ἀποέργει.
αἱ μὲν ἄρ' ἔνθ' ἦλθον, σπουδῇ δ' ἤλυξαν ὄλεθρον
ἄνδρες, ἀτὰρ νῆάς γε ποτὶ σπιλάδεσσιν ἔαξαν
κύματ'· ἀτὰρ τὰς πέντε νέας κυανοπρωρείους

300   Αἰγύπτῳ ἐπέλασσε φέρων ἄνεμός τε καὶ ὕδωρ.
ὣς ὁ μὲν ἔνθα πολὺν βίοτον καὶ χρυσὸν ἀγείρων
ἠλᾶτο ξὺν νηυσὶ κατ' ἀλλοθρόους ἀνθρώπους·
τόφρα δὲ ταῦτ' Αἴγισθος ἐμήσατο οἴκοθι λυγρά.

305   ἑπτάετες δ' ἤνασσε πολυχρύσοιο Μυκήνης,
304   κτείνας Ἀτρεΐδην, δέδμητο δὲ λαὸς ὑπ' αὐτῷ.
τῷ δέ οἱ ὀγδοάτῳ κακὸν ἤλυθε δῖος Ὀρέστης
ἂψ ἀπ' Ἀθηνάων,[2] κατὰ δ' ἔκτανε πατροφονῆα,
Αἴγισθον δολόμητιν, ὅ οἱ πατέρα κλυτὸν ἔκτα.
ἦ τοι ὁ τὸν κτείνας δαίνυ τάφον Ἀργείοισιν

310   μητρός τε στυγερῆς καὶ ἀνάλκιδος Αἰγίσθοιο·
αὐτῆμαρ δέ οἱ ἦλθε βοὴν ἀγαθὸς Μενέλαος
πολλὰ κτήματ' ἄγων, ὅσα οἱ νέες ἄχθος ἄειραν.

    "καὶ σύ, φίλος, μὴ δηθὰ δόμων ἄπο τῆλ' ἀλάλησο,
κτήματά τε προλιπὼν ἄνδρας τ' ἐν σοῖσι δόμοισι

315   οὕτω ὑπερφιάλους, μή τοι κατὰ πάντα φάγωσιν

Zeus, whose voice is borne afar, planned for him a hateful path and poured upon him the blasts of shrill winds, and the waves were swollen to huge size, like mountains. Then he split the fleet in two, bringing some ships to Crete where the Cydonians dwelt about the streams of Iardanus. Now there is a smooth cliff, sheer toward the sea, on the border of Gortyn in the misty deep, where the Southwest Wind drives the great wave against the headland on the left toward Phaestus, and a little rock holds back a great wave. Thither came some of the ships, and the men with much difficulty escaped destruction, but the ships the waves dashed to pieces against the reef. But the five other dark-prowed ships the wind, as it bore them, and wave brought to Egypt. So he was wandering there with his ships among men of strange speech, gathering much livelihood and gold; but meanwhile Aegisthus devised this woeful work at home, slaying the son of Atreus, and the people were subdued under him. Seven years he reigned over Mycenae, rich in gold, but in the eighth came as his bane the noble Orestes back from Athens, and slew his father's murderer, the guileful Aegisthus, because he had slain his glorious father. Now when he had slain him, he made a funeral feast for the Argives over his hateful mother and the craven Aegisthus; and on the selfsame day there came to him Menelaus, good at the war cry, bringing much treasure, all the burden that his ships could bear.

"So do not you, my friend, wander long far from home, leaving your wealth behind you and men in your house so insolent, for fear they divide and devour all your wealth,

---

[1] τροφέοντο Aristarchus: τροφόεντα
[2] Ἀθηνάων: Ἀθηναίης Aristarchus, Φωκήων Zenodotus

103

κτήματα δασσάμενοι, σὺ δὲ τηϋσίην ὁδὸν ἔλθῃς.
ἀλλ᾽ ἐς μὲν Μενέλαον ἐγὼ κέλομαι καὶ ἄνωγα
ἐλθεῖν· κεῖνος γὰρ νέον ἄλλοθεν εἰλήλουθεν,
ἐκ τῶν ἀνθρώπων, ὅθεν οὐκ ἔλποιτό γε θυμῷ
320   ἐλθέμεν, ὅν τινα πρῶτον ἀποσφήλωσιν ἄελλαι
ἐς πέλαγος μέγα τοῖον, ὅθεν τέ περ οὐδ᾽ οἰωνοὶ
αὐτόετες οἰχνεῦσιν, ἐπεὶ μέγα τε δεινόν τε.
ἀλλ᾽ ἴθι νῦν σὺν νηΐ τε σῇ καὶ σοῖς ἑτάροισιν·
εἰ δ᾽ ἐθέλεις πεζός, πάρα τοι δίφρος τε καὶ ἵπποι,
325   πὰρ δὲ τοι υἷες ἐμοί, οἵ τοι πομπῆες ἔσονται
ἐς Λακεδαίμονα δῖαν, ὅθι ξανθὸς Μενέλαος.
λίσσεσθαι δέ μιν αὐτός, ἵνα νημερτὲς ἐνίσπῃ·
ψεῦδος δ᾽ οὐκ ἐρέει· μάλα γὰρ πεπνυμένος ἐστίν."
ὣς ἔφατ᾽, ἠέλιος δ᾽ ἄρ᾽ ἔδυ καὶ ἐπὶ κνέφας ἦλθε.
330   τοῖσι δὲ καὶ μετέειπε θεά, γλαυκῶπις Ἀθήνη·
"ὦ γέρον, ἦ τοι ταῦτα κατὰ μοῖραν κατέλεξας·
ἀλλ᾽ ἄγε τάμνετε μὲν γλώσσας, κεράσθε δὲ οἶνον,
ὄφρα Ποσειδάωνι καὶ ἄλλοις ἀθανάτοισιν
σπείσαντες κοίτοιο μεδώμεθα· τοῖο γὰρ ὥρη.
335   ἤδη γὰρ φάος οἴχεθ᾽ ὑπὸ ζόφον, οὐδὲ ἔοικεν
δηθὰ θεῶν ἐν δαιτὶ θαασσέμεν, ἀλλὰ νέεσθαι."
ἦ ῥα Διὸς θυγάτηρ, οἱ δ᾽ ἔκλυον αὐδησάσης.
τοῖσι δὲ κήρυκες μὲν ὕδωρ ἐπὶ χεῖρας ἔχευαν,
κοῦροι δὲ κρητῆρας ἐπεστέψαντο ποτοῖο,
340   νώμησαν δ᾽ ἄρα πᾶσιν ἐπαρξάμενοι δεπάεσσι·
γλώσσας δ᾽ ἐν πυρὶ βάλλον, ἀνιστάμενοι δ᾽ ἐπέλειβον.
αὐτὰρ ἐπεὶ σπεῖσάν τ᾽ ἔπιον θ᾽, ὅσον ἤθελε θυμός,
δὴ τότ᾽ Ἀθηναίη καὶ Τηλέμαχος θεοειδὴς

and you shall have gone on a fruitless journey. But to Menelaus I bid and command you to go, for he has but lately come from abroad, from a folk whence no one would hope in his heart to return, once the storms had driven him astray into a sea so great that the very birds do not return from it in the space of a year, so great is it and terrible. But now go your way with your ship and your comrades, or, if you will go by land, here are chariot and horses at hand for you, and here at your service are my sons, who will be your guides to splendid Lacedaemon, where lives fair-haired Menelaus. And do you beseech him yourself that he may tell you the very truth. A lie will he not utter, for he is wise indeed."

So he spoke, and the sun set, and darkness came on. Then among them spoke the goddess, flashing-eyed Athene: "Old man, truly have you told this tale. But come, first cut the tongues, then mix the wine, that when we have poured libations to Poseidon and the other immortals, we may think of sleep; for it is time for that. Already the light has gone down beneath the darkness, and it is not right to sit long at the feast of the gods, but to go home."

So spoke the daughter of Zeus, and they hearkened to her voice. Heralds poured water over their hands, and youths filled the bowls brimful of drink, and served out to all, pouring first drops for libation into the cups. Then they cast the tongues upon the fire, and, rising up, poured libations upon them. But when they had poured libations and had drunk to their hearts' content, then Athene and godlike Telemachus were both eager to return to the hollow

ἄμφω ἱέσθην κοίλην ἐπὶ νῆα νέεσθαι.
345 Νέστωρ δ' αὖ κατέρυκε καθαπτόμενος ἐπέεσσιν·
"Ζεὺς τό γ' ἀλεξήσειε καὶ ἀθάνατοι θεοὶ ἄλλοι,
ὡς ὑμεῖς παρ' ἐμεῖο θοὴν ἐπὶ νῆα κίοιτε
ὥς τέ τευ ἦ παρὰ πάμπαν ἀνείμονος ἠδὲ πενιχροῦ,
ᾧ οὔ τι χλαῖναι καὶ ῥήγεα πόλλ' ἐνὶ οἴκῳ,
350 οὔτ' αὐτῷ μαλακῶς οὔτε ξείνοισιν ἐνεύδειν.
αὐτὰρ ἐμοὶ πάρα μὲν χλαῖναι καὶ ῥήγεα καλά.
οὔ θην δὴ τοῦδ' ἀνδρὸς Ὀδυσσῆος φίλος υἱὸς
νηὸς ἐπ' ἰκριόφιν καταλέξεται, ὄφρ' ἂν ἐγώ γε
ζώω, ἔπειτα δὲ παῖδες ἐνὶ μεγάροισι λίπωνται,
355 ξείνους ξεινίζειν, ὅς τίς κ' ἐμὰ δώμαθ' ἵκηται."
    τὸν δ' αὖτε προσέειπε θεά, γλαυκῶπις Ἀθήνη·
"εὖ δὴ ταῦτά γ' ἔφησθα, γέρον φίλε· σοὶ δὲ ἔοικεν
Τηλέμαχον πείθεσθαι, ἐπεὶ πολὺ κάλλιον οὕτως.
ἀλλ' οὗτος μὲν νῦν σοὶ ἅμ' ἕψεται, ὄφρα κεν εὕδῃ
360 σοῖσιν ἐνὶ μεγάροισιν· ἐγὼ δ' ἐπὶ νῆα μέλαιναν
εἶμ', ἵνα θαρσύνω θ' ἑτάρους εἴπω τε ἕκαστα.
οἶος γὰρ μετὰ τοῖσι γεραίτερος εὔχομαι εἶναι·
οἱ δ' ἄλλοι φιλότητι νεώτεροι ἄνδρες ἕπονται,
πάντες ὁμηλικίη μεγαθύμου Τηλεμάχοιο.
365 ἔνθα κε λεξαίμην κοίλῃ παρὰ νηὶ μελαίνῃ
νῦν· ἀτὰρ ἠῶθεν μετὰ Καύκωνας μεγαθύμους
εἶμ' ἔνθα χρεῖός μοι ὀφέλλεται, οὔ τι νέον γε
οὐδ' ὀλίγον. σὺ δὲ τοῦτον, ἐπεὶ τεὸν ἵκετο δῶμα,
πέμψον σὺν δίφρῳ τε καὶ υἱέι· δὸς δέ οἱ ἵππους,
370 οἵ τοι ἐλαφρότατοι θείειν καὶ κάρτος ἄριστοι."
    ὣς ἄρα φωνήσασ' ἀπέβη γλαυκῶπις Ἀθήνη

106

ship; but Nestor on his part sought to detain them, and he spoke to them, saying:

"This may Zeus forbid, and the other immortal gods, that you should go from my house to your swift ship as from one utterly without raiment and poor, who has not cloaks and blankets in plenty in his house, whereon both he and his guests may sleep softly. In my house are both cloaks and fair blankets. Never surely shall the staunch son of this man Odysseus lie down upon the deck of a ship, while I yet live and children after me are left in my halls to entertain strangers, whosoever shall come to my house."

Then the goddess, flashing-eyed Athene, answered him: "Well indeed have you spoken in this, old friend, and it is fitting for Telemachus to hearken to you, since it is far better thus. But while he shall now follow with you, that he may sleep in your halls, I for my part will go to the black ship, that I may hearten my comrades and tell them everything. For alone among them I claim to be an older man; the others are younger who follow in friendship, all of them of like age with great-hearted Telemachus. There will I lie down by the hollow black ship this night, but in the morning I will go to the great-hearted Cauconians, where a debt is owing to me, by no means new or small. But send this man on his way with a chariot and with your son, since he has come to your house, and give him horses, the fleetest you have in running and the best in strength."

So spoke the goddess, flashing-eyed Athene, and she

φήνῃ εἰδομένη· θάμβος δ' ἕλε πάντας ἰδόντας.[1]
θαύμαζεν δ' ὁ γεραιός, ὅπως ἴδεν ὀφθαλμοῖσι·
Τηλεμάχου δ' ἕλε χεῖρα, ἔπος τ' ἔφατ' ἔκ τ' ὀνόμαζεν·

375 "ὦ φίλος, οὔ σε ἔολπα κακὸν καὶ ἄναλκιν ἔσεσθαι,
εἰ δή τοι νέῳ ὧδε θεοὶ πομπῆες ἕπονται.
οὐ μὲν γάρ τις ὅδ' ἄλλος Ὀλύμπια δώματ' ἐχόντων,
ἀλλὰ Διὸς θυγάτηρ, κυδίστη[2] τριτογένεια,
ἥ τοι καὶ πατέρ' ἐσθλὸν ἐν Ἀργείοισιν ἐτίμα.

380 ἀλλὰ ἄνασσ' ἵληθι, δίδωθι δέ μοι κλέος ἐσθλόν,
αὐτῷ καὶ παίδεσσι καὶ αἰδοίῃ παρακοίτι·
σοὶ δ' αὖ ἐγὼ ῥέξω βοῦν ἦνιν εὐρυμέτωπον
ἀδμήτην, ἣν οὔ πω ὑπὸ ζυγὸν ἤγαγεν ἀνήρ·
τήν τοι ἐγὼ ῥέξω χρυσὸν κέρασιν περιχεύας."

385 ὣς ἔφατ' εὐχόμενος, τοῦ δ' ἔκλυε Παλλὰς Ἀθήνη.
τοῖσιν δ' ἡγεμόνευε Γερήνιος ἱππότα Νέστωρ,
υἱάσι καὶ γαμβροῖσιν, ἑὰ πρὸς δώματα καλά.
ἀλλ' ὅτε δώμαθ' ἵκοντο ἀγακλυτὰ τοῖο ἄνακτος,
ἑξείης ἕζοντο κατὰ κλισμούς τε θρόνους τε·

390 τοῖς δ' ὁ γέρων ἐλθοῦσιν ἀνὰ κρητῆρα κέρασσεν
οἴνου ἡδυπότοιο, τὸν ἑνδεκάτῳ ἐνιαυτῷ
ὤιξεν ταμίη καὶ ἀπὸ κρήδεμνον ἔλυσε·
τοῦ ὁ γέρων κρητῆρα κεράσσατο, πολλὰ δ' Ἀθήνῃ
εὔχετ' ἀποσπένδων, κούρῃ Διὸς αἰγιόχοιο.

395 αὐτὰρ ἐπεὶ σπεῖσάν τ' ἔπιον θ', ὅσον ἤθελε θυμός,
οἱ μὲν κακκείοντες ἔβαν οἰκόνδε ἕκαστος,
τὸν δ' αὐτοῦ κοίμησε Γερήνιος ἱππότα Νέστωρ,

---

[1] ἰδόντας: Ἀχαιούς
[2] κυδίστη Zenodotus: ἀγελείη

departed in the likeness of a sea eagle; and amazement fell upon everyone at the sight, and the old man marveled, when his eyes beheld it. And he grasped the hand of Telemachus, and spoke, and addressed him:

"Friend, I do not think you will prove a base man or a craven if truly when you are so young the gods follow you to be your guides. For truly this is no other of those who have their dwellings on Olympus but the daughter of Zeus, Tritogeneia, the maid most glorious, she that honored also your noble father among the Argives. Be gracious, Queen, and grant to me fair renown, to me and to my sons and to my revered wife; and to you in return will I sacrifice a yearling heifer, broad of brow, unbroken, which no man has yet led beneath the yoke. Her will I sacrifice, and I will overlay her horns with gold."

So he spoke in prayer, and Pallas Athene heard him. Then the horseman, Nestor of Gerenia, led them, his sons and the husbands of his daughters, to his beautiful palace. And when they reached the glorious palace of the king, they sat down in rows on the chairs and high seats; and on their coming the old man mixed for them a bowl of sweet wine, which now in the eleventh year the housekeeper opened, when she had broken the seal upon it. Of this the old man bade mix a bowl, and earnestly he prayed, as he poured libations, to Athene, the daughter of Zeus who bears the aegis.

But when they had poured libations, and had drunk to their hearts' content, they went, each to his home, to take their rest. But the horseman, Nestor of Gerenia, bade

Τηλέμαχον, φίλον υἱὸν Ὀδυσσῆος θείοιο,
τρητοῖς ἐν λεχέεσσιν ὑπ' αἰθούσῃ ἐριδούπῳ,
400 πὰρ δ' ἄρ' ἐυμμελίην Πεισίστρατον, ὄρχαμον ἀνδρῶν,
ὅς οἱ ἔτ' ἠίθεος παίδων ἦν ἐν μεγάροισιν·
αὐτὸς δ' αὖτε καθεῦδε μυχῷ δόμου ὑψηλοῖο,
τῷ δ' ἄλοχος δέσποινα λέχος πόρσυνε καὶ εὐνήν.
ἦμος δ' ἠριγένεια φάνη ῥοδοδάκτυλος Ἠώς,
405 ὤρνυτ' ἄρ' ἐξ εὐνῆφι Γερήνιος ἱππότα Νέστωρ,
ἐκ δ' ἐλθὼν κατ' ἄρ' ἕζετ' ἐπὶ ξεστοῖσι λίθοισιν·
οἵ οἱ ἔσαν προπάροιθε θυράων ὑψηλάων,
λευκοί, ἀποστίλβοντες ἀλείφατος· οἷς ἔπι μὲν πρὶν
Νηλεὺς ἵζεσκεν, θεόφιν μήστωρ ἀτάλαντος·
410 ἀλλ' ὁ μὲν ἤδη κηρὶ δαμεὶς Ἄιδόσδε βεβήκει,
Νέστωρ αὖ τότ' ἐφῖζε Γερήνιος, οὖρος Ἀχαιῶν,
σκῆπτρον ἔχων. περὶ δ' υἷες ἀολλέες ἠγερέθοντο
ἐκ θαλάμων ἐλθόντες, Ἐχέφρων τε Στρατίος τε
Περσεύς τ' Ἄρητός τε καὶ ἀντίθεος Θρασυμήδης.
415 τοῖσι δ' ἔπειθ' ἕκτος Πεισίστρατος ἤλυθεν ἥρως,
πὰρ δ' ἄρα Τηλέμαχον θεοείκελον εἷσαν ἄγοντες.
τοῖσι δὲ μύθων ἦρχε Γερήνιος ἱππότα Νέστωρ·
"καρπαλίμως μοι, τέκνα φίλα, κρηήνατ' ἐέλδωρ,
ὄφρ' ἦ τοι πρώτιστα θεῶν ἱλάσσομ' Ἀθήνην,
420 ἥ μοι ἐναργὴς ἦλθε θεοῦ ἐς δαῖτα θάλειαν.
ἀλλ' ἄγ' ὁ μὲν πεδίονδ' ἐπὶ βοῦν ἴτω, ὄφρα τάχιστα
ἔλθῃσιν, ἐλάσῃ δὲ βοῶν ἐπιβουκόλος ἀνήρ·
εἷς δ' ἐπὶ Τηλεμάχου μεγαθύμου νῆα μέλαιναν
πάντας ἰὼν ἑτάρους ἀγέτω, λιπέτω δὲ δύ' οἴους·
425 εἷς δ' αὖ χρυσοχόον Λαέρκεα δεῦρο κελέσθω

Telemachus, the staunch son of divine Odysseus, to sleep there on a corded bedstead under the echoing portico, and by him Peisistratus, of the good ashen spear, a leader of men, who among his sons was still unwed in the palace. But he himself slept in the inmost chamber of the lofty house, and beside him the lady his wife brought him love and comfort.

As soon as early Dawn appeared, the rosy-fingered, up from his bed rose the horseman, Nestor of Gerenia, and went forth and sat down on the polished stones which were before his lofty doors, white and glistening as with oil. On these of old was accustomed to sit Neleus, the peer of the gods in counsel; but before this he had been stricken by fate and had gone down to the house of Hades, and now there sat upon them in his turn Nestor of Gerenia, the warder of the Achaeans, holding a scepter in his hands. About him his sons gathered in a throng as they came forth from their chambers, Echephron and Stratius and Perseus and Aretus and godlike Thrasymedes; to these then came as sixth the hero Peisistratus, and they brought godlike Telemachus and made him sit beside him; and the horseman, Nestor of Gerenia, was first to speak among them:

"Quickly, my dear children, fulfill my desire, that first of all the gods I may propitiate Athene, who came to me in manifest presence to the rich feast of the god. Come now, let someone go to the plain for a heifer, that she may come speedily, and that the cowherd may drive her; and let another go to the black ship of great-hearted Telemachus and bring all his comrades, and let him leave two men only; and let another again bid the goldsmith Laërces come

ἐλθεῖν, ὄφρα βοὸς χρυσὸν κέρασιν περιχεύῃ.
οἱ δ' ἄλλοι μένετ' αὐτοῦ ἀολλέες, εἴπατε δ' εἴσω
δμῳῇσιν κατὰ δώματ' ἀγακλυτὰ δαῖτα πένεσθαι,
ἕδρας τε ξύλα τ' ἀμφὶ καὶ ἀγλαὸν οἰσέμεν ὕδωρ."

430 ὣς ἔφαθ', οἱ δ' ἄρα πάντες ἐποίπνυον. ἦλθε μὲν ἂρ
βοῦς
ἐκ πεδίου, ἦλθον δὲ θοῆς παρὰ νηὸς ἐίσης
Τηλεμάχου ἕταροι μεγαλήτορος, ἦλθε δὲ χαλκεὺς
ὅπλ' ἐν χερσὶν ἔχων χαλκήια, πείρατα τέχνης,
ἄκμονά τε σφῦράν τ' εὐποίητόν τε πυράγρην,

435 οἷσίν τε χρυσὸν εἰργάζετο· ἦλθε δ' Ἀθήνη
ἱρῶν ἀντιόωσα. γέρων δ' ἱππηλάτα Νέστωρ
χρυσὸν ἔδωχ'· ὁ δ' ἔπειτα βοὸς κέρασιν περίχευεν
ἀσκήσας, ἵν' ἄγαλμα θεὰ κεχάροιτο ἰδοῦσα.
βοῦν δ' ἀγέτην κεράων Στρατίος καὶ δῖος Ἐχέφρων.

440 χέρνιβα δέ σφ' Ἄρητος ἐν ἀνθεμόεντι λέβητι
ἤλυθεν ἐκ θαλάμοιο φέρων, ἑτέρῃ δ' ἔχεν οὐλὰς
ἐν κανέῳ· πέλεκυν δὲ μενεπτόλεμος Θρασυμήδης
ὀξὺν ἔχων ἐν χειρὶ παρίστατο βοῦν ἐπικόψων.
Περσεὺς δ' ἀμνίον εἶχε· γέρων δ' ἱππηλάτα Νέστωρ

445 χέρνιβά τ' οὐλοχύτας τε κατήρχετο, πολλὰ δ' Ἀθήνῃ
εὔχετ' ἀπαρχόμενος, κεφαλῆς τρίχας ἐν πυρὶ βάλλων.
αὐτὰρ ἐπεί ῥ' εὔξαντο καὶ οὐλοχύτας προβάλοντο,
αὐτίκα Νέστορος υἱὸς ὑπέρθυμος Θρασυμήδης
ἤλασεν ἄγχι στάς· πέλεκυς δ' ἀπέκοψε τένοντας

450 αὐχενίους, λῦσεν δὲ βοὸς μένος. αἱ δ' ὀλόλυξαν
θυγατέρες τε νυοί τε καὶ αἰδοίη παράκοιτις

hither, that he may overlay the heifer's horns with gold. Remain here together, the rest of you, and bid the handmaids within to make ready a feast throughout our glorious halls, to bring seats, and logs to set on either side of the altar, and to bring clear water."

So he spoke, and they all set busily to work. The heifer came from the plain, and from the swift, shapely ship came the comrades of great-hearted Telemachus; the smith came, bearing in his hands his tools of bronze, the implements of his craft, anvil and hammer and well-made tongs, with which he wrought the gold; and Athene came to accept the sacrifice. Then the old man, Nestor, driver of chariots, gave gold, and the smith prepared it, and overlaid with it the horns of the heifer, that the goddess might rejoice when she beheld the offering. And Stratius and noble Echephron led the heifer by the horns, and Aretus came from the chamber, bringing them water for the hands in a basin embossed with flowers, and in the other hand he held barley grains in a basket; and Thrasymedes, steadfast in fight, stood by, holding in his hands a sharp axe, to fell the heifer; and Perseus held the bowl for the blood. Then the old man, Nestor, driver of chariots, began the opening rite of hand-washing and sprinkling with barley grains, and earnestly he prayed to Athene, cutting off as first offering the hair from the head, and casting it into the fire.

Now when they had prayed, and had strewn the barley grains, at once the son of Nestor, Thrasymedes, high of heart, came near and dealt the blow; and the axe cut through the sinews of the neck, and loosened the strength of the heifer, and the women raised the sacred cry, the daughters and the sons' wives and the revered wife of Nes-

Νέστορος, Εὐρυδίκη, πρέσβα Κλυμένοιο θυγατρῶν.
οἱ μὲν ἔπειτ᾽ ἀνελόντες ἀπὸ χθονὸς εὐρυοδείης
ἔσχον· ἀτὰρ σφάξεν Πεισίστρατος, ὄρχαμος ἀνδρῶν.
455 τῆς δ᾽ ἐπεὶ ἐκ μέλαν αἷμα ῥύη, λίπε δ᾽ ὀστέα θυμός,
αἶψ᾽ ἄρα μιν διέχευαν, ἄφαρ δ᾽ ἐκ μηρία τάμνον
πάντα κατὰ μοῖραν, κατά τε κνίσῃ ἐκάλυψαν
δίπτυχα ποιήσαντες, ἐπ᾽ αὐτῶν δ᾽ ὠμοθέτησαν.
καῖε δ᾽ ἐπὶ σχίζῃς ὁ γέρων, ἐπὶ δ᾽ αἴθοπα οἶνον
460 λεῖβε· νέοι δὲ παρ᾽ αὐτὸν ἔχον πεμπώβολα χερσίν.
αὐτὰρ ἐπεὶ κατὰ μῆρ᾽ ἐκάη καὶ σπλάγχνα πάσαντο,
μίστυλλόν τ᾽ ἄρα τἆλλα καὶ ἀμφ᾽ ὀβελοῖσιν ἔπειραν,
ὤπτων δ᾽ ἀκροπόρους ὀβελοὺς ἐν χερσὶν ἔχοντες.
      τόφρα δὲ Τηλέμαχον λοῦσεν καλὴ Πολυκάστη,
465 Νέστορος ὁπλοτάτη θυγάτηρ Νηληϊάδαο.
αὐτὰρ ἐπεὶ λοῦσέν τε καὶ ἔχρισεν λίπ᾽ ἐλαίῳ,
ἀμφὶ δέ μιν φᾶρος καλὸν βάλεν ἠδὲ χιτῶνα,
ἔκ ῥ᾽ ἀσαμίνθου βῆ δέμας ἀθανάτοισιν ὁμοῖος·
πὰρ δ᾽ ὅ γε Νέστορ᾽ ἰὼν κατ᾽ ἄρ᾽ ἕζετο, ποιμένα λαῶν.
470 οἱ δ᾽ ἐπεὶ ὤπτησαν κρέ᾽ ὑπέρτερα καὶ ἐρύσαντο,
δαίνυνθ᾽ ἑζόμενοι· ἐπὶ δ᾽ ἀνέρες ἐσθλοὶ ὄροντο
οἶνον οἰνοχοεῦντες ἐνὶ χρυσέοις δεπάεσσιν.
αὐτὰρ ἐπεὶ πόσιος καὶ ἐδητύος ἐξ ἔρον ἕντο,
τοῖσι δὲ μύθων ἦρχε Γερήνιος ἱππότα Νέστωρ·
475   "παῖδες ἐμοί, ἄγε Τηλεμάχῳ καλλίτριχας ἵππους
ζεύξαθ᾽ ὑφ᾽ ἅρματ᾽ ἄγοντες, ἵνα πρήσσῃσιν ὁδοῖο."

---

[a] Apparently the original purpose of this rite, no longer under-
stood in Homer's time, was to reconstitute the animal symbolically

tor, Eurydice, the eldest of the daughters of Clymenus. Then the men raised the heifer's head from the broad-wayed earth and held it, and Peisistratus, leader of men, cut the throat. And when the black blood had flowed from her and the life had left the bones, at once they cut up the body and straightway cut out the thigh pieces all in due order, and covered them with a double layer of fat, and laid the raw bits upon them.[a] Then the old man burned them on billets of wood, and poured over them sparkling wine, and beside him the young men held in their hands the five-pronged forks. But when the thigh pieces were wholly burned, and they had tasted the inner parts, they cut up the rest and spitted and roasted it, holding the pointed spits in their hands.

Meanwhile the fair Polycaste, the youngest daughter of Nestor, son of Neleus, bathed Telemachus. And when she had bathed him and anointed him with oil, and had cast about him a fair cloak and a tunic, forth he came from the bath in form like the immortals; and he went and sat down by Nestor, the shepherd of the people.

Now when they had roasted the outer flesh and had drawn it off the spits, they sat down and feasted, and worthy men waited on them, pouring wine into golden cups. But when they had put from them the desire of food and drink, the horseman, Nestor of Gerenia, was first to speak, saying:

"My sons, up, yoke for Telemachus horses with beautiful mane beneath the chariot, that he may get forward on his journey."

by burning representative bits of its several members together with the bones and fat. Walter Burkert, *Greek Religion* (Cambridge, Mass., and Oxford, 1985), p. 57. Cf. *Odyssey*, 14.427–28. D.

ὣς ἔφαθ', οἱ δ' ἄρα τοῦ μάλα μὲν κλύον ἠδ' ἐπίθοντο,
καρπαλίμως δ' ἔζευξαν ὑφ' ἅρμασιν ὠκέας ἵππους.
ἐν δὲ γυνὴ ταμίη σῖτον καὶ οἶνον ἔθηκεν
480 ὄψα τε, οἷα ἔδουσι διοτρεφέες βασιλῆες.
ἂν δ' ἄρα Τηλέμαχος περικαλλέα βήσετο δίφρον·
πὰρ δ' ἄρα Νεστορίδης Πεισίστρατος, ὄρχαμος ἀνδρῶν,
ἐς δίφρον τ' ἀνέβαινε καὶ ἡνία λάζετο χερσί,
μάστιξεν δ' ἐλάαν, τὼ δ' οὐκ ἀέκοντε πετέσθην
485 ἐς πεδίον, λιπέτην δὲ Πύλου αἰπὺ πτολίεθρον.
οἱ δὲ πανημέριοι σεῖον ζυγὸν ἀμφὶς ἔχοντες.

    δύσετό τ' ἠέλιος σκιόωντό τε πᾶσαι ἀγυιαί,
ἐς Φηρὰς δ' ἵκοντο Διοκλῆος ποτὶ δῶμα,
υἱέος Ὀρτιλόχοιο, τὸν Ἀλφειὸς τέκε παῖδα.
490 ἔνθα δὲ νύκτ' ἄεσαν, ὁ δὲ τοῖς πὰρ ξείνια θῆκεν.

    ἦμος δ' ἠριγένεια φάνη ῥοδοδάκτυλος Ἠώς,
ἵππους τε ζεύγνυντ' ἀνά θ' ἅρματα ποικίλ' ἔβαινον·
ἐκ δ' ἔλασαν προθύροιο καὶ αἰθούσης ἐριδούπου·[1]
μάστιξεν δ' ἐλάαν, τὼ δ' οὐκ ἀέκοντε πετέσθην·
495 ἷξον δ' ἐς πεδίον πυρηφόρον, ἔνθα δ' ἔπειτα
ἦνον ὁδόν· τοῖον γὰρ ὑπέκφερον ὠκέες ἵπποι.
δύσετό τ' ἠέλιος σκιόωντό τε πᾶσαι ἀγυιαί.

[1] Line 493 is omitted in most MSS.

So he spoke, and they readily hearkened and obeyed; and quickly they yoked beneath the chariot the swift horses. And the housewife placed in the chariot bread and wine and dainties, such as kings, fostered by Zeus, are accustomed to eat. Then Telemachus mounted the beautiful chariot, and Peisistratus, son of Nestor, a leader of men, mounted beside him, and took the reins in his hands. He touched the horses with the whip to start them, and nothing loath the pair sped on to the plain, and left the steep citadel of Pylos. So all day long they shook the yoke which spanned their necks.

Now the sun set and all the ways grew dark. And they came to Pherae, to the house of Diocles, son of Ortilochus, whom Alpheus begot. There they spent the night, and before them he set the entertainment due to strangers.

As soon as early Dawn appeared, the rosy-fingered, they yoked the horses and mounted the inlaid chariot, and drove forth from the gateway and the echoing portico. Then Peisistratus touched the horses with the whip to start them, and nothing loath the pair sped onward. So they came to the wheat-bearing plain, and thereafter pressed on toward their journey's end, so well did their swift horses bear them on. And the sun set and all the ways grew dark.

Δ

Οἱ δ' ἷξον κοίλην Λακεδαίμονα κητώεσσαν,
πρὸς δ' ἄρα δώματ' ἔλων Μενελάου κυδαλίμοιο.
τὸν δ' εὗρον δαινύντα γάμον πολλοῖσιν ἔτησιν
υἱέος ἠδὲ θυγατρὸς ἀμύμονος ᾧ ἐνὶ οἴκῳ.
5   τὴν μὲν Ἀχιλλῆος ρηξήνορος υἱέι πέμπεν·
ἐν Τροίῃ γὰρ πρῶτον ὑπέσχετο καὶ κατένευσε
δωσέμεναι, τοῖσιν δὲ θεοὶ γάμον ἐξετέλειον.
τὴν ἄρ' ὅ γ' ἔνθ' ἵπποισι καὶ ἅρμασι πέμπε νέεσθαι
Μυρμιδόνων προτὶ ἄστυ περικλυτόν, οἷσιν ἄνασσεν.
10   υἱέι δὲ Σπάρτηθεν Ἀλέκτορος ἤγετο κούρην,
ὅς οἱ τηλύγετος γένετο κρατερὸς Μεγαπένθης
ἐκ δούλης· Ἑλένῃ δὲ θεοὶ γόνον οὐκέτ' ἔφαινον,
ἐπεὶ δὴ τὸ πρῶτον ἐγείνατο παῖδ' ἐρατεινήν,
Ἑρμιόνην, ἣ εἶδος ἔχε χρυσέης Ἀφροδίτης.
15   ὣς οἱ μὲν δαίνυντο καθ' ὑψερεφὲς μέγα δῶμα
γείτονες ἠδὲ ἔται Μενελάου κυδαλίμοιο,
τερπόμενοι· μετὰ δέ σφιν ἐμέλπετο θεῖος ἀοιδὸς
φορμίζων, δοιὼ δὲ κυβιστητῆρε κατ' αὐτούς,
μολπῆς ἐξάρχοντος,[1] ἐδίνευον κατὰ μέσσους.
20   τὼ δ' αὖτ' ἐν προθύροισι δόμων αὐτώ τε καὶ ἵππω,

---

[1] ἐξάρχοντος: ἐξάρχοντες

118

BOOK 4

And they came to the hollow land of Lacedaemon with
its many ravines, and drove to the palace of glorious
Menelaus. Him they found giving a marriage feast to his
many kinsfolk for his flawless son and daughter within his
house. His daughter he was sending to the son of Achilles,
breaker of the ranks of men, for in the land of Troy he first
had promised and pledged that he would give her, and now
the gods were bringing their marriage to pass. Her then he
was sending forth with horses and chariots to go her way to
the glorious city of the Myrmidons, over whom her lord
was king; but for his son he was bringing to his home from
Sparta the daughter of Alector, to wed the stalwart Mega-
penthes, who was his son well-beloved, born of a slave
woman; for to Helen the gods vouchsafed issue no more
after she had at the first borne her lovely child, Hermione,
who had the beauty of golden Aphrodite. So they were
feasting in the great high-roofed hall, the neighbors and
kinsfolk of glorious Menelaus, and making merry; and
among them a divine minstrel was singing to the lyre, and
two tumblers whirled up and down through the midst of
them, leading the dance.

Then the two, the hero Telemachus and the glorious

Τηλέμαχός θ' ἥρως καὶ Νέστορος ἀγλαὸς υἱός,
στῆσαν· ὁ δὲ προμολὼν ἴδετο κρείων Ἐτεωνεύς,
ὀτρηρὸς θεράπων Μενελάου κυδαλίμοιο,
βῆ δ' ἴμεν ἀγγελέων διὰ δώματα ποιμένι λαῶν,
25   ἀγχοῦ δ' ἱστάμενος ἔπεα πτερόεντα προσηύδα·
      "ξείνω δή τινε τώδε, διοτρεφὲς ὦ Μενέλαε,
ἄνδρε δύω, γενεῇ δὲ Διὸς μεγάλοιο ἔικτον.
ἀλλ' εἴπ', ἦ σφωιν καταλύσομεν ὠκέας ἵππους,
ἦ ἄλλον πέμπωμεν ἱκανέμεν, ὅς κε φιλήσῃ."
30   τὸν δὲ μέγ' ὀχθήσας προσέφη ξανθὸς Μενέλαος·
"οὐ μὲν νήπιος ἦσθα, Βοηθοΐδη Ἐτεωνεῦ,
τὸ πρίν· ἀτὰρ μὲν νῦν γε πάις ὣς νήπια βάζεις.
ἦ μὲν δὴ νῶι ξεινήια πολλὰ φαγόντε
ἄλλων ἀνθρώπων δεῦρ' ἱκόμεθ', αἴ κέ ποθι Ζεὺς
35   ἐξοπίσω περ παύσῃ ὀιζύος. ἀλλὰ λύ' ἵππους
ξείνων, ἐς δ' αὐτοὺς προτέρω ἄγε θοινηθῆναι."
      ὣς φάθ', ὁ δὲ μεγάροιο διέσσυτο, κέκλετο δ' ἄλλους
ὀτρηροὺς θεράποντας ἅμα σπέσθαι ἑοῖ αὐτῷ.
οἱ δ' ἵππους μὲν λῦσαν ὑπὸ ζυγοῦ ἱδρώοντας,
40   καὶ τοὺς μὲν κατέδησαν ἐφ' ἱππείῃσι κάπῃσι,
πὰρ δ' ἔβαλον ζειάς, ἀνὰ δὲ κρῖ λευκὸν ἔμιξαν,
ἅρματα δ' ἔκλιναν πρὸς ἐνώπια παμφανόωντα,
αὐτοὺς δ' εἰσῆγον θεῖον δόμον. οἱ δὲ ἰδόντες
θαύμαζον κατὰ δῶμα διοτρεφέος βασιλῆος·
45   ὥς τε γὰρ ἠελίου αἴγλη πέλεν ἠὲ σελήνης
δῶμα καθ' ὑψερεφὲς Μενελάου κυδαλίμοιο.
αὐτὰρ ἐπεὶ τάρπησαν ὁρώμενοι ὀφθαλμοῖσιν,
ἔς ῥ' ἀσαμίνθους βάντες ἐυξέστας λούσαντο.

son of Nestor, halted at the gateway of the palace, they and
their two horses. And the lord Eteoneus came forth and
saw them, the eager squire of glorious Menelaus; and he
went through the hall to bear the tidings to the shepherd of
the people. So he came near and spoke to him winged
words:

"Here are two strangers, Menelaus, fostered of Zeus,
two men that are like the seed of great Zeus. But tell me,
shall we unyoke for them their swift horses, or send them
on their way to some other host, who will give them enter-
tainment?"

Then, stirred to exceeding displeasure, fair-haired
Menelaus spoke to him: "Before this it was not your cus-
tom to be a fool, Eteoneus, son of Boethous, but now like a
child you talk folly. Surely we two many times ate the
hospitable cheer of other men on our way here, hoping
that Zeus would some day grant us respite from pain. No,
unyoke the strangers' horses, and bring the men in, that
they may feast."

So he spoke, and the other hastened through the hall,
and called to the other eager squires to follow along with
him. They loosed the sweating horses from beneath the
yoke and tied them at the stalls of the horses, and flung
before them spelt, and mixed with it white barley. Then
they tilted the chariot against the shining entrance walls,
and led the men into the divine palace. But at the sight
they marveled as they passed through the palace of the
king, fostered by Zeus; for there was a gleam as of sun or
moon over the high-roofed house of glorious Menelaus.
But when they had satisfied their eyes with gazing they
went into the polished baths and bathed. And when the

τοὺς δ' ἐπεὶ οὖν δμῳαὶ λοῦσαν καὶ χρῖσαν ἐλαίῳ,
50 ἀμφὶ δ' ἄρα χλαίνας οὔλας βάλον ἠδὲ χιτῶνας,
ἔς ῥα θρόνους ἕζοντο παρ' Ἀτρεΐδην Μενέλαον.
χέρνιβα δ' ἀμφίπολος προχόῳ ἐπέχευε φέρουσα
καλῇ χρυσείῃ ὑπὲρ ἀργυρέοιο λέβητος,
νίψασθαι· παρὰ δὲ ξεστὴν ἐτάνυσσε τράπεζαν.
55 σῖτον δ' αἰδοίη ταμίη παρέθηκε φέρουσα,
εἴδατα πόλλ' ἐπιθεῖσα, χαριζομένη παρεόντων.
δαιτρὸς δὲ κρειῶν πίνακας παρέθηκεν ἀείρας
παντοίων, παρὰ δέ σφι τίθει χρύσεια κύπελλα.[1]
τὼ καὶ δεικνύμενος προσέφη ξανθὸς Μενέλαος·
60 "σίτου θ' ἅπτεσθον καὶ χαίρετον. αὐτὰρ ἔπειτα
δείπνου πασσαμένω εἰρησόμεθ', οἵ τινές ἐστον
ἀνδρῶν· οὐ γὰρ σφῶν γε γένος ἀπόλωλε τοκήων,
ἀλλ' ἀνδρῶν γένος ἐστὲ διοτρεφέων βασιλήων
σκηπτούχων, ἐπεὶ οὔ κε κακοὶ τοιούσδε τέκοιεν."[2]
65 ὣς φάτο, καί σφιν νῶτα βοὸς παρὰ πίονα θῆκεν
ὄπτ' ἐν χερσὶν ἑλών, τά ῥά οἱ γέρα πάρθεσαν αὐτῷ.
οἱ δ' ἐπ' ὀνείαθ' ἑτοῖμα προκείμενα χεῖρας ἴαλλον.
αὐτὰρ ἐπεὶ πόσιος καὶ ἐδητύος ἐξ ἔρον ἕντο,
δὴ τότε Τηλέμαχος προσεφώνεε Νέστορος υἱόν,
70 ἄγχι σχὼν κεφαλήν, ἵνα μὴ πευθοίαθ' οἱ ἄλλοι·
"φράζεο, Νεστορίδη, τῷ ἐμῷ κεχαρισμένε θυμῷ,
χαλκοῦ τε στεροπὴν κὰδ δώματα ἠχήεντα
χρυσοῦ τ' ἠλέκτρου τε καὶ ἀργύρου ἠδ' ἐλέφαντος.

[1] Lines 57 and 58 are omitted in many MSS.
[2] Lines 62–64, rejected by Zenodotus, Aristophanes, and Aristarchus, are bracketed by many editors.

maids had bathed them and anointed them with oil, and had cast about them fleecy cloaks and tunics, they sat down on chairs beside Menelaus, son of Atreus. Then a hand-maid brought water for the hands in a beautiful pitcher of gold, and poured it over a silver basin for them to wash, and beside them drew up a polished table. And the revered housekeeper brought and set before them bread, and with it dainties in abundance, giving freely of what she had. And a carver lifted up and set before them platters of all sorts of meats, and set by them golden goblets. Then fair-haired Menelaus greeted the two and said:

"Take the food, and be glad, and then when you have partaken of supper, we will ask you who among men you are; for in you two the line of your sires is not lost, but you are of the race of men that are sceptered kings, fostered by Zeus; for no commoner could beget such sons as you."

So saying he took in his hands roast meat and set it before them, the same fat ox chine which they had set before himself as a mark of honor. So they put forth their hands to the good cheer lying ready before them. But when they had put from them the desire for food and drink, then Telemachus spoke to the son of Nestor, hold-ing his head close to him, that the others might not hear:

"Son of Nestor, dear to this heart of mine, you see the flashing of bronze throughout these echoing halls, and the flashing of gold, of electrum,[a] of silver, and of ivory? Of

[a] Probably here the metal is meant, an alloy of gold and silver. In 15.460 and 18.296 the word, in the plural, means "amber beads." M.

Ζηνός που τοιήδε γ' Ὀλυμπίου ἔνδοθεν αὐλή,
75 ὅσσα τάδ' ἄσπετα πολλά· σέβας μ' ἔχει εἰσορόωντα."
    τοῦ δ' ἀγορεύοντος ξύνετο ξανθὸς Μενέλαος,
    καί σφεας φωνήσας ἔπεα πτερόεντα προσηύδα·
    "τέκνα φίλ', ἦ τοι Ζηνὶ βροτῶν οὐκ ἄν τις ἐρίζοι·
    ἀθάνατοι γὰρ τοῦ γε δόμοι καὶ κτήματ' ἔασιν·
80 ἀνδρῶν δ' ἤ κέν τίς μοι ἐρίσσεται, ἠὲ καὶ οὐκί,
    κτήμασιν. ἦ γὰρ πολλὰ παθὼν καὶ πόλλ' ἐπαληθεὶς
    ἠγαγόμην ἐν νηυσὶ καὶ ὀγδοάτῳ ἔτει ἦλθον,
    Κύπρον Φοινίκην τε καὶ Αἰγυπτίους ἐπαληθείς,
    Αἰθίοπάς θ' ἱκόμην καὶ Σιδονίους καὶ Ἐρεμβοὺς
85 καὶ Λιβύην, ἵνα τ' ἄρνες ἄφαρ κεραοὶ τελέθουσι.
    τρὶς γὰρ τίκτει μῆλα τελεσφόρον εἰς ἐνιαυτόν.
    ἔνθα μὲν οὔτε ἄναξ ἐπιδευὴς οὔτε τι ποιμὴν
    τυροῦ καὶ κρειῶν οὐδὲ γλυκεροῖο γάλακτος,
    ἀλλ' αἰεὶ παρέχουσιν ἐπηετανὸν γάλα θῆσθαι.
90 ἧος ἐγὼ περὶ κεῖνα πολὺν βίοτον συναγείρων
    ἠλώμην, τῆός μοι ἀδελφεὸν ἄλλος ἔπεφνεν
    λάθρη, ἀνωιστί, δόλῳ οὐλομένης ἀλόχοιο·
    ὣς οὔ τοι χαίρων τοῖσδε κτεάτεσσιν ἀνάσσω.
    καὶ πατέρων τάδε μέλλετ' ἀκουέμεν, οἵ τινες ὑμῖν
95 εἰσίν, ἐπεὶ μάλα πολλὰ πάθον, καὶ ἀπώλεσα οἶκον
    εὖ μάλα ναιετάοντα, κεχανδότα πολλὰ καὶ ἐσθλά.
    ὧν ὄφελον τριτάτην περ ἔχων ἐν δώμασι μοῖραν
    ναίειν, οἱ δ' ἄνδρες σόοι ἔμμεναι, οἳ τότ' ὄλοντο
    Τροίῃ ἐν εὐρείῃ ἑκὰς Ἄργεος ἱπποβότοιο.

such sort must be the court of Olympian Zeus within, such untold wealth is here; amazement holds me as I look."

Now as he spoke fair-haired Menelaus heard him, and he spoke and addressed them with winged words:

"Dear children, with Zeus, you may be sure, no mortal man could vie, for everlasting are his halls and his possessions; but of men another might vie with me in wealth or perhaps might not. For true it is that after many woes and wide wanderings I brought my wealth home in my ships and came in the eighth year. Over Cyprus and Phoenicia I wandered, and Egypt, and I came to the Ethiopians and the Sidonians and the Erembi, and to Libya, where the lambs are horned from their birth.[a] For there the ewes bear their young thrice within the full course of the year; there neither master nor shepherd has any lack of cheese or of meat or of sweet milk, but the flocks ever yield milk to the milking the year through. While I wandered in those lands gathering much livelihood, meanwhile another slew my brother by stealth and off his guard, by the guile of his accursed wife. Thus, you may understand, I have no joy in being lord of this wealth; and you may well have heard of this from your fathers, whosoever they may be, for greatly indeed did I suffer, and saw the ruin of a stately house, stored with much excellent treasure.[b] Would that I dwelt in my halls with but a third part of this wealth, and that those men were safe who then perished in the broad land

[a] So Aristotle understood the passage (*History of Animals* 7.28); Herodotus, on the contrary, took the meaning to be "begin at once to become horned" (4.29). Eustathius agrees with Herodotus. M.

[b] Paris stole not only Helen, but much property as well, *Iliad* 3.72, 92, 255, 282, 285; 7.350, 361–64. D.

100 ἀλλ' ἔμπης πάντας μὲν ὀδυρόμενος καὶ ἀχεύων
πολλάκις ἐν μεγάροισι καθήμενος ἡμετέροισιν
ἄλλοτε μέν τε γόῳ φρένα τέρπομαι, ἄλλοτε δ' αὖτε
παύομαι· αἰψηρὸς δὲ κόρος κρυεροῖο γόοιο.
τῶν πάντων οὐ τόσσον ὀδύρομαι, ἀχνύμενός περ,
105 ὡς ἑνός, ὅς τέ μοι ὕπνον ἀπεχθαίρει καὶ ἐδωδὴν
μνωομένῳ, ἐπεὶ οὔ τις Ἀχαιῶν τόσσ' ἐμόγησεν,
ὅσσ' Ὀδυσεὺς ἐμόγησε καὶ ἤρατο. τῷ δ' ἄρ' ἔμελλεν
αὐτῷ κήδε' ἔσεσθαι, ἐμοὶ δ' ἄχος αἰὲν ἄλαστον
κείνου, ὅπως δὴ δηρὸν ἀποίχεται, οὐδέ τι ἴδμεν,
110 ζώει ὅ γ' ἦ τέθνηκεν. ὀδύρονταί νύ που αὐτὸν
Λαέρτης θ' ὁ γέρων καὶ ἐχέφρων Πηνελόπεια
Τηλέμαχός θ', ὃν ἔλειπε νέον γεγαῶτ' ἐνὶ οἴκῳ."
    ὣς φάτο, τῷ δ' ἄρα πατρὸς ὑφ' ἵμερον ὦρσε γόοιο.
δάκρυ δ' ἀπὸ βλεφάρων χαμάδις βάλε πατρὸς ἀκούσας,
115 χλαῖναν πορφυρέην ἄντ' ὀφθαλμοῖιν ἀνασχὼν
ἀμφοτέρῃσιν χερσί. νόησε δέ μιν Μενέλαος,
μερμήριξε δ' ἔπειτα κατὰ φρένα καὶ κατὰ θυμόν,
ἠέ μιν αὐτὸν πατρὸς ἐάσειε μνησθῆναι
ἦ πρῶτ' ἐξερέοιτο ἕκαστά τε πειρήσαιτο.
120   ἧος ὁ ταῦθ' ὥρμαινε κατὰ φρένα καὶ κατὰ θυμόν,
ἐκ δ' Ἑλένη θαλάμοιο θυώδεος ὑψορόφοιο
ἤλυθεν Ἀρτέμιδι χρυσηλακάτῳ εἰκυῖα.
τῇ δ' ἄρ' ἅμ' Ἀδρήστη κλισίην εὔτυκτον ἔθηκεν,
Ἀλκίππη δὲ τάπητα φέρεν μαλακοῦ ἐρίοιο,
125 Φυλὼ δ' ἀργύρεον τάλαρον φέρε, τόν οἱ ἔθηκεν
Ἀλκάνδρη, Πολύβοιο δάμαρ, ὃς ἔναι' ἐνὶ Θήβῃς
Αἰγυπτίῃς, ὅθι πλεῖστα δόμοις ἐν κτήματα κεῖται·

126

of Troy far from horse-pasturing Argos. And yet, though I often sit in my halls weeping and sorrowing for them all— one moment indeed I ease my heart with weeping, and then again I cease, for men soon have surfeit of chill lament—yet for them all I mourn not so much, despite my grief, as for one only, who makes me loathe both sleep and food, when I think of him; for no one of the Achaeans toiled so much as Odysseus toiled and endured. But for himself, as it seems, his portion was to be only woe, and for me there is sorrow never to be forgotten for him, in that he is gone so long, nor do we know at all whether he is alive or dead. Mourned must he be by the old man Laertes, and by steadfast Penelope, and by Telemachus, whom he left a newborn child in his house."

So he spoke, and in Telemachus he roused the desire to weep for his father. Tears from his eyelids he let fall upon the ground, when he heard his father's name, and with both hands held up his purple cloak before his eyes. And Menelaus noted him, and debated in mind and heart whether he should leave him to speak of his father himself, or whether he should first question him and test him in each thing.

While he pondered thus in mind and heart, forth then from her fragrant high-roofed chamber came Helen, like Artemis of the golden distaff; and with her came Adraste, and placed for her a chair, beautifully wrought, and Alcippe brought a rug of soft wool and Phylo a silver basket, which Alcandre had given her, the wife of Polybus, who dwelt in Thebes of Egypt, where greatest store of wealth is laid up in men's houses. He gave to Menelaus

ὃς Μενελάῳ δῶκε δύ᾽ ἀργυρέας ἀσαμίνθους,
δοιοὺς δὲ τρίποδας, δέκα δὲ χρυσοῖο τάλαντα.
130 χωρὶς δ᾽ αὖθ᾽ Ἑλένῃ ἄλοχος πόρε κάλλιμα δῶρα ·
χρυσέην τ᾽ ἠλακάτην τάλαρόν θ᾽ ὑπόκυκλον ὄπασσεν
ἀργύρεον, χρυσῷ δ᾽ ἐπὶ χείλεα κεκράαντο.
τόν ῥά οἱ ἀμφίπολος Φυλὼ παρέθηκε φέρουσα
νήματος ἀσκητοῖο βεβυσμένον · αὐτὰρ ἐπ᾽ αὐτῷ
135 ἠλακάτη τετάνυστο ἰοδνεφὲς εἶρος ἔχουσα.
ἕζετο δ᾽ ἐν κλισμῷ, ὑπὸ δὲ θρῆνυς ποσὶν ἦεν.
αὐτίκα δ᾽ ἥ γ᾽ ἐπέεσσι πόσιν ἐρέεινεν ἕκαστα ·

"ἴδμεν δή, Μενέλαε διοτρεφές, οἵ τινες οἵδε
ἀνδρῶν εὐχετόωνται ἱκανέμεν ἡμέτερον δῶ;
140 ψεύσομαι ἦ ἔτυμον ἐρέω; κέλεται δέ με θυμός.
οὐ γάρ πώ τινά φημι ἐοικότα ὧδε ἰδέσθαι
οὔτ᾽ ἄνδρ᾽ οὔτε γυναῖκα, σέβας μ᾽ ἔχει εἰσορόωσαν,
ὡς ὅδ᾽ Ὀδυσσῆος μεγαλήτορος υἷι ἔοικε,
Τηλεμάχῳ, τὸν ἔλειπε νέον γεγαῶτ᾽ ἐνὶ οἴκῳ
145 κεῖνος ἀνήρ, ὅτ᾽ ἐμεῖο κυνώπιδος εἵνεκ᾽ Ἀχαιοὶ
ἤλθεθ᾽ ὑπὸ Τροίην πόλεμον θρασὺν ὁρμαίνοντες."

τὴν δ᾽ ἀπαμειβόμενος προσέφη ξανθὸς Μενέλαος ·
"οὕτω νῦν καὶ ἐγὼ νοέω, γύναι, ὡς σὺ ἐΐσκεις ·
κείνου γὰρ τοιοίδε πόδες τοιαίδε τε χεῖρες
150 ὀφθαλμῶν τε βολαὶ κεφαλή τ᾽ ἐφύπερθέ τε χαῖται.
καὶ νῦν ἦ τοι ἐγὼ μεμνημένος ἀμφ᾽ Ὀδυσῆι
μυθεόμην, ὅσα κεῖνος ὀιζύσας ἐμόγησεν
ἀμφ᾽ ἐμοί, αὐτὰρ ὁ πικρὸν[1] ὑπ᾽ ὀφρύσι δάκρυον εἶβε,
χλαῖναν πορφυρέην ἄντ᾽ ὀφθαλμοῖιν ἀνασχών."

---

[1] πικρὸν: πυκνὸν

128

two silver baths and two tripods and ten talents of gold. And besides these, his wife gave to Helen also beautiful gifts—a golden distaff and a basket with wheels did she give, a basket of silver, and its rims were gilded with gold. This then the handmaid Phylo brought and placed beside her, filled with finely spun yarn, and across it was laid the distaff laden with violet-dark wool. So Helen sat down upon the chair, and below was a footstool for the feet; and at once she questioned her husband on each matter, and said:

"Do we know, Menelaus, fostered by Zeus, who these men declare themselves to be who have come to our house? Shall I disguise my thought, or speak the truth? My heart bids me speak. For never yet, I declare, saw I one so like another, whether man or woman—amazement holds me, as I look—as this man is like the son of great-hearted Odysseus, Telemachus, whom that warrior left a newborn child in his house when for the sake of shameless me you Achaeans came up under the walls of Troy, pondering in your hearts fierce war."

Then fair-haired Menelaus answered her: "Even so do I myself now note it, wife, as you perceive the likeness. Such were his feet, such his hands, and the glances of his eyes, and his head and hair above. On my word, just now, as I made mention of Odysseus and was telling of all the woe and toil he endured for my sake, this youth let fall a bitter tear from beneath his brows, holding up his purple cloak before his eyes."

155　τὸν δ' αὖ Νεστορίδης Πεισίστρατος ἀντίον ηὔδα·
　　"Ἀτρεΐδη Μενέλαε διοτρεφές, ὄρχαμε λαῶν,
　　κείνου μέν τοι ὅδ' υἱὸς ἐτήτυμον, ὡς ἀγορεύεις·
　　ἀλλὰ σαόφρων ἐστί, νεμεσσᾶται δ' ἐνὶ θυμῷ
　　ὧδ' ἐλθὼν τὸ πρῶτον ἐπεσβολίας ἀναφαίνειν
160　ἄντα σέθεν, τοῦ νῶι θεοῦ ὣς τερπόμεθ' αὐδῇ.
　　αὐτὰρ ἐμὲ προέηκε Γερήνιος ἱππότα Νέστωρ
　　τῷ ἅμα πομπὸν ἕπεσθαι· ἐέλδετο γάρ σε ἰδέσθαι,
　　ὄφρα οἱ ἤ τι ἔπος ὑποθήσεαι ἠέ τι ἔργον.
　　πολλὰ γὰρ ἄλγε' ἔχει πατρὸς πάις οἰχομένοιο
165　ἐν μεγάροις, ᾧ μὴ ἄλλοι ἀοσσητῆρες ἔωσιν,
　　ὡς νῦν Τηλεμάχῳ ὁ μὲν οἴχεται, οὐδέ οἱ ἄλλοι
　　εἴσ' οἵ κεν κατὰ δῆμον ἀλάλκοιεν κακότητα."
　　τὸν δ' ἀπαμειβόμενος προσέφη ξανθὸς Μενέλαος·
　　"ὢ πόποι, ἦ μάλα δὴ φίλου ἀνέρος υἱὸς ἐμὸν δῶ
170　ἵκεθ', ὃς εἵνεκ' ἐμεῖο πολέας ἐμόγησεν ἀέθλους·
　　καί μιν ἔφην ἐλθόντα φιλησέμεν ἔξοχον ἄλλων
　　Ἀργείων, εἰ νῶιν ὑπεὶρ ἅλα νόστον ἔδωκε
　　νηυσὶ θοῇσι γενέσθαι Ὀλύμπιος εὐρύοπα Ζεύς.
　　καί κέ οἱ Ἀργεῖ νάσσα πόλιν καὶ δώματ' ἔτευξα,
175　ἐξ Ἰθάκης ἀγαγὼν σὺν κτήμασι καὶ τέκεϊ ᾧ
　　καὶ πᾶσιν λαοῖσι, μίαν πόλιν ἐξαλαπάξας,
　　αἳ περιναιετάουσιν, ἀνάσσονται δ' ἐμοὶ αὐτῷ.
　　καί κε θάμ' ἐνθάδ' ἐόντες ἐμισγόμεθ'· οὐδέ κεν ἡμέας
　　ἄλλο διέκρινεν φιλέοντέ τε τερπομένω τε,
180　πρίν γ' ὅτε δὴ θανάτοιο μέλαν νέφος ἀμφεκάλυψεν.
　　ἀλλὰ τὰ μέν που μέλλεν ἀγάσσεσθαι θεὸς αὐτός,
　　ὃς κεῖνον δύστηνον ἀνόστιμον οἶον ἔθηκεν."

BOOK 4

Then Peisistratus, son of Nestor, answered him: "Menelaus, son of Atreus, fostered by Zeus, leader of hosts, indeed this youth is his son, as you say. But he is of prudent mind and feels shame at heart thus on his first coming to make a show of forward words in the presence of you, in whose voice we both take delight as in a god's. But the horseman, Nestor of Gerenia, sent me forth to go with him as his guide, for he was eager to see you, that you might put in his heart some word or some deed. For many sorrows has a son in his halls when his father is gone, when there are no others to be his helpers, just as it is now with Telemachus; his father is gone, and there are no others among the people who might ward off his ruin."

Then fair-haired Menelaus answered him and said: "Will wonders never cease! Truly has there come to my house the son of a man well-beloved, who for my sake endured many toils. And I thought that if he came back I should give him welcome beyond all the other Argives, if Olympian Zeus, whose voice is borne afar, had granted to us two a return in our swift ships over the sea. And in Argos I would have given him a city to dwell in, and would have built him a house, when I had brought him from Ithaca with his goods and his son and all his people, driving out the dwellers of some one city among those that lie round about and obey me myself as their lord. Then, living here, should we often have met together, nor would anything have parted us, loving and joying in one another, until the black cloud of death enfolded us. But of this, I suppose, the god himself must have been jealous, who to that unfortunate man alone vouchsafed no return."

ὣς φάτο, τοῖσι δὲ πᾶσιν ὑφ' ἵμερον ὦρσε γόοιο.
κλαῖε μὲν Ἀργείη Ἑλένη, Διὸς ἐκγεγαυῖα,
185 κλαῖε δὲ Τηλέμαχός τε καὶ Ἀτρεΐδης Μενέλαος,
οὐδ' ἄρα Νέστορος υἱὸς ἀδακρύτω ἔχεν ὄσσε·
μνήσατο γὰρ κατὰ θυμὸν ἀμύμονος Ἀντιλόχοιο,
τόν ῥ' Ἠοῦς ἔκτεινε φαεινῆς ἀγλαὸς υἱός·
τοῦ ὅ γ' ἐπιμνησθεὶς ἔπεα πτερόεντ' ἀγόρευεν·
190 "Ἀτρεΐδη, περὶ μέν σε βροτῶν πεπνυμένον εἶναι
Νέστωρ φάσχ' ὁ γέρων, ὅτ' ἐπιμνησαίμεθα σεῖο
οἶσιν ἐνὶ μεγάροισι, καὶ ἀλλήλους ἐρέοιμεν.
καὶ νῦν, εἴ τί που ἔστι, πίθοιό μοι· οὐ γὰρ ἐγώ γε
τέρπομ' ὀδυρόμενος μεταδόρπιος, ἀλλὰ καὶ ἠὼς
195 ἔσσεται ἠριγένεια· νεμεσσῶμαί γε μὲν οὐδὲν
κλαίειν ὅς κε θάνῃσι βροτῶν καὶ πότμον ἐπίσπῃ.
τοῦτό νυ καὶ γέρας οἶον ὀιζυροῖσι βροτοῖσιν,
κείρασθαί τε κόμην βαλέειν τ' ἀπὸ δάκρυ παρειῶν.
καὶ γὰρ ἐμὸς τέθνηκεν ἀδελφεός, οὔ τι κάκιστος
200 Ἀργείων· μέλλεις δὲ σὺ ἴδμεναι· οὐ γὰρ ἐγώ γε
ἤντησ' οὐδὲ ἴδον· περὶ δ' ἄλλων φασὶ γενέσθαι
Ἀντίλοχον, πέρι μὲν θείειν ταχὺν ἠδὲ μαχητήν."
τὸν δ' ἀπαμειβόμενος προσέφη ξανθὸς Μενέλαος·
"ὦ φίλ', ἐπεὶ τόσα εἶπες, ὅσ' ἂν πεπνυμένος ἀνὴρ
205 εἴποι καὶ ῥέξειε, καὶ ὃς προγενέστερος εἴη·
τοίου γὰρ καὶ πατρός, ὃ καὶ πεπνυμένα βάζεις,
ῥεῖα δ' ἀρίγνωτος γόνος ἀνέρος ᾧ τε Κρονίων
ὄλβον ἐπικλώσῃ γαμέοντί τε γεινομένῳ τε,
ὡς νῦν Νέστορι δῶκε διαμπερὲς ἤματα πάντα
210 αὐτὸν μὲν λιπαρῶς γηρασκέμεν ἐν μεγάροισιν,

132

So he spoke, and in them all aroused the desire of lament. Argive Helen wept, the daughter of Zeus, Telemachus wept, and Menelaus, the son of Atreus, nor could the son of Nestor keep his eyes tearless. For he thought in his heart of flawless Antilochus, whom the glorious son of the bright Dawn[a] had slain. Thinking of him he spoke winged words:

"Son of Atreus, old Nestor used always to say that you were understanding above all men, whenever we made mention of you in his halls and questioned one another. So now, if it is at all possible, grant my request, for I take no joy in weeping after supper—and moreover early dawn will soon be here. I count it indeed no blame to weep for any mortal who has died and met his fate. This is, to be sure, the only due we pay to miserable mortals, to cut our hair and to let a tear fall from our cheeks. For a brother of mine, too, is dead, not at all the meanest of the Argives, and you may well have known him. As for me, I never met him nor saw him; but men say that Antilochus was above all others preeminent in speed of foot and as a warrior."

Then fair-haired Menelaus answered him and said: "My friend, truly you have said everything that an understanding man could say or do, even one that was older than you; for from such a father are you sprung, as your wise speech shows. Easily known is that man for whom the son of Cronos spins the thread of good fortune in his marriage and in begetting children, just as now he has granted to Nestor throughout all his days continually that he should himself reach a sleek old age in his halls, and that his sons in their

---

[a] Memnon, leader of the Ethiopians. M.

υἵέας αὖ πινυτούς τε καὶ ἔγχεσιν εἶναι ἀρίστους.
ἡμεῖς δὲ κλαυθμὸν μὲν ἐάσομεν, ὃς πρὶν ἐτύχθη,
δόρπου δ' ἐξαῦτις μνησώμεθα, χερσὶ δ' ἐφ' ὕδωρ
χευάντων. μῦθοι δὲ καὶ ἠῶθέν περ ἔσονται
215   Τηλεμάχῳ καὶ ἐμοὶ διαειπέμεν ἀλλήλοισιν."
      ὣς ἔφατ', Ἀσφαλίων δ' ἄρ' ὕδωρ ἐπὶ χεῖρας ἔχευεν,
ὀτρηρὸς θεράπων Μενελάου κυδαλίμοιο.
οἱ δ' ἐπ' ὀνείαθ' ἑτοῖμα προκείμενα χεῖρας ἴαλλον.
      ἔνθ' αὖτ' ἄλλ' ἐνόησ' Ἑλένη Διὸς ἐκγεγαυῖα·
220   αὐτίκ' ἄρ' εἰς οἶνον βάλε φάρμακον, ἔνθεν ἔπινον,
νηπενθές τ' ἄχολόν τε, κακῶν ἐπίληθον ἁπάντων.
ὃς τὸ καταβρόξειεν, ἐπὴν κρητῆρι μιγείη,
οὔ κεν ἐφημέριός γε βάλοι κατὰ δάκρυ παρειῶν,
οὐδ' εἴ οἱ κατατεθναίη μήτηρ τε πατήρ τε,
225   οὐδ' εἴ οἱ προπάροιθεν ἀδελφεὸν ἢ φίλον υἱὸν
χαλκῷ δηιόῳεν, ὁ δ' ὀφθαλμοῖσιν ὁρῷτο.
τοῖα Διὸς θυγάτηρ ἔχε φάρμακα μητιόεντα,
ἐσθλά, τά οἱ Πολύδαμνα πόρεν, Θῶνος παράκοιτις
Αἰγυπτίη, τῇ πλεῖστα φέρει ζείδωρος ἄρουρα
230   φάρμακα, πολλὰ μὲν ἐσθλὰ μεμιγμένα πολλὰ δὲ λυγρά·
ἰητρὸς δὲ ἕκαστος ἐπιστάμενος περὶ πάντων
ἀνθρώπων· ἦ γὰρ Παιήονός εἰσι γενέθλης.
αὐτὰρ ἐπεί ῥ' ἐνέηκε κέλευσέ τε οἰνοχοῆσαι,
ἐξαῦτις μύθοισιν ἀμειβομένη προσέειπεν·
235   "Ἀτρεΐδη Μενέλαε διοτρεφὲς ἠδὲ καὶ οἵδε
ἀνδρῶν ἐσθλῶν παῖδες· ἀτὰρ θεὸς ἄλλοτε ἄλλῳ
Ζεὺς ἀγαθόν τε κακόν τε διδοῖ· δύναται γὰρ ἅπαντα·
ἦ τοι νῦν δαίνυσθε καθήμενοι ἐν μεγάροισι

turn should be wise and most valiant with the spear. But we will cease the weeping which just now took place, and let us once more think of our supper, and let them pour water over our hands. Words there will be in the morning also for Telemachus and me to exchange with one another to the full."

So he spoke, and Asphalion poured water over their hands, the eager squire of glorious Menelaus. And they put forth their hands to the good cheer lying ready before them.

Then Helen, daughter of Zeus, took other counsel. At once she cast into the wine of which they were drinking a drug to quiet all pain and strife, and bring forgetfulness of every ill. Whoever should drink this down, when it is mingled in the bowl, would not in the course of that day let a tear fall down over his cheeks, no, not though his mother and father should lie there dead, or though before his face men should slay with the sword his brother or dear son and his own eyes behold it. Such cunning drugs had the daughter of Zeus, drugs of healing, which Polydamna, the wife of Thon, had given her, a woman of Egypt, for there the earth, the giver of grain, bears greatest store of drugs, many that are healing when mixed, and many that are baneful; there every man is a physician, wise above humankind; for they are of the race of Paeëon. Now when she had cast in the drug, and had bidden pour forth the wine, again she made answer, and said:

"Menelaus, son of Atreus, fostered by Zeus, and you that are here, sons of noble men—though now to one and now to another Zeus gives good and ill, for he can do all things—sit now in the halls and feast, and take joy in telling

καὶ μύθοις τέρπεσθε· ἐοικότα γὰρ καταλέξω.
240　πάντα μὲν οὐκ ἂν ἐγὼ μυθήσομαι οὐδ' ὀνομήνω,
ὅσσοι Ὀδυσσῆς ταλασίφρονός εἰσιν ἄεθλοι·
ἀλλ' οἷον τόδ' ἔρεξε καὶ ἔτλη καρτερὸς ἀνὴρ
δήμῳ ἔνι Τρώων, ὅθι πάσχετε πήματ' Ἀχαιοί.
αὐτόν μιν πληγῇσιν ἀεικελίῃσι δαμάσσας,
245　σπεῖρα κάκ' ἀμφ' ὤμοισι βαλών, οἰκῆι ἐοικώς,
ἀνδρῶν δυσμενέων κατέδυ πόλιν εὐρυάγυιαν·
ἄλλῳ δ' αὐτὸν φωτὶ κατακρύπτων ἤισκε,
δέκτῃ, ὃς οὐδὲν τοῖος ἔην ἐπὶ νηυσὶν Ἀχαιῶν.
τῷ ἴκελος κατέδυ Τρώων πόλιν, οἱ δ' ἀβάκησαν
250　πάντες· ἐγὼ δέ μιν οἴη ἀνέγνων τοῖον ἐόντα,
καί μιν ἀνηρώτων· ὁ δὲ κερδοσύνῃ ἀλέεινεν.
ἀλλ' ὅτε δή μιν ἐγὼ λόεον καὶ χρῖον ἐλαίῳ,
ἀμφὶ δὲ εἵματα ἕσσα καὶ ὤμοσα καρτερὸν ὅρκον
μὴ μὲν πρὶν Ὀδυσῆα μετὰ Τρώεσσ' ἀναφῆναι,
255　πρίν γε τὸν ἐς νῆάς τε θοὰς κλισίας τ' ἀφικέσθαι,
καὶ τότε δή μοι πάντα νόον κατέλεξεν Ἀχαιῶν.
πολλοὺς δὲ Τρώων κτείνας ταναήκεϊ χαλκῷ
ἦλθε μετ' Ἀργείους, κατὰ δὲ φρόνιν ἤγαγε πολλήν.
ἔνθ' ἄλλαι Τρῳαὶ λίγ' ἐκώκυον· αὐτὰρ ἐμὸν κῆρ
260　χαῖρ', ἐπεὶ ἤδη μοι κραδίη τέτραπτο νέεσθαι
ἂψ οἶκόνδ', ἄτην δὲ μετέστενον, ἣν Ἀφροδίτη
δῶχ', ὅτε μ' ἤγαγε κεῖσε φίλης ἀπὸ πατρίδος αἴης,
παῖδά τ' ἐμὴν νοσφισσαμένην θάλαμόν τε πόσιν τε
οὔ τευ δευόμενον, οὔτ' ἂρ φρένας οὔτε τι εἶδος."
265　　τὴν δ' ἀπαμειβόμενος προσέφη ξανθὸς Μενέλαος·
"ναὶ δὴ ταῦτά γε πάντα, γύναι, κατὰ μοῖραν ἔειπες.

tales, for I will tell something appropriate. All the labors of steadfast Odysseus I cannot tell or recount; but what a thing was this which that mighty man wrought and endured in the land of the Trojans, where you Achaeans suffered woes! Marring his own body with cruel blows, and flinging a wretched garment about his shoulders, in the fashion of a slave he entered the broad-wayed city of the foe, and he hid himself under the likeness of another, a beggar, he who was not at all such at the ships of the Achaeans. In this likeness he entered the city of the Trojans, and all of them were deceived.[a] I alone recognized him in this disguise, and questioned him, but he in his cunning sought to avoid me. But when I was bathing him and anointing him with oil, and had put clothes upon him, and sworn a mighty oath not to make him known among the Trojans as Odysseus before he reached the swift ships and the huts, then at last he told me all the purpose of the Achaeans. And when he had slain many of the Trojans with the long sword, he returned to the company of the Argives and brought back plentiful tidings. Then the other Trojan women wailed aloud, but my soul was glad, for already my heart was turned to go back to my home, and I groaned for the blindness that Aphrodite gave me, when she led me there from my dear native land, forsaking my child and my bridal chamber, and my husband, a man who lacked nothing, whether in wisdom or in looks."

Then fair-haired Menelaus answered her and said: "Truly, all this, wife, have you told properly. Before this

---

[a] A reasonable guess by the ancient commentators at the meaning of the otherwise unattested verb ἀβακέω. D.

ἤδη μὲν πολέων ἐδάην βουλήν τε νόον τε
ἀνδρῶν ἡρώων, πολλὴν δ' ἐπελήλυθα γαῖαν·
ἀλλ' οὔ πω τοιοῦτον ἐγὼν ἴδον ὀφθαλμοῖσιν,
270   οἷον Ὀδυσσῆος ταλασίφρονος ἔσκε φίλον κῆρ.
οἷον καὶ τόδ' ἔρεξε καὶ ἔτλη καρτερὸς ἀνὴρ
ἵππῳ ἔνι ξεστῷ, ἵν' ἐνήμεθα πάντες ἄριστοι
Ἀργείων Τρώεσσι φόνον καὶ κῆρα φέροντες.
ἦλθες ἔπειτα σὺ κεῖσε· κελευσέμεναι δέ σ' ἔμελλε
275   δαίμων, ὃς Τρώεσσιν ἐβούλετο κῦδος ὀρέξαι·
καί τοι Δηΐφοβος θεοείκελος ἕσπετ' ἰούσῃ.
τρὶς δὲ περίστειξας κοῖλον λόχον ἀμφαφόωσα,
ἐκ δ' ὀνομακλήδην Δαναῶν ὀνόμαζες ἀρίστους,
πάντων Ἀργείων φωνὴν ἴσκουσ' ἀλόχοισιν.
280   αὐτὰρ ἐγὼ καὶ Τυδεΐδης καὶ δῖος Ὀδυσσεὺς
ἥμενοι ἐν μέσσοισιν ἀκούσαμεν ὡς ἐβόησας.
νῶι μὲν ἀμφοτέρω μενεήναμεν ὁρμηθέντε
ἢ ἐξελθέμεναι, ἢ ἔνδοθεν αἶψ' ὑπακοῦσαι·
ἀλλ' Ὀδυσεὺς κατέρυκε καὶ ἔσχεθεν ἱεμένω περ.
285   ἔνθ' ἄλλοι μὲν πάντες ἀκὴν ἔσαν υἷες Ἀχαιῶν,
Ἄντικλος δὲ σέ γ' οἶος ἀμείψασθαι ἐπέεσσιν
ἤθελεν. ἀλλ' Ὀδυσεὺς ἐπὶ μάστακα χερσὶ πίεζεν
νωλεμέως κρατερῇσι, σάωσε δὲ πάντας Ἀχαιούς·
τόφρα δ' ἔχ', ὄφρα σε νόσφιν ἀπήγαγε Παλλὰς Ἀθήνη."
290   τὸν δ' αὖ Τηλέμαχος πεπνυμένος ἀντίον ηὔδα·
"Ἀτρεΐδη Μενέλαε διοτρεφές, ὄρχαμε λαῶν,
ἄλγιον· οὐ γάρ οἵ τι τάδ' ἤρκεσε λυγρὸν ὄλεθρον,
οὐδ' εἰ οἱ κραδίη γε σιδηρέη ἔνδοθεν ἦεν.
ἀλλ' ἄγετ' εἰς εὐνὴν τράπεθ' ἡμέας, ὄφρα καὶ ἤδη

have I come to know the counsel and the mind of many heroes, and have traveled over the wide earth, but never yet have my eyes beheld such a one as was steadfast Odysseus in heart. What a thing was this, too, which that mighty man performed and endured in the carved horse, wherein all we chiefs of the Argives were sitting, bearing to the Trojans slaughter and death! You came there then, and it must be that you were bidden by some god who wished to grant glory to the Trojans; and godlike Deiphobus followed you on your way. Three times did you circle the hollow ambush, trying it with your touch, and you named aloud the chieftains of the Danaans by their names, likening your voice to the voices of the wives of all the Argives. Now I and the son of Tydeus and noble Odysseus sat there in the midst and heard how you called, and we two were eager to rise up and come out, or else to answer at once from inside, but Odysseus held us back and stopped us, in spite of our eagerness. Then all the other sons of the Achaeans kept quiet, but Anticlus alone wished to speak and answer you; but Odysseus firmly closed his mouth with strong hands, and saved all the Achaeans, and held him thus until Pallas Athene led you away."

Then wise Telemachus answered him: "Menelaus, son of Atreus, fostered by Zeus, leader of hosts, all the more grievous is it; for in no way did this ward off from him woeful destruction, no, not though the heart within him had been of iron. But come, send us to bed, that lulled now by

295 ὕπνῳ ὕπο γλυκερῷ ταρπώμεθα κοιμηθέντες."

ὣς ἔφατ᾽, Ἀργείη δ᾽ Ἑλένη δμῳῆσι κέλευσεν
δέμνι᾽ ὑπ᾽ αἰθούσῃ θέμεναι καὶ ῥήγεα καλὰ
πορφύρε᾽ ἐμβαλέειν στορέσαι τ᾽ ἐφύπερθε τάπητας,
χλαίνας τ᾽ ἐνθέμεναι οὔλας καθύπερθεν ἕσασθαι.

300 αἱ δ᾽ ἴσαν ἐκ μεγάροιο δάος μετὰ χερσὶν ἔχουσαι,
δέμνια δὲ στόρεσαν· ἐκ δὲ ξείνους ἄγε κῆρυξ.
οἱ μὲν ἄρ᾽ ἐν προδόμῳ δόμου αὐτόθι κοιμήσαντο,
Τηλέμαχός θ᾽ ἥρως καὶ Νέστορος ἀγλαὸς υἱός·
Ἀτρεΐδης δὲ καθεῦδε μυχῷ δόμου ὑψηλοῖο,

305 πὰρ δ᾽ Ἑλένη τανύπεπλος ἐλέξατο, δῖα γυναικῶν.

ἦμος δ᾽ ἠριγένεια φάνη ῥοδοδάκτυλος Ἠώς,
ὤρνυτ᾽ ἄρ᾽ ἐξ εὐνῆφι βοὴν ἀγαθὸς Μενέλαος
εἵματα ἑσσάμενος, περὶ δὲ ξίφος ὀξὺ θέτ᾽ ὤμῳ,
ποσσὶ δ᾽ ὑπὸ λιπαροῖσιν ἐδήσατο καλὰ πέδιλα,

310 βῆ δ᾽ ἴμεν ἐκ θαλάμοιο θεῷ ἐναλίγκιος ἄντην,
Τηλεμάχῳ δὲ παρῖζεν, ἔπος τ᾽ ἔφατ᾽ ἔκ τ᾽ ὀνόμαζεν·

"τίπτε δέ σε χρειὼ δεῦρ᾽ ἤγαγε, Τηλέμαχ᾽ ἥρως,
ἐς Λακεδαίμονα δῖαν, ἐπ᾽ εὐρέα νῶτα θαλάσσης;
δήμιον ἦ ἴδιον; τόδε μοι νημερτὲς ἐνίσπες."

315 τὸν δ᾽ αὖ Τηλέμαχος πεπνυμένος ἀντίον ηὔδα·
"Ἀτρεΐδη Μενέλαε διοτρεφές, ὄρχαμε λαῶν,
ἤλυθον, εἴ τινά μοι κληηδόνα πατρὸς ἐνίσποις.
ἐσθίεταί μοι οἶκος, ὄλωλε δὲ πίονα ἔργα,
δυσμενέων δ᾽ ἀνδρῶν πλεῖος δόμος, οἵ τέ μοι αἰεὶ

320 μῆλ᾽ ἁδινὰ σφάζουσι καὶ εἰλίποδας ἕλικας βοῦς,
μητρὸς ἐμῆς μνηστῆρες ὑπέρβιον ὕβριν ἔχοντες.
τούνεκα νῦν τὰ σὰ γούναθ᾽ ἱκάνομαι, αἴ κ᾽ ἐθέλῃσθα

sweet sleep we may rest and take our joy."

Thus he spoke, and Argive Helen bade her handmaids place bedsteads beneath the portico, and to lay on them beautiful purple blankets, and to spread above them coverlets, and on these to put fleecy cloaks for clothing. The maids went forth from the hall with torches in their hands and strewed the couches, and a herald led forth the guests. So they slept there in the porch of the palace, the hero Telemachus and the glorious son of Nestor; but the son of Atreus slept in the inmost chamber of the lofty house, and beside him lay long-robed Helen, peerless among women.

As soon as early Dawn appeared, the rosy-fingered, up from his bed rose Menelaus, good at the war cry, and put on his clothing. About his shoulders he slung his sharp sword, and beneath his shining feet bound his beautiful sandals, and went forth from his chamber like a god to look upon. Then he sat down beside Telemachus, and spoke, and addressed him:

"What need has brought you here, hero Telemachus, to splendid Lacedaemon over the broad back of the sea? Is it a public matter, or your own? Tell me the truth of this."

Then wise Telemachus answered him: "Menelaus, son of Atreus, fostered by Zeus, leader of hosts, I came in hope that you might tell me some tidings of my father. My home is being devoured and my rich lands are ruined; my house is filled with men that are foes, who continue to slay my thronging sheep and my spiral-horned cattle of shambling gait—the suitors, these, of my mother, overweening in their insolence. Therefore have I now come to your knees, if perchance you will be willing to tell me of his woeful

κείνου λυγρὸν ὄλεθρον ἐνισπεῖν, εἴ που ὄπωπας
ὀφθαλμοῖσι τεοῖσιν ἢ ἄλλου μῦθον ἄκουσας
325 πλαζομένου· περὶ γάρ μιν ὀιζυρὸν τέκε μήτηρ.
μηδέ τί μ' αἰδόμενος μείλισσεο μηδ' ἐλεαίρων,
ἀλλ' εὖ μοι κατάλεξον ὅπως ἤντησας ὀπωπῆς.
λίσσομαι, εἴ ποτέ τοί τι πατὴρ ἐμός, ἐσθλὸς Ὀδυσσεὺς
ἢ ἔπος ἠέ τι ἔργον ὑποστὰς ἐξετέλεσσε
330 δήμῳ ἔνι Τρώων, ὅθι πάσχετε πήματ' Ἀχαιοί,
τῶν νῦν μοι μνῆσαι, καί μοι νημερτὲς ἐνίσπες."
    τὸν δὲ μέγ' ὀχθήσας προσέφη ξανθὸς Μενέλαος·
"ὢ πόποι, ἦ μάλα δὴ κρατερόφρονος ἀνδρὸς ἐν εὐνῇ
ἤθελον εὐνηθῆναι ἀνάλκιδες αὐτοὶ ἐόντες.
335 ὡς δ' ὁπότ' ἐν ξυλόχῳ ἔλαφος κρατεροῖο λέοντος
νεβροὺς κοιμήσασα νεηγενέας γαλαθηνοὺς
κνημοὺς ἐξερέῃσι καὶ ἄγκεα ποιήεντα
βοσκομένη, ὁ δ' ἔπειτα ἑὴν εἰσήλυθεν εὐνήν,
ἀμφοτέροισι δὲ τοῖσιν ἀεικέα πότμον ἐφῆκεν,
340 ὣς Ὀδυσεὺς κείνοισιν ἀεικέα πότμον ἐφήσει.
αἲ γάρ, Ζεῦ τε πάτερ καὶ Ἀθηναίη καὶ Ἄπολλον,
τοῖος ἐών, οἷός ποτ' ἐυκτιμένῃ ἐνὶ Λέσβῳ
ἐξ ἔριδος Φιλομηλεΐδῃ ἐπάλαισεν ἀναστάς,
κὰδ δ' ἔβαλε κρατερῶς, κεχάροντο δὲ πάντες Ἀχαιοί,
345 τοῖος ἐὼν μνηστῆρσιν ὁμιλήσειεν Ὀδυσσεύς·
πάντες κ' ὠκύμοροί τε γενοίατο πικρόγαμοί τε.
ταῦτα δ' ἅ μ' εἰρωτᾷς καὶ λίσσεαι, οὐκ ἂν ἐγώ γε
ἄλλα παρὲξ εἴποιμι παρακλιδόν, οὐδ' ἀπατήσω,
ἀλλὰ τὰ μέν μοι ἔειπε γέρων ἅλιος νημερτής,
350 τῶν οὐδέν τοι ἐγὼ κρύψω ἔπος οὐδ' ἐπικεύσω.

death, whether you saw it, it may be, with your own eyes, or heard the report of some other wanderer; for beyond all men did his mother bear him to sorrow. And do not out of consideration or pity for me, speak soothing words, but tell me truly what evidence you came upon. I beseech you, if ever my father, noble Odysseus, promised you any word or deed and fulfilled it in the land of the Trojans, where you Achaeans suffered woes, be mindful of it now, I pray you, and tell me the very truth."

Then, deeply indignant, fair-haired Menelaus spoke to him: "Out upon them! For truly they who are themselves of little prowess undertook to lie in the bed of a man of valiant heart. Just as when in the thicket lair of a powerful lion a doe has laid to sleep her newborn suckling fawns, and roams over the mountain slopes and grassy vales seeking pasture, and then the lion comes to his lair and upon her two fawns lets loose a cruel doom, so will Odysseus let loose a cruel doom upon these men. I would, father Zeus and Athene and Apollo, that in such strength as when once in well-ordered Lesbos he rose up and wrestled a match with Philomeleides and threw him violently, and all the Achaeans rejoiced, in just such strength Odysseus might come among the suitors; then should they all meet with a swift death and a bitter marriage. But in this matter of which you ask and beseech me, be sure I shall not swerve aside to speak of other things, nor will I deceive you; on the contrary, of all that the unerring old man of the sea told me not one thing will I hide from you or conceal.

"Αἰγύπτῳ μ' ἔτι δεῦρο θεοὶ μεμαῶτα νέεσθαι
ἔσχον, ἐπεὶ οὔ σφιν ἔρεξα τεληέσσας ἑκατόμβας.
οἱ δ' αἰεὶ βούλοντο θεοὶ μεμνῆσθαι ἐφετμέων.[1]
νῆσος ἔπειτά τις ἔστι πολυκλύστῳ ἐνὶ πόντῳ
355 Αἰγύπτου προπάροιθε, Φάρον δέ ἑ κικλήσκουσι,
τόσσον ἄνευθ' ὅσσον τε πανημερίη γλαφυρὴ νηῦς
ἤνυσεν, ᾗ λιγὺς οὖρος ἐπιπνείῃσιν ὄπισθεν·
ἐν δὲ λιμὴν ἐύορμος, ὅθεν τ' ἀπὸ νῆας ἐίσας
ἐς πόντον βάλλουσιν, ἀφυσσάμενοι μέλαν ὕδωρ.
360 ἔνθα μ' ἐείκοσιν ἤματ' ἔχον θεοί, οὐδέ ποτ' οὖροι
πνείοντες φαίνονθ' ἁλιάεες, οἵ ῥά τε νηῶν
πομπῆες γίγνονται ἐπ' εὐρέα νῶτα θαλάσσης.
καί νύ κεν ἤια πάντα κατέφθιτο καὶ μένε' ἀνδρῶν,
εἰ μή τίς με θεῶν ὀλοφύρατο καί μ' ἐσάωσε,[2]
365 Πρωτέος ἰφθίμου θυγάτηρ ἁλίοιο γέροντος,
Εἰδοθέη· τῇ γάρ ῥα μάλιστά γε θυμὸν ὄρινα.
ἥ μ' οἴῳ ἔρροντι συνήντετο νόσφιν ἑταίρων·
αἰεὶ γὰρ περὶ νῆσον ἀλώμενοι ἰχθυάασκον
γναμπτοῖς ἀγκίστροισιν, ἔτειρε δὲ γαστέρα λιμός.
370 ἡ δέ μευ ἄγχι στᾶσα ἔπος φάτο φώνησέν τε·

"'νήπιός εἰς, ὦ ξεῖνε, λίην τόσον ἠδὲ χαλίφρων,
ἦε ἑκὼν μεθίεις καὶ τέρπεαι ἄλγεα πάσχων;
ὡς δὴ δήθ' ἐνὶ νήσῳ ἐρύκεαι, οὐδέ τι τέκμωρ
εὑρέμεναι δύνασαι, μινύθει δέ τοι ἦτορ ἑταίρων.'

---

[1] Line 353, rejected by Zenodotus, is bracketed by many editors.

[2] μ' ἐσάωσε: μ' ἐλέησε

"In Egypt, eager though I was to return here, the gods still held me back, because I did not offer them perfect hecatombs, and the gods always wish that men should be mindful of their commands. Now there is an island in the surging sea in front of Egypt, and men call it Pharos, distant as far as a hollow ship runs in a whole day when the shrill wind blows behind her. There is a harbor there with good anchorage, from which men launch the shapely ships into the sea, when they have drawn supplies of black[a] water. There for twenty days the gods kept me, nor ever did the winds that blow over the deep spring up, which speed men's ships over the broad back of the sea. And now would all my stores have been spent and the strength of my men, had not one of the gods taken pity on me and saved me: Eidothea, daughter of mighty Proteus, the old man of the sea; for her heart above all others had I moved. She met me as I wandered alone apart from my comrades, who continually roamed about the island fishing with bent hooks, for hunger pinched their bellies; and she came close to me, and spoke, and said:

"'Are you so very foolish, stranger, and slack of wit, or are you of your own will remiss, and have pleasure in suffering woes? So long are you pent in the isle and can find no appointed end, and the heart of your comrades grows faint.'

[a] The epithet "black" is applied to water in deep places, where the light cannot reach it, and to water trickling down the face of a rock covered with lichens (*Iliad*, 16.4ff). M.

375   "ὣς ἔφατ', αὐτὰρ ἐγώ μιν ἀμειβόμενος προσέειπον·
    'ἐκ μέν τοι ἐρέω, ἥ τις σύ πέρ ἐσσι θεάων,
    ὡς ἐγὼ οὔ τι ἑκὼν κατερύκομαι, ἀλλά νυ μέλλω
    ἀθανάτους ἀλιτέσθαι, οἳ οὐρανὸν εὐρὺν ἔχουσιν.
    ἀλλὰ σύ πέρ μοι εἰπέ, θεοὶ δέ τε πάντα ἴσασιν,
380   ὅς τίς μ' ἀθανάτων πεδάᾳ καὶ ἔδησε κελεύθου,
    νόστον θ', ὡς ἐπὶ πόντον ἐλεύσομαι ἰχθυόεντα.'
     "ὣς ἐφάμην, ἡ δ' αὐτίκ' ἀμείβετο δῖα θεάων·
    'τοιγὰρ ἐγώ τοι, ξεῖνε, μάλ' ἀτρεκέως ἀγορεύσω.
    πωλεῖταί τις δεῦρο γέρων ἅλιος νημερτὴς
385   ἀθάνατος Πρωτεὺς Αἰγύπτιος, ὅς τε θαλάσσης
    πάσης βένθεα οἶδε, Ποσειδάωνος ὑποδμώς·
    τὸν δέ τ' ἐμόν φασιν πατέρ' ἔμμεναι ἠδὲ τεκέσθαι.
    τόν γ' εἴ πως σὺ δύναιο λοχησάμενος λελαβέσθαι,
    ὅς κέν τοι εἴπῃσιν ὁδὸν καὶ μέτρα κελεύθου
390   νόστον θ', ὡς ἐπὶ πόντον ἐλεύσεαι ἰχθυόεντα.
    καὶ δέ κέ τοι εἴπῃσι, διοτρεφές, αἴ κ' ἐθέλησθα,
    ὅττι τοι ἐν μεγάροισι κακόν τ' ἀγαθόν τε τέτυκται
    οἰχομένοιο σέθεν δολιχὴν ὁδὸν ἀργαλέην τε.'
     "ὣς ἔφατ', αὐτὰρ ἐγώ μιν ἀμειβόμενος προσέειπον·
395   'αὐτὴ νῦν φράζευ σὺ λόχον θείοιο γέροντος,
    μή πώς με προϊδὼν ἠὲ προδαεὶς ἀλέηται·
    ἀργαλέος γάρ τ' ἐστὶ θεὸς βροτῷ ἀνδρὶ δαμῆναι.'
     "ὣς ἐφάμην, ἡ δ' αὐτίκ' ἀμείβετο δῖα θεάων·
    'τοιγὰρ ἐγώ τοι, ξεῖνε,[1] μάλ' ἀτρεκέως ἀγορεύσω.
400   ἦμος δ' ἠέλιος μέσον οὐρανὸν ἀμφιβεβήκῃ,
    τῆμος ἄρ' ἐξ ἁλὸς εἶσι γέρων ἅλιος νημερτὴς
    πνοιῇ ὕπο Ζεφύροιο μελαίνῃ φρικὶ καλυφθείς,

"So she spoke, and I made answer and said: 'I will speak out and tell you, whosoever among goddesses you are, that in no way am I pent here of my own will, but it must be that I have sinned against the immortals, who hold broad heaven. But tell me—for the gods know all things—who of the immortals fetters me here, and has hindered me from my path, and tell me of my return, how I may go over the fish-filled sea.'

"So I spoke, and the beautiful goddess at once made answer: 'Since you ask, stranger, I will frankly tell you all. There comes here from habit a certain unerring old man of the sea, immortal Proteus of Egypt, who knows the depths of every sea, and is the servant of Poseidon. He, they say, is my father that begot me. If you could somehow lie in wait and catch him, he will tell you your way and the measure of your path, and of your return, how you may go over the fish-filled sea. And he will tell you, fostered by Zeus, if so you wish, what evil and what good has been done in your halls, while you have been gone on your long and grievous way.'

"So she spoke, and I made answer and said: 'Do you yourself now devise a means of lying in wait for the divine old man, lest perchance he see me beforehand and avoid me. For hard is a god for a mortal man to master.'

"So I spoke, and the beautiful goddess at once made answer: 'Since you ask, stranger, I will frankly tell you all. When the sun has reached mid heaven, the unerring old man of the sea comes forth from the salt water at the breath of the West Wind, hidden by the dark ripple. And

---

[1] ξεῖνε: ταῦτα

ἐκ δ' ἐλθὼν κοιμᾶται ὑπὸ σπέσσι γλαφυροῖσιν·
ἀμφὶ δέ μιν φῶκαι νέποδες καλῆς ἁλοσύδνης
405 ἀθρόαι εὕδουσιν, πολιῆς ἁλὸς ἐξαναδῦσαι,
πικρὸν ἀποπνείουσαι ἁλὸς πολυβενθέος ὀδμήν.
ἔνθα σ' ἐγὼν ἀγαγοῦσα ἅμ' ἠοῖ φαινομένηφιν
εὐνάσω ἐξείης· σὺ δ' ἐὺ κρίνασθαι ἑταίρους
τρεῖς, οἵ τοι παρὰ νηυσὶν ἐυσσέλμοισιν ἄριστοι.
410 πάντα δέ τοι ἐρέω ὀλοφώια τοῖο γέροντος.
φώκας μέν τοι πρῶτον ἀριθμήσει καὶ ἔπεισιν·
αὐτὰρ ἐπὴν πάσας πεμπάσσεται ἠδὲ ἴδηται,
λέξεται ἐν μέσσῃσι νομεὺς ὣς πώεσι μήλων.
τὸν μὲν ἐπὴν δὴ πρῶτα κατευνηθέντα ἴδησθε,
415 καὶ τότ' ἔπειθ' ὑμῖν μελέτω κάρτος τε βίη τε,
αὖθι δ' ἔχειν μεμαῶτα καὶ ἐσσύμενόν περ ἀλύξαι.
πάντα δὲ γιγνόμενος πειρήσεται, ὅσσ' ἐπὶ γαῖαν
ἑρπετὰ γίγνονται, καὶ ὕδωρ καὶ θεσπιδαὲς πῦρ·
ὑμεῖς δ' ἀστεμφέως ἐχέμεν μᾶλλόν τε πιέζειν.
420 ἀλλ' ὅτε κεν δή σ' αὐτὸς ἀνείρηται ἐπέεσσι,
τοῖος ἐὼν οἷόν κε κατευνηθέντα ἴδησθε,
καὶ τότε δὴ σχέσθαι τε βίης λῦσαί τε γέροντα,
ἥρως, εἴρεσθαι δέ, θεῶν ὅς τίς σε χαλέπτει,
νόστον θ', ὡς ἐπὶ πόντον ἐλεύσεαι ἰχθυόεντα.'
425   ὣς εἰποῦσ' ὑπὸ πόντον ἐδύσετο κυμαίνοντα.
αὐτὰρ ἐγὼν ἐπὶ νῆας, ὅθ' ἕστασαν ἐν ψαμάθοισιν,
ἤια· πολλὰ δέ μοι κραδίη πόρφυρε κιόντι.
αὐτὰρ ἐπεί ῥ' ἐπὶ νῆα κατήλυθον ἠδὲ θάλασσαν,
δόρπον θ' ὁπλισάμεσθ', ἐπί τ' ἤλυθεν ἀμβροσίη νύξ·
430 δὴ τότε κοιμήθημεν ἐπὶ ῥηγμῖνι θαλάσσης.

when he has come forth, he lies down to sleep in the hollow caves; and around him the seals, the brood of the fair daughter of the sea, sleep in a herd, coming out from the gray water, and bitter is the smell they breathe forth of the depths of the sea. There I will lead you at break of day and lay you down all in a row; for you must choose carefully three of your companions, who are the best you have in your well-benched ships. And I will tell you all the wizard wiles of that old man. First, he will count the seals, and go over them; but when he has told them all off by fives, and beheld them, he will lay himself down in their midst, like a shepherd among his flocks of sheep. Now as soon as you see him laid to rest, then let your hearts be filled with strength and courage, and hold him there despite his striving and struggling to escape. For try he will, and will assume all shapes of all things that move upon the earth, and of water, and of wondrous blazing fire. Yet hold him unflinchingly and grip him more tightly still. But when at length of his own will he speaks and questions you in that shape in which you saw him laid to rest, then, hero, cease from force, and set the old man free, and ask him who of the gods is angry with you, and of your return, how you may go over the fish-filled sea.'

"So saying she plunged beneath the surging sea, but I went to my ships, where they stood on the sand, and many things did my heart darkly ponder as I went. But when I had come down to the ship and to the sea, and we had made ready our supper, and immortal night had come on, then we laid down to rest on the shore of the sea. And as

ἦμος δ' ἠριγένεια φάνη ῥοδοδάκτυλος Ἠώς,
καὶ τότε δὴ παρὰ θῖνα θαλάσσης εὐρυπόροιο
ἤια πολλὰ θεοὺς γουνούμενος· αὐτὰρ ἑταίρους
τρεῖς ἄγον, οἷσι μάλιστα πεποίθεα πᾶσαν ἐπ' ἰθύν.

435   "τόφρα δ' ἄρ' ἥ γ' ὑποδῦσα θαλάσσης εὐρέα κόλπον
τέσσαρα φωκάων ἐκ πόντου δέρματ' ἔνεικε·
πάντα δ' ἔσαν νεόδαρτα· δόλον δ' ἐπεμήδετο πατρί.
εὐνὰς δ' ἐν ψαμάθοισι διαγλάψασ' ἁλίῃσιν
ἧστο μένουσ'· ἡμεῖς δὲ μάλα σχεδὸν ἤλθομεν αὐτῆς·
440   ἑξείης δ' εὔνησε, βάλεν δ' ἐπὶ δέρμα ἑκάστῳ.
ἔνθα κεν¹ αἰνότατος λόχος ἔπλετο· τεῖρε γὰρ αἰνῶς
φωκάων ἁλιοτρεφέων ὀλοώτατος ὀδμή·
τίς γάρ κ' εἰναλίῳ παρὰ κήτεϊ κοιμηθείη;
ἀλλ' αὐτὴ ἐσάωσε καὶ ἐφράσατο μέγ' ὄνειαρ·
445   ἀμβροσίην ὑπὸ ῥῖνα ἑκάστῳ θῆκε φέρουσα
ἡδὺ μάλα πνείουσαν, ὄλεσσε δὲ κήτεος ὀδμήν.
πᾶσαν δ' ἠοίην μένομεν τετληότι θυμῷ·
φῶκαι δ' ἐξ ἁλὸς ἦλθον ἀολλέες. αἱ μὲν ἔπειτα
ἑξῆς εὐνάζοντο παρὰ ῥηγμῖνι θαλάσσης·
450   ἔνδιος δ' ὁ γέρων ἦλθ' ἐξ ἁλός, εὗρε δὲ φώκας
ζατρεφέας, πάσας δ' ἄρ' ἐπώχετο, λέκτο δ' ἀριθμόν·
ἐν δ' ἡμέας πρώτους λέγε κήτεσιν, οὐδέ τι θυμῷ
ὠίσθη δόλον εἶναι· ἔπειτα δὲ λέκτο καὶ αὐτός.
ἡμεῖς δὲ ἰάχοντες ἐπεσσύμεθ', ἀμφὶ δὲ χεῖρας
455   βάλλομεν· οὐδ' ὁ γέρων δολίης ἐπελήθετο τέχνης,
ἀλλ' ἦ τοι πρώτιστα λέων γένετ' ἠυγένειος,
αὐτὰρ ἔπειτα δράκων καὶ πάρδαλις ἠδὲ μέγας σῦς·
γίγνετο δ' ὑγρὸν ὕδωρ καὶ δένδρεον ὑψιπέτηλον·

150

soon as early Dawn appeared, the rosy-fingered, I went along the shore of the broad-wayed sea, praying earnestly to the gods; and I took with me three of my comrades, in whom I trusted most for every adventure.

"She meanwhile had plunged beneath the broad bosom of the sea, and had brought forth from the deep the skins of the four seals, and all were newly flayed; and she devised a plot against her father. She had scooped out lairs in the sand of the sea, and sat waiting; and we came very near to her, and she made us to lie down in a row, and cast a skin over each. Then would our ambush have proved most terrible, for terribly did the stench of the brine-bred seals distress us—who would lay himself down by a beast of the sea?—but she of herself delivered us, and devised a great boon; she brought and placed ambrosia beneath each man's nose, extremely fragrant, and destroyed the stench of the beast. So all the morning we waited with steadfast heart, and the seals came forth from the sea in throngs. These then laid themselves down in rows along the shore of the sea, and at noon the old man came forth from the sea and found the fatted seals; and he went over all, and counted their number. Among the seals he counted us first, nor did his heart guess that there was guile; and then he too laid himself down. We rushed upon him with a shout, and threw our arms about him; nor did that old man forget his crafty wiles, but first he turned into a bearded lion, and then into a serpent, and a leopard, and a huge boar; then he turned into flowing water, and into a tree,

---

[1] ἔνθα κεν: κεῖθι δή

151

ἡμεῖς δ' ἀστεμφέως ἔχομεν τετληότι θυμῷ.

460 ἀλλ' ὅτε δή ῥ' ἀνίαζ' ὁ γέρων ὀλοφώϊα εἰδώς,
καὶ τότε δή μ' ἐπέεσσιν ἀνειρόμενος προσέειπε·

"'τίς νύ τοι, Ἀτρέος υἱέ, θεῶν συμφράσσατο βουλάς,
ὄφρα μ' ἕλοις ἀέκοντα λοχησάμενος; τέο σε χρή;'

"ὣς ἔφατ', αὐτὰρ ἐγώ μιν ἀμειβόμενος προσέειπον·

465 'οἶσθα, γέρον, τί με ταῦτα παρατροπέων ἐρεείνεις,[1]
ὡς δὴ δήθ' ἐνὶ νήσῳ ἐρύκομαι, οὐδέ τι τέκμωρ
εὑρέμεναι δύναμαι, μινύθει δέ μοι ἔνδοθεν ἦτορ.
ἀλλὰ σύ πέρ μοι εἰπέ, θεοὶ δέ τε πάντα ἴσασιν,
ὅς τίς μ' ἀθανάτων πεδάᾳ καὶ ἔδησε κελεύθου,

470 νόστον θ', ὡς ἐπὶ πόντον ἐλεύσομαι ἰχθυόεντα.'

"ὣς ἐφάμην, ὁ δέ μ' αὐτίκ' ἀμειβόμενος
προσέειπεν·

'ἀλλὰ μάλ' ὤφελλες Διί τ' ἄλλοισίν τε θεοῖσι
ῥέξας ἱερὰ κάλ' ἀναβαινέμεν, ὄφρα τάχιστα
σὴν ἐς πατρίδ' ἵκοιο πλέων ἐπὶ οἴνοπα πόντον.

475 οὐ γάρ τοι πρὶν μοῖρα φίλους τ' ἰδέειν καὶ ἱκέσθαι
οἶκον ἐϋκτίμενον καὶ σὴν ἐς πατρίδα γαῖαν,
πρίν γ' ὅτ' ἂν Αἰγύπτοιο, διιπετέος ποταμοῖο,
αὖτις ὕδωρ ἔλθῃς ῥέξῃς θ' ἱερὰς ἑκατόμβας
ἀθανάτοισι θεοῖσι, τοὶ οὐρανὸν εὐρὺν ἔχουσι·

480 καὶ τότε τοι δώσουσιν ὁδὸν θεοί, ἣν σὺ μενοινᾷς.'

"ὣς ἔφατ', αὐτὰρ ἐμοί γε κατεκλάσθη φίλον ἦτορ,
οὕνεκά μ' αὖτις ἄνωγεν ἐπ' ἠεροειδέα πόντον
Αἴγυπτόνδ' ἰέναι, δολιχὴν ὁδὸν ἀργαλέην τε.
ἀλλὰ καὶ ὣς μύθοισιν[2] ἀμειβόμενος προσέειπον·

[1] ἐρεείνεις Aristarchus: ἀγορεύεις

high and leafy; but we held on unflinchingly with steadfast heart. But when at last that old man, skilled in wizard arts, grew weary, then he questioned me, and spoke, and said:

"'Who of the gods, son of Atreus, took counsel with you that you might lie in wait for me, and take me against my will? Of what have you need?' So he spoke, and I made answer and said: 'You know, old man—why do you seek to put me off with this question?—how long a time I am pent in this isle, and can find no sign of deliverance, and my heart grows faint within me. But tell me—for the gods know all things—who of the immortals fetters me here, and has hindered me from my path, and tell me of my return, how I may go over the fish-filled sea.'

"So I spoke, and he at once made answer and said: 'But surely you ought to have made choice offerings to Zeus and the other gods before embarking, that with greatest speed you might have come to your country, sailing over the wine-dark sea. For it is not your fate to see your friends, and reach your well-ordered household and your native land, before you have once more gone to the waters of Aegyptus, the heaven-fed river, and have offered holy hecatombs to the immortal gods who hold broad heaven. Then at length shall the gods grant you the journey you desire.'

"So he spoke, and my spirit was broken within me, because he bade me go again over the misty deep to Aegyptus, a long and weary way. Yet even so I made answer, and said:

---

[2] μύθοισιν: μιν ἔπεσσιν

485   "'ταῦτα μὲν οὕτω δὴ τελέω, γέρον, ὡς σὺ κελεύεις.
ἀλλ' ἄγε μοι τόδε εἰπὲ καὶ ἀτρεκέως κατάλεξον,
ἢ πάντες σὺν νηυσὶν ἀπήμονες ἦλθον Ἀχαιοί,
οὓς Νέστωρ καὶ ἐγὼ λίπομεν Τροίηθεν ἰόντες,
ἠέ τις ὤλετ' ὀλέθρῳ ἀδευκέι ἧς ἐπὶ νηὸς
490   ἠὲ φίλων ἐν χερσίν, ἐπεὶ πόλεμον τολύπευσεν.'
      "ὣς ἐφάμην, ὁ δέ μ' αὐτίκ' ἀμειβόμενος
        προσέειπεν·
"Ἀτρεΐδη, τί με ταῦτα διείρεαι; οὐδέ τί σε χρὴ
ἴδμεναι, οὐδὲ δαῆναι ἐμὸν νόον· οὐδέ σέ φημι
δὴν ἄκλαυτον ἔσεσθαι, ἐπὴν εὖ πάντα πύθηαι.
495   πολλοὶ μὲν γὰρ τῶν γε δάμεν, πολλοὶ δὲ λίποντο·
ἀρχοὶ δ' αὖ δύο μοῦνοι Ἀχαιῶν χαλκοχιτώνων
ἐν νόστῳ ἀπόλοντο· μάχῃ δέ τε καὶ σὺ παρῆσθα.
εἷς δ' ἔτι που ζωὸς κατερύκεται εὐρέι πόντῳ.
      "'Αἴας μὲν μετὰ νηυσὶ δάμη δολιχηρέτμοισι.
500   Γυρῇσίν μιν πρῶτα Ποσειδάων ἐπέλασσεν
πέτρῃσιν μεγάλῃσι καὶ ἐξεσάωσε θαλάσσης·
καί νύ κεν ἔκφυγε κῆρα καὶ ἐχθόμενός περ Ἀθήνῃ,
εἰ μὴ ὑπερφίαλον ἔπος ἔκβαλε καὶ μέγ' ἀάσθη·
φῆ ῥ' ἀέκητι θεῶν φυγέειν μέγα λαῖτμα θαλάσσης.
505   τοῦ δὲ Ποσειδάων μεγάλ' ἔκλυεν αὐδήσαντος·
αὐτίκ' ἔπειτα τρίαιναν ἑλὼν χερσὶ στιβαρῇσιν
ἤλασε Γυραίην πέτρην, ἀπὸ δ' ἔσχισεν αὐτήν·
καὶ τὸ μὲν αὐτόθι μεῖνε, τὸ δὲ τρύφος ἔμπεσε πόντῳ,
τῷ ῥ' Αἴας τὸ πρῶτον ἐφεζόμενος μέγ' ἀάσθη·
510   τὸν δ' ἐφόρει κατὰ πόντον ἀπείρονα κυμαίνοντα.
ὣς ὁ μὲν ἔνθ' ἀπόλωλεν, ἐπεὶ πίεν ἁλμυρὸν ὕδωρ.

154

"'All this will I perform, old man, even as you bid. But come, tell me this, and declare it truly. Did all the Achaeans return unscathed in their ships, all those whom Nestor and I left, as we set out from Troy? Or did any perish by a cruel death on board his ship, or in the arms of his friends, when he had wound up the skein of war?'

"So I spoke, and he at once made answer, and said: 'Son of Atreus, why do you question me about this? In no way does it behoove you to know, or to learn my mind; nor, I think, will you long be free from tears, when you have heard all fairly. For many of them were slain, and many were left; but two chieftains alone of the brazen-shirted Achaeans perished on their homeward way (as for the fighting, you yourself were there), and one, I suppose, still lives, and is held back on the broad deep.

"'Aias was lost amid his long-oared ships. Poseidon at first drove him upon the great rocks of Gyrae, but saved him from the sea; and he would have escaped his doom, hated by Athene though he was, had he not uttered a boastful word in great blindness of heart. He declared that it was in spite of the gods that he had escaped the great gulf of the sea; and Poseidon heard his boastful speech, and at once took his trident in his mighty hands, and smote the rock of Gyrae and broke it asunder. And one part remained in its place, but the sundered part fell into the sea, that on which Aias sat at the first when his heart was greatly blinded, and it bore him down into the boundless surging deep. So there he perished, when he had drunk the salt water.

"'σὸς δέ που ἔκφυγε κῆρας ἀδελφεὸς ἠδ' ὑπάλυξεν
ἐν νηυσὶ γλαφυρῇσι· σάωσε δὲ πότνια Ἥρη.
ἀλλ' ὅτε δὴ τάχ' ἔμελλε Μαλειάων ὄρος αἰπὺ
515 ἵξεσθαι, τότε δή μιν ἀναρπάξασα θύελλα
πόντον ἐπ' ἰχθυόεντα φέρεν βαρέα στενάχοντα,
ἀγροῦ ἐπ' ἐσχατιήν, ὅθι δώματα ναῖε Θυέστης
τὸ πρίν, ἀτὰρ τότ' ἔναιε Θυεστιάδης Αἴγισθος.
ἀλλ' ὅτε δὴ καὶ κεῖθεν ἐφαίνετο νόστος ἀπήμων,
520 ἂψ δὲ θεοὶ οὖρον στρέψαν, καὶ οἴκαδ' ἵκοντο,
ἦ τοι ὁ μὲν χαίρων ἐπεβήσετο πατρίδος αἴης
καὶ κύνει ἁπτόμενος ἣν πατρίδα· πολλὰ δ' ἀπ' αὐτοῦ
δάκρυα θερμὰ χέοντ', ἐπεὶ ἀσπασίως ἴδε γαῖαν.
τὸν δ' ἄρ' ἀπὸ σκοπιῆς εἶδε σκοπός, ὅν ῥα καθεῖσεν
525 Αἴγισθος δολόμητις ἄγων, ὑπὸ δ' ἔσχετο μισθὸν
χρυσοῦ δοιὰ τάλαντα· φύλασσε δ' ὅ γ' εἰς ἐνιαυτόν,
μή ἑ λάθοι παριών, μνήσαιτο δὲ θούριδος ἀλκῆς.
βῆ δ' ἴμεν ἀγγελέων πρὸς δώματα ποιμένι λαῶν.
αὐτίκα δ' Αἴγισθος δολίην ἐφράσσατο τέχνην·
530 κρινάμενος κατὰ δῆμον ἐείκοσι φῶτας ἀρίστους
εἷσε λόχον, ἑτέρωθι δ' ἀνώγει δαῖτα πένεσθαι.
αὐτὰρ ὁ βῆ καλέων Ἀγαμέμνονα, ποιμένα λαῶν
ἵπποισιν καὶ ὄχεσφιν, ἀεικέα μερμηρίζων.
τὸν δ' οὐκ εἰδότ' ὄλεθρον ἀνήγαγε καὶ κατέπεφνεν
535 δειπνίσσας, ὥς τίς τε κατέκτανε βοῦν ἐπὶ φάτνῃ.
οὐδέ τις Ἀτρεΐδεω ἑτάρων λίπεθ' οἵ οἱ ἕποντο,
οὐδέ τις Αἰγίσθου, ἀλλ' ἔκταθεν ἐν μεγάροισιν.'

"'But your brother, indeed, escaped the fates and shunned them with his hollow ships, for queenly Hera saved him. But when he was now about to reach the steep height of Malea, then the storm wind caught him up and bore him over the fish-filled sea, groaning heavily, to the end of the land,[a] where in the time before Thyestes dwelt, but where now dwelt Thyestes' son Aegisthus. But when from here too a safe return was showed him, and the gods changed the course of the wind so that it blew fair, and they reached home, then indeed with rejoicing did Agamemnon set foot on his native land, and laying hold of his land he kissed it, and many were the hot tears that streamed from his eyes, for welcome to him was the sight of his land. Now from his place of watch a watchman saw him, whom guileful Aegisthus took and set there, promising him as a reward two talents of gold; and he had been keeping guard for a year, for fear Agamemnon should pass by him unseen, and be mindful of his furious might. So he went to the palace to bear the tidings to the shepherd of the people, and Aegisthus at once planned a treacherous device. He chose out twenty men, the best in the land, and set them to lie in wait, but on the further side of the hall he bade prepare a feast. Then he went with chariot and horses to summon Agamemnon, shepherd of the people, his mind pondering a dastardly deed. So he brought him up all unaware of his doom, and when he had feasted him he slew him, as one slays an ox at the corn crib. And not one of the comrades of the son of Atreus was left, of all that followed him, nor one of the men of Aegisthus, but they were all slain in the halls.'

[a] Probably the Argolic promontory. D.

"ὣς ἔφατ᾽, αὐτὰρ ἐμοί γε κατεκλάσθη φίλον ἦτορ,
κλαῖον δ᾽ ἐν ψαμάθοισι καθήμενος, οὐδέ νύ μοι κῆρ
540   ἤθελ᾽ ἔτι ζώειν καὶ ὁρᾶν φάος ἠελίοιο.
αὐτὰρ ἐπεὶ κλαίων τε κυλινδόμενός τε κορέσθην,
δὴ τότε με προσέειπε γέρων ἅλιος νημερτής·

"'μηκέτι, Ἀτρέος υἱέ, πολὺν χρόνον ἀσκελὲς οὕτω
κλαῖ᾽, ἐπεὶ οὐκ ἄνυσίν τινα δήομεν· ἀλλὰ τάχιστα
545   πείρα ὅπως κεν δὴ σὴν πατρίδα γαῖαν ἵκηαι.
ἢ γάρ μιν ζωόν γε κιχήσεαι, ἤ κεν Ὀρέστης
κτεῖνεν ὑποφθάμενος, σὺ δέ κεν τάφου ἀντιβολήσαις.'

"ὣς ἔφατ᾽, αὐτὰρ ἐμοὶ κραδίη καὶ θυμὸς ἀγήνωρ
αὖτις ἐνὶ στήθεσσι καὶ ἀχνυμένῳ περ ἰάνθη,
550   καί μιν φωνήσας ἔπεα πτερόεντα προσηύδων·

"'τούτους μὲν δὴ οἶδα· σὺ δὲ τρίτον ἄνδρ᾽ ὀνόμαζε,
ὅς τις ἔτι ζωὸς κατερύκεται εὐρέι πόντῳ
ἠὲ θανών· ἐθέλω δὲ καὶ ἀχνύμενός περ ἀκοῦσαι.'[1]

"ὣς ἐφάμην, ὁ δέ μ᾽ αὐτίκ᾽ ἀμειβόμενος
    προσέειπεν·
555   'υἱὸς Λαέρτεω, Ἰθάκῃ ἔνι οἰκία ναίων·
τὸν δ᾽ ἴδον ἐν νήσῳ θαλερὸν κατὰ δάκρυ χέοντα,
νύμφης ἐν μεγάροισι Καλυψοῦς, ἥ μιν ἀνάγκῃ
ἴσχει· ὁ δ᾽ οὐ δύναται ἣν πατρίδα γαῖαν ἱκέσθαι·
οὐ γάρ οἱ πάρα νῆες ἐπήρετμοι καὶ ἑταῖροι,
560   οἵ κέν μιν πέμποιεν ἐπ᾽ εὐρέα νῶτα θαλάσσης.
σοὶ δ᾽ οὐ θέσφατόν ἐστι, διοτρεφὲς ὦ Μενέλαε,
Ἄργει ἐν ἱπποβότῳ θανέειν καὶ πότμον ἐπισπεῖν,
ἀλλά σ᾽ ἐς Ἠλύσιον πεδίον καὶ πείρατα γαίης
ἀθάνατοι πέμψουσιν, ὅθι ξανθὸς Ῥαδάμανθυς,

158

"So he spoke, and my spirit was broken within me, and I wept, as I sat on the sands, nor had my heart any longer desire to live and to behold the light of the sun. But when I had had my fill of weeping and writhing, then the unerring old man of the sea said to me:

"'No more, son of Atreus, weep thus so long a time without ceasing, for in it we shall find no help. Rather, with all the speed you can, strive to come to your native land for either you will find Aegisthus alive, or Orestes may have forestalled you and slain him, and you may chance upon his funeral feast.'

"So he spoke, and my heart and spirit were again warmed with comfort in my breast despite my grief, and I spoke, and addressed him with winged words:

"'Of these men now I know, but name the third man, who he is that still lives, and is held back upon the broad sea, or is perhaps dead. I wish to hear, despite my grief.'

"So I spoke, and he at once made answer, and said: 'It is the son of Laertes, whose home is in Ithaca. Him I saw in an island, shedding big tears, in the halls of the nymph Calypso, who keeps him there perforce, and he cannot come to his native land, for he has at hand no ships with oars, and no comrades, to send him on his way over the broad back of the sea. But for yourself, Menelaus, fostered by Zeus, it is not ordained that you should die and meet your fate in horse-pasturing Argos, but to the Elysian plain and the ends of the earth will the immortals convey you, where dwells fair-haired Rhadamanthus, and where life is

---

[1] Line 553 was rejected by all ancient critics.

565 τῇ περ ῥηίστη βιοτὴ πέλει ἀνθρώποισιν·
οὐ νιφετός, οὔτ' ἄρ χειμὼν πολὺς οὔτε ποτ' ὄμβρος,
ἀλλ' αἰεὶ Ζεφύροιο λιγὺ πνείοντος ἀήτας
Ὠκεανὸς ἀνίησιν ἀναψύχειν ἀνθρώπους·
οὕνεκ' ἔχεις Ἑλένην καί σφιν γαμβρὸς Διός ἐσσι.'

570   "ὣς εἰπὼν ὑπὸ πόντον ἐδύσετο κυμαίνοντα.
αὐτὰρ ἐγὼν ἐπὶ νῆας ἅμ' ἀντιθέοις ἑτάροισιν
ἤια, πολλὰ δέ μοι κραδίη πόρφυρε κιόντι.
αὐτὰρ ἐπεί ῥ' ἐπὶ νῆα κατήλθομεν ἠδὲ θάλασσαν,
δόρπον θ' ὁπλισάμεσθ', ἐπί τ' ἤλυθεν ἀμβροσίη νύξ,

575 δὴ τότε κοιμήθημεν ἐπὶ ῥηγμῖνι θαλάσσης.
ἦμος δ' ἠριγένεια φάνη ῥοδοδάκτυλος Ἠώς,
νῆας μὲν πάμπρωτον ἐρύσσαμεν εἰς ἅλα δῖαν,
ἐν δ' ἱστοὺς τιθέμεσθα καὶ ἱστία νηυσὶν ἐίσης,
ἂν δὲ καὶ αὐτοὶ βάντες ἐπὶ κληῖσι καθῖζον·

580 ἑξῆς δ' ἑζόμενοι πολιὴν ἅλα τύπτον ἐρετμοῖς.
ἂψ δ' εἰς Αἰγύπτοιο διιπετέος ποταμοῖο
στῆσα νέας, καὶ ἔρεξα τεληέσσας ἑκατόμβας.
αὐτὰρ ἐπεὶ κατέπαυσα θεῶν χόλον αἰὲν ἐόντων,
χεῦ' Ἀγαμέμνονι τύμβον, ἵν' ἄσβεστον κλέος εἴη.

585 ταῦτα τελευτήσας νεόμην, ἔδοσαν δέ μοι οὖρον
ἀθάνατοι, τοί μ' ὦκα φίλην ἐς πατρίδ' ἔπεμψαν.
ἀλλ' ἄγε νῦν ἐπίμεινον ἐνὶ μεγάροισιν ἐμοῖσιν,
ὄφρα κεν ἑνδεκάτη τε δυωδεκάτη τε γένηται·
καὶ τότε σ' εὖ πέμψω, δώσω δέ τοι ἀγλαὰ δῶρα,

590 τρεῖς ἵππους καὶ δίφρον ἐύξοον· αὐτὰρ ἔπειτα
δώσω καλὸν ἄλεισον, ἵνα σπένδησθα θεοῖσιν
ἀθανάτοις ἐμέθεν μεμνημένος ἤματα πάντα."

easiest for men. No snow is there, nor heavy storm, nor ever rain, but always Ocean sends up blasts of the shrill-blowing West Wind that they may give cooling to men; for you have Helen to wife, and are in their eyes the husband of the daughter of Zeus.'

"So saying he plunged beneath the surging sea, but I went to my ships with my godlike comrades, and many things did my heart darkly ponder as I went. But when I had come down to the ship and to the sea and we had made ready our supper, and immortal night had come on, then we lay down to rest on the shore of the sea. And as soon as early Dawn appeared, the rosy-fingered, our ships first of all we drew down to the bright sea, and set the masts and the sails in the shapely ships, and the men, too, went on board and sat down upon the benches, and sitting well in order struck the gray sea with their oars. So back again to the waters of Aegyptus, the heaven-fed river, I sailed, and there moored my ships and offered perfect hecatombs. But when I had stayed the wrath of the gods that are forever, I heaped up a mound to Agamemnon, that his fame might be unquenchable. Then, when I had made an end of this, I set out for home, and the immortals gave me a fair wind, and brought me swiftly to my dear native land. But come now, tarry in my halls until the eleventh or the twelfth day is come. Then will I send you forth with honor and give you splendid gifts, three horses and a well-polished chariot; and besides I will give you a beautiful cup, that you may pour libations to the immortal gods, and remember me all your days."

τὸν δ' αὖ Τηλέμαχος πεπνυμένος ἀντίον ηὔδα·
"Ἀτρεΐδη, μὴ δή με πολὺν χρόνον ἐνθάδ' ἔρυκε.
595 καὶ γάρ κ' εἰς ἐνιαυτὸν ἐγὼ παρὰ σοί γ' ἀνεχοίμην
ἥμενος, οὐδέ κέ μ' οἴκου ἕλοι πόθος οὐδὲ τοκήων·
αἰνῶς γὰρ μύθοισιν ἔπεσσί τε σοῖσιν ἀκούων
τέρπομαι. ἀλλ' ἤδη μοι ἀνιάζουσιν ἑταῖροι
ἐν Πύλῳ ἠγαθέῃ· σὺ δέ με χρόνον ἐνθάδ' ἐρύκεις.
600 δῶρον δ' ὅττι κέ μοι δοίης, κειμήλιον ἔστω·
ἵππους δ' εἰς Ἰθάκην οὐκ ἄξομαι, ἀλλὰ σοὶ αὐτῷ
ἐνθάδε λείψω ἄγαλμα· σὺ γὰρ πεδίοιο ἀνάσσεις
εὐρέος, ᾧ ἔνι μὲν λωτὸς πολύς, ἐν δὲ κύπειρον
πυροί τε ζειαί τε ἰδ' εὐρυφυὲς κρῖ λευκόν.
605 ἐν δ' Ἰθάκῃ οὔτ' ἂρ δρόμοι εὐρέες οὔτε τι λειμών·
αἰγίβοτος, καὶ μᾶλλον ἐπήρατος ἱπποβότοιο.
οὐ γάρ τις νήσων ἱππήλατος οὐδ' εὐλείμων,
αἵ θ' ἁλὶ κεκλίαται· Ἰθάκη δέ τε καὶ περὶ πασέων."
ὣς φάτο, μείδησεν δὲ βοὴν ἀγαθὸς Μενέλαος,
610 χειρί τέ μιν κατέρεξεν ἔπος τ' ἔφατ' ἔκ τ' ὀνόμαζεν·
"αἵματός εἰς ἀγαθοῖο, φίλον τέκος, οἷ' ἀγορεύεις·
τοιγὰρ ἐγώ τοι ταῦτα μεταστήσω· δύναμαι γάρ.
δώρων δ' ὅσσ' ἐν ἐμῷ οἴκῳ κειμήλια κεῖται,
δώσω ὃ κάλλιστον καὶ τιμήεστατόν ἐστιν·
615 δώσω τοι κρητῆρα τετυγμένον· ἀργύρεος δὲ
ἔστιν ἅπας, χρυσῷ δ' ἐπὶ χείλεα κεκράανται,
ἔργον δ' Ἡφαίστοιο. πόρεν δέ ἑ Φαίδιμος ἥρως,
Σιδονίων βασιλεύς, ὅθ' ἑὸς δόμος ἀμφεκάλυψε
κεῖσέ με νοστήσαντα· τεῒν δ' ἐθέλω τόδ' ὀπάσσαι."
620 ὣς οἱ μὲν τοιαῦτα πρὸς ἀλλήλους ἀγόρευον,

Then wise Telemachus answered him: "Son of Atreus, keep me no long time here, for truly for a year would I be content to sit in your house, nor would desire for home or parents come upon me; for wondrous is the pleasure I take in listening to your tales and your speech. But even now my comrades are chafing in sacred Pylos, and you are keeping me long here. And whatever gift you would give me, let it be some treasure; but horses I will not take to Ithaca, but will leave them here for you to delight in, for you are lord of a wide plain, where there is lotus in abundance, and galingale and wheat and spelt, and broad-eared white barley. But in Ithaca there are no broad courses nor meadow land at all. It is a pasture land of goats and more lovely than one that pastures horses. For not one of the islands is fit for driving horses, or rich in meadows, of those that slope abruptly to the sea, and Ithaca least of all."

So he spoke, and Menelaus, good at the war cry, smiled, and stroked him with his hand, and spoke, and addressed him:

"You are of good blood, dear child, that you speak thus. Therefore will I change these gifts, for I can do so. Of all the gifts that lie stored as treasures in my house, I will give you that one that is most beautiful and costliest. I will give you a well-wrought mixing bowl. All of silver it is, and the rims of it are finished off with gold, the work of Hephaestus; and the hero Phaedimus, king of the Sidonians, gave it to me, when his house sheltered me when I came there on my way home, and now I am minded to give it to you."

Thus they spoke to one another, and meanwhile the

δαιτυμόνες δ' ἐς δώματ' ἴσαν θείου βασιλῆος.
οἱ δ' ἦγον μὲν μῆλα, φέρον δ' εὐήνορα οἶνον·
σῖτον δέ σφ' ἄλοχοι καλλικρήδεμνοι ἔπεμπον.[1]
ὣς οἱ μὲν περὶ δεῖπνον ἐνὶ μεγάροισι πένοντο.

625 μνηστῆρες δὲ πάροιθεν Ὀδυσσῆος μεγάροιο
δίσκοισιν τέρποντο καὶ αἰγανέῃσιν ἱέντες
ἐν τυκτῷ δαπέδῳ, ὅθι περ πάρος, ὕβριν ἔχοντες.[2]
Ἀντίνοος δὲ καθῆστο καὶ Εὐρύμαχος θεοειδής,
ἀρχοὶ μνηστήρων, ἀρετῇ δ' ἔσαν ἔξοχ' ἄριστοι.

630 τοῖς δ' υἱὸς Φρονίοιο Νοήμων ἐγγύθεν ἐλθὼν
Ἀντίνοον μύθοισιν ἀνειρόμενος προσέειπεν·

"Ἀντίνο', ἦ ῥά τι ἴδμεν ἐνὶ φρεσίν, ἦε καὶ οὐκί,
ὁππότε Τηλέμαχος νεῖτ' ἐκ Πύλου ἠμαθόεντος;
νῆά μοι οἴχετ' ἄγων· ἐμὲ δὲ χρεὼ γίγνεται αὐτῆς

635 Ἤλιδ' ἐς εὐρύχορον διαβήμεναι, ἔνθα μοι ἵπποι
δώδεκα θήλειαι, ὑπὸ δ' ἡμίονοι ταλαεργοὶ
ἀδμῆτες· τῶν κέν τιν' ἐλασσάμενος δαμασαίμην."

ὣς ἔφαθ', οἱ δ' ἀνὰ θυμὸν ἐθάμβεον· οὐ γὰρ ἔφαντο
ἐς Πύλον οἴχεσθαι Νηλήιον, ἀλλά που αὐτοῦ

640 ἀγρῶν ἢ μήλοισι παρέμμεναι ἠὲ συβώτῃ.

τὸν δ' αὖτ' Ἀντίνοος προσέφη Εὐπείθεος υἱός·
"νημερτές μοι ἔνισπε, πότ' ᾤχετο καὶ τίνες αὐτῷ
κοῦροι ἕποντ'; Ἰθάκης ἐξαίρετοι, ἦ ἑοὶ αὐτοῦ
θῆτές τε δμῶές τε; δύναιτό κε καὶ τὸ τελέσσαι.

645 καί μοι τοῦτ' ἀγόρευσον ἐτήτυμον, ὄφρ' ἐὺ εἰδῶ,
ἦ σε βίῃ ἀέκοντος ἀπηύρα νῆα μέλαιναν,
ἦε ἑκὼν οἱ δῶκας, ἐπεὶ προσπτύξατο μύθῳ."

[1] ἔπεμπον: ἔνεικαν

164

banqueters came to the palace of the divine king. They drove up sheep, and brought strengthening wine, and their beautifully veiled wives brought bread. Thus they were busied about the feast in the halls.

But the suitors in front of the palace of Odysseus were making merry, throwing the discus and the javelin in a leveled place, as their custom was, in insolence of heart; and Antinous and godlike Eurymachus were sitting there, the leaders of the suitors, who in ability were far the best of all. To them Noemon, son of Phronius, drew near, and he questioned Antinous, and spoke, and said:

"Antinous, know we at all in our hearts, or do we not, when Telemachus will return from sandy Pylos? He is gone, taking a ship of mine, and I have need of her to cross over to spacious Elis, where I have twelve brood mares, and at the teat sturdy mules as yet unbroken. Of these I mean to drive one off and break him in."

So he spoke, and they marveled at heart, for they did not imagine that Telemachus had gone to Neleian Pylos, but that he was somewhere there on his lands, among the flocks or with the swineherd.

Then Antinous, son of Eupeithes, spoke to him, saying: "Tell me the truth; when did he go, and what youths went with him? Were they chosen youths of Ithaca, or hirelings and slaves of his own? That too he could have done. And tell me this truly, that I may be sure. Was it perforce and against your will that he took from you the black ship? or did you give it to him freely of your own will, because he besought you?"

---

[2] ἔχοντες Aristarchus: ἔχεσκον

τὸν δ' υἱὸς Φρονίοιο Νοήμων ἀντίον ηὔδα·
"αὐτὸς ἑκών οἱ δῶκα· τί κεν ῥέξειε καὶ ἄλλος,
650 ὁππότ' ἀνὴρ τοιοῦτος ἔχων μελεδήματα θυμῷ
αἰτίζῃ; χαλεπόν κεν ἀνήνασθαι δόσιν εἴη.
κοῦροι δ', οἳ κατὰ δῆμον ἀριστεύουσι μεθ' ἡμέας,
οἵ οἱ ἔποντ'· ἐν δ' ἀρχὸν ἐγὼ βαίνοντ' ἐνόησα
Μέντορα, ἠὲ θεόν, τῷ δ' αὐτῷ πάντα ἐῴκει.
655 ἀλλὰ τὸ θαυμάζω· ἴδον ἐνθάδε Μέντορα δῖον
χθιζὸν ὑπηοῖον, τότε δ' ἔμβη νηὶ Πύλονδε."
ὣς ἄρα φωνήσας ἀπέβη πρὸς δώματα πατρός,
τοῖσιν δ' ἀμφοτέροισιν ἀγάσσατο θυμὸς ἀγήνωρ.
μνηστῆρας δ' ἄμυδις κάθισαν καὶ παῦσαν ἀέθλων.
660 τοῖσιν δ' Ἀντίνοος μετέφη Εὐπείθεος υἱός,
ἀχνύμενος· μένεος δὲ μέγα φρένες ἀμφιμέλαιναι
πίμπλαντ', ὄσσε δέ οἱ πυρὶ λαμπετόωντι ἐΐκτην·[1]
"ὢ πόποι, ἦ μέγα ἔργον ὑπερφιάλως ἐτελέσθη
Τηλεμάχῳ ὁδὸς ἥδε· φάμεν δέ οἱ οὐ τελέεσθαι.
665 ἐκ τοσσῶνδ' ἀέκητι νέος πάις οἴχεται αὔτως
νῆα ἐρυσσάμενος, κρίνας τ' ἀνὰ δῆμον ἀρίστους.
ἄρξει καὶ προτέρω κακὸν ἔμμεναι· ἀλλά οἱ αὐτῷ
Ζεὺς ὀλέσειε βίην, πρὶν ἥβης μέτρον ἱκέσθαι.[2]
ἀλλ' ἄγε μοι δότε νῆα θοὴν καὶ εἴκοσ' ἑταίρους,
670 ὄφρα μιν αὐτὸν ἰόντα λοχήσομαι ἠδὲ φυλάξω
ἐν πορθμῷ Ἰθάκης τε Σάμοιό τε παιπαλοέσσης,
ὡς ἂν ἐπισμυγερῶς ναυτίλλεται εἵνεκα πατρός."

---

[1] Lines 661 and 662 were rejected by Aristarchus, as borrowed from *Iliad* 1.103 f.

[2] ἥβης μέτρον ἱκέσθαι Aristarchus: ἡμῖν πῆμα γενέσθαι

Then Noemon, son of Phronius, answered him: "I myself freely gave it to him. What else could any man do, when a man like him, his heart laden with care, makes entreaty? Hard it would be to deny the gift. The youths that are the ablest in the land after ourselves, these are they who have gone with him; and among them I noted one going on board as their leader, Mentor, or a god who was in all things like Mentor. But at this I marvel. I saw noble Mentor here yesterday at early dawn; but at that time he embarked for Pylos."

So saying he departed to his father's house, but of the other two the proud hearts were angered. They at once made the suitors sit down and cease from their games; and among them Antinous, son of Eupeithes, spoke in displeasure; and with rage was his black heart wholly filled, and his eyes were like blazing fire.

"Out upon him, truly a proud deed has been insolently brought to pass by Telemachus, this journey, and we imagined that he would never see it accomplished. In despite of all of us here the lad is gone without more ado, launching a ship, and choosing the best men in the land. He will begin by and by to give us trouble; but to his own undoing may Zeus destroy his might before ever he reaches the measure of manhood. But come, give me a swift ship and twenty men, that I may watch in ambush for him as he makes his lonely passage in the straight between Ithaca and rugged Samos, so that he will have a sorry voyage of it in search of his father."

ὣς ἔφαθ᾽, οἱ δ᾽ ἄρα πάντες ἐπήνεον ἠδ᾽ ἐκέλευον.
αὐτίκ᾽ ἔπειτ᾽ ἀναστάντες ἔβαν δόμον εἰς Ὀδυσῆος.
675   οὐδ᾽ ἄρα Πηνελόπεια πολὺν χρόνον ἦεν ἄπυστος
μύθων, οὓς μνηστῆρες ἐνὶ φρεσὶ βυσσοδόμευον·
κῆρυξ γάρ οἱ ἔειπε Μέδων, ὃς ἐπεύθετο βουλὰς
αὐλῆς ἐκτὸς ἐών· οἱ δ᾽ ἔνδοθι μῆτιν ὕφαινον.
βῆ δ᾽ ἴμεν ἀγγελέων διὰ δώματα Πηνελοπείῃ·
680 τὸν δὲ κατ᾽ οὐδοῦ βάντα προσηύδα Πηνελόπεια·
    "κῆρυξ, τίπτε δέ σε πρόεσαν μνηστῆρες ἀγαυοί;
ἦ εἰπέμεναι δμῳῇσιν Ὀδυσσῆος θείοιο
ἔργων παύσασθαι, σφίσι δ᾽ αὐτοῖς δαῖτα πένεσθαι;
μὴ μνηστεύσαντες μηδ᾽ ἄλλοθ᾽ ὁμιλήσαντες
685 ὕστατα καὶ πύματα νῦν ἐνθάδε δειπνήσειαν·
οἳ θάμ᾽ ἀγειρόμενοι βίοτον κατακείρετε πολλόν,
κτῆσιν Τηλεμάχοιο δαΐφρονος· οὐδέ τι πατρῶν
ὑμετέρων τὸ πρόσθεν ἀκούετε, παῖδες ἐόντες,
οἷος Ὀδυσσεὺς ἔσκε μεθ᾽ ὑμετέροισι τοκεῦσιν,
690 οὔτε τινὰ ῥέξας ἐξαίσιον οὔτε τι εἰπὼν
ἐν δήμῳ, ἥ τ᾽ ἐστὶ δίκη θείων βασιλήων·
ἄλλον κ᾽ ἐχθαίρῃσι βροτῶν, ἄλλον κε φιλοίη.
κεῖνος δ᾽ οὔ ποτε πάμπαν ἀτάσθαλον ἄνδρα ἐώργει.
ἀλλ᾽ ὁ μὲν ὑμέτερος θυμὸς καὶ ἀεικέα ἔργα
695 φαίνεται, οὐδέ τίς ἐστι χάρις μετόπισθ᾽ εὐεργέων."
    τὴν δ᾽ αὖτε προσέειπε Μέδων πεπνυμένα εἰδώς·
"αἲ γὰρ δή, βασίλεια, τόδε πλεῖστον κακὸν εἴη.
ἀλλὰ πολὺ μεῖζόν τε καὶ ἀργαλεώτερον ἄλλο
μνηστῆρες φράζονται, ὃ μὴ τελέσειε Κρονίων·
700 Τηλέμαχον μεμάασι κατακτάμεν ὀξέι χαλκῷ

So he spoke, and they all praised his words, and bade him act. And at once they rose up and went to the house of Odysseus.

Now Penelope was not long without knowledge of the plans which the suitors were plotting deep in their hearts; for the herald Medon told her, who heard their counsel as he stood outside the court and they within were weaving their plot. So he went through the hall to bear the tidings to Penelope; and as he stepped across the threshold Penelope spoke to him and said:

"Herald, why have the lordly suitors sent you here? Was it to tell the handmaids of divine Odysseus to cease from their tasks, and make ready a feast for them? Neither wooing any more, nor consorting together elsewhere, may they now feast here their latest and their last—you who are ever thronging here and wasting much livelihood, the wealth of wise Telemachus. Surely you hearkened not at all in olden days when you were children, when your fathers told what manner of man Odysseus was among them that begot you, in that he did no wrong in deed or word to any man in the land as the custom is of divine kings—one man they hate and another they love. Yet he never dealt intemperately at all with any man. But your mind and your unseemly deeds are plain to see, nor is there in later days any gratitude for good deeds done."

Then Medon, wise of heart, answered her: "I would, my queen, that this were the greatest evil. But another far greater and more grievous are the suitors planning, which I pray that the son of Cronos may never bring to pass. They mean to slay Telemachus with the sharp sword on his

οἴκαδε νισόμενον· ὁ δ' ἔβη μετὰ πατρὸς ἀκουὴν
ἐς Πύλον ἠγαθέην ἠδ' ἐς Λακεδαίμονα δῖαν."

ὣς φάτο, τῆς δ' αὐτοῦ λύτο γούνατα καὶ φίλον ἦτορ,
δὴν δέ μιν ἀμφασίη ἐπέων λάβε· τὼ δέ οἱ ὄσσε
705 δακρυόφι πλῆσθεν, θαλερὴ δέ οἱ ἔσχετο φωνή.
ὀψὲ δὲ δή μιν ἔπεσσιν ἀμειβομένη προσέειπε·

"κῆρυξ, τίπτε δέ μοι πάις οἴχεται; οὐδέ τί μιν χρεὼ
νηῶν ὠκυπόρων ἐπιβαινέμεν, αἵ θ' ἁλὸς ἵπποι
ἀνδράσι γίγνονται, περόωσι δὲ πουλὺν ἐφ' ὑγρήν.
710 ἦ ἵνα μηδ' ὄνομ' αὐτοῦ ἐν ἀνθρώποισι λίπηται;"

τὴν δ' ἠμείβετ' ἔπειτα Μέδων πεπνυμένα εἰδώς·
"οὐκ οἶδ' ἤ τίς μιν θεὸς ὤρορεν, ἦε καὶ αὐτοῦ
θυμὸς ἐφωρμήθη ἴμεν ἐς Πύλον, ὄφρα πύθηται
πατρὸς ἑοῦ ἢ νόστον ἢ ὅν τινα πότμον ἐπέσπεν."

715 ὣς ἄρα φωνήσας ἀπέβη κατὰ δῶμ' Ὀδυσῆος.
τὴν δ' ἄχος ἀμφεχύθη θυμοφθόρον, οὐδ' ἄρ' ἔτ' ἔτλη
δίφρῳ ἐφέζεσθαι πολλῶν κατὰ οἶκον ἐόντων,
ἀλλ' ἄρ' ἐπ' οὐδοῦ ἷζε πολυκμήτου θαλάμοιο
οἴκτρ' ὀλοφυρομένη· περὶ δὲ δμωαὶ μινύριζον
720 πᾶσαι, ὅσαι κατὰ δώματ' ἔσαν νέαι ἠδὲ παλαιαί.
τῆς δ' ἁδινὸν γοόωσα μετηύδα Πηνελόπεια·

"κλῦτε, φίλαι· πέρι γάρ μοι Ὀλύμπιος ἄλγε'
 ἔδωκεν

ἐκ πασέων, ὅσσαι μοι ὁμοῦ τράφεν ἠδ' ἐγένοντο·
ἢ πρὶν μὲν πόσιν ἐσθλὸν ἀπώλεσα θυμολέοντα,
725 παντοίης ἀρετῇσι κεκασμένον ἐν Δαναοῖσιν,
ἐσθλόν, τοῦ κλέος εὐρὺ καθ' Ἑλλάδα καὶ μέσον
 Ἄργος.[1]

homeward way; for he went in quest of tidings of his father to sacred Pylos and to stately Lacedaemon."

So he spoke, and her knees were loosened where she sat, and her heart melted. For long she was speechless, and both her eyes were filled with tears, and the flow of her voice was checked. But at last she made answer and said to him:

"Herald, why is my son gone? He had no need to go on board swift-faring ships, which serve men as horses of the deep, and cross over the wide waters of the sea. Was it that not even his name should be left among men?"

Then Medon, wise of heart, answered her: "I do not know whether some god impelled him, or whether his own heart was moved to go to Pylos, that he might learn either of his father's return or what fate he had met."

So he spoke and departed through the house of Odysseus, and on her fell a cloud of soul-consuming grief, and she had no more the heart to sit upon one of the many seats that were in the room, but down upon the threshold of her beautifully wrought chamber she sank, moaning piteously, and round about her wailed her handmaids, all that were in the house, both young and old. To them with sobs of lamentation spoke Penelope:

"Hear me, my friends, for to me the Olympian has given sorrow above all the women who were bred and born with me. Long since I lost my splendid husband of the lion heart, preeminent among the Danaans in all the virtues there are, splendid, whose fame is wide through Hellas and

---

[1] Line 726 was rejected by Aristarchus; cf. 1.344 and, below, 816.

νῦν αὖ παῖδ' ἀγαπητὸν ἀνηρείψαντο θύελλαι
ἀκλέα ἐκ μεγάρων, οὐδ' ὁρμηθέντος ἄκουσα.
σχέτλιαι, οὐδ' ὑμεῖς περ ἐνὶ φρεσὶ θέσθε ἑκάστη
730 ἐκ λεχέων μ' ἀνεγεῖραι, ἐπιστάμεναι σάφα θυμῷ,
ὁππότ' ἐκεῖνος ἔβη κοίλην ἐπὶ νῆα μέλαιναν.
εἰ γὰρ ἐγὼ πυθόμην ταύτην ὁδὸν ὁρμαίνοντα,
τῷ κε μάλ' ἤ κεν ἔμεινε καὶ ἐσσύμενός περ ὁδοῖο,
ἤ κέ με τεθνηκυῖαν ἐνὶ μεγάροισιν ἔλειπεν.
735 ἀλλά τις ὀτρηρῶς Δολίον καλέσειε γέροντα,
δμῶ' ἐμόν, ὅν μοι δῶκε πατὴρ ἔτι δεῦρο κιούσῃ,
καί μοι κῆπον ἔχει πολυδένδρεον, ὄφρα τάχιστα
Λαέρτῃ τάδε πάντα παρεζόμενος καταλέξῃ,
εἰ δή πού τινα κεῖνος ἐνὶ φρεσὶ μῆτιν ὑφήνας
740 ἐξελθὼν λαοῖσιν ὀδύρεται, οἳ μεμάασιν
ὃν καὶ 'Οδυσσῆος φθῖσαι γόνον ἀντιθέοιο."
    τὴν δ' αὖτε προσέειπε φίλη τροφὸς Εὐρύκλεια·
"νύμφα φίλη, σὺ μὲν ἄρ με κατάκτανε νηλέι χαλκῷ
ἤ ἔα ἐν μεγάρῳ· μῦθον δέ τοι οὐκ ἐπικεύσω.
745 ᾔδε' ἐγὼ τάδε πάντα, πόρον δέ οἱ ὅσσ' ἐκέλευε,
σῖτον καὶ μέθυ ἡδύ· ἐμεῦ δ' ἕλετο μέγαν ὅρκον
μὴ πρὶν σοὶ ἐρέειν, πρὶν δωδεκάτην γε γενέσθαι
ἤ σ' αὐτὴν ποθέσαι καὶ ἀφορμηθέντος ἀκοῦσαι,
ὡς ἂν μὴ κλαίουσα κατὰ χρόα καλὸν ἰάπτῃς.
750 ἀλλ' ὑδρηναμένη, καθαρὰ χροῒ εἵμαθ' ἑλοῦσα,
εἰς ὑπερῷ' ἀναβᾶσα σὺν ἀμφιπόλοισι γυναιξὶν
εὔχε' 'Αθηναίῃ κούρῃ Διὸς αἰγιόχοιο·
ἡ γάρ κέν μιν ἔπειτα καὶ ἐκ θανάτοιο σαώσαι.
μηδὲ γέροντα κάκου κεκακωμένον· οὐ γὰρ ὀίω

mid-Argos. And now again my well-loved son have the
storm winds swept away from our halls without tidings, nor
did I hear of his departure. Cruel, that you are! Not even
you took thought, any of you, to rouse me from my couch,
though in your hearts you knew full well when he went on
board the hollow black ship. For had I learned that he was
pondering this journey, he would by all means have stayed
here, however eager to be gone, or he would have left me
dead in the halls. But now let someone hasten to summon
the aged Dolius, my servant, whom my father gave me as I
was about to come here, and who keeps my garden of many
trees, that he may at once go and sit by Laertes, and tell
him of all these things. So perhaps may Laertes weave
some plan in his heart, and show himself and with weeping
make his plea to the people, who are bent on destroying his
race and that of godlike Odysseus."

Then the loyal nurse Eurycleia answered her: "Dear
bride of Odysseus, you may slay me with the pitiless sword
or let me abide in the house, yet I will not hide my word
from you. I knew all this, and gave him whatever he bade
me, bread and sweet wine. But he took from me a mighty
oath not to tell you until at least the twelfth day should
come, or you should yourself miss him and hear that he was
gone, that you might not mar your beautiful flesh with
weeping. But now bathe yourself, and take clean clothing
for your body and then go up to your upper chamber with
your handmaids and pray to Athene, the daughter of Zeus
who bears the aegis; for she may then save him even from
death. And do not trouble a troubled old man; for I do not

755 πάγχυ θεοῖς μακάρεσσι γονὴν Ἀρκεισιάδαο
ἔχθεσθ᾽, ἀλλ᾽ ἔτι πού τις ἐπέσσεται ὅς κεν ἔχῃσι
δώματά θ᾽ ὑψερεφέα καὶ ἀπόπροθι πίονας ἀγρούς."

ὣς φάτο, τῆς δ᾽ εὔνησε γόον, σχέθε δ᾽ ὄσσε γόοιο.
ἡ δ᾽ ὑδρηναμένη, καθαρὰ χροῒ εἵμαθ᾽ ἑλοῦσα
760 εἰς ὑπερῷ᾽ ἀνέβαινε σὺν ἀμφιπόλοισι γυναιξίν,
ἐν δ᾽ ἔθετ᾽ οὐλοχύτας κανέῳ, ἠρᾶτο δ᾽ Ἀθήνη·

"κλῦθί μευ, αἰγιόχοιο Διὸς τέκος, ἀτρυτώνη,
εἰ ποτέ τοι πολύμητις ἐνὶ μεγάροισιν Ὀδυσσεὺς
ἢ βοὸς ἢ ὄιος κατὰ πίονα μηρί᾽ ἔκηε,
765 τῶν νῦν μοι μνῆσαι, καί μοι φίλον υἷα σάωσον,
μνηστῆρας δ᾽ ἀπάλαλκε κακῶς ὑπερηνορέοντας."

ὣς εἰποῦσ᾽ ὀλόλυξε, θεὰ δέ οἱ ἔκλυεν ἀρῆς.
μνηστῆρες δ᾽ ὁμάδησαν ἀνὰ μέγαρα σκιόεντα·
ὧδε δέ τις εἴπεσκε νέων ὑπερηνορεόντων·
770 "ἦ μάλα δὴ γάμον ἄμμι πολυμνήστη βασίλεια
ἀρτύει, οὐδέ τι οἶδεν ὅ οἱ φόνος υἷι τέτυκται."

ὣς ἄρα τις εἴπεσκε, τὰ δ᾽ οὐκ ἴσαν ὡς ἐτέτυκτο.
τοῖσιν δ᾽ Ἀντίνοος ἀγορήσατο καὶ μετέειπε·

"δαιμόνιοι, μύθους μὲν ὑπερφιάλους ἀλέασθε
775 πάντας ὁμῶς, μή πού τις ἀπαγγείλῃσι[1] καὶ εἴσω.
ἀλλ᾽ ἄγε σιγῇ τοῖον ἀναστάντες τελέωμεν
μῦθον, ὃ δὴ καὶ πᾶσιν ἐνὶ φρεσὶν ἤραρεν ἡμῖν."

ὣς εἰπὼν ἐκρίνατ᾽ ἐείκοσι φῶτας ἀρίστους,

---

[1] ἀπαγγείλῃσι: ἐπαγγείλῃσι

---

[a] The word δαιμόνιος properly means "under the influence of a divinity." It is used in the vocative in cases where the person

think the race of the son of Arceisius is utterly hated by the blessed gods, but surely there shall still be one to possess the high-roofed halls and the rich fields in the distance."

So she spoke, and lulled Penelope's laments, and made her eyes to cease from weeping. She then bathed, and took clean clothing for her body, and went up to her upper chamber with her handmaids, and placing barley grains in a basket prayed to Athene:

"Hear me, child of Zeus who bears the aegis, Atrytone. If ever resourceful Odysseus burned for you in his halls fat thigh pieces of heifer or ewe, remember these things now, I pray you, and save my dear son, and ward off from him the suitors in their evil insolence."

So saying she raised the sacred cry, and the goddess heard her prayer. But the suitors broke into uproar throughout the shadowy halls, and thus would one of the proud youths speak:

"Now surely the queen, wooed of many, is preparing our marriage, nor does she know at all that death has been made ready for her son."

So would one of them speak; but they did not know how these things were to be. And Antinous addressed their company and said:

"God-touched sirs,[a] shun over-confident speech of every kind alike, for fear someone report your speech even within the house. But come, in silence thus let us arise and put into effect our plan which pleased us one and all at heart."

So he spoke, and chose twenty men that were best, and

addressed is acting in some unaccountable or ill-omened way. Hence the tone varies from angry remonstrance to gentle expostulation, or even pity. M.

βὰν δ' ἰέναι ἐπὶ νῆα θοὴν καὶ θῖνα θαλάσσης.
780 νῆα μὲν οὖν πάμπρωτον ἁλὸς βένθοσδε ἔρυσσαν,
ἐν δ' ἱστόν τ' ἐτίθεντο καὶ ἱστία νηὶ μελαίνῃ,
ἠρτύναντο δ' ἐρετμὰ τροποῖς ἐν δερματίνοισιν,
πάντα κατὰ μοῖραν, ἀνά θ' ἱστία λευκὰ πέτασσαν·[1]
τεύχεα δέ σφ' ἤνεικαν ὑπέρθυμοι θεράποντες.
785 ὑψοῦ δ' ἐν νοτίῳ τήν γ' ὥρμισαν, ἐκ δ' ἔβαν αὐτοί·
ἔνθα δὲ δόρπον ἕλοντο, μένον δ' ἐπὶ ἕσπερον ἐλθεῖν.

ἡ δ' ὑπερῴῳ αὖθι περίφρων Πηνελόπεια
κεῖτ' ἄρ' ἄσιτος, ἄπαστος ἐδητύος ἠδὲ ποτῆτος,
ὁρμαίνουσ' ἤ οἱ θάνατον φύγοι υἱὸς ἀμύμων,
790 ἦ ὅ γ' ὑπὸ μνηστῆρσιν ὑπερφιάλοισι δαμείη.
ὅσσα δὲ μερμήριξε λέων ἀνδρῶν ἐν ὁμίλῳ
δείσας, ὁππότε μιν δόλιον περὶ κύκλον ἄγωσι,
τόσσα μιν ὁρμαίνουσαν ἐπήλυθε νήδυμος ὕπνος·
εὗδε δ' ἀνακλινθεῖσα, λύθεν δέ οἱ ἅψεα πάντα.

795 ἔνθ' αὖτ' ἄλλ' ἐνόησε θεά, γλαυκῶπις Ἀθήνη·
εἴδωλον ποίησε, δέμας δ' ἤικτο γυναικί,
Ἰφθίμῃ, κούρῃ μεγαλήτορος Ἰκαρίοιο,
τὴν Εὔμηλος ὄπυιε Φερῇς ἔνι οἰκία ναίων.
πέμπε δέ μιν πρὸς δώματ' Ὀδυσσῆος θείοιο,
800 ἧος Πηνελόπειαν ὀδυρομένην γοόωσαν
παύσειε κλαυθμοῖο γόοιό τε δακρυόεντος.
ἐς θάλαμον δ' εἰσῆλθε παρὰ κληῖδος ἱμάντα,
στῆ δ' ἄρ' ὑπὲρ κεφαλῆς, καί μιν πρὸς μῦθον ἔειπεν·
"εὕδεις, Πηνελόπεια, φίλον τετιημένη ἦτορ;
805 οὐ μέν σ' οὐδὲ ἐῶσι θεοὶ ῥεῖα ζώοντες
κλαίειν οὐδ' ἀκάχησθαι, ἐπεί ῥ' ἔτι νόστιμός ἐστι

176

they went their way to the swift ship and the shore of the
sea. The ship first of all they drew down to the deep water,
and set the mast and sail in the black ship, and fitted the
oars in the leather thole straps, all in due order, and spread
the white sail. And proud squires brought them their
weapons. Well out in the channel they moored the ship,
and themselves disembarked. There then they took
supper, and waited till evening should come.

But she, the wise Penelope, lay there in her upper
chamber, touching no food, tasting neither meat nor drink,
pondering whether her flawless son would escape death, or
be slain by the insolent suitors. And just as a lion is seized
with fear and broods among a throng of men, when they
draw their crafty ring about him, so was she pondering
when sweet sleep came upon her. And she sank back and
slept, and all her joints relaxed.

Then the goddess, flashing-eyed Athene, had another
thought. She made a phantom, and likened it in form to a
woman, Iphthime, daughter of great-hearted Icarius,
whom Eumelus wedded, whose home was in Pherae. And
she sent it to the house of divine Odysseus, to Penelope in
the midst of her wailing and lamenting, to bid her cease
from weeping and tearful lamentation. So into the
chamber it passed by the thong of the bolt, and stood
above her head, and spoke to her, and said:

"Do you sleep, Penelope, troubled at heart? The gods
that live at ease are unwilling that you should weep or be

---

[1] Line 783 (= 8.54) is omitted in many MSS.

σὸς παῖς· οὐ μὲν γάρ τι θεοῖς ἀλιτήμενός ἐστι."

τὴν δ' ἠμείβετ' ἔπειτα περίφρων Πηνελόπεια,
ἡδὺ μάλα κνώσσουσ' ἐν ὀνειρείῃσι πύλῃσιν·

810 "τίπτε, κασιγνήτη, δεῦρ' ἤλυθες; οὔ τι πάρος γε
πωλέ', ἐπεὶ μάλα πολλὸν ἀπόπροθι δώματα ναίεις·
καί με κέλεαι παύσασθαι ὀιζύος ἠδ' ὀδυνάων
πολλέων, αἵ μ' ἐρέθουσι κατὰ φρένα καὶ κατὰ θυμόν,
ἣ πρὶν μὲν πόσιν ἐσθλὸν ἀπώλεσα θυμολέοντα,

815 παντοίῃς ἀρετῇσι κεκασμένον ἐν Δαναοῖσιν,
ἐσθλόν, τοῦ κλέος εὐρὺ καθ' Ἑλλάδα καὶ μέσον
          Ἄργος·[1]
νῦν αὖ παῖς ἀγαπητὸς ἔβη κοίλης ἐπὶ νηός,
νήπιος, οὔτε πόνων εὖ εἰδὼς οὔτ' ἀγοράων.
τοῦ δὴ ἐγὼ καὶ μᾶλλον ὀδύρομαι ἤ περ ἐκείνου·

820 τοῦ δ' ἀμφιτρομέω καὶ δείδια, μή τι πάθῃσιν,
ἢ ὅ γε τῶν ἐνὶ δήμῳ, ἵν' οἴχεται, ἢ ἐνὶ πόντῳ·
δυσμενέες γὰρ πολλοὶ ἐπ' αὐτῷ μηχανόωνται,
ἱέμενοι κτεῖναι πρὶν πατρίδα γαῖαν ἱκέσθαι."

τὴν δ' ἀπαμειβόμενον προσέφη εἴδωλον ἀμαυρόν·

825 "θάρσει, μηδέ τι πάγχυ μετὰ φρεσὶ δείδιθι λίην·
τοίη γάρ οἱ πομπὸς ἅμ' ἔρχεται, ἥν τε καὶ ἄλλοι
ἀνέρες ἠρήσαντο παρεστάμεναι, δύναται γάρ,
Παλλὰς Ἀθηναίη· σὲ δ' ὀδυρομένην ἐλεαίρει·
ἣ νῦν με προέηκε τεῒν τάδε μυθήσασθαι."

830 τὴν δ' αὖτε προσέειπε περίφρων Πηνελόπεια·
"εἰ μὲν δὴ θεός ἐσσι θεοῖό τε ἔκλυες αὐδῆς,
εἰ δ' ἄγε μοι καὶ κεῖνον ὀιζυρὸν κατάλεξον,
ἦ που ἔτι ζώει καὶ ὁρᾷ φάος ἠελίοιο,

distressed, seeing that your son is yet to return; for in no way is he a sinner in the eyes of the gods."

Then wise Penelope answered her, as she slumbered very sweetly at the gates of dreams:

"Why, sister, have you come here? Before this it has not been your habit to come, for you swell in a home far away. And you bid me cease from my grief and the many pains that distress me in mind and heart. Long since I lost my noble husband of the lion heart, preeminent among the Danaans in all the virtues there are, noble, whose fame is wide through Hellas and mid-Argos. And now again my well-loved son has gone away in a hollow ship, a mere child, knowing nothing of toils or the gatherings of men. For him I sorrow even more than for that other, and tremble for him, and fear lest anything befall him, whether it be in the land of the men to whom he is gone, or on the sea. For many foes are plotting against him, eager to slay him before he comes back to his native land."

Then the dim phantom answered her and said: "Take heart and be not in your mind too greatly afraid; since such a guide goes with him as other men too have prayed to stand by their side, for she has power—Pallas Athene herself and she pities you in your sorrow, for she it is who has sent me forth to tell you this."

Then again wise Penelope answered her: "If you are indeed a god, and have listened to the voice of a god, come, tell me, I pray you, also of that man of sorrows, whether he still lives and beholds the light of the sun, or whether he is

---

[1] Line 816 was rejected by Aristarchus; cf. 726 and 1.344.

ἢ ἤδη τέθνηκε καὶ εἰν Ἀΐδαο δόμοισι."

835   τὴν δ' ἀπαμειβόμενον προσέφη εἴδωλον ἀμαυρόν·
"οὐ μέν τοι κεῖνόν γε διηνεκέως ἀγορεύσω,
ζώει ὅ γ' ἦ τέθνηκε· κακὸν δ' ἀνεμώλια βάζειν."
  ὣς εἰπὸν σταθμοῖο παρὰ κληῖδα λιάσθη
ἐς πνοιὰς ἀνέμων. ἡ δ' ἐξ ὕπνου ἀνόρουσε

840 κούρη Ἰκαρίοιο· φίλον δέ οἱ ἦτορ ἰάνθη,
ὣς οἱ ἐναργὲς ὄνειρον ἐπέσσυτο νυκτὸς ἀμολγῷ.
  μνηστῆρες δ' ἀναβάντες ἐπέπλεον ὑγρὰ κέλευθα
Τηλεμάχῳ φόνον αἰπὺν ἐνὶ φρεσὶν ὁρμαίνοντες.
ἔστι δέ τις νῆσος μέσσῃ ἁλὶ πετρήεσσα,

845 μεσσηγὺς Ἰθάκης τε Σάμοιό τε παιπαλοέσσης,
Ἀστερίς, οὐ μεγάλη· λιμένες δ' ἔνι ναύλοχοι αὐτῇ
ἀμφίδυμοι· τῇ τόν γε μένον λοχόωντες Ἀχαιοί.

already dead and in the house of Hades."

And the dim phantom answered her and said: "No, of him I shall not speak explicitly, whether he be alive or dead; it is an ill thing to speak words vain as wind."

So saying the phantom glided away by the bolt of the door into the breath of the winds. And the daughter of Icarius started up from sleep, and her heart was warmed with comfort, that so clear a vision had sped to her in the darkness of night.

But the suitors embarked, and sailed over the watery ways, pondering in their hearts utter murder for Telemachus. There is a rocky isle in the midst of the sea, midway between Ithaca and rugged Samos, Asteris, of no great size, but in it is a harbor where ships may lie, with an entrance on either side. There, in ambush, the Achaeans waited for him.

E

Ἠὼς δ' ἐκ λεχέων παρ' ἀγαυοῦ Τιθωνοῖο
ὤρνυθ', ἵν' ἀθανάτοισι φόως φέροι ἠδὲ βροτοῖσιν·
οἱ δὲ θεοὶ θῶκόνδε καθίζανον, ἐν δ' ἄρα τοῖσι
Ζεὺς ὑψιβρεμέτης, οὗ τε κράτος ἐστὶ μέγιστον.
5 τοῖσι δ' Ἀθηναίη λέγε κήδεα πόλλ' Ὀδυσῆος
μνησαμένη· μέλε γάρ οἱ ἐὼν ἐν δώμασι νύμφης·
   "Ζεῦ πάτερ ἠδ' ἄλλοι μάκαρες θεοὶ αἰὲν ἐόντες,
μή τις ἔτι πρόφρων ἀγανὸς καὶ ἤπιος ἔστω
σκηπτοῦχος βασιλεύς, μηδὲ φρεσὶν αἴσιμα εἰδώς,
10 ἀλλ' αἰεὶ χαλεπός τ' εἴη καὶ αἴσυλα ῥέζοι·
ὡς οὔ τις μέμνηται Ὀδυσσῆος θείοιο
λαῶν οἷσιν ἄνασσε, πατὴρ δ' ὣς ἤπιος ἦεν.
ἀλλ' ὁ μὲν ἐν νήσῳ κεῖται κρατέρ' ἄλγεα πάσχων
νύμφης ἐν μεγάροισι Καλυψοῦς, ἥ μιν ἀνάγκῃ
15 ἴσχει· ὁ δ' οὐ δύναται ἣν πατρίδα γαῖαν ἱκέσθαι·
οὐ γάρ οἱ πάρα νῆες ἐπήρετμοι καὶ ἑταῖροι,
οἵ κέν μιν πέμποιεν ἐπ' εὐρέα νῶτα θαλάσσης.
νῦν αὖ παῖδ' ἀγαπητὸν ἀποκτεῖναι μεμάασιν
οἴκαδε νισόμενον· ὁ δ' ἔβη μετὰ πατρὸς ἀκουὴν
20 ἐς Πύλον ἠγαθέην ἠδ' ἐς Λακεδαίμονα δῖαν."
   τὴν δ' ἀπαμειβόμενος προσέφη νεφεληγερέτα Ζεύς·
"τέκνον ἐμόν, ποῖόν σε ἔπος φύγεν ἕρκος ὀδόντων.

BOOK 5

Now Dawn arose from her couch from beside lordly Tithonus, to bear light to the immortals and to mortal men. And the gods were sitting down to counsel, and among them Zeus, who thunders on high, whose might is supreme. To them Athene was recounting the many woes of Odysseus, as she called them to mind; for it troubled her that he remained in the dwelling of the nymph:

"Father Zeus, and you other blessed gods that are forever, never hence forward let sceptered king with a ready heart be kind and gentle, nor let him heed righteousness in his mind; but let him ever be harsh, and deal unjustly, seeing that no one remembers divine Odysseus of the people whose lord he was, although gentle was he as a father. Yet he lies in an island suffering grievous pains, in the halls of the nymph Calypso, who keeps him perforce, and he cannot return to his own land, for he has at hand no ships with oars and no comrades to send him on his way over the broad back of the sea; and now again they are minded to slay his well-loved son on his homeward way, for he went in quest of tidings of his father to sacred Pylos and to splendid Lacedaemon."

Then Zeus, the cloud-gatherer, answered her, and said: "My child, what a word has escaped the barrier of your

οὐ γὰρ δὴ τοῦτον μὲν ἐβούλευσας νόον αὐτή,
ὡς ἦ τοι κείνους Ὀδυσεὺς ἀποτίσεται ἐλθών;
25 Τηλέμαχον δὲ σὺ πέμψον ἐπισταμένως, δύνασαι γάρ,
ὥς κε μάλ᾽ ἀσκηθὴς ἣν πατρίδα γαῖαν ἵκηται,
μνηστῆρες δ᾽ ἐν νηὶ παλιμπετὲς ἀπονέωνται."

ἦ ῥα καὶ Ἑρμείαν, υἱὸν φίλον, ἀντίον ηὔδα·
"Ἑρμεία, σὺ γὰρ αὖτε τά τ᾽ ἄλλα περ ἄγγελός ἐσσι,
30 νύμφῃ ἐυπλοκάμῳ εἰπεῖν νημερτέα βουλήν,
νόστον Ὀδυσσῆος ταλασίφρονος, ὥς κε νέηται
οὔτε θεῶν πομπῇ οὔτε θνητῶν ἀνθρώπων·
ἀλλ᾽ ὅ γ᾽ ἐπὶ σχεδίης πολυδέσμου πήματα πάσχων
ἤματί κ᾽ εἰκοστῷ Σχερίην ἐρίβωλον ἵκοιτο,
35 Φαιήκων ἐς γαῖαν, οἳ ἀγχίθεοι γεγάασιν,
οἵ κέν μιν περὶ κῆρι θεὸν ὣς τιμήσουσιν,
πέμψουσιν δ᾽ ἐν νηὶ φίλην ἐς πατρίδα γαῖαν,
χαλκόν τε χρυσόν τε ἅλις ἐσθῆτά τε δόντες,
πόλλ᾽, ὅσ᾽ ἂν οὐδέ ποτε Τροίης ἐξήρατ᾽ Ὀδυσσεύς,
40 εἴ περ ἀπήμων ἦλθε, λαχὼν ἀπὸ ληίδος αἶσαν.
ὣς γάρ οἱ μοῖρ᾽ ἐστὶ φίλους τ᾽ ἰδέειν καὶ ἱκέσθαι
οἶκον ἐς ὑψόροφον καὶ ἑὴν ἐς πατρίδα γαῖαν."

ὣς ἔφατ᾽, οὐδ᾽ ἀπίθησε διάκτορος ἀργεϊφόντης.
αὐτίκ᾽ ἔπειθ᾽ ὑπὸ ποσσὶν ἐδήσατο καλὰ πέδιλα,
45 ἀμβρόσια χρύσεια, τά μιν φέρον ἠμὲν ἐφ᾽ ὑγρὴν
ἠδ᾽ ἐπ᾽ ἀπείρονα γαῖαν ἅμα πνοιῇς ἀνέμοιο.
εἵλετο δὲ ῥάβδον, τῇ τ᾽ ἀνδρῶν ὄμματα θέλγει,
ὧν ἐθέλει, τοὺς δ᾽ αὖτε καὶ ὑπνώοντας ἐγείρει.
τὴν μετὰ χερσὶν ἔχων πέτετο κρατὺς ἀργεϊφόντης.
50 Πιερίην δ᾽ ἐπιβὰς ἐξ αἰθέρος ἔμπεσε πόντῳ·

teeth! Did you not yourself devise this plan, that in all truth Odysseus might take vengeance on these men at his coming? But concerning Telemachus, guide him in your wisdom, for you have the power, that all unscathed he may reach his native land, and the suitors may come back in their ship baffled in their purpose."

He spoke, and said to Hermes, his loyal son: "Hermes, seeing that you are at other times our messenger, declare to the fair-tressed nymph our fixed resolve, the return of steadfast Odysseus, that he may return with guidance neither of gods nor of mortal men, but that on a stoutly bound raft, suffering woes, he may come on the twentieth day to deep-soiled Scheria, the land of the Phaeacians, who are near of kin to the gods. These shall heartily show him all honor, as if he were a god, and shall send him in a ship to his own native land, after giving him stores of bronze and gold and clothing, more than Odysseus would ever have won for himself from Troy, if he had returned unscathed with his due share of the spoil. For in this manner it is his fate to see his own people, and reach his high-roofed house and his native land."

So he spoke, and the guide, Argeïphontes, did not fail to obey. At once he bound beneath his feet his beautiful sandals, immortal, golden, which bore him over the waters of the sea and over the boundless land swift as the blasts of the wind. And he took the wand, with which he lulls to sleep the eyes of whom he will, while others again he rouses even out of slumber. With this in his hand the strong Argeïphontes flew. On to Pieria he stepped from the upper air, and swooped down upon the sea, and then

σεύατ' ἔπειτ' ἐπὶ κῦμα λάρῳ ὄρνιθι ἐοικώς,
ὅς τε κατὰ δεινοὺς κόλπους ἁλὸς ἀτρυγέτοιο
ἰχθῦς ἀγρώσσων πυκινὰ πτερὰ δεύεται ἅλμῃ·
τῷ ἴκελος πολέεσσιν ὀχήσατο κύμασιν Ἑρμῆς.

55 ἀλλ' ὅτε δὴ τὴν νῆσον ἀφίκετο τηλόθ' ἐοῦσαν,
ἔνθ' ἐκ πόντου βὰς ἰοειδέος ἤπειρόνδε
ἤιεν, ὄφρα μέγα σπέος ἵκετο, τῷ ἔνι νύμφη
ναῖεν ἐυπλόκαμος· τὴν δ' ἔνδοθι τέτμεν ἐοῦσαν.
πῦρ μὲν ἐπ' ἐσχαρόφιν μέγα καίετο, τηλόσε δ' ὀδμὴ

60 κέδρου τ' εὐκεάτοιο θύου τ' ἀνὰ νῆσον ὀδώδει
δαιομένων· ἡ δ' ἔνδον ἀοιδιάουσ' ὀπὶ καλῇ
ἱστὸν ἐποιχομένη χρυσείῃ κερκίδ' ὕφαινεν.
ὕλη δὲ σπέος ἀμφὶ πεφύκει τηλεθόωσα,
κλήθρη τ' αἴγειρός τε καὶ εὐώδης κυπάρισσος.

65 ἔνθα δέ τ' ὄρνιθες τανυσίπτεροι εὐνάζοντο,
σκῶπές τ' ἴρηκές τε τανύγλωσσοί τε κορῶναι
εἰνάλιαι, τῇσίν τε θαλάσσια ἔργα μέμηλεν.
ἡ δ' αὐτοῦ τετάνυστο περὶ σπείους γλαφυροῖο
ἡμερὶς ἡβώωσα, τεθήλει δὲ σταφυλῇσι.

70 κρῆναι δ' ἑξείης πίσυρες ῥέον ὕδατι λευκῷ,
πλησίαι ἀλλήλων τετραμμέναι ἄλλυδις ἄλλη.
ἀμφὶ δὲ λειμῶνες μαλακοὶ ἴου ἠδὲ σελίνου
θήλεον. ἔνθα κ' ἔπειτα καὶ ἀθάνατός περ ἐπελθὼν
θηήσαιτο ἰδὼν καὶ τερφθείη φρεσὶν ᾗσιν.

75 ἔνθα στὰς θηεῖτο διάκτορος ἀργεϊφόντης.
αὐτὰρ ἐπεὶ δὴ πάντα ἑῷ θηήσατο θυμῷ,
αὐτίκ' ἄρ' εἰς εὐρὺ σπέος ἤλυθεν. οὐδέ μιν ἄντην
ἠγνοίησεν ἰδοῦσα Καλυψώ, δῖα θεάων·

sped over the waves like a bird, the cormorant, which in quest of fish over the frightening gulfs of the unresting sea wets its thick plumage in the salt water. In such fashion did Hermes convey himself over the multitudinous waves. But when he had reached the island which lay afar, then forth from the violet sea he came to land, and went his way until he came to a great cave, wherein dwelt the fair-tressed nymph; and he found her within. A great fire was burning on the hearth, and far over the isle spread the fragrance of split cedar and citronwood, as they burned; but she within was singing with a sweet voice as she went to and fro before the loom, weaving with a golden shuttle. Round about the cave grew a luxuriant wood, alder and poplar and sweet-smelling cypress, in which long-winged birds made their nests, owls and falcons and sea crows with chattering tongues, who ply their business on the sea. And right there about the hollow cave ran trailing a garden vine, in pride of its prime, richly laden with clusters. And four springs in a row were flowing with bright water close by one another, turned one this way, one that, and round about soft meadows of violets and celery were blooming. There even an immortal, who chanced to come, might gaze and marvel, and delight his soul, and there the guide Argeïphontes stood and marveled. But when he had marveled in his heart at all things, he went straight into the wide cave; nor did Calypso, the beautiful goddess, fail to know

οὐ γάρ τ᾽ ἀγνῶτες θεοὶ ἀλλήλοισι πέλονται
80 ἀθάνατοι, οὐδ᾽ εἴ τις ἀπόπροθι δώματα ναίει.
οὐδ᾽ ἄρ᾽ Ὀδυσσῆα μεγαλήτορα ἔνδον ἔτετμεν,
ἀλλ᾽ ὅ γ᾽ ἐπ᾽ ἀκτῆς κλαῖε καθήμενος, ἔνθα πάρος περ,
δάκρυσι καὶ στοναχῇσι καὶ ἄλγεσι θυμὸν ἐρέχθων.
πόντον ἐπ᾽ ἀτρύγετον δερκέσκετο δάκρυα λείβων.[1]
85 Ἑρμείαν δ᾽ ἐρέεινε Καλυψώ, δῖα θεάων,
ἐν θρόνῳ ἱδρύσασα φαεινῷ σιγαλόεντι·
    "τίπτε μοι, Ἑρμεία χρυσόρραπι, εἰλήλουθας
αἰδοῖός τε φίλος τε; πάρος γε μὲν οὔ τι θαμίζεις.
αὔδα ὅ τι φρονέεις· τελέσαι δέ με θυμὸς ἄνωγεν,
90 εἰ δύναμαι τελέσαι γε καὶ εἰ τετελεσμένον ἐστίν.
ἀλλ᾽ ἕπεο προτέρω, ἵνα τοι πὰρ ξείνια θείω."[2]
    ὣς ἄρα φωνήσασα θεὰ παρέθηκε τράπεζαν
ἀμβροσίης πλήσασα, κέρασσε δὲ νέκταρ ἐρυθρόν.
αὐτὰρ ὁ πῖνε καὶ ἦσθε διάκτορος ἀργεϊφόντης.
95 αὐτὰρ ἐπεὶ δείπνησε καὶ ἤραρε θυμὸν ἐδωδῇ,
καὶ τότε δή μιν ἔπεσσιν ἀμειβόμενος προσέειπεν·
    "εἰρωτᾷς μ᾽ ἐλθόντα θεὰ θεόν· αὐτὰρ ἐγώ τοι
νημερτέως τὸν μῦθον ἐνισπήσω· κέλεαι γάρ.
Ζεὺς ἐμέ γ᾽ ἠνώγει δεῦρ᾽ ἐλθέμεν οὐκ ἐθέλοντα·
100 τίς δ᾽ ἂν ἑκὼν τοσσόνδε διαδράμοι ἁλμυρὸν ὕδωρ
ἄσπετον; οὐδέ τις ἄγχι βροτῶν πόλις, οἵ τε θεοῖσιν
ἱερά τε ῥέζουσι καὶ ἐξαίτους ἑκατόμβας.
ἀλλὰ μάλ᾽ οὔ πως ἔστι Διὸς νόον αἰγιόχοιο
οὔτε παρεξελθεῖν ἄλλον θεὸν οὔθ᾽ ἁλιῶσαι.
105 φησί τοι ἄνδρα παρεῖναι ὀιζυρώτατον ἄλλων,

---

[1] Line 84 (= 158) was rejected by Aristarchus.

him, when she saw him face to face; for not unknown are the immortal gods to one another, even though one dwells in a home far away. But the great-hearted Odysseus he found not within; for he sat weeping on the shore, in his accustomed place, racking his heart with tears and groans and griefs. There he would look out over the unresting sea, shedding tears. And Calypso, the beautiful goddess, questioned Hermes, when she had made him sit on a bright shining chair:

"Why, pray, Hermes of the golden wand, have you come, a revered guest and a welcome one? Before this your visits have not been frequent. Speak what is in your mind; my heart bids me fulfill it, if fulfill it I can and it is a thing that has fulfillment. But follow me further, that I may set before you entertainment."

So saying the goddess set before him a table laden with ambrosia, and mixed the red nectar. So he drank and ate, the guide Argeïphontes. But when he had dined and satisfied his heart with food, then he made answer, and addressed her, saying:

"You, a goddess, have questioned me, a god, upon my coming, and I will speak my word truly, since you ask me to. It was Zeus who bade me come here against my will. Who of his own will would speed over so great space of salt seawater, great past telling? Nor is there at hand any city of mortals who offer to the gods sacrifice and choice hecatombs. But it is in no way possible for any other god to evade or make void the will of Zeus, who bears the aegis. He says that there is here with you a man most wretched

---

[2] Line 91 is omitted in the best MSS.

τῶν ἀνδρῶν, οἳ ἄστυ πέρι Πριάμοιο μάχοντο
εἰνάετες, δεκάτῳ δὲ πόλιν πέρσαντες ἔβησαν
οἴκαδ᾽· ἀτὰρ ἐν νόστῳ Ἀθηναίην ἀλίτοντο,
ἥ σφιν ἐπῶρσ᾽ ἄνεμόν τε κακὸν καὶ κύματα μακρά.
110 ἔνθ᾽ ἄλλοι μὲν πάντες ἀπέφθιθεν ἐσθλοὶ ἑταῖροι,
τὸν δ᾽ ἄρα δεῦρ᾽ ἄνεμός τε φέρων καὶ κῦμα πέλασσε.[1]
τὸν νῦν σ᾽ ἠνώγειν ἀποπεμπέμεν ὅττι τάχιστα·
οὐ γάρ οἱ τῇδ᾽ αἶσα φίλων ἀπονόσφιν ὀλέσθαι,
ἀλλ᾽ ἔτι οἱ μοῖρ᾽ ἐστὶ φίλους τ᾽ ἰδέειν καὶ ἱκέσθαι
115 οἶκον ἐς ὑψόροφον καὶ ἑὴν ἐς πατρίδα γαῖαν."
      ὣς φάτο, ῥίγησεν δὲ Καλυψώ, δῖα θεάων,
καί μιν φωνήσασ᾽ ἔπεα πτερόεντα προσηύδα·
"σχέτλιοί ἐστε, θεοί, ζηλήμονες ἔξοχον ἄλλων,
οἵ τε θεαῖς ἀγάασθε παρ᾽ ἀνδράσιν εὐνάζεσθαι
120 ἀμφαδίην, ἤν τίς τε φίλον ποιήσετ᾽ ἀκοίτην.
ὣς μὲν ὅτ᾽ Ὠρίων᾽ ἕλετο ῥοδοδάκτυλος Ἠώς,
τόφρα οἱ ἠγάασθε θεοὶ ῥεῖα ζώοντες,
ἧος ἐν Ὀρτυγίῃ χρυσόθρονος Ἄρτεμις ἁγνὴ
οἷς ἀγανοῖς βελέεσσιν ἐποιχομένη κατέπεφνεν.
125 ὣς δ᾽ ὁπότ᾽ Ἰασίωνι ἐυπλόκαμος Δημήτηρ,
ᾧ θυμῷ εἴξασα, μίγη φιλότητι καὶ εὐνῇ
νειῷ ἔνι τριπόλῳ· οὐδὲ δὴν ἦεν ἄπυστος
Ζεύς, ὅς μιν κατέπεφνε βαλὼν ἀργῆτι κεραυνῷ.
ὥς δ᾽ αὖ νῦν μοι ἄγασθε, θεοί, βροτὸν ἄνδρα παρεῖναι.
130 τὸν μὲν ἐγὼν ἐσάωσα περὶ τρόπιος βεβαῶτα
οἶον, ἐπεί οἱ νῆα θοὴν ἀργῆτι κεραυνῷ
Ζεὺς ἔλσας[2] ἐκέασσε μέσῳ ἐνὶ οἴνοπι πόντῳ.

above all those warriors who around the city of Priam fought for nine years, and in the tenth year sacked the city and departed homeward. But on the way they sinned against Athene, and she sent upon them an evil wind and towering waves. There all the rest of his noble comrades perished, but as for him, the wind and the waves, as they bore him, brought him here. Him Zeus now bids you to send on his way with all speed, for it is not his fate to perish here far from his friends, but it is still his lot to see his friends and reach his high-roofed house and his native land."

So he spoke, and Calypso, the beautiful goddess, shuddered, and she spoke, and addressed him with winged words: "Cruel are you, you gods, and quick to envy above all others, seeing that you begrudge goddesses that they should mate with men openly, if any takes a mortal as her own bedfellow. Thus, when rosy-fingered Dawn took to herself Orion, you gods that live at ease begrudged her, till in Ortygia chaste Artemis of the golden throne assailed him with her gentle shafts and slew him. Thus too, when fair-tressed Demeter, yielding to her passion, lay in love with Iasion in the thrice-plowed fallow land, Zeus was not long without knowledge of it, but smote him with his bright thunderbolt and slew him. And in this way again do you now begrudge me, you gods, that a mortal man should be my companion. Him I saved when he was bestriding the keel and all alone, for Zeus had struck his swift ship with his bright thunderbolt and had shattered it in the midst of

---

[1] Lines 110f (= 133f) cannot be genuine in this place. Aristarchus rejected the whole passage 105 (107?)–111.

[2] ἔλσας: ἐλάσας Zenodotus; cf. 7.250

ἔνθ' ἄλλοι μὲν πάντες ἀπέφθιθεν ἐσθλοὶ ἑταῖροι,
τὸν δ' ἄρα δεῦρ' ἄνεμός τε φέρων καὶ κῦμα πέλασσε.
135 τὸν μὲν ἐγὼ φίλεόν τε καὶ ἔτρεφον, ἠδὲ ἔφασκον
θήσειν ἀθάνατον καὶ ἀγήραον ἤματα πάντα.
ἀλλ' ἐπεὶ οὔ πως ἔστι Διὸς νόον αἰγιόχοιο
οὔτε παρεξελθεῖν ἄλλον θεὸν οὔθ' ἁλιῶσαι,
ἐρρέτω, εἴ μιν κεῖνος ἐποτρύνει καὶ ἀνώγει,
140 πόντον ἐπ' ἀτρύγετον· πέμψω δέ μιν οὔ πη ἐγώ γε·
οὐ γάρ μοι πάρα νῆες ἐπήρετμοι καὶ ἑταῖροι,
οἵ κέν μιν πέμποιεν ἐπ' εὐρέα νῶτα θαλάσσης.
αὐτάρ οἱ πρόφρων ὑποθήσομαι, οὐδ' ἐπικεύσω,
ὥς κε μάλ' ἀσκηθὴς ἣν πατρίδα γαῖαν ἵκηται."
145   τὴν δ' αὖτε προσέειπε διάκτορος ἀργεϊφόντης·
"οὕτω νῦν ἀπόπεμπε, Διὸς δ' ἐποπίζεο μῆνιν,
μή πώς τοι μετόπισθε κοτεσσάμενος χαλεπήνῃ."
    ὣς ἄρα φωνήσας ἀπέβη κρατὺς ἀργεϊφόντης·
ἡ δ' ἐπ' Ὀδυσσῆα μεγαλήτορα πότνια νύμφη
150 ἤι', ἐπεὶ δὴ Ζηνὸς ἐπέκλυεν ἀγγελιάων.
τὸν δ' ἄρ' ἐπ' ἀκτῆς εὗρε καθήμενον· οὐδέ ποτ' ὄσσε
δακρυόφιν τέρσοντο, κατείβετο δὲ γλυκὺς αἰὼν
νόστον ὀδυρομένῳ, ἐπεὶ οὐκέτι ἥνδανε νύμφη.
ἀλλ' ἦ τοι νύκτας μὲν ἰαύεσκεν καὶ ἀνάγκῃ
155 ἐν σπέσσι γλαφυροῖσι παρ' οὐκ ἐθέλων ἐθελούσῃ·
ἤματα δ' ἂμ πέτρῃσι καὶ ἠιόνεσσι καθίζων
δάκρυσι καὶ στοναχῇσι καὶ ἄλγεσι θυμὸν ἐρέχθων[1]
πόντον ἐπ' ἀτρύγετον δερκέσκετο δάκρυα λείβων.
ἀγχοῦ δ' ἱσταμένη προσεφώνεε δῖα θεάων·

the wine-dark sea. There all the rest of his noble comrades perished, but as for him, the wind and the waves, as they bore him, brought him here. Him I welcomed kindly and gave him food, and said that I would make him immortal and ageless all his days. But since it is in no way possible for any other god to evade or make void the will of Zeus who bears the aegis, let him go his way, if Zeus thus orders and commands, over the unresting sea. But it is not I that shall give him convoy, for I have at hand no ships with oars and no men to send him on his way over the broad back of the sea. But with a ready heart will I give him counsel, and will hide nothing, that all unscathed he may return to his native land."

Then again the messenger Argeïphontes answered her: "As you propose, then, send him forth now, and beware of the wrath of Zeus, for fear he may become angry and visit his wrath upon you hereafter."

So saying, the strong Argeïphontes departed, and the queenly nymph went to the great-hearted Odysseus, when she had heard the message of Zeus. Him she found sitting on the shore, and his eyes were never dry of tears, and his sweet life was ebbing away, as he grieved for his return, for the nymph no longer pleased him. By night indeed he would sleep by her side perforce in the hollow caves, unwilling beside the willing nymph, but by day he would sit on the rocks and the sands, racking his heart with tears and groans and griefs, and he would look out over the unresting sea, shedding tears. Then coming close to him, the beautiful goddess addressed him:

---

[1] Line 157 (= 83), omitted in many MSS, seems to have been unknown to Aristarchus.

160   "κάμμορε, μή μοι ἔτ' ἐνθάδ' ὀδύρεο, μηδέ τοι αἰὼν
φθινέτω· ἤδη γάρ σε μάλα πρόφρασσ' ἀποπέμψω.
ἀλλ' ἄγε δούρατα μακρὰ ταμὼν ἁρμόζεο χαλκῷ
εὐρεῖαν σχεδίην· ἀτὰρ ἴκρια πῆξαι ἐπ' αὐτῆς
ὑψοῦ, ὥς σε φέρῃσιν ἐπ' ἠεροειδέα πόντον.
165   αὐτὰρ ἐγὼ σῖτον καὶ ὕδωρ καὶ οἶνον ἐρυθρὸν
ἐνθήσω μενοεικέ', ἅ κέν τοι λιμὸν ἐρύκοι,
εἵματά τ' ἀμφιέσω· πέμψω δέ τοι οὖρον ὄπισθεν,
ὥς κε μάλ' ἀσκηθὴς σὴν πατρίδα γαῖαν ἵκηαι,
αἴ κε θεοί γ' ἐθέλωσι, τοὶ οὐρανὸν εὐρὺν ἔχουσιν,
170   οἵ μευ φέρτεροί εἰσι νοῆσαί τε κρῆναί τε."
    ὣς φάτο, ῥίγησεν δὲ πολύτλας δῖος Ὀδυσσεύς,
καί μιν φωνήσας ἔπεα πτερόεντα προσηύδα·
"ἄλλο τι δὴ σύ, θεά, τόδε μήδεαι, οὐδέ τι πομπήν,
ἥ με κέλεαι σχεδίῃ περάαν μέγα λαῖτμα θαλάσσης,
175   δεινόν τ' ἀργαλέον τε· τὸ δ' οὐδ' ἐπὶ νῆες ἐῖσαι
ὠκύποροι περόωσιν, ἀγαλλόμεναι Διὸς οὔρῳ.
οὐδ' ἂν ἐγὼν ἀέκητι σέθεν σχεδίης ἐπιβαίην,
εἰ μή μοι τλαίης γε, θεά, μέγαν ὅρκον ὀμόσσαι
μή τί μοι αὐτῷ πῆμα κακὸν βουλευσέμεν ἄλλο."
180   ὣς φάτο, μείδησεν δὲ Καλυψὼ δῖα θεάων,
χειρί τέ μιν κατέρεξεν ἔπος τ' ἔφατ' ἔκ τ' ὀνόμαζεν·
"ἦ δὴ ἀλιτρός γ' ἐσσὶ καὶ οὐκ ἀποφώλια εἰδώς,
οἷον δὴ τὸν μῦθον ἐπεφράσθης ἀγορεῦσαι.
ἴστω νῦν τόδε γαῖα καὶ οὐρανὸς εὐρὺς ὕπερθε
185   καὶ τὸ κατειβόμενον Στυγὸς ὕδωρ, ὅς τε μέγιστος
ὅρκος δεινότατός τε πέλει μακάρεσσι θεοῖσι,
μή τί τοι αὐτῷ πῆμα κακὸν βουλευσέμεν ἄλλο.

"Unhappy man, sorrow no longer here, I pray you, nor let your life pine away; for now with a ready heart I will send you on your way. Come, hew with the axe long timbers, and make a broad raft, and fasten upon it cross planks for a deck well above it, that it may bear you over the misty sea. And I will place in it bread and water and red wine to satisfy your heart, to keep hunger from you, and I will give you clothes to wear. Also I will send a fair wind behind you, that all unscathed you may return to your native land, if it be the will of the gods who hold broad heaven; for they are more powerful than I both to purpose and to fulfill."

So she spoke, and much-enduring noble Odysseus shuddered, and he spoke, and addressed her with winged words: "Some other thing, goddess, are you planning in this, and not my sending, seeing that you bid me cross on a raft the great gulf of the sea, dangerous and dismaying, over which not even the shapely, swift-faring ships pass, rejoicing in the wind of Zeus. But I will not set foot on a raft against your will, unless you, goddess, will bring yourself to swear a mighty oath that you will not plot against me any fresh mischief to my hurt."

So he spoke, but Calypso, the beautiful goddess, smiled, and stroked him with her hand, and spoke, and addressed him: "Truly you are a rogue, and not stunted in wit, that it has occurred to you to utter such a word. Now therefore let Earth be witness to this, and the broad Heaven above, and the down-flowing water of the Styx, which is the greatest and most fearful oath for the blessed gods, that I will not plot against you any fresh mischief to

ἀλλὰ τὰ μὲν νοέω καὶ φράσσομαι, ἅσσ' ἂν ἐμοί περ
αὐτῇ μηδοίμην, ὅτε με χρειὼ τόσον ἵκοι·
190 καὶ γὰρ ἐμοὶ νόος ἐστὶν ἐναίσιμος, οὐδέ μοι αὐτῇ
θυμὸς ἐνὶ στήθεσσι σιδήρεος, ἀλλ' ἐλεήμων."
ὣς ἄρα φωνήσασ' ἡγήσατο δῖα θεάων
καρπαλίμως· ὁ δ' ἔπειτα μετ' ἴχνια βαῖνε θεοῖο.
ἷξον δὲ σπεῖος γλαφυρὸν θεὸς ἠδὲ καὶ ἀνήρ,
195 καί ῥ' ὁ μὲν ἔνθα καθέζετ' ἐπὶ θρόνου ἔνθεν ἀνέστη
Ἑρμείας, νύμφη δ' ἐτίθει πάρα πᾶσαν ἐδωδήν,
ἔσθειν καὶ πίνειν, οἷα βροτοὶ ἄνδρες ἔδουσιν·
αὐτὴ δ' ἀντίον ἷζεν Ὀδυσσῆος θείοιο,
τῇ δὲ παρ' ἀμβροσίην δμωαὶ καὶ νέκταρ ἔθηκαν.
200 οἱ δ' ἐπ' ὀνείαθ' ἑτοῖμα προκείμενα χεῖρας ἴαλλον.
αὐτὰρ ἐπεὶ τάρπησαν ἐδητύος ἠδὲ ποτῆτος,
τοῖς ἄρα μύθων ἦρχε Καλυψώ, δῖα θεάων·
"διογενὲς Λαερτιάδη, πολυμήχαν' Ὀδυσσεῦ,
οὕτω δὴ οἶκόνδε φίλην ἐς πατρίδα γαῖαν
205 αὐτίκα νῦν ἐθέλεις ἰέναι; σὺ δὲ χαῖρε καὶ ἔμπης.
εἴ γε μὲν εἰδείης σῇσι φρεσὶν ὅσσα τοι αἶσα
κήδε' ἀναπλῆσαι, πρὶν πατρίδα γαῖαν ἱκέσθαι,
ἐνθάδε κ' αὖθι μένων σὺν ἐμοὶ τόδε δῶμα φυλάσσοις
ἀθάνατός τ' εἴης, ἱμειρόμενός περ ἰδέσθαι
210 σὴν ἄλοχον, τῆς τ' αἰὲν ἐέλδεαι ἤματα πάντα.
οὐ μέν θην κείνης γε χερείων εὔχομαι εἶναι,
οὐ δέμας οὐδὲ φυήν, ἐπεὶ οὔ πως οὐδὲ ἔοικεν
θνητὰς ἀθανάτῃσι δέμας καὶ εἶδος ἐρίζειν."
τὴν δ' ἀπαμειβόμενος προσέφη πολύμητις
Ὀδυσσεύς·

your hurt. On the contrary, I have such thoughts in mind, and will give such counsel, as I should devise for my own self, if such need should come on me. For my intentions are honest, and the heart in my own breast is not of iron, but feels pity."

So saying, the beautiful goddess led the way quickly, and he followed in the footsteps of the goddess. And they came to the hollow cave, the goddess and the man, and he sat down upon the chair from which Hermes had arisen, and the nymph set before him all kinds of food to eat and drink, of such sort as mortal men eat. But she herself sat opposite divine Odysseus, and before her the handmaids set ambrosia and nectar. So they put forth their hands to the good cheer lying ready before them. But when they had had their fill of food and drink, Calypso, the beautiful goddess, was the first to speak, and said:

"Son of Laertes, sprung from Zeus, Odysseus of many devices, must you, just like that, go home to your own native land forthwith? Yet, even so, may you fare well. If, however, in your heart you knew all the measure of woe it is your fate to fulfill before you come to your native land, you would remain here and keep this house with me, and would be immortal, for all your desire to see your wife for whom you long day in and day out. Surely not inferior to her do I declare myself to be, either in form or in stature, since in no way is it reasonable that mortal women should vie with immortals in form or looks."

Then resourceful Odysseus answered her and said:

215 "πότνα θεά, μή μοι τόδε χώεο· οἶδα καὶ αὐτὸς
πάντα μάλ᾽, οὕνεκα σεῖο περίφρων Πηνελόπεια
εἶδος ἀκιδνοτέρη μέγεθός τ᾽ εἰσάντα ἰδέσθαι·
ἡ μὲν γὰρ βροτός ἐστι, σὺ δ᾽ ἀθάνατος καὶ ἀγήρως.
ἀλλὰ καὶ ὣς ἐθέλω καὶ ἐέλδομαι ἤματα πάντα
220 οἴκαδέ τ᾽ ἐλθέμεναι καὶ νόστιμον ἦμαρ ἰδέσθαι.
εἰ δ᾽ αὖ τις ῥαίῃσι θεῶν ἐνὶ οἴνοπι πόντῳ,
τλήσομαι ἐν στήθεσσιν ἔχων ταλαπενθέα θυμόν·
ἤδη γὰρ μάλα πολλὰ πάθον καὶ πολλὰ μόγησα
κύμασι καὶ πολέμῳ· μετὰ καὶ τόδε τοῖσι γενέσθω."
225 ὣς ἔφατ᾽, ἠέλιος δ᾽ ἄρ᾽ ἔδυ καὶ ἐπὶ κνέφας ἦλθεν·
ἐλθόντες δ᾽ ἄρα τώ γε μυχῷ σπείους γλαφυροῖο
τερπέσθην φιλότητι, παρ᾽ ἀλλήλοισι μένοντες.
ἦμος δ᾽ ἠριγένεια φάνη ῥοδοδάκτυλος Ἠώς,
αὐτίχ᾽ ὁ μὲν χλαῖνάν τε χιτῶνά τε ἔννυτ᾽ Ὀδυσσεύς,
230 αὐτὴ δ᾽ ἀργύφεον φᾶρος μέγα ἔννυτο νύμφη,
λεπτὸν καὶ χαρίεν, περὶ δὲ ζώνην βάλετ᾽ ἰξυῖ
καλὴν χρυσείην, κεφαλῇ δ᾽ ἐφύπερθε[1] καλύπτρην.
καὶ τότ᾽ Ὀδυσσῆι μεγαλήτορι μήδετο πομπήν·
δῶκέν οἱ πέλεκυν μέγαν, ἄρμενον ἐν παλάμῃσι,
235 χάλκεον, ἀμφοτέρωθεν ἀκαχμένον· αὐτὰρ ἐν αὐτῷ
στειλειὸν περικαλλὲς ἐλάινον, εὖ ἐναρηρός·
δῶκε δ᾽ ἔπειτα σκέπαρνον ἐύξοον· ἦρχε δ᾽ ὁδοῖο
νήσου ἐπ᾽ ἐσχατιῆς, ὅθι δένδρεα μακρὰ πεφύκει,
κλήθρη τ᾽ αἴγειρός τ᾽, ἐλάτη τ᾽ ἦν οὐρανομήκης,
240 αὖα πάλαι, περίκηλα, τά οἱ πλώοιεν ἐλαφρῶς.
αὐτὰρ ἐπεὶ δὴ δεῖξ᾽, ὅθι δένδρεα μακρὰ πεφύκει,
ἡ μὲν ἔβη πρὸς δῶμα Καλυψώ, δῖα θεάων,

"Mighty goddess, do not be angry with me for this. I know very well myself that wise Penelope is less impressive to look upon than you in looks and stature, for she is a mortal, while you are immortal and ageless. But even so I wish and long day in and day out to reach my home, and to see the day of my return. And if again some god shall smite me on the wine-dark sea, I will endure it, having in my breast a heart that endures affliction. For before now I have suffered much and toiled much amid the waves and in war; let this trouble be added to those."

So he spoke, and the sun set and darkness came on. And the two went into the innermost recess of the hollow cave, and took their joy of love, remaining by each other.

As soon as early Dawn appeared, the rosy-fingered, at once Odysseus put on a cloak and a tunic, and the nymph clothed herself in a long white robe, finely woven and beautiful, and about her waist she threw a beautiful girdle of gold, and on her head she placed a veil. Then she set herself to plan the departure of great-hearted Odysseus. She gave him a big axe, well fitted to his hands, an axe of bronze, sharpened on both sides; and in it was a beautiful handle of olive wood, securely fastened; and thereafter she gave him a polished adz. Then she led the way to the borders of the island where tall trees were standing, alder and poplar and fir, reaching to the skies, long dry and well-seasoned, which would float for him lightly. But when she had shown him where the tall trees grew, Calypso, the beautiful goddess, returned homeward, while he fell to

---

[1] ἐφύπερθε Aristarchus: ἐπέθηκε

αὐτὰρ ὁ τάμνετο δοῦρα· θοῶς δέ οἱ ἤνυτο ἔργον.
εἴκοσι δ' ἔκβαλε πάντα, πελέκκησεν δ' ἄρα χαλκῷ,
245 ξέσσε δ' ἐπισταμένως καὶ ἐπὶ στάθμην ἴθυνεν.
τόφρα δ' ἔνεικε τέρετρα Καλυψώ, δῖα θεάων·
τέτρηνεν δ' ἄρα πάντα καὶ ἥρμοσεν ἀλλήλοισιν,
γόμφοισιν δ' ἄρα τήν γε καὶ ἁρμονίῃσιν ἄρασσεν.
ὅσσον τίς τ' ἔδαφος νηὸς τορνώσεται ἀνὴρ
250 φορτίδος εὐρείης, ἐὺ εἰδὼς τεκτοσυνάων,
τόσσον ἔπ' εὐρεῖαν σχεδίην ποιήσατ' Ὀδυσσεύς.
ἴκρια δὲ στήσας, ἀραρὼν θαμέσι σταμίνεσσι,
ποίει· ἀτὰρ μακρῇσιν ἐπηγκενίδεσσι τελεύτα.
ἐν δ' ἱστὸν ποίει καὶ ἐπίκριον ἄρμενον αὐτῷ·
255 πρὸς δ' ἄρα πηδάλιον ποιήσατο, ὄφρ' ἰθύνοι.
φράξε δέ μιν ῥίπεσσι διαμπερὲς οἰσυΐνῃσι
κύματος εἶλαρ ἔμεν· πολλὴν δ' ἐπεχεύατο ὕλην.
τόφρα δὲ φάρε' ἔνεικε Καλυψώ, δῖα θεάων,
ἱστία ποιήσασθαι· ὁ δ' εὖ τεχνήσατο καὶ τά.
260 ἐν δ' ὑπέρας τε κάλους τε πόδας τ' ἐνέδησεν ἐν αὐτῇ,
μοχλοῖσιν δ' ἄρα τήν γε κατείρυσεν εἰς ἅλα δῖαν.

    τέτρατον ἦμαρ ἔην, καὶ τῷ τετέλεστο ἅπαντα·
τῷ δ' ἄρα πέμπτῳ πέμπ' ἀπὸ νήσου δῖα Καλυψώ,
εἵματά τ' ἀμφιέσασα θυώδεα καὶ λούσασα.
265 ἐν δέ οἱ ἀσκὸν ἔθηκε θεὰ μέλανος οἴνοιο
τὸν ἕτερον, ἕτερον δ' ὕδατος μέγαν, ἐν δὲ καὶ ᾖα
κωρύκῳ· ἐν δέ οἱ ὄψα τίθει μενοεικέα πολλά·
οὖρον δὲ προέηκεν ἀπήμονά τε λιαρόν τε.
γηθόσυνος δ' οὔρῳ πέτας' ἱστία δῖος Ὀδυσσεύς.
270 αὐτὰρ ὁ πηδαλίῳ ἰθύνετο τεχνηέντως

cutting timbers, and his work went forward speedily. Twenty trees in all did he fell, and trimmed them with the axe; then he cunningly smoothed them all and trued them to the line. Meanwhile Calypso, the beautiful goddess, brought him augers; and he bored all the pieces and fitted them to one another, and with pegs and morticings he hammered it together. Wide as a man well-skilled in carpentry marks out the curve of the hull of a freight ship, broad of beam, just so wide did Odysseus make his raft. And he set in place the decks, bolting them to the close-set ribs, as he continued the work; and he finished the raft[a] with long gunwales. In it he set a mast and a yard arm, fitted to it, and furthermore made him a steering oar, with which to steer. Then he fenced in the whole from stem to stern with willow withes to be a defense against the waves, and covered the bottom with brush. Meanwhile Calypso, the beautiful goddess, brought him cloth to make him a sail, and he fashioned that too with skill. And he made fast in the raft braces and halyards and sheets, and then with levers worked it down into the bright sea.

Now the fourth day came and all his work was done. And on the fifth the beautiful Calypso sent him on his way from the island after she had bathed him and dressed him in fragrant clothing. On the raft the goddess put a skin of dark wine, and another, a large one, of water, and provisions, too, in a bag. In it she put many good things to satisfy his heart, and sent him, too, a fair wind, gentle and warm. Gladly then did noble Odysseus spread his sail to the breeze; and he sat and guided his raft skillfully with the

[a] In describing the construction of Odysseus' raft, Homer seems to have made use of a traditional poetic description of the building of a ship. D.

ἥμενος, οὐδέ οἱ ὕπνος ἐπὶ βλεφάροισιν ἔπιπτεν
Πληιάδας τ᾽ ἐσορῶντι καὶ ὀψὲ δύοντα Βοώτην
Ἄρκτον θ᾽, ἣν καὶ ἅμαξαν ἐπίκλησιν καλέουσιν,
ἥ τ᾽ αὐτοῦ στρέφεται καί τ᾽ Ὠρίωνα δοκεύει,
275 οἴη δ᾽ ἄμμορός ἐστι λοετρῶν Ὠκεανοῖο·
τὴν γὰρ δή μιν ἄνωγε Καλυψώ, δῖα θεάων,
ποντοπορευέμεναι ἐπ᾽ ἀριστερὰ χειρὸς ἔχοντα.
ἑπτὰ δὲ καὶ δέκα μὲν πλέεν ἤματα ποντοπορεύων,
ὀκτωκαιδεκάτῃ δ᾽ ἐφάνη ὄρεα σκιόεντα
280 γαίης Φαιήκων, ὅθι τ᾽ ἄγχιστον πέλεν αὐτῷ·
εἴσατο δ᾽ ὡς ὅτε ῥινὸν[1] ἐν ἠεροειδέι πόντῳ.

τὸν δ᾽ ἐξ Αἰθιόπων ἀνιὼν κρείων ἐνοσίχθων
τηλόθεν ἐκ Σολύμων ὀρέων ἴδεν· εἴσατο γάρ οἱ
πόντον ἐπιπλώων. ὁ δ᾽ ἐχώσατο κηρόθι μᾶλλον,
285 κινήσας δὲ κάρη προτὶ ὃν μυθήσατο θυμόν·
"ὢ πόποι, ἦ μάλα δὴ μετεβούλευσαν θεοὶ ἄλλως
ἀμφ᾽ Ὀδυσῆι ἐμεῖο μετ᾽ Αἰθιόπεσσιν ἐόντος,
καὶ δὴ Φαιήκων γαίης σχεδόν, ἔνθα οἱ αἶσα
ἐκφυγέειν μέγα πεῖραρ ὀιζύος, ἥ μιν ἱκάνει.
290 ἀλλ᾽ ἔτι μέν μίν φημι ἅδην ἐλάαν κακότητος."

ὣς εἰπὼν σύναγεν νεφέλας, ἐτάραξε δὲ πόντον
χερσὶ τρίαιναν ἑλών· πάσας δ᾽ ὀρόθυνεν ἀέλλας
παντοίων ἀνέμων, σὺν δὲ νεφέεσσι κάλυψε
γαῖαν ὁμοῦ καὶ πόντον· ὀρώρει δ᾽ οὐρανόθεν νύξ.
295 σὺν δ᾽ Εὖρός τε Νότος τ᾽ ἔπεσον Ζέφυρός τε δυσαὴς
καὶ Βορέης αἰθρηγενέτης, μέγα κῦμα κυλίνδων.
καὶ τότ᾽ Ὀδυσσῆος λύτο γούνατα καὶ φίλον ἦτορ,

---

[1] ὅτε ῥινὸν MSS: ὅτ᾽ ἐρινὸν Aristarchus

steering oar, nor did sleep fall upon his eyelids, as he watched the Pleiades, and late-setting Boötes, and the Bear, which men also call the Wain, which ever circles where it is and watches Orion, and alone has no part in the baths of Ocean. For this star Calypso, the beautiful goddess, had bidden him to keep on the left hand as he sailed over the sea. For seventeen days then he sailed over the sea, and on the eighteenth appeared the shadowy mountains of the land of the Phaeacians, where it lay nearest to him; and it looked like a shield in the misty sea.

But the lordly earth-shaker, as he came back from the Ethiopians,[a] beheld him from afar, from the mountains of the Solymi: for he came into his sight sailing over the sea; and he became the more angry in spirit, and shook his head, and thus he spoke to his own heart:

"Out on it! The gods have certainly changed their purpose regarding Odysseus, while I was among the Ethiopians. Here he is near to the land of the Phaeacians, where it is his fate to escape the trial of misery which has come upon him. Nevertheless, even yet, I think I shall give him his fill of evil."

So saying, he gathered the clouds, and seizing his trident in his hands troubled the sea, and roused all blasts of every sort of wind, and hid with clouds land and sea alike; and down from heaven night came rushing. Together the East Wind and the South Wind dashed, and the fierce-blowing West Wind and the North Wind, born in the bright heaven, rolling before him a great wave. Then were the knees of Odysseus loosened, and the heart within him

[a] See 1.22f. M.

ὀχθήσας δ' ἄρα εἶπε πρὸς ὃν μεγαλήτορα θυμόν·

"ὤ μοι ἐγὼ δειλός, τί νύ μοι μήκιστα γένηται;

300 δείδω μὴ δὴ πάντα θεὰ νημερτέα εἶπεν,

ἥ μ' ἔφατ' ἐν πόντῳ, πρὶν πατρίδα γαῖαν ἱκέσθαι,

ἄλγε' ἀναπλήσειν· τὰ δὲ δὴ νῦν πάντα τελεῖται.

οἵοισιν νεφέεσσι περιστέφει οὐρανὸν εὐρὺν

Ζεύς, ἐτάραξε δὲ πόντον, ἐπισπέρχουσι δ' ἄελλαι

305 παντοίων ἀνέμων. νῦν μοι σῶς αἰπὺς ὄλεθρος.

τρὶς μάκαρες Δαναοὶ καὶ τετράκις, οἳ τότ' ὄλοντο

Τροίῃ ἐν εὐρείῃ χάριν Ἀτρεΐδῃσι φέροντες.

ὡς¹ δὴ ἐγώ γ' ὄφελον θανέειν καὶ πότμον ἐπισπεῖν

ἤματι τῷ ὅτε μοι πλεῖστοι χαλκήρεα δοῦρα

310 Τρῶες ἐπέρριψαν περὶ Πηλεΐωνι θανόντι.

τῷ κ' ἔλαχον κτερέων, καί μευ κλέος ἦγον Ἀχαιοί·

νῦν δέ λευγαλέῳ θανάτῳ εἵμαρτο ἁλῶναι."

ὣς ἄρα μιν εἰπόντ' ἔλασεν μέγα κῦμα κατ' ἄκρης

δεινὸν ἐπεσσύμενον, περὶ δὲ σχεδίην ἐλέλιξε.

315 τῆλε δ' ἀπὸ σχεδίης αὐτὸς πέσε, πηδάλιον δὲ

ἐκ χειρῶν προέηκε· μέσον δέ οἱ ἱστὸν ἔαξεν

δεινὴ μισγομένων ἀνέμων ἐλθοῦσα θύελλα,

τηλοῦ δὲ σπεῖρον καὶ ἐπίκριον ἔμπεσε πόντῳ.

τὸν δ' ἄρ' ὑπόβρυχα θῆκε πολὺν χρόνον, οὐδ' ἐδυνάσθη

320 αἶψα μάλ' ἀνσχεθέειν μεγάλου ὑπὸ κύματος ὁρμῆς·

εἵματα γάρ ῥ' ἐβάρυνε, τά οἱ πόρε δῖα Καλυψώ.

ὀψὲ δὲ δή ῥ' ἀνέδυ, στόματος δ' ἐξέπτυσεν ἅλμην

πικρήν, ἥ οἱ πολλὴ ἀπὸ κρατὸς κελάρυζεν.

ἀλλ' οὐδ' ὣς σχεδίης ἐπελήθετο, τειρόμενός περ,

---

¹ ὡς: καὶ

204

melted, and deeply shaken he spoke to his own great-hearted spirit:

"Ah me, wretch that I am! What in the end will befall me? I fear that all that the goddess said was true, when she declared that on the sea, before I came to my native land, I should fill up my measure of woes; now all this is being brought to pass. Such are the clouds with which Zeus over-casts the broad heaven, and so has he stirred up the sea, and the blasts of every kind of wind sweep upon me; now is my utter destruction sure. Thrice blessed those Danaans and four times blessed who perished in those days in the wide land of Troy, doing the pleasure of the sons of Atreus. Would that like them I too had died and met my fate on that day when the throngs of the Trojans hurled upon me bronze-tipped spears, fighting around the body of the dead son of Peleus. Then should I have got funeral rites, and the Achaeans would have spread my fame, but now it is by a miserable death that it was my fate to be cut off."

Even as he was saying this the great wave struck him from above, rushing upon him with terrible force, and spun his raft in a circle. Far from the raft he fell, and let fall the steering oar from his hand; his mast was broken in the middle by the fierce blast of tumultuous winds that came upon it, and far in the sea sail and yardarm fell. As for him, for long the wave held him under, nor could he rise at once from beneath the onrush of the great wave, for the garments which beautiful Calypso had given him weighed him down. At length, however, he came up, and spat forth from his mouth the bitter brine which flowed in streams from his head. Yet even so he did not forget his

325 ἀλλὰ μεθορμηθεὶς ἐνὶ κύμασιν ἐλλάβετ' αὐτῆς,
ἐν μέσσῃ δὲ καθῖζε τέλος θανάτου ἀλεείνων.
τὴν δ' ἐφόρει μέγα κῦμα κατὰ ῥόον ἔνθα καὶ ἔνθα.
ὡς δ' ὅτ' ὀπωρινὸς Βορέης φορέῃσιν ἀκάνθας
ἂμ πεδίον, πυκιναὶ δὲ πρὸς ἀλλήλῃσιν ἔχονται,
330 ὣς τὴν ἂμ πέλαγος ἄνεμοι φέρον ἔνθα καὶ ἔνθα·
ἄλλοτε μέν τε Νότος Βορέῃ προβάλεσκε φέρεσθαι,
ἄλλοτε δ' αὖτ' Εὖρος Ζεφύρῳ εἴξασκε διώκειν.

τὸν δὲ ἴδεν Κάδμου θυγάτηρ, καλλίσφυρος Ἰνώ,
Λευκοθέη, ἣ πρὶν μὲν ἔην βροτὸς αὐδήεσσα,
335 νῦν δ' ἁλὸς ἐν πελάγεσσι θεῶν ἒξ ἔμμορε τιμῆς.
ἥ ῥ' Ὀδυσῆ' ἐλέησεν ἀλώμενον, ἄλγε' ἔχοντα,
αἰθυίῃ δ' ἐικυῖα ποτῇ ἀνεδύσετο λίμνης,
ἷζε δ' ἐπὶ σχεδίης πολυδέσμου εἶπέ τε μῦθον·[1]
"κάμμορε, τίπτε τοι ὧδε Ποσειδάων ἐνοσίχθων
340 ὠδύσατ' ἐκπάγλως, ὅτι τοι κακὰ πολλὰ φυτεύει;
οὐ μὲν δή σε καταφθίσει μάλα περ μενεαίνων.
ἀλλὰ μάλ' ὧδ' ἔρξαι, δοκέεις δέ μοι οὐκ ἀπινύσσειν·
εἴματα ταῦτ' ἀποδὺς σχεδίην ἀνέμοισι φέρεσθαι
κάλλιπ', ἀτὰρ χείρεσσι νέων ἐπιμαίεο νόστου
345 γαίης Φαιήκων, ὅθι τοι μοῖρ' ἐστὶν ἀλύξαι.
τῇ δέ, τόδε κρήδεμνον ὑπὸ στέρνοιο τανύσσαι
ἄμβροτον· οὐδέ τί τοι παθέειν δέος οὐδ' ἀπολέσθαι.
αὐτὰρ ἐπὴν χείρεσσιν ἐφάψεαι ἠπείροιο,
ἂψ ἀπολυσάμενος βαλέειν εἰς οἴνοπα πόντον
350 πολλὸν ἀπ' ἠπείρου, αὐτὸς δ' ἀπονόσφι τραπέσθαι."

[1] πολυδέσμου εἶπέ τε μῦθον: καί μιν πρὸς μῦθον ἔειπε

raft, in distress though he was, but lunged after it amid the waves, and laid hold of it, and sat down in the middle of it, seeking to escape the doom of death; and the great seas bore the raft this way and that along their course. As when in autumn the North Wind bears the thistle tufts over the plain, and close they cling to one another, so did the winds bear the raft this way and that over the sea. Now the South Wind would fling it to the North Wind to be driven on, and now again the East Wind would yield it to the West Wind to drive.

But the daughter of Cadmus, Ino of the beautiful ankles, saw him, that is, Leukothea, who formerly was a mortal of human speech, but now in the depths of the sea has won a share of honor from the gods. She was touched with pity for Odysseus, as he wandered beset with troubles, and she rose up from the waters like a sea mew on the wing, and sat on the stoutly bound raft, and spoke, saying:

"Unhappy man, how is it that Poseidon, the earth-shaker, has so astoundingly willed your pain,[a] in that he sows for you the seeds of so many evils? Yet certainly he shall not utterly destroy you for all his rage. Instead, do as I say; you seem not to lack understanding. Strip off these garments, and leave your raft to be driven by the winds, while you by swimming with your hands strive to reach the land of the Phaeacians, where it is your fate to escape. Come, take this veil, and stretch it beneath your breast. It is immortal, and there is no fear that you shall suffer any hurt, or perish. But when with your hands you have laid hold of the land, untie it again and throw it into the wine-dark sea far from the land and yourself turn away."

[a] $\dot{\omega}\delta\acute{\nu}\sigma a\tau$' : a pun on Odysseus' name, as noted at 1.62.

ὣς ἄρα φωνήσασα θεὰ κρήδεμνον ἔδωκεν,
αὐτὴ δ' ἂψ ἐς πόντον ἐδύσετο κυμαίνοντα
αἰθυίῃ ἐικυῖα· μέλαν δέ ἑ κῦμα κάλυψεν.
αὐτὰρ ὁ μερμήριξε πολύτλας δῖος Ὀδυσσεύς,
355   ὀχθήσας δ' ἄρα εἶπε πρὸς ὃν μεγαλήτορα θυμόν·
"ὤ μοι ἐγώ, μή τίς μοι ὑφαίνῃσιν δόλον αὖτε
ἀθανάτων, ὅ τέ με σχεδίης ἀποβῆναι ἀνώγει.
ἀλλὰ μάλ' οὔ πω πείσομ', ἐπεὶ ἑκὰς ὀφθαλμοῖσιν
γαῖαν ἐγὼν ἰδόμην, ὅθι μοι φάτο φύξιμον εἶναι.
360   ἀλλὰ μάλ' ὧδ' ἔρξω, δοκέει δέ μοι εἶναι ἄριστον·
ὄφρ' ἂν μέν κεν δούρατ' ἐν ἁρμονίῃσιν ἀρήρῃ,
τόφρ' αὐτοῦ μενέω καὶ τλήσομαι ἄλγεα πάσχων·
αὐτὰρ ἐπὴν δή μοι σχεδίην διὰ κῦμα τινάξῃ,
νήξομ', ἐπεὶ οὐ μέν τι πάρα προνοῆσαι ἄμεινον."
365   ἧος ὁ ταῦθ' ὥρμαινε κατὰ φρένα καὶ κατὰ θυμόν,
ὦρσε δ' ἐπὶ μέγα κῦμα Ποσειδάων ἐνοσίχθων,
δεινόν τ' ἀργαλέον τε, κατηρεφές, ἤλασε δ' αὐτόν.
ὡς δ' ἄνεμος ζαὴς ἠίων θημῶνα τινάξῃ
καρφαλέων· τὰ μὲν ἄρ τε διεσκέδασ' ἄλλυδις ἄλλη·
370   ὣς τῆς δούρατα μακρὰ διεσκέδασ'. αὐτὰρ Ὀδυσσεὺς
ἀμφ' ἑνὶ δούρατι βαῖνε, κέληθ' ὡς ἵππον ἐλαύνων,
εἵματα δ' ἐξαπέδυνε, τά οἱ πόρε δῖα Καλυψώ.
αὐτίκα δὲ κρήδεμνον ὑπὸ στέρνοιο τάνυσσεν,
αὐτὸς δὲ πρηνὴς ἁλὶ κάππεσε, χεῖρε πετάσσας,
375   νηχέμεναι μεμαώς. ἴδε δὲ κρείων ἐνοσίχθων,
κινήσας δὲ κάρη προτὶ ὃν μυθήσατο θυμόν·
"οὕτω νῦν κακὰ πολλὰ παθὼν ἀλόω κατὰ πόντον,
εἰς ὅ κεν ἀνθρώποισι διοτρεφέεσσι μιγήῃς.

So saying the goddess gave him the veil, and herself plunged again into the surging sea, like a sea mew; and the dark wave hid her. Then the much-enduring, noble Odysseus pondered, and deeply shaken he spoke to his own great-hearted spirit:

"Woe is me! Let it not be that some one of the immortals is again weaving a snare for me, that she bids me leave my raft. I shall not in any case obey her yet, for far off was the land my eyes beheld, where she said I was to escape. This is what I shall do, and it seems to me to be the best: as long as the timbers hold firm in their fastenings, so long will I remain here and endure the troubles I have; but when the waves shall have shattered the raft to pieces, I will swim, seeing that there is nothing better to devise."

While he pondered thus in mind and heart, Poseidon, the earth-shaker, made to rise up a great wave, dangerous and dismaying, arching over from above, and drove it upon him. And as when a strong wind tosses a heap of straw that is dry, and some it scatters here, some there, just so the wave scattered the timbers of the raft. But Odysseus bestrode one plank, as though he were riding a horse, and stripped off the garments which the beautiful Calypso had given him. Then at once he stretched the veil beneath his breast, and flung himself into the sea with hands outstretched, ready to swim. And the lordly earth-shaker saw him, and, shaking his head, thus he spoke to his own heart:

"So now, after you have suffered many ills, go wandering over the sea, until you come among men fostered by

ἀλλ' οὐδ' ὥς σε ἔολπα ὀνόσσεσθαι κακότητος."

380 ὣς ἄρα φωνήσας ἵμασεν καλλίτριχας ἵππους,
ἵκετο δ' εἰς Αἰγάς, ὅθι οἱ κλυτὰ δώματ' ἔασιν.

αὐτὰρ Ἀθηναίη κούρη Διὸς ἄλλ' ἐνόησεν.
ἦ τοι τῶν ἄλλων ἀνέμων κατέδησε κελεύθους,
παύσασθαι δ' ἐκέλευσε καὶ εὐνηθῆναι ἅπαντας·

385 ὦρσε δ' ἐπὶ κραιπνὸν Βορέην, πρὸ δὲ κύματ' ἔαξεν,
ἧος ὃ Φαιήκεσσι φιληρέτμοισι μιγείη
διογενὴς Ὀδυσεὺς θάνατον καὶ κῆρας ἀλύξας.

ἔνθα δύω νύκτας δύο τ' ἤματα κύματι πηγῷ
πλάζετο, πολλὰ δέ οἱ κραδίη προτιόσσετ' ὄλεθρον.

390 ἀλλ' ὅτε δὴ τρίτον ἦμαρ ἐυπλόκαμος τέλεσ' Ἠώς,
καὶ τότ' ἔπειτ' ἄνεμος μὲν ἐπαύσατο ἠδὲ γαλήνη
ἔπλετο νηνεμίη· ὁ δ' ἄρα σχεδὸν εἴσιδε γαῖαν
ὀξὺ μάλα προϊδών, μεγάλου ὑπὸ κύματος ἀρθείς.
ὡς δ' ὅτ' ἂν ἀσπάσιος βίοτος παίδεσσι φανήῃ

395 πατρός, ὃς ἐν νούσῳ κεῖται κρατέρ' ἄλγεα πάσχων,
δηρὸν τηκόμενος, στυγερὸς δέ οἱ ἔχραε δαίμων,
ἀσπάσιον δ' ἄρα τόν γε θεοὶ κακότητος ἔλυσαν,
ὣς Ὀδυσεῖ ἀσπαστὸν ἐείσατο γαῖα καὶ ὕλη,
νῆχε δ' ἐπειγόμενος ποσὶν ἠπείρου ἐπιβῆναι.

400 ἀλλ' ὅτε τόσσον ἀπῆν ὅσσον τε γέγωνε βοήσας,
καὶ δὴ δοῦπον ἄκουσε ποτὶ σπιλάδεσσι θαλάσσης·
ῥόχθει γὰρ μέγα κῦμα ποτὶ ξερὸν ἠπείροιο
δεινὸν ἐρευγόμενον, εἴλυτο δὲ πάνθ' ἁλὸς ἄχνῃ·
οὐ γὰρ ἔσαν λιμένες νηῶν ὄχοι, οὐδ' ἐπιωγαί·

405 ἀλλ' ἀκταὶ προβλῆτες ἔσαν σπιλάδες τε πάγοι τε·
καὶ τότ' Ὀδυσσῆος λύτο γούνατα καὶ φίλον ἦτορ,

Zeus. Yet even so, I think, you shall not make light of your suffering."

So saying, he lashed his beautifully maned horses and came to Aegae, where is his glorious palace.

But Athene, daughter of Zeus, had another thought. She checked the paths of the other winds, and bade them all cease and be lulled to rest; but she roused the swift North Wind, and broke the waves before him, to the end that Zeus-born Odysseus might come among the Phaeacians, lovers of the oar, escaping from death and doom.

Then for two nights and two days he was driven about over the swollen waves, and many times his heart foresaw destruction. But when fair-tressed Dawn brought to its birth the third day, then the wind ceased and there was a windless calm, and he caught sight of the shore close at hand, casting a quick glance forward, as he was raised up by a great wave. And in the same way as when most welcome to his children appears the life of a father who lies in sickness, bearing strong pains, long wasting away, and some cruel god assails him, but then to their joy the gods free him from his woe, so to Odysseus did the land and the wood seem welcome; and he swam on, eager to set foot on the land. But when he was as far away as a man's voice carries when he shouts, and heard the boom of the sea upon the reefs—for the great wave thundered against the dry land, belching upon it in terrible fashion, and all things were wrapped in the foam of the sea; for there were neither harbors where ships might ride, nor roadsteads, but projecting headlands, and reefs, and cliffs—then were the knees of Odysseus loosened and the heart within him

ὀχθήσας δ' ἄρα εἶπε πρὸς ὃν μεγαλήτορα θυμόν·
"ὤ μοι, ἐπεὶ δὴ γαῖαν ἀελπέα δῶκεν ἰδέσθαι
Ζεύς, καὶ δὴ τόδε λαῖτμα διατμήξας ἐπέρησα,[1]
410 ἔκβασις οὔ πη φαίνεθ' ἁλὸς πολιοῖο θύραζε·
ἔκτοσθεν μὲν γὰρ πάγοι ὀξέες, ἀμφὶ δὲ κῦμα
βέβρυχεν ῥόθιον, λισσὴ δ' ἀναδέδρομε πέτρη,
ἀγχιβαθὴς δὲ θάλασσα, καὶ οὔ πως ἔστι πόδεσσι
στήμεναι ἀμφοτέροισι καὶ ἐκφυγέειν κακότητα·
415 μή πώς μ' ἐκβαίνοντα βάλῃ λίθακι ποτὶ πέτρῃ
κῦμα μέγ' ἁρπάξαν· μελέη δέ μοι ἔσσεται ὁρμή.
εἰ δέ κ' ἔτι προτέρω παρανήξομαι, ἤν που ἐφεύρω
ἠιόνας τε παραπλῆγας λιμένας τε θαλάσσης,
δείδω μή μ' ἐξαῦτις ἀναρπάξασα θύελλα
420 πόντον ἐπ' ἰχθυόεντα φέρῃ βαρέα στενάχοντα,
ἠέ τί μοι καὶ κῆτος ἐπισσεύῃ μέγα δαίμων
ἐξ ἁλός, οἷά τε πολλὰ τρέφει κλυτὸς Ἀμφιτρίτη·
οἶδα γάρ, ὥς μοι ὀδώδυσται κλυτὸς ἐννοσίγαιος."
ἧος ὁ ταῦθ' ὥρμαινε κατὰ φρένα καὶ κατὰ θυμόν,
425 τόφρα δέ μιν μέγα κῦμα φέρε τρηχεῖαν ἐπ' ἀκτήν.
ἔνθα κ' ἀπὸ ῥινοὺς δρύφθη, σὺν δ' ὀστέ' ἀράχθη,
εἰ μὴ ἐπὶ φρεσὶ θῆκε θεά, γλαυκῶπις Ἀθήνη·
ἀμφοτέρῃσι δὲ χερσὶν ἐπεσσύμενος λάβε πέτρης,
τῆς ἔχετο στενάχων, ἧος μέγα κῦμα παρῆλθε.
430 καὶ τὸ μὲν ὣς ὑπάλυξε, παλιρρόθιον δέ μιν αὖτις
πλῆξεν ἐπεσσύμενον, τηλοῦ δέ μιν ἔμβαλε πόντῳ.
ὡς δ' ὅτε πουλύποδος θαλάμης ἐξελκομένοιο

---

[1] ἐπέρησα: ἐτέλεσσα

melted, and deeply shaken he spoke to his own great-hearted spirit:

"Ah me, when Zeus has at last granted me to see the land beyond my hopes, and I have prevailed to cleave my way and to cross this gulf, nowhere does there appear a way to come out from the gray sea. For outside are sharp crags, and around them the wave roars foaming, and the rock runs up sheer, and the water is deep close in shore, so that there is no way to stand firm on both feet and escape evil. As I try to come ashore a great wave may seize me and dash me against the jagged rock, and so shall my effort be in vain. But if I swim on yet further in hope of finding shelving beaches and harbors of the sea, I fear that the storm wind may catch me up again, and bear me, groaning heavily, over the fish-filled sea; or that some god may even send forth upon me some great monster out of the sea, like those that glorious Amphitrite breeds in such numbers. For I know how the great Earth-shaker wills me pain."[a]

While he pondered these things in mind and heart, a great wave bore him against the rugged shore. There would his skin have been stripped off and his bones broken, had not the goddess, flashing-eyed Athene, put a thought in his mind. On he rushed and seized the rock with both hands, and clung to it, groaning, until the great wave went by. Thus he escaped this wave, but in its backward flow it once more rushed upon him and struck him, and flung him far out in the sea. And just as, when a cuttlefish is dragged from its hole, many pebbles cling to its

[a] ὀδώδυσται: another instance of the pun on Odysseus' name noted at 1.62.

πρὸς κοτυληδονόφιν πυκιναὶ λάιγγες ἔχονται,
ὣς τοῦ πρὸς πέτρῃσι θρασειάων ἀπὸ χειρῶν
435   ρινοὶ ἀπέδρυφθεν· τὸν δὲ μέγα κῦμα κάλυψεν.
ἔνθα κε δὴ δύστηνος ὑπὲρ μόρον ὤλετ' Ὀδυσσεύς,
εἰ μὴ ἐπιφροσύνην δῶκε γλαυκῶπις Ἀθήνη.
κύματος ἐξαναδύς, τά τ' ἐρεύγεται ἤπειρόνδε,
νῆχε παρέξ, ἐς γαῖαν ὁρώμενος, εἴ που ἐφεύροι
440   ἠιόνας τε παραπλῆγας λιμένας τε θαλάσσης.
ἀλλ' ὅτε δὴ ποταμοῖο κατὰ στόμα καλλιρόοιο
ἷξε νέων, τῇ δή οἱ ἐείσατο χῶρος ἄριστος,
λεῖος πετράων, καὶ ἐπὶ σκέπας ἦν ἀνέμοιο,
ἔγνω δὲ προρέοντα καὶ εὔξατο ὃν κατὰ θυμόν·
445   "κλῦθι, ἄναξ, ὅτις ἐσσί· πολύλλιστον δέ σ' ἱκάνω,
φεύγων ἐκ πόντοιο Ποσειδάωνος ἐνιπάς.
αἰδοῖος μέν τ' ἐστὶ καὶ ἀθανάτοισι θεοῖσιν
ἀνδρῶν ὅς τις ἵκηται ἀλώμενος, ὡς καὶ ἐγὼ νῦν
σόν τε ρόον σά τε γούναθ' ἱκάνω πολλὰ μογήσας.
450   ἀλλ' ἐλέαιρε, ἄναξ· ἱκέτης δέ τοι εὔχομαι εἶναι."
ὣς φάθ', ὁ δ' αὐτίκα παῦσεν ἑὸν ρόον, ἔσχε δὲ κῦμα,
πρόσθε δέ οἱ ποίησε γαλήνην, τὸν δ' ἐσάωσεν
ἐς ποταμοῦ προχοάς. ὁ δ' ἄρ' ἄμφω γούνατ' ἔκαμψε
χεῖράς τε στιβαράς. ἁλὶ γὰρ δέδμητο φίλον κῆρ.
455   ᾤδεε δὲ χρόα πάντα, θάλασσα δὲ κήκιε πολλὴ
ἂν στόμα τε ρῖνάς θ'· ὁ δ' ἄρ' ἄπνευστος καὶ ἄναυδος
κεῖτ' ὀλιγηπελέων, κάματος δέ μιν αἰνὸς ἵκανεν.
ἀλλ' ὅτε δή ρ' ἄμπνυτο καὶ ἐς φρένα θυμὸς ἀγέρθη,
καὶ τότε δὴ κρήδεμνον ἀπὸ ἕο λῦσε θεοῖο.
460   καὶ τὸ μὲν ἐς ποταμὸν ἁλιμυρήεντα μεθῆκεν,

suckers, so from his valiant hands were bits of skin stripped off against the rocks; and the great wave covered him. Then surely would unfortunate Odysseus have perished beyond his fate, had not flashing-eyed Athene given him presence of mind. Making his way out of the surge where it belched upon the shore, he swam outside, looking continually toward the land in hope to find shelving beaches and harbors of the sea. But when, as he swam, he came to the mouth of a fair-flowing river, where seemed to him the best place, since it was smooth of stones, and there was shelter from the wind there, he knew the river as he flowed forth, and prayed to him in his heart:

"Hear me, king, whoever you are. As to one greatly longed-for do I come to you seeking to escape out of the sea from the threats of Poseidon. Reverend even in the eyes of the immortal gods is that man who comes as a wanderer, as I have come to your stream and to your knees, after many toils. Pity me, king; I declare myself your suppliant."

So he spoke, and the god at once made his current cease, and checked the waves, and made a calm before him, and brought him safely to the mouth of the river. And he let his two knees bend and his strong hands fall, for the heart within him was crushed by the sea. And all his flesh was swollen, and seawater oozed in streams up through his mouth and nostrils. So he lay breathless and speechless, with hardly strength to move; for terrible weariness had come upon him. But when he revived, and his spirit returned again into his breast, then he unbound from him the veil of the goddess and let it fall into the seaward-

ἂψ δ' ἔφερεν μέγα κῦμα κατὰ ρόον, αἶψα δ' ἄρ' Ἰνὼ
δέξατο χερσὶ φίλῃσιν· ὁ δ' ἐκ ποταμοῖο λιασθεὶς
σχοίνῳ ὑπεκλίνθη, κύσε δὲ ζείδωρον ἄρουραν.
ὀχθήσας δ' ἄρα εἶπε πρὸς ὃν μεγαλήτορα θυμόν·

465   "ὤ μοι ἐγώ, τί πάθω; τί νύ μοι μήκιστα γένηται;
εἰ μέν κ' ἐν ποταμῷ δυσκηδέα νύκτα φυλάσσω,
μή μ' ἄμυδις στίβη τε κακὴ καὶ θῆλυς ἐέρση
ἐξ ὀλιγηπελίης δαμάσῃ κεκαφηότα θυμόν·
αὔρη δ' ἐκ ποταμοῦ ψυχρὴ πνέει ἠῶθι πρό.

470   εἰ δέ κεν ἐς κλιτὺν ἀναβὰς καὶ δάσκιον ὕλην
θάμνοις ἐν πυκινοῖσι καταδράθω, εἴ με μεθείη
ῥῖγος καὶ κάματος, γλυκερὸς δέ μοι ὕπνος ἐπέλθῃ,
δείδω, μὴ θήρεσσιν ἕλωρ καὶ κύρμα γένωμαι."

ὣς ἄρα οἱ φρονέοντι δοάσσατο κέρδιον εἶναι·

475   βῆ ῥ' ἴμεν εἰς ὕλην· τὴν δὲ σχεδὸν ὕδατος εὗρεν
ἐν περιφαινομένῳ· δοιοὺς δ' ἄρ' ὑπήλυθε θάμνους,
ἐξ ὁμόθεν πεφυῶτας· ὁ μὲν φυλίης, ὁ δ' ἐλαίης.
τοὺς μὲν ἄρ' οὔτ' ἀνέμων διάη μένος ὑγρὸν ἀέντων,
οὔτε ποτ' ἠέλιος φαέθων ἀκτῖσιν ἔβαλλεν,

480   οὔτ' ὄμβρος περάασκε διαμπερές· ὣς ἄρα πυκνοὶ
ἀλλήλοισιν ἔφυν ἐπαμοιβαδίς· οὓς ὑπ' Ὀδυσσεὺς
δύσετ'. ἄφαρ δ' εὐνὴν ἐπαμήσατο χερσὶ φίλῃσιν
εὐρεῖαν· φύλλων γὰρ ἔην χύσις ἤλιθα πολλή,
ὅσσον τ' ἠὲ δύω ἠὲ τρεῖς ἄνδρας ἔρυσθαι

485   ὥρῃ χειμερίῃ, εἰ καὶ μάλα περ χαλεπαίνοι.
τὴν μὲν ἰδὼν γήθησε πολύτλας δῖος Ὀδυσσεύς,
ἐν δ' ἄρα μέσσῃ λέκτο, χύσιν δ' ἐπεχεύατο φύλλων.
ὡς δ' ὅτε τις δαλὸν σποδιῇ ἐνέκρυψε μελαίνῃ

flowing river; and the great wave bore it back down the stream, and Ino quickly received it in her hands. Odysseus, going back from the river, sank down in the reeds and kissed the earth, the giver of grain; and deeply shaken he spoke to his own great-hearted spirit:

"Ah me, what will become of me? What in the end will befall me? If here in the river bed I keep watch throughout the weary night, I fear that together the bitter frost and the fresh dew may overcome in my feebleness my gasping spirit; and the breeze from the river blows cold in the early morning. But if I climb up the slope to the shady wood and lie down to rest in the thick bushes, in the hope that the cold and the weariness might leave me, and if sweet sleep comes over me, I fear I may become a prey and spoil to wild beasts."

Then, as he pondered, this thing seemed to him the better: he set out for the wood, and he found his spot near the water beside a clearing; there he crept beneath two bushes which grew from the same place, one of thorn and one of olive. Through these the strength of the wet winds could never blow, nor the rays of the bright sun beat, nor could the rain pierce through them, so closely did they grow, intertwining one with the other. Beneath these Odysseus crept. Without delay he swept together with his hands a broad bed, for fallen leaves were there in plenty, enough to shelter two men or three in winter time, however bitter the weather. Seeing it, much-enduring, noble Odysseus was glad, and lay down in the middle of it, and heaped over him the fallen leaves. And as a man hides a

ἀγροῦ ἐπ' ἐσχατιῆς, ᾧ μὴ πάρα γείτονες ἄλλοι,
490 σπέρμα πυρὸς σῴζων, ἵνα μή ποθεν ἄλλοθεν αὕοι,
ὣς Ὀδυσεὺς φύλλοισι καλύψατο· τῷ δ' ἄρ' Ἀθήνη
ὕπνον ἐπ' ὄμμασι χεῦ', ἵνα μιν παύσειε τάχιστα
δυσπονέος καμάτοιο φίλα βλέφαρ' ἀμφικαλύψας.

brand beneath the dark embers in an outlying farm, a man who has no neighbors, and so saves a seed of fire, that he may not have to kindle it from some other source, so Odysseus covered himself with leaves. And Athene shed sleep upon his eyes, that it might enfold his lids and speedily free him from toilsome weariness.

Z

Ὡς ὁ μὲν ἔνθα καθεῦδε πολύτλας δῖος Ὀδυσσεὺς
ὕπνῳ καὶ καμάτῳ ἀρημένος· αὐτὰρ Ἀθήνη
βῆ ῥ᾽ ἐς Φαιήκων ἀνδρῶν δῆμόν τε πόλιν τε,
οἳ πρὶν μέν ποτ᾽ ἔναιον ἐν εὐρυχόρῳ Ὑπερείῃ,
5 ἀγχοῦ Κυκλώπων ἀνδρῶν ὑπερηνορεόντων,
οἵ σφεας σινέσκοντο, βίηφι δὲ φέρτεροι ἦσαν.
ἔνθεν ἀναστήσας ἄγε Ναυσίθοος θεοειδής,
εἷσεν δὲ Σχερίῃ, ἑκὰς ἀνδρῶν ἀλφηστάων,
ἀμφὶ δὲ τεῖχος ἔλασσε πόλει, καὶ ἐδείματο οἴκους,
10 καὶ νηοὺς ποίησε θεῶν, καὶ ἐδάσσατ᾽ ἀρούρας.
ἀλλ᾽ ὁ μὲν ἤδη κηρὶ δαμεὶς Ἀιδόσδε βεβήκει,
Ἀλκίνοος δὲ τότ᾽ ἦρχε, θεῶν ἄπο μήδεα εἰδώς.
τοῦ μὲν ἔβη πρὸς δῶμα θεά, γλαυκῶπις Ἀθήνη,
νόστον Ὀδυσσῆι μεγαλήτορι μητιόωσα.
15 βῆ δ᾽ ἴμεν ἐς θάλαμον πολυδαίδαλον, ᾧ ἔνι κούρη
κοιμᾶτ᾽ ἀθανάτῃσι φυὴν καὶ εἶδος ὁμοίη,
Ναυσικάα, θυγάτηρ μεγαλήτορος Ἀλκινόοιο,
πὰρ δὲ δύ᾽ ἀμφίπολοι, Χαρίτων ἄπο κάλλος ἔχουσαι,
σταθμοῖιν ἑκάτερθε· θύραι δ᾽ ἐπέκειντο φαειναί.
20 ἡ δ᾽ ἀνέμου ὡς πνοιὴ ἐπέσσυτο δέμνια κούρης,
στῆ δ᾽ ἄρ᾽ ὑπὲρ κεφαλῆς, καί μιν πρὸς μῦθον ἔειπεν,

BOOK 6

So he lay there asleep, the much-enduring, noble Odysseus, overcome with sleep and weariness; but Athene went to the land and city of the Phaeacians. These dwelt of old in spacious Hypereia near the Cyclopes, men overweening in pride who plundered them continually and were mightier than they. From there Nausithous, the godlike, had removed them, and led and settled them in Scheria far from bread-eating mankind. About the city he had drawn a wall, he had built houses and made temples for the gods, and divided the plowlands; but he by this time had been stricken by fate and had gone to the house of Hades, and Alcinous was now king, made wise in counsel by the gods. To his house went the goddess, flashing-eyed Athene, to contrive the return of great-hearted Odysseus. She went to the chamber, richly wrought, wherein slept a maiden like the immortal goddesses in form and looks, Nausicaa, the daughter of great-hearted Alcinous; by her slept two handmaids, gifted with beauty by the Graces, one on either side of the doorposts, and the bright doors were shut.

Like a breath of air the goddess sped to the couch of the maiden, and stood above her head, and spoke to her, taking

εἰδομένη κούρῃ ναυσικλειτοῖο Δύμαντος,
ἥ οἱ ὁμηλικίη μὲν ἔην, κεχάριστο δὲ θυμῷ.
τῇ μιν ἐεισαμένη προσέφη γλαυκῶπις Ἀθήνη·

25   "Ναυσικάα, τί νύ σ' ὧδε μεθήμονα γείνατο μήτηρ;
εἵματα μέν τοι κεῖται ἀκηδέα σιγαλόεντα,
σοὶ δὲ γάμος σχεδόν ἐστιν, ἵνα χρὴ καλὰ μὲν αὐτὴν
ἕννυσθαι, τὰ δὲ τοῖσι παρασχεῖν, οἵ κέ σ' ἄγωνται.
ἐκ γάρ τοι τούτων φάτις ἀνθρώπους ἀναβαίνει

30   ἐσθλή, χαίρουσιν δὲ πατὴρ καὶ πότνια μήτηρ.
ἀλλ' ἴομεν πλυνέουσαι ἅμ' ἠοῖ φαινομένηφι·
καί τοι ἐγὼ συνέριθος ἅμ' ἕψομαι, ὄφρα τάχιστα
ἐντύνεαι, ἐπεὶ οὔ τοι ἔτι δὴν παρθένος ἔσσεαι·
ἤδη γάρ σε μνῶνται ἀριστῆες κατὰ δῆμον

35   πάντων Φαιήκων, ὅθι τοι γένος ἐστὶ καὶ αὐτῇ.
ἀλλ' ἄγ' ἐπότρυνον πατέρα κλυτὸν ἠῶθι πρὸ
ἡμιόνους καὶ ἄμαξαν ἐφοπλίσαι, ἥ κεν ἄγῃσι
ζῶστρά τε καὶ πέπλους καὶ ῥήγεα σιγαλόεντα.
καὶ δὲ σοὶ ὧδ' αὐτῇ πολὺ κάλλιον ἠὲ πόδεσσιν

40   ἔρχεσθαι· πολλὸν γὰρ ἀπὸ πλυνοί εἰσι πόληος."

ἡ μὲν ἄρ' ὣς εἰποῦσ' ἀπέβη γλαυκῶπις Ἀθήνη
Οὔλυμπόνδ', ὅθι φασὶ θεῶν ἕδος ἀσφαλὲς αἰεὶ
ἔμμεναι. οὔτ' ἀνέμοισι τινάσσεται οὔτε ποτ' ὄμβρῳ
δεύεται οὔτε χιὼν ἐπιπίλναται, ἀλλὰ μάλ' αἴθρη

45   πέπταται ἀνέφελος, λευκὴ δ' ἐπιδέδρομεν αἴγλη·
τῷ ἔνι τέρπονται μάκαρες θεοὶ ἤματα πάντα.
ἔνθ' ἀπέβη γλαυκῶπις, ἐπεὶ διεπέφραδε κούρῃ.

αὐτίκα δ' Ἠὼς ἦλθεν ἐΰθρονος, ἥ μιν ἔγειρε
Ναυσικάαν εὔπεπλον· ἄφαρ δ' ἀπεθαύμασ' ὄνειρον,

the form of the daughter of Dymas, famed for his ships, a girl who was of like age with Nausicaa, and was dear to her heart. Likening herself to her, the flashing-eyed Athene spoke and said:

"Nausicaa, how comes it that your mother bore you so heedless? Your bright clothes are lying uncared for; yet your marriage is near at hand, when you will need not only to be dressed in beautiful garments yourself, but to provide others like them for those who escort you. It is from things like these, you know, that good report arises among men, and the father and honored mother rejoice. Come, let us go to wash them at break of day, for I will go with you to help you so that you may make yourself ready without delay; for you shall not long remain a maiden. Even now you have suitors in the land, the noblest of all the Phaeacians, from whom is your own lineage also. But come, urge your noble father early this morning to make ready mules and a wagon for you, to carry the girdles and robes and bright coverlets. And for yourself too it is much better to go in this way than on foot, for the washing tanks are far from the city."

So saying, the goddess, flashing-eyed Athene, departed to Olympus, where, they say, is the abode of the gods that stands fast forever. Neither is it shaken by winds nor ever wet with rain, nor does snow fall upon it, but the air is outspread clear and cloudless, and over it hovers a radiant whiteness; here the blessed gods are happy all their days. Thither went the flashing-eyed one, when she had made her proposal to the maiden.

At once then came fair-throned Dawn and awakened Nausicaa of the beautiful robes, and immediately she won-

223

50 βῆ δ' ἰέναι διὰ δώμαθ', ἵν' ἀγγείλειε τοκεῦσιν,
    πατρὶ φίλῳ καὶ μητρί· κιχήσατο δ' ἔνδον ἐόντας·
    ἡ μὲν ἐπ' ἐσχάρῃ ἧστο σὺν ἀμφιπόλοισι γυναιξὶν
    ἠλάκατα στρωφῶσ' ἁλιπόρφυρα· τῷ δὲ θύραζε
    ἐρχομένῳ ξύμβλητο μετὰ κλειτοὺς βασιλῆας
55 ἐς βουλήν, ἵνα μιν κάλεον Φαίηκες ἀγαυοί.
    ἡ δὲ μάλ' ἄγχι στᾶσα φίλον πατέρα προσέειπε·
    "πάππα φίλ', οὐκ ἂν δή μοι ἐφοπλίσσειας ἀπήνην
    ὑψηλὴν ἐύκυκλον, ἵνα κλυτὰ εἵματ' ἄγωμαι
    ἐς ποταμὸν πλυνέουσα, τά μοι ῥερυπωμένα κεῖται;
60 καὶ δὲ σοὶ αὐτῷ ἔοικε μετὰ πρώτοισιν ἐόντα
    βουλὰς βουλεύειν καθαρὰ χροΐ εἵματ' ἔχοντα.
    πέντε δέ τοι φίλοι υἷες ἐνὶ μεγάροις γεγάασιν,
    οἱ δύ' ὀπυίοντες, τρεῖς δ' ἤίθεοι θαλέθοντες·
    οἱ δ' αἰεὶ ἐθέλουσι νεόπλυτα εἵματ' ἔχοντες
65 ἐς χορὸν ἔρχεσθαι· τὰ δ' ἐμῇ φρενὶ πάντα μέμηλεν."
    ὣς ἔφατ'· αἴδετο γὰρ θαλερὸν γάμον ἐξονομῆναι
    πατρὶ φίλῳ. ὁ δὲ πάντα νόει καὶ ἀμείβετο μύθῳ·
    "οὔτε τοι ἡμιόνων φθονέω, τέκος, οὔτε τευ ἄλλου.
    ἔρχευ· ἀτάρ τοι δμῶες ἐφοπλίσσουσιν ἀπήνην
70 ὑψηλὴν ἐύκυκλον, ὑπερτερίῃ ἀραρυῖαν."
    ὣς εἰπὼν δμώεσσιν ἐκέκλετο, τοὶ δ' ἐπίθοντο.
    οἱ μὲν ἄρ' ἐκτὸς ἄμαξαν ἐύτροχον ἡμιονείην
    ὥπλεον, ἡμιόνους θ' ὕπαγον ζεῦξάν θ' ὑπ' ἀπήνῃ·
    κούρη δ' ἐκ θαλάμοιο φέρεν ἐσθῆτα φαεινήν.
75 καὶ τὴν μὲν κατέθηκεν ἐυξέστῳ ἐπ' ἀπήνῃ,
    μήτηρ δ' ἐν κίστῃ ἐτίθει μενοεικέ' ἐδωδὴν
    παντοίην, ἐν δ' ὄψα τίθει, ἐν δ' οἶνον ἔχευεν

dered at her dream, and went through the house to tell her parents, her staunch father and her mother; and she found them both within. Her mother sat at the hearth with her handmaids, spinning the yarn of purple dye, and her father she met as he was going out to join the glorious kings in the place of council, to which the lordly Phaeacians called him. She came up close to her dear father, and said:

"Papa dear, will you not make ready for me a wagon, high and with strong wheels, so that I may take my fine clothes, which are lying here soiled, to the river for washing? For you yourself, too, it is proper, when you are at council with the princes, that you should have clean clothes upon you; and you have five sons living in your halls—two are wedded, but three are sturdy bachelors—and these always wish to put on freshly washed clothes and go to the dance. All this I have to think about."

So she spoke, for she was ashamed to name the joys of marriage to her father; but he understood all, and answered, saying: "Neither the mules do I begrudge you, my child, nor anything else. Go your way; the slaves shall make ready for you the wagon, high and with strong wheels and fitted with a box above."

With this he called to the slaves, and they obeyed him. Outside the palace they made ready the light-running mule wagon, and led up the mules and yoked them to it; and the maiden brought from her chamber the bright clothes, and placed them upon the polished wagon, while her mother put in a chest food of all sorts to satisfy the heart. In it she put dainties, and poured wine in a goatskin flask; and the maiden mounted upon the wagon. Her mother gave her also soft olive oil in a flask of gold, that she

ἀσκῷ ἐν αἰγείῳ· κούρη δ' ἐπεβήσετ' ἀπήνης.
δῶκεν δὲ χρυσέῃ ἐν ληκύθῳ ὑγρὸν ἔλαιον,
80   ἧος χυτλώσαιτο σὺν ἀμφιπόλοισι γυναιξίν.
ἡ δ' ἔλαβεν μάστιγα καὶ ἡνία σιγαλόεντα,
μάστιξεν δ' ἐλάαν· καναχὴ δ' ἦν ἡμιόνοιιν.
αἱ δ' ἄμοτον τανύοντο, φέρον δ' ἐσθῆτα καὶ αὐτήν,
οὐκ οἴην, ἅμα τῇ γε καὶ ἀμφίπολοι κίον ἄλλαι.
85   αἱ δ' ὅτε δὴ ποταμοῖο ῥόον περικαλλέ' ἵκοντο,
ἔνθ' ἦ τοι πλυνοὶ ἦσαν ἐπηετανοί, πολὺ δ' ὕδωρ
καλὸν ὑπεκπρόρεεν[1] μάλα περ ῥυπόωντα καθῆραι,
ἔνθ' αἵ γ' ἡμιόνους μὲν ὑπεκπροέλυσαν ἀπήνης.
καὶ τὰς μὲν σεῦαν ποταμὸν πάρα δινήεντα
90   τρώγειν ἄγρωστιν μελιηδέα· ταὶ δ' ἀπ' ἀπήνης
εἵματα χερσὶν ἕλοντο καὶ ἐσφόρεον μέλαν ὕδωρ,
στεῖβον δ' ἐν βόθροισι θοῶς ἔριδα προφέρουσαι.
αὐτὰρ ἐπεὶ πλῦνάν τε κάθηράν τε ῥύπα πάντα,
ἑξείης πέτασαν παρὰ θῖν' ἁλός, ἧχι μάλιστα
95   λάιγγας ποτὶ χέρσον ἀποπλύνεσκε[2] θάλασσα.
αἱ δὲ λοεσσάμεναι καὶ χρισάμεναι λίπ' ἐλαίῳ
δεῖπνον ἔπειθ' εἵλοντο παρ' ὄχθῃσιν ποταμοῖο,
εἵματα δ' ἠελίοιο μένον τερσήμεναι αὐγῇ.
αὐτὰρ ἐπεὶ σίτου τάρφθεν δμῳαί τε καὶ αὐτή,
100   σφαίρῃ ταὶ δ' ἄρ' ἔπαιζον, ἀπὸ κρήδεμνα βαλοῦσαι·
τῇσι δὲ Ναυσικάα λευκώλενος ἤρχετο μολπῆς.
οἵη δ' Ἄρτεμις εἶσι κατ' οὔρεα[3] ἰοχέαιρα,

---

[1] ὑπεκπρόρεεν: ὑπεκπρορέει MSS
[2] ἀποπλύνεσκε: ἀποπτύεσκε
[3] οὔρεα: οὔρεος

and her maidens might have it for the bath. Then Nausicaa took the whip and the bright reins, and struck the mules to start them; and there was a clatter of the mules as they sped on swiftly, bearing the clothing and the maiden; nor did she go alone, for with her went her handmaids as well.

Now when they came to the beautiful streams of the river, where were the washing tanks that never failed—for abundant clear water welled up from beneath and flowed over, to cleanse garments however soiled—there they unhitched the mules from the wagon and drove them along the eddying river to graze on the honey-sweet water grass, and themselves took in their arms the clothes from the wagon, and bore them into the dark water, and trampled them in the trenches, busily vying each with one another. Now when they had washed the garments, and had cleansed them of all stains, they spread them out in rows on the shore of the sea where the waves dashing against the land washed the pebbles cleanest; and they, after they had bathed and anointed themselves richly with oil, took their meal on the river's banks, and waited for the clothes to dry in the bright sunshine. Then when they had had their joy of food, she and her handmaids, they threw off their headgear and fell to playing at ball, and white-armed Nausicaa was leader in the song.[a] And even as Artemis, the archer, roves over the mountains, along the

[a] They sing while tossing the ball to one another. M.

ἢ κατὰ Τηΰγετον περιμήκετον ἢ Ἐρύμανθον,
τερπομένη κάπροισι καὶ ὠκείῃς ἐλάφοισι·
105 τῇ δέ θ' ἅμα νύμφαι, κοῦραι Διὸς αἰγιόχοιο,
ἀγρονόμοι παίζουσι, γέγηθε δέ τε φρένα Λητώ·
πασάων δ' ὑπὲρ ἥ γε κάρη ἔχει ἠδὲ μέτωπα,
ῥεῖά τ' ἀριγνώτη πέλεται, καλαὶ δέ τε πᾶσαι·
ὣς ἥ γ' ἀμφιπόλοισι μετέπρεπε παρθένος ἀδμής.
110 ἀλλ' ὅτε δὴ ἄρ' ἔμελλε πάλιν οἰκόνδε νέεσθαι
ζεύξασ' ἡμιόνους πτύξασά τε εἵματα καλά,
ἔνθ' αὖτ' ἄλλ' ἐνόησε θεά, γλαυκῶπις Ἀθήνη,
ὡς Ὀδυσεὺς ἔγροιτο, ἴδοι τ' ἐυώπιδα κούρην,
ἥ οἱ Φαιήκων ἀνδρῶν πόλιν ἡγήσαιτο.
115 σφαῖραν ἔπειτ' ἔρριψε μετ' ἀμφίπολον βασίλεια·
ἀμφιπόλου μὲν ἅμαρτε, βαθείῃ δ' ἔμβαλε δίνῃ·
αἱ δ' ἐπὶ μακρὸν ἄυσαν· ὁ δ' ἔγρετο δῖος Ὀδυσσεύς,
ἑζόμενος δ' ὥρμαινε κατὰ φρένα καὶ κατὰ θυμόν·
"ὤ μοι ἐγώ, τέων αὖτε βροτῶν ἐς γαῖαν ἱκάνω;
120 ἦ ῥ' οἵ γ' ὑβρισταί τε καὶ ἄγριοι οὐδὲ δίκαιοι,
ἦε φιλόξεινοι καί σφιν νόος ἐστὶ θεουδής;
ὥς τέ με κουράων ἀμφήλυθε θῆλυς ἀυτή·
νυμφάων, αἳ ἔχουσ' ὀρέων αἰπεινὰ κάρηνα
καὶ πηγὰς ποταμῶν καὶ πίσεα ποιήεντα.
125 ἦ νύ που ἀνθρώπων εἰμὶ σχεδὸν αὐδηέντων;
ἀλλ' ἄγ' ἐγὼν αὐτὸς πειρήσομαι ἠδὲ ἴδωμαι."
ὣς εἰπὼν θάμνων ὑπεδύσετο δῖος Ὀδυσσεύς,
ἐκ πυκινῆς δ' ὕλης πτόρθον κλάσε χειρὶ παχείῃ
φύλλων, ὡς ῥύσαιτο περὶ χροῒ μήδεα φωτός.
130 βῆ δ' ἴμεν ὥς τε λέων ὀρεσίτροφος ἀλκὶ πεποιθώς,

ridges of lofty Taÿgetus or Erymanthus, joying in the pursuit of boars and swift deer, and the wood nymphs, daughters of Zeus who bears the aegis, share her sport, and Leto is glad at heart—high above them all Artemis holds her head and brows, and easily may she be known, though all are beautiful—so amid her handmaids shone the unwed maiden.

But when she was about to yoke the mules, and fold the handsome clothes, in order to return homeward, then the goddess, flashing-eyed Athene, had another thought, that Odysseus might awake and see the fair-faced maiden, who should lead him to the city of the Phaeacians. So then the princess tossed the ball to one of her maids; the maid indeed she missed, but threw it into a deep eddy, whereupon they cried aloud, and noble Odysseus awoke, and sat up, and thus he pondered in mind and heart:

"Alas, to the land of what mortals have I now come? Are they cruel, and wild and unjust? or are they kind to strangers and fear the gods in their thoughts? There rang in my ears a cry as of maidens, of nymphs who haunt the towering peaks of the mountains, the springs that feed the rivers, and the grassy meadows! Can it be that I am somewhere near men of human speech? But come, I will myself make trial and see."

So saying the noble Odysseus came forth from beneath the bushes, and with his stout hand he broke from the thick wood a leafy branch, that he might hold it about him and thereby hide his genitals. Forth he came like a mountain-nurtured lion trusting in his strength, who goes forth,

ὅς τ᾽ εἶσ᾽ ὑόμενος καὶ ἀήμενος, ἐν δέ οἱ ὄσσε
δαίεται· αὐτὰρ ὁ βουσὶ μετέρχεται ἢ ὀίεσσιν
ἠὲ μετ᾽ ἀγροτέρας ἐλάφους· κέλεται δέ ἑ γαστὴρ
μήλων πειρήσοντα καὶ ἐς πυκινὸν δόμον ἐλθεῖν·

135   ὣς Ὀδυσεὺς κούρῃσιν ἐυπλοκάμοισιν ἔμελλε
μίξεσθαι, γυμνός περ ἐών· χρειὼ γὰρ ἵκανε.
σμερδαλέος δ᾽ αὐτῇσι φάνη κεκακωμένος ἅλμῃ,
τρέσσαν δ᾽ ἄλλυδις ἄλλη ἐπ᾽ ἠιόνας προὐχούσας·
οἴη δ᾽ Ἀλκινόου θυγάτηρ μένε· τῇ γὰρ Ἀθήνη

140   θάρσος ἐνὶ φρεσὶ θῆκε καὶ ἐκ δέος εἵλετο γυίων.
στῆ δ᾽ ἄντα σχομένη· ὁ δὲ μερμήριξεν Ὀδυσσεύς,
ἢ γούνων λίσσοιτο λαβὼν ἐυώπιδα κούρην,
ἢ αὔτως ἐπέεσσιν ἀποσταδὰ μειλιχίοισι
λίσσοιτ᾽, εἰ δείξειε πόλιν καὶ εἵματα δοίη.

145   ὣς ἄρα οἱ φρονέοντι δοάσσατο κέρδιον εἶναι,
λίσσεσθαι ἐπέεσσιν ἀποσταδὰ μειλιχίοισι,
μή οἱ γοῦνα λαβόντι χολώσαιτο φρένα κούρη.
αὐτίκα μειλίχιον καὶ κερδαλέον φάτο μῦθον.

    "γουνοῦμαί σε, ἄνασσα· θεός νύ τις, ἦ βροτός ἐσσι;

150   εἰ μέν τις θεός ἐσσι, τοὶ οὐρανὸν εὐρὺν ἔχουσιν,
Ἀρτέμιδί σε ἐγώ γε, Διὸς κούρῃ μεγάλοιο,
εἶδός τε μέγεθός τε φυήν τ᾽ ἄγχιστα ἐίσκω·
εἰ δέ τίς ἐσσι βροτῶν, τοὶ ἐπὶ χθονὶ ναιετάουσιν,
τρὶς μάκαρες μὲν σοί γε πατὴρ καὶ πότνια μήτηρ,

155   τρὶς μάκαρες δὲ κασίγνητοι· μάλα πού σφισι θυμὸς
αἰὲν ἐυφροσύνῃσιν ἰαίνεται εἵνεκα σεῖο,
λευσσόντων τοιόνδε θάλος χορὸν εἰσοιχνεῦσαν.
κεῖνος δ᾽ αὖ περὶ κῆρι μακάρτατος ἔξοχον ἄλλων,

230

beaten with rain and wind, his two eyes blazing in his head: into the midst of the cattle he goes, or of the sheep, or on the track of the wild deer, and his belly bids him go even into the close-built fold, to make an attack upon the flocks. Even so Odysseus was about to enter the company of the fair-tressed maidens, naked though he was, for need had come upon him. And terrible he seemed to them, all befouled with brine, and they fled in fear, one here, one there, along the jutting sand spits. Alone the daughter of Alcinous kept her place, for in her heart Athene put courage, and took fear from her limbs. She stood and faced him; and Odysseus pondered whether he should clasp the knees of the fair-faced maiden, and make his prayer, or whether, standing apart as he was, he should beseech her with winning words, in hope that she might show him the way to the city and give him clothes. And, as he pondered, it seemed to him better to stand apart and beseech her with winning words, fearing that the maiden's heart might take offense if he should lay hold of her knees; so at once he made a speech both winning and crafty:

"I clasp your knees, my queen—are you a goddess, or are you mortal? If you are a goddess, one of those who hold broad heaven, to Artemis, the daughter of great Zeus, I liken you most nearly in looks and in stature and in form. But if you are one of mortals who dwell upon the earth, thrice-blessed then are your father and your honored mother, and thrice-blessed your brothers. Great must be the joy with which their hearts are always warmed because of you, as they see you entering the dance, a flower so fair. But that man in his turn is blessed in heart above all others,

ὅς κέ σ' ἐέδνοισι βρίσας οἰκόνδ' ἀγάγηται.
160 οὐ γάρ πω τοιοῦτον ἴδον βροτὸν[1] ὀφθαλμοῖσιν,
οὔτ' ἄνδρ' οὔτε γυναῖκα· σέβας μ' ἔχει εἰσορόωντα.
Δήλῳ δή ποτε τοῖον Ἀπόλλωνος παρὰ βωμῷ
φοίνικος νέον ἔρνος ἀνερχόμενον ἐνόησα·
ἦλθον γὰρ καὶ κεῖσε, πολὺς δέ μοι ἕσπετο λαός,
165 τὴν ὁδὸν ᾗ δὴ μέλλεν ἐμοὶ κακὰ κήδε' ἔσεσθαι.
ὣς δ' αὔτως καὶ κεῖνο ἰδὼν ἐτεθήπεα θυμῷ
δήν, ἐπεὶ οὔ πω τοῖον ἀνήλυθεν ἐκ δόρυ γαίης,
ὡς σέ, γύναι, ἄγαμαί τε τέθηπά τε, δείδια δ' αἰνῶς
γούνων ἅψασθαι· χαλεπὸν δέ με πένθος ἱκάνει.
170 χθιζὸς ἐεικοστῷ φύγον ἤματι οἴνοπα πόντον·
τόφρα δέ μ' αἰεὶ κῦμ' ἐφόρει κραιπναί τε θύελλαι
νήσου ἀπ' Ὠγυγίης. νῦν δ' ἐνθάδε κάββαλε δαίμων,
ὄφρ' ἔτι που καὶ τῇδε πάθω κακόν· οὐ γὰρ ὀίω
παύσεσθ', ἀλλ' ἔτι πολλὰ θεοὶ τελέουσι πάροιθεν.
175 ἀλλά, ἄνασσ', ἐλέαιρε· σὲ γὰρ κακὰ πολλὰ μογήσας
ἐς πρώτην ἱκόμην, τῶν δ' ἄλλων οὔ τινα οἶδα
ἀνθρώπων, οἳ τήνδε πόλιν καὶ γαῖαν ἔχουσιν.
ἄστυ δέ μοι δεῖξον, δὸς δὲ ῥάκος ἀμφιβαλέσθαι,
εἴ τί που εἴλυμα σπείρων ἔχες ἐνθάδ' ἰοῦσα.
180 σοὶ δὲ θεοὶ τόσα δοῖεν ὅσα φρεσὶ σῇσι μενοινᾷς,
ἄνδρα τε καὶ οἶκον, καὶ ὁμοφροσύνην ὀπάσειαν
ἐσθλήν· οὐ μὲν γὰρ τοῦ γε κρεῖσσον καὶ ἄρειον,
ἢ ὅθ' ὁμοφρονέοντε νοήμασιν οἶκον ἔχητον
ἀνὴρ ἠδὲ γυνή· πόλλ' ἄλγεα δυσμενέεσσι,
185 χάρματα δ' εὐμενέτῃσι, μάλιστα δέ τ' ἔκλυον αὐτοί."

who shall prevail with his gifts of wooing and lead you to his home. For never yet have my eyes looked upon a mortal such as you, whether man or woman; awe holds me as I look on you. Now in Delos once I saw such a thing, a young shoot of a palm springing up beside the altar of Apollo— for there, too, I went, and many men followed with me, on that journey on which evil woes were to be my portion—in the same way, when I saw that, I marveled long at heart, for never yet did such a tree spring up from the earth. In like manner, lady, I marvel at you, and am amazed, and fear greatly to touch your knees; and hard is the trouble which has come upon me. Yesterday, on the twentieth day, I escaped from the wine-dark sea: during all that time the waves and the swift winds were carrying me from the island of Ogygia; and now fate has cast me ashore here, that here, too, no doubt, I may suffer some ill. For not yet, I think, will my troubles cease, but the gods before that will bring many more to pass. Instead, my queen, have pity; for it is to you first that I have come after many grievous toils, and of the others who possess this city and land I know not one. Show me the way to the city, and give me some rag to throw about me, if perhaps you had any wrapping for the clothes when you came here. And for yourself, may the gods grant you all your heart desires, a husband and a home, and may they bestow on you as well oneness of heart in all its excellence. For nothing is greater or better than this, than when a man and a woman keep house together sharing one heart and mind, a great grief to their foes and a joy to their friends; while their own fame is unsurpassed."

---

[1] ἴδον βροτὸν· ἐγὼν ἴδον

233

τὸν δ᾽ αὖ Ναυσικάα λευκώλενος ἀντίον ηὔδα·
"ξεῖν᾽, ἐπεὶ οὔτε κακῷ οὔτ᾽ ἄφρονι φωτὶ ἔοικας·
Ζεὺς δ᾽ αὐτὸς νέμει ὄλβον Ὀλύμπιος ἀνθρώποισιν,
ἐσθλοῖς ἠδὲ κακοῖσιν, ὅπως ἐθέλῃσιν, ἑκάστῳ·
190 καί που σοὶ τάδ᾽ ἔδωκε, σὲ δὲ χρὴ τετλάμεν ἔμπης.
νῦν δ᾽, ἐπεὶ ἡμετέρην τε πόλιν καὶ γαῖαν ἱκάνεις,
οὔτ᾽ οὖν ἐσθῆτος δευήσεαι οὔτε τευ ἄλλου,
ὧν ἐπέοιχ᾽ ἱκέτην ταλαπείριον ἀντιάσαντα.
ἄστυ δέ τοι δείξω, ἐρέω δέ τοι οὔνομα λαῶν.
195 Φαίηκες μὲν τήνδε πόλιν καὶ γαῖαν ἔχουσιν,
εἰμὶ δ᾽ ἐγὼ θυγάτηρ μεγαλήτορος Ἀλκινόοιο,
τοῦ δ᾽ ἐκ Φαιήκων ἔχεται κάρτος τε βίη τε."
ἦ ῥα καὶ ἀμφιπόλοισιν ἐϋπλοκάμοισι κέλευσε·
"στῆτέ μοι, ἀμφίπολοι· πόσε φεύγετε φῶτα ἰδοῦσαι;
200 ἦ μή πού τινα δυσμενέων φάσθ᾽ ἔμμεναι ἀνδρῶν;
οὐκ ἔσθ᾽ οὗτος ἀνὴρ διερὸς βροτὸς οὐδὲ γένηται,
ὅς κεν Φαιήκων ἀνδρῶν ἐς γαῖαν ἵκηται
δηϊοτῆτα φέρων· μάλα γὰρ φίλοι ἀθανάτοισιν.
οἰκέομεν δ᾽ ἀπάνευθε πολυκλύστῳ ἐνὶ πόντῳ,
205 ἔσχατοι, οὐδέ τις ἄμμι βροτῶν ἐπιμίσγεται ἄλλος.
ἀλλ᾽ ὅδε τις δύστηνος ἀλώμενος ἐνθάδ᾽ ἱκάνει,
τὸν νῦν χρὴ κομέειν· πρὸς γὰρ Διός εἰσιν ἅπαντες
ξεῖνοί τε πτωχοί τε, δόσις δ᾽ ὀλίγη τε φίλη τε.
ἀλλὰ δότ᾽, ἀμφίπολοι, ξείνῳ βρῶσίν τε πόσιν τε,
210 λούσατέ τ᾽ ἐν ποταμῷ, ὅθ᾽ ἐπὶ σκέπας ἔστ᾽ ἀνέμοιο."
ὣς ἔφαθ᾽, αἱ δ᾽ ἔσταν τε καὶ ἀλλήλῃσι κέλευσαν,
κὰδ δ᾽ ἄρ᾽ Ὀδυσσῆ᾽ εἷσαν ἐπὶ σκέπας, ὡς ἐκέλευσεν
Ναυσικάα θυγάτηρ μεγαλήτορος Ἀλκινόοιο·

Then white-armed Nausicaa answered him: "Stranger, since you seem to be neither a bad man nor without understanding, and it is Zeus himself, the Olympian, that gives happy fortune to men, both to the good and the bad, to each man as he will; so to you, it seems, he has given this lot, and you must in any case endure it. But now, since you have come to our city and land, you shall not lack clothing nor anything else of those things which befit a sore-tried suppliant when he appears. I will show you the way to the city, and will tell you the name of the people. The Phaeacians possess this city and land, and I am the daughter of great-hearted Alcinous, in whom are vested the power and might of the Phaeacians."

She spoke, and called to her fair-tressed handmaids: "Stop, my maidens. Where are you running to at the sight of a man? You do not think, surely, that he is an enemy? There is no mortal man so slippery, nor will there ever be one, as to come to the land of the Phaeacians bringing hostility, for we are very dear to the immortals. Far off we dwell in the surging sea, the farthermost of men, and no other mortals have dealings with us. On the contrary, this is some unfortunate wanderer that has come here. Him must we now tend; for from Zeus are all strangers and beggars, and a gift, though small, is welcome. Come, then, my maidens, give to the stranger food and drink, and bathe him in the river in a spot where there is shelter from the wind."

So she spoke, and they halted and called to each other. Then they set Odysseus in a sheltered place, as Nausicaa, the daughter of great-hearted Alcinous, bade, and beside

πὰρ δ' ἄρα οἱ φᾶρός τε χιτῶνά τε εἵματ' ἔθηκαν,
215   δῶκαν δὲ χρυσέῃ ἐν ληκύθῳ ὑγρὸν ἔλαιον,
ἤνωγον δ' ἄρα μιν λοῦσθαι ποταμοῖο ῥοῇσιν.
δή ῥα τότ' ἀμφιπόλοισι μετηύδα δῖος Ὀδυσσεύς·
"ἀμφίπολοι, στῆθ' οὕτω ἀπόπροθεν, ὄφρ' ἐγὼ αὐτὸς
ἅλμην ὤμοιιν ἀπολούσομαι, ἀμφὶ δ' ἐλαίῳ
220   χρίσομαι· ἦ γὰρ δηρὸν ἀπὸ χροός ἐστιν ἀλοιφή.
ἄντην δ' οὐκ ἂν ἐγώ γε λοέσσομαι· αἰδέομαι γὰρ
γυμνοῦσθαι κούρῃσιν ἐυπλοκάμοισι μετελθών."
    ὣς ἔφαθ', αἱ δ' ἀπάνευθεν ἴσαν, εἶπον δ' ἄρα κούρῃ.
αὐτὰρ ὁ ἐκ ποταμοῦ χρόα νίζετο δῖος Ὀδυσσεὺς
225   ἅλμην, ἥ οἱ νῶτα καὶ εὐρέας ἄμπεχεν ὤμους,
ἐκ κεφαλῆς δ' ἔσμηχεν ἁλὸς χνόον ἀτρυγέτοιο.
αὐτὰρ ἐπεὶ δὴ πάντα λοέσσατο καὶ λίπ' ἄλειψεν,
ἀμφὶ δὲ εἵματα ἕσσαθ' ἅ οἱ πόρε παρθένος ἀδμής,
τὸν μὲν Ἀθηναίη θῆκεν Διὸς ἐκγεγαυῖα
230   μείζονά τ' εἰσιδέειν καὶ πάσσονα, κὰδ δὲ κάρητος
οὔλας ἧκε κόμας, ὑακινθίνῳ ἄνθει ὁμοίας.
ὡς δ' ὅτε τις χρυσὸν περιχεύεται ἀργύρῳ ἀνὴρ
ἴδρις, ὃν Ἥφαιστος δέδαεν καὶ Παλλὰς Ἀθήνη
τέχνην παντοίην, χαρίεντα δὲ ἔργα τελείει,
235   ὣς ἄρα τῷ κατέχευε χάριν κεφαλῇ τε καὶ ὤμοις.
ἕζετ' ἔπειτ' ἀπάνευθε κιὼν ἐπὶ θῖνα θαλάσσης,
κάλλεϊ καὶ χάρισι στίλβων· θηεῖτο δὲ κούρη.
δή ῥα τότ' ἀμφιπόλοισιν ἐυπλοκάμοισι μετηύδα·
    "κλῦτέ μέν, ἀμφίπολοι λευκώλενοι, ὄφρα τι εἴπω.
240   οὐ πάντων ἀέκητι θεῶν, οἳ Ὄλυμπον ἔχουσιν,
Φαιήκεσσ' ὅδ' ἀνὴρ ἐπιμίσγεται ἀντιθέοισι·

him they put a cloak and tunic for him to wear, and gave him soft olive oil in the flask of gold, and bade him bathe in the streams of the river. Then among the maidens spoke noble Odysseus: "Maidens, stand yonder apart, that by myself I may wash the brine from my shoulders, and anoint myself with olive oil; for indeed it is long since oil came near my skin. But in your presence I will not bathe, and I am ashamed to be naked in the midst of fair-tressed maidens."

So he said and they went apart and told the princess. But with water from the river noble Odysseus washed from his skin the brine which covered his back and broad shoulders, and from his head he wiped the scurf of the barren sea. But when he had washed his whole body and anointed himself with oil, and had put on him the clothes which the unwed maiden had given him, then Athene, the daughter of Zeus, made him taller to look upon and stronger, and from his head she made the locks to flow in curls like the hyacinth flower. And as when a man overlays silver with gold, a cunning workman whom Hephaestus and Pallas Athene have taught all kinds of craft, and full of grace is the work he produces, even so the goddess shed grace upon his head and shoulders. Then he went apart and sat down on the shore of the sea, gleaming with beauty and grace; and the maiden marveled at him, and spoke to her fair-tressed handmaids, saying:

"Listen, white-armed maidens, to what I am about to say. Not without the will of all the gods who hold Olympus does this man come among the godlike Phaeacians.

πρόσθεν μὲν γὰρ δή μοι ἀεικέλιος δέατ' εἶναι,
νῦν δὲ θεοῖσιν ἔοικε, τοὶ οὐρανὸν εὐρὺν ἔχουσιν.
αἲ γὰρ ἐμοὶ τοιόσδε πόσις κεκλημένος εἴη
245 ἐνθάδε ναιετάων, καὶ οἱ ἅδοι αὐτόθι μίμνειν.
ἀλλὰ δότ', ἀμφίπολοι, ξείνῳ βρῶσίν τε πόσιν τε."
        ὣς ἔφαθ', αἱ δ' ἄρα τῆς μάλα μὲν κλύον ἠδ'
        ἐπίθοντο,
πὰρ δ' ἄρ' Ὀδυσσῆι ἔθεσαν βρῶσίν τε πόσιν τε.
ἦ τοι ὁ πῖνε καὶ ἦσθε πολύτλας δῖος Ὀδυσσεὺς
250 ἁρπαλέως· δηρὸν γὰρ ἐδητύος ἦεν ἄπαστος.
        αὐτὰρ Ναυσικάα λευκώλενος ἄλλ' ἐνόησεν·
εἵματ' ἄρα πτύξασα τίθει καλῆς ἐπ' ἀπήνης,
ζεῦξεν δ' ἡμιόνους κρατερώνυχας, ἂν δ' ἔβη αὐτή,
ὤτρυνεν δ' Ὀδυσῆα, ἔπος τ' ἔφατ' ἔκ τ' ὀνόμαζεν·
255 "ὄρσεο δὴ νῦν, ξεῖνε, πόλινδ' ἴμεν, ὄφρα σε πέμψω
πατρὸς ἐμοῦ πρὸς δῶμα δαΐφρονος, ἔνθα σέ φημι
πάντων Φαιήκων εἰδησέμεν ὅσσοι ἄριστοι.
ἀλλὰ μάλ' ὧδ' ἔρδειν, δοκέεις δέ μοι οὐκ ἀπινύσσειν·
ὄφρ' ἂν μέν κ' ἀγροὺς ἴομεν καὶ ἔργ' ἀνθρώπων,
260 τόφρα σὺν ἀμφιπόλοισι μεθ' ἡμιόνους καὶ ἄμαξαν
καρπαλίμως ἔρχεσθαι· ἐγὼ δ' ὁδὸν ἡγεμονεύσω.
αὐτὰρ ἐπὴν πόλιος ἐπιβήομεν, ἣν πέρι πύργος
ὑψηλός, καλὸς δὲ λιμὴν ἑκάτερθε πόληος,
λεπτὴ δ' εἰσίθμη· νῆες δ' ὁδὸν ἀμφιέλισσαι
265 εἰρύαται· πᾶσιν γὰρ ἐπίστιόν ἐστιν ἑκάστῳ.
ἔνθα δέ τέ σφ' ἀγορὴ καλὸν Ποσιδήιον ἀμφίς,
ῥυτοῖσιν λάεσσι κατωρυχέεσσ' ἀραρυῖα.
ἔνθα δὲ νηῶν ὅπλα μελαινάων ἀλέγουσι,

Before, he seemed to me uncouth, but now he is like the gods, who hold broad heaven. Would that such a man as he might be called my husband, dwelling here, and that it might please him to remain here. But come, my maidens; give to the stranger food and drink."

So she spoke, and they readily listened and obeyed, and set before Odysseus food and drink. Then indeed did the much-enduring noble Odysseus drink and eat, ravenously; for long had he been without taste of food.

But white-armed Nausicaa had another thought. She folded the clothes and put them in the beautiful wagon, and yoked the stout-hoofed mules, and mounted the wagon herself. Then she hailed Odysseus, and spoke and addressed him: "Prepare yourself, now, stranger, to go to the city, that I may set you on the way to the house of my wise father, where, I promise you, you shall come to know all the noblest of the Phaeacians. But be sure to do as I suggest, and I think you do not lack understanding: so long as we are passing through the country and the tilled fields of men, go along quickly with the handmaids behind the mules and the wagon, and I will lead the way. But when we are about to enter the city, about which runs a high wall, a handsome harbor lies on either side of the city and the way between is narrow, and curved ships are drawn up along the road, for they all have stations for their ships, each man one for himself. There, too, is their place of assembly around the beautiful temple of Poseidon, marked by huge stones set deep in the earth. Here the men are busied with

πείσματα καὶ σπεῖρα, καὶ ἀποξύνουσιν ἐρετμά.
270 οὐ γὰρ Φαιήκεσσι μέλει βιὸς οὐδὲ φαρέτρη,
ἀλλ' ἱστοὶ καὶ ἐρετμὰ νεῶν καὶ νῆες ἐῖσαι,
ᾗσιν ἀγαλλόμενοι πολιὴν περόωσι θάλασσαν.
τῶν ἀλεείνω φῆμιν ἀδευκέα, μή τις ὀπίσσω
μωμεύῃ· μάλα δ' εἰσὶν ὑπερφίαλοι κατὰ δῆμον·
275 καί νύ τις ὧδ' εἴπῃσι κακώτερος ἀντιβολήσας·
'τίς δ' ὅδε Ναυσικάᾳ ἕπεται καλός τε μέγας τε
ξεῖνος; ποῦ δέ μιν εὗρε; πόσις νύ οἱ ἔσσεται αὐτῇ.
ἦ τινά που πλαγχθέντα κομίσσατο ἧς ἀπὸ νηὸς
ἀνδρῶν τηλεδαπῶν, ἐπεὶ οὔ τινες ἐγγύθεν εἰσίν·
280 ἤ τίς οἱ εὐξαμένῃ πολυάρητος θεὸς ἦλθεν
οὐρανόθεν καταβάς, ἕξει δέ μιν ἤματα πάντα.
βέλτερον, εἰ καὐτή περ ἐποιχομένη πόσιν εὗρεν
ἄλλοθεν· ἦ γὰρ τούσδε γ' ἀτιμάζει κατὰ δῆμον
Φαίηκας, τοί μιν μνῶνται πολέες τε καὶ ἐσθλοί.'
285 ὣς ἐρέουσιν, ἐμοὶ δέ κ' ὀνείδεα ταῦτα γένοιτο.
καὶ δ' ἄλλῃ νεμεσῶ, ἥ τις τοιαῦτά γε ῥέζοι,
ἥ τ' ἀέκητι φίλων πατρὸς καὶ μητρὸς ἐόντων,
ἀνδράσι μίσγηται, πρίν γ' ἀμφάδιον γάμον ἐλθεῖν.
ξεῖνε, σὺ δ' ὦκ'[1] ἐμέθεν ξυνίει ἔπος, ὄφρα τάχιστα
290 πομπῆς καὶ νόστοιο τύχῃς παρὰ πατρὸς ἐμοῖο.
δήεις ἀγλαὸν ἄλσος Ἀθήνης ἄγχι κελεύθου
αἰγείρων· ἐν δὲ κρήνη νάει, ἀμφὶ δὲ λειμών·
ἔνθα δὲ πατρὸς ἐμοῦ τέμενος τεθαλυῖά τ' ἀλωή,
τόσσον ἀπὸ πτόλιος, ὅσσον τε γέγωνε βοήσας.
295 ἔνθα καθεζόμενος μεῖναι χρόνον, εἰς ὅ κεν ἡμεῖς
ἄστυδε ἔλθωμεν καὶ ἱκώμεθα δώματα πατρός.

the tackle of their black ships, with cables and sails, and here they shape the thin oar blades. For the Phaeacians care not for bow or quiver, but for masts and oars of ships, and for the shapely ships, rejoicing in which they cross over the gray sea. It is their evil speech I shun, that hereafter some man may taunt me, for indeed there are insolent folk among the people, and thus might one of the commoner sort say, should he meet us: 'Who is this that follows Nausicaa, a handsome man and tall, a stranger? Where did she find him? No doubt she is about to marry him. She must have brought some storm-tossed fellow from his ship, a distant foreigner, for none are near us—or some god, long prayed for, has come down from heaven in answer to her prayers, and she will have him as her husband all her days. Better so, even if she has gone off and found a husband from another people; for truly she scorns the Phaeacians here in the land, where she has wooers many and noble!' So will they say, and this would become a reproach to me. I, too, would blame another maiden who should do likewise, and in despite of her own father and mother, while they still live, should consort with men before the day of public marriage. No, stranger, quickly hearken to my words, that with all speed you may win from my father an escort and a return to your land. You will find a handsome grove of Athene close to the road, a grove of poplar trees. In it a spring wells up, and round about is a meadow. There is my father's estate and fruitful vineyard, as far from the city as a man's voice carries when he shouts. Sit down there, and wait for a time, until we come to the city and reach the house of my father. But when you think that

---

[1] ὥκ' Aristarchus: ὥδ' MSS

αὐτὰρ ἐπὴν ἡμέας ἔλπῃ ποτὶ δώματ' ἀφῖχθαι,
καὶ τότε Φαιήκων ἴμεν ἐς πόλιν ἠδ' ἐρέεσθαι
δώματα πατρὸς ἐμοῦ μεγαλήτορος Ἀλκινόοιο.

300 ῥεῖα δ' ἀρίγνωτ' ἐστί, καὶ ἂν πάϊς ἡγήσαιτο
νήπιος· οὐ μὲν γάρ τι ἐοικότα τοῖσι τέτυκται
δώματα Φαιήκων, οἷος δόμος Ἀλκινόοιο
ἥρωος. ἀλλ' ὁπότ' ἄν σε δόμοι κεκύθωσι καὶ αὐλή,
ὦκα μάλα μεγάροιο διελθέμεν, ὄφρ' ἂν ἵκηαι

305 μητέρ' ἐμήν· ἡ δ' ἧσται ἐπ' ἐσχάρῃ ἐν πυρὸς αὐγῇ,
ἠλάκατα στρωφῶσ' ἁλιπόρφυρα, θαῦμα ἰδέσθαι,
κίονι κεκλιμένη· δμωαὶ δέ οἱ εἵατ' ὄπισθεν.
ἔνθα δὲ πατρὸς ἐμοῖο θρόνος ποτικέκλιται αὐτῇ,
τῷ ὅ γε οἰνοποτάζει ἐφήμενος ἀθάνατος ὥς.

310 τὸν παραμειψάμενος μητρὸς περὶ γούνασι χεῖρας
βάλλειν ἡμετέρης, ἵνα νόστιμον ἦμαρ ἴδηαι
χαίρων καρπαλίμως, εἰ καὶ μάλα τηλόθεν ἐσσί.
εἴ κέν τοι κείνη γε φίλα φρονέῃσ' ἐνὶ θυμῷ,
ἐλπωρή τοι ἔπειτα φίλους τ' ἰδέειν καὶ ἱκέσθαι

315 οἶκον ἐϋκτίμενον καὶ σὴν ἐς πατρίδα γαῖαν."[1]

ὣς ἄρα φωνήσασ' ἵμασεν μάστιγι φαεινῇ
ἡμιόνους· αἱ δ' ὦκα λίπον ποταμοῖο ῥέεθρα.
αἱ δ' ἐῢ μὲν τρώχων, ἐῢ δὲ πλίσσοντο πόδεσσιν·
ἡ δὲ μάλ' ἡνιόχευεν, ὅπως ἅμ' ἑποίατο πεζοὶ

320 ἀμφίπολοί τ' Ὀδυσεύς τε, νόῳ δ' ἐπέβαλλεν ἱμάσθλην.
δύσετό τ' ἠέλιος καὶ τοὶ κλυτὸν ἄλσος ἵκοντο
ἱρὸν Ἀθηναίης, ἵν' ἄρ' ἕζετο δῖος Ὀδυσσεύς.
αὐτίκ' ἔπειτ' ἠρᾶτο Διὸς κούρῃ μεγάλοιο·
"κλῦθί μευ, αἰγιόχοιο Διὸς τέκος, Ἀτρυτώνη·

we have reached the house, then go to the city of the
Phaeacians and ask for the house of my father, great-
hearted Alcinous. Easily may it be recognized, and even a
child could guide you, a mere infant; for the houses of the
Phaeacians are in no way built of such a kind as is the
palace of the hero Alcinous. But when the house and the
court enclose you, pass quickly through the great hall, till
you come to my mother, who sits at the hearth in the light
of the fire, spinning the purple yarn, a wonder to behold,
leaning against a pillar, and her handmaids sit behind her.
There, too, leaning against the selfsame pillar, is set the
throne of my father, whereon he sits and quaffs his wine,
like an immortal. Pass him by, and throw your arms about
my mother's knees, that you may quickly see with rejoicing
the day of your return, though you have come from never
so far. If in her sight you win favor, then there is hope that
you will see your people, and return to your well-built
house and to your native land."

So saying, she struck the mules with the shining whip,
and they quickly left the streams of the river. Well did they
trot, well did they ply their ambling feet, and she drove
with care that the maidens and Odysseus might follow on
foot, and with judgment did she ply the lash. Then the sun
set, and they came to the glorious grove, sacred to Athene.
There Odysseus sat himself down, and at once made
prayer to the daughter of great Zeus: "Hear me, child of
aegis-bearing Zeus, unwearied one. Listen now to my

---

[1] Lines 313–15 are omitted in many MSS; cf. 7.75–77.

325 νῦν δή πέρ μευ ἄκουσον, ἐπεὶ πάρος οὔ ποτ᾽ ἄκουσας
ῥαιομένου, ὅτε μ᾽ ἔρραιε κλυτὸς ἐννοσίγαιος.
δός μ᾽ ἐς Φαίηκας φίλον ἐλθεῖν ἠδ᾽ ἐλεεινόν."
ὣς ἔφατ᾽ εὐχόμενος, τοῦ δ᾽ ἔκλυε Παλλὰς Ἀθήνη.
αὐτῷ δ᾽ οὔ πω φαίνετ᾽ ἐναντίη· αἴδετο γάρ ῥα
330 πατροκασίγνητον· ὁ δ᾽ ἐπιζαφελῶς μενέαινεν
ἀντιθέῳ Ὀδυσῆι πάρος ἦν γαῖαν ἱκέσθαι.

prayer, since before this you did not listen when I was wrecked, when the glorious Earth-shaker wrecked me. Grant that I may come to the Phaeacians as one to be cherished and pitied."

So he spoke in prayer, and Pallas Athene heard him; but she did not yet appear to him face to face, for she respected her father's brother; he furiously raged against godlike Odysseus, until he reached his own land.

H

ᾮς ὁ μὲν ἔνθ' ἠρᾶτο πολύτλας δῖος Ὀδυσσεύς,
κούρην δὲ προτὶ ἄστυ φέρεν μένος ἡμιόνοιιν.
ἡ δ' ὅτε δὴ οὗ πατρὸς ἀγακλυτὰ δώμαθ' ἵκανε,
στῆσεν ἄρ' ἐν προθύροισι, κασίγνητοι δέ μιν ἀμφὶς
5 ἵσταντ' ἀθανάτοις ἐναλίγκιοι, οἵ ῥ' ὑπ' ἀπήνης
ἡμιόνους ἔλυον ἐσθῆτά τε ἔσφερον εἴσω.
αὐτὴ δ' ἐς θάλαμον ἑὸν ἤιε· δαῖε δέ οἱ πῦρ
γρῆυς Ἀπειραίη, θαλαμηπόλος Εὐρυμέδουσα,
τήν ποτ' Ἀπείρηθεν νέες ἤγαγον ἀμφιέλισσαι·
10 Ἀλκινόῳ δ' αὐτὴν γέρας ἔξελον, οὕνεκα πᾶσιν
Φαιήκεσσιν ἄνασσε, θεοῦ δ' ὣς δῆμος ἄκουεν·
ἡ τρέφε Ναυσικάαν λευκώλενον ἐν μεγάροισιν.
ἡ οἱ πῦρ ἀνέκαιε καὶ εἴσω δόρπον ἐκόσμει.
    καὶ τότ' Ὀδυσσεὺς ὦρτο πόλινδ' ἴμεν· ἀμφὶ δ'
            Ἀθήνη
15 πολλὴν ἠέρα χεῦε φίλα φρονέουσ' Ὀδυσῆι,
μή τις Φαιήκων μεγαθύμων ἀντιβολήσας
κερτομέοι τ' ἐπέεσσι καὶ ἐξερέοιθ' ὅτις εἴη.
ἀλλ' ὅτε δὴ ἄρ' ἔμελλε πόλιν δύσεσθαι ἐραννήν,
ἔνθα οἱ ἀντεβόλησε θεά, γλαυκῶπις Ἀθήνη,
20 παρθενικῇ ἐικυῖα νεήνιδι, κάλπιν ἐχούσῃ.
στῆ δὲ πρόσθ' αὐτοῦ, ὁ δ' ἀνείρετο δῖος Ὀδυσσεύς·

BOOK 7

So he prayed there, the much-enduring noble Odysseus, while the two strong mules bore the maiden to the city. When she had come to the glorious palace of her father, she halted the mules at the outer gate, and her brothers crowded about her, men like the immortals, and unhitched the mules from the wagon, and took the clothing inside; and she herself went to her chamber. There a fire was kindled for her by her waiting-woman, Eurymedusa, an aged lady from Apeirê. Long ago the curved ships had brought her from Apeirê, and men had chosen her from the spoil as a gift of honor for Alcinous, because he was king over all the Phaeacians, and the people hearkened to him as to a god. She it was who had reared the white-armed Nausicaa in the palace, and she it was who kindled a fire for her, and made ready her supper in the chamber.

Then Odysseus roused himself to go to the city, and Athene, with kindly purpose, poured about him a thick mist, that no one of the great-hearted Phaeacians, meeting him, should challenge him, and ask him who he was. But when he was about to enter the lovely city, then the goddess, flashing-eyed Athene, met him in the guise of a young maiden carrying a pitcher, and she stood before him; and noble Odysseus questioned her, saying:

"ὦ τέκος, οὐκ ἄν μοι δόμον ἀνέρος ἡγήσαιο
Ἀλκινόου, ὃς τοῖσδε μετ' ἀνθρώποισι ἀνάσσει;
καὶ γὰρ ἐγὼ ξεῖνος ταλαπείριος ἐνθάδ' ἱκάνω
25 τηλόθεν ἐξ ἀπίης γαίης· τῷ οὔ τινα οἶδα
ἀνθρώπων, οἳ τήνδε πόλιν καὶ γαῖαν ἔχουσιν."[1]
τὸν δ' αὖτε προσέειπε θεά, γλαυκῶπις Ἀθήνη·
"τοιγὰρ ἐγώ τοι, ξεῖνε πάτερ, δόμον, ὅν με κελεύεις,
δείξω, ἐπεί μοι πατρὸς ἀμύμονος ἐγγύθι ναίει.
30 ἀλλ' ἴθι σιγῇ τοῖον, ἐγὼ δ' ὁδὸν ἡγεμονεύσω,
μηδέ τιν' ἀνθρώπων προτιόσσεο μηδ' ἐρέεινε.
οὐ γὰρ ξείνους οἷδε μάλ' ἀνθρώπους ἀνέχονται,
οὐδ' ἀγαπαζόμενοι φιλέουσ' ὅς κ' ἄλλοθεν ἔλθῃ.
νηυσὶ θοῇσιν τοί γε πεποιθότες ὠκείῃσι
35 λαῖτμα μέγ' ἐκπερόωσιν, ἐπεί σφισι δῶκ' ἐνοσίχθων·
τῶν νέες ὠκεῖαι ὡς εἰ πτερὸν ἠὲ νόημα."
ὣς ἄρα φωνήσασ' ἡγήσατο Παλλὰς Ἀθήνη
καρπαλίμως· ὁ δ' ἔπειτα μετ' ἴχνια βαῖνε θεοῖο.
τὸν δ' ἄρα Φαίηκες ναυσικλυτοὶ οὐκ ἐνόησαν
40 ἐρχόμενον κατὰ ἄστυ διὰ σφέας· οὐ γὰρ Ἀθήνη
εἴα ἐυπλόκαμος, δεινὴ θεός, ἥ ῥά οἱ ἀχλὺν
θεσπεσίην κατέχευε φίλα φρονέουσ' ἐνὶ θυμῷ.
θαύμαζεν δ' Ὀδυσεὺς λιμένας καὶ νῆας ἐίσας
αὐτῶν θ' ἡρώων ἀγορὰς καὶ τείχεα μακρὰ
45 ὑψηλά, σκολόπεσσιν ἀρηρότα, θαῦμα ἰδέσθαι.
ἀλλ' ὅτε δὴ βασιλῆος ἀγακλυτὰ δώμαθ' ἵκοντο,
τοῖσι δὲ μύθων ἦρχε θεά, γλαυκῶπις Ἀθήνη·
"οὗτος δή τοι, ξεῖνε πάτερ, δόμος, ὅν με κελεύεις

[1] γαῖαν ἔχουσιν: ἔργα νέμονται

248

BOOK 7

"My child, could you not guide me to the house of him they call Alcinous, who is lord among the people here? For I come here a much-tried stranger from afar, from a distant country; therefore I know no one of the people who possess this city and land."

Then the goddess, flashing-eyed Athene, answered him: "Then indeed, father stranger, I will show you the house you ask for, for Alcinous lives close by my flawless father. Only go in silence, and I will lead the way; do not turn your eyes on any man nor question any, for the people here have not much patience with strangers, nor do they give kindly welcome to him who comes from another land. Relying on the speed of their ships, these people cross over the great gulf of the sea, for this the Earth-shaker has granted them; and their ships are swift as a bird on the wing or as a thought."

So speaking, Pallas Athene led the way quickly, and he followed in the footsteps of the goddess. Nor did the Phaeacians, famed for their ships, notice him as he went through the city in the midst of them, for Athene, the dread goddess, did not allow it, but poured about him a magic mist, for her heart was kind toward him. And Odysseus marveled at the harbors and the shapely ships, at the meeting places where the heroes themselves gathered, and the walls, long and high and crowned with palisades, a wonder to behold. But when they had come to the glorious palace of the king, the goddess, flashing-eyed Athene, was the first to speak, saying:

"Here, father stranger, is the house which you asked me

πεφραδέμεν· δήεις δὲ διοτρεφέας βασιλῆας
50 δαίτην δαινυμένους· σὺ δ' ἔσω κίε, μηδέ τι θυμῷ
τάρβει· θαρσαλέος γὰρ ἀνὴρ ἐν πᾶσιν ἀμείνων
ἔργοισιν τελέθει, εἰ καί ποθεν ἄλλοθεν ἔλθοι.
δέσποιναν μὲν πρῶτα κιχήσεαι ἐν μεγάροισιν·
Ἀρήτη δ' ὄνομ' ἐστὶν ἐπώνυμον, ἐκ δὲ τοκήων
55 τῶν αὐτῶν οἵ περ τέκον Ἀλκίνοον βασιλῆα.
Ναυσίθοον μὲν πρῶτα Ποσειδάων ἐνοσίχθων
γείνατο καὶ Περίβοια, γυναικῶν εἶδος ἀρίστη,
ὁπλοτάτη θυγάτηρ μεγαλήτορος Εὐρυμέδοντος,
ὅς ποθ' ὑπερθύμοισι Γιγάντεσσιν βασίλευεν.
60 ἀλλ' ὁ μὲν ὤλεσε λαὸν ἀτάσθαλον, ὤλετο δ' αὐτός·
τῇ δὲ Ποσειδάων ἐμίγη καὶ ἐγείνατο παῖδα
Ναυσίθοον μεγάθυμον, ὃς ἐν Φαίηξιν ἄνασσε·
Ναυσίθοος δ' ἔτεκεν Ῥηξήνορά τ' Ἀλκίνοόν τε.
τὸν μὲν ἄκουρον ἐόντα βάλ' ἀργυρότοξος Ἀπόλλων
65 νυμφίον ἐν μεγάρῳ, μίαν οἴην παῖδα λιπόντα
Ἀρήτην· τὴν δ' Ἀλκίνοος ποιήσατ' ἄκοιτιν,
καί μιν ἔτισ', ὡς οὔ τις ἐπὶ χθονὶ τίεται ἄλλη,
ὅσσαι νῦν γε γυναῖκες ὑπ' ἀνδράσιν οἶκον ἔχουσιν.
ὣς κείνη περὶ κῆρι τετίμηταί τε καὶ ἔστιν
70 ἔκ τε φίλων παίδων ἔκ τ' αὐτοῦ Ἀλκινόοιο
καὶ λαῶν, οἵ μίν ῥα θεὸν ὣς εἰσορόωντες
δειδέχαται μύθοισιν, ὅτε στείχῃσ' ἀνὰ ἄστυ.
οὐ μὲν γάρ τι νόου γε καὶ αὐτὴ δεύεται ἐσθλοῦ·
οἷσι τ' ἐὺ φρονέῃσι καὶ ἀνδράσι νείκεα λύει.
75 εἴ κέν τοι κείνη γε φίλα φρονέῃσ' ἐνὶ θυμῷ,
ἐλπωρή τοι ἔπειτα φίλους τ' ἰδέειν καὶ ἱκέσθαι

to show to you, and you will find the kings, fostered by Zeus, feasting at the banquet. Go inside, and let your heart fear nothing; for a bold man does better in all things, even when he is a stranger from another land. The first person you will come upon in the palace hall is the queen; Arete is the name by which she is called, and she is sprung from the same line as the king Alcinous. First Nausithous was born from the earth-shaker Poseidon and Periboea, the best in looks of women, youngest daughter of great-hearted Eurymedon, who once was king over the insolent Giants. But he brought destruction on his reckless people, and was himself destroyed. But Poseidon lay with Periboea and begat a son, great-hearted Nausithous, who ruled over the Phaeacians; and Nausithous begat Rhexenor and Alcinous. Rhexenor, when as yet he had no son, Apollo of the silver bow struck down in his hall while yet a bridegroom, and he left only one daughter, Arete. Her Alcinous made his wife, and honored her as no other woman on earth is honored, of all those who in these days direct their households in subjection to their husbands; so heartily is she honored, and has ever been, by her children and by Alcinous himself and by the people, who look upon her as upon a goddess, and greet her as she goes through the city. For she of herself is in no way lacking in good understanding, and settles the quarrels of those to whom she has good will, even if they are men. If in her sight you win favor, then there is hope that you will see your own people, and will return to your

οἶκον ἐς ὑψόροφον καὶ σὴν ἐς πατρίδα γαῖαν."

ὣς ἄρα φωνήσασ' ἀπέβη γλαυκῶπις Ἀθήνη
πόντον ἐπ' ἀτρύγετον, λίπε δὲ Σχερίην ἐρατεινήν,
80 ἵκετο δ' ἐς Μαραθῶνα καὶ εὐρυάγυιαν Ἀθήνην,
δῦνε δ' Ἐρεχθῆος πυκινὸν δόμον. αὐτὰρ Ὀδυσσεὺς
Ἀλκινόου πρὸς δώματ' ἴε κλυτά· πολλὰ δέ οἱ κῆρ
ὥρμαιν' ἱσταμένῳ, πρὶν χάλκεον οὐδὸν ἱκέσθαι.
ὥς τε γὰρ ἠελίου αἴγλη πέλεν ἠὲ σελήνης
85 δῶμα καθ' ὑψερεφὲς μεγαλήτορος Ἀλκινόοιο.
χάλκεοι μὲν γὰρ τοῖχοι ἐληλέδατ' ἔνθα καὶ ἔνθα,
ἐς μυχὸν ἐξ οὐδοῦ, περὶ δὲ θριγκὸς κυάνοιο·
χρύσειαι δὲ θύραι πυκινὸν δόμον ἐντὸς ἔεργον·
σταθμοὶ δ' ἀργύρεοι ἐν χαλκέῳ ἕστασαν οὐδῷ,
90 ἀργύρεον δ' ἐφ' ὑπερθύριον, χρυσέη δὲ κορώνη.
χρύσειοι δ' ἑκάτερθε καὶ ἀργύρεοι κύνες ἦσαν,
οὓς Ἥφαιστος ἔτευξεν ἰδυίῃσι πραπίδεσσι
δῶμα φυλασσέμεναι μεγαλήτορος Ἀλκινόοιο,
ἀθανάτους ὄντας καὶ ἀγήρως ἤματα πάντα.
95 ἐν δὲ θρόνοι περὶ τοῖχον ἐρηρέδατ' ἔνθα καὶ ἔνθα,
ἐς μυχὸν ἐξ οὐδοῖο διαμπερές, ἔνθ' ἐνὶ πέπλοι
λεπτοὶ ἐΰννητοι βεβλήατο, ἔργα γυναικῶν.
ἔνθα δὲ Φαιήκων ἡγήτορες ἑδριόωντο
πίνοντες καὶ ἔδοντες· ἐπηετανὸν γὰρ ἔχεσκον.
100 χρύσειοι δ' ἄρα κοῦροι ἐϋδμήτων ἐπὶ βωμῶν
ἕστασαν αἰθομένας δαΐδας μετὰ χερσὶν ἔχοντες,
φαίνοντες νύκτας κατὰ δώματα δαιτυμόνεσσι.
πεντήκοντα δέ οἱ δμωαὶ κατὰ δῶμα γυναῖκες
αἱ μὲν ἀλετρεύουσι μύλῃς ἔπι μήλοπα καρπόν,

high-roofed house and to your native land."

So saying, flashing-eyed Athene departed over the barren sea, and left lovely Scheria. She came to Marathon and broad-wayed Athens, and entered the well-built house of Erectheus; but Odysseus went to the glorious palace of Alcinous. There he stood, and his heart pondered much before he reached the threshold of bronze; for there was a gleam as of sun or moon over the high-roofed house of great-hearted Alcinous. Of bronze were the walls that stretched this way and that from the threshold to the innermost chamber, surmounted by a cornice of cyanus.[a] Golden were the doors that shut in the well-built house, and doorposts of silver were set in a threshold of bronze. Of silver was the lintel above, and of gold the handle. On either side of the door there stood gold and silver dogs, which Hephaestus had fashioned with cunning skill to guard the palace of great-hearted Alcinous; immortal they were and ageless all their days.[b] Within, seats were fixed along the wall on either hand, from the threshold to the innermost chamber, and on them were thrown robes of soft fabric, cunningly woven, the handiwork of women. On these the leaders of the Phaeacians were wont to sit drinking and eating, for they lived in unfailing abundance. And golden youths stood on well-built pedestals, holding lighted torches in their hands to give light by night to the banqueters in the hall. And fifty slave women he had in the house, of whom some grind the yellow grain on the mill-

[a] A blue enamel, or glass paste, imitating lapis lazuli. M.

[b] The dogs, though wrought of gold and silver, are thought of as alive. The Phaeacians live in fairyland. M.

105 αἱ δ' ἱστοὺς ὑφόωσι καὶ ἠλάκατα στρωφῶσιν
    ἥμεναι, οἷά τε φύλλα μακεδνῆς αἰγείροιο·
    καιρουσσέων δ' ὀθονέων ἀπολείβεται ὑγρὸν ἔλαιον.
    ὅσσον Φαίηκες περὶ πάντων ἴδριες ἀνδρῶν
    νῆα θοὴν ἐνὶ πόντῳ ἐλαυνέμεν, ὣς δὲ γυναῖκες
110 ἱστῶν τεχνῆσσαι· πέρι γάρ σφισι δῶκεν Ἀθήνη
    ἔργα τ' ἐπίστασθαι περικαλλέα καὶ φρένας ἐσθλάς.
    ἔκτοσθεν δ' αὐλῆς μέγας ὄρχατος ἄγχι θυράων
    τετράγυος· περὶ δ' ἕρκος ἐλήλαται ἀμφοτέρωθεν.
    ἔνθα δὲ δένδρεα μακρὰ πεφύκασι τηλεθόωντα,
115 ὄγχναι καὶ ῥοιαὶ καὶ μηλέαι ἀγλαόκαρποι
    συκέαι τε γλυκεραὶ καὶ ἐλαῖαι τηλεθόωσαι.
    τάων οὔ ποτε καρπὸς ἀπόλλυται οὐδ' ἀπολείπει
    χείματος οὐδὲ θέρευς, ἐπετήσιος· ἀλλὰ μάλ' αἰεὶ
    Ζεφυρίη πνείουσα τὰ μὲν φύει, ἄλλα δὲ πέσσει.
120 ὄγχνη ἐπ' ὄγχνῃ γηράσκει, μῆλον δ' ἐπὶ μήλῳ,
    αὐτὰρ ἐπὶ σταφυλῇ σταφυλή, σῦκον δ' ἐπὶ σύκῳ.
    ἔνθα δέ οἱ πολύκαρπος ἀλωὴ ἐρρίζωται,
    τῆς ἕτερον μὲν θειλόπεδον λευρῷ ἐνὶ χώρῳ
    τέρσεται ἠελίῳ, ἑτέρας δ' ἄρα τε τρυγόωσιν,
125 ἄλλας δὲ τραπέουσι· πάροιθε δέ τ' ὄμφακές εἰσιν
    ἄνθος ἀφιεῖσαι, ἕτεραι δ' ὑποπερκάζουσιν.
    ἔνθα δὲ κοσμηταὶ πρασιαὶ παρὰ νείατον ὄρχον
    παντοῖαι πεφύασιν, ἐπηετανὸν γανόωσαι·
    ἐν δὲ δύω κρῆναι ἡ μέν τ' ἀνὰ κῆπον ἅπαντα
130 σκίδναται, ἡ δ' ἑτέρωθεν ὑπ' αὐλῆς οὐδὸν ἵησι
    πρὸς δόμον ὑψηλόν, ὅθεν ὑδρεύοντο πολῖται.
    τοῖ' ἄρ' ἐν Ἀλκινόοιο θεῶν ἔσαν ἀγλαὰ δῶρα.

stone, and others weave fabrics, or, as they sit, twirl the yarn, busy as the leaves of a tall poplar tree; and from the closely woven fabrics the soft olive oil drips down. For as the Phaeacian men above all others are skilled in speeding a swift ship upon the sea, so are the women cunning workers at the loom; for Athene has given to them above all others knowledge of beautiful handiwork, and excellent character. Outside the courtyard, close to the doors, is a great orchard of four acres, and a hedge runs about it on each side. In it grow trees tall and luxuriant, pears and pomegranates and apple trees with their bright fruit, and sweet figs, and luxuriant olives. The fruit of these neither perishes nor fails in winter or in summer, but lasts throughout the year; and continually the West Wind, as it blows, quickens to life some fruits, and ripens others; pear upon pear waxes ripe, apple upon apple, grape bunch upon grape bunch, and fig upon fig. There, too, is his fruitful vineyard planted, one part of which, a warm spot on level ground, is for drying in the sun, while other grapes men are gathering, and others, too, they are treading; but in front are unripe grapes that are shedding the blossom, and others that are turning purple. There again, by the last row of the vines, grow trim garden beds of every sort, blooming the year through, and in the orchard are two springs, one of which sends its water throughout all the garden, while the other, opposite to it, flows beneath the threshold of the court toward the high house; from this the townsfolk draw their water. Such were the glorious gifts of the gods at the dwelling of Alcinous.

ἔνθα στὰς θηεῖτο πολύτλας δῖος Ὀδυσσεύς.
αὐτὰρ ἐπεὶ δὴ πάντα ἑῷ θηήσατο θυμῷ,
135　καρπαλίμως ὑπὲρ οὐδὸν ἐβήσετο δώματος εἴσω.
εὗρε δὲ Φαιήκων ἡγήτορας ἠδὲ μέδοντας
σπένδοντας δεπάεσσιν ἐυσκόπῳ ἀργεϊφόντῃ,
ᾧ πυμάτῳ σπένδεσκον, ὅτε μνησαίατο κοίτου.
αὐτὰρ ὁ βῆ διὰ δῶμα πολύτλας δῖος Ὀδυσσεὺς
140　πολλὴν ἠέρ' ἔχων, ἥν οἱ περίχευεν Ἀθήνη,
ὄφρ' ἵκετ' Ἀρήτην τε καὶ Ἀλκίνοον βασιλῆα.
ἀμφὶ δ' ἄρ' Ἀρήτης βάλε γούνασι χεῖρας Ὀδυσσεύς,
καὶ τότε δή ῥ' αὐτοῖο πάλιν χύτο θέσφατος ἀήρ.
οἱ δ' ἄνεῳ ἐγένοντο, δόμον κάτα φῶτα ἰδόντες·
145　θαύμαζον δ' ὁρόωντες. ὁ δὲ λιτάνευεν Ὀδυσσεύς·

"Ἀρήτη, θύγατερ Ῥηξήνορος ἀντιθέοιο,
σόν τε πόσιν σά τε γούναθ' ἱκάνω πολλὰ μογήσας
τούσδε τε δαιτυμόνας· τοῖσιν θεοὶ ὄλβια δοῖεν
ζωέμεναι, καὶ παισὶν ἐπιτρέψειεν ἕκαστος
150　κτήματ' ἐνὶ μεγάροισι γέρας θ' ὅ τι δῆμος ἔδωκεν·
αὐτὰρ ἐμοὶ πομπὴν ὀτρύνετε πατρίδ' ἱκέσθαι
θᾶσσον, ἐπεὶ δὴ δηθὰ φίλων ἄπο πήματα πάσχω."

ὣς εἰπὼν κατ' ἄρ' ἕζετ' ἐπ' ἐσχάρῃ ἐν κονίῃσιν
πὰρ πυρί· οἱ δ' ἄρα πάντες ἀκὴν ἐγένοντο σιωπῇ.
155　ὀψὲ δὲ δὴ μετέειπε γέρων ἥρως Ἐχένηος,
ὃς δὴ Φαιήκων ἀνδρῶν προγενέστερος ἦεν
καὶ μύθοισι κέκαστο, παλαιά τε πολλά τε εἰδώς·
ὅ σφιν ἐὺ φρονέων ἀγορήσατο καὶ μετέειπεν·

"Ἀλκίνο', οὐ μέν τοι τόδε κάλλιον, οὐδὲ ἔοικε,
160　ξεῖνον μὲν χαμαὶ ἧσθαι ἐπ' ἐσχάρῃ ἐν κονίῃσιν,

There the much-enduring noble Odysseus stood and gazed. But when he had marveled in his heart at all this, he passed quickly over the threshold into the house. There he found the leaders and counselors of the Phaeacians pouring libations from their cups to the keen-sighted Argeïphontes,[a] to whom they were accustomed to pour the wine last of all, when it seemed to them time to go to their rest. But the much-enduring noble Odysseus went through the hall, wrapped in the thick mist which Athene had shed upon him, till he came to Arete and to Alcinous the king. About the knees of Arete Odysseus threw his arms, and there and then the wondrous mist melted from him, and a hush fell upon all that were in the room at the sight of the man, and they marveled as they looked upon him. Odysseus then made his prayer:

"Arete, daughter of godlike Rhexenor, to your husband and to your knees have I come suppliant after many toils, and to these banqueters, too, to whom may the gods grant happiness in life, and may each of them hand down to his children the wealth in his halls, and the dues of honor which the people have given him. But grant me speedy conveyance, that I may come to my native land, and quickly; for it is a long time that I have been suffering woes far from my people."

So saying he sat down on the hearth in the ashes by the fire, and they were all hushed in silence. At length there spoke among them the hero Echeneüs, who was an elder among the Phaeacians, well skilled in speech, and understanding all the wisdom of old. He with good intent addressed the assembly, and said: "Alcinous, lo, this is not the better way, nor is it proper, that a stranger should sit

[a] Hermes. D.

οἵδε δὲ σὸν μῦθον ποτιδέγμενοι ἰσχανόωνται.
ἀλλ' ἄγε δὴ ξεῖνον μὲν ἐπὶ θρόνου ἀργυροήλου
εἶσον ἀναστήσας, σὺ δὲ κηρύκεσσι κέλευσον
οἶνον ἐπικρῆσαι, ἵνα καὶ Διὶ τερπικεραύνῳ
165　σπείσομεν, ὅς θ' ἱκέτῃσιν ἅμ' αἰδοίοισιν ὀπηδεῖ·
δόρπον δὲ ξείνῳ ταμίη δότω ἔνδον ἐόντων."
　　αὐτὰρ ἐπεὶ τό γ' ἄκουσ' ἱερὸν μένος Ἀλκινόοιο,
χειρὸς ἑλὼν Ὀδυσῆα δαΐφρονα ποικιλομήτην
ὦρσεν ἀπ' ἐσχαρόφιν καὶ ἐπὶ θρόνου εἷσε φαεινοῦ,
170　υἱὸν ἀναστήσας ἀγαπήνορα Λαοδάμαντα,
ὅς οἱ πλησίον ἷζε, μάλιστα δέ μιν φιλέεσκεν.
χέρνιβα δ' ἀμφίπολος προχόῳ ἐπέχευε φέρουσα
καλῇ χρυσείῃ ὑπὲρ ἀργυρέοιο λέβητος,
νίψασθαι· παρὰ δὲ ξεστὴν ἐτάνυσσε τράπεζαν.
175　σῖτον δ' αἰδοίη ταμίη παρέθηκε φέρουσα,
εἴδατα πόλλ' ἐπιθεῖσα, χαριζομένη παρεόντων.
αὐτὰρ ὁ πῖνε καὶ ἦσθε πολύτλας δῖος Ὀδυσσεύς.
καὶ τότε κήρυκα προσέφη μένος Ἀλκινόοιο·
　　"Ποντόνοε, κρητῆρα κερασσάμενος μέθυ νεῖμον
180　πᾶσιν ἀνὰ μέγαρον, ἵνα καὶ Διὶ τερπικεραύνῳ
σπείσομεν, ὅς θ' ἱκέτῃσιν ἅμ' αἰδοίοισιν ὀπηδεῖ."
　　ὣς φάτο, Ποντόνοος δὲ μελίφρονα οἶνον ἐκίρνα,
νώμησεν δ' ἄρα πᾶσιν ἐπαρξάμενος δεπάεσσιν.
αὐτὰρ ἐπεὶ σπεῖσάν τ' ἔπιόν θ', ὅσον ἤθελε θυμός,
185　τοῖσιν δ' Ἀλκίνοος ἀγορήσατο καὶ μετέειπε·
　　"κέκλυτε, Φαιήκων ἡγήτορες ἠδὲ μέδοντες
ὄφρ' εἴπω τά με θυμὸς ἐνὶ στήθεσσι κελεύει.

upon the ground on the hearth in the ashes; but these others hold back waiting for your word. Come, raise the stranger to his feet and set him upon a silver-studded chair; bid the heralds mix wine, that we may pour libations also to Zeus, who hurls the thunderbolt; for he walks in the footsteps of reverend suppliants. And let the housekeeper give supper to the stranger from what she has within."

When the divine might of Alcinous[a] heard this, he took by the hand Odysseus, the wise and crafty-minded, and raised him from the hearth, and set him upon a bright chair from which he bade his son, the kindly Laodamas, to rise; for he sat next to him, and was his best beloved. Then a handmaid brought water for the hands in a beautiful pitcher of gold, and poured it over a silver basin, for him to wash, and beside him drew up a polished table. And the revered housekeeper brought and set before him bread, and with it dainties in abundance, giving freely of what she had. So the much-enduring noble Odysseus drank and ate; and then the divine might of Alcinous spoke to the herald, and said:

"Pontonous, mix the bowl, and serve wine to all in the hall, that we may pour libations also to Zeus, who hurls the thunderbolt; for he walks in the footsteps of reverend suppliants."

He spoke, and Pontonous mixed the honey-hearted wine, and served out to all, pouring first drops for libation into the cups. But when they had poured libations, and had drunk to their heart's content, Alcinous addressed the assembly, and spoke among them:

"Listen to me, leaders and counselors of the Phaeacians, that I may say what the heart in my breast bids me.

[a] See note on 2.409.

νῦν μὲν δαισάμενοι κατακείετε οἴκαδ' ἰόντες·
ἠῶθεν δὲ γέροντας ἐπὶ πλέονας καλέσαντες
190 ξεῖνον ἐνὶ μεγάροις ξεινίσσομεν ἠδὲ θεοῖσιν
ῥέξομεν ἱερὰ καλά, ἔπειτα δὲ καὶ περὶ πομπῆς
μνησόμεθ', ὥς χ' ὁ ξεῖνος ἄνευθε πόνου καὶ ἀνίης
πομπῇ ὑφ' ἡμετέρῃ ἥν πατρίδα γαῖαν ἵκηται
χαίρων καρπαλίμως, εἰ καὶ μάλα τηλόθεν ἐστί,
195 μηδέ τι μεσσηγύς γε κακὸν καὶ πῆμα πάθῃσι,
πρίν γε τὸν ἧς γαίης ἐπιβήμεναι· ἔνθα δ' ἔπειτα
πείσεται, ἅσσα οἱ αἶσα κατὰ κλῶθές τε βαρεῖαι
γιγνομένῳ νήσαντο λίνῳ, ὅτε μιν τέκε μήτηρ.
εἰ δέ τις ἀθανάτων γε κατ' οὐρανοῦ εἰλήλουθεν,
200 ἄλλο τι δὴ τόδ' ἔπειτα θεοὶ περιμηχανόωνται.
αἰεὶ γὰρ τὸ πάρος γε θεοὶ φαίνονται ἐναργεῖς
ἡμῖν, εὖτ' ἔρδωμεν ἀγακλειτὰς ἑκατόμβας,
δαίνυνταί τε παρ' ἄμμι καθήμενοι ἔνθα περ ἡμεῖς.
εἰ δ' ἄρα τις καὶ μοῦνος ἰὼν ξύμβληται ὁδίτης,
205 οὔ τι κατακρύπτουσιν, ἐπεί σφισιν ἐγγύθεν εἰμέν,
ὥς περ Κύκλωπές τε καὶ ἄγρια φῦλα Γιγάντων."
    τὸν δ' ἀπαμειβόμενος προσέφη πολύμητις Ὀδυσσεύς·
"Ἀλκίνο', ἄλλο τί τοι μελέτω φρεσίν· οὐ γὰρ ἐγώ γε
ἀθανάτοισιν ἔοικα, τοὶ οὐρανὸν εὐρὺν ἔχουσιν,
210 οὐ δέμας οὐδὲ φυήν, ἀλλὰ θνητοῖσι βροτοῖσιν.
οὕς τινας ὑμεῖς ἴστε μάλιστ' ὀχέοντας ὀιζὺν
ἀνθρώπων, τοῖσίν κεν ἐν ἄλγεσιν ἰσωσαίμην.
καὶ δ' ἔτι κεν καὶ μᾶλλον[1] ἐγὼ κακὰ μυθησαίμην,
ὅσσα γε δὴ ξύμπαντα θεῶν ἰότητι μόγησα.
215 ἀλλ' ἐμὲ μὲν δορπῆσαι ἐάσατε κηδόμενόν περ·

Now that you have finished your feast, go each of you to his house to rest. In the morning we will call more of the elders together, and will entertain the stranger in our halls and offer choice victims to the gods. After that we will take thought also of his conveyance, that without toil or pain the stranger may under our conveyance come to his native land speedily and with rejoicing, though he come from never so far. Nor shall he meanwhile suffer any evil or harm, until he sets foot upon his own land; but thereafter he shall suffer whatever fate and the dread spinners spun with their thread for him at his birth, when his mother bore him. But if he is one of the immortals come down from heaven, then this is some new thing which the gods are planning; for always before this they have appeared before us in manifest form, when we sacrifice to them glorious hecatombs, and they feast among us, sitting where we sit. Not only that, but if one of us walking the roads alone meets them, they use no concealment, for we are near of kin to them, as are the Cyclopes and the wild tribes of the Giants."

The resourceful Odysseus answered him and said: "Alcinous, far from you be that thought; for I am not like the immortals, who hold broad heaven, either in stature or in form, but like mortal men. Whoever you know of men who bear the greatest burden of woe, to them might I liken myself in my sorrows. Yes, and I could tell a yet longer tale of all the evils which I have endured by the will of the gods. But as for me, allow me now to eat, despite my grief; for

---

[1] μᾶλλον: πλεῖον'

οὐ γάρ τι στυγερῇ ἐπὶ γαστέρι κύντερον ἄλλο
ἔπλετο, ἥ τ᾽ ἐκέλευσεν ἕο μνήσασθαι ἀνάγκῃ
καὶ μάλα τειρόμενον καὶ ἐνὶ φρεσὶ πένθος ἔχοντα,
ὡς καὶ ἐγὼ πένθος μὲν ἔχω φρεσίν, ἡ δὲ μάλ᾽ αἰεὶ
220   ἐσθέμεναι κέλεται καὶ πινέμεν, ἐκ δέ με πάντων
ληθάνει ὅσσ᾽ ἔπαθον, καὶ ἐνιπλησθῆναι ἀνώγει.
ὑμεῖς δ᾽ ὀτρύνεσθαι ἅμ᾽ ἠοῖ φαινομένηφιν,
ὥς κ᾽ ἐμὲ τὸν δύστηνον ἐμῆς ἐπιβήσετε πάτρης
καί περ πολλὰ παθόντα· ἰδόντα με καὶ λίποι αἰὼν
225   κτῆσιν ἐμήν, δμῶάς τε καὶ ὑψερεφὲς μέγα δῶμα."
   ὣς ἔφαθ᾽, οἱ δ᾽ ἄρα πάντες ἐπήνεον ἠδ᾽ ἐκέλευον
πεμπέμεναι τὸν ξεῖνον, ἐπεὶ κατὰ μοῖραν ἔειπεν.
αὐτὰρ ἐπεὶ σπεῖσάν τ᾽ ἔπιον θ᾽ ὅσον ἤθελε θυμός,
οἱ μὲν κακκείοντες ἔβαν οἰκόνδε ἕκαστος,
230   αὐτὰρ ὁ ἐν μεγάρῳ ὑπελείπετο δῖος Ὀδυσσεύς,
πὰρ δέ οἱ Ἀρήτη τε καὶ Ἀλκίνοος θεοειδὴς
ἥσθην· ἀμφίπολοι δ᾽ ἀπεκόσμεον ἔντεα δαιτός.
τοῖσιν δ᾽ Ἀρήτη λευκώλενος ἤρχετο μύθων·
ἔγνω γὰρ φᾶρός τε χιτῶνά τε εἵματ᾽ ἰδοῦσα
235   καλά, τά ῥ᾽ αὐτὴ τεῦξε σὺν ἀμφιπόλοισι γυναιξί·
καί μιν φωνήσασ᾽ ἔπεα πτερόεντα προσηύδα·
   "ξεῖνε, τὸ μέν σε πρῶτον ἐγὼν εἰρήσομαι αὐτή·
τίς πόθεν εἰς ἀνδρῶν; τίς τοι τάδε εἵματ᾽ ἔδωκεν;
οὐ δὴ φῂς ἐπὶ πόντον ἀλώμενος ἐνθάδ᾽ ἱκέσθαι;"
240   τὴν δ᾽ ἀπαμειβόμενος προσέφη πολύμητις Ὀδυσσεύς·
"ἀργαλέον, βασίλεια, διηνεκέως ἀγορεῦσαι
κήδε᾽, ἐπεί μοι πολλὰ δόσαν θεοὶ Οὐρανίωνες·
τοῦτο δέ τοι ἐρέω ὅ μ᾽ ἀνείρεαι ἠδὲ μεταλλᾷς.

there is nothing more shameless than one's hateful belly, which bids a man perforce take thought of it, be he never so sadly distressed and laden with grief at heart, even as I too am laden with grief at heart, yet constantly does my belly bid me eat and drink, and makes me forget all that I have suffered, and commands that it be filled. But do you make haste at break of day, that you may set me, unfortunate that I am, on the soil of my native land, even after many woes. Yes, even let life leave me, once I have seen my possessions, my slaves, and my great high-roofed house."

So he spoke, and they all praised his words, and urged sending the stranger on his way, since he had spoken fittingly. Then when they had poured libations, and had drunk to their hearts' content, they went each man to his home, to take their rest, and noble Odysseus was left behind in the hall, and beside him sat Arete and godlike Alcinous; and the handmaids cleared away the dishes of the feast. Then white-armed Arete was the first to speak; for she recognized his mantle and tunic as soon as she saw the beautiful clothes which she herself had made with the help of her handmaids. And she spoke, and addressed him with winged words.

"Stranger, this question will I myself ask you first. Who are you among men, and from where? Who gave you these clothes? Did you not say that you came here wandering over the sea?"

Then resourceful Odysseus answered her and said: "Hard it would be, my queen, to tell to the end the tale of my woes, since the heavenly gods have given me many. But this will I tell you, of which you ask and inquire. There

Ὠγυγίη τις νῆσος ἀπόπροθεν εἰν ἁλὶ κεῖται ·
245 ἔνθα μὲν Ἄτλαντος θυγάτηρ, δολόεσσα Καλυψὼ
ναίει ἐυπλόκαμος, δεινὴ θεός · οὐδέ τις αὐτῇ
μίσγεται οὔτε θεῶν οὔτε θνητῶν ἀνθρώπων.
ἀλλ' ἐμὲ τὸν δύστηνον ἐφέστιον ἤγαγε δαίμων
οἶον, ἐπεί μοι νῆα θοὴν ἀργῆτι κεραυνῷ
250 Ζεὺς ἔλσας[1] ἐκέασσε μέσῳ ἐνὶ οἴνοπι πόντῳ.
ἔνθ' ἄλλοι μὲν πάντες ἀπέφθιθεν ἐσθλοὶ ἑταῖροι,
αὐτὰρ ἐγὼ τρόπιν ἀγκὰς ἑλὼν νεὸς ἀμφιελίσσης
ἐννῆμαρ φερόμην · δεκάτῃ δέ με νυκτὶ μελαίνῃ
νῆσον ἐς Ὠγυγίην πέλασαν θεοί, ἔνθα Καλυψὼ
255 ναίει ἐυπλόκαμος, δεινὴ θεός, ἥ με λαβοῦσα
ἐνδυκέως ἐφίλει τε καὶ ἔτρεφεν ἠδὲ ἔφασκε
θήσειν ἀθάνατον καὶ ἀγήραον ἤματα πάντα ·
ἀλλ' ἐμὸν οὔ ποτε θυμὸν ἐνὶ στήθεσσιν ἔπειθεν.[2]
ἔνθα μὲν ἑπτάετες μένον ἔμπεδον, εἵματα δ' αἰεὶ
260 δάκρυσι δεύεσκον, τά μοι ἄμβροτα δῶκε Καλυψώ ·
ἀλλ' ὅτε δὴ ὀγδόατόν μοι ἐπιπλόμενον ἔτος ἦλθεν,
καὶ τότε δή μ' ἐκέλευσεν ἐποτρύνουσα νέεσθαι
Ζηνὸς ὑπ' ἀγγελίης, ἢ καὶ νόος ἐτράπετ' αὐτῆς.
πέμπε δ' ἐπὶ σχεδίης πολυδέσμου, πολλὰ δ' ἔδωκε,
265 σῖτον καὶ μέθυ ἡδύ, καὶ ἄμβροτα εἵματα ἔσσεν,
οὖρον δὲ προέηκεν ἀπήμονά τε λιαρόν τε.
ἑπτὰ δὲ καὶ δέκα μὲν πλέον ἤματα ποντοπορεύων,
ὀκτωκαιδεκάτῃ δ' ἐφάνη ὄρεα σκιόεντα
γαίης ὑμετέρης, γήθησε δέ μοι φίλον ἦτορ
270 δυσμόρῳ · ἦ γὰρ ἔμελλον ἔτι ξυνέσεσθαι ὀιζυῖ
πολλῇ, τήν μοι ἐπῶρσε Ποσειδάων ἐνοσίχθων,

is an island, Ogygia, which lies far off in the sea. There dwells the fair-tressed daughter of Atlas, guileful Calypso, a dread goddess, and no one either of gods or mortals has anything to do with her; but, unfortunate that I am, fate brought me to her hearth alone, for Zeus had struck my ship with his bright thunderbolt, and had shattered it in the midst of the wine-dark sea. There all the rest of my trusty comrades perished, but I clasped in my arms the keel of my curved ship and was borne drifting for nine days, and on the tenth black night the gods brought me to the island, Ogygia, where the fair-tressed Calypso dwells, a dread goddess. She took me to her home with kindly welcome, and gave me food, and said she would make me immortal and ageless all my days; but she could never persuade the heart in my breast. There for seven years I remained continually, and always with my tears I kept wet the immortal clothes which Calypso gave me. But when the eighth year came in its circling course, then she urged me and told me to go, either because of some message from Zeus, or because her own mind was turned. And she sent me on my way on a raft, stoutly bound, and gave me abundant provisions, bread and sparkling wine, and clad me in immortal clothes, and made a favorable wind to blow, gentle and warm. So for seventeen days I sailed over the sea, and on the eighteenth appeared the shadowy mountains of your land; and my heart was glad, ill-fated that I was; for truly I was still to have fellowship with great woe, which Poseidon,

---

[1] ἔλσας: ἐλάσας; cf. 5.132

[2] Lines 251–58 were rejected by Aristarchus.

ὅς μοι ἐφορμήσας ἀνέμους κατέδησε κέλευθον,
ὤρινεν δὲ θάλασσαν ἀθέσφατον, οὐδέ τι κῦμα
εἴα ἐπὶ σχεδίης ἁδινὰ στενάχοντα φέρεσθαι.
275 τὴν μὲν ἔπειτα θύελλα διεσκέδασ᾽· αὐτὰρ ἐγώ γε
νηχόμενος τόδε λαῖτμα διέτμαγον, ὄφρα με γαίῃ
ὑμετέρῃ ἐπέλασσε φέρων ἄνεμός τε καὶ ὕδωρ.
ἔνθα κέ μ᾽ ἐκβαίνοντα βιήσατο κῦμ᾽ ἐπὶ χέρσου,
πέτρῃς πρὸς μεγάλῃσι βαλὸν καὶ ἀτερπέι χώρῳ·
280 ἀλλ᾽ ἀναχασσάμενος νῆχον πάλιν, ἧος ἐπῆλθον
ἐς ποταμόν, τῇ δή μοι ἐείσατο χῶρος ἄριστος,
λεῖος πετράων, καὶ ἐπὶ σκέπας ἦν ἀνέμοιο.
ἐκ δ᾽ ἔπεσον θυμηγερέων, ἐπὶ δ᾽ ἀμβροσίη νὺξ
ἤλυθ᾽. ἐγὼ δ᾽ ἀπάνευθε διιπετέος ποταμοῖο
285 ἐκβὰς ἐν θάμνοισι κατέδραθον, ἀμφὶ δὲ φύλλα
ἠφυσάμην· ὕπνον δὲ θεὸς κατ᾽ ἀπείρονα χεῦεν.
ἔνθα μὲν ἐν φύλλοισι φίλον τετιημένος ἦτορ
εὗδον παννύχιος καὶ ἐπ᾽ ἠῶ καὶ μέσον ἦμαρ.
δείλετό[1] τ᾽ ἠέλιος καί με γλυκὺς ὕπνος ἀνῆκεν.
290 ἀμφιπόλους δ᾽ ἐπὶ θινὶ τεῆς ἐνόησα θυγατρὸς
παιζούσας, ἐν δ᾽ αὐτὴ ἔην ἐικυῖα θεῇσι·
τὴν ἱκέτευσ᾽· ἡ δ᾽ οὔ τι νοήματος ἤμβροτεν ἐσθλοῦ,
ὡς οὐκ ἂν ἔλποιο νεώτερον ἀντιάσαντα
ἐρξέμεν· αἰεὶ γάρ τε νεώτεροι ἀφραδέουσιν.
295 ἥ μοι σῖτον ἔδωκεν ἅλις ἠδ᾽ αἴθοπα οἶνον
καὶ λοῦσ᾽ ἐν ποταμῷ καί μοι τάδε εἵματ᾽ ἔδωκε.
ταῦτά τοι ἀχνύμενός περ ἀληθείην κατέλεξα.”

---

[1] δείλετο Aristarchus: δύσετο.

the earth-shaker, sent upon me. For he stirred up the winds against me and hindered my course, and monstrously roused the sea, nor would the wave let me be borne upon my raft, groaning without cease. My raft indeed the storm shattered, but by swimming I made my way through this great gulf of the sea here, until the wind and the waves, bearing me along, brought me to your shores. There, had I sought to land, the waves would have hurled me upon the shore, dashing me upon the great crags in a most unwelcome spot; but I retreated, and swam back until I came to a river, where seemed to me the best place, since it was smooth of rocks, and besides there was shelter from the wind. Out then I staggered, and sank down, gasping for breath, and immortal night came on. Then I emerged from the heaven-fed river, and lay down to sleep in the bushes, gathering leaves about me; and a god shed over me infinite sleep. So there among the leaves I slept, my heart much troubled, the whole night through, until morning and until midday; and the sun turned to his setting before sweet sleep released me. Then I saw the handmaids of your daughter upon the shore at play, and amid them was she, looking like a goddess. To her I made my prayer; and she in no way fell short of excellent understanding, such as you would not expect a young person meeting you to act upon; for younger people are always thoughtless. She gave bread in plenty and sparkling wine, and bathed me in the river, and gave me these clothes. In this, despite my sorrows, I have told you the truth."

τὸν δ' αὖτ' Ἀλκίνοος ἀπαμείβετο φώνησέν τε·
"ξεῖν', ἦ τοι μὲν τοῦτό γ' ἐναίσιμον οὐκ ἐνόησε
300 παῖς ἐμή, οὕνεκά σ' οὔ τι μετ' ἀμφιπόλοισι γυναιξὶν
ἦγεν ἐς ἡμέτερον, σὺ δ' ἄρα πρώτην ἱκέτευσας."
τὸν δ' ἀπαμειβόμενος προσέφη πολύμητις Ὀδυσσεύς·
"ἥρως, μή τοι τούνεκ' ἀμύμονα νείκεε κούρην·
ἡ μὲν γάρ μ' ἐκέλευε σὺν ἀμφιπόλοισιν ἕπεσθαι,
305 ἀλλ' ἐγὼ οὐκ ἔθελον δείσας αἰσχυνόμενός τε,
μή πως καὶ σοὶ θυμὸς ἐπισκύσσαιτο ἰδόντι·
δύσζηλοι γάρ τ' εἰμὲν ἐπὶ χθονὶ φῦλ' ἀνθρώπων."
τὸν δ' αὖτ' Ἀλκίνοος ἀπαμείβετο φώνησέν τε·
"ξεῖν', οὔ μοι τοιοῦτον ἐνὶ στήθεσσι φίλον κῆρ
310 μαψιδίως κεχολῶσθαι· ἀμείνω δ' αἴσιμα πάντα.
αἲ γάρ, Ζεῦ τε πάτερ καὶ Ἀθηναίη καὶ Ἄπολλον,
τοῖος ἐὼν οἷός ἐσσι, τά τε φρονέων ἅ τ' ἐγώ περ,
παῖδά τ' ἐμὴν ἐχέμεν καὶ ἐμὸς γαμβρὸς καλέεσθαι
αὖθι μένων· οἶκον δέ κ' ἐγὼ καὶ κτήματα δοίην,
315 εἴ κ' ἐθέλων γε μένοις· ἀέκοντα δέ σ' οὔ τις ἐρύξει
Φαιήκων· μὴ τοῦτο φίλον Διὶ πατρὶ γένοιτο.
πομπὴν δ' ἐς τόδ' ἐγὼ τεκμαίρομαι, ὄφρ' ἐὺ εἰδῇς,
αὔριον ἔς· τῆμος δὲ σὺ μὲν δεδμημένος ὕπνῳ
λέξεαι, οἱ δ' ἐλόωσι γαλήνην, ὄφρ' ἂν ἵκηαι
320 πατρίδα σὴν καὶ δῶμα, καὶ εἴ πού τοι φίλον ἐστίν,
εἴ περ καὶ μάλα πολλὸν ἑκαστέρω ἔστ' Εὐβοίης,
τήν περ τηλοτάτω φάσ' ἔμμεναι, οἵ μιν ἴδοντο
λαῶν ἡμετέρων, ὅτε τε ξανθὸν Ῥαδάμανθυν
ἦγον ἐποψόμενον Τιτυὸν Γαιήιον υἱόν.
325 καὶ μὲν οἱ ἔνθ' ἦλθον καὶ ἄτερ καμάτοιο τέλεσσαν

Then in turn Alcinous answered him, and said: "Stranger, truly my daughter did not judge rightly in this, that she did not bring you to our house with her maidens, when it was to her first that you made your prayer."

Then resourceful Odysseus answered him, and said: "Hero, do not rebuke for this your flawless daughter, I pray you. She did indeed bid me follow with her maidens, but I refused for fear and shame, thinking perchance your heart might darken with wrath when you saw it; for we are quick to anger, we tribes of men upon the earth."

And again Alcinous answered him and said: "Stranger, not such is the heart in my breast, to be filled with anger without a cause. Better is due measure in all things. I would, father Zeus, and Athene and Apollo, that you, being the kind of man you are, and like-minded with me, would have my daughter to wife, and be called my son, and remain here; a house and possessions would I give you, if you should choose to remain, but against your will shall no one of the Phaeacians keep you; may such a thing never please father Zeus. But as for your conveyance, that you may know it surely, I appoint a time for it, namely, tomorrow. Then shall you lie down, overcome by sleep, and they shall row you over the calm sea until you come to your country and your house, or to whatever place you will, even if it is much farther off than Euboea, which those of our people who saw it when they carried fair-haired Rhadamanthus to visit Tityus, the son of Earth, say is the farthest of lands. Thither they went, and without toil accomplished their journey, and on the selfsame day came

ἤματι τῷ αὐτῷ καὶ ἀπήνυσαν οἴκαδ᾽ ὀπίσσω.
εἰδήσεις δὲ καὶ αὐτὸς ἐνὶ φρεσὶν ὅσσον ἄρισται
νῆες ἐμαὶ καὶ κοῦροι ἀναρρίπτειν ἅλα πηδῷ.”

   ὣς φάτο, γήθησεν δὲ πολύτλας δῖος Ὀδυσσεύς,
330 εὐχόμενος δ᾽ ἄρα εἶπεν, ἔπος τ᾽ ἔφατ᾽ ἔκ τ᾽ ὀνόμαζεν·[1]
“Ζεῦ πάτερ, αἴθ᾽ ὅσα εἶπε τελευτήσειεν ἅπαντα
Ἀλκίνοος· τοῦ μέν κεν ἐπὶ ζείδωρον ἄρουραν
ἄσβεστον κλέος εἴη, ἐγὼ δέ κε πατρίδ᾽ ἱκοίμην.”

   ὣς οἱ μὲν τοιαῦτα πρὸς ἀλλήλους ἀγόρευον·
335 κέκλετο δ᾽ Ἀρήτη λευκώλενος ἀμφιπόλοισιν
δέμνι᾽ ὑπ᾽ αἰθούσῃ θέμεναι καὶ ῥήγεα καλὰ
πορφύρε᾽ ἐμβαλέειν, στορέσαι τ᾽ ἐφύπερθε τάπητας
χλαίνας τ᾽ ἐνθέμεναι οὔλας καθύπερθεν ἕσασθαι.
αἱ δ᾽ ἴσαν ἐκ μεγάροιο δάος μετὰ χερσὶν ἔχουσαι·
340 αὐτὰρ ἐπεὶ στόρεσαν πυκινὸν λέχος ἐγκονέουσαι,
ὤτρυνον δ᾽ Ὀδυσῆα παριστάμεναι ἐπέεσσιν·
“ὄρσο κέων, ὦ ξεῖνε· πεποίηται δέ τοι εὐνή.”

   ὣς φάν, τῷ δ᾽ ἀσπαστὸν ἐείσατο κοιμηθῆναι.
ὣς ὁ μὲν ἔνθα καθεῦδε πολύτλας δῖος Ὀδυσσεὺς
345 τρητοῖς ἐν λεχέεσσιν ὑπ᾽ αἰθούσῃ ἐριδούπῳ·
Ἀλκίνοος δ᾽ ἄρα λέκτο μυχῷ δόμου ὑψηλοῖο,
πὰρ δὲ γυνὴ δέσποινα λέχος πόρσυνε καὶ εὐνήν.

---

[1] ἔπος . . . ὀνόμαζεν: πρὸς ὃν μεγαλήτορα θυμόν.

back home. So shall you, too, know for yourself how much my ships are the best, and my young men at tossing the brine with the oar blade."

So said he, and the much-enduring noble Odysseus was glad; and he spoke in prayer and said: "Father Zeus, grant that Alcinous may bring to pass all that he has said. So shall his fame be unquenchable over the earth, the giver of grain, and I shall reach my native land."

Thus they spoke to one another, and white-armed Arete told her maids to place a bedstead beneath the portico, and to lay on it beautiful purple blankets, and to spread above them coverlets, and on these to put fleecy cloaks for clothing. The maids went forth from the hall with torches in their hands. But when they had busily spread the stout-built bedstead, they came to Odysseus, and called to him and said: "Rouse yourself now, stranger, to go to your rest; your bed is made."

So they spoke, and welcome it seemed to him to lie down to sleep. So there he slept, the much-enduring noble Odysseus, on the corded bedstead under the echoing portico. But Alcinous lay down in the inmost chamber of the lofty house, and beside him the lady his wife brought him love and comfort.

Θ

Ἦμος δ᾽ ἠριγένεια φάνη ῥοδοδάκτυλος Ἠώς,
ὤρνυτ᾽ ἄρ᾽ ἐξ εὐνῆς ἱερὸν μένος Ἀλκινόοιο,
ἂν δ᾽ ἄρα διογενὴς ὦρτο πτολίπορθος Ὀδυσσεύς.
τοῖσιν δ᾽ ἡγεμόνευ᾽ ἱερὸν μένος Ἀλκινόοιο
5   Φαιήκων ἀγορήνδ᾽, ἥ σφιν παρὰ νηυσὶ τέτυκτο.
ἐλθόντες δὲ καθῖζον ἐπὶ ξεστοῖσι λίθοισι
πλησίον. ἡ δ᾽ ἀνὰ ἄστυ μετῴχετο Παλλὰς Ἀθήνη
εἰδομένη κήρυκι δαΐφρονος Ἀλκινόοιο,
νόστον Ὀδυσσῆι μεγαλήτορι μητιόωσα,
10   καί ῥα ἑκάστῳ φωτὶ παρισταμένη φάτο μῦθον·
"δεῦτ᾽ ἄγε, Φαιήκων ἡγήτορες ἠδὲ μέδοντες,
εἰς ἀγορὴν ἰέναι, ὄφρα ξείνοιο πύθησθε,
ὃς νέον Ἀλκινόοιο δαΐφρονος ἵκετο δῶμα
πόντον ἐπιπλαγχθείς, δέμας ἀθανάτοισιν ὁμοῖος."
15   ὣς εἰποῦσ᾽ ὤτρυνε μένος καὶ θυμὸν ἑκάστου.
καρπαλίμως δ᾽ ἔμπληντο βροτῶν ἀγοραί τε καὶ ἕδραι
ἀγρομένων· πολλοὶ δ᾽ ἄρ᾽ ἐθηήσαντο ἰδόντες
υἱὸν Λαέρταο δαΐφρονα· τῷ δ᾽ ἄρ᾽ Ἀθήνη
θεσπεσίην κατέχευε χάριν κεφαλῇ τε καὶ ὤμοις
20   καί μιν μακρότερον καὶ πάσσονα θῆκεν ἰδέσθαι,
ὥς κεν Φαιήκεσσι φίλος πάντεσσι γένοιτο
δεινός τ᾽ αἰδοῖός τε καὶ ἐκτελέσειεν ἀέθλους

BOOK 8

As soon as early Dawn appeared, the rosy-fingered, the divine might of Alcinous rose from his couch, and up rose also Zeus-born Odysseus, sacker of cities. And the divine might of Alcinous led the way to the place of assembly of the Phaeacians, which was built for them close by their ships. To this place they came and sat down on the polished stones close by one another; and Pallas Athene went throughout the city, in the likeness of the herald of wise Alcinous, devising a return for great-hearted Odysseus. To each man's side she came, and spoke and said:

"Come here now, leaders and counselors of the Phaeacians, and go to the place of assembly, so that you may learn of the stranger who has newly come to the palace of wise Alcinous driven astray over the sea; in form he is like the immortals."

So saying she roused the spirit and heart of each man, and speedily the place of assembly and the seats were filled with gathering men. And many marveled at the sight of the wise son of Laertes, for wondrous was the grace that Athene shed upon his head and shoulders; and she made him taller and sturdier to behold, that he might be welcomed by all the Phaeacians, and win awe and reverence, and might accomplish the many feats in which the Phaea-

πολλούς, τοὺς Φαίηκες ἐπειρήσαντ' Ὀδυσῆος.
αὐτὰρ ἐπεί ῥ' ἤγερθεν ὁμηγερέες τ' ἐγένοντο,
25 τοῖσιν δ' Ἀλκίνοος ἀγορήσατο καὶ μετέειπε·
    "κέκλυτε, Φαιήκων ἡγήτορες ἠδὲ μέδοντες,
ὄφρ' εἴπω τά με θυμὸς ἐνὶ στήθεσσι κελεύει.
ξεῖνος ὅδ', οὐκ οἶδ' ὅς τις, ἀλώμενος ἵκετ' ἐμὸν δῶ,
ἠὲ πρὸς ἠοίων ἦ ἑσπερίων ἀνθρώπων·
30 πομπὴν δ' ὀτρύνει, καὶ λίσσεται ἔμπεδον εἶναι.
ἡμεῖς δ', ὡς τὸ πάρος περ, ἐποτρυνώμεθα πομπήν.
οὐδὲ γὰρ οὐδέ τις ἄλλος, ὅτις κ' ἐμὰ δώμαθ' ἵκηται,
ἐνθάδ' ὀδυρόμενος δηρὸν μένει εἵνεκα πομπῆς.
ἀλλ' ἄγε νῆα μέλαιναν ἐρύσσομεν εἰς ἅλα δῖαν
35 πρωτόπλοον, κούρω δὲ δύω καὶ πεντήκοντα
κρινάσθων κατὰ δῆμον, ὅσοι πάρος εἰσὶν ἄριστοι.
δησάμενοι δ' ἐῢ πάντες ἐπὶ κληῖσιν ἐρετμὰ
ἔκβητ'· αὐτὰρ ἔπειτα θοὴν ἀλεγύνετε δαῖτα
ἡμέτερόνδ' ἐλθόντες· ἐγὼ δ' ἐῢ πᾶσι παρέξω.
40 κούροισιν μὲν ταῦτ' ἐπιτέλλομαι· αὐτὰρ οἱ ἄλλοι
σκηπτοῦχοι βασιλῆες ἐμὰ πρὸς δώματα καλὰ
ἔρχεσθ', ὄφρα ξεῖνον ἐνὶ μεγάροισι φιλέωμεν,
μηδέ τις ἀρνείσθω. καλέσασθε δὲ θεῖον ἀοιδὸν
Δημόδοκον· τῷ γάρ ῥα θεὸς πέρι δῶκεν ἀοιδὴν
45 τέρπειν, ὅππῃ θυμὸς ἐποτρύνῃσιν ἀείδειν."
    ὣς ἄρα φωνήσας ἡγήσατο, τοὶ δ' ἅμ' ἕποντο
σκηπτοῦχοι· κῆρυξ δὲ μετῴχετο θεῖον ἀοιδόν.
κούρω δὲ κρινθέντε δύω καὶ πεντήκοντα
βήτην, ὡς ἐκέλευσ', ἐπὶ θῖν' ἁλὸς ἀτρυγέτοιο.
50 αὐτὰρ ἐπεί ῥ' ἐπὶ νῆα κατήλυθον ἠδὲ θάλασσαν,

cians made trial of Odysseus. Now when they were assembled and met together, Alcinous addressed their assembly and spoke among them:

"Listen to me, leaders and counselors of the Phaeacians, so that I may speak what the heart in my breast prompts me. This stranger—who he is I do not know—has come to my house in his wanderings, whether from men of the east or of the west. He urges that he be sent on his way, and prays for assurance. Let us, as in the past, speed on his conveyance. For no other man, certainly, who comes to my house, waits here long in sorrow for lack of conveyance. No, come, let us draw a black ship down to the bright sea for her first voyage, and let men choose two and fifty youths from the people, all who before were the best. And when you all have duly lashed the oars at the benches, go ashore, and then quickly go your way to my house and prepare for a feast; and I will provide bountifully for all. To the youths this is my command, but do you others, the sceptered kings, come to my beautiful palace, that we may entertain the stranger in the halls; and let no man refuse me. And summon the divine minstrel, Demodocus; for to him above all others has the god granted skill in song, to give delight in whatever way his spirit prompts him to sing."

So saying, he led the way, and the sceptered kings followed him, while a herald went for the divine minstrel. And chosen youths, two and fifty, went, as he commanded, to the shore of the barren sea. And when they had come down to the ship and to the sea, they drew the black ship

νῆα μὲν οἵ γε μέλαιναν ἁλὸς βένθοσδε ἔρυσσαν,
ἐν δ' ἱστόν τ' ἐτίθεντο καὶ ἱστία νηὶ μελαίνῃ,
ἠρτύναντο δ' ἐρετμὰ τροποῖς ἐν δερματίνοισι,
πάντα κατὰ μοῖραν, ἀνά θ' ἱστία λευκὰ πέτασσαν.
55 ὑψοῦ δ' ἐν νοτίῳ τήν γ' ὥρμισαν· αὐτὰρ ἔπειτα
βάν ῥ' ἴμεν Ἀλκινόοιο δαΐφρονος ἐς μέγα δῶμα.
πλῆντο δ' ἄρ' αἴθουσαί τε καὶ ἔρκεα καὶ δόμοι ἀνδρῶν
ἀγρομένων· πολλοὶ δ' ἄρ' ἔσαν, νέοι ἠδὲ παλαιοί.[1]
τοῖσιν δ' Ἀλκίνοος δυοκαίδεκα μῆλ' ἱέρευσεν,
60 ὀκτὼ δ' ἀργιόδοντας ὕας, δύο δ' εἰλίποδας βοῦς·
τοὺς δέρον ἀμφί θ' ἕπον, τετύκοντό τε δαῖτ' ἐρατεινήν.
    κῆρυξ δ' ἐγγύθεν ἦλθεν ἄγων ἐρίηρον ἀοιδόν,
τὸν πέρι μοῦσ' ἐφίλησε, δίδου δ' ἀγαθόν τε κακόν τε·
ὀφθαλμῶν μὲν ἄμερσε, δίδου δ' ἡδεῖαν ἀοιδήν.
65 τῷ δ' ἄρα Ποντόνοος θῆκε θρόνον ἀργυρόηλον
μέσσῳ δαιτυμόνων, πρὸς κίονα μακρὸν ἐρείσας·
κὰδ δ' ἐκ πασσαλόφι κρέμασεν φόρμιγγα λίγειαν
αὐτοῦ ὑπὲρ κεφαλῆς καὶ ἐπέφραδε χερσὶν ἑλέσθαι
κῆρυξ· πὰρ δ' ἐτίθει κάνεον καλήν τε τράπεζαν,
70 πὰρ δὲ δέπας οἴνοιο, πιεῖν ὅτε θυμὸς ἀνώγοι.
οἱ δ' ἐπ' ὀνείαθ' ἑτοῖμα προκείμενα χεῖρας ἴαλλον.
αὐτὰρ ἐπεὶ πόσιος καὶ ἐδητύος ἐξ ἔρον ἕντο,
μοῦσ' ἄρ' ἀοιδὸν ἀνῆκεν ἀειδέμεναι κλέα ἀνδρῶν,
οἴμης τῆς τότ' ἄρα κλέος οὐρανὸν εὐρὺν ἵκανε,
75 νεῖκος Ὀδυσσῆος καὶ Πηλεΐδεω Ἀχιλῆος,
ὥς ποτε δηρίσαντο θεῶν ἐν δαιτὶ θαλείῃ
ἐκπάγλοις ἐπέεσσιν, ἄναξ δ' ἀνδρῶν Ἀγαμέμνων
χαῖρε νόῳ, ὅ τ' ἄριστοι Ἀχαιῶν δηριόωντο.

down to the deep water, and placed the mast and sail in the black ship, and fitted the oars in the leather thole straps, all in due order, and spread the white sail. Well out in the channel they moored the ship, and then went their way to the great palace of the wise Alcinous. Filled were the porticoes and courts and rooms with the men that gathered, for many there were, both young and old. For them Alcinous slaughtered twelve sheep, and eight white-tusked boars, and two oxen of shambling gait. These they flayed and dressed, and prepared a tempting feast.

Then the herald approached leading the good minstrel, whom the Muse loved above all other men, and gave him both good and evil; of his sight she deprived him, but gave him the gift of sweet song. For him, Pontonous, the herald, set a silver-studded chair in the midst of the banqueters, leaning it against a tall pillar, and he hung the clear-toned lyre from a peg close above his head, and showed him how to reach it with his hands. And beside him he placed a basket and a beautiful table, and a cup of wine, to drink when his heart should bid him. So they put forth their hands to the good cheer lying ready before them. But when they had put from them the desire for food and drink, the Muse moved the minstrel to sing of the glorious deeds of men, from that lay the fame of which had then reached broad heaven, the quarrel of Odysseus and Achilles, son of Peleus, how once they strove with violent words at a rich feast of the gods, and Agamemnon, king of men, was glad at heart that the best of the Achaeans were

---

[1] Line 58 is omitted in most MSS.

ὡς γὰρ οἱ χρείων μυθήσατο Φοῖβος Ἀπόλλων
80   Πυθοῖ ἐν ἠγαθέῃ, ὅθ᾽ ὑπέρβη λάινον οὐδὸν
χρησόμενος· τότε γάρ ῥα κυλίνδετο πήματος ἀρχὴ
Τρωσί τε καὶ Δαναοῖσι Διὸς μεγάλου διὰ βουλάς.
    ταῦτ᾽ ἄρ᾽ ἀοιδὸς ἄειδε περικλυτός· αὐτὰρ Ὀδυσσεὺς
πορφύρεον μέγα φᾶρος ἑλὼν χερσὶ στιβαρῇσι
85   κὰκ κεφαλῆς εἴρυσσε, κάλυψε δὲ καλὰ πρόσωπα·
αἴδετο γὰρ Φαίηκας ὑπ᾽ ὀφρύσι δάκρυα λείβων.
ἦ τοι ὅτε λήξειεν ἀείδων θεῖος ἀοιδός,
δάκρυ ὀμορξάμενος κεφαλῆς ἄπο φᾶρος ἔλεσκε
καὶ δέπας ἀμφικύπελλον ἑλὼν σπείσασκε θεοῖσιν·
90   αὐτὰρ ὅτ᾽ ἂψ ἄρχοιτο καὶ ὀτρύνειαν ἀείδειν
Φαιήκων οἱ ἄριστοι, ἐπεὶ τέρποντ᾽ ἐπέεσσιν,
ἂψ Ὀδυσεὺς κατὰ κρᾶτα καλυψάμενος γοάασκεν.
ἔνθ᾽ ἄλλους μὲν πάντας ἐλάνθανε δάκρυα λείβων,
Ἀλκίνοος δέ μιν οἶος ἐπεφράσατ᾽ ἠδ᾽ ἐνόησεν
95   ἥμενος ἄγχ᾽ αὐτοῦ, βαρὺ δὲ στενάχοντος ἄκουσεν.
αἶψα δὲ Φαιήκεσσι φιληρέτμοισι μετηύδα·
    "κέκλυτε, Φαιήκων ἡγήτορες ἠδὲ μέδοντες.
ἤδη μὲν δαιτὸς κεκορήμεθα θυμὸν ἐίσης
φόρμιγγός θ᾽, ἣ δαιτὶ συνήορός ἐστι θαλείῃ·
100   νῦν δ᾽ ἐξέλθωμεν καὶ ἀέθλων πειρηθῶμεν
πάντων, ὥς χ᾽ ὁ ξεῖνος ἐνίσπῃ οἷσι φίλοισιν
οἴκαδε νοστήσας, ὅσσον περιγιγνόμεθ᾽ ἄλλων
πύξ τε παλαιμοσύνῃ τε καὶ ἅλμασιν ἠδὲ πόδεσσιν."
    ὣς ἄρα φωνήσας ἡγήσατο, τοὶ δ᾽ ἅμ᾽ ἕποντο.
105   κὰδ δ᾽ ἐκ πασσαλόφι κρέμασεν φόρμιγγα λίγειαν,
Δημοδόκου δ᾽ ἕλε χεῖρα καὶ ἔξαγεν ἐκ μεγάροιο

quarreling; for thus Phoebus Apollo, in giving his response, had told him that it should be, in sacred Pytho, when he crossed the threshold of stone to inquire of the oracle. For then the beginning of woe was rolling upon Trojans and Danaans alike through the will of great Zeus.

This song the famous minstrel sang; but Odysseus grasped his great purple cloak with his stout hands, and drew it down over his head, and hid his handsome face; for he felt shame before the Phaeacians as he let fall tears from beneath his eyebrows. Indeed, as often as the divine minstrel ceased his singing, Odysseus would wipe away his tears and draw the cloak from off his head, and taking the two-handled cup would pour libations to the gods. But as often as he began again, and the Phaeacian nobles urged him to sing, because they took pleasure in his song, Odysseus would again cover his head and groan. Now from all the rest he concealed the tears that he shed, but Alcinous alone was aware of him and noticed, for he sat by him, and heard him groaning heavily. And at once he spoke among the Phaeacians, lovers of the oar:

"Hear me, leaders and counselors of the Phaeacians, already have we satisfied our hearts with the feast we share and with the lyre, which is the companion of the rich feast. But now let us go out, and make trial of all sorts of games, that this stranger may tell his friends, when he returns home, how far we excel other men in boxing and wrestling and jumping and speed of foot."

So saying, he led the way, and they followed him. From the peg the herald hung the clear-toned lyre, and took Demodocus by the hand, and led him out of the hall, guid-

κῆρυξ· ἦρχε δὲ τῷ αὐτὴν ὁδὸν ἥν περ οἱ ἄλλοι
Φαιήκων οἱ ἄριστοι, ἀέθλια θαυμανέοντες.
βὰν δ᾽ ἴμεν εἰς ἀγορήν, ἅμα δ᾽ ἕσπετο πουλὺς ὅμιλος,
110   μυρίοι· ἂν δ᾽ ἵσταντο νέοι πολλοί τε καὶ ἐσθλοί.
ὦρτο μὲν Ἀκρόνεώς τε καὶ Ὠκύαλος καὶ Ἐλατρεύς,
Ναυτεύς τε Πρυμνεύς τε καὶ Ἀγχίαλος καὶ Ἐρετμεύς,
Ποντεύς τε Πρωρεύς τε, Θόων Ἀναβησίνεώς τε
Ἀμφίαλός θ᾽, υἱὸς Πολυνήου Τεκτονίδαο·
115   ἂν δὲ καὶ Εὐρύαλος, βροτολοιγῷ ἶσος Ἄρηι,
Ναυβολίδης, ὃς ἄριστος ἔην εἶδός τε δέμας τε
πάντων Φαιήκων μετ᾽ ἀμύμονα Λαοδάμαντα.
ἂν δ᾽ ἔσταν τρεῖς παῖδες ἀμύμονος Ἀλκινόοιο,
Λαοδάμας θ᾽ Ἅλιός τε καὶ ἀντίθεος Κλυτόνηος.
120   οἱ δ᾽ ἦ τοι πρῶτον μὲν ἐπειρήσαντο πόδεσσι.
τοῖσι δ᾽ ἀπὸ νύσσης τέτατο δρόμος· οἱ δ᾽ ἅμα πάντες
καρπαλίμως ἐπέτοντο κονίοντες πεδίοιο·
τῶν δὲ θέειν ὄχ᾽ ἄριστος ἔην Κλυτόνηος ἀμύμων·
ὅσσον τ᾽ ἐν νειῷ οὖρον πέλει ἡμιόνοιιν,
125   τόσσον ὑπεκπροθέων λαοὺς ἵκεθ᾽, οἱ δ᾽ ἐλίποντο.
οἱ δὲ παλαιμοσύνης ἀλεγεινῆς πειρήσαντο·
τῇ δ᾽ αὖτ᾽ Εὐρύαλος ἀπεκαίνυτο πάντας ἀρίστους.
ἅλματι δ᾽ Ἀμφίαλος πάντων προφερέστατος ἦεν·
δίσκῳ δ᾽ αὖ πάντων πολὺ φέρτατος ἦεν Ἐλατρεύς,
130   πὺξ δ᾽ αὖ Λαοδάμας, ἀγαθὸς πάις Ἀλκινόοιο.
αὐτὰρ ἐπεὶ δὴ πάντες ἐτέρφθησαν φρέν᾽ ἀέθλοις,
τοῖς ἄρα Λαοδάμας μετέφη πάις Ἀλκινόοιο·
    "δεῦτε, φίλοι, τὸν ξεῖνον ἐρώμεθα εἴ τιν᾽ ἄεθλον
οἶδέ τε καὶ δεδάηκε. φυήν γε μὲν οὐ κακός ἐστι,

ing him by the selfsame road by which the others, the nobles of the Phaeacians, had gone to admire the games. They went their way to the place of assembly, and with them went a great throng, past counting; and up rose many noble youths. There rose Acroneüs, and Ocyalus, and Elatreus, and Nauteus, and Prymneus, and Anchialus, and Eretmeus, and Ponteus, and Proreus, Thoön and Anabesineüs, and Amphialus, son of Polyneüs, son of Tecton; and up rose also Euryalus, the peer of man-destroying Ares, the son of Naubolus, who in looks and form was the best of all the Phaeacians after peerless Laodamas; and up rose the three sons of flawless Alcinous, Laodamas, and Halius, and godlike Clytoneüs. These then first tested themselves in the foot race: a course was laid out for them from the mark, and they all sped swiftly, raising the dust of the plain; but among them flawless Clytoneüs was far the best at running, and by as far as is the range[a] of a team of mules in fallow land, by so far he shot to the front and reached the crowd, and the others were left behind. Then they tested themselves in painful wrestling, and here in turn Euryalus excelled all the princes. And in jumping Amphialus was best of all, and with the discus again far the best of all was Elatreus, and in boxing Laodamas, the good son of Alcinous. But when the hearts of all had taken pleasure in the contests, Laodamas, the son of Alcinous, spoke among them:

"Come, friends, let us ask this stranger whether he knows and has learned any contests. In build, surely, he is

[a] The word probably denotes the length of the furrow cut before a turn was made. M.

135 μηρούς τε κνήμας τε καὶ ἄμφω χεῖρας ὕπερθεν
αὐχένα τε στιβαρὸν μέγα τε σθένος· οὐδέ τι ἥβης
δεύεται, ἀλλὰ κακοῖσι συνέρρηκται πολέεσσιν·
οὐ γὰρ ἐγώ γέ τί φημι κακώτερον ἄλλο θαλάσσης
ἄνδρα γε συγχεῦαι, εἰ καὶ μάλα καρτερὸς εἴη."

140 τὸν δ' αὖτ' Εὐρύαλος ἀπαμείβετο φώνησέν τε·
"Λαοδάμα, μάλα τοῦτο ἔπος κατὰ μοῖραν ἔειπες.
αὐτὸς νῦν προκάλεσσαι ἰὼν καὶ πέφραδε μῦθον."[1]

αὐτὰρ ἐπεὶ τό γ' ἄκουσ' ἀγαθὸς πάϊς Ἀλκινόοιο,
στῆ ῥ' ἐς μέσσον ἰὼν καὶ Ὀδυσσῆα προσέειπε·

145 "δεῦρ' ἄγε καὶ σύ, ξεῖνε πάτερ, πείρησαι ἀέθλων,
εἴ τινά που δεδάηκας· ἔοικε δέ σ' ἴδμεν ἀέθλους·
οὐ μὲν γὰρ μεῖζον κλέος ἀνέρος ὄφρα κ' ἔῃσιν,
ἤ ὅ τι ποσσίν τε ῥέξῃ καὶ χερσὶν ἑῇσιν.
ἀλλ' ἄγε πείρησαι, σκέδασον δ' ἀπὸ κήδεα θυμοῦ.

150 σοὶ δ' ὁδὸς οὐκέτι δηρὸν ἀπέσσεται, ἀλλά τοι ἤδη
νηῦς τε κατείρυσται καὶ ἐπαρτέες εἰσὶν ἑταῖροι."

τὸν δ' ἀπαμειβόμενος προσέφη πολύμητις Ὀδυσσεύς·
"Λαοδάμα, τί με ταῦτα κελεύετε κερτομέοντες;
κήδεά μοι καὶ μᾶλλον ἐνὶ φρεσὶν ἤ περ ἄεθλοι,

155 ὃς πρὶν μὲν μάλα πολλὰ πάθον καὶ πολλὰ μόγησα,
νῦν δὲ μεθ' ὑμετέρῃ ἀγορῇ νόστοιο χατίζων
ἧμαι, λισσόμενος βασιλῆά τε πάντα τε δῆμον."

τὸν δ' αὖτ' Εὐρύαλος ἀπαμείβετο νείκεσέ τ' ἄντην·
"οὐ γάρ σ' οὐδέ, ξεῖνε, δαήμονι φωτὶ ἐΐσκω

160 ἄθλων, οἷά τε πολλὰ μετ' ἀνθρώποισι πέλονται,
ἀλλὰ τῷ, ὅς θ' ἄμα νηὶ πολυκληΐδι θαμίζων,

---

[1] Line 142 was unknown to Alexandrian critics.

no mean man, in thighs and calves, and in his two arms above, his stout neck, and his great strength. Nor has he lost any of the vigor of youth, but he has been broken by much suffering. For to my mind there is nothing worse than the sea to confound a man, however strong he may be."

And Euryalus in turn answered him, and said: "Laodamas, this word of yours is most fitly spoken. Go now yourself and challenge him, and make your challenge public."

Now when the good son of Alcinous heard this he came and took his stand among them all and spoke to Odysseus: "You, too, father stranger, come forward and try the contests, if perchance you are skilled in any; and it is likely that you are skilled in contests, for there is no greater glory for a man so long as he lives than that which he achieves by his own hands and feet. So come, make test yourself, and cast away care from your heart. No more shall your journey be long delayed; your ship is already launched and the crew prepared."

Then resourceful Odysseus answered him, and said: "Laodamas, why do you mock me with this challenge? Sorrow is in my mind far more than contests, seeing that in time past I have suffered much and toiled much, and now I sit in the midst of your assembly, longing for my return home, and making my prayer to the king and to all the people."

Then Euryalus in his turn made answer and taunted him to his face: "No, stranger, for you do not look to me like a man who knows contests, such as abound among men, but like one who, faring to and fro with his benched

ἀρχὸς ναυτάων οἵ τε πρηκτῆρες ἔασιν,
φόρτου τε μνήμων καὶ ἐπίσκοπος ᾖσιν ὁδαίων
κερδέων θ' ἁρπαλέων· οὐδ' ἀθλητῆρι ἔοικας."

165   τὸν δ' ἄρ' ὑπόδρα ἰδὼν προσέφη πολύμητις Ὀδυσσεύς·
"ξεῖν', οὐ καλὸν ἔειπες· ἀτασθάλῳ ἀνδρὶ ἔοικας.
οὕτως οὐ πάντεσσι θεοὶ χαρίεντα διδοῦσιν
ἀνδράσιν, οὔτε φυὴν οὔτ' ἂρ φρένας οὔτ' ἀγορητύν.
ἄλλος μὲν γάρ τ' εἶδος ἀκιδνότερος πέλει ἀνήρ,

170   ἀλλὰ θεὸς μορφὴν ἔπεσι στέφει, οἱ δέ τ' ἐς αὐτὸν
τερπόμενοι λεύσσουσιν· ὁ δ' ἀσφαλέως ἀγορεύει
αἰδοῖ μειλιχίῃ, μετὰ δὲ πρέπει ἀγρομένοισιν,
ἐρχόμενον δ' ἀνὰ ἄστυ θεὸν ὣς εἰσορόωσιν.
ἄλλος δ' αὖ εἶδος μὲν ἀλίγκιος ἀθανάτοισιν,

175   ἀλλ' οὔ οἱ χάρις ἀμφιπεριστέφεται ἐπέεσσιν,
ὡς καὶ σοὶ εἶδος μὲν ἀριπρεπές, οὐδέ κεν ἄλλως
οὐδὲ θεὸς τεύξειε, νόον δ' ἀποφώλιός ἐσσι.
ὤρινάς μοι θυμὸν ἐνὶ στήθεσσι φίλοισιν
εἰπὼν οὐ κατὰ κόσμον. ἐγὼ δ' οὐ νῇις ἀέθλων,

180   ὡς σύ γε μυθεῖαι, ἀλλ' ἐν πρώτοισιν ὀίω
ἔμμεναι, ὄφρ' ἥβῃ τε πεποίθεα χερσί τ' ἐμῇσι.
νῦν δ' ἔχομαι κακότητι καὶ ἄλγεσι· πολλὰ γὰρ ἔτλην
ἀνδρῶν τε πτολέμους ἀλεγεινά τε κύματα πείρων.
ἀλλὰ καὶ ὥς, κακὰ πολλὰ παθών, πειρήσομ' ἀέθλων·

185   θυμοδακὴς γὰρ μῦθος, ἐπώτρυνας δέ με εἰπών."
ἦ ῥα καὶ αὐτῷ φάρει ἀναΐξας λάβε δίσκον
μείζονα καὶ πάχετον, στιβαρώτερον οὐκ ὀλίγον περ
ἢ οἵῳ Φαίηκες ἐδίσκεον ἀλλήλοισι.
τόν ῥα περιστρέψας ἧκε στιβαρῆς ἀπὸ χειρός,

ship, is a captain of sailors who are merchantmen, one who
is mindful of his freight and keeps close watch on his cargo
and the gains of his greed. No, you do not seem an ath-
lete."

Then with an angry glance from beneath his brows
resourceful Odysseus answered him: "Stranger, you have
not spoken well; you seem like a man blind with folly.
So true is it that the gods do not give gracious gifts to all
alike, not form, nor mind, nor eloquence. For one man is
inferior in looks, but the god sets a crown of beauty upon
his words, and men look upon him with delight, and he
speaks on unfalteringly with sweet modesty, and is conspic-
uous among the gathered people, and as he goes through
the city men gaze upon him as upon a god. Another again
is in looks like the immortals, but no crown of grace is set
about his words. So also in your case your looks are preem-
inent, nor could a god himself improve them, but in mind
you are stunted. You have stirred the spirit in my breast by
speaking without manners. I am not a novice in sports as
you say; on the contrary, I think I was among the first so
long as I trusted in my youth and in my hands. But now I
am bound by suffering and pains; for much have I endured
in passing through wars of men and the grievous waves.
But even so, though I have suffered much, I will make trial
of the contests, for your word has stung me to the heart,
and you have provoked me with your speech."

He spoke, and, leaping up with his cloak about him as it
was, seized a discus larger than the rest, and thick, heavier
by no slight amount than those with which the Phaeacians
were accustomed to contend one with another. This, spin-
ning about, he sent from his stout hand, and the stone

190 βόμβησεν δὲ λίθος · κατὰ δ' ἔπτηξαν ποτὶ γαίῃ
Φαίηκες δολιχήρετμοι, ναυσίκλυτοι ἄνδρες,
λᾶος ὑπὸ ῥιπῆς · ὁ δ' ὑπέρπτατο σήματα πάντων
ῥίμφα θέων ἀπὸ χειρός. ἔθηκε δὲ τέρματ' Ἀθήνη
ἀνδρὶ δέμας ἐικυῖα, ἔπος τ' ἔφατ' ἔκ τ' ὀνόμαζεν ·

195 "καί κ' ἀλαός τοι, ξεῖνε, διακρίνειε τὸ σῆμα
ἀμφαφόων, ἐπεὶ οὔ τι μεμιγμένον ἐστὶν ὁμίλῳ,
ἀλλὰ πολὺ πρῶτον. σὺ δὲ θάρσει τόνδε γ' ἄεθλον ·
οὔ τις Φαιήκων τόδε γ' ἵξεται, οὐδ' ὑπερήσει."

ὣς φάτο, γήθησεν δὲ πολύτλας δῖος Ὀδυσσεύς,
200 χαίρων, οὕνεχ' ἑταῖρον ἐνηέα λεῦσσ' ἐν ἀγῶνι.
καὶ τότε κουφότερον μετεφώνεε Φαιήκεσσιν ·

"τοῦτον νῦν ἀφίκεσθε, νέοι. τάχα δ' ὕστερον ἄλλον
ἥσειν ἢ τοσσοῦτον ὀίομαι ἢ ἔτι μᾶσσον.
τῶν δ' ἄλλων ὅτινα κραδίη θυμός τε κελεύει,
205 δεῦρ' ἄγε πειρηθήτω, ἐπεί μ' ἐχολώσατε λίην,
ἢ πὺξ ἠὲ πάλῃ ἢ καὶ ποσίν, οὔ τι μεγαίρω,
πάντων Φαιήκων, πλήν γ' αὐτοῦ Λαοδάμαντος.
ξεῖνος γάρ μοι ὅδ' ἐστί · τίς ἂν φιλέοντι μάχοιτο;
ἄφρων δὴ κεῖνός γε καὶ οὐτιδανὸς πέλει ἀνήρ,
210 ὅς τις ξεινοδόκῳ ἔριδα προφέρηται ἀέθλων
δήμῳ ἐν ἀλλοδαπῷ · ἕο δ' αὐτοῦ πάντα κολούει.
τῶν δ' ἄλλων οὔ πέρ τιν' ἀναίνομαι οὐδ' ἀθερίζω,
ἀλλ' ἐθέλω ἴδμεν καὶ πειρηθήμεναι ἄντην.
πάντα γὰρ οὐ κακός εἰμι, μετ' ἀνδράσιν ὅσσοι ἄεθλοι ·
215 εὖ μὲν τόξον οἶδα ἐΰξοον ἀμφαφάασθαι ·
πρῶτός κ' ἄνδρα βάλοιμι ὀιστεύσας ἐν ὁμίλῳ
ἀνδρῶν δυσμενέων, εἰ καὶ μάλα πολλοὶ ἑταῖροι

hummed as it flew; and down they cowered to the earth, the Phaeacians of the long oars, men famed for their ships, beneath the rush of the stone. Past the marks of all it flew, speeding lightly from his hand, and Athene, in the likeness of a man, set the mark, and she spoke and addressed him:

"Even a blind man, stranger, could distinguish this mark, groping for it with his hands, for it is in no way confused in the throng of the others, but is far the first. You may take confidence from this throw, at any rate: no one of the Phaeacians will reach this, or surpass it."

So she spoke, and the much-enduring noble Odysseus was glad, rejoicing that he had found a true supporter at the games. Then with a lighter heart he spoke among the Phaeacians.

"Reach this now, young men; soon, I think, I will send another after it, as far or even farther. Of the rest, if any man's heart and spirit bid him, let him come here and be tested—for you have greatly angered me—be it in boxing or in wrestling, yes, or in running, I care not; let any one come of all the Phaeacians, except Laodamas alone. For he is my host, and who would quarrel with one that entertains him? Foolish is that man and worthless, who challenges to a contest the host who receives him in a strange land; he only mars his own fortunes. But of all the rest I refuse none, and make light of none, but rather wish to know their skill and be tested against them. For in all things I am no weakling, not in any of the contests that are practiced among men. Well do I know how to handle the polished bow, and always would I be the first to shoot and hit my man in the throng of the foe, even though many

ἄγχι παρασταῖεν καὶ τοξαζοίατο φωτῶν.
οἷος δή με Φιλοκτήτης ἀπεκαίνυτο τόξῳ
220 δήμῳ ἔνι Τρώων, ὅτε τοξαζοίμεθ᾽ Ἀχαιοί.
τῶν δ᾽ ἄλλων ἐμέ φημι πολὺ προφερέστερον εἶναι,
ὅσσοι νῦν βροτοί εἰσιν ἐπὶ χθονὶ σῖτον ἔδοντες.
ἀνδράσι δὲ προτέροισιν ἐριζέμεν οὐκ ἐθελήσω,
οὔθ᾽ Ἡρακλῆι οὔτ᾽ Εὐρύτῳ Οἰχαλιῆι,
225 οἵ ῥα καὶ ἀθανάτοισιν ἐρίζεσκον περὶ τόξων.
τῷ ῥα καὶ αἶψ᾽ ἔθανεν μέγας Εὔρυτος, οὐδ᾽ ἐπὶ γῆρας
ἵκετ᾽ ἐνὶ μεγάροισι· χολωσάμενος γὰρ Ἀπόλλων
ἔκτανεν, οὕνεκά μιν προκαλίζετο τοξάζεσθαι.
δουρὶ δ᾽ ἀκοντίζω ὅσον οὐκ ἄλλος τις ὀιστῷ.
230 οἴοισιν δείδοικα ποσὶν μή τίς με παρέλθῃ
Φαιήκων· λίην γὰρ ἀεικελίως ἐδαμάσθην
κύμασιν ἐν πολλοῖς, ἐπεὶ οὐ κομιδὴ κατὰ νῆα
ἦεν ἐπηετανός· τῷ μοι φίλα γυῖα λέλυνται."
    ὣς ἔφαθ᾽, οἱ δ᾽ ἄρα πάντες ἀκὴν ἐγένοντο σιωπῇ.
235 Ἀλκίνοος δέ μιν οἶος ἀμειβόμενος προσέειπεν·
    "ξεῖν᾽, ἐπεὶ οὐκ ἀχάριστα μεθ᾽ ἡμῖν ταῦτ᾽ ἀγορεύεις,
ἀλλ᾽ ἐθέλεις ἀρετὴν σὴν φαινέμεν, ἥ τοι ὀπηδεῖ,
χωόμενος ὅτι σ᾽ οὗτος ἀνὴρ ἐν ἀγῶνι παραστὰς
νείκεσεν, ὡς ἂν σὴν ἀρετὴν βροτὸς οὔ τις ὄνοιτο,
240 ὅς τις ἐπίσταιτο ᾗσι φρεσὶν ἄρτια βάζειν·
ἀλλ᾽ ἄγε νῦν ἐμέθεν ξυνίει ἔπος, ὄφρα καὶ ἄλλῳ
εἴπῃς ἡρώων, ὅτε κεν σοῖς ἐν μεγάροισι
δαινύῃ παρὰ σῇ τ᾽ ἀλόχῳ καὶ σοῖσι τέκεσσιν,
ἡμετέρης ἀρετῆς μεμνημένος, οἷα καὶ ἡμῖν
245 Ζεὺς ἐπὶ ἔργα τίθησι διαμπερὲς ἐξ ἔτι πατρῶν.

comrades stood by me and were shooting at the men. Only Philoctetes excelled me in the land of the Trojans, when we Achaeans shot. But of all the others I declare that I am best by far, of all mortals that are now upon the earth and eat bread. Yet with men of former days I will not seek to vie, with Heracles or with Eurytus of Oechalia, who strove even with the immortals in archery. Therefore great Eurytus died soon, nor did old age come upon him in his halls, for Apollo became angry and killed him, because he had challenged him to a contest with the bow. And the spear I throw farther than any other man can shoot with an arrow. In the foot race alone I fear that someone of the Phaeacians may outstrip me, for cruelly have I been broken amid the many waves, since aboard my craft there was no steady care for the body; therefore my limbs are loosened."

So he spoke and they were all hushed in silence; Alcinous alone answered him and said:

"Stranger, since not ungraciously you speak thus in our midst, but rather desire to make clear the prowess with which you are endowed, in anger that this man came up to you at the games and taunted you in a way that no mortal would make light of your prowess who knew in his heart how to speak fitly; come, now, listen to my words, that you may tell to another hero, when in your halls you are feasting with your wife and children, and remember our skill, what feats Zeus has vouchsafed to us from our fathers' days

THE ODYSSEY

οὐ γὰρ πυγμάχοι εἰμὲν ἀμύμονες οὐδὲ παλαισταί,
ἀλλὰ ποσὶ κραιπνῶς θέομεν καὶ νηυσὶν ἄριστοι,
αἰεὶ δ' ἡμῖν δαίς τε φίλη κίθαρίς τε χοροί τε
εἵματά τ' ἐξημοιβὰ λοετρά τε θερμὰ καὶ εὐναί.
250 ἀλλ' ἄγε, Φαιήκων βητάρμονες ὅσσοι ἄριστοι,
παίσατε, ὥς χ' ὁ ξεῖνος ἐνίσπῃ οἷσι φίλοισιν
οἴκαδε νοστήσας, ὅσσον περιγιγνόμεθ' ἄλλων
ναυτιλίῃ καὶ ποσσὶ καὶ ὀρχηστυῖ καὶ ἀοιδῇ.
Δημοδόκῳ δέ τις αἶψα κιὼν φόρμιγγα λίγειαν
255 οἰσέτω, ἥ που κεῖται ἐν ἡμετέροισι δόμοισιν."
ὣς ἔφατ' Ἀλκίνοος θεοείκελος, ὦρτο δὲ κῆρυξ
οἴσων φόρμιγγα γλαφυρὴν δόμου ἐκ βασιλῆος.
αἰσυμνῆται δὲ κριτοὶ ἐννέα πάντες ἀνέσταν
δήμιοι, οἳ κατ' ἀγῶνας ἐὺ πρήσσεσκον ἕκαστα,
260 λείηναν δὲ χορόν, καλὸν δ' εὔρυναν ἀγῶνα.
κῆρυξ δ' ἐγγύθεν ἦλθε φέρων φόρμιγγα λίγειαν
Δημοδόκῳ· ὁ δ' ἔπειτα κί' ἐς μέσον· ἀμφὶ δὲ κοῦροι
πρωθῆβαι ἵσταντο, δαήμονες ὀρχηθμοῖο,
πέπληγον δὲ χορὸν θεῖον ποσίν. αὐτὰρ Ὀδυσσεὺς
265 μαρμαρυγὰς θηεῖτο ποδῶν, θαύμαζε δὲ θυμῷ.
αὐτὰρ[1] ὁ φορμίζων ἀνεβάλλετο καλὸν ἀείδειν
ἀμφ' Ἄρεος φιλότητος εὐστεφάνου τ' Ἀφροδίτης,
ὡς τὰ πρῶτα μίγησαν ἐν Ἡφαίστοιο δόμοισι
λάθρῃ, πολλὰ δ' ἔδωκε, λέχος δ' ᾔσχυνε καὶ εὐνὴν
270 Ἡφαίστοιο ἄνακτος. ἄφαρ δέ οἱ ἄγγελος ἦλθεν
Ἥλιος, ὅ σφ' ἐνόησε μιγαζομένους φιλότητι.

[1] The whole passage 266–369 (or 267–366) was on moral grounds rejected by some ancient critics.

even until now. For we are not flawless boxers or wrestlers, but in the foot race we run swiftly, and we are the best seamen; and always to us is the banquet dear, and the lyre, and the dance, and changes of clothes, and warm baths, and the couch. But come now, all you who are the best dancers of the Phaeacians, make sport, that the stranger may tell his friends on reaching home how far we surpass others in seamanship and in fleetness of foot, and in the dance and in song. And let someone go at once and fetch for Demodocus the clear-toned lyre which lies somewhere in our halls."

So spoke Alcinous the godlike, and the herald rose to fetch the hollow lyre from the palace of the king. Then stood up officials, nine in all, men chosen from the people, who at the games arranged everything properly. They leveled a place for the dance, and marked out a fair wide ring, and the herald came near, bearing the clear-toned lyre for Demodocus. He then moved into the midst, and around him stood boys in the first bloom of youth, well skilled in the dance, and they struck the sacred dancing floor with their feet. And Odysseus gazed at the flashing of their feet and marveled in spirit.

Next the minstrel struck the chords in prelude to his sweet lay and sang of the love of Ares and fair-crowned Aphrodite, how first they lay together in the house of Hephaestus secretly; and Ares gave her many gifts, and shamed the bed of the lord Hephaestus. But immediately Helios came to him to tell him, for he had seen them lying

Ἥφαιστος δ' ὡς οὖν θυμαλγέα μῦθον ἄκουσε,
βῆ ῥ' ἴμεν ἐς χαλκεῶνα κακὰ φρεσὶ βυσσοδομεύων,
ἐν δ' ἔθετ' ἀκμοθέτῳ μέγαν ἄκμονα, κόπτε δὲ δεσμοὺς
275 ἀρρήκτους ἀλύτους, ὄφρ' ἔμπεδον αὖθι μένοιεν.
αὐτὰρ ἐπεὶ δὴ τεῦξε δόλον κεχολωμένος Ἄρει,
βῆ ῥ' ἴμεν ἐς θάλαμον, ὅθι οἱ φίλα δέμνι' ἔκειτο,
ἀμφὶ δ' ἄρ' ἑρμῖσιν χέε δέσματα κύκλῳ ἁπάντῃ·
πολλὰ δὲ καὶ καθύπερθε μελαθρόφιν ἐξεκέχυντο,
280 ἠΰτ' ἀράχνια λεπτά, τά γ' οὔ κέ τις οὐδὲ ἴδοιτο,
οὐδὲ θεῶν μακάρων· πέρι γὰρ δολόεντα τέτυκτο.
αὐτὰρ ἐπεὶ δὴ πάντα δόλον περὶ δέμνια χεῦεν,
εἴσατ' ἴμεν ἐς Λῆμνον, ἐϋκτίμενον πτολίεθρον,
ἥ οἱ γαιάων πολὺ φιλτάτη ἐστὶν ἁπασέων.
285 οὐδ' ἀλαοσκοπιὴν εἶχε χρυσήνιος Ἄρης,
ὡς ἴδεν Ἥφαιστον κλυτοτέχνην νόσφι κιόντα·
βῆ δ' ἰέναι πρὸς δῶμα περικλυτοῦ Ἡφαίστοιο
ἰσχανόων φιλότητος ἐϋστεφάνου Κυθερείης.
ἡ δὲ νέον παρὰ πατρὸς ἐρισθενέος Κρονίωνος
290 ἐρχομένη κατ' ἄρ' ἕζεθ'· ὁ δ' εἴσω δώματος ἦει,
ἔν τ' ἄρα οἱ φῦ χειρί, ἔπος τ' ἔφατ' ἔκ τ' ὀνόμαζε·
"δεῦρο, φίλη, λέκτρονδε τραπείομεν εὐνηθέντες·
οὐ γὰρ ἔθ' Ἥφαιστος μεταδήμιος, ἀλλά που ἤδη
οἴχεται ἐς Λῆμνον μετὰ Σίντιας ἀγριοφώνους."
295 ὣς φάτο, τῇ δ' ἀσπαστὸν ἐείσατο κοιμηθῆναι.
τὼ δ' ἐς δέμνια βάντε κατέδραθον· ἀμφὶ δὲ δεσμοὶ
τεχνήεντες ἔχυντο πολύφρονος Ἡφαίστοιο,
οὐδέ τι κινῆσαι μελέων ἦν οὐδ' ἀναεῖραι.
καὶ τότε δὴ γίγνωσκον, ὅ τ' οὐκέτι φυκτὰ πέλοντο.

together in love. And when Hephaestus heard the heart-stinging tale, he went his way to his smithy, pondering evil in the deep of his heart, and set on the anvil block the great anvil and forged bonds which could not be broken or loosed, that they might stay firmly in place. But when he had fashioned the snare in his wrath against Ares, he went to his chamber where lay his bed, and everywhere round about the bedposts he spread the bonds, and many, too, were hung from above, from the roofbeams, fine as spiders' webs, so that no one even of the blessed gods could see them, so cunningly were they fashioned. But when he had spread all his snare about the couch, he made as though he would go to Lemnos, that well-ordered citadel, which is in his eyes far the dearest of all lands. And no blind watch did Ares of the golden rein keep, when he saw Hephaestus, famed for his handicraft, departing, but he went his way to the house of famous Hephaestus, eager for the love of fair-crowned Cytherea. Now she had just come from the presence of her father, the mighty son of Cronos, and had sat down. And Ares came into the house and clasped her hand and spoke and addressed her:

"Come, love, let us to bed and take our joy, couched together. For Hephaestus is no longer here in the land, but has now gone, no doubt, to Lemnos, to visit the Sintians of savage speech."

So he spoke, and a welcome thing it seemed to her to lie with him. So they two went to the couch and laid them down to sleep, and about them fell the cunning bonds of the wise Hephaestus, nor could they in any way stir their limbs or raise them up. Then at length they realized that there was no more escaping. And near to them came the

300 ἀγχίμολον δέ σφ' ἦλθε περικλυτὸς ἀμφιγυήεις,
αὖτις ὑποστρέψας πρὶν Λήμνου γαῖαν ἱκέσθαι·
Ἥλιος γάρ οἱ σκοπιὴν ἔχεν εἶπέ τε μῦθον.
βῆ δ' ἴμεναι πρὸς δῶμα φίλον τετιημένος ἦτορ·[1]
ἔστη δ' ἐν προθύροισι, χόλος δέ μιν ἄγριος ᾕρει·
305 σμερδαλέον δ' ἐβόησε, γέγωνέ τε πᾶσι θεοῖσιν·

    "Ζεῦ πάτερ ἠδ' ἄλλοι μάκαρες θεοὶ αἰὲν ἐόντες,
δεῦθ', ἵνα ἔργα γελαστὰ καὶ οὐκ ἐπιεικτὰ ἴδησθε,
ὡς ἐμὲ χωλὸν ἐόντα Διὸς θυγάτηρ Ἀφροδίτη
αἰὲν ἀτιμάζει, φιλέει δ' ἀΐδηλον Ἄρηα,
310 οὕνεχ' ὁ μὲν καλός τε καὶ ἀρτίπος, αὐτὰρ ἐγώ γε
ἠπεδανὸς γενόμην. ἀτὰρ οὔ τί μοι αἴτιος ἄλλος,
ἀλλὰ τοκῆε δύω, τὼ μὴ γείνασθαι ὄφελλον.
ἀλλ' ὄψεσθ', ἵνα τώ γε καθεύδετον ἐν φιλότητι
εἰς ἐμὰ δέμνια βάντες, ἐγὼ δ' ὁρόων ἀκάχημαι.
315 οὐ μέν σφεας ἔτ' ἔολπα μίνυνθά γε κείμεν οὕτως
καὶ μάλα περ φιλέοντε· τάχ' οὐκ ἐθελήσετον ἄμφω
εὕδειν· ἀλλά σφωε δόλος καὶ δεσμὸς ἐρύξει,
εἰς ὅ κέ μοι μάλα πάντα πατὴρ ἀποδῷσιν ἔεδνα,
ὅσσα οἱ ἐγγυάλιξα κυνώπιδος εἵνεκα κούρης,
320 οὕνεκά οἱ καλὴ θυγάτηρ, ἀτὰρ οὐκ ἐχέθυμος."

    ὣς ἔφαθ', οἱ δ' ἀγέροντο θεοὶ ποτὶ χαλκοβατὲς δῶ·
ἦλθε Ποσειδάων γαιήοχος, ἦλθ' ἐριούνης
Ἑρμείας, ἦλθεν δὲ ἄναξ ἑκάεργος Ἀπόλλων.
θηλύτεραι δὲ θεαὶ μένον αἰδοῖ οἴκοι ἑκάστη.
325 ἔσταν δ' ἐν προθύροισι θεοί, δωτῆρες ἑάων·
ἄσβεστος δ' ἄρ' ἐνῶρτο γέλως μακάρεσσι θεοῖσι
τέχνας εἰσορόωσι πολύφρονος Ἡφαίστοιο.

famous god of the two lame legs, having turned back before he reached the land of Lemnos; for Helios had kept watch for him and brought him word. So he went to his house troubled at heart, and stood in the gateway, and fierce anger seized him. And terribly he cried out and called to all the gods:

"Father Zeus, and you other blessed gods that are forever, come hither that you may see a matter laughable and unendurable, how Aphrodite, daughter of Zeus, scorns me for being lame and loves hateful Ares because he is handsome and strong of limb, whereas I was born misshapen. Yet for this is none other to blame but my two parents—would they had never begotten me! But you shall see where these two have gone up into my bed and sleep together in love, while I am filled with grief at the sight. Yet I think they will not wish to lie longer like this, no, not for a moment, no matter how loving they are. Soon shall both lose their desire to sleep; instead the snare and the bonds shall hold them until her father pays back to me all the gifts of wooing that I gave him for his shameless girl, since his daughter is beautiful but faithless."

So he spoke, and the gods gathered to his house with its bronze threshold. Poseidon came, the earth-bearer, and the helper Hermes came, and the lord Apollo who works from afar. The goddesses stayed behind for shame, each in her own house, but the gods, the givers of good things, stood in the gateway; and unquenchable laughter arose among the blessed gods as they saw the craft of wise

---

[1] Line 303 is omitted in most MSS; cf. 2.298.

ὧδε δέ τις εἴπεσκεν ἰδὼν ἐς πλησίον ἄλλον·

"οὐκ ἀρετᾷ κακὰ ἔργα· κιχάνει τοι βραδὺς ὠκύν,

330 ὡς καὶ νῦν Ἥφαιστος ἐὼν βραδὺς εἷλεν Ἄρηα

ὠκύτατόν περ ἐόντα θεῶν οἳ Ὄλυμπον ἔχουσιν,

χωλὸς ἐὼν τέχνῃσι· τὸ καὶ μοιχάγρι' ὀφέλλει."

ὣς οἱ μὲν τοιαῦτα πρὸς ἀλλήλους ἀγόρευον·

Ἑρμῆν δὲ προσέειπεν ἄναξ Διὸς υἱὸς Ἀπόλλων·

335 "Ἑρμεία, Διὸς υἱέ, διάκτορε, δῶτορ ἑάων,

ἦ ῥά κεν ἐν δεσμοῖς ἐθέλοις κρατεροῖσι πιεσθεὶς

εὕδειν ἐν λέκτροισι παρὰ χρυσέῃ Ἀφροδίτῃ;"

τὸν δ' ἠμείβετ' ἔπειτα διάκτορος ἀργεϊφόντης·

"αἲ γὰρ τοῦτο γένοιτο, ἄναξ ἑκατηβόλ' Ἄπολλον·

340 δεσμοὶ μὲν τρὶς τόσσοι ἀπείρονες ἀμφὶς ἔχοιεν,

ὑμεῖς δ' εἰσορόῳτε θεοὶ πᾶσαί τε θέαιναι,

αὐτὰρ ἐγὼν εὕδοιμι παρὰ χρυσέῃ Ἀφροδίτῃ."

ὣς ἔφατ', ἐν δὲ γέλως ὦρτ' ἀθανάτοισι θεοῖσιν.

οὐδὲ Ποσειδάωνα γέλως ἔχε, λίσσετο δ' αἰεὶ

345 Ἥφαιστον κλυτοεργὸν ὅπως λύσειεν Ἄρηα.

καί μιν φωνήσας ἔπεα πτερόεντα προσηύδα·

"λῦσον· ἐγὼ δέ τοι αὐτὸν ὑπίσχομαι, ὡς σὺ κελεύεις,

τίσειν αἴσιμα πάντα μετ' ἀθανάτοισι θεοῖσιν."

τὸν δ' αὖτε προσέειπε περικλυτὸς ἀμφιγυήεις·

350 "μή με, Ποσείδαον γαιήοχε, ταῦτα κέλευε·

δειλαί τοι δειλῶν γε καὶ ἐγγύαι ἐγγυάασθαι.

πῶς ἂν ἐγώ σε δέοιμι μετ' ἀθανάτοισι θεοῖσιν,

εἴ κεν Ἄρης οἴχοιτο χρέος καὶ δεσμὸν ἀλύξας;"

τὸν δ' αὖτε προσέειπε Ποσειδάων ἐνοσίχθων·

355 "Ἥφαιστ', εἴ περ γάρ κεν Ἄρης χρεῖος ὑπαλύξας

Hephaestus. And thus would one speak, with a glance at his neighbor:

"Ill deeds do not win out. The slow catches the swift; just as now Hephaestus, slow as he is, has caught Ares even though he is the swiftest of the gods who hold Olympus. Lame, he has caught him by craft. Ares must pay for his adultery."

Thus they spoke to one another. But to Hermes the lord Apollo, son of Zeus, said:

"Hermes, son of Zeus, guide, giver of good things, would you be willing, even though ensnared with strong bonds, to lie on a couch by the side of golden Aphrodite?"

Then the messenger Argeïphontes answered him: "Would that this might happen, lord Apollo, far-shooter—that thrice as many ineluctable bonds might clasp me about and you gods, yes, and all the goddesses too might be looking on, but that I might sleep by the side of golden Aphrodite."

So he spoke and laughter arose among the immortal gods. But Poseidon did not laugh, but kept beseeching Hephaestus, the famous craftsman, to set Ares free; and he spoke, and addressed him with winged words:

"Free him, and I promise, as you demand, that he shall himself pay you all that is right in the presence of the immortal gods."

Then the famous god of the two lame legs answered him: "Do not ask this of me, Poseidon, earth-bearer. A sorry thing to be sure of is the surety for a sorry rascal. How could I put you in bonds among the immortal gods, if Ares should avoid both the debt and the bonds and depart?"

Then again Poseidon, the earth-shaker, answered him: "Hephaestus, even if Ares shall avoid the debt and escape,

οἴχηται φεύγων, αὐτός τοι ἐγὼ τάδε τίσω."

    τὸν δ' ἠμείβετ' ἔπειτα περικλυτὸς ἀμφιγυήεις·
"οὐκ ἔστ' οὐδὲ ἔοικε τεὸν ἔπος ἀρνήσασθαι."

    ὣς εἰπὼν δεσμὸν ἀνίει μένος Ἡφαίστοιο.

360 τὼ δ' ἐπεὶ ἐκ δεσμοῖο λύθεν, κρατεροῦ περ ἐόντος,
αὐτίκ' ἀναΐξαντε ὁ μὲν Θρήκηνδε βεβήκει,
ἡ δ' ἄρα Κύπρον ἵκανε φιλομμειδὴς Ἀφροδίτη,
ἐς Πάφον· ἔνθα δέ οἱ τέμενος βωμός τε θυήεις.
ἔνθα δέ μιν Χάριτες λοῦσαν καὶ χρῖσαν ἐλαίῳ

365 ἀμβρότῳ, οἷα θεοὺς ἐπενήνοθεν αἰὲν ἐόντας,
ἀμφὶ δὲ εἵματα ἕσσαν ἐπήρατα, θαῦμα ἰδέσθαι.

    ταῦτ' ἄρ' ἀοιδὸς ἄειδε περικλυτός· αὐτὰρ Ὀδυσσεὺς
τέρπετ' ἐνὶ φρεσὶν ᾗσιν ἀκούων ἠδὲ καὶ ἄλλοι
Φαίηκες δολιχήρετμοι, ναυσίκλυτοι ἄνδρες.

370 Ἀλκίνοος δ' Ἅλιον καὶ Λαοδάμαντα κέλευσεν
μουνὰξ ὀρχήσασθαι, ἐπεί σφισιν οὔ τις ἔριζεν.
οἱ δ' ἐπεὶ οὖν σφαῖραν καλὴν μετὰ χερσὶν ἕλοντο,
πορφυρέην, τήν σφιν Πόλυβος ποίησε δαΐφρων,
τὴν ἕτερος ῥίπτασκε ποτὶ νέφεα σκιόεντα

375 ἰδνωθεὶς ὀπίσω, ὁ δ' ἀπὸ χθονὸς ὑψόσ' ἀερθεὶς
ῥηιδίως μεθέλεσκε, πάρος ποσὶν οὖδας ἱκέσθαι.
αὐτὰρ ἐπεὶ δὴ σφαίρῃ ἀν' ἰθὺν πειρήσαντο,
ὠρχείσθην δὴ ἔπειτα ποτὶ χθονὶ πουλυβοτείρῃ
ταρφέ' ἀμειβομένω· κοῦροι δ' ἐπελήκεον ἄλλοι

380 ἑσταῶτες κατ' ἀγῶνα, πολὺς δ' ὑπὸ κόμπος ὀρώρει.

    δὴ τότ' ἄρ' Ἀλκίνοον προσεφώνεε δῖος Ὀδυσσεύς·
"Ἀλκίνοε κρεῖον, πάντων ἀριδείκετε λαῶν,
ἠμὲν ἀπείλησας βητάρμονας εἶναι ἀρίστους,

I will myself pay you this."

Then the famous god of the two lame legs answered him: "I cannot refuse you, nor would it be right."

So saying the mighty Hephaestus loosed the bonds and the two, when they were freed from that bond so strong, sprang up instantly. And Ares departed to Thrace, but she, the laughter-loving Aphrodite, went to Cyprus, to Paphos, where she has a precinct and fragrant altar. There the Graces bathed her and anointed her with immortal oil, such as adorns the skin of the gods who are forever. And they dressed her in lovely garments, a wonder to behold.

This song the famous minstrel sang; and Odysseus was glad at heart as he listened, and so too were the Phaeacians of the long oars, men famed for their ships.

Then Alcinous made Halius and Laodamas dance alone, for no one could vie with them. And when they had taken in their hands the beautiful ball of purple, which wise Polybus had made for them, the one would lean backward and toss it toward the shadowy clouds, and the other would leap up from the earth and skillfully catch it before his feet touched the ground again. But when they had tried their skill in tossing the ball straight up, the two fell to dancing on the bounteous earth, constantly tossing the ball to and fro, and the other youths stood in the place of contests and beat time, and loud was the applause that arose.

Then to Alcinous spoke noble Odysseus: "Lord Alcinous, renowned above all men, you boasted that your dancers were the best, and lo, your words were made

ἠδ' ἄρ' ἑτοῖμα τέτυκτο· σέβας μ' ἔχει εἰσορόωντα."

385 ὣς φάτο, γήθησεν δ' ἱερὸν μένος Ἀλκινόοιο,
αἶψα δὲ Φαιήκεσσι φιληρέτμοισι μετηύδα·
"κέκλυτε, Φαιήκων ἡγήτορες ἠδὲ μέδοντες.
ὁ ξεῖνος μάλα μοι δοκέει πεπνυμένος εἶναι.
ἀλλ' ἄγε οἱ δῶμεν ξεινήιον, ὡς ἐπιεικές.

390 δώδεκα γὰρ κατὰ δῆμον ἀριπρεπέες βασιλῆες
ἀρχοὶ κραίνουσι, τρισκαιδέκατος δ' ἐγὼ αὐτός·
τῶν οἱ ἕκαστος φᾶρος ἐυπλυνὲς ἠδὲ χιτῶνα
καὶ χρυσοῖο τάλαντον ἐνείκατε τιμήεντος.
αἶψα δὲ πάντα φέρωμεν ἀολλέα, ὄφρ' ἐνὶ χερσὶν

395 ξεῖνος ἔχων ἐπὶ δόρπον ἴῃ χαίρων ἐνὶ θυμῷ.
Εὐρύαλος δέ ἑ αὐτὸν ἀρεσσάσθω ἐπέεσσι
καὶ δώρῳ, ἐπεὶ οὔ τι ἔπος κατὰ μοῖραν ἔειπεν."
ὣς ἔφαθ', οἱ δ' ἄρα πάντες ἐπῄνεον ἠδ' ἐκέλευον,
δῶρα δ' ἄρ' οἰσέμεναι πρόεσαν κήρυκα ἕκαστος.

400 τὸν δ' αὖτ' Εὐρύαλος ἀπαμείβετο φωνήσέν τε·
"Ἀλκίνοε κρεῖον, πάντων ἀριδείκετε λαῶν,
τοιγὰρ ἐγὼ τὸν ξεῖνον ἀρέσσομαι, ὡς σὺ κελεύεις.
δώσω οἱ τόδ' ἄορ παγχάλκεον, ᾧ ἔπι κώπη
ἀργυρέη, κολεὸν δὲ νεοπρίστου ἐλέφαντος

405 ἀμφιδεδίνηται· πολέος δέ οἱ ἄξιον ἔσται."
ὣς εἰπὼν ἐν χερσὶ τίθει ξίφος ἀργυρόηλον
καί μιν φωνήσας ἔπεα πτερόεντα προσηύδα·
"χαῖρε, πάτερ ὦ ξεῖνε· ἔπος δ' εἴ πέρ τι βέβακται
δεινόν, ἄφαρ τὸ φέροιεν ἀναρπάξασαι ἄελλαι.

410 σοὶ δὲ θεοὶ ἄλοχόν τ' ἰδέειν καὶ πατρίδ' ἱκέσθαι
δοῖεν, ἐπεὶ δὴ δηθὰ φίλων ἄπο πήματα πάσχεις."

good; amazement holds me as I look on them."

So he spoke, and the divine might of Alcinous was glad; and instantly he spoke among the Phaeacians, lovers of the oar:

"Hear me, leaders and counselors of the Phaeacians. This stranger seems to me in the highest degree a man of understanding. Come then, let us give him a gift of friendship, as is fitting; for twelve glorious kings hold sway in our land as rulers, and I myself am the thirteenth. Now do you, each of the twelve, bring a newly washed cloak and tunic, and a talent of precious gold, and let us quickly bring it all together, that the stranger with our gifts in his hands may go to his supper glad at heart. And let Euryalus make amends to the stranger himself with words and with a gift, for the word that he spoke was in no way suitable."

So he spoke, and they all praised his words and bade that so it should be, and sent forth each of them a herald to bring the gifts. And Euryalus in turn made answer and said:

"Lord Alcinous, renowned above all men, I will indeed make amends to the stranger as you bid me. I will give him this sword, all of bronze, on which is a hilt of silver, and a scabbard of new-sawn ivory is worked about it; it will be a thing of great worth to him."

So saying, he put into his hands the silver-studded sword, and spoke, and addressed him with winged words: "Hail, father stranger; and if any word has been spoken that was harsh, may the storm winds instantly snatch it and bear it away. And for yourself, may the gods grant you to see your wife, and to come to your native land, since it is a long time indeed that you have been suffering woes far from your people."

τὸν δ' ἀπαμειβόμενος προσέφη πολύμητις Ὀδυσσεύς·
"καὶ σὺ φίλος μάλα χαῖρε, θεοὶ δέ τοι ὄλβια δοῖεν.
μηδέ τι τοι ξίφεός γε ποθὴ μετόπισθε γένοιτο
415 τούτου, ὃ δή μοι δῶκας ἀρεσσάμενος ἐπέεσσιν."
ἦ ῥα καὶ ἀμφ' ὤμοισι θέτο ξίφος ἀργυρόηλον.
δύσετό τ' ἠέλιος, καὶ τῷ κλυτὰ δῶρα παρῆεν.
καὶ τά γ' ἐς Ἀλκινόοιο φέρον κήρυκες ἀγαυοί·
δεξάμενοι δ' ἄρα παῖδες ἀμύμονος Ἀλκινόοιο
420 μητρὶ παρ' αἰδοίῃ ἔθεσαν περικαλλέα δῶρα.
τοῖσιν δ' ἡγεμόνευ' ἱερὸν μένος Ἀλκινόοιο,
ἐλθόντες δὲ καθῖζον ἐν ὑψηλοῖσι θρόνοισι.
δή ῥα τότ' Ἀρήτην προσέφη μένος Ἀλκινόοιο·
"δεῦρο, γύναι, φέρε χηλὸν ἀριπρεπέ', ἥ τις ἀρίστη·
425 ἐν δ' αὐτὴ θὲς φᾶρος ἐϋπλυνὲς ἠδὲ χιτῶνα.
ἀμφὶ δέ οἱ πυρὶ χαλκὸν ἰήνατε, θέρμετε δ' ὕδωρ,
ὄφρα λοεσσάμενός τε ἰδών τ' ἐῢ κείμενα πάντα
δῶρα, τά οἱ Φαίηκες ἀμύμονες ἐνθάδ' ἔνεικαν,
δαιτί τε τέρπηται καὶ ἀοιδῆς ὕμνον ἀκούων.
430 καί οἱ ἐγὼ τόδ' ἄλεισον ἐμὸν περικαλλὲς ὀπάσσω,
χρύσεον, ὄφρ' ἐμέθεν μεμνημένος ἤματα πάντα
σπένδῃ ἐνὶ μεγάρῳ Διί τ' ἄλλοισίν τε θεοῖσιν."
ὣς ἔφατ', Ἀρήτη δὲ μετὰ δμῳῆσιν ἔειπεν
ἀμφὶ πυρὶ στῆσαι τρίποδα μέγαν ὅττι τάχιστα.
435 αἱ δὲ λοετροχόον τρίποδ' ἵστασαν ἐν πυρὶ κηλέῳ,
ἔν δ' ἄρ' ὕδωρ ἔχεαν, ὑπὸ δὲ ξύλα δαῖον ἑλοῦσαι.
γάστρην μὲν τρίποδος πῦρ ἄμφεπε, θέρμετο δ' ὕδωρ·
τόφρα δ' ἄρ' Ἀρήτη ξείνῳ περικαλλέα χηλὸν
ἐξέφερεν θαλάμοιο, τίθει δ' ἐνὶ κάλλιμα δῶρα,

And resourceful Odysseus answered him, and said: "All hail to you, too, friend; and may the gods grant you happiness, and may you never hereafter miss this sword which you have given me, making amends with gentle speech."

He spoke, and about his shoulders hung the silver-studded sword. And the sun set, and the glorious gifts were brought him. These the lordly heralds bore to the palace of Alcinous, and the sons of the flawless Alcinous took the beautiful gifts and set them before their revered mother. And the divine might of Alcinous led the way, and they came in and sat down on the high seats. Then to Arete spoke the mighty Alcinous:

"Bring hither, wife, a handsome chest, the best you have, and yourself place in it a newly washed cloak and tunic; and heat for the stranger a cauldron on the fire, and warm water, that when he has bathed and seen well bestowed all the gifts which the flawless Phaeacians have brought here, he may take pleasure in the feast, and in hearing the strains of the song. And I will give him this beautiful cup of mine, wrought of gold, that he may remember me all his days as he pours libations in his halls to Zeus and to the other gods."

So he spoke, and Arete bade her handmaids to set a great cauldron on the fire with all speed. And they set on the blazing fire the cauldron for filling the bath, and poured in water, and took billets of wood and kindled them beneath it. Then the fire played about the belly of the cauldron, and the water grew warm; but meanwhile Arete brought forth for the stranger a beautiful chest from the treasure chamber, and placed in it the handsome gifts, the

440 ἐσθῆτα χρυσόν τε, τά οἱ Φαίηκες ἔδωκαν·
ἐν δ᾽ αὐτῇ φᾶρος θῆκεν καλόν τε χιτῶνα,
καί μιν φωνήσασ᾽ ἔπεα πτερόεντα προσηύδα·
"αὐτὸς νῦν ἴδε πῶμα, θοῶς δ᾽ ἐπὶ δεσμὸν ἴηλον,
μή τίς τοι καθ᾽ ὁδὸν δηλήσεται, ὁππότ᾽ ἂν αὖτε
445 εὕδῃσθα γλυκὺν ὕπνον ἰὼν ἐν νηὶ μελαίνῃ."
αὐτὰρ ἐπεὶ τό γ᾽ ἄκουσε πολύτλας δῖος Ὀδυσσεύς,
αὐτίκ᾽ ἐπήρτυε πῶμα, θοῶς δ᾽ ἐπὶ δεσμὸν ἴηλεν
ποικίλον, ὅν ποτέ μιν δέδαε φρεσὶ πότνια Κίρκη·
αὐτόδιον δ᾽ ἄρα μιν ταμίη λούσασθαι ἀνώγει
450 ἔς ῥ᾽ ἀσάμινθον βάνθ᾽· ὁ δ᾽ ἄρ ἀσπασίως ἴδε θυμῷ
θερμὰ λοέτρ᾽, ἐπεὶ οὔ τι κομιζόμενός γε θάμιζεν,
ἐπεὶ δὴ λίπε δῶμα Καλυψοῦς ἠυκόμοιο.
τόφρα δέ οἱ κομιδή γε θεῷ ὣς ἔμπεδος ἦεν.
τὸν δ᾽ ἐπεὶ οὖν δμωαὶ λοῦσαν καὶ χρῖσαν ἐλαίῳ,
455 ἀμφὶ δέ μιν χλαῖναν καλὴν βάλον ἠδὲ χιτῶνα,
ἔκ ῥ᾽ ἀσαμίνθου βὰς ἄνδρας μέτα οἰνοποτῆρας
ἤιε· Ναυσικάα δὲ θεῶν ἄπο κάλλος ἔχουσα
στῆ ῥα παρὰ σταθμὸν τέγεος πύκα ποιητοῖο,
θαύμαζεν δ᾽ Ὀδυσῆα ἐν ὀφθαλμοῖσιν ὁρῶσα,
460 καί μιν φωνήσασ᾽ ἔπεα πτερόεντα προσηύδα·
"χαῖρε, ξεῖν᾽, ἵνα καί ποτ᾽ ἐὼν ἐν πατρίδι γαίῃ
μνήσῃ ἐμεῦ, ὅτι μοι πρώτῃ ζωάγρι᾽ ὀφέλλεις."
τὴν δ᾽ ἀπαμειβόμενος προσέφη πολύμητις Ὀδυσσεύς.
"Ναυσικάα θύγατερ μεγαλήτορος Ἀλκινόοιο,
465 οὕτω νῦν Ζεὺς θείη, ἐρίγδουπος πόσις Ἥρης,
οἴκαδέ τ᾽ ἐλθέμεναι καὶ νόστιμον ἦμαρ ἰδέσθαι·
τῷ κέν τοι καὶ κεῖθι θεῷ ὣς εὐχετοώμην

clothes and the gold, which the Phaeacians gave. And in it she herself placed a cloak and a beautiful tunic; and she spoke and addressed Odysseus with winged words:

"Look now yourself to the lid, and quickly fasten a cord upon it, for fear some one rob you of your goods on the way, when later on you are lying in sweet sleep, as you travel in the black ship."

Now when the much-enduring noble Odysseus heard these words, he at once fitted on the lid, and quickly fastened a cord upon it—a cunning knot which queenly Circe had once taught him. Then forthwith the house-keeper bade him go to the bath and bathe; and his heart was glad when he saw the warm bath, for such tendance had been by no means frequent from the time that he left the dwelling of lovely-haired Calypso, but until then he had tendance continually, like a god.

Now when the handmaids had bathed him and anointed him with oil, and had put upon him a handsome cloak and tunic, he came forth from the bath, and went to join the men at their wine. And Nausicaa, gifted with beauty by the gods, stood by the doorpost of the well-built hall, and she marveled at Odysseus, as her eyes beheld him, and she spoke, and addressed him with winged words:

"Farewell, stranger, and hereafter even in your own native land may you remember me, for to me first you owe the price of your life."

And resourceful Odysseus answered her, and said: "Nausicaa, daughter of great-hearted Alcinous, so may Zeus, the loud-thundering spouse of Hera, grant that I may reach my home and see the day of my returning. Then I

αἰεὶ ἤματα πάντα· σὺ γάρ μ' ἐβιώσαο, κούρη."

ἦ ῥα καὶ ἐς θρόνον ἷζε παρ' Ἀλκίνοον βασιλῆα·

470 οἱ δ' ἤδη μοίρας τ' ἔνεμον κερόωντό τε οἶνον.
κῆρυξ δ' ἐγγύθεν ἦλθεν ἄγων ἐρίηρον ἀοιδόν,
Δημόδοκον λαοῖσι τετιμένον· εἷσε δ' ἄρ' αὐτὸν
μέσσῳ δαιτυμόνων, πρὸς κίονα μακρὸν ἐρείσας.
δὴ τότε κήρυκα προσέφη πολύμητις Ὀδυσσεύς,

475 νώτου ἀποπροταμών, ἐπὶ δὲ πλεῖον ἐλέλειπτο,
ἀργιόδοντος ὑός, θαλερὴ δ' ἦν ἀμφὶς ἀλοιφή·

"κῆρυξ, τῇ δή, τοῦτο πόρε κρέας, ὄφρα φάγῃσιν,
Δημοδόκῳ· καί μιν προσπτύξομαι ἀχνύμενός περ·
πᾶσι γὰρ ἀνθρώποισιν ἐπιχθονίοισιν ἀοιδοὶ

480 τιμῆς ἔμμοροί εἰσι καὶ αἰδοῦς, οὕνεκ' ἄρα σφέας
οἴμας μοῦσ' ἐδίδαξε, φίλησε δὲ φῦλον ἀοιδῶν."

ὣς ἄρ' ἔφη, κῆρυξ δὲ φέρων ἐν χερσὶν ἔθηκεν
ἥρῳ Δημοδόκῳ· ὁ δ' ἐδέξατο, χαῖρε δὲ θυμῷ.
οἱ δ' ἐπ' ὀνείαθ' ἑτοῖμα προκείμενα χεῖρας ἴαλλον.

485 αὐτὰρ ἐπεὶ πόσιος καὶ ἐδητύος ἐξ ἔρον ἕντο,
δὴ τότε Δημόδοκον προσέφη πολύμητις Ὀδυσσεύς·

"Δημόδοκ', ἔξοχα δή σε βροτῶν αἰνίζομ' ἀπάντων.
ἢ σέ γε μοῦσ' ἐδίδαξε, Διὸς πάις, ἢ σέ γ' Ἀπόλλων·
λίην γὰρ κατὰ κόσμον Ἀχαιῶν οἶτον ἀείδεις,

490 ὅσσ' ἔρξαν τ' ἔπαθόν τε καὶ ὅσσ' ἐμόγησαν Ἀχαιοί,
ὥς τέ που ἢ αὐτὸς παρεὼν ἢ ἄλλου ἀκούσας.
ἀλλ' ἄγε δὴ μετάβηθι καὶ ἵππου κόσμον ἄεισον
δουρατέου, τὸν Ἐπειὸς ἐποίησεν σὺν Ἀθήνῃ,
ὅν ποτ' ἐς ἀκρόπολιν δόλον ἤγαγε δῖος Ὀδυσσεὺς

495 ἀνδρῶν ἐμπλήσας οἵ ῥ' Ἴλιον ἐξαλάπαξαν.

will there, too, pray to you as to a god all my days, for you, maiden, have given me life."

He spoke, and sat down on a chair beside king Alcinous. And now they were serving out portions and mixing the wine. Then the herald came near, leading the good minstrel, Demodocus, held in honor by the people, and seated him in the midst of the banqueters, leaning his chair against a high pillar. Then to the herald said resourceful Odysseus, cutting off a portion of the chine of a white-tusked boar, of which still more was left, and there was rich fat on either side:

"Herald, take and give this portion to Demodocus, that he may eat, and I will greet him, despite my grief. For among all men that are upon the earth minstrels win honor and reverence, for the Muse has taught them the paths of song, and loves the tribe of minstrels."

So he spoke, and the herald took the portion and placed it in the hands of the hero Demodocus, and he took it and was glad at heart. So they put forth their hands to the good cheer lying ready before them. But when they had put from them the desire for food and drink, then to Demodocus said resourceful Odysseus:

"Demodocus, truly above all mortal men do I praise you, whether it was the Muse, daughter of Zeus, that taught you, or Apollo; for well and truly do you sing of the fate of the Achaeans, all that they did and suffered, and all the toils they endured, as perhaps one who had yourself been present, or had heard the tale from another. But come now, change your theme, and sing of the building of the horse of wood, which Epeius made with Athene's help, the horse which once Odysseus led up into the citadel as a thing of guile, when he had filled it with the men who

αἴ κεν δή μοι ταῦτα κατὰ μοῖραν καταλέξῃς,
αὐτίκ᾽ ἐγὼ πᾶσιν μυθήσομαι ἀνθρώποισιν,
ὡς ἄρα τοι πρόφρων θεὸς ὤπασε θέσπιν ἀοιδήν."
   ὣς φάθ᾽, ὁ δ᾽ ὁρμηθεὶς θεοῦ ἤρχετο, φαῖνε δ᾽ ἀοιδήν,
500 ἔνθεν ἑλὼν ὡς οἱ μὲν ἐυσσέλμων ἐπὶ νηῶν
βάντες ἀπέπλειον, πῦρ ἐν κλισίῃσι βαλόντες,
Ἀργεῖοι, τοὶ δ᾽ ἤδη ἀγακλυτὸν ἀμφ᾽ Ὀδυσῆα
ἥατ᾽ ἐνὶ Τρώων ἀγορῇ κεκαλυμμένοι ἵππῳ·
αὐτοὶ γάρ μιν Τρῶες ἐς ἀκρόπολιν ἐρύσαντο.
505 ὣς ὁ μὲν ἑστήκει, τοὶ δ᾽ ἄκριτα πόλλ᾽ ἀγόρευον
ἥμενοι ἀμφ᾽ αὐτόν· τρίχα δέ σφισιν ἥνδανε βουλή,
ἠὲ διαπλῆξαι[1] κοῖλον δόρυ νηλέι χαλκῷ,
ἢ κατὰ πετράων βαλέειν ἐρύσαντας ἐπ᾽ ἄκρης,
ἢ ἐάαν μέγ᾽ ἄγαλμα θεῶν θελκτήριον εἶναι,
510 τῇ περ δὴ καὶ ἔπειτα τελευτήσεσθαι ἔμελλεν·
αἶσα γὰρ ἦν ἀπολέσθαι, ἐπὴν πόλις ἀμφικαλύψῃ
δουράτεον μέγαν ἵππον, ὅθ᾽ ἥατο πάντες ἄριστοι
Ἀργείων Τρώεσσι φόνον καὶ κῆρα φέροντες.
ἤειδεν δ᾽ ὡς ἄστυ διέπραθον υἷες Ἀχαιῶν
515 ἱππόθεν ἐκχύμενοι, κοῖλον λόχον ἐκπρολιπόντες.
ἄλλον δ᾽ ἄλλῃ ἄειδε πόλιν κεραϊζέμεν αἰπήν,
αὐτὰρ Ὀδυσσῆα προτὶ δώματα Δηιφόβοιο
βήμεναι, ἠύτ᾽ Ἄρηα σὺν ἀντιθέῳ Μενελάῳ.
κεῖθι δὴ αἰνότατον πόλεμον φάτο τολμήσαντα
520 νικῆσαι καὶ ἔπειτα διὰ μεγάθυμον Ἀθήνην.
   ταῦτ᾽ ἄρ᾽ ἀοιδὸς ἄειδε περικλυτός· αὐτὰρ Ὀδυσσεὺς
τήκετο, δάκρυ δ᾽ ἔδευεν ὑπὸ βλεφάροισι παρειάς.

---

[1] διαπλῆξαι Aristarchus: διατμῆξαι MSS

sacked Ilium, no less. If you indeed tell me this tale rightly, I will declare to all mankind that the god has with a ready heart granted you the gift of divine song."

So he spoke, and the minstrel, moved by the god, began, and let his song be heard, taking up the tale where the Argives had embarked on their benched ships and were sailing away, after throwing fire on their huts, while those others led by glorious Odysseus were now sitting in the place of assembly of the Trojans, hidden in the horse; for the Trojans had themselves dragged it into the citadel. So there it stood, while the people talked long as they sat about it, and could form no resolve. Three counsels found favor in their minds: either to cleave the hollow timber with the pitiless bronze, or to drag it to the height and throw it down the rocks, or to let it stand as a great offering to propitiate the gods, just as in the end it was to be brought to pass; for it was their fate to perish when their city should enclose the great horse of wood, in which were sitting all the best of the Argives, bearing to the Trojans slaughter and death. And he sang how the sons of the Achaeans poured forth from the horse and, leaving their hollow ambush, sacked the city. Of the others he sang how, some here, some there, they wasted the lofty city, but of Odysseus, how he went like Ares to the house of Deiphobus together with godlike Menelaus. There it was, he said, that Odysseus dared the most terrible fight and in the end conquered by the aid of great-hearted Athene.

This song the famous minstrel sang. But the heart of Odysseus was melted and tears wet his cheeks beneath his

ὡς δὲ γυνὴ κλαίῃσι φίλον πόσιν ἀμφιπεσοῦσα,
ὅς τε ἑῆς πρόσθεν πόλιος λαῶν τε πέσῃσιν,
525 ἄστεϊ καὶ τεκέεσσιν ἀμύνων νηλεὲς ἦμαρ·
ἡ μὲν τὸν θνήσκοντα καὶ ἀσπαίροντα ἰδοῦσα
ἀμφ' αὐτῷ χυμένη λίγα κωκύει· οἱ δέ τ' ὄπισθε
κόπτοντες δούρεσσι μετάφρενον ἠδὲ καὶ ὤμους
εἴρερον εἰσανάγουσι, πόνον τ' ἐχέμεν καὶ ὀϊζύν·
530 τῆς δ' ἐλεεινοτάτῳ ἄχεϊ φθινύθουσι παρειαί·
ὣς Ὀδυσεὺς ἐλεεινὸν ὑπ' ὀφρύσι δάκρυον εἶβεν.
ἔνθ' ἄλλους μὲν πάντας ἐλάνθανε δάκρυα λείβων,
Ἀλκίνοος δέ μιν οἶος ἐπεφράσατ' ἠδ' ἐνόησεν,
ἥμενος ἄγχ' αὐτοῦ, βαρὺ δὲ στενάχοντος ἄκουσεν.
535 αἶψα δὲ Φαιήκεσσι φιληρέτμοισι μετηύδα·
    "κέκλυτε, Φαιήκων ἡγήτορες ἠδὲ μέδοντες,
Δημόδοκος δ' ἤδη σχεθέτω φόρμιγγα λίγειαν·
οὐ γάρ πως πάντεσσι χαριζόμενος τάδ' ἀείδει.
ἐξ οὗ δορπέομέν τε καὶ ὦρορε θεῖος ἀοιδός,
540 ἐκ τοῦ δ' οὔ πω παύσατ' ὀϊζυροῖο γόοιο
ὁ ξεῖνος· μάλα πού μιν ἄχος φρένας ἀμφιβέβηκεν.
ἀλλ' ἄγ' ὁ μὲν σχεθέτω, ἵν' ὁμῶς τερπώμεθα πάντες,
ξεινοδόκοι καὶ ξεῖνος, ἐπεὶ πολὺ κάλλιον οὕτως·
εἵνεκα γὰρ ξείνοιο τάδ' αἰδοίοιο τέτυκται,
545 πομπὴ καὶ φίλα δῶρα, τά οἱ δίδομεν φιλέοντες.
ἀντὶ κασιγνήτου ξεῖνός θ' ἱκέτης τε τέτυκται
ἀνέρι, ὅς τ' ὀλίγον περ ἐπιψαύῃ πραπίδεσσι.
τῷ νῦν μηδὲ σὺ κεῦθε νοήμασι κερδαλέοισιν
ὅττι κέ σ' εἴρωμαι· φάσθαι δέ σε κάλλιόν ἐστιν.
550 εἴπ' ὄνομ' ὅττι σε κεῖθι κάλεον μήτηρ τε πατήρ τε

eyelids. And as a woman wails and throws herself upon her dear husband, who has fallen in front of his city and his people, seeking to ward off from his city and his children the pitiless day; and as she beholds him dying and gasping for breath, she clings to him and shrieks aloud, while the foe behind her beat her back and shoulders with their spears, and lead her away to captivity to bear toil and woe, while with most pitiful grief her cheeks are wasted—so did Odysseus let fall pitiful tears from beneath his brows. Now from all the rest he concealed the tears that he shed, but Alcinous alone was aware of him and noticed, for he sat by him and heard him groaning heavily. And at once he spoke among the Phaeacians, lovers of the oar:

"Hear me, leaders and counselors of the Phaeacians, and let Demodocus now check his clear-toned lyre, for in no way to all alike does he give pleasure with this song. Ever since we began to feast and the divine minstrel was moved to sing, from that time our stranger has never ceased from sorrowful lamentation; surely grief must have encompassed his heart. No, let the minstrel cease, that we all may make merry, hosts and guest alike, since it is much better so. For it is for the revered stranger's sake that all these things have been made ready, his sending and the gifts of friendship which we give him of our love. Dear as a brother is the stranger and the suppliant to a man whose wits have even the slightest reach. Therefore do not you on your part hide with crafty intention whatever I shall ask you; to speak out plainly is the better course. Tell me the name by which they called you at home, your mother and

ἄλλοι θ' οἳ κατὰ ἄστυ καὶ οἳ περιναιετάουσιν.
οὐ μὲν γάρ τις πάμπαν ἀνώνυμός ἐστ' ἀνθρώπων,
οὐ κακὸς οὐδὲ μὲν ἐσθλός, ἐπὴν τὰ πρῶτα γένηται,
ἀλλ' ἐπὶ πᾶσι τίθενται, ἐπεί κε τέκωσι, τοκῆες.
555 εἰπὲ δέ μοι γαῖάν τε τεὴν δῆμόν τε πόλιν τε,
ὄφρα σε τῇ πέμπωσι τιτυσκόμεναι φρεσὶ νῆες·
οὐ γὰρ Φαιήκεσσι κυβερνητῆρες ἔασιν,
οὐδέ τι πηδάλι' ἔστι, τά τ' ἄλλαι νῆες ἔχουσιν·
ἀλλ' αὐταὶ ἴσασι νοήματα καὶ φρένας ἀνδρῶν,
560 καὶ πάντων ἴσασι πόλιας καὶ πίονας ἀγροὺς
ἀνθρώπων, καὶ λαῖτμα τάχισθ' ἁλὸς ἐκπερόωσιν
ἠέρι καὶ νεφέλῃ κεκαλυμμέναι· οὐδέ ποτέ σφιν
οὔτε τι πημανθῆναι ἔπι δέος οὔτ' ἀπολέσθαι.
ἀλλὰ τόδ' ὥς ποτε πατρὸς ἐγὼν εἰπόντος ἄκουσα
565 Ναυσιθόου, ὃς ἔφασκε Ποσειδάων' ἀγάσασθαι
ἡμῖν, οὕνεκα πομποὶ ἀπήμονές εἰμεν ἁπάντων.
φῆ ποτὲ Φαιήκων ἀνδρῶν εὐεργέα νῆα
ἐκ πομπῆς ἀνιοῦσαν ἐν ἠεροειδέι πόντῳ
ῥαισέμεναι, μέγα δ' ἧμιν ὄρος πόλει ἀμφικαλύψειν.
570 ὣς ἀγόρευ' ὁ γέρων· τὰ δέ κεν θεὸς ἢ τελέσειεν
ἤ κ' ἀτέλεστ' εἴη, ὥς οἱ φίλον ἔπλετο θυμῷ·
ἀλλ' ἄγε μοι τόδε εἰπὲ καὶ ἀτρεκέως κατάλεξον,
ὅππῃ ἀπεπλάγχθης τε καὶ ἅς τινας ἵκεο χώρας
ἀνθρώπων, αὐτούς τε πόλιάς τ' ἐὺ ναιετοώσας,
575 ἠμὲν ὅσοι χαλεποί τε καὶ ἄγριοι οὐδὲ δίκαιοι,
οἵ τε φιλόξεινοι, καί σφιν νόος ἐστὶ θεουδής.
εἰπὲ δ' ὅ τι κλαίεις καὶ ὀδύρεαι ἔνδοθι θυμῷ
Ἀργείων Δαναῶν ἠδ' Ἰλίου οἶτον ἀκούων.

your father and other folk besides, your townsmen and the dwellers round about. For there is no one of all mankind who is nameless, be he base man or noble, when once he has been born, but parents bestow names on all when they give them birth. And tell me your country, your people, and your city, that our ships may convey you there, discerning the course by their wits. For the Phaeacians have no pilots, nor steering oars such as other ships have, but the ships themselves understand the thoughts and minds of men, and they know the cities and rich fields of all peoples, and the gulf of the sea they cross most quickly, hidden in mist and cloud, nor ever have they fear of damage or shipwreck. Yet this story I once heard thus told by my father Nausithous, who used to say that Poseidon was indignant with us because we give safe convoy to all men. He said that some day, as a well-built ship of the Phaeacians was returning from a convoy over the misty deep, Poseidon would smite her and would hide our city behind a huge encircling mountain. So that old man spoke, and these things the god will bring to pass, or will leave unfulfilled, as may be his good pleasure. But come, tell me this and declare it truly: whither you have wandered and to what countries of men you have come; tell me of the people and of their populous cities, both of those who are cruel and wild and unjust, and of those who are kind to strangers and fear the gods in their thoughts. And tell me why you weep and wail in spirit as you hear the doom of the Argives and Danaans, and of Ilium. This the gods brought about,

τὸν δὲ θεοὶ μὲν τεῦξαν, ἐπεκλώσαντο δ' ὄλεθρον
580 ἀνθρώποις, ἵνα ᾖσι καὶ ἐσσομένοισιν ἀοιδή.
ἦ τίς τοι καὶ πηὸς ἀπέφθιτο Ἰλιόθι πρὸ
ἐσθλὸς ἐών, γαμβρὸς ἢ πενθερός, οἵ τε μάλιστα
κήδιστοι τελέθουσι μεθ' αἷμά τε καὶ γένος αὐτῶν;
ἦ τίς που καὶ ἑταῖρος ἀνὴρ κεχαρισμένα εἰδώς,
585 ἐσθλός; ἐπεὶ οὐ μέν τι κασιγνήτοιο χερείων
γίγνεται, ὅς κεν ἑταῖρος ἐὼν πεπνυμένα εἰδῇ."

and spun the skein of ruin for men, that there might be a song for those yet to be born. Did some kinsman of yours fall before Ilium, some good, true man, your daughter's husband or your wife's father, such as are nearest to one after one's own kin and blood? Or was it perhaps some comrade dear to your heart, some good, true man? For no whit worse than a brother is a comrade who knows what is right."

I

Τὸν δ' ἀπαμειβόμενος προσέφη πολύμητις Ὀδυσσεύς·
"Ἀλκίνοε κρεῖον, πάντων ἀριδείκετε λαῶν,
ἦ τοι μὲν τόδε καλὸν ἀκουέμεν ἐστὶν ἀοιδοῦ
τοιοῦδ' οἷος ὅδ' ἐστί, θεοῖς ἐναλίγκιος αὐδήν.
5   οὐ γὰρ ἐγώ γέ τί φημι τέλος χαριέστερον εἶναι
ἢ ὅτ' ἐυφροσύνη μὲν ἔχῃ κάτα δῆμον ἅπαντα,
δαιτυμόνες δ' ἀνὰ δώματ' ἀκουάζωνται ἀοιδοῦ
ἥμενοι ἑξείης, παρὰ δὲ πλήθωσι τράπεζαι
σίτου καὶ κρειῶν, μέθυ δ' ἐκ κρητῆρος ἀφύσσων
10 οἰνοχόος φορέῃσι καὶ ἐγχείῃ δεπάεσσι·
τοῦτό τί μοι κάλλιστον ἐνὶ φρεσὶν εἴδεται εἶναι.
σοὶ δ' ἐμὰ κήδεα θυμὸς ἐπετράπετο στονόεντα
εἴρεσθ', ὄφρ' ἔτι μᾶλλον ὀδυρόμενος στεναχίζω·
τί πρῶτόν τοι ἔπειτα, τί δ' ὑστάτιον καταλέξω;
15 κήδε' ἐπεί μοι πολλὰ δόσαν θεοὶ Οὐρανίωνες.
νῦν δ' ὄνομα πρῶτον μυθήσομαι, ὄφρα καὶ ὑμεῖς
εἴδετ', ἐγὼ δ' ἂν ἔπειτα φυγὼν ὕπο νηλεὲς ἦμαρ
ὑμῖν ξεῖνος ἔω καὶ ἀπόπροθι δώματα ναίων.
εἴμ' Ὀδυσεὺς Λαερτιάδης, ὃς πᾶσι δόλοισιν
20 ἀνθρώποισι μέλω, καί μευ κλέος οὐρανὸν ἵκει.
ναιετάω δ' Ἰθάκην ἐυδείελον· ἐν δ' ὄρος αὐτῇ
Νήριτον εἰνοσίφυλλον, ἀριπρεπές· ἀμφὶ δὲ νῆσοι

BOOK 9

Then resourceful Odysseus answered him, and said:
"Lord Alcinous, renowned above all men, truly this is a
good thing, to listen to a minstrel such as this man is, like to
the gods in voice. For myself I declare that there is no
greater fulfillment of delight than when joy possesses a
whole people, and banqueters in the halls listen to a min-
strel as they sit side by side, and the cupbearer draws wine
from the bowl and bears it round and pours it into the
cups. This seems to my mind a thing surpassingly lovely.
But your heart is turned to ask of my grievous woes, that I
may weep and groan the more. What, then, shall I tell you
first, what last? For woes uncounted have the heavenly
gods given me. First now will I tell my name, that you all
also may know of it, and that I hereafter escaping the piti-
less day of doom may be your host, far off though my home
is. I am Odysseus, son of Laertes, known to all men for my
stratagems, and my fame reaches the heavens. I dwell in
clear-seen Ithaca; on it is a mountain, Neriton, covered
with waving forests, conspicuous from afar; and round it lie

πολλαὶ ναιετάουσι μάλα σχεδὸν ἀλλήλῃσι,
Δουλίχιόν τε Σάμη τε καὶ ὑλήεσσα Ζάκυνθος.
25 αὐτὴ δὲ χθαμαλὴ πανυπερτάτη εἰν ἁλὶ κεῖται
πρὸς ζόφον, αἱ δέ τ' ἄνευθε πρὸς ἠῶ τ' ἠέλιόν τε,
τρηχεῖ', ἀλλ' ἀγαθὴ κουροτρόφος· οὔ τοι ἐγώ γε
ἧς γαίης δύναμαι γλυκερώτερον ἄλλο ἰδέσθαι.
ἦ μέν μ' αὐτόθ' ἔρυκε Καλυψώ, δῖα θεάων,
30 ἐν σπέσσι γλαφυροῖσι, λιλαιομένη πόσιν εἶναι·[1]
ὣς δ' αὔτως Κίρκη κατερήτυεν ἐν μεγάροισιν
Αἰαίη δολόεσσα, λιλαιομένη πόσιν εἶναι·
ἀλλ' ἐμὸν οὔ ποτε θυμὸν ἐνὶ στήθεσσιν ἔπειθον.
ὣς οὐδὲν γλύκιον ἧς πατρίδος οὐδὲ τοκήων
35 γίγνεται, εἴ περ καί τις ἀπόπροθι πίονα οἶκον
γαίῃ ἐν ἀλλοδαπῇ ναίει ἀπάνευθε τοκήων.
εἰ δ' ἄγε τοι καὶ νόστον ἐμὸν πολυκηδέ' ἐνίσπω,
ὅν μοι Ζεὺς ἐφέηκεν ἀπὸ Τροίηθεν ἰόντι.

"Ἰλιόθεν με φέρων ἄνεμος Κικόνεσσι πέλασσεν,
40 Ἰσμάρῳ. ἔνθα δ' ἐγὼ πόλιν ἔπραθον, ὤλεσα δ' αὐτούς·
ἐκ πόλιος δ' ἀλόχους καὶ κτήματα πολλὰ λαβόντες
δασσάμεθ', ὡς μή τίς μοι ἀτεμβόμενος κίοι ἴσης.
ἔνθ' ἦ τοι μὲν ἐγὼ διερῷ ποδὶ φευγέμεν ἡμέας
ἠνώγεα, τοὶ δὲ μέγα νήπιοι οὐκ ἐπίθοντο.
45 ἔνθα δὲ πολλὸν μὲν μέθυ πίνετο, πολλὰ δὲ μῆλα
ἔσφαζον παρὰ θῖνα καὶ εἰλίποδας ἕλικας βοῦς·
τόφρα δ' ἄρ' οἰχόμενοι Κίκονες Κικόνεσσι γεγώνευν,
οἵ σφιν γείτονες ἦσαν, ἅμα πλέονες καὶ ἀρείους,
ἤπειρον ναίοντες, ἐπιστάμενοι μὲν ἀφ' ἵππων
50 ἀνδράσι μάρνασθαι καὶ ὅθι χρὴ πεζὸν ἐόντα.

many islands close by one another, Dulichium, and Same and wooded Zacynthus. Ithaca itself lies low in the sea, farthest of all toward the dark, but the others lie apart toward the Dawn and the sun—a rugged island, but a good nurse of young men; and for myself no other thing can I see sweeter than one's own land. It is true that Calypso, the beautiful goddess, kept me by her in her hollow caves, yearning that I should be her husband; and in the same way Circe held me back in her halls, the guileful lady of Aeaea, yearning that I should be her husband; but they could never persuade the heart in my breast. So true is it that nothing is sweeter than a man's own land and his parents, even though it is in a rich house that he dwells afar in a foreign land away from his parents. But come, let me tell also of my woeful homecoming, which Zeus laid upon me as I came from Troy.

"From Ilium the wind bore me and brought me to the Cicones, to Ismarus. There I sacked the city and slew the men; and from the city we took their wives and much treasure, and divided it among us, that so far as lay in me no man might go defrauded of an equal share. Then you may be sure I for my part ordered that we should flee with a quick foot, but the others in their great folly did not listen. There much wine was drunk, and many sheep they slew by the shore, and spiral-horned cattle of shambling gait. Meanwhile the Cicones went and called to other Cicones who were their neighbors, at once more numerous and braver than they—men that lived inland and were skilled at fighting their foes from chariots, and, where necessary,

---

[1] Line 30 is omitted in most MSS.

ἦλθον ἔπειθ' ὅσα φύλλα καὶ ἄνθεα γίγνεται ὥρῃ,
ἠέριοι· τότε δή ῥα κακὴ Διὸς αἶσα παρέστη
ἡμῖν αἰνομόροισιν, ἵν' ἄλγεα πολλὰ πάθοιμεν.
στησάμενοι δ' ἐμάχοντο μάχην παρὰ νηυσὶ θοῇσι,
55   βάλλον δ' ἀλλήλους χαλκήρεσιν ἐγχείῃσιν.
ὄφρα μὲν ἠὼς ἦν καὶ ἀέξετο ἱερὸν ἦμαρ,
τόφρα δ' ἀλεξόμενοι μένομεν πλέονάς περ ἐόντας.
ἦμος δ' ἠέλιος μετενίσσετο βουλυτόνδε,
καὶ τότε δὴ Κίκονες κλῖναν δαμάσαντες Ἀχαιούς.
60   ἓξ δ' ἀφ' ἑκάστης νηὸς ἐυκνήμιδες ἑταῖροι
ὤλονθ'· οἱ δ' ἄλλοι φύγομεν θάνατόν τε μόρον τε.
     ἔνθεν δὲ προτέρω πλέομεν ἀκαχήμενοι ἦτορ,
ἄσμενοι ἐκ θανάτοιο, φίλους ὀλέσαντες ἑταίρους.
οὐδ' ἄρα μοι προτέρω νῆες κίον ἀμφιέλισσαι,
65   πρίν τινα τῶν δειλῶν ἑτάρων τρὶς ἕκαστον ἀῦσαι,
οἳ θάνον ἐν πεδίῳ Κικόνων ὕπο δῃωθέντες.
νηυσὶ δ' ἐπῶρσ' ἄνεμον Βορέην νεφεληγερέτα Ζεὺς
λαίλαπι θεσπεσίῃ, σὺν δὲ νεφέεσσι κάλυψε
γαῖαν ὁμοῦ καὶ πόντον· ὀρώρει δ' οὐρανόθεν νύξ.
70   αἱ μὲν ἔπειτ' ἐφέροντ' ἐπικάρσιαι, ἱστία δέ σφιν
τριχθά τε καὶ τετραχθὰ διέσχισεν ἲς ἀνέμοιο.
καὶ τὰ μὲν ἐς νῆας κάθεμεν, δείσαντες ὄλεθρον,
αὐτὰς δ' ἐσσυμένως προερέσσαμεν ἤπειρόνδε.
ἔνθα δύω νύκτας δύο τ' ἤματα συνεχὲς αἰεὶ
75   κείμεθ', ὁμοῦ καμάτῳ τε καὶ ἄλγεσι θυμὸν ἔδοντες.
ἀλλ' ὅτε δὴ τρίτον ἦμαρ ἐυπλόκαμος τέλεσ' Ἠώς,
ἱστοὺς στησάμενοι ἀνά θ' ἱστία λεύκ' ἐρύσαντες
ἥμεθα, τὰς δ' ἄνεμός τε κυβερνῆταί τ' ἴθυνον.

on foot. Soon they arrived, in numbers like the leaves and flowers that bloom in the spring, at dawn; then it was that an evil fate from Zeus beset us, luckless as we were, that we might suffer many woes. Setting their line of battle by the swift ships, they fought, and each side hurled at the other with bronze-tipped spears. As long as it was morning and the sacred day was waxing, so long we held our ground and beat them off, though they were more than we. But when the sun turned to the time for the unyoking of oxen, then the Cicones prevailed and routed the Achaeans, and six of my well-greaved comrades perished from each ship; but the rest of us escaped death and fate.

"From there we sailed on, grieved at heart, glad to have escaped death, though we had lost our staunch comrades; nor did I let my curved ships go on their way until we had all called three times on each of those luckless comrades of ours who died on the plain, cut down by the Cicones. But against our ships Zeus, the cloud-gatherer, roused the North Wind with a wondrous tempest, and hid with clouds the land and the sea alike, and night rushed down from heaven. Then the ships were driven headlong, and their sails were torn to shreds by the violence of the wind. So we lowered the sails and stowed them aboard, in fear of death, and rowed the ships hurriedly toward the land. There for two nights and two days continuously we lay, eating our hearts for weariness and sorrow. But when now fair-tressed Dawn brought to its birth the third day, we set up the masts and hoisted the white sails, and took our seats, and the wind and the helmsmen steered the ships. And

καί νύ κεν ἀσκηθὴς ἱκόμην ἐς πατρίδα γαῖαν·
80 ἀλλά με κῦμα ῥόος τε περιγνάμπτοντα Μάλειαν
καὶ Βορέης ἀπέωσε, παρέπλαγξεν δὲ Κυθήρων.

"ἔνθεν δ' ἐννῆμαρ φερόμην ὀλοοῖς ἀνέμοισιν
πόντον ἐπ' ἰχθυόεντα· ἀτὰρ δεκάτῃ ἐπέβημεν
γαίης Λωτοφάγων, οἵ τ' ἄνθινον εἶδαρ ἔδουσιν.
85 ἔνθα δ' ἐπ' ἠπείρου βῆμεν καὶ ἀφυσσάμεθ' ὕδωρ,
αἶψα δὲ δεῖπνον ἕλοντο θοῆς παρὰ νηυσὶν ἑταῖροι.
αὐτὰρ ἐπεὶ σίτοιό τ' ἐπασσάμεθ' ἠδὲ ποτῆτος,
δὴ τότ' ἐγὼν ἑτάρους προΐειν πεύθεσθαι ἰόντας,
οἵ τινες ἀνέρες εἶεν ἐπὶ χθονὶ σῖτον ἔδοντες
90 ἄνδρε δύω κρίνας, τρίτατον κήρυχ' ἅμ' ὀπάσσας.[1]
οἱ δ' αἶψ' οἰχόμενοι μίγεν ἀνδράσι Λωτοφάγοισιν·
οὐδ' ἄρα Λωτοφάγοι μήδονθ' ἑτάροισιν ὄλεθρον
ἡμετέροις, ἀλλά σφι δόσαν λωτοῖο πάσασθαι.
τῶν δ' ὅς τις λωτοῖο φάγοι μελιηδέα καρπόν,
95 οὐκέτ' ἀπαγγεῖλαι πάλιν ἤθελεν οὐδὲ νέεσθαι,
ἀλλ' αὐτοῦ βούλοντο μετ' ἀνδράσι Λωτοφάγοισι
λωτὸν ἐρεπτόμενοι μενέμεν νόστου τε λαθέσθαι.
τοὺς μὲν ἐγὼν ἐπὶ νῆας ἄγον κλαίοντας ἀνάγκῃ,
νηυσὶ δ' ἐνὶ γλαφυρῇσιν ὑπὸ ζυγὰ δῆσα ἐρύσσας.
100 αὐτὰρ τοὺς ἄλλους κελόμην ἐρίηρας ἑταίρους
σπερχομένους νηῶν ἐπιβαινέμεν ὠκειάων,
μή πώς τις λωτοῖο φαγὼν νόστοιο λάθηται.
οἱ δ' αἶψ' εἴσβαινον καὶ ἐπὶ κληῖσι καθῖζον,
ἑξῆς δ' ἑζόμενοι πολιὴν ἅλα τύπτον ἐρετμοῖς.
105 "ἔνθεν δὲ προτέρω πλέομεν ἀκαχήμενοι ἦτορ·
Κυκλώπων δ' ἐς γαῖαν ὑπερφιάλων ἀθεμίστων

now all unscathed would I have reached my native land,
but the waves and the current and the North Wind beat me
back as I was rounding Malea, and drove me off-course
past Cythera.

"Thence for nine days' time I was borne by savage
winds over the fish-filled sea; but on the tenth we set foot
on the land of the Lotus-eaters, who eat a flowery food.
There we went on shore and drew water, and without
further ado my comrades took their meal by the swift ships.
But when we had tasted food and drink, I sent out some of
my comrades to go and learn who the men were, who here
ate bread upon the earth; two men I chose, sending with
them a third as herald. They departed at once and mingled
with the Lotus-eaters; nor did the Lotus-eaters think of
killing my comrades, but gave them lotus to eat. And who-
ever of them ate the honey-sweet fruit of the lotus had no
longer any wish to bring back word or return, but there
they wished to remain among the Lotus-eaters, champing
on the lotus, and to forget their homecoming. These men I
myself brought back to the ships under compulsion, weep-
ing, and dragged them beneath the benches and bound
them fast in the hollow ships; and I bade the rest of my
trusty comrades to embark with speed on the swift ships,
for fear that perchance anyone should eat the lotus and for-
get his homecoming. So they went on board quickly and
sat down upon the benches, and sitting well in order struck
the gray sea with their oars.

"Thence we sailed on, grieved at heart, and we came to
the land of the Cyclopes, an insolent and lawless folk, who,

---

[1] Line 90 (= 10.102) is placed before 89 in most MSS. It seems
inconsistent with 94.

ἱκόμεθ᾽, οἵ ῥα θεοῖσι πεποιθότες ἀθανάτοισιν
οὔτε φυτεύουσιν χερσὶν φυτὸν οὔτ᾽ ἀρόωσιν,
ἀλλὰ τά γ᾽ ἄσπαρτα καὶ ἀνήροτα πάντα φύονται,
110 πυροὶ καὶ κριθαὶ ἠδ᾽ ἄμπελοι, αἵ τε φέρουσιν
οἶνον ἐρισταφυλον, καί σφιν Διὸς ὄμβρος ἀέξει.
τοῖσιν δ᾽ οὔτ᾽ ἀγοραὶ βουληφόροι οὔτε θέμιστες,
ἀλλ᾽ οἵ γ᾽ ὑψηλῶν ὀρέων ναίουσι κάρηνα
ἐν σπέσσι γλαφυροῖσι, θεμιστεύει δὲ ἕκαστος
115 παίδων ἠδ᾽ ἀλόχων, οὐδ᾽ ἀλλήλων ἀλέγουσιν.
    "νῆσος ἔπειτα λάχεια[1] παρὲκ λιμένος τετάνυσται,
γαίης Κυκλώπων οὔτε σχεδὸν οὔτ᾽ ἀποτηλοῦ,
ὑλήεσσ᾽· ἐν δ᾽ αἶγες ἀπειρέσιαι γεγάασιν
ἄγριαι· οὐ μὲν γὰρ πάτος ἀνθρώπων ἀπερύκει,
120 οὐδέ μιν εἰσοιχνεῦσι κυνηγέται, οἵ τε καθ᾽ ὕλην
ἄλγεα πάσχουσιν κορυφὰς ὀρέων ἐφέποντες.
οὔτ᾽ ἄρα ποίμνῃσιν καταΐσχεται οὔτ᾽ ἀρότοισιν,
ἀλλ᾽ ἥ γ᾽ ἄσπαρτος καὶ ἀνήροτος ἤματα πάντα
ἀνδρῶν χηρεύει, βόσκει δέ τε μηκάδας αἶγας.
125 οὐ γὰρ Κυκλώπεσσι νέες πάρα μιλτοπάρῃοι,
οὐδ᾽ ἄνδρες νηῶν ἔνι τέκτονες, οἵ κε κάμοιεν
νῆας ἐυσσέλμους, αἵ κεν τελέοιεν ἕκαστα
ἄστε᾽ ἐπ᾽ ἀνθρώπων ἱκνεύμεναι, οἷά τε πολλὰ
ἄνδρες ἐπ᾽ ἀλλήλους νηυσὶν περόωσι θάλασσαν·
130 οἵ κέ σφιν καὶ νῆσον ἐυκτιμένην ἐκάμοντο.
οὐ μὲν γάρ τι κακή γε, φέροι δέ κεν ὥρια πάντα·
ἐν μὲν γὰρ λειμῶνες ἁλὸς πολιοῖο παρ᾽ ὄχθας
ὑδρηλοὶ μαλακοί· μάλα κ᾽ ἄφθιτοι ἄμπελοι εἶεν.

trusting in the immortal gods, plant nothing with their hands, nor plow; but all these things spring up for them without sowing or plowing, wheat, and barley, and vines, which bear the rich clusters of wine, and Zeus's rain makes these grow for them. Neither assemblies for council have they, nor appointed laws, but they dwell on the peaks of mountains in hollow caves, and each one is lawgiver to his children and his wives, and they have no regard for one another.

"Now there is a fertile island that stretches slantwise outside the harbor, neither close to the shore of the land of the Cyclopes, nor yet far off, well-wooded. On it live wild goats innumerable, for no traffic of men prevents them, nor do hunters come there, men who suffer hardship in the woodland as they course over the peaks of the mountains. Neither with flocks is it occupied, nor with plowed lands, but unsown and untilled all its days it is bereft of mankind, but feeds the bleating goats. For the Cyclopes have at hand no ships with vermilion cheeks,[a] nor are there shipwrights in their land who might build them well-benched ships, which could perform all their wants, passing to the cities of other men, as men often cross the sea in ships to visit one another—craftsmen, who would also have made of this island a well-arranged settlement for them. For the island is not at all a poor one, but would bear all things in season. On it are meadows by the shores of the gray sea, well-watered and soft, where vines would never fail, and on

---

[a] That is, with bows painted red. M.

---

[1] ἔπειτα λάχεια: ἔππειτ' ἐλάχεια Zenodotus; cf. 10.509

ἐν δ' ἄροσις λείη· μάλα κεν βαθὺ λήιον αἰεὶ
135 εἰς ὥρας ἀμῷεν, ἐπεὶ μάλα πῖαρ ὑπ' οὖδας.
ἐν δὲ λιμὴν ἐύορμος, ἵν' οὐ χρεὼ πείσματός ἐστιν,
οὔτ' εὐνὰς βαλέειν οὔτε πρυμνήσι' ἀνάψαι,
ἀλλ' ἐπικέλσαντας μεῖναι χρόνον εἰς ὅ κε ναυτέων
θυμὸς ἐποτρύνῃ καὶ ἐπιπνεύσωσιν ἀῆται.
140 αὐτὰρ ἐπὶ κρατὸς λιμένος ῥέει ἀγλαὸν ὕδωρ,
κρήνη ὑπὸ σπείους· περὶ δ' αἴγειροι πεφύασιν.
ἔνθα κατεπλέομεν, καί τις θεὸς ἡγεμόνευεν
νύκτα δι' ὀρφναίην, οὐδὲ προυφαίνετ' ἰδέσθαι·
ἀὴρ γὰρ περὶ νηυσὶ βαθεῖ' ἦν, οὐδὲ σελήνη
145 οὐρανόθεν προύφαινε, κατείχετο δὲ νεφέεσσιν.
ἔνθ' οὔ τις τὴν νῆσον ἐσέδρακεν ὀφθαλμοῖσιν,
οὔτ' οὖν κύματα μακρὰ κυλινδόμενα προτὶ χέρσον
εἰσίδομεν, πρὶν νῆας ἐυσσέλμους ἐπικέλσαι.
κελσάσῃσι δὲ νηυσὶ καθείλομεν ἱστία πάντα,
150 ἐκ δὲ καὶ αὐτοὶ βῆμεν ἐπὶ ῥηγμῖνι θαλάσσης·
ἔνθα δ' ἀποβρίξαντες ἐμείναμεν Ἠῶ δῖαν.

       "ἦμος δ' ἠριγένεια φάνη ῥοδοδάκτυλος Ἠώς,
νῆσον θαυμάζοντες ἐδινεόμεσθα κατ' αὐτήν.
ὦρσαν δὲ νύμφαι, κοῦραι Διὸς αἰγιόχοιο,
155 αἶγας ὀρεσκῴους, ἵνα δειπνήσειαν ἑταῖροι.
αὐτίκα καμπύλα τόξα καὶ αἰγανέας δολιχαύλους
εἱλόμεθ' ἐκ νηῶν, διὰ δὲ τρίχα κοσμηθέντες
βάλλομεν· αἶψα δ' ἔδωκε θεὸς μενοεικέα θήρην.
νῆες μέν μοι ἕποντο δυώδεκα, ἐς δὲ ἑκάστην
160 ἐννέα λάγχανον αἶγες· ἐμοὶ δὲ δέκ' ἔξελον οἴῳ.

       "ὣς τότε μὲν πρόπαν ἦμαρ ἐς ἠέλιον καταδύντα

it level plowlands, from which they might reap from season to season very deep harvests, so rich is the soil beneath; and in it, too, is a harbor giving safe anchorage, where there is no need of moorings, either to throw out anchor stones or to make fast stern cables, but one may beach one's ship and wait until the sailors' minds bid them put out, and the breezes blow fair. Now at the head of the harbor a spring of bright water flows out from beneath a cave, and round about it poplars grow. There we sailed in, and some god guided us through the murky night; for there was no light to see, but a mist lay deep about the ships and the moon showed no light from heaven, but was shut in by clouds. Then no man's eyes beheld that island, nor did we see the long waves rolling on the beach, until we ran our well-benched ships on the shore. And when we had beached the ships we lowered all the sails and ourselves disembarked on the shore of the sea, and there we fell asleep and waited for the bright Dawn.

"As soon as early Dawn appeared, the rosy-fingered, we roamed throughout the island, marveling at it; and the nymphs, the daughters of Zeus who bears the aegis, roused the mountain goats, that my comrades might have something of which to make their meal. Instantly we took from the ships our curved bows and long javelins, and forming three groups we took to shooting; and at once the god gave us a bag to satisfy our hearts. The ships that followed me were twelve, and to each nine goats fell by lot, but for me alone they chose out ten.

"So then all day long till set of sun we sat feasting on

ἥμεθα δαινύμενοι κρέα τ' ἄσπετα καὶ μέθυ ἡδύ·
οὐ γάρ πω νηῶν ἐξέφθιτο οἶνος ἐρυθρός,
ἀλλ' ἐνέην· πολλὸν γὰρ ἐν ἀμφιφορεῦσιν ἕκαστοι
165 ἠφύσαμεν Κικόνων ἱερὸν πτολίεθρον ἑλόντες.
Κυκλώπων δ' ἐς γαῖαν ἐλεύσσομεν ἐγγὺς ἐόντων,
καπνόν τ' αὐτῶν τε φθογγὴν ὀίων τε καὶ αἰγῶν.
ἦμος δ' ἠέλιος κατέδυ καὶ ἐπὶ κνέφας ἦλθε,
δὴ τότε κοιμήθημεν ἐπὶ ῥηγμῖνι θαλάσσης.
170 ἦμος δ' ἠριγένεια φάνη ῥοδοδάκτυλος Ἠώς,
καὶ τότ' ἐγὼν ἀγορὴν θέμενος μετὰ πᾶσιν ἔειπον·

"'ἄλλοι μὲν νῦν μίμνετ', ἐμοὶ ἐρίηρες ἑταῖροι·
αὐτὰρ ἐγὼ σὺν νηί τ' ἐμῇ καὶ ἐμοῖς ἑτάροισιν
ἐλθὼν τῶνδ' ἀνδρῶν πειρήσομαι, οἵ τινές εἰσιν,
175 ἦ ῥ' οἵ γ' ὑβρισταί τε καὶ ἄγριοι οὐδὲ δίκαιοι,
ἦε φιλόξεινοι, καί σφιν νόος ἐστὶ θεουδής.'

"ὣς εἰπὼν ἀνὰ νηὸς ἔβην, ἐκέλευσα δ' ἑταίρους
αὐτούς τ' ἀμβαίνειν ἀνά τε πρυμνήσια λῦσαι.
οἱ δ' αἶψ' εἴσβαινον καὶ ἐπὶ κληῖσι καθῖζον,
180 ἑξῆς δ' ἑζόμενοι πολιὴν ἅλα τύπτον ἐρετμοῖς.
ἀλλ' ὅτε δὴ τὸν χῶρον ἀφικόμεθ' ἐγγὺς ἐόντα,
ἔνθα δ' ἐπ' ἐσχατιῇ σπέος εἴδομεν ἄγχι θαλάσσης,
ὑψηλόν, δάφνῃσι κατηρεφές. ἔνθα δὲ πολλὰ
μῆλ', ὄιές τε καὶ αἶγες, ἰαύεσκον· περὶ δ' αὐλὴ
185 ὑψηλὴ δέδμητο κατωρυχέεσσι λίθοισι
μακρῇσίν τε πίτυσσιν ἰδὲ δρυσὶν ὑψικόμοισιν.
ἔνθα δ' ἀνὴρ ἐνίαυε πελώριος, ὅς ῥα τὰ μῆλα
οἶος ποιμαίνεσκεν ἀπόπροθεν· οὐδὲ μετ' ἄλλους
πωλεῖτ', ἀλλ' ἀπάνευθεν ἐὼν ἀθεμίστια ᾔδη.

abundant meat and sweet wine. For not yet was the red wine spent from our ships, but some was still left, for each crew had drawn a large quantity in jars when we took the sacred citadel of the Cicones. And we looked across to the land of the Cyclopes, who dwelt close at hand, and noticed smoke, and the voices of the Cyclopes, and of their sheep and goats. But when the sun set and darkness came on, then we lay down to rest on the shore of the sea. And as soon as early Dawn appeared, the rosy-fingered, I called my men together and spoke among them all:

"'Remain here now, all the rest of you, my trusty comrades, while I with my own ship and my own crew will go and make trial of these men, to learn who they are, whether they are cruel, and wild, and unjust, or whether they are kind to strangers and fear the gods in their thoughts.'

"So saying, I went on board the ship and told my comrades themselves to embark, and to loose the stern cables. So they went on board quickly and sat down upon the benches, and sitting well in order struck the gray sea with their oars. But when we had reached the place, which lay close at hand, there on the land's edge close by the sea we saw a high cave, roofed over with laurels, and there many flocks, sheep and goats alike, were penned at night. Round about it a high courtyard was built with stones set deep in the earth, and with tall pines and high-crested oaks. There a monstrous man spent his nights, who shepherded his flocks alone and afar, and did not mingle with others, but lived apart, obedient to no law. For he was created a mon-

190 καὶ γὰρ θαῦμ᾽ ἐτέτυκτο πελώριον, οὐδὲ ἐῴκει
ἀνδρί γε σιτοφάγῳ, ἀλλὰ ῥίῳ ὑλήεντι
ὑψηλῶν ὀρέων, ὅ τε φαίνεται οἷον ἀπ᾽ ἄλλων.

"δὴ τότε τοὺς ἄλλους κελόμην ἐρίηρας ἑταίρους
αὐτοῦ πὰρ νηΐ τε μένειν καὶ νῆα ἔρυσθαι,
195 αὐτὰρ ἐγὼ κρίνας ἑτάρων δυοκαίδεκ᾽ ἀρίστους
βῆν· ἀτὰρ αἴγεον ἀσκὸν ἔχον μέλανος οἴνοιο
ἡδέος, ὅν μοι ἔδωκε Μάρων, Εὐάνθεος υἱός,
ἱρεὺς Ἀπόλλωνος, ὃς Ἴσμαρον ἀμφιβεβήκει,
οὕνεκά μιν σὺν παιδὶ περισχόμεθ᾽ ἠδὲ γυναικὶ
200 ἁζόμενοι· ᾤκει γὰρ ἐν ἄλσεϊ δενδρήεντι
Φοίβου Ἀπόλλωνος. ὁ δέ μοι πόρεν ἀγλαὰ δῶρα·
χρυσοῦ μέν μοι ἔδωκ᾽ ἐυεργέος ἑπτὰ τάλαντα,
δῶκε δέ μοι κρητῆρα πανάργυρον, αὐτὰρ ἔπειτα
οἶνον ἐν ἀμφιφορεῦσι δυώδεκα πᾶσιν ἀφύσσας
205 ἡδὺν ἀκηράσιον, θεῖον ποτόν· οὐδέ τις αὐτὸν
ἠείδη δμώων οὐδ᾽ ἀμφιπόλων ἐνὶ οἴκῳ,
ἀλλ᾽ αὐτὸς ἄλοχός τε φίλη ταμίη τε μί᾽ οἴη.
τὸν δ᾽ ὅτε πίνοιεν μελιηδέα οἶνον ἐρυθρόν,
ἓν δέπας ἐμπλήσας ὕδατος ἀνὰ εἴκοσι μέτρα
210 χεῦ᾽, ὀδμὴ δ᾽ ἡδεῖα ἀπὸ κρητῆρος ὀδώδει
θεσπεσίη· τότ᾽ ἂν οὔ τοι ἀποσχέσθαι φίλον ἦεν.
τοῦ φέρον ἐμπλήσας ἀσκὸν μέγαν, ἐν δὲ καὶ ᾖα
κωρύκῳ· αὐτίκα γάρ μοι ὀίσατο θυμὸς ἀγήνωρ
ἄνδρ᾽ ἐπελεύσεσθαι μεγάλην ἐπιειμένον ἀλκήν,
215 ἄγριον, οὔτε δίκας ἐῢ εἰδότα οὔτε θέμιστας.

"καρπαλίμως δ᾽ εἰς ἄντρον ἀφικόμεθ᾽, οὐδέ μιν
ἔνδον

330

strous marvel, and was not like a man that lives by bread, but like a wooded peak of lofty mountains, which stands out to view alone, apart from the rest.

"Then I bade the rest of my comrades to remain there by the ship and to guard the ship, but I chose twelve of the best of my comrades and went my way. With me I had a goatskin of the dark, sweet wine, which Maro, son of Euanthes, had given me, the priest of Apollo, the god who watched over Ismarus. And he had given me it because we had protected him with his child and wife out of reverence; for he lived in a wooded grove of Phoebus Apollo. And he gave me splendid gifts: of well-wrought gold he gave me seven talents, and he gave me a mixing bowl all of silver; and besides these, wine, with which he filled twelve jars in all, wine sweet and unmixed, a drink divine. Not one of his slaves nor of the maids in his halls knew of it, but himself and his loyal wife, and one housekeeper only. And as often as they drank that honey-sweet red wine he would fill one cup and pour it into twenty measures of water, and a smell would rise from the mixing bowl marvelously sweet; then truly would one not choose to hold back. With this wine I filled and took with me a great skin, and also provisions in a bag; for my proud spirit told me that very soon a man would come upon us clothed in tremendous strength, a savage man that knew nothing of rights or laws.

"Speedily we came to the cave, nor did we find him

εὕρομεν, ἀλλ' ἐνόμευε νομὸν κάτα πίονα μῆλα.
ἐλθόντες δ' εἰς ἄντρον ἐθηεύμεσθα ἕκαστα.
ταρσοὶ μὲν τυρῶν βρῖθον, στείνοντο δὲ σηκοὶ
220   ἀρνῶν ἠδ' ἐρίφων· διακεκριμέναι δὲ ἕκασται
ἔρχατο, χωρὶς μὲν πρόγονοι, χωρὶς δὲ μέτασσαι,
χωρὶς δ' αὖθ' ἕρσαι. ναῖον δ' ὀρῷ ἄγγεα πάντα,
γαυλοί τε σκαφίδες τε, τετυγμένα, τοῖς ἐνάμελγεν.
ἔνθ' ἐμὲ μὲν πρώτισθ' ἕταροι λίσσοντ' ἐπέεσσιν
225   τυρῶν αἰνυμένους ἰέναι πάλιν, αὐτὰρ ἔπειτα
καρπαλίμως ἐπὶ νῆα θοὴν ἐρίφους τε καὶ ἄρνας
σηκῶν ἐξελάσαντας ἐπιπλεῖν ἁλμυρὸν ὕδωρ·
ἀλλ' ἐγὼ οὐ πιθόμην, ἦ τ' ἂν πολὺ κέρδιον ἦεν,
ὄφρ' αὐτόν τε ἴδοιμι, καὶ εἴ μοι ξείνια δοίη.
230   οὐδ' ἄρ' ἔμελλ' ἑτάροισι φανεὶς ἐρατεινὸς ἔσεσθαι.
    "ἔνθα δὲ πῦρ κήαντες ἐθύσαμεν ἠδὲ καὶ αὐτοὶ
τυρῶν αἰνύμενοι φάγομεν, μένομέν τέ μιν ἔνδον
ἥμενοι, ἧος ἐπῆλθε νέμων. φέρε δ' ὄβριμον ἄχθος
ὕλης ἀζαλέης, ἵνα οἱ ποτιδόρπιον εἴη,
235   ἔντοσθεν[1] δ' ἄντροιο βαλὼν ὀρυμαγδὸν ἔθηκεν·
ἡμεῖς δὲ δείσαντες ἀπεσσύμεθ' ἐς μυχὸν ἄντρου.
αὐτὰρ ὅ γ' εἰς εὐρὺ σπέος ἤλασε πίονα μῆλα
πάντα μάλ' ὅσσ' ἤμελγε, τὰ δ' ἄρσενα λεῖπε θύρηφιν,
ἀρνειούς τε τράγους τε, βαθείης ἔκτοθεν[2] αὐλῆς.
240   αὐτὰρ ἔπειτ' ἐπέθηκε θυρεὸν μέγαν ὑψόσ' ἀείρας,
ὄβριμον· οὐκ ἂν τόν γε δύω καὶ εἴκοσ' ἄμαξαι
ἐσθλαὶ τετράκυκλοι ἀπ' οὔδεος ὀχλίσσειαν·
τόσσην ἠλίβατον πέτρην ἐπέθηκε θύρῃσιν.
ἑζόμενος δ' ἤμελγεν ὄις καὶ μηκάδας αἶγας,

within, but he was pasturing his fat flocks in the fields. So we entered the cave and gazed in wonder at all things there. The crates were laden with cheeses, and the pens were crowded with lambs and kids. Each kind was penned separately; by themselves the firstlings, by themselves the later lambs, and by themselves again the newly born. And with whey were swimming all the well-wrought vessels, the milk pails and the bowls into which he milked. Then my comrades spoke and besought me first of all to take some of the cheeses and depart, and then speedily to drive to the swift ship the kids and lambs out of the pens, and to sail over the salt water. But I did not listen to them—truly it would have been far better—to the end that I might see the man himself, and whether he would give me gifts of entertainment. And in truth, when he appeared, he proved no joy to my comrades.

"Then we kindled a fire and offered sacrifice, and ourselves, too, took some of the cheeses and ate, and thus we sat in the cave and waited for him until he came back, herding his flocks. He carried a mighty weight of dry wood to serve him at supper time, and flung it down with a crash inside the cave, but we, seized with terror, shrank back into a recess of the cave. He drove his fat flocks into the wide cavern—all those that he milked; but the males—the rams and the goats—he left outside in the deep courtyard. Then he lifted up and set in place the great doorstone, a mighty rock; two and twenty stout four-wheeled wagons could not lift it from the ground, such a towering mass of rock he set in the doorway. Thereafter he sat down and milked the

---

[1] ἔντοσθεν: ἔκτοσθεν

[2] ἔκτοθεν: ἔντοθεν most editors; cf. 338

245 πάντα κατὰ μοῖραν, καὶ ὑπ' ἔμβρυον ἧκεν ἑκάστῃ.
αὐτίκα δ' ἥμισυ μὲν θρέψας λευκοῖο γάλακτος
πλεκτοῖς ἐν ταλάροισιν ἀμησάμενος κατέθηκεν,
ἥμισυ δ' αὖτ' ἔστησεν ἐν ἄγγεσιν, ὄφρα οἱ εἴη
πίνειν αἰνυμένῳ καί οἱ ποτιδόρπιον εἴη.
250 αὐτὰρ ἐπεὶ δὴ σπεῦσε πονησάμενος τὰ ἃ ἔργα,
καὶ τότε πῦρ ἀνέκαιε καὶ εἴσιδεν, εἴρετο δ' ἡμέας·
    "'ὦ ξεῖνοι, τίνες ἐστέ; πόθεν πλεῖθ' ὑγρὰ κέλευθα;
ἦ τι κατὰ πρῆξιν ἦ μαψιδίως ἀλάλησθε,
οἷά τε ληιστῆρες, ὑπεὶρ ἅλα, τοί τ' ἀλόωνται
255 ψυχὰς παρθέμενοι κακὸν ἀλλοδαποῖσι φέροντες;'
    "ὣς ἔφαθ', ἡμῖν δ' αὖτε κατεκλάσθη φίλον ἦτορ,
δεισάντων φθόγγον τε βαρὺν αὐτόν τε πέλωρον.
ἀλλὰ καὶ ὣς μιν ἔπεσσιν ἀμειβόμενος προσέειπον·
    "'ἡμεῖς τοι Τροίηθεν ἀποπλαγχθέντες Ἀχαιοὶ
260 παντοίοις ἀνέμοισιν ὑπὲρ μέγα λαῖτμα θαλάσσης,
οἴκαδε ἱέμενοι, ἄλλην ὁδὸν ἄλλα κέλευθα
ἤλθομεν· οὕτω που Ζεὺς ἤθελε μητίσασθαι.
λαοὶ δ' Ἀτρεΐδεω Ἀγαμέμνονος εὐχόμεθ' εἶναι,
τοῦ δὴ νῦν γε μέγιστον ὑπουράνιον κλέος ἐστί·
265 τόσσην γὰρ διέπερσε πόλιν καὶ ἀπώλεσε λαοὺς
πολλούς. ἡμεῖς δ' αὖτε κιχανόμενοι τὰ σὰ γοῦνα
ἱκόμεθ', εἴ τι πόροις ξεινήιον ἠὲ καὶ ἄλλως
δοίης δωτίνην, ἥ τε ξείνων θέμις ἐστίν.
ἀλλ' αἰδεῖο, φέριστε, θεούς· ἱκέται δέ τοί εἰμεν,
270 Ζεὺς δ' ἐπιτιμήτωρ ἱκετάων τε ξείνων τε,
ξείνιος, ὃς ξείνοισιν ἅμ' αἰδοίοισιν ὀπηδεῖ.'
    "ὣς ἐφάμην, ὁ δέ μ' αὐτίκ' ἀμείβετο νηλέι θυμῷ·

ewes and bleating goats all in turn, and beneath each dam he placed her young. Next he curdled half the white milk and gathered it in wicker baskets and stored it away, and the other half he set in vessels that he might have it to take and drink, and that it might serve him for supper. But when he had busily performed his tasks, then he rekindled the fire, and caught sight of us, and asked:

"'Strangers, who are you? Whence do you sail over the watery ways? Is it on some business, or do you wander at random over the sea, as pirates do, who wander hazarding their lives and bringing evil to men of other lands?'

"So he spoke, and in our breasts our spirit was broken for terror of his deep voice and monstrous self; yet even so I made answer and spoke to him saying:

"'We, you must know, are from Troy, Achaeans, driven by all the winds there are over the great gulf of the sea. Seeking our home, we have come by another way, by other paths. So, I suppose, Zeus was pleased to devise. And we declare that we are the men of Agamemnon, son of Atreus, whose fame is now the greatest under heaven, so great a city did he sack, and slew many people; but we on our part, thus visiting you, have come as suppliants to your knees, in the hope that you will give us entertainment, or in some other manner be generous to us, as is the due of strangers. Do not deny us, good sir, but reverence the gods; we are your suppliants; and Zeus is the avenger of suppliants and strangers—Zeus, the strangers' god—who walks in the footsteps of reverend strangers.'

"So I spoke, and at once he made answer with pitiless

'νήπιός εἰς, ὦ ξεῖν', ἢ τηλόθεν εἰλήλουθας,
ὅς με θεοὺς κέλεαι ἢ δειδίμεν ἢ ἀλέασθαι·
275 οὐ γὰρ Κύκλωπες Διὸς αἰγιόχου ἀλέγουσιν
οὐδὲ θεῶν μακάρων, ἐπεὶ ἦ πολὺ φέρτεροί εἰμεν·
οὐδ' ἂν ἐγὼ Διὸς ἔχθος ἀλευάμενος πεφιδοίμην
οὔτε σεῦ οὔθ' ἑτάρων, εἰ μὴ θυμός με κελεύοι.
ἀλλά μοι εἴφ' ὅπη ἔσχες ἰὼν ἐνεργέα νῆα,
280 ἤ που ἐπ' ἐσχατιῆς, ἦ καὶ σχεδόν, ὄφρα δαείω.'
   "ὣς φάτο πειράζων, ἐμὲ δ' οὐ λάθεν εἰδότα πολλά,
ἀλλά μιν ἄψορρον προσέφην δολίοις ἐπέεσσι·
   "'νέα μέν μοι κατέαξε Ποσειδάων ἐνοσίχθων
πρὸς πέτρηισι βαλὼν ὑμῆς ἐπὶ πείρασι γαίης,
285 ἄκρη προσπελάσας· ἄνεμος δ' ἐκ πόντου ἔνεικεν·
αὐτὰρ ἐγὼ σὺν τοῖσδε ὑπέκφυγον αἰπὺν ὄλεθρον.'
   "ὣς ἐφάμην, ὁ δέ μ' οὐδὲν ἀμείβετο νηλέι θυμῷ,
ἀλλ' ὅ γ' ἀναΐξας ἑτάροις ἐπὶ χεῖρας ἴαλλε,
σὺν δὲ δύω μάρψας ὥς τε σκύλακας ποτὶ γαίη
290 κόπτ'· ἐκ δ' ἐγκέφαλος χαμάδις ῥέε, δεῦε δὲ γαῖαν.
τοὺς δὲ διὰ μελεϊστὶ ταμὼν ὡπλίσσατο δόρπον·
ἤσθιε δ' ὥς τε λέων ὀρεσίτροφος, οὐδ' ἀπέλειπεν,
ἔγκατά τε σάρκας τε καὶ ὀστέα μυελόεντα.
ἡμεῖς δὲ κλαίοντες ἀνεσχέθομεν Διὶ χεῖρας,
295 σχέτλια ἔργ' ὁρόωντες, ἀμηχανίη δ' ἔχε θυμόν.
αὐτὰρ ἐπεὶ Κύκλωψ μεγάλην ἐμπλήσατο νηδὺν
ἀνδρόμεα κρέ' ἔδων καὶ ἐπ' ἄκρητον γάλα πίνων,
κεῖτ' ἔντοσθ' ἄντροιο τανυσσάμενος διὰ μήλων.
τὸν μὲν ἐγὼ βούλευσα κατὰ μεγαλήτορα θυμὸν
300 ἆσσον ἰών, ξίφος ὀξὺ ἐρυσσάμενος παρὰ μηροῦ,

heart: 'You are a fool, stranger, or have come from afar, seeing that you bid me either to fear or to avoid the gods. For the Cyclopes pay no heed to Zeus, who bears the aegis, nor to the blessed gods, since truly we are better far than they. Nor would I, to shun the wrath of Zeus, spare either you or your comrades, unless my own heart should bid me. But tell me where you moored your well-wrought ship when you came here. Was it perchance at a remote part of the land, or close by? I would like to know.'

"So he spoke, tempting me, but he did not fool me—I knew too much for that; and I made answer again in crafty words:

"'My ship Poseidon, the earth-shaker, dashed to pieces, throwing her upon the rocks at the border of your land; for he brought her close to the headland, and the wind drove her in from the sea. But I, with these men here, escaped sheer destruction.'

"So I spoke, but from his pitiless heart he made no answer, but sprang up and laid his hands upon my comrades. Two of them together he seized and dashed to the earth like puppies, and their brains flowed forth upon the ground and wetted the earth. Then he cut them limb from limb and made ready his supper, and ate them like a mountain-nurtured lion, leaving nothing—ate the entrails, and the flesh, and the bones and marrow. And we with wailing held up our hands to Zeus, beholding his cruel deeds; and helplessness possessed our spirits. But when the Cyclops had filled his huge belly by eating human flesh and thereafter drinking pure milk, he lay down within the cave, stretched out among the sheep. And I formed a plan in my great heart to steal near him, and draw my sharp sword from beside my thigh and stab him in the breast,

οὐτάμεναι πρὸς στῆθος, ὅθι φρένες ἧπαρ ἔχουσι,
χεῖρ' ἐπιμασσάμενος· ἕτερος δέ με θυμὸς ἔρυκεν.
αὐτοῦ γάρ κε καὶ ἄμμες ἀπωλόμεθ' αἰπὺν ὄλεθρον·
οὐ γάρ κεν δυνάμεσθα θυράων ὑψηλάων
305 χερσὶν ἀπώσασθαι λίθον ὄβριμον, ὃν προσέθηκεν.
ὣς τότε μὲν στενάχοντες ἐμείναμεν Ἠῶ δῖαν.

"ἦμος δ' ἠριγένεια φάνη ῥοδοδάκτυλος Ἠώς,
καὶ τότε πῦρ ἀνέκαιε καὶ ἤμελγε κλυτὰ μῆλα,
πάντα κατὰ μοῖραν, καὶ ὑπ' ἔμβρυον ἧκεν ἑκάστῃ.
310 αὐτὰρ ἐπεὶ δὴ σπεῦσε πονησάμενος τὰ ἃ ἔργα,
σὺν δ' ὅ γε δὴ αὖτε δύω μάρψας ὡπλίσσατο δεῖπνον.
δειπνήσας δ' ἄντρου ἐξήλασε πίονα μῆλα,
ῥηιδίως ἀφελὼν θυρεὸν μέγαν· αὐτὰρ ἔπειτα
ἂψ ἐπέθηχ', ὡς εἴ τε φαρέτρῃ πῶμ' ἐπιθείη.
315 πολλῇ δὲ ῥοίζῳ πρὸς ὄρος τρέπε πίονα μῆλα
Κύκλωψ· αὐτὰρ ἐγὼ λιπόμην κακὰ βυσσοδομεύων,
εἴ πως τισαίμην, δοίη δέ μοι εὖχος Ἀθήνη.

"ἥδε δέ μοι κατὰ θυμὸν ἀρίστη φαίνετο βουλή.
Κύκλωπος γὰρ ἔκειτο μέγα ῥόπαλον παρὰ σηκῷ,
320 χλωρὸν ἐλαΐνεον· τὸ μὲν ἔκταμεν, ὄφρα φοροίη
αὐανθέν. τὸ μὲν ἄμμες ἐΐσκομεν εἰσορόωντες
ὅσσον θ' ἱστὸν νηὸς ἐεικοσόροιο μελαίνης,
φορτίδος εὐρείης, ἥ τ' ἐκπεράᾳ μέγα λαῖτμα·
τόσσον ἔην μῆκος, τόσσον πάχος εἰσοράασθαι.
325 τοῦ μὲν ὅσον τ' ὄργυιαν ἐγὼν ἀπέκοψα παραστὰς
καὶ παρέθηχ' ἑτάροισιν, ἀποξῦναι δ' ἐκέλευσα·
οἱ δ' ὁμαλὸν ποίησαν· ἐγὼ δ' ἐθόωσα παραστὰς
ἄκρον, ἄφαρ δὲ λαβὼν ἐπυράκτεον ἐν πυρὶ κηλέῳ.

where the midriff holds the liver, feeling for the place with my hand. But a second thought checked me, for there in the cave should we too have perished in utter ruin. For we should not have been able to thrust back with our hands from the high door the mighty stone which he had set there. So then, with wailing, we waited for the bright Dawn.

"As soon as early Dawn appeared, the rosy-fingered, he rekindled the fire and milked his fine flocks all in turn, and beneath each dam placed her young. Then, when he had busily performed his tasks, again he seized two men together and made ready his meal. And when he had made his meal he drove his fat flocks forth from the cave, easily moving away the great doorstone; and then he put it in place again, as one might set the lid upon a quiver. Then with loud whistling the Cyclops turned his fat flocks toward the mountain, and I was left there, devising evil in the depths of my heart, if in any way I might take vengeance on him, and Athene grant me glory.

"Now this seemed to my mind the best plan. There lay beside a sheep pen a great club of the Cyclops, a staff of green olivewood, which he had cut to carry with him when dry; and as we looked at it we thought it as large as is the mast of a black ship of twenty oars, a merchantman, broad of beam, which crosses over the great gulf; so huge it was in length and breadth to look upon. Going up to it, I cut off from this about a fathom's length and handed it to my comrades, bidding them dress it down; and they made it smooth, and I, standing by, sharpened it at the point, and then took it at once and hardened it in the blazing fire.

καὶ τὸ μὲν εὖ κατέθηκα κατακρύψας ὑπὸ κόπρῳ,
330   ἥ ῥα κατὰ σπείους κέχυτο μεγάλ' ἤλιθα πολλή·
αὐτὰρ τοὺς ἄλλους κλήρῳ πεπαλάσθαι[1] ἄνωγον,
ὅς τις τολμήσειεν ἐμοὶ σὺν μοχλὸν ἀείρας
τρῖψαι ἐν ὀφθαλμῷ, ὅτε τὸν γλυκὺς ὕπνος ἱκάνοι.
οἱ δ' ἔλαχον τοὺς ἄν κε καὶ ἤθελον αὐτὸς ἑλέσθαι,
335   τέσσαρες, αὐτὰρ ἐγὼ πέμπτος μετὰ τοῖσιν ἐλέγμην.
ἑσπέριος δ' ἦλθεν καλλίτριχα μῆλα νομεύων.
αὐτίκα δ' εἰς εὐρὺ σπέος ἤλασε πίονα μῆλα
πάντα μάλ', οὐδέ τι λεῖπε βαθείης ἔκτοθεν[2] αὐλῆς,
ἤ τι ὀισάμενος, ἢ καὶ θεὸς ὣς ἐκέλευσεν.
340   αὐτὰρ ἔπειτ' ἐπέθηκε θυρεὸν μέγαν ὑψόσ' ἀείρας,
ἑζόμενος δ' ἤμελγεν ὄις καὶ μηκάδας αἶγας,
πάντα κατὰ μοῖραν, καὶ ὑπ' ἔμβρυον ἧκεν ἑκάστῃ.
αὐτὰρ ἐπεὶ δὴ σπεῦσε πονησάμενος τὰ ἃ ἔργα,
σὺν δ' ὅ γε δὴ αὖτε δύω μάρψας ὡπλίσσατο δόρπον.
345   καὶ τότ' ἐγὼ Κύκλωπα προσηύδων ἄγχι παραστάς,
κισσύβιον μετὰ χερσὶν ἔχων μέλανος οἴνοιο·

   "'Κύκλωψ, τῆ, πίε οἶνον, ἐπεὶ φάγες ἀνδρόμεα κρέα,
ὄφρ' εἰδῇς οἷόν τι ποτὸν τόδε νηῦς ἐκεκεύθει
ἡμετέρη. σοὶ δ' αὖ λοιβὴν φέρον, εἴ μ' ἐλεήσας
350   οἴκαδε πέμψειας· σὺ δὲ μαίνεαι οὐκέτ' ἀνεκτῶς.
σχέτλιε, πῶς κέν τίς σε καὶ ὕστερον ἄλλος ἵκοιτο
ἀνθρώπων πολέων, ἐπεὶ οὐ κατὰ μοῖραν ἔρεξας;'

   "ὣς ἐφάμην, ὁ δ' ἔδεκτο καὶ ἔκπιεν· ἥσατο δ' αἰνῶς
ἡδὺ ποτὸν πίνων καί μ' ᾔτεε δεύτερον αὖτις·

---

[1] πεπαλάσθαι Aristarchus, πεπαλάχθαι

Then I laid it carefully away, hiding it beneath the dung, which lay in great heaps about the cave. And I told my comrades to cast lots among them, which of them should have the hardihood with me to lift the stake and grind it into his eye when sweet sleep should come upon him. And the lot fell upon those whom I myself would have wished to choose; four they were, and I was numbered with them as the fifth. At evening he came, herding his fine-fleeced sheep. Without delay he drove into the wide cave his fat flocks one and all, and left not one outside in the deep courtyard, either from some foreboding or because a god so bade him. Then he lifted up and set in place the great doorstone, and sitting down he milked the ewes and bleating goats all in turn, and beneath each dam he placed her young. But when he had busily performed his tasks, again he seized two men together and made ready his supper. Then I drew near and spoke to the Cyclops, holding in my hands an ivy-wood bowl of dark wine:

"'Cyclops, here; drink wine, now that you have had your meal of human flesh, that you may know what kind of drink this is which our ship contained. It was to you that I was bringing it as a drink offering, in the hope that, touched with pity, you might send me on my way home; but you rage in a way that is past all bearing. Cruel man, how shall anyone of all the men there are ever come to you again hereafter, since what you have done is not right?'

"So I spoke, and he took the cup and drained it, and was wondrously pleased as he drank the sweet draught, and asked me for it again a second time:

---

[2] ἔκτοθεν: ἔντοθεν most editors; cf. 239

355 "'δός μοι ἔτι πρόφρων, καί μοι τεὸν οὔνομα εἰπὲ
αὐτίκα νῦν, ἵνα τοι δῶ ξείνιον, ᾧ κε σὺ χαίρῃς·
καὶ γὰρ Κυκλώπεσσι φέρει ζείδωρος ἄρουρα
οἶνον ἐρισταφυλον, καί σφιν Διὸς ὄμβρος ἀέξει·
ἀλλὰ τόδ' ἀμβροσίης καὶ νέκταρός ἐστιν ἀπορρώξ.'

360 "ὣς φάτ', ἀτάρ οἱ αὖτις ἐγὼ πόρον αἴθοπα οἶνον.
τρὶς μὲν ἔδωκα φέρων, τρὶς δ' ἔκπιεν ἀφραδίῃσιν.
αὐτὰρ ἐπεὶ Κύκλωπα περὶ φρένας ἤλυθεν οἶνος,
καὶ τότε δή μιν ἔπεσσι προσηύδων μειλιχίοισι·

"'Κύκλωψ, εἰρωτᾷς μ' ὄνομα κλυτόν, αὐτὰρ ἐγώ τοι
365 ἐξερέω· σὺ δέ μοι δὸς ξείνιον, ὥς περ ὑπέστης.
Οὖτις ἐμοί γ' ὄνομα· Οὖτιν δέ με κικλήσκουσι
μήτηρ ἠδὲ πατὴρ ἠδ' ἄλλοι πάντες ἑταῖροι.'

"ὣς ἐφάμην, ὁ δέ μ' αὐτίκ' ἀμείβετο νηλέι θυμῷ·
'Οὖτιν ἐγὼ πύματον ἔδομαι μετὰ οἷς ἑτάροισιν,
370 τοὺς δ' ἄλλους πρόσθεν· τὸ δέ τοι ξεινήιον ἔσται.'

"ἦ καὶ ἀνακλινθεὶς πέσεν ὕπτιος, αὐτὰρ ἔπειτα
κεῖτ' ἀποδοχμώσας παχὺν αὐχένα, κὰδ δέ μιν ὕπνος
ᾕρει πανδαμάτωρ· φάρυγος δ' ἐξέσσυτο οἶνος
ψωμοί τ' ἀνδρόμεοι· ὁ δ' ἐρεύγετο οἰνοβαρείων.
375 καὶ τότ' ἐγὼ τὸν μοχλὸν ὑπὸ σποδοῦ ἤλασα πολλῆς,
ἧος θερμαίνοιτο· ἔπεσσι δὲ πάντας ἑταίρους
θάρσυνον, μή τίς μοι ὑποδείσας ἀναδύη.
ἀλλ' ὅτε δὴ τάχ' ὁ μοχλὸς ἐλάινος ἐν πυρὶ μέλλεν
ἅψεσθαι, χλωρός περ ἐών, διεφαίνετο δ' αἰνῶς,
380 καὶ τότ' ἐγὼν ἆσσον φέρον ἐκ πυρός, ἀμφὶ δ' ἑταῖροι
ἵσταντ'· αὐτὰρ θάρσος ἐνέπνευσεν μέγα δαίμων.
οἱ μὲν μοχλὸν ἑλόντες ἐλάινον, ὀξὺν ἐπ' ἄκρῳ,

"'Give me it again with a ready heart, and tell me your name at once, that I may give you a stranger's gift at which you may be glad. For among the Cyclopes the earth, the giver of grain, bears the rich clusters of wine, and the rain of Zeus gives them increase; but this is a draught from a stream of ambrosia and nectar.'

"So he spoke, and again I handed him the sparkling wine. Three times I brought and gave it to him, and three times he drained it in his folly. But when the wine had got round the wits of the Cyclops, then I spoke to him with winning words:

"'Cyclops, you ask me of my glorious name, and I will tell you it; and do you give me a stranger's gift, even as you promised. Nobody is my name, Nobody they call me—my mother and my father, and all my comrades as well.'

"So I spoke, and at once he answered me with pitiless heart: 'Nobody will I eat last among his comrades, and the others before him; this shall be your gift.'

"He spoke, and reeling fell upon his back, and lay there with his thick neck bent aslant, and sleep that conquers all laid hold on him. And from his gullet came forth wine and bits of human flesh, and he vomited in his drunken sleep. Then it was I who thrust in the stake under the deep ashes until it should grow hot, and heartened all my comrades with cheering words, so that no man might falter from fear. But when presently that stake of olivewood was about to catch fire, green though it was, and began to glow terribly, then it was I who brought it near from the fire, and my comrades stood round me and a god breathed into us great courage. They took the stake of olivewood, sharp at the

ὀφθαλμῷ ἐνέρεισαν· ἐγὼ δ' ἐφύπερθεν ἐρεισθεὶς[1]
δίνεον, ὡς ὅτε τις τρυπῷ δόρυ νήιον ἀνὴρ
385   τρυπάνῳ, οἱ δέ τ' ἔνερθεν ὑποσσείουσιν ἱμάντι
ἁψάμενοι ἑκάτερθε, τὸ δὲ τρέχει ἐμμενὲς αἰεί.
ὣς τοῦ ἐν ὀφθαλμῷ πυριήκεα μοχλὸν ἑλόντες
δινέομεν, τὸν δ' αἷμα περίρρεε θερμὸν ἐόντα.
πάντα δέ οἱ βλέφαρ' ἀμφὶ καὶ ὀφρύας εὗσεν ἀυτμὴ
390   γλήνης καιομένης, σφαραγεῦντο δέ οἱ πυρὶ ῥίζαι.
ὡς δ' ὅτ' ἀνὴρ χαλκεὺς πέλεκυν μέγαν ἠὲ σκέπαρνον
εἰν ὕδατι ψυχρῷ βάπτῃ μεγάλα ἰάχοντα
φαρμάσσων· τὸ γὰρ αὖτε σιδήρου γε κράτος ἐστίν·
ὣς τοῦ σίζ' ὀφθαλμὸς ἐλαϊνέῳ περὶ μοχλῷ.
395   σμερδαλέον δὲ μέγ' ᾤμωξεν, περὶ δ' ἴαχε πέτρη,
ἡμεῖς δὲ δείσαντες ἀπεσσύμεθ'· αὐτὰρ ὁ μοχλὸν
ἐξέρυσ' ὀφθαλμοῖο πεφυρμένον αἵματι πολλῷ.
τὸν μὲν ἔπειτ' ἔρριψεν ἀπὸ ἕο χερσὶν ἀλύων,
αὐτὰρ ὁ Κύκλωπας μεγάλ' ἤπυεν, οἵ ῥά μιν ἀμφὶς
400   ᾤκεον ἐν σπήεσσι δι' ἄκριας ἠνεμοέσσας.
οἱ δὲ βοῆς ἀίοντες ἐφοίτων ἄλλοθεν ἄλλος,
ἱστάμενοι δ' εἴροντο περὶ σπέος ὅττι ἑ κήδοι·
    "'τίπτε τόσον, Πολύφημ', ἀρημένος ὧδ' ἐβόησας
νύκτα δι' ἀμβροσίην καὶ ἀύπνους ἄμμε τίθησθα;
405   ἦ μή τίς σευ μῆλα βροτῶν ἀέκοντος ἐλαύνει;
ἦ μή τίς σ' αὐτὸν κτείνει δόλῳ ἠὲ βίηφιν;'
    "τοὺς δ' αὖτ' ἐξ ἄντρου προσέφη κρατερὸς
      Πολύφημος·
'ὦ φίλοι, Οὖτίς με κτείνει δόλῳ οὐδὲ βίηφιν.'
    "οἱ δ' ἀπαμειβόμενοι ἔπεα πτερόεντ' ἀγόρευον·

point, and thrust it into his eye, while I, throwing my
weight upon it from above, whirled it round, as a man
bores a ship's timber with a drill, while those below keep it
spinning with the strap, which they lay hold of by either
end, and the drill runs unceasingly. Even so we took the
fiery-pointed stake and whirled it around in his eye, and
the blood flowed round it, all hot as it was. His eyelids
above and below and his brows were all singed by the flame
from the burning eyeball, and its roots crackled in the fire.
And as when a smith dips a great axe or an adze in cold
water to temper it and it makes a great hissing—for from
this comes the strength of iron—so did his eye hiss round
the stake of olivewood. Terribly then did he cry aloud, and
the rock rang around; and we, seized with terror, shrank
back, while he wrenched from his eye the stake, all
befouled with blood. Then with both arms he flung it from
him, beside himself, and shouted to the Cyclopes, who
dwelt round about him in caves among the windy heights,
and they heard his cry and came thronging from every side,
and standing around the cave asked him what ailed him:

"'What sore distress is this, Polyphemus, that you cry
out thus through the immortal night, and make us sleep-
less? Can it be that some mortal man is driving off your
flocks against your will, or killing you yourself by guile or by
strength?'

"Then from inside the cave strong Polyphemus
answered them: 'My friends, it is Nobody that is slaying
me by guile and not by force.'

"And they made answer and addressed him with

---

[1] ἐρεισθείς Aristarchus: ἀερθείς

410   εἰ μὲν δὴ μή τίς σε βιάζεται οἶον ἐόντα,
     νοῦσον γ᾽ οὔ πως ἔστι Διὸς μεγάλου ἀλέασθαι,
     ἀλλὰ σύ γ᾽ εὔχεο πατρὶ Ποσειδάωνι ἄνακτι.᾽
     "ὣς ἄρ᾽ ἔφαν ἀπιόντες, ἐμὸν δ᾽ ἐγέλασσε φίλον κῆρ,
     ὡς ὄνομ᾽ ἐξαπάτησεν ἐμὸν καὶ μῆτις ἀμύμων.
415   Κύκλωψ δὲ στενάχων τε καὶ ὠδίνων ὀδύνῃσι
     χερσὶ ψηλαφόων ἀπὸ μὲν λίθον εἷλε θυράων,
     αὐτὸς δ᾽ εἰνὶ θύρῃσι καθέζετο χεῖρε πετάσσας,
     εἴ τινά που μετ᾽ ὄεσσι λάβοι στείχοντα θύραζε·
     οὕτω γάρ πού μ᾽ ἤλπετ᾽ ἐνὶ φρεσὶ νήπιον εἶναι.
420   αὐτὰρ ἐγὼ βούλευον, ὅπως ὄχ᾽ ἄριστα γένοιτο,
     εἴ τιν᾽ ἑταίροισιν θανάτου λύσιν ἠδ᾽ ἐμοὶ αὐτῷ
     εὑροίμην· πάντας δὲ δόλους καὶ μῆτιν ὕφαινον
     ὥς τε περὶ ψυχῆς· μέγα γὰρ κακὸν ἐγγύθεν ἦεν.
     ἥδε δέ μοι κατὰ θυμὸν ἀρίστη φαίνετο βουλή.
425   ἄρσενες ὄιες ἦσαν ἐυτρεφέες, δασύμαλλοι,
     καλοί τε μεγάλοι τε, ἰοδνεφὲς εἶρος ἔχοντες·
     τοὺς ἀκέων συνέεργον ἐυστρεφέεσσι λύγοισι,
     τῆς ἔπι Κύκλωψ εὗδε πέλωρ, ἀθεμίστια εἰδώς,
     σύντρεις αἰνύμενος· ὁ μὲν ἐν μέσῳ ἄνδρα φέρεσκε,
430   τὼ δ᾽ ἑτέρω ἑκάτερθεν ἴτην σώοντες ἑταίρους.
     τρεῖς δὲ ἕκαστον φῶτ᾽ ὄιες φέρον· αὐτὰρ ἐγώ γε—
     ἀρνειὸς γὰρ ἔην μήλων ὄχ᾽ ἄριστος ἁπάντων,
     τοῦ κατὰ νῶτα λαβών, λασίην ὑπὸ γαστέρ᾽ ἐλυσθεὶς
     κείμην· αὐτὰρ χερσὶν ἀώτου θεσπεσίοιο
435   νωλεμέως στρεφθεὶς ἐχόμην τετληότι θυμῷ.
     ὣς τότε μὲν στενάχοντες ἐμείναμεν Ἠῶ δῖαν.
     "ἦμος δ᾽ ἠριγένεια φάνη ῥοδοδάκτυλος Ἠώς,

winged words: 'If, then, nobody does violence to you all alone as you are, sickness which comes from Zeus there is no way you can escape; you must pray to our father the lord Poseidon.'

"So they spoke and went their way; and my heart laughed within me that my name and flawless scheme had so beguiled. But the Cyclops, groaning and toiling in anguish, groped with his hands and took away the stone from the door, and himself sat in the doorway with arms outstretched in the hope of catching any one who tried to go out with the sheep—so foolish, I suppose, in his heart he expected to find me. But I took thought how all might be the very best, if I might find some way of escape from death for my comrades and for myself. And I wove all sorts of wiles and schemes, as a man will in a matter of life and death; for great was the evil that was close upon us. And this seemed to my mind the best plan. Rams there were, well-fed and thick of fleece, fine beasts and large, with wool as dark as the violet. These I silently bound together with twisted withes on which the Cyclops, that monster obedient to no law, was accustomed to sleep. Three at a time I took. The one in the middle in each case bore a man, and the other two went, one on either side, saving my comrades. Thus every three sheep bore a man. But as for me—there was a ram, far the best of the flock; him I grasped by the back, and, curled beneath his shaggy belly, lay there face upwards with steadfast heart, clinging fast with my hands to his wondrous fleece. So then, with groaning, we waited for the bright dawn.

"As soon as early Dawn appeared, the rosy-fingered,

καὶ τότ' ἔπειτα νομόνδ' ἐξέσσυτο ἄρσενα μῆλα,
θήλειαι δὲ μέμηκον ἀνήμελκτοι περὶ σηκούς·
440 οὔθατα γὰρ σφαραγεῦντο. ἄναξ δ' ὀδύνῃσι κακῇσι
τειρόμενος πάντων ὀίων ἐπεμαίετο νῶτα
ὀρθῶν ἑσταότων· τὸ δὲ νήπιος οὐκ ἐνόησεν,
ὥς οἱ ὑπ' εἰροπόκων ὀίων στέρνοισι δέδεντο.
ὕστατος ἀρνειὸς μήλων ἔστειχε θύραζε
445 λάχνῳ στεινόμενος καὶ ἐμοὶ πυκινὰ φρονέοντι.
τὸν δ' ἐπιμασσάμενος προσέφη κρατερὸς Πολύφημος·

"'κριὲ πέπον, τί μοι ὧδε διὰ σπέος ἔσσυο μήλων
ὕστατος; οὔ τι πάρος γε λελειμμένος ἔρχεαι οἰῶν,
ἀλλὰ πολὺ πρῶτος νέμεαι τέρεν' ἄνθεα ποίης
450 μακρὰ βιβάς, πρῶτος δὲ ῥοὰς ποταμῶν ἀφικάνεις,
πρῶτος δὲ σταθμόνδε λιλαίεαι ἀπονέεσθαι
ἑσπέριος· νῦν αὖτε πανύστατος. ἦ σύ γ' ἄνακτος
ὀφθαλμὸν ποθέεις, τὸν ἀνὴρ κακὸς ἐξαλάωσε
σὺν λυγροῖς ἑτάροισι δαμασσάμενος φρένας οἴνῳ,
455 Οὖτις, ὃν οὔ πώ φημι πεφυγμένον εἶναι ὄλεθρον.
εἰ δὴ ὁμοφρονέοις ποτιφωνήεις τε γένοιο
εἰπεῖν ὅππῃ κεῖνος ἐμὸν μένος ἠλασκάζει·
τῷ κέ οἱ ἐγκέφαλός γε διὰ σπέος ἄλλυδις ἄλλῃ
θεινομένου ῥαίοιτο πρὸς οὔδεϊ, κὰδ δέ κ' ἐμὸν κῆρ
460 λωφήσειε κακῶν, τά μοι οὐτιδανὸς πόρεν Οὖτις.'

"ὣς εἰπὼν τὸν κριὸν ἀπὸ ἕο πέμπε θύραζε.
ἐλθόντες δ' ἠβαιὸν ἀπὸ σπείους τε καὶ αὐλῆς
πρῶτος ὑπ' ἀρνειοῦ λυόμην, ὑπέλυσα δ' ἑταίρους.
καρπαλίμως δὲ τὰ μῆλα ταναύποδα, πίονα δημῷ,
465 πολλὰ περιτροπέοντες ἐλαύνομεν, ὄφρ' ἐπὶ νῆα

then the males of the flock hastened forth to pasture and the females bleated unmilked about the pens, for their udders were bursting. And their master, oppressed by hard pangs, felt along the backs of all the sheep as they stood up before him, but in his folly he did not perceive this, that my men were bound beneath the breasts of his fleecy sheep. Last of all the flock the ram went out, burdened with the weight of his fleece and of me with my teeming brain. And mighty Polyphemus, as he felt along his back, spoke to him saying:

"'Beloved ram, why is it that you go out through the cave like this, the last of the flock? Never before have you been left behind by the sheep, but are always far the first to graze on the tender bloom of the grass, stepping high, and the first to reach the streams of the river, and the first to show your longing to return to the fold at evening. But now you are last of all. Surely you are sorrowing for the eye of your master, which an evil man blinded along with his miserable fellows, when he had overpowered my wits with wine, Nobody, who, I tell you, has not yet escaped destruction. If only you could feel as I do, and could get for yourself the power of speech to tell me where he skulks away from my wrath, then would his brains be dashed on the ground throughout the cave, some here, some there, once I had struck him, and my heart would be lightened of the woes which good-for-nothing Nobody has brought me.'

"So saying he sent the ram away from him out the door. And when we had gone a little way from the cave and the courtyard, I first loosed myself from under the ram and untied my comrades. Quickly then we drove off those long-shanked sheep, rich with fat, looking behind us often until we came to the ship. And welcome to our dear com-

ἱκόμεθ'. ἀσπάσιοι δὲ φίλοις ἑτάροισι φάνημεν,
οἳ φύγομεν θάνατον, τοὺς δὲ στενάχοντο γοῶντες.
ἀλλ' ἐγὼ οὐκ εἴων, ἀνὰ δ' ὀφρύσι νεῦον ἑκάστῳ,
κλαίειν, ἀλλ' ἐκέλευσα θοῶς καλλίτριχα μῆλα
470 πόλλ' ἐν νηὶ βαλόντας ἐπιπλεῖν ἁλμυρὸν ὕδωρ.
οἱ δ' αἶψ' εἴσβαινον καὶ ἐπὶ κληῖσι καθῖζον,
ἑξῆς δ' ἑζόμενοι πολιὴν ἅλα τύπτον ἐρετμοῖς.
ἀλλ' ὅτε τόσσον ἀπῆν, ὅσσον τε γέγωνε βοήσας,
καὶ τότ' ἐγὼ Κύκλωπα προσηύδων κερτομίοισι·
475 "'Κύκλωψ, οὐκ ἄρ' ἔμελλες ἀνάλκιδος ἀνδρὸς
       ἑταίρους
ἔδμεναι ἐν σπῆι γλαφυρῷ κρατερῆφι βίηφι.
καὶ λίην σέ γ' ἔμελλε κιχήσεσθαι κακὰ ἔργα,
σχέτλι', ἐπεὶ ξείνους οὐχ ἅζεο σῷ ἐνὶ οἴκῳ
ἐσθέμεναι· τῷ σε Ζεὺς τίσατο καὶ θεοὶ ἄλλοι.'
480 "ὣς ἐφάμην, ὁ δ' ἔπειτα χολώσατο κηρόθι μᾶλλον,
ἧκε δ' ἀπορρήξας κορυφὴν ὄρεος μεγάλοιο,
κὰδ δ' ἔβαλε προπάροιθε νεὸς κυανοπρώροιο
τυτθόν, ἐδεύησεν δ' οἰήιον ἄκρον ἱκέσθαι,[1]
ἐκλύσθη δὲ θάλασσα κατερχομένης ὑπὸ πέτρης·
485 τὴν δ' αἶψ' ἤπειρόνδε παλιρρόθιον φέρε κῦμα,
πλημυρὶς ἐκ πόντοιο, θέμωσε δὲ χέρσον ἱκέσθαι.

---

[1] Line 483 (= 540) was rejected by Aristarchus.

[a] Murray omitted verse 483 in the translation as "ruinous to the sense," but the following interpretation convinces me that it is well in place.

At line 472 the men take their places and proceed to row, or rather to backwater, since the ship was presumably beached or tied

350

rades was the sight of us who had escaped death, but for the others they wept and groaned; yet I would not allow them to weep, but with an upward nod forbade each man. Rather I bade them to fling on board with speed the many fine-fleeced sheep and to sail over the salt water. So they went on board quickly and sat down upon the benches, and sitting well in order struck the gray sea with their oars. But when I was as far away as a man's voice carries when he shouts, then I spoke to the Cyclops with mocking words:

"'Cyclops, that man, it seems, was no weakling, whose comrades you intended to devour violently in your hollow cave. Only too surely were your evil deeds to fall on your own head, you stubborn wretch, who did not shrink from eating your guests in your own house. Therefore has Zeus taken vengeance on you, and the other gods.'

"So I spoke, whereupon he became all the more angry at heart, and broke off the peak of a high mountain and hurled it at us, and it fell a little in front of the dark-prowed ship[a] and barely missed the end of the steering oar. And the sea surged beneath the stone as it fell, and the backward flow, like a tidal wave, bore the ship swiftly landwards and drove it upon the shore. But I seized a long pole in my

up bow-first; the ship is still proceeding stern-first when the Cyclops hurls his first rock, which lands "in front of the dark prowed ship" and thus just misses "hitting the tip of the steering oar" (482–83) at the stern. The wave produced by this rock drives the ship back toward the shore. By line 491 they are twice as far out, and so have managed to bring the ship about when the Cyclops' second rock falls a little *behind* the ship, just missing the tip of the steering oar (540). This time the wave carries the ship forward, to the shore of the island where the rest of Odysseus' fleet is waiting. D.

αὐτὰρ ἐγὼ χείρεσσι λαβὼν περιμήκεα κοντὸν
ὦσα παρέξ, ἑτάροισι δ' ἐποτρύνας ἐκέλευσα
ἐμβαλέειν κώπῃς, ἵν' ὑπὲκ κακότητα φύγοιμεν,
490 κρατὶ κατανεύων· οἱ δὲ προπεσόντες ἔρεσσον.
ἀλλ' ὅτε δὴ δὶς τόσσον ἅλα πρήσσοντες ἀπῆμεν,
καὶ τότε δὴ Κύκλωπα προσηύδων· ἀμφὶ δ' ἑταῖροι
μειλιχίοις ἐπέεσσιν ἐρήτυον ἄλλοθεν ἄλλος·
  "'σχέτλιε, τίπτ' ἐθέλεις ἐρεθιζέμεν ἄγριον ἄνδρα;
495 ὃς καὶ νῦν πόντονδε βαλὼν βέλος ἤγαγε νῆα
αὖτις ἐς ἤπειρον, καὶ δὴ φάμεν αὐτόθ' ὀλέσθαι.
εἰ δὲ φθεγξαμένου τευ ἢ αὐδήσαντος ἄκουσε,
σύν κεν ἄραξ' ἡμέων κεφαλὰς καὶ νήια δοῦρα
μαρμάρῳ ὀκριόεντι βαλών· τόσσον γὰρ ἵησιν.'
500   "ὣς φάσαν, ἀλλ' οὐ πεῖθον ἐμὸν μεγαλήτορα θυμόν,
ἀλλά μιν ἄψορρον προσέφην κεκοτηότι θυμῷ·
  "'Κύκλωψ, αἴ κέν τίς σε καταθνητῶν ἀνθρώπων
ὀφθαλμοῦ εἴρηται ἀεικελίην ἀλαωτύν,
φάσθαι Ὀδυσσῆα πτολιπόρθιον ἐξαλαῶσαι,
505 υἱὸν Λαέρτεω, Ἰθάκῃ ἔνι οἰκί' ἔχοντα.'
  "ὣς ἐφάμην, ὁ δέ μ' οἰμώξας ἠμείβετο μύθῳ·
'ὢ πόποι, ἦ μάλα δή με παλαίφατα θέσφαθ' ἱκάνει.
ἔσκε τις ἐνθάδε μάντις ἀνὴρ ἠΰς τε μέγας τε,
Τήλεμος Εὐρυμίδης, ὃς μαντοσύνῃ ἐκέκαστο
510 καὶ μαντευόμενος κατεγήρα Κυκλώπεσσιν·
ὅς μοι ἔφη τάδε πάντα τελευτήσεσθαι ὀπίσσω,
χειρῶν ἐξ Ὀδυσῆος ἁμαρτήσεσθαι ὀπωπῆς.
ἀλλ' αἰεί τινα φῶτα μέγαν καὶ καλὸν ἐδέγμην
ἐνθάδ' ἐλεύσεσθαι, μεγάλην ἐπιειμένον ἀλκήν·

hands and shoved the ship off and along the shore, and I roused my comrades and bade them fall to their oars that we might escape out of our evil plight, by nodding with my head. And they bent to their oars and rowed. But when, putting sea behind us, we were twice as far distant, then I began to call to the Cyclops, though round about me my comrades, one after another, tried to check me with winning words:

"'Stubborn man, why will you provoke to anger a savage, who just now hurled his missile into the sea and drove our ship back to the land, and indeed we thought to perish there? And had he heard one of us uttering a sound or speaking, he would have hurled a jagged rock and crushed our heads and the timbers of our ship, so strongly does he throw.'

"So they spoke, but they could not persuade my greathearted spirit; and I answered him again with angry heart:

"'Cyclops, if any one of mortal men shall ask you about the shameful blinding of your eye, say that Odysseus, the sacker of cities, blinded it, the son of Laertes, whose home is in Ithaca.'

"So I spoke, and he groaned and said in answer: 'Woe is me! How true it is that a prophecy uttered long ago has come upon me! There lived here a soothsayer, a good man and tall, Telemus, son of Eurymus, who excelled all men in soothsaying, and grew old as a seer among the Cyclopes. He told me that all these things should be brought to pass in days to come, that by the hands of Odysseus I should lose my sight. But I always looked for some tall and handsome man to come here, clothed in great strength, but now

515 νῦν δέ μ' ἐὼν ὀλίγος τε καὶ οὐτιδανὸς καὶ ἄκικυς
ὀφθαλμοῦ ἀλάωσεν, ἐπεί μ' ἐδαμάσσατο οἴνῳ.
ἀλλ' ἄγε δεῦρ', Ὀδυσεῦ, ἵνα τοι πὰρ ξείνια θείω
πομπήν τ' ὀτρύνω δόμεναι κλυτὸν ἐννοσίγαιον·
τοῦ γὰρ ἐγὼ πάις εἰμί, πατὴρ δ' ἐμὸς εὔχεται εἶναι.
520 αὐτὸς δ', αἴ κ' ἐθέλῃσ', ἰήσεται, οὐδέ τις ἄλλος
οὔτε θεῶν μακάρων οὔτε θνητῶν ἀνθρώπων.'
    "ὣς ἔφατ', αὐτὰρ ἐγώ μιν ἀμειβόμενος προσέειπον·
'αἲ γὰρ δὴ ψυχῆς τε καὶ αἰῶνός σε δυναίμην
εὖνιν ποιήσας πέμψαι δόμον Ἄιδος εἴσω,
525 ὡς οὐκ ὀφθαλμόν γ' ἰήσεται οὐδ' ἐνοσίχθων.'
    "ὣς ἐφάμην, ὁ δ' ἔπειτα Ποσειδάωνι ἄνακτι
εὔχετο χεῖρ' ὀρέγων εἰς οὐρανὸν ἀστερόεντα·
'κλῦθι, Ποσείδαον γαιήοχε κυανοχαῖτα,
εἰ ἐτεόν γε σός εἰμι, πατὴρ δ' ἐμὸς εὔχεαι εἶναι,
530 δὸς μὴ Ὀδυσσῆα πτολιπόρθιον οἴκαδ' ἱκέσθαι
υἱὸν Λαέρτεω, Ἰθάκῃ ἔνι οἰκί' ἔχοντα.[1]
ἀλλ' εἴ οἱ μοῖρ' ἐστὶ φίλους τ' ἰδέειν καὶ ἱκέσθαι
οἶκον ἐυκτίμενον καὶ ἑὴν ἐς πατρίδα γαῖαν,
ὀψὲ κακῶς ἔλθοι, ὀλέσας ἄπο πάντας ἑταίρους,
535 νηὸς ἐπ' ἀλλοτρίης, εὕροι δ' ἐν πήματα οἴκῳ.'
    "ὣς ἔφατ' εὐχόμενος, τοῦ δ' ἔκλυε κυανοχαίτης.
αὐτὰρ ὅ γ' ἐξαῦτις πολὺ μείζονα λᾶαν ἀείρας
ἧκ' ἐπιδινήσας, ἐπέρεισε δὲ ἶν' ἀπέλεθρον,
κὰδ' δ' ἔβαλεν μετόπισθε νεὸς κυανοπρώροιο
540 τυτθόν, ἐδεύησεν δ' οἰήιον ἄκρον ἱκέσθαι.
ἐκλύσθη δὲ θάλασσα κατερχομένης ὑπὸ πέτρης·
τὴν δὲ πρόσω φέρε κῦμα, θέμωσε δὲ χέρσον ἱκέσθαι.

one that is puny, a no-good and a weakling, has blinded me
of my eye when he had overpowered me with wine. Yet
come here, Odysseus, that I may set before you gifts of
entertainment, and may urge the glorious Earth-shaker to
give you conveyance hence. For I am his son, and he
declares himself my father; and he himself will heal me, if
he will, but no one else either of the blessed gods or of
mortal men.'

"So he spoke, and I answered him and said: 'Would
that I were able to rob you of soul and survival, and to send
you to the house of Hades, as surely as not even the Earth-
shaker shall heal your eye.'

"So I spoke, and he then prayed to the lord Poseidon,
stretching out both his hands to the starry heaven: 'Hear
me Poseidon, earth-bearer, dark-haired god, if indeed I am
your son and you declare yourself my father; grant that
Odysseus, the sacker of cities, may never reach his home,
the son of Laertes, whose home is in Ithaca; but if it is his
fate to see his people and to reach his well-built house and
his native land, late may he come, and in distress, after los-
ing all his comrades, in a ship that is another's; and may he
find trouble in his house.'

"So he spoke in prayer, and the dark-haired god heard
him. But the Cyclops lifted up again a far greater stone,
and swung and hurled it, putting into the throw infinite
strength. He threw it a little behind the dark-prowed ship,
and barely missed the end of the steering oar. And the sea
surged beneath the stone as it fell, and the wave bore the
ship onward and drove it to the shore.

---

[1] Line 531 is omitted in most MSS.

"ἀλλ' ὅτε δὴ τὴν νῆσον ἀφικόμεθ', ἔνθα περ ἄλλαι
νῆες ἐΰσσελμοι μένον ἁθρόαι, ἀμφὶ δ' ἑταῖροι
545   ἥατ' ὀδυρόμενοι, ἡμέας ποτιδέγμενοι αἰεί,
νῆα μὲν ἔνθ' ἐλθόντες ἐκέλσαμεν ἐν ψαμάθοισιν,
ἐκ δὲ καὶ αὐτοὶ βῆμεν ἐπὶ ῥηγμῖνι θαλάσσης.
μῆλα δὲ Κύκλωπος γλαφυρῆς ἐκ νηὸς ἑλόντες
δασσάμεθ', ὡς μή τίς μοι ἀτεμβόμενος κίοι ἴσης.
550   ἀρνειὸν δ' ἐμοὶ οἴῳ ἐϋκνήμιδες ἑταῖροι
μήλων δαιομένων δόσαν ἔξοχα· τὸν δ' ἐπὶ θινὶ
Ζηνὶ κελαινεφέϊ Κρονίδῃ, ὃς πᾶσιν ἀνάσσει,
ῥέξας μηρί' ἔκαιον· ὁ δ' οὐκ ἐμπάζετο ἱρῶν,
ἀλλ' ὅ γε μερμήριξεν ὅπως ἀπολοίατο πᾶσαι
555   νῆες ἐΰσσελμοι καὶ ἐμοὶ ἐρίηρες ἑταῖροι.

"ὣς τότε μὲν πρόπαν ἦμαρ ἐς ἠέλιον καταδύντα
ἥμεθα δαινύμενοι κρέα τ' ἄσπετα καὶ μέθυ ἡδύ·
ἦμος δ' ἠέλιος κατέδυ καὶ ἐπὶ κνέφας ἦλθε,
δὴ τότε κοιμήθημεν ἐπὶ ῥηγμῖνι θαλάσσης.
560   ἦμος δ' ἠριγένεια φάνη ῥοδοδάκτυλος Ἠώς,
δὴ τότ' ἐγὼν ἑτάροισιν ἐποτρύνας ἐκέλευσα
αὐτούς τ' ἀμβαίνειν ἀνά τε πρυμνήσια λῦσαι·
οἱ δ' αἶψ' εἴσβαινον καὶ ἐπὶ κληῖσι καθῖζον,
ἑξῆς δ' ἑζόμενοι πολιὴν ἅλα τύπτον ἐρετμοῖς.
565   "ἔνθεν δὲ προτέρω πλέομεν ἀκαχήμενοι ἦτορ,
ἄσμενοι ἐκ θανάτοιο, φίλους ὀλέσαντες ἑταίρους."

"Now when we had come to the island, where our other well-benched ships lay all together, and round about them our comrades, ever expecting us, sat weeping, then, on coming there, we beached our ship on the sands, and ourselves disembarked upon the shore of the sea. Then we took out of the hollow ship the flocks of the Cyclops, and divided them, that so far as lay in me no man might go defrauded of an equal share. But the ram my well-greaved comrades gave to me alone, when the flocks were divided, as a gift; and on the shore I sacrificed him to Zeus, son of Cronos, god of the dark clouds, who is lord of all, and burned the thigh pieces. But he did not heed my sacrifice, but was planning how all my well-benched ships might perish and my trusty comrades.

"So, then, all day long till sunset we sat feasting on abundant flesh and sweet wine; but when the sun set and darkness came on, then we lay down to rest on the shore of the sea. And as soon as early Dawn appeared, the rosy-fingered, I roused my comrades, and bade them themselves to embark and to loose the stern cables. So they went on board quickly and sat down upon the benches, and sitting well in order struck the gray sea with their oars.

"From there we sailed on, grieved at heart, glad to have escaped death, though we had lost our staunch comrades."

Κ

"Αἰολίην δ᾽ ἐς νῆσον ἀφικόμεθ᾽· ἔνθα δ᾽ ἔναιεν
Αἴολος Ἱπποτάδης, φίλος ἀθανάτοισι θεοῖσιν,
πλωτῇ ἐνὶ νήσῳ· πᾶσαν δέ τέ μιν πέρι τεῖχος
χάλκεον ἄρρηκτον, λισσὴ δ᾽ ἀναδέδρομε πέτρη.
5 τοῦ καὶ δώδεκα παῖδες ἐνὶ μεγάροις γεγάασιν,
ἓξ μὲν θυγατέρες, ἓξ δ᾽ υἱέες ἡβώοντες·
ἔνθ᾽ ὅ γε θυγατέρας πόρεν υἱάσιν εἶναι ἀκοίτις.
οἱ δ᾽ αἰεὶ παρὰ πατρὶ φίλῳ καὶ μητέρι κεδνῇ
δαίνυνται, παρὰ δέ σφιν ὀνείατα μυρία κεῖται,
10 κνισῆεν δέ τε δῶμα περιστεναχίζεται αὐλῇ
ἤματα· νύκτας δ᾽ αὖτε παρ᾽ αἰδοίῃς ἀλόχοισιν
εὕδουσ᾽ ἔν τε τάπησι καὶ ἐν τρητοῖσι λέχεσσι.
καὶ μὲν τῶν ἱκόμεσθα πόλιν καὶ δώματα καλά.
μῆνα δὲ πάντα φίλει με καὶ ἐξερέεινεν ἕκαστα,
15 Ἴλιον Ἀργείων τε νέας καὶ νόστον Ἀχαιῶν·
καὶ μὲν ἐγὼ τῷ πάντα κατὰ μοῖραν κατέλεξα.
ἀλλ᾽ ὅτε δὴ καὶ ἐγὼν ὁδὸν ᾔτεον ἠδ᾽ ἐκέλευον
πεμπέμεν, οὐδέ τι κεῖνος ἀνήνατο, τεῦχε δὲ πομπήν.
δῶκε δέ μ᾽ ἐκδείρας ἀσκὸν βοὸς ἐννεώροιο,
20 ἔνθα δὲ βυκτάων ἀνέμων κατέδησε κέλευθα·
κεῖνον γὰρ ταμίην ἀνέμων ποίησε Κρονίων,
ἠμὲν παυέμεναι ἠδ᾽ ὀρνύμεν, ὅν κ᾽ ἐθέλῃσι.

BOOK 10

"Then we came to the island of Aeolia, where dwelt Aeolus, son of Hippotas, dear to the immortal gods, on a floating island, and all around it is a wall of unbreakable bronze, and the cliff runs up sheer. Twelve children of his, too, there are in the halls, six daughters and six sturdy sons, and he gave his daughters to his sons to wife. These, then, feast continually by their staunch father and good mother, and before them lies boundless good cheer. And the house, filled with the savor of feasting, resounds all about in the courtyard by day, whereas at night they sleep by their revered wives on blankets and on corded bedsteads. To their city, then, and the fine palace we came, and for a full month he made me welcome and questioned me about each thing, about Ilium, and the ships of the Argives, and the return of the Achaeans. And I told him the whole tale in due order. But when I, in my turn, asked him that I might depart and requested that he send me on my way, he, too, denied me nothing, but gave me conveyance. He gave me a bag, made of the hide of an ox nine years old, which he skinned, and in it he bound the paths of the blustering winds; for the son of Cronos had made him keeper of the winds, both to still and to rouse whatever one he will.

νηὶ δ᾽ ἐνὶ γλαφυρῇ κατέδει μέρμιθι φαεινῇ
ἀργυρέῃ, ἵνα μή τι παραπνεύσῃ ὀλίγον περ·
25 αὐτὰρ ἐμοὶ πνοιὴν Ζεφύρου προέηκεν ἀῆναι,
ὄφρα φέροι νῆάς τε καὶ αὐτούς· οὐδ᾽ ἄρ᾽ ἔμελλεν
ἐκτελέειν· αὐτῶν γὰρ ἀπωλόμεθ᾽ ἀφραδίῃσιν.

"ἐννῆμαρ μὲν ὁμῶς πλέομεν νύκτας τε καὶ ἦμαρ,
τῇ δεκάτῃ δ᾽ ἤδη ἀνεφαίνετο πατρὶς ἄρουρα,
30 καὶ δὴ πυρπολέοντας ἐλεύσσομεν ἐγγὺς ἐόντες·[1]
ἔνθ᾽ ἐμὲ μὲν γλυκὺς ὕπνος ἐπήλυθε κεκμηῶτα,
αἰεὶ γὰρ πόδα νηὸς ἐνώμων, οὐδέ τῳ ἄλλῳ
δῶχ᾽ ἑτάρων, ἵνα θᾶσσον ἱκοίμεθα πατρίδα γαῖαν·
οἱ δ᾽ ἕταροι ἐπέεσσι πρὸς ἀλλήλους ἀγόρευον,
35 καί μ᾽ ἔφασαν χρυσόν τε καὶ ἄργυρον οἴκαδ᾽ ἄγεσθαι
δῶρα παρ᾽ Αἰόλου μεγαλήτορος Ἱπποτάδαο.
ὧδε δέ τις εἴπεσκεν ἰδὼν ἐς πλησίον ἄλλον·

"'ὦ πόποι, ὡς ὅδε πᾶσι φίλος καὶ τίμιός ἐστιν
ἀνθρώποις, ὁτέων τε πόλιν καὶ γαῖαν ἵκηται.
40 πολλὰ μὲν ἐκ Τροίης ἄγεται κειμήλια καλὰ
ληΐδος, ἡμεῖς δ᾽ αὖτε ὁμὴν ὁδὸν ἐκτελέσαντες
οἴκαδε νισσόμεθα κενεὰς σὺν χείρας ἔχοντες·
καὶ νῦν οἱ τάδ᾽ ἔδωκε χαριζόμενος φιλότητι
Αἴολος. ἀλλ᾽ ἄγε θᾶσσον ἰδώμεθα ὅττι τάδ᾽ ἐστίν,
45 ὅσσος τις χρυσός τε καὶ ἄργυρος ἀσκῷ ἔνεστιν.'

"ὣς ἔφασαν, βουλὴ δὲ κακὴ νίκησεν ἑταίρων·
ἀσκὸν μὲν λῦσαν, ἄνεμοι δ᾽ ἐκ πάντες ὄρουσαν.
τοὺς δ᾽ αἶψ᾽ ἁρπάξασα φέρεν πόντονδε θύελλα
κλαίοντας, γαίης ἄπο πατρίδος. αὐτὰρ ἐγώ γε
50 ἐγρόμενος κατὰ θυμὸν ἀμύμονα μερμήριξα,

And in my hollow ship he bound it fast with a bright cord of silver, that not a breath might escape, no matter how slight. But for me he sent forth the breath of the West Wind to blow, that it might bear on their way both ships and men. Yet this he was not to bring to pass, for we were lost through our own folly.

"For nine days we sailed, night and day alike, and now on the tenth our native land came in sight, and indeed we were so near that we saw men tending their fires. Then upon me came sweet sleep in my weariness, for I had never ceased tending the sheet of the ship, and had yielded it to no one else of my comrades, that we might come the sooner to our native land. But my comrades meanwhile began to speak to one another, and said that I was bringing home for myself gold and silver as gifts from Aeolus, the great-hearted son of Hippotas. And thus would one speak, with a glance at his neighbor:

"'How beloved and honored this man is by all men to whose city and land he comes! Much beautiful treasure is he carrying with him from the land of Troy from the booty, while we, who have accomplished the same journey as he, are coming home bearing empty hands. And now Aeolus has given him these gifts, granting them freely out of love. No, come, let us quickly see what is here, how much gold and silver in the bag.'

"So they spoke, and the evil counsel of my comrades prevailed. They opened the bag, and all the winds rushed out, and swiftly the storm wind seized them and bore them weeping out to sea away from their native land; but as for me, I awoke, and pondered in my flawless heart whether I

---

[1] ἐόντες: ἐόντας

ἠὲ πεσὼν ἐκ νηὸς ἀποφθίμην ἐνὶ πόντῳ,
ἦ ἀκέων τλαίην καὶ ἔτι ζωοῖσι μετείην.
ἀλλ' ἔτλην καὶ ἔμεινα, καλυψάμενος δ' ἐνὶ νηὶ
κείμην. αἱ δ' ἐφέροντο κακῇ ἀνέμοιο θυέλλῃ
55 αὖτις ἐπ' Αἰολίην νῆσον, στενάχοντο δ' ἑταῖροι.

  "ἔνθα δ' ἐπ' ἠπείρου βῆμεν καὶ ἀφυσσάμεθ' ὕδωρ,
αἶψα δὲ δεῖπνον ἕλοντο θοῆς παρὰ νηυσὶν ἑταῖροι.
αὐτὰρ ἐπεὶ σίτοιό τ' ἐπασσάμεθ' ἠδὲ ποτῆτος,
δὴ τότ' ἐγὼ κήρυκά τ' ὀπασσάμενος καὶ ἑταῖρον
60 βῆν εἰς Αἰόλου κλυτὰ δώματα· τὸν δ' ἐκίχανον
δαινύμενον παρὰ ᾗ τ' ἀλόχῳ καὶ οἷσι τέκεσσιν.
ἐλθόντες δ' ἐς δῶμα παρὰ σταθμοῖσιν ἐπ' οὐδοῦ
ἑζόμεθ'· οἱ δ' ἀνὰ θυμὸν ἐθάμβεον ἔκ τ' ἐρέοντο·

  "'πῶς ἦλθες, Ὀδυσεῦ; τίς τοι κακὸς ἔχραε δαίμων;
65 ἦ μέν σ' ἐνδυκέως ἀπεπέμπομεν, ὄφρ' ἀφίκοιο
πατρίδα σὴν καὶ δῶμα καὶ εἴ πού τοι φίλον ἐστίν.'

  "ὣς φάσαν, αὐτὰρ ἐγὼ μετεφώνεον ἀχνύμενος κῆρ·
'ἄασάν μ' ἕταροί τε κακοὶ πρὸς τοῖσί τε ὕπνος
σχέτλιος. ἀλλ' ἀκέσασθε, φίλοι· δύναμις γὰρ ἐν ὑμῖν.'

70 "ὣς ἐφάμην μαλακοῖσι καθαπτόμενος ἐπέεσσιν,
οἱ δ' ἄνεῳ ἐγένοντο· πατὴρ δ' ἠμείβετο μύθῳ·

  "'ἔρρ' ἐκ νήσου θᾶσσον, ἐλέγχιστε ζωόντων·
οὐ γάρ μοι θέμις ἐστὶ κομιζέμεν οὐδ' ἀποπέμπειν
ἄνδρα τόν, ὅς κε θεοῖσιν ἀπέχθηται μακάρεσσιν·
75 ἔρρε, ἐπεὶ ἄρα θεοῖσιν ἀπεχθόμενος τόδ' ἱκάνεις.'

  "ὣς εἰπὼν ἀπέπεμπε δόμων βαρέα στενάχοντα.
ἔνθεν δὲ προτέρω πλέομεν ἀκαχήμενοι ἦτορ.
τείρετο δ' ἀνδρῶν θυμὸς ὑπ' εἰρεσίης ἀλεγεινῆς

should throw myself off the ship and perish in the sea, or endure in silence and still remain among the living. However, I endured and I remained; wrapping my head in my cloak I lay down in the ship. But the ships were borne by an evil blast of wind back to the Aeolian island; and my comrades groaned.

"There we went ashore and drew water, and quickly my comrades took their meal by the swift ships. But when we had tasted food and drink, I took with me a herald and one companion and went to the glorious palace of Aeolus, and I found him feasting beside his wife and children. So we entered the house and sat down by the doorposts on the threshold, and they were amazed at heart, and questioned us:

"'How have you come here, Odysseus? What cruel god attacked you? Surely we sent you off with kindly care, that you might reach your native land and your home, and whatever place you wished.'

"So said they, but I with sorrowing heart spoke among them and said: 'My evil comrades ruined me, and with them cruel sleep; but bring healing, my friends, for in you is the power.'

"So I spoke, addressing them with winning words, but they were silent. Then their father answered and said:

"'Begone from our island instantly, you vilest of all that live. It would be against all religion for me to help or send upon his way that man who is hated by the blessed gods. Begone, for you come here as one hated by the immortals.'

"So saying, he sent me away from the house, groaning heavily. From there we sailed on, grieved at heart. And worn was the spirit of the men by the grievous rowing,

ἡμετέρῃ ματίῃ, ἐπεὶ οὐκέτι φαίνετο πομπή.
80 ἐξῆμαρ μὲν ὁμῶς πλέομεν νύκτας τε καὶ ἦμαρ,
ἑβδομάτῃ δ' ἱκόμεσθα Λάμου αἰπὺ πτολίεθρον,
Τηλέπυλον Λαιστρυγονίην, ὅθι ποιμένα ποιμὴν
ἠπύει εἰσελάων, ὁ δέ τ' ἐξελάων ὑπακούει.
ἔνθα κ' ἄυπνος ἀνὴρ δοιοὺς ἐξήρατο μισθούς,
85 τὸν μὲν βουκολέων, τὸν δ' ἄργυφα μῆλα νομεύων·
ἐγγὺς γὰρ νυκτός τε καὶ ἤματός εἰσι κέλευθοι.
ἔνθ' ἐπεὶ ἐς λιμένα κλυτὸν ἤλθομεν, ὃν πέρι πέτρη
ἠλίβατος τετύχηκε διαμπερὲς ἀμφοτέρωθεν,
ἀκταὶ δὲ προβλῆτες ἐναντίαι ἀλλήλῃσιν
90 ἐν στόματι προύχουσιν, ἀραιὴ δ' εἴσοδός ἐστιν,
ἔνθ' οἵ γ' εἴσω πάντες ἔχον νέας ἀμφιελίσσας.
αἱ μὲν ἄρ' ἔντοσθεν λιμένος κοίλοιο δέδεντο
πλησίαι· οὐ μὲν γάρ ποτ' ἀέξετο κῦμά γ' ἐν αὐτῷ,
οὔτε μέγ' οὔτ' ὀλίγον, λευκὴ δ' ἦν ἀμφὶ γαλήνη·
95 αὐτὰρ ἐγὼν οἶος σχέθον ἔξω νῆα μέλαιναν,
αὐτοῦ ἐπ' ἐσχατιῇ, πέτρης ἐκ πείσματα δήσας·
ἔστην δὲ σκοπιὴν ἐς παιπαλόεσσαν ἀνελθών.
ἔνθα μὲν οὔτε βοῶν οὔτ' ἀνδρῶν φαίνετο ἔργα,
καπνὸν δ' οἶον ὁρῶμεν ἀπὸ χθονὸς ἀίσσοντα.
100 δὴ τότ' ἐγὼν ἑτάρους προΐειν πεύθεσθαι ἰόντας,
οἵ τινες ἀνέρες εἶεν ἐπὶ χθονὶ σῖτον ἔδοντες,
ἄνδρε δύω κρίνας, τρίτατον κήρυχ' ἅμ' ὀπάσσας.
οἱ δ' ἴσαν ἐκβάντες λείην ὁδόν, ᾗ περ ἅμαξαι

because of our own folly, since no longer appeared any breeze to help us on our way. So for six days we sailed, night and day alike, and on the seventh we came to the lofty citadel of Lamus, to Telepylus of the Laestrygonians, where herdsman calls to herdsman as he drives in his flock, and the other answers as he drives his out. There a man who never slept could have earned a double wage, one by herding cattle, and one by pasturing white sheep, for the paths of the night and the day are close together.[a] When we had come there into the fine harbor, about which on both sides a sheer cliff runs continuously, and projecting headlands opposite to one another stretch out at the mouth, and the entrance is narrow, then all the rest steered their curved ships in, and the ships were moored within the hollow harbor close together; for in it no wave ever swelled, great or small, but all about was a bright calm. But I alone moored my black ship outside, there on the border of the land, making the cables fast to the rock. Then I climbed to a rugged height, a point of outlook, and there took my stand; from there no works of men or oxen appeared; smoke alone we saw springing up from the land. So then I sent forth some of my comrades to go and learn who the men were, who here ate bread upon the earth— two men I chose, and sent them a third as a herald. Now when they had gone ashore, they went along a smooth road

[a] The meaning appears to be that the interval between nightfall and daybreak is so short that a herdsman returning from his day's task meets his fellow already driving his flock forth for the following day. Thus a man who could do without sleep could earn a double wage. The passage is plainly due to some vague knowledge of the land of the midnight sun. M.

ἄστυδ᾽ ἀφ᾽ ὑψηλῶν ὀρέων καταγίνεον ὕλην,
105 κούρῃ δὲ ξύμβληντο πρὸ ἄστεος ὑδρευούσῃ,
θυγατέρ᾽ ἰφθίμῃ Λαιστρυγόνος Ἀντιφάταο.
ἡ μὲν ἄρ᾽ ἐς κρήνην κατεβήσετο καλλιρέεθρον
Ἀρτακίην· ἔνθεν γὰρ ὕδωρ προτὶ ἄστυ φέρεσκον·
οἱ δὲ παριστάμενοι προσεφώνεον ἔκ τ᾽ ἐρέοντο
110 ὅς τις τῶνδ᾽ εἴη βασιλεὺς καὶ οἷσιν ἀνάσσοι·
ἡ δὲ μάλ᾽ αὐτίκα πατρὸς ἐπέφραδεν ὑψερεφὲς δῶ.
οἱ δ᾽ ἐπεὶ εἰσῆλθον κλυτὰ δώματα, τὴν δὲ γυναῖκα
εὗρον, ὅσην τ᾽ ὄρεος κορυφήν, κατὰ δ᾽ ἔστυγον αὐτήν.
ἡ δ᾽ αἶψ᾽ ἐξ ἀγορῆς ἐκάλει κλυτὸν Ἀντιφατῆα,
115 ὃν πόσιν, ὃς δὴ τοῖσιν ἐμήσατο λυγρὸν ὄλεθρον.
αὐτίχ᾽ ἕνα μάρψας ἑτάρων ὡπλίσσατο δεῖπνον·
τὼ δὲ δύ᾽ ἀίξαντε φυγῇ ἐπὶ νῆας ἱκέσθην.
αὐτὰρ ὁ τεῦχε βοὴν διὰ ἄστεος· οἱ δ᾽ ἀίοντες
φοίτων ἴφθιμοι Λαιστρυγόνες ἄλλοθεν ἄλλος,
120 μυρίοι, οὐκ ἄνδρεσσιν ἐοικότες, ἀλλὰ Γίγασιν.
οἵ ῥ᾽ ἀπὸ πετράων ἀνδραχθέσι χερμαδίοισιν
βάλλον· ἄφαρ δὲ κακὸς κόναβος κατὰ νῆας ὀρώρει
ἀνδρῶν τ᾽ ὀλλυμένων νηῶν θ᾽ ἅμα ἀγνυμενάων·
ἰχθῦς δ᾽ ὣς πείροντες ἀτερπέα δαῖτα φέροντο.[1]
125 ὄφρ᾽ οἱ τοὺς ὄλεκον λιμένος πολυβενθέος ἐντός,
τόφρα δ᾽ ἐγὼ ξίφος ὀξὺ ἐρυσσάμενος παρὰ μηροῦ
τῷ ἀπὸ πείσματ᾽ ἔκοψα νεὸς κυανοπρώοιο.
αἶψα δ᾽ ἐμοῖς ἑτάροισιν ἐποτρύνας ἐκέλευσα
ἐμβαλέειν κώπῃς, ἵν᾽ ὑπὲκ κακότητα φύγοιμεν·
130 οἱ δ᾽ ἅλα[2] πάντες ἀνέρριψαν, δείσαντες ὄλεθρον.

---

[1] φέροντο Zenodotus, Aristarchus: πένοντο

by which wagons brought wood down to the city from the high mountains. And in front of the city they met a girl drawing water, the stalwart daughter of Laestrygonian Antiphates, who had come down to the fair-flowing spring Artacia, from which they carried water to the town. So they came up to her and spoke to her, and asked her who was king of this people, and who they were of whom he was lord. And she showed them forthwith the high-roofed house of her father. Now when they had entered the glorious house, they found there his wife, huge as the peak of a mountain, and they were aghast at her. At once she called from the place of assembly the glorious Antiphates, her husband, and he devised for them woeful destruction. Instantly he seized one of my comrades and made ready his meal, but the other two sprang up and came in flight to the ships. Then he raised a cry throughout the city, and as they heard it the mighty Laestrygonians came thronging from all sides, a host past counting, not like men, but like the Giants. They pelted us from the cliffs with rocks huge as a man could lift, and at once there rose throughout the ships a dreadful din, alike from men that were dying and from ships that were being crushed. And spearing them like fishes, they carried them home for their loathsome meal. While they were slaying those within the deep harbor, I meanwhile drew my sharp sword from beside my thigh and with it cut the cables of my dark-prowed ship; and quickly calling to my comrades bade them fall to their oars, that we might escape from our evil plight. And they all tossed the sea with their oar blades in fear of death, and joyfully out to

---

[2] ἄλα Rhianus, Callistratus: ἄμα Aristarchus: ἄρα

ἀσπασίως δ' ἐς πόντον ἐπηρεφέας φύγε πέτρας
νηῦς ἐμή· αὐτὰρ αἱ ἄλλαι ἀολλέες αὐτόθ' ὄλοντο.

"ἔνθεν δὲ προτέρω πλέομεν ἀκαχήμενοι ἦτορ,
ἄσμενοι ἐκ θανάτοιο, φίλους ὀλέσαντες ἑταίρους.

135 Αἰαίην δ' ἐς νῆσον ἀφικόμεθ'· ἔνθα δ' ἔναιε
Κίρκη ἐυπλόκαμος, δεινὴ θεὸς αὐδήεσσα,
αὐτοκασιγνήτη ὀλοόφρονος Αἰήταο·
ἄμφω δ' ἐκγεγάτην φαεσιμβρότου Ἠελίοιο
μητρός τ' ἐκ Πέρσης, τὴν Ὠκεανὸς τέκε παῖδα.

140 ἔνθα δ' ἐπ' ἀκτῆς νηὶ κατηγαγόμεσθα σιωπῇ
ναύλοχον ἐς λιμένα, καί τις θεὸς ἡγεμόνευεν.
ἔνθα τότ' ἐκβάντες δύο τ' ἤματα καὶ δύο νύκτας
κείμεθ' ὁμοῦ καμάτῳ τε καὶ ἄλγεσι θυμὸν ἔδοντες.
ἀλλ' ὅτε δὴ τρίτον ἦμαρ ἐυπλόκαμος τέλεσ' Ἠώς,

145 καὶ τότ' ἐγὼν ἐμὸν ἔγχος ἑλὼν καὶ φάσγανον ὀξὺ
καρπαλίμως παρὰ νηὸς ἀνήιον ἐς περιωπήν,
εἴ πως ἔργα ἴδοιμι βροτῶν ἐνοπήν τε πυθοίμην.
ἔστην δὲ σκοπιὴν ἐς παιπαλόεσσαν ἀνελθών,
καί μοι ἐείσατο καπνὸς ἀπὸ χθονὸς εὐρυοδείης,

150 Κίρκης ἐν μεγάροισι, διὰ δρυμὰ πυκνὰ καὶ ὕλην.
μερμήριξα δ' ἔπειτα κατὰ φρένα καὶ κατὰ θυμὸν
ἐλθεῖν ἠδὲ πυθέσθαι, ἐπεὶ ἴδον αἴθοπα καπνόν.
ὧδε δέ μοι φρονέοντι δοάσσατο κέρδιον εἶναι,
πρῶτ' ἐλθόντ' ἐπὶ νῆα θοὴν καὶ θῖνα θαλάσσης

155 δεῖπνον ἑταίροισιν δόμεναι προέμεν τε πυθέσθαι.
ἀλλ' ὅτε δὴ σχεδὸν ἦα κιὼν νεὸς ἀμφιελίσσης,
καὶ τότε τίς με θεῶν ὀλοφύρατο μοῦνον ἐόντα,
ὅς ῥά μοι ὑψίκερων ἔλαφον μέγαν εἰς ὁδὸν αὐτὴν

sea my ship sped away from the beetling cliffs; but the other ships, all together, perished where they were.

"From there we sailed on, grieved at heart, glad to have escaped death, though we had lost our staunch comrades. And we came to the island of Aeaea, where fair-tressed Circe lived, a dread goddess of human speech, own sister to Aeetes of baneful mind; and both are sprung from Helios, who gives light to mortals, and from Perse, their mother, whom Oceanus begot. Here we put in to shore with our ship in silence, into a harbor where ships can lie, and some god guided us. Then we disembarked, and lay there for two days and two nights, eating our hearts for weariness and sorrow. But when fair-tressed Dawn brought to its birth the third day, then I took my spear and my sharp sword, and quickly went up from the ship to a place of wide prospect, in the hope that I might see the works of men, and hear their voice. So I climbed to a rugged height, a place of outlook, and there took my stand, and saw smoke rising from the broad-wayed earth in the halls of Circe, through the thick brush and the wood. And I debated in mind and heart whether I should go and investigate, when I had seen the fire and smoke. And as I pondered, this seemed to me to be the better way, to go first to the swift ship and the shore of the sea, and give to my comrades their meal, and send them forth to investigate. But when, as I went, I was near to the curved ship, then some god took pity on me in my loneliness, and sent a great, high-horned stag into my very path. He was coming

ἧκεν. ὁ μὲν ποταμόνδε κατήιεν ἐκ νομοῦ ὕλης
160 πιόμενος· δὴ γάρ μιν ἔχεν μένος ἠελίοιο.
τὸν δ' ἐγὼ ἐκβαίνοντα κατ' ἄκνηστιν μέσα νῶτα
πλῆξα· τὸ δ' ἀντικρὺ δόρυ χάλκεον ἐξεπέρησε,
κὰδ δ' ἔπεσ' ἐν κονίῃσι μακών, ἀπὸ δ' ἔπτατο θυμός.
τῷ δ' ἐγὼ ἐμβαίνων δόρυ χάλκεον ἐξ ὠτειλῆς
165 εἰρυσάμην· τὸ μὲν αὖθι κατακλίνας ἐπὶ γαίῃ
εἴασ'· αὐτὰρ ἐγὼ σπασάμην ῥῶπάς τε λύγους τε,
πεῖσμα δ', ὅσον τ' ὄργυιαν, ἐυστρεφὲς ἀμφοτέρωθεν
πλεξάμενος συνέδησα πόδας δεινοῖο πελώρου,
βῆν δὲ καταλοφάδεια φέρων ἐπὶ νῆα μέλαιναν
170 ἔγχει ἐρειδόμενος, ἐπεὶ οὔ πως ἦεν ἐπ' ὤμου
χειρὶ φέρειν ἑτέρῃ· μάλα γὰρ μέγα θηρίον ἦεν.
κὰδ δ' ἔβαλον προπάροιθε νεός, ἀνέγειρα δ' ἑταίρους
μειλιχίοις ἐπέεσσι παρασταδὸν ἄνδρα ἕκαστον·

"'ὦ φίλοι, οὐ γάρ πω καταδυσόμεθ' ἀχνύμενοί περ
175 εἰς Ἀίδαο δόμους, πρὶν μόρσιμον ἦμαρ ἐπέλθῃ·
ἀλλ' ἄγετ', ὄφρ' ἐν νηὶ θοῇ βρῶσίς τε πόσις τε,
μνησόμεθα βρώμης, μηδὲ τρυχώμεθα λιμῷ.'

"ὣς ἐφάμην, οἱ δ' ὦκα ἐμοῖς ἐπέεσσι πίθοντο,
ἐκ δὲ καλυψάμενοι παρὰ θῖν' ἁλὸς ἀτρυγέτοιο
180 θηήσαντ' ἔλαφον· μάλα γὰρ μέγα θηρίον ἦεν.
αὐτὰρ ἐπεὶ τάρπησαν ὁρώμενοι ὀφθαλμοῖσιν,
χεῖρας νιψάμενοι τεύχοντ' ἐρικυδέα δαῖτα.
ὣς τότε μὲν πρόπαν ἦμαρ ἐς ἠέλιον καταδύντα
ἥμεθα δαινύμενοι κρέα τ' ἄσπετα καὶ μέθυ ἡδύ·
185 ἦμος δ' ἠέλιος κατέδυ καὶ ἐπὶ κνέφας ἦλθε,
δὴ τότε κοιμήθημεν ἐπὶ ῥηγμῖνι θαλάσσης.

down to the river from his pasture in the wood to drink, for the power of the sun oppressed him; and as he came out I struck him on the spine in the middle of the back, and the bronze spear passed right through him, and down he fell in the dust with a moan, and his spirit flew from him. Then I planted my foot upon him, and drew the bronze spear from the wound, and left it there to lie on the ground. But for my part, I plucked twigs and osiers, and weaving a rope about a fathom in length, well twisted from end to end, I bound together the feet of the monstrous beast, and went my way to the black ship, bearing him across my back and leaning on my spear, since in no way could I hold him on my shoulder with one hand, for he was a very large beast. Down I flung him before the ship, and heartened my comrades with winning words, coming up to each man in turn:

"'Friends, not yet shall we go down to the house of Hades, despite our sorrows, before the day of fate comes upon us. No, come, while there is still food and drink in our swift ship, let us take thought of food, and not waste away from hunger.'

"So I spoke, and they quickly hearkened to my words. From their faces they drew their cloaks,[a] and marveled at the stag on the shore of the barren sea, for he was a very large beast. But when they had satisfied their eyes with gazing, they washed their hands and made ready a glorious feast. So then all day long till set of sun we sat feasting on abundant flesh and sweet wine. But when the sun set and darkness came on, then we lay down to rest on the shore of

[a] The Greek veiled his face under stress of despairing sorrow. M.

ἦμος δ' ἠριγένεια φάνη ῥοδοδάκτυλος Ἠώς,
καὶ τότ' ἐγὼν ἀγορὴν θέμενος μετὰ πᾶσιν ἔειπον·
    "'κέκλυτέ μευ μύθων, κακά περ πάσχοντες ἑταῖροι·[1]

190 ὦ φίλοι, οὐ γάρ τ' ἴδμεν, ὅπῃ ζόφος οὐδ' ὅπῃ ἠώς,
οὐδ' ὅπῃ ἠέλιος φαεσίμβροτος εἶσ' ὑπὸ γαῖαν,
οὐδ' ὅπῃ ἀννεῖται· ἀλλὰ φραζώμεθα θᾶσσον
εἴ τις ἔτ' ἔσται μῆτις. ἐγὼ δ' οὔκ οἴομαι εἶναι.
εἶδον γὰρ σκοπιὴν ἐς παιπαλόεσσαν ἀνελθὼν

195 νῆσον, τὴν πέρι πόντος ἀπείριτος ἐστεφάνωται·
αὐτὴ δὲ χθαμαλὴ κεῖται· καπνὸν δ' ἐνὶ μέσσῃ
ἔδρακον ὀφθαλμοῖσι διὰ δρυμὰ πυκνὰ καὶ ὕλην.'

    "ὣς ἐφάμην, τοῖσιν δὲ κατεκλάσθη φίλον ἦτορ
μνησαμένοις ἔργων Λαιστρυγόνος Ἀντιφάταο

200 Κύκλωπός τε βίης μεγαλήτορος, ἀνδροφάγοιο.
κλαῖον δὲ λιγέως θαλερὸν κατὰ δάκρυ χέοντες·
ἀλλ' οὐ γάρ τις πρῆξις ἐγίγνετο μυρομένοισιν.

    "αὐτὰρ ἐγὼ δίχα πάντας ἐυκνήμιδας ἑταίρους
ἠρίθμεον, ἀρχὸν δὲ μετ' ἀμφοτέροισιν ὄπασσα·

205 τῶν μὲν ἐγὼν ἦρχον, τῶν δ' Εὐρύλοχος θεοειδής.
κλήρους δ' ἐν κυνέῃ χαλκήρεϊ πάλλομεν ὦκα·
ἐκ δ' ἔθορε κλῆρος μεγαλήτορος Εὐρυλόχοιο.
βῆ δ' ἰέναι, ἅμα τῷ γε δύω καὶ εἴκοσ' ἑταῖροι
κλαίοντες· κατὰ δ' ἄμμε λίπον γοόωντες ὄπισθεν.

210 εὗρον δ' ἐν βήσσῃσι τετυγμένα δώματα Κίρκης
ξεστοῖσιν λάεσσι, περισκέπτῳ ἐνὶ χώρῳ·
ἀμφὶ δέ μιν λύκοι ἦσαν ὀρέστεροι ἠδὲ λέοντες,
τοὺς αὐτὴ κατέθελξεν, ἐπεὶ κακὰ φάρμακ' ἔδωκεν.
οὐδ' οἵ γ' ὡρμήθησαν ἐπ' ἀνδράσιν, ἀλλ' ἄρα τοί γε

the sea. And as soon as early Dawn appeared, the rosy-
fingered, I called my men together and spoke among them
all:

"'Listen to my words, comrades, for all your evil plight.
My friends, we know not where darkness is, or where the
dawn, neither where the sun, who gives light to mortals,
goes beneath the earth, or where he rises; but let us at once
take thought if any device is still left for us. As for me, I do
not think there is. For I climbed to a rugged point of
outlook, and beheld the island, about which the boundless
sea lies like a wreath. The island itself lies low, and in the
midst of it my eyes saw smoke through the thick brush and
the wood.'

"So I spoke, and their spirit was broken within them, as
they remembered the deeds of the Laestrygonian, Anti-
phates, and the violence of the great-hearted Cyclops, the
man-eater. And they wailed aloud, and shed big tears. But
their mourning did no good.

"Then I told off in two bands all my well-greaved com-
rades, and appointed a leader for each band. Of the one I
took command, and of the other godlike Eurylochus.
Quickly then we shook lots in a brazen helmet, and out
leapt the lot of great-hearted Eurylochus. So he set out,
and with him went two and twenty comrades, all weeping;
and they left us behind, lamenting. Within the forest
glades they found the house of Circe, built of polished
stone in a place of wide outlook, and round about it were
mountain wolves and lions, whom Circe herself had
bewitched; for she gave them evil drugs. Yet these beasts
did not rush upon my men, but indeed, wagging their long

---

[1] Line 189 was rejected in antiquity.

215 οὐρῇσιν μακρῇσι περισσαίνοντες ἀνέσταν.
ὡς δ' ὅτ' ἂν ἀμφὶ ἄνακτα κύνες δαίτηθεν ἰόντα
σαίνωσ', αἰεὶ γάρ τε φέρει μειλίγματα θυμοῦ,
ὣς τοὺς ἀμφὶ λύκοι κρατερώνυχες ἠδὲ λέοντες
σαῖνον· τοὶ δ' ἔδεισαν, ἐπεὶ ἴδον αἰνὰ πέλωρα.
220 ἔσταν δ' ἐν προθύροισι θεᾶς καλλιπλοκάμοιο,
Κίρκης δ' ἔνδον ἄκουον ἀειδούσης ὀπὶ καλῇ,
ἱστὸν ἐποιχομένης μέγαν ἄμβροτον, οἷα θεάων
λεπτά τε καὶ χαρίεντα καὶ ἀγλαὰ ἔργα πέλονται.
τοῖσι δὲ μύθων ἦρχε Πολίτης ὄρχαμος ἀνδρῶν,
225 ὅς μοι κήδιστος ἑτάρων ἦν κεδνότατός τε·
    "'ὦ φίλοι, ἔνδον γάρ τις ἐποιχομένη μέγαν ἱστὸν
καλὸν ἀοιδιάει, δάπεδον δ' ἅπαν ἀμφιμέμυκεν,
ἢ θεὸς ἠὲ γυνή· ἀλλὰ φθεγγώμεθα θᾶσσον.'
    "ὣς ἄρ' ἐφώνησεν, τοὶ δὲ φθέγγοντο καλεῦντες.
230 ἡ δ' αἶψ' ἐξελθοῦσα θύρας ὤιξε φαεινὰς
καὶ κάλει· οἱ δ' ἅμα πάντες ἀιδρείῃσιν ἕποντο·
Εὐρύλοχος δ' ὑπέμεινεν, ὀισάμενος δόλον εἶναι.
εἷσεν δ' εἰσαγαγοῦσα κατὰ κλισμούς τε θρόνους τε,
ἐν δέ σφιν τυρόν τε καὶ ἄλφιτα καὶ μέλι χλωρὸν
235 οἴνῳ Πραμνείῳ ἐκύκα· ἀνέμισγε δὲ σίτῳ
φάρμακα λύγρ', ἵνα πάγχυ λαθοίατο πατρίδος αἴης.
αὐτὰρ ἐπεὶ δῶκέν τε καὶ ἔκπιον, αὐτίκ' ἔπειτα
ῥάβδῳ πεπληγυῖα κατὰ συφεοῖσιν ἐέργνυ.
οἱ δὲ συῶν μὲν ἔχον κεφαλὰς φωνήν τε τρίχας τε
240 καὶ δέμας, αὐτὰρ νοῦς ἦν ἔμπεδος, ὡς τὸ πάρος περ.
ὣς οἱ μὲν κλαίοντες ἐέρχατο, τοῖσι δὲ Κίρκη
πάρ ῥ' ἄκυλον βάλανόν τε βάλεν καρπόν τε κρανείης

tails, stood on their hind legs. And as when dogs fawn
around their master as he comes from a feast, for he always
brings them bits to delight their hearts, so about them
fawned the stout-clawed wolves and lions; but they were
seized with fear when they saw the dread monsters. So
they stood in the gateway of the fair-tressed goddess, and
within they heard Circe singing with sweet voice, as she
went to and fro before a great imperishable web, such as is
the handiwork of goddesses, finely woven and beautiful,
and glorious. Then among them spoke Polites, a leader of
men, dearest to me of my comrades, and trustiest:

"'Friends, within someone goes to and fro before a
great web, singing sweetly, so that all the floor echoes;
some goddess it is, or some woman. Come, let us quickly
call to her.'

"So he spoke, and they cried aloud and called to her.
And she at once came forth and opened the bright doors,
and invited them in; and they all, in their innocence, fol-
lowed her inside. Only Eurylochus remained behind, for
he suspected that this was a snare. She brought them in
and made them all sit on chairs and seats, and made for
them a potion of cheese and barley meal and yellow honey
with Pramnian wine; but in the food she mixed evil drugs,
that they might utterly forget their native land. Now when
she had given them the potion, and they had drunk it off,
then she immediately struck them with her wand, and
penned them in the pigsties. And they had the heads, and
voice, and bristles, and shape of swine, but their minds
remained unchanged, just as they were before. So they
were penned there weeping, and before them Circe flung
mast, and acorns, and the fruit of the cornel tree to eat,

ἔδμεναι, οἷα σύες χαμαιευνάδες αἰὲν ἔδουσιν.

"Εὐρύλοχος δ' αἶψ' ἦλθε θοὴν ἐπὶ νῆα μέλαιναν
245 ἀγγελίην ἑτάρων ἐρέων καὶ ἀδευκέα πότμον.
οὐδέ τι ἐκφάσθαι δύνατο ἔπος ἱέμενός περ,
κῆρ ἄχεϊ μεγάλῳ βεβολημένος· ἐν δέ οἱ ὄσσε
δακρυόφιν πίμπλαντο, γόον δ' ὠίετο θυμός.
ἀλλ' ὅτε δή μιν πάντες ἀγασσάμεθ' ἐξερέοντες,
250 καὶ τότε τῶν ἄλλων ἑτάρων κατέλεξεν ὄλεθρον·

"'ἤιομεν, ὡς ἐκέλευες, ἀνὰ δρυμά, φαίδιμ' Ὀδυσσεῦ·
εὕρομεν ἐν βήσσῃσι τετυγμένα δώματα καλὰ
ξεστοῖσιν λάεσσι, περισκέπτῳ ἐνὶ χώρῳ.[1]
ἔνθα δέ τις μέγαν ἱστὸν ἐποιχομένη λίγ' ἄειδεν,
255 ἢ θεὸς ἠὲ γυνή· τοὶ δὲ φθέγγοντο καλεῦντες.
ἡ δ' αἶψ' ἐξελθοῦσα θύρας ὤιξε φαεινὰς
καὶ κάλει· οἱ δ' ἅμα πάντες ἀιδρείῃσιν ἕποντο·
αὐτὰρ ἐγὼν ὑπέμεινα, ὀισάμενος δόλον εἶναι.
οἱ δ' ἅμ' ἀιστώθησαν ἀολλέες, οὐδέ τις αὐτῶν
260 ἐξεφάνη· δηρὸν δὲ καθήμενος ἐσκοπίαζον.'

"ὣς ἔφατ', αὐτὰρ ἐγὼ περὶ μὲν ξίφος ἀργυρόηλον
ὤμοιιν βαλόμην, μέγα χάλκεον, ἀμφὶ δὲ τόξα·
τὸν δ' αἶψ' ἠνώγεα αὐτὴν ὁδὸν ἡγήσασθαι.
αὐτὰρ ὅ γ' ἀμφοτέρῃσι λαβὼν ἐλλίσσετο γούνων
265 καί μ' ὀλοφυρόμενος ἔπεα πτερόεντα προσηύδα·[2]

"'μή μ' ἄγε κεῖσ' ἀέκοντα, διοτρεφές, ἀλλὰ λίπ'
αὐτοῦ.
οἶδα γάρ, ὡς οὔτ' αὐτὸς ἐλεύσεαι οὔτε τιν' ἄλλον

---

[1] Line 253 is omitted in most MSS.

such things as wallowing swine are accustomed to feed upon.

"But Eurylochus at once came back to the swift, black ship, to tell the news of his comrades and their shameful fate. Not a word could he utter, for all his desire, so stricken to the heart was he with great distress, and his eyes were filled with tears, and his spirit was set on lamentation. But when we questioned him in amazement, then he told the fate of the others, his comrades:

"'We went through the thickets, as you told us to, glorious Odysseus. We found in the forest glades a beautiful palace, built of polished stones, in a place of wide outlook. There someone was going to and fro before a great web, and singing with a clear voice, some goddess or some woman, and they cried aloud and called to her. And she at once came forth and opened the bright doors, and invited them in; and they all, in their innocence, followed her inside. But I remained behind, for I suspected that there was a snare. Then they all vanished together, nor did one of them appear again, though I sat long and watched.'

"So he spoke, and I cast my silver-studded sword about my shoulders, a great sword of bronze, and slung my bow about me, and bade him lead me back by the selfsame road. But he clasped me with both hands, and besought me by my knees, and with wailing he spoke to me winged words:

"'Do not take me there against my will, O fostered by Zeus, but leave me here. For I know that you will neither

---

[2] Line 265 is omitted in most MSS.

ἄξεις σῶν ἑτάρων. ἀλλὰ ξὺν τοίσδεσι θᾶσσον
φεύγωμεν· ἔτι γάρ κεν ἀλύξαιμεν κακὸν ἦμαρ.'
270 "ὣς ἔφατ', αὐτὰρ ἐγώ μιν ἀμειβόμενος προσέειπον·
'Εὐρύλοχ', ἦ τοι μὲν σὺ μέν' αὐτοῦ τῷδ' ἐνὶ χώρῳ
ἔσθων καὶ πίνων κοίλῃ παρὰ νηὶ μελαίνῃ·
αὐτὰρ ἐγὼν εἶμι, κρατερὴ δέ μοι ἔπλετ' ἀνάγκη.'
"ὣς εἰπὼν παρὰ νηὸς ἀνήιον ἠδὲ θαλάσσης.
275 ἀλλ' ὅτε δὴ ἄρ' ἔμελλον ἰὼν ἱερὰς ἀνὰ βήσσας
Κίρκης ἵξεσθαι πολυφαρμάκου ἐς μέγα δῶμα,
ἔνθα μοι Ἑρμείας χρυσόρραπις ἀντεβόλησεν
ἐρχομένῳ πρὸς δῶμα, νεηνίῃ ἀνδρὶ ἐοικώς,
πρῶτον ὑπηνήτῃ, τοῦ περ χαριεστάτη ἥβη·
280 ἔν τ' ἄρα μοι φῦ χειρί, ἔπος τ' ἔφατ' ἔκ τ' ὀνόμαζε·
"'πῇ δὴ αὖτ', ὦ δύστηνε, δι' ἄκριας ἔρχεαι οἶος,
χώρου ἄιδρις ἐών; ἕταροι δέ τοι οἵδ' ἐνὶ Κίρκης
ἔρχαται ὥς τε σύες πυκινοὺς κευθμῶνας ἔχοντες.
ἦ τοὺς λυσόμενος δεῦρ' ἔρχεαι; οὐδέ σέ φημι
285 αὐτὸν νοστήσειν, μενέεις δὲ σύ γ', ἔνθα περ ἄλλοι.
ἀλλ' ἄγε δή σε κακῶν ἐκλύσομαι ἠδὲ σαώσω.
τῆ, τόδε φάρμακον ἐσθλὸν ἔχων ἐς δώματα Κίρκης
ἔρχευ, ὅ κέν τοι κρατὸς ἀλάλκῃσιν κακὸν ἦμαρ.
πάντα δέ τοι ἐρέω ὀλοφώια δήνεα Κίρκης.
290 τεύξει τοι κυκεῶ, βαλέει δ' ἐν φάρμακα σίτῳ.
ἀλλ' οὐδ' ὣς θέλξαι σε δυνήσεται· οὐ γὰρ ἐάσει
φάρμακον ἐσθλόν, ὅ τοι δώσω, ἐρέω δὲ ἕκαστα.
ὁππότε κεν Κίρκη σ' ἐλάσῃ περιμήκεϊ ῥάβδῳ,
δὴ τότε σὺ ξίφος ὀξὺ ἐρυσσάμενος παρὰ μηροῦ
295 Κίρκῃ ἐπαΐξαι, ὥς τε κτάμεναι μενεαίνων.

come back yourself, nor bring anyone of your comrades. No, with those that are here let us flee with all speed, for we still may escape the evil day.'

"So he spoke, and I answered him and said: 'Eurylochus, by all means stay here in this spot eating and drinking by the hollow black ship; but I will go; strong necessity is laid upon me.'

"So saying, I went up from the ship and the sea. But when, as I went through the sacred glades, I was about to come to the great house of Circe, expert in poisons, then Hermes, of the golden wand, met me as I went toward the house, in the likeness of a young man with the first down upon his lip, in whom the charm of youth is fairest. He clasped my hand, and spoke, and addressed me:

"'Where now again, unfortunate man, do you go alone through the hills, knowing nothing of the country? Those comrades of yours in Circe's house are penned like pigs in close-barred sties. And have you come here to release them? No, I tell you, you yourself will not return, but will remain there with the others. But come, I will free you from harm, and save you. Here, take this potent herb, and go to the house of Circe, and it shall ward off from your head the evil day. And I will tell you all the deadly wiles of Circe. She will mix you a potion, and cast drugs into the food; but even so she will not be able to bewitch you, for the potent herb that I shall give you will not permit it. And I will tell you all. When Circe shall smite you with her long wand, then draw your sharp sword from beside your thigh, and rush upon Circe, as though meaning to kill her. And

ἡ δέ σ' ὑποδείσασα κελήσεται εὐνηθῆναι·
ἔνθα σὺ μηκέτ' ἔπειτ' ἀπανήνασθαι θεοῦ εὐνήν,
ὄφρα κέ τοι λύσῃ θ' ἑτάρους αὐτόν τε κομίσσῃ·
ἀλλὰ κέλεσθαί μιν μακάρων μέγαν ὅρκον ὀμόσσαι,
300 μή τί τοι αὐτῷ πῆμα κακὸν βουλευσέμεν ἄλλο,
μή σ' ἀπογυμνωθέντα κακὸν καὶ ἀνήνορα θήῃ.'
    "ὣς ἄρα φωνήσας πόρε φάρμακον ἀργεϊφόντης
ἐκ γαίης ἐρύσας, καί μοι φύσιν αὐτοῦ ἔδειξε.
ῥίζῃ μὲν μέλαν ἔσκε, γάλακτι δὲ εἴκελον ἄνθος·
305 μῶλυ δέ μιν καλέουσι θεοί· χαλεπὸν δέ τ' ὀρύσσειν
ἀνδράσι γε θνητοῖσι, θεοὶ δέ τε πάντα δύνανται.[1]
Ἑρμείας μὲν ἔπειτ' ἀπέβη πρὸς μακρὸν Ὄλυμπον
νῆσον ἀν' ὑλήεσσαν, ἐγὼ δ' ἐς δώματα Κίρκης
ἤια, πολλὰ δέ μοι κραδίη πόρφυρε κιόντι.
310 ἔστην δ' εἰνὶ θύρῃσι θεᾶς καλλιπλοκάμοιο·
ἔνθα στὰς ἐβόησα, θεὰ δέ μευ ἔκλυεν αὐδῆς.
ἡ δ' αἶψ' ἐξελθοῦσα θύρας ὤιξε φαεινὰς
καὶ κάλει· αὐτὰρ ἐγὼν ἑπόμην ἀκαχήμενος ἦτορ.
εἷσε δέ μ' εἰσαγαγοῦσα ἐπὶ θρόνου ἀργυροήλου
315 καλοῦ δαιδαλέου· ὑπὸ δὲ θρῆνυς ποσὶν ἦεν·
τεῦχε δέ μοι κυκεῶ χρυσέῳ δέπαι, ὄφρα πίοιμι,
ἐν δέ τε φάρμακον ἧκε, κακὰ φρονέουσ' ἐνὶ θυμῷ.
αὐτὰρ ἐπεὶ δῶκέν τε καὶ ἔκπιον, οὐδέ μ' ἔθελξε,
ῥάβδῳ πεπληγυῖα ἔπος τ' ἔφατ' ἔκ τ' ὀνόμαζεν·
320 'ἔρχεο νῦν συφεόνδε, μετ' ἄλλων λέξο ἑταίρων.'
    "ὣς φάτ', ἐγὼ δ' ἄορ ὀξὺ ἐρυσσάμενος παρὰ μηροῦ
Κίρκῃ ἐπήιξα ὥς τε κτάμεναι μενεαίνων.

----

[1] δύνανται: ἴσασιν; cf. 4.379

she will be seized with fear and will bid you lie with her. Whereupon do you in your turn no longer refuse the couch of the goddess, that she may set free your comrades and give you yourself tendance. But bid her swear a great oath by the blessed gods that she will not plot against you any fresh mischief to your hurt, for fear that when she has you stripped she may deprive you of your courage and your manhood.'

"So saying, Argeïphontes gave me the herb, pulling it out of the ground, and showed me its nature. At the root it was black, but its flower was like milk. Moly the gods call it, and it is hard for mortal men to dig; but the gods can do anything. Hermes then departed to high Olympus through the wooded island, and I went my way to the house of Circe, and many things did my heart darkly ponder as I went. So I stood at the gates of the fair-tressed goddess. There I stood and called, and the goddess heard my voice. She came out at once and opened the bright doors and called me in; and I went with her, my heart deeply troubled. She brought me in and made me sit on a silver-studded chair, a beautiful chair, richly wrought, and beneath was a footstool for the feet. And she prepared me a potion in a golden cup, that I might drink, and put in it a drug, with evil purpose in her heart. But when she had given it to me, and I had drunk it off, yet was not bewitched, she struck me with her wand, and spoke, and addressed me: 'Begone now to your sty, and lie with the rest of your comrades.'

"So she spoke, but I, drawing my sharp sword from beside my thigh, rushed upon Circe, as though meaning to

ἡ δὲ μέγα ἰάχουσα ὑπέδραμε καὶ λάβε γούνων,
καί μ' ὀλοφυρομένη ἔπεα πτερόεντα προσηύδα·

325 "'τίς πόθεν εἰς ἀνδρῶν; πόθι τοι πόλις ἠδὲ τοκῆες;
θαῦμά μ' ἔχει ὡς οὔ τι πιὼν τάδε φάρμακ' ἐθέλχθης·
οὐδὲ γὰρ οὐδέ τις ἄλλος ἀνὴρ τάδε φάρμακ' ἀνέτλη,
ὅς κε πίῃ καὶ πρῶτον ἀμείψεται ἕρκος ὀδόντων.
σοὶ δέ τις ἐν στήθεσσιν ἀκήλητος νόος ἐστίν.

330 ἦ σύ γ' Ὀδυσσεύς ἐσσι πολύτροπος, ὅν τέ μοι αἰεὶ
φάσκεν ἐλεύσεσθαι χρυσόρραπις ἀργεϊφόντης,
ἐκ Τροίης ἀνιόντα θοῇ σὺν νηὶ μελαίνῃ.
ἀλλ' ἄγε δὴ κολεῷ μὲν ἄορ θέο, νῶι δ' ἔπειτα
εὐνῆς ἡμετέρης ἐπιβείομεν, ὄφρα μιγέντε

335 εὐνῇ καὶ φιλότητι πεποίθομεν ἀλλήλοισιν.'
"ὣς ἔφατ', αὐτὰρ ἐγώ μιν ἀμειβόμενος προσέειπον·
'ὦ Κίρκη, πῶς γάρ με κέλεαι σοὶ ἤπιον εἶναι,
ἥ μοι σῦς μὲν ἔθηκας ἐνὶ μεγάροισιν ἑταίρους,
αὐτὸν δ' ἐνθάδ' ἔχουσα δολοφρονέουσα κελεύεις

340 ἐς θάλαμόν τ' ἰέναι καὶ σῆς ἐπιβήμεναι εὐνῆς,
ὄφρα με γυμνωθέντα κακὸν καὶ ἀνήνορα θήῃς.
οὐδ' ἂν ἐγώ γ' ἐθέλοιμι τεῆς ἐπιβήμεναι εὐνῆς,
εἰ μή μοι τλαίης γε, θεά, μέγαν ὅρκον ὀμόσσαι
μή τί μοι αὐτῷ πῆμα κακὸν βουλευσέμεν ἄλλο.'

345 "ὣς ἐφάμην, ἡ δ' αὐτίκ' ἀπώμνυεν, ὡς ἐκέλευον.
αὐτὰρ ἐπεί ῥ' ὅμοσέν τε τελεύτησέν τε τὸν ὅρκον,
καὶ τότ' ἐγὼ Κίρκης ἐπέβην περικαλλέος εὐνῆς.
"ἀμφίπολοι δ' ἄρα τέως μὲν ἐνὶ μεγάροισι πένοντο
τέσσαρες, αἵ οἱ δῶμα κάτα δρήστειραι ἔασι·

350 γίγνονται δ' ἄρα ταί γ' ἔκ τε κρηνέων ἀπό τ' ἀλσέων

382

kill her. But she, with a loud cry, ran beneath, and clasped my knees, and beseeching me with wailing addressed me with winged words:

"'Who are you among men, and from where? Where is your city, and your parents? Amazement holds me that you have drunk this charm and were in no way bewitched. For no other man has ever withstood this charm, when once he has drunk it, and it has passed the barrier of his teeth. No, but the mind in your breast is not one to be beguiled. Surely you are Odysseus, the man of many devices, who Argeïphontes of the golden wand always said to me would come here on his way home from Troy with his swift, black ship. No, come, put up your sword in its sheath, and let us two then go up into my bed, that mingling in the bed of love we may come to trust one another.'

"So she spoke, and I answered her and said: 'Circe, how can you ask me to be gentle to you, who have turned my comrades into swine in your halls, and now keep me here, and with guileful purpose bid me go to your chamber, and go up into your bed, that when you have me stripped you may deprive me of my courage and my manhood? For my part I would not wish to go up into your bed, unless you, goddess, will consent to swear a mighty oath that you will not plot against me any fresh mischief to my hurt.'

"So I spoke, and she at once swore the oath to do me no harm, as I bade her. But when she had sworn, and made an end of the oath, then I went up to the beautiful bed of Circe.

"But her handmaids meanwhile were busied in the halls, four maidens who are her serving women in the house. Children are they of the springs and groves, and of

ἔκ θ' ἱερῶν ποταμῶν, οἵ τ' εἰς ἅλαδε προρέουσι.
τάων ἥ μὲν ἔβαλλε θρόνοις ἔνι ῥήγεα καλὰ
πορφύρεα καθύπερθ', ὑπένερθε δὲ λῖθ' ὑπέβαλλεν·
ἥ δ' ἑτέρη προπάροιθε θρόνων ἐτίταινε τραπέζας
355 ἀργυρέας, ἐπὶ δέ σφι τίθει χρύσεια κάνεια·
ἥ δὲ τρίτη κρητῆρι μελίφρονα οἶνον ἐκίρνα
ἡδὺν ἐν ἀργυρέῳ, νέμε δὲ χρύσεια κύπελλα·
ἥ δὲ τετάρτη ὕδωρ ἐφόρει καὶ πῦρ ἀνέκαιε
πολλὸν ὑπὸ τρίποδι μεγάλῳ· ἰαίνετο δ' ὕδωρ.
360 αὐτὰρ ἐπεὶ δὴ ζέσσεν ὕδωρ ἐνὶ ἤνοπι χαλκῷ,
ἔς ῥ' ἀσάμινθον ἕσασα λό' ἐκ τρίποδος μεγάλοιο,
θυμῆρες κεράσασα, κατὰ κρατός τε καὶ ὤμων,
ὄφρα μοι ἐκ κάματον θυμοφθόρον εἵλετο γυίων.
αὐτὰρ ἐπεὶ λοῦσέν τε καὶ ἔχρισεν λίπ' ἐλαίῳ,
365 ἀμφὶ δέ με χλαῖναν καλὴν βάλεν ἠδὲ χιτῶνα,
εἷσε δέ μ' εἰσαγαγοῦσα ἐπὶ θρόνου ἀργυροήλου
καλοῦ δαιδαλέου, ὑπὸ δὲ θρῆνυς ποσὶν ἦεν·
χέρνιβα δ' ἀμφίπολος προχόῳ ἐπέχευε φέρουσα
καλῇ χρυσείῃ, ὑπὲρ ἀργυρέοιο λέβητος,
370 νίψασθαι· παρὰ δὲ ξεστὴν ἐτάνυσσε τράπεζαν.
σῖτον δ' αἰδοίη ταμίη παρέθηκε φέρουσα,
εἴδατα πόλλ' ἐπιθεῖσα, χαριζομένη παρεόντων.[1]
ἐσθέμεναι δ' ἐκέλευεν· ἐμῷ δ' οὐχ ἥνδανε θυμῷ,
ἀλλ' ἥμην ἀλλοφρονέων, κακὰ δ' ὄσσετο θυμός.
375   "Κίρκη δ' ὡς ἐνόησεν ἔμ' ἥμενον οὐδ' ἐπὶ σίτῳ
χεῖρας ἰάλλοντα, κρατερὸν[2] δέ με πένθος ἔχοντα,
ἄγχι παρισταμένη ἔπεα πτερόεντα προσηύδα·

the sacred rivers that flow forth to the sea, and one of them
threw upon chairs beautiful rugs of purple above, and
spread beneath them a linen cloth; another drew up before
the chairs tables of silver, and set upon them golden
baskets; and the third mixed sweet, honey-hearted wine in
a bowl of silver, and served out golden cups; and the fourth
brought water, and kindled a great fire beneath a large
cauldron, and the water grew warm. But when the water
boiled in the bright bronze, she set me in a bath, and
bathed me with water from the great cauldron, mixing it to
my liking, and pouring it over my head and shoulders, till
she took from my limbs the soul-consuming weariness.
But when she had bathed me, and anointed me richly with
oil, and had thrown about me a beautiful cloak and a tunic,
she brought me into the hall, and made me sit upon a
silver-studded chair—a beautiful chair, richly wrought,
and beneath was a footstool for the feet. Then a handmaid
brought water for the hands in a beautiful pitcher of gold,
and poured it over a silver basin for me to wash, and beside
me drew up a polished table. And the revered house-
keeper brought and set before me bread, and with it meats
in abundance, giving freely of what she had. Then she
bade me eat, but this did not please my heart. Rather, I sat
with other thoughts, and my spirit boded ill.

"Now when Circe noticed that I sat thus, and did not
put forth my hands to the food, but was burdened with
strong grief, she came close to me, and spoke winged
words:

---

[1] Lines 368–72 are omitted in most MSS.

[2] κρατερὸν: στυγερὸν

"'τίφθ' οὕτως, Ὀδυσεῦ, κατ' ἄρ' ἕζεαι ἶσος ἀναύδῳ,
θυμὸν ἔδων, βρώμης δ' οὐχ ἅπτεαι οὐδὲ ποτῆτος;
380 ἦ τινά που δόλον ἄλλον ὀίεαι· οὐδέ τί σε χρὴ
δειδίμεν· ἤδη γάρ τοι ἀπώμοσα καρτερὸν ὅρκον.'

"ὣς ἔφατ', αὐτὰρ ἐγώ μιν ἀμειβόμενος προσέειπον·
'ὦ Κίρκη, τίς γάρ κεν ἀνήρ, ὃς ἐναίσιμος εἴη,
πρὶν τλαίη πάσσασθαι ἐδητύος ἠδὲ ποτῆτος,
385 πρὶν λύσασθ' ἑτάρους καὶ ἐν ὀφθαλμοῖσιν ἰδέσθαι;
ἀλλ' εἰ δὴ πρόφρασσα πιεῖν φαγέμεν τε κελεύεις,
λῦσον, ἵν' ὀφθαλμοῖσιν ἴδω ἐρίηρας ἑταίρους.'

"ὣς ἐφάμην, Κίρκη δὲ διὲκ μεγάροιο βεβήκει
ῥάβδον ἔχουσ' ἐν χειρί, θύρας δ' ἀνέῳξε συφειοῦ,
390 ἐκ δ' ἔλασεν σιάλοισιν ἐοικότας ἐννεώροισιν.
οἱ μὲν ἔπειτ' ἔστησαν ἐναντίοι, ἡ δὲ δι' αὐτῶν
ἐρχομένη προσάλειφεν ἑκάστῳ φάρμακον ἄλλο.
τῶν δ' ἐκ μὲν μελέων τρίχες ἔρρεον, ἃς πρὶν ἔφυσε
φάρμακον οὐλόμενον, τό σφιν πόρε πότνια Κίρκη·
395 ἄνδρες δ' ἂψ ἐγένοντο νεώτεροι ἢ πάρος ἦσαν,
καὶ πολὺ καλλίονες καὶ μείζονες εἰσοράασθαι.
ἔγνωσαν δέ μ' ἐκεῖνοι ἔφυν τ' ἐν χερσὶν ἕκαστος.
πᾶσιν δ' ἱμερόεις ὑπέδυ γόος, ἀμφὶ δὲ δῶμα
σμερδαλέον κονάβιζε· θεὰ δ' ἐλέαιρε καὶ αὐτή.
400 "ἡ δέ μευ ἄγχι στᾶσα προσηύδα δῖα θεάων·
'Διογενὲς Λαερτιάδη, πολυμήχαν' Ὀδυσσεῦ,
ἔρχεο νῦν ἐπὶ νῆα θοὴν καὶ θῖνα θαλάσσης.
νῆα μὲν ἂρ πάμπρωτον ἐρύσσατε ἤπειρόνδε,
κτήματα δ' ἐν σπήεσσι πελάσσατε ὅπλα τε πάντα·
405 αὐτὸς δ' ἂψ ἰέναι καὶ ἄγειν ἐρίηρας ἑταίρους.'

"'Why, Odysseus, do you sit thus like one that is dumb, eating your heart, and do not touch food or drink? Do you perhaps forebode some other guile? You have no need to fear. I have already sworn you a mighty oath to do you no harm.'

"So she spoke, and I answered her and said: 'Circe, what man that is right-minded could bring himself to taste of food and drink, before he had yet won freedom for his comrades, and beheld them before his face? But if you truly mean it when you bid me drink and eat, set them free, that with my own eyes I may see my trusty comrades.'

"So I spoke, and Circe went out through the hall holding her wand in her hand, and opened the doors of the sty, and drove them out in the form of swine nine years old. So they stood there before her, and she went through the midst of them, and anointed each man with another charm. Then from their limbs the bristles fell away which the hateful drug that Circe gave them had before made to grow, and they became men again, younger than they were before, and far handsomer and taller to look upon. They knew me, and clung to my hands, each man of them, and upon them all came a passionate sobbing, and the house about them rang terribly, and the goddess herself was moved to pity.

"Then the beautiful goddess drew near me, and said: 'Son of Laertes, sprung from Zeus, Odysseus of many devices, go now to your swift ship and to the shore of the sea. First of all draw the ship up on the land, and store your goods and all the tackle in caves. Then come back yourself, and bring your trusty comrades.'

387

"ὣς ἔφατ', αὐτὰρ ἐμοί γ' ἐπεπείθετο θυμὸς ἀγήνωρ,
βῆν δ' ἰέναι ἐπὶ νῆα θοὴν καὶ θῖνα θαλάσσης.
εὗρον ἔπειτ' ἐπὶ νηὶ θοῇ ἐρίηρας ἑταίρους
οἴκτρ' ὀλοφυρομένους, θαλερὸν κατὰ δάκρυ χέοντας.
410 ὡς δ' ὅτ' ἂν ἄγραυλοι πόριες περὶ βοῦς ἀγελαίας,
ἐλθούσας ἐς κόπρον, ἐπὴν βοτάνης κορέσωνται,
πᾶσαι ἅμα σκαίρουσιν ἐναντίαι· οὐδ' ἔτι σηκοὶ
ἴσχουσ', ἀλλ' ἁδινὸν μυκώμεναι ἀμφιθέουσι
μητέρας· ὣς ἔμ' ἐκεῖνοι ἐπεὶ ἴδον ὀφθαλμοῖσι,
415 δακρυόεντες ἔχυντο· δόκησε δ' ἄρα σφίσι θυμὸς
ὣς ἔμεν, ὡς εἰ πατρίδ' ἱκοίατο καὶ πόλιν αὐτὴν
τρηχείης Ἰθάκης, ἵνα τ' ἔτραφεν ἠδ' ἐγένοντο.
καί μ' ὀλοφυρόμενοι ἔπεα πτερόεντα προσηύδων·

"'σοὶ μὲν νοστήσαντι, διοτρεφές, ὡς ἐχάρημεν,
420 ὡς εἴ τ' εἰς Ἰθάκην ἀφικοίμεθα πατρίδα γαῖαν·
ἀλλ' ἄγε, τῶν ἄλλων ἑτάρων κατάλεξον ὄλεθρον.'

"ὣς ἔφαν, αὐτὰρ ἐγὼ προσέφην μαλακοῖς ἐπέεσσι·
'νῆα μὲν ἂρ πάμπρωτον ἐρύσσομεν ἤπειρόνδε,
κτήματα δ' ἐν σπήεσσι πελάσσομεν ὅπλα τε πάντα·
425 αὐτοὶ δ' ὀτρύνεσθε ἐμοὶ ἅμα πάντες ἔπεσθαι,
ὄφρα ἴδηθ' ἑτάρους ἱεροῖς ἐν δώμασι Κίρκης
πίνοντας καὶ ἔδοντας· ἐπηετανὸν γὰρ ἔχουσιν.'

"ὣς ἐφάμην, οἱ δ' ὦκα ἐμοῖς ἐπέεσσι πίθοντο.
Εὐρύλοχος δέ μοι οἶος ἐρύκανε πάντας ἑταίρους·
430 καί σφεας φωνήσας ἔπεα πτερόεντα προσηύδα·[1]

"'ἆ δειλοί, πόσ' ἴμεν; τί κακῶν ἱμείρετε τούτων;
Κίρκης ἐς μέγαρον καταβήμεναι, ἥ κεν ἅπαντας
ἢ σῦς ἠὲ λύκους ποιήσεται ἠὲ λέοντας,

"So she spoke, and my proud heart consented. I went my way to the swift ship and the shore of the sea, and there I found my trusty comrades by the swift ship, wailing piteously, shedding big tears. And as when calves in a farmstead sport about the droves of cows returning to the yard, when they have had their fill of grazing—all together they frisk before them, and the pens no longer hold them, but with constant lowing they run about their mothers—so those men, when their eyes beheld me, thronged about me weeping, and it seemed to their hearts as though they had got to their native land, and the very city of rugged Ithaca, where they were bred and born. And with wailing they spoke to me winged words:

"'At your return, O fostered by Zeus, we are as glad as though we had returned to Ithaca, our native land. But come, tell the fate of the others, our comrades.'

"So they spoke, and I answered them with gentle words: 'First of all let us draw the ship up on the land, and store our goods and all the tackle in caves. Then yourselves hasten one and all to follow me so that you may see your comrades in the sacred halls of Circe, drinking and eating, for they have enough to last forever.'

"So I spoke, and they quickly hearkened to my words. Eurylochus alone sought to hold back all my comrades, and he spoke, and addressed them with winged words:

"'Ah, wretched men, where are we going? Why are you so enamored of these woes, as to go down to the house of Circe, who will change us all to swine, or wolves, or lions,

---

[1] Line 430 is omitted in many MSS.

οἵ κέν οἱ μέγα δῶμα φυλάσσοιμεν καὶ ἀνάγκῃ,
435 ὥς περ Κύκλωψ ἔρξ᾽, ὅτε οἱ μέσσαυλον ἵκοντο
ἡμέτεροι ἕταροι, σὺν δ᾽ ὁ θρασὺς εἵπετ᾽ Ὀδυσσεύς·
τούτου γὰρ καὶ κεῖνοι ἀτασθαλίῃσιν ὄλοντο.᾽

"ὣς ἔφατ᾽, αὐτὰρ ἐγώ γε μετὰ φρεσὶ μερμήριξα,
σπασσάμενος τανύηκες ἄορ παχέος παρὰ μηροῦ,
440 τῷ οἱ ἀποπλήξας[1] κεφαλὴν οὐδάσδε πελάσσαι,
καὶ πηῷ περ ἐόντι μάλα σχεδόν· ἀλλά μ᾽ ἑταῖροι
μειλιχίοις ἐπέεσσιν ἐρήτυον ἄλλοθεν ἄλλος·

"᾽διογενές, τοῦτον μὲν ἐάσομεν, εἰ σὺ κελεύεις,
αὐτοῦ πὰρ νηΐ τε μένειν καὶ νῆα ἔρυσθαι·
445 ἡμῖν δ᾽ ἡγεμόνευ᾽ ἱερὰ πρὸς δώματα Κίρκης.᾽

"ὣς φάμενοι παρὰ νηὸς ἀνήιον ἠδὲ θαλάσσης.
οὐδὲ μὲν Εὐρύλοχος κοίλῃ παρὰ νηὶ λέλειπτο,
ἀλλ᾽ ἕπετ᾽· ἔδεισεν γὰρ ἐμὴν ἔκπαγλον ἐνιπήν.

"τόφρα δὲ τοὺς ἄλλους ἑτάρους ἐν δώμασι Κίρκη
450 ἐνδυκέως λοῦσέν τε καὶ ἔχρισεν λίπ᾽ ἐλαίῳ,
ἀμφὶ δ᾽ ἄρα χλαίνας οὔλας βάλεν ἠδὲ χιτῶνας·
δαινυμένους δ᾽ εὖ πάντας ἐφεύρομεν ἐν μεγάροισιν.
οἱ δ᾽ ἐπεὶ ἀλλήλους εἶδον φράσσαντό τ᾽ ἐσάντα,
κλαῖον ὀδυρόμενοι, περὶ δὲ στεναχίζετο δῶμα.
455 ἡ δέ μευ ἄγχι στᾶσα προσηύδα δῖα θεάων·

"᾽Διογενὲς Λαερτιάδη, πολυμήχαν᾽ Ὀδυσσεῦ[2]
μηκέτι νῦν θαλερὸν γόον ὄρνυτε· οἶδα καὶ αὐτὴ
ἡμὲν ὅσ᾽ ἐν πόντῳ πάθετ᾽ ἄλγεα ἰχθυόεντι,
ἠδ᾽ ὅσ᾽ ἀνάρσιοι ἄνδρες ἐδηλήσαντ᾽ ἐπὶ χέρσου.
460 ἀλλ᾽ ἄγετ᾽ ἐσθίετε βρώμην καὶ πίνετε οἶνον,
εἰς ὅ κεν αὖτις θυμὸν ἐνὶ στήθεσσι λάβητε,

to guard her great house under compulsion? Just so did the Cyclops, when our comrades went to his fold, and with them went this reckless Odysseus. For it was through this man's folly that they too perished.'

"So he spoke, and I pondered in my heart, whether to draw my long sword from beside my stout thigh, and with it strike off his head and bring it to the ground, near kinsman of mine by marriage though he was; but my comrades one after another sought to check me with winning words:

"'Sprung from Zeus, let us leave this man, if you so bid us, to stay here by the ship and to guard the ship; but as for us, lead us to the sacred house of Circe.'

"So saying, they went up from the ship and the sea. Nor was Eurylochus left beside the hollow ship, but he went with us, for he feared my fierce reproof.

"Meanwhile in her halls Circe bathed the rest of my comrades with kindly care, and anointed them richly with oil, and threw about them fleecy cloaks and tunics; and we found them all feasting bountifully in the halls. But when they saw and recognized one another, face to face, they wept and wailed, and the house rang round about them. Then the beautiful goddess drew near me, and said:

"'Son of Laertes, sprung from Zeus, Odysseus of many devices, no longer now rouse this swelling lament. Of myself I know both all the woes you have suffered on the fish-filled deep, and all the wrong that hostile men have done you on the land. No, come, eat food and drink wine, until you once more get spirit in your breasts such as when

---

[1] ἀποπλήξας Aristarchus (?): ἀποτμήξας
[2] Line 456 occurs in some MSS.

οἷον ὅτε πρώτιστον ἐλείπετε πατρίδα γαῖαν
τρηχείης Ἰθάκης. νῦν δ' ἀσκελέες καὶ ἄθυμοι,
αἰὲν ἄλης χαλεπῆς μεμνημένοι, οὐδέ ποθ' ὕμιν
465   θυμὸς ἐν εὐφροσύνῃ, ἐπεὶ ἦ μάλα πολλὰ πέποσθε.'
      "ὣς ἔφαθ', ἡμῖν δ' αὖτ' ἐπεπείθετο θυμὸς ἀγήνωρ.
ἔνθα μὲν ἤματα πάντα τελεσφόρον εἰς ἐνιαυτὸν
ἥμεθα δαινύμενοι κρέα τ' ἄσπετα καὶ μέθυ ἡδύ·
ἀλλ' ὅτε δή ῥ' ἐνιαυτὸς ἔην, περὶ δ' ἔτραπον ὧραι
470   μηνῶν φθινόντων, περὶ δ' ἤματα μακρὰ τελέσθη,[1]
καὶ τότε μ' ἐκκαλέσαντες ἔφαν ἐρίηρες ἑταῖροι·
      "'δαιμόνι', ἤδη νῦν μιμνήσκεο πατρίδος αἴης,
εἴ τοι θέσφατόν ἐστι σαωθῆναι καὶ ἱκέσθαι
οἶκον ἐς ὑψόροφον[2] καὶ σὴν ἐς πατρίδα γαῖαν.'
475   "ὣς ἔφαν, αὐτὰρ ἐμοί γ' ἐπεπείθετο θυμὸς ἀγήνωρ.
ὣς τότε μὲν πρόπαν ἦμαρ ἐς ἠέλιον καταδύντα
ἥμεθα, δαινύμενοι κρέα τ' ἄσπετα καὶ μέθυ ἡδύ·
ἦμος δ' ἠέλιος κατέδυ καὶ ἐπὶ κνέφας ἦλθεν,
οἱ μὲν κοιμήσαντο κατὰ μέγαρα σκιόεντα.
480   αὐτὰρ ἐγὼ Κίρκης ἐπιβὰς περικαλλέος εὐνῆς
γούνων ἐλλιτάνευσα, θεὰ δέ μευ ἔκλυεν αὐδῆς·
καί μιν φωνήσας ἔπεα πτερόεντα προσηύδων·
      "'ὦ Κίρκη, τέλεσόν μοι ὑπόσχεσιν ἥν περ ὑπέστης,
οἴκαδε πεμψέμεναι· θυμὸς δέ μοι ἔσσυται ἤδη,
485   ἠδ' ἄλλων ἑτάρων, οἵ μευ φθινύθουσι φίλον κῆρ
ἀμφ' ἔμ' ὀδυρόμενοι, ὅτε που σύ γε νόσφι γένηαι.'
      "ὣς ἐφάμην, ἡ δ' αὐτίκ' ἀμείβετο δῖα θεάων·
'διογενὲς Λαερτιάδη, πολυμήχαν' Ὀδυσσεῦ,
μηκέτι νῦν ἀέκοντες ἐμῷ ἐνὶ μίμνετε οἴκῳ.
490   ἀλλ' ἄλλην χρὴ πρῶτον ὁδὸν τελέσαι καὶ ἱκέσθαι

first you left your native land of rugged Ithaca; but now you are withered and spiritless, always thinking of your harsh wanderings, nor are your hearts ever joyful, for in truth you have suffered much.'

"So she spoke, and our proud hearts consented. So there day after day for a full year we sat, feasting on abundant flesh and sweet wine. But when a year was gone and the seasons turned, as the months waned and the long days came round in their course, then my trusty comrades called me out, and said:

"'God-touched man, remember now at last your native land, if it is fated for you to be saved, and to reach your high-roofed house and your native soil.'

"So they spoke and my proud heart consented. So then all day long till set of sun we sat feasting on abundant flesh and sweet wine. But when the sun set and darkness came on, they lay down to sleep throughout the shadowy halls, but I went up to the beautiful bed of Circe, and besought her by her knees; and the goddess heard my voice, and I spoke, and addressed her with winged words:

"'Circe, fulfill for me the promise which you gave to send me home; for my spirit is now eager to be gone, and the spirit of my comrades, who wear out my heart as they sit about me mourning, whenever by chance you are not there.'

"So I spoke, and the beautiful goddess at once made answer: 'Son of Laertes, sprung from Zeus, Odysseus of many devices, remain now no longer in my house against your will; but you must first complete another journey, and

---

[1] Line 470 is omitted in many MSS.

[2] ἐς ὑψόροφον: ἐυκτίμενον

εἰς Ἀίδαο δόμους καὶ ἐπαινῆς Περσεφονείης,
ψυχῇ χρησομένους Θηβαίου Τειρεσίαο,
μάντηος ἀλαοῦ, τοῦ τε φρένες ἔμπεδοί εἰσι·
τῷ καὶ τεθνηῶτι νόον πόρε Περσεφόνεια,
495   οἴῳ πεπνῦσθαι, τοὶ δὲ σκιαὶ ἀίσσουσιν.'

       "ὣς ἔφατ', αὐτὰρ ἐμοί γε κατεκλάσθη φίλον ἦτορ·
κλαῖον δ' ἐν λεχέεσσι καθήμενος, οὐδέ νύ μοι κῆρ[1]
ἤθελ' ἔτι ζώειν καὶ ὁρᾶν φάος ἠελίοιο.
αὐτὰρ ἐπεὶ κλαίων τε κυλινδόμενός τ' ἐκορέσθην,
500   καὶ τότε δή μιν ἔπεσσιν ἀμειβόμενος προσέειπον·

       "'ὦ Κίρκη, τίς γὰρ ταύτην ὁδὸν ἡγεμονεύσει;
εἰς Ἄιδος δ' οὔ πώ τις ἀφίκετο νηὶ μελαίνῃ.'

       "ὣς ἐφάμην, ἡ δ' αὐτίκ' ἀμείβετο δῖα θεάων·
'διογενὲς Λαερτιάδη, πολυμήχαν' Ὀδυσσεῦ,
505   μή τί τοι ἡγεμόνος γε ποθὴ παρὰ νηὶ μελέσθω,
ἱστὸν δὲ στήσας, ἀνά θ' ἱστία λευκὰ πετάσσας
ἧσθαι· τὴν δέ κέ τοι πνοιὴ Βορέαο φέρῃσιν.
ἀλλ' ὁπότ' ἂν δὴ νηὶ δι' Ὠκεανοῖο περήσῃς,
ἔνθ' ἀκτή τε λάχεια[2] καὶ ἄλσεα Περσεφονείης,
510   μακραί τ' αἴγειροι καὶ ἰτέαι ὠλεσίκαρποι,
νῆα μὲν αὐτοῦ κέλσαι ἐπ' Ὠκεανῷ βαθυδίνῃ,
αὐτὸς δ' εἰς Ἀίδεω ἰέναι δόμον εὐρώεντα.
ἔνθα μὲν εἰς Ἀχέροντα Πυριφλεγέθων τε ῥέουσιν
Κώκυτός θ', ὃς δὴ Στυγὸς ὕδατός ἐστιν ἀπορρώξ,
515   πέτρη τε ξύνεσίς τε δύω ποταμῶν ἐριδούπων·
ἔνθα δ' ἔπειθ', ἥρως, χριμφθεὶς πέλας, ὥς σε κελεύω,
βόθρον ὀρύξαι, ὅσον τε πυγούσιον ἔνθα καὶ ἔνθα,
ἀμφ' αὐτῷ δὲ χοὴν χεῖσθαι πᾶσιν νεκύεσσιν,

come to the house of Hades and dread Persephone, to seek
prophecy from the ghost of Theban Teiresias, the blind
seer, whose mind remains steadfast. To him even in death
Persephone has granted reason, that he alone should have
understanding, but the others flit about as shadows.'

"So she spoke, and my spirit was broken within me, and
I wept as I sat on the bed, nor had my heart any longer
desire to live and behold the light of the sun. But when I
had had my fill of weeping and writhing, then I made
answer, and addressed her, saying:

"'Who, Circe, will guide us on this journey? To Hades
no man ever yet went in a black ship.'

"So I spoke, and the beautiful goddess at once made
answer: 'Son of Laertes, sprung from Zeus, Odysseus of
many devices, let there be in your mind no concern for a
pilot to guide your ship, but set up your mast, and spread
the white sail, and sit yourself down; and the breath of the
North Wind will bear her onward. But when in your ship
you have now crossed the stream of Oceanus, where is a
level shore and the groves of Persephone—tall poplars,
and willows that shed their fruit—there beach your ship by
the deep eddying Oceanus, but go yourself to the dank
house of Hades. There into Acheron flow Puriphlegethon
and Cocytus, which is a branch of the water of the Styx; and
there is a rock, and the meeting place of the two roaring
rivers. Then there, hero, draw yourself close, as I bid you,
and dig a pit of a cubit's length this way and that, and
around it pour a libation to all the dead, first with milk and

---

[1] οὐδέ νύ μοι κῆρ: οὐδέ τι θυμὸς
[2] τε λάχεια: τ᾽ ἐλάχεια: τ᾽ ἐλαχεῖα; cf. 9.116

πρῶτα μελικρήτῳ, μετέπειτα δὲ ἡδέι οἴνῳ,
520 τὸ τρίτον αὖθ᾽ ὕδατι· ἐπὶ δ᾽ ἄλφιτα λευκὰ παλύνειν.
πολλὰ δὲ γουνοῦσθαι νεκύων ἀμενηνὰ κάρηνα,
ἐλθὼν εἰς Ἰθάκην στεῖραν βοῦν, ἥ τις ἀρίστη,
ῥέξειν ἐν μεγάροισι πυρήν τ᾽ ἐμπλησέμεν ἐσθλῶν,
Τειρεσίῃ δ᾽ ἀπάνευθεν ὄιν ἱερευσέμεν οἴῳ
525 παμμέλαν᾽, ὃς μήλοισι μεταπρέπει ὑμετέροισιν.
αὐτὰρ ἐπὴν εὐχῇσι λίσῃ κλυτὰ ἔθνεα νεκρῶν,
ἔνθ᾽ ὄιν ἀρνειὸν ῥέζειν θῆλύν τε μέλαιναν
εἰς Ἔρεβος στρέψας, αὐτὸς δ᾽ ἀπονόσφι τραπέσθαι
ἱέμενος ποταμοῖο ῥοάων· ἔνθα δὲ πολλαὶ
530 ψυχαὶ ἐλεύσονται νεκύων κατατεθνηώτων.
δὴ τότ᾽ ἔπειθ᾽ ἑτάροισιν ἐποτρῦναι καὶ ἀνῶξαι
μῆλα, τὰ δὴ κατάκειτ᾽ ἐσφαγμένα νηλέι χαλκῷ,
δείραντας κατακῆαι, ἐπεύξασθαι δὲ θεοῖσιν,
ἰφθίμῳ τ᾽ Ἀίδῃ καὶ ἐπαινῇ Περσεφονείῃ·
535 αὐτὸς δὲ ξίφος ὀξὺ ἐρυσσάμενος παρὰ μηροῦ
ἧσθαι, μηδὲ ἐᾶν νεκύων ἀμενηνὰ κάρηνα
αἵματος ἆσσον ἴμεν, πρὶν Τειρεσίαο πυθέσθαι.
ἔνθα τοι αὐτίκα μάντις ἐλεύσεται, ὄρχαμε λαῶν,
ὅς κέν τοι εἴπῃσιν ὁδὸν καὶ μέτρα κελεύθου
540 νόστον θ᾽, ὡς ἐπὶ πόντον ἐλεύσεαι ἰχθυόεντα.᾽
    ᾽ὣς ἔφατ᾽, αὐτίκα δὲ χρυσόθρονος ἤλυθεν Ἠώς.
ἀμφὶ δέ με χλαῖνάν τε χιτῶνά τε εἵματα ἕσσεν·
αὐτὴ δ᾽ ἀργύφεον φᾶρος μέγα ἕννυτο νύμφη,
λεπτὸν καὶ χαρίεν, περὶ δὲ ζώνην βάλετ᾽ ἰξυῖ
545 καλὴν χρυσείην, κεφαλῇ δ᾽ ἐπέθηκε καλύπτρην.
αὐτὰρ ἐγὼ διὰ δώματ᾽ ἰὼν ὤτρυνον ἑταίρους

honey, thereafter with sweet wine, and in the third place with water, and sprinkle on it white barley meal. And earnestly entreat the strengthless heads of the dead, vowing that when you come to Ithaca you will sacrifice in your halls a barren heifer, the best you have, and will load the altar with rich gifts, and that to Teiresias alone you will sacrifice separately a ram, wholly black, the finest of your flocks. But when with prayers you have made supplication to the glorious tribes of the dead, then sacrifice a ram and a black ewe, turning their heads toward Erebus but yourself turning backward, and setting your face toward the streams of the river. Then many ghosts of men that are dead will come forth. Thereupon call to your comrades, and bid them flay and burn the sheep that lie there, slain by the pitiless bronze, and make prayer to the gods, to mighty Hades and to dread Persephone. You yourself, drawing your sharp sword from beside your thigh, must sit there, and not allow the strengthless heads of the dead to draw near to the blood till you have inquired of Teiresias. Then the seer will quickly come to you, leader of men, and he will tell you your way, and the measures of your path, and of your return, how you may go over the fish-filled deep.'

"So she spoke, and at once came golden-throned Dawn. Round about me then she threw a cloak and tunic to wear, and the nymph put on a long white robe, finely woven and lovely, and about her waist she threw a beautiful girdle of gold, and upon her head she set a veil. But I went through

μειλιχίοις ἐπέεσσι παρασταδὸν ἄνδρα ἕκαστον·

"'μηκέτι νῦν εὕδοντες ἀωτεῖτε γλυκὺν ὕπνον,
ἀλλ' ἴομεν· δὴ γάρ μοι ἐπέφραδε πότνια Κίρκη.'

550   "ὣς ἐφάμην, τοῖσιν δ' ἐπεπείθετο θυμὸς ἀγήνωρ.
οὐδὲ μὲν οὐδ' ἔνθεν περ ἀπήμονας ἦγον ἑταίρους.
Ἐλπήνωρ δέ τις ἔσκε νεώτατος, οὔτε τι λίην
ἄλκιμος ἐν πολέμῳ οὔτε φρεσὶν ᾗσιν ἀρηρώς·
ὅς μοι ἄνευθ' ἑτάρων ἱεροῖς ἐν δώμασι Κίρκης,

555   ψύχεος ἱμείρων, κατελέξατο οἰνοβαρείων.
κινυμένων δ' ἑτάρων ὅμαδον καὶ δοῦπον ἀκούσας
ἐξαπίνης ἀνόρουσε καὶ ἐκλάθετο φρεσὶν ᾗσιν
ἄψορρον καταβῆναι ἰὼν ἐς κλίμακα μακρήν,
ἀλλὰ καταντικρὺ τέγεος πέσεν· ἐκ δέ οἱ αὐχὴν

560   ἀστραγάλων ἐάγη, ψυχὴ δ' Ἄιδόσδε κατῆλθεν.

"ἐρχομένοισι δὲ τοῖσιν ἐγὼ μετὰ μῦθον ἔειπον·
'φάσθε νύ που οἰκόνδε φίλην ἐς πατρίδα γαῖαν
ἔρχεσθ'· ἄλλην δ' ἧμιν ὁδὸν τεκμήρατο Κίρκη,
εἰς Ἀίδαο δόμους καὶ ἐπαινῆς Περσεφονείης

565   ψυχῇ χρησομένους Θηβαίου Τειρεσίαο.'

"ὣς ἐφάμην, τοῖσιν δὲ κατεκλάσθη φίλον ἦτορ,
ἑζόμενοι δὲ κατ' αὖθι γόων τίλλοντό τε χαίτας·
ἀλλ' οὐ γάρ τις πρῆξις ἐγίγνετο μυρομένοισιν.

"ἀλλ' ὅτε δή ῥ' ἐπὶ νῆα θοὴν καὶ θῖνα θαλάσσης

570   ᾔομεν ἀχνύμενοι θαλερὸν κατὰ δάκρυ χέοντες,
τόφρα δ' ἄρ' οἰχομένη Κίρκη παρὰ νηὶ μελαίνῃ
ἀρνειὸν κατέδησεν ὄιν θῆλύν τε μέλαιναν,
ῥεῖα παρεξελθοῦσα· τίς ἂν θεὸν οὐκ ἐθέλοντα
ὀφθαλμοῖσιν ἴδοιτ' ἢ ἔνθ' ἢ ἔνθα κιόντα;"

the halls, and roused my men with winning words, coming up to each man in turn:

"'No longer on your beds pluck the flower of sweet sleep, but let us go; queenly Circe has told me all.'

"So I spoke, and their proud hearts consented. But not even from there could I lead my men unscathed. There was one, Elpenor, the youngest of all, not over valiant in war nor sound of understanding, who had lain down apart from his comrades in the sacred house of Circe, seeking the cool air, for he was heavy with wine. He heard the noise and bustle of his comrades as they moved about, and suddenly sprang up, and forgot to go to the long ladder that he might come down again, but fell headlong from the roof, and his neck was broken away from the spine, and his ghost went down to the house of Hades.

"But as my men were going on their way, I spoke among them, saying: 'You think, no doubt, that you are going to your own native land; but Circe has pointed out for us another journey, to the house of Hades and dread Persephone, to seek prophecy from the ghost of Theban Teiresias.'

"So I spoke, and their spirit was broken within them, and sitting down right where they were, they wept and tore their hair. But no good came of their lamenting.

"But when we were on our way to the swift ship and the shore of the sea, sorrowing and shedding big tears, meanwhile Circe had gone out and made fast beside the black ship a ram and a black ewe, for easily she passed us by. Who with his eyes could behold a god against his will, whether going to or fro?"

Λ

"Αὐτὰρ ἐπεί ῥ' ἐπὶ νῆα κατήλθομεν ἠδὲ θάλασσαν,
νῆα μὲν ἂρ πάμπρωτον ἐρύσσαμεν εἰς ἅλα δῖαν,
ἐν δ' ἱστὸν τιθέμεσθα καὶ ἱστία νηὶ μελαίνῃ,
ἐν δὲ τὰ μῆλα λαβόντες ἐβήσαμεν, ἂν δὲ καὶ αὐτοὶ
5   βαίνομεν ἀχνύμενοι θαλερὸν κατὰ δάκρυ χέοντες.
ἡμῖν δ' αὖ κατόπισθε νεὸς κυανοπρώροιο
ἴκμενον οὖρον ἵει πλησίστιον, ἐσθλὸν ἑταῖρον,
Κίρκη εὐπλόκαμος, δεινὴ θεὸς αὐδήεσσα.
ἡμεῖς δ' ὅπλα ἕκαστα πονησάμενοι κατὰ νῆα
10   ἥμεθα· τὴν δ' ἄνεμός τε κυβερνήτης τ' ἴθυνε.
τῆς δὲ πανημερίης τέταθ' ἱστία ποντοπορούσης·
δύσετό τ' ἠέλιος σκιόωντό τε πᾶσαι ἀγυιαί.

"ἡ δ' ἐς πείραθ' ἵκανε βαθυρρόου Ὠκεανοῖο.
ἔνθα δὲ Κιμμερίων ἀνδρῶν δῆμός τε πόλις τε,
15   ἠέρι καὶ νεφέλῃ κεκαλυμμένοι· οὐδέ ποτ' αὐτοὺς
ἠέλιος φαέθων καταδέρκεται ἀκτίνεσσιν,
οὔθ' ὁπότ' ἂν στείχῃσι πρὸς οὐρανὸν ἀστερόεντα,
οὔθ' ὅτ' ἂν ἂψ ἐπὶ γαῖαν ἀπ' οὐρανόθεν προτράπηται,
ἀλλ' ἐπὶ νὺξ ὀλοὴ τέταται δειλοῖσι βροτοῖσι.
20   νῆα μὲν ἔνθ' ἐλθόντες ἐκέλσαμεν, ἐκ δὲ τὰ μῆλα
εἱλόμεθ'· αὐτοὶ δ' αὖτε παρὰ ῥόον Ὠκεανοῖο
ᾖομεν, ὄφρ' ἐς χῶρον ἀφικόμεθ', ὃν φράσε Κίρκη.

400

BOOK 11

"But when we had come down to the ship and to the sea, first of all we drew the ship down to the bright sea, and set the mast and sail in the black ship, and took the sheep and put them aboard, and ourselves embarked, sorrowing, and shedding big tears. And for our aid in the wake of our dark-prowed ship a fair wind that filled the sail, a good comrade, was sent by fair-tressed Circe, dread goddess of human speech. So when we had made fast all the tackling throughout the ship, we sat down, and the wind and the helmsman made straight her course. All the day long her sail was stretched as she sped over the sea; and the sun set and all the ways grew dark.

"She came to deep-flowing Oceanus, that bounds the earth, where is the land and city of the Cimmerians, wrapped in mist and cloud. Never does the bright sun look down on them with his rays either when he mounts the starry heaven or when he turns again to earth from heaven, but instead horrid night is spread over wretched mortals. There we came and beached our ship, and took out the sheep, and ourselves went along beside the stream of Oceanus until we came to the place of which Circe had told us.

"ἔνθ' ἱερήια μὲν Περιμήδης Εὐρύλοχός τε
ἔσχον· ἐγὼ δ' ἄορ ὀξὺ ἐρυσσάμενος παρὰ μηροῦ
25 βόθρον ὄρυξ' ὅσσον τε πυγούσιον ἔνθα καὶ ἔνθα,
ἀμφ' αὐτῷ δὲ χοὴν χεόμην πᾶσιν νεκύεσσι,
πρῶτα μελικρήτῳ, μετέπειτα δὲ ἡδέι οἴνῳ,
τὸ τρίτον αὖθ' ὕδατι· ἐπὶ δ' ἄλφιτα λευκὰ πάλυνον.
πολλὰ δὲ γουνούμην νεκύων ἀμενηνὰ κάρηνα,
30 ἐλθὼν εἰς Ἰθάκην στεῖραν βοῦν, ἥ τις ἀρίστη,
ῥέξειν ἐν μεγάροισι πυρήν τ' ἐμπλησέμεν ἐσθλῶν,
Τειρεσίῃ δ' ἀπάνευθεν ὄιν ἱερευσέμεν οἴῳ
παμμέλαν', ὃς μήλοισι μεταπρέπει ἡμετέροισι.
τοὺς δ' ἐπεὶ εὐχωλῇσι λιτῇσί τε, ἔθνεα νεκρῶν,
35 ἐλλισάμην, τὰ δὲ μῆλα λαβὼν ἀπεδειροτόμησα
ἐς βόθρον, ῥέε δ' αἷμα κελαινεφές· αἱ δ' ἀγέροντο
ψυχαὶ ὑπὲξ Ἐρέβευς νεκύων κατατεθνηώτων.
νύμφαι τ' ἠίθεοί τε πολύτλητοί τε γέροντες
παρθενικαί τ' ἀταλαὶ νεοπενθέα θυμὸν ἔχουσαι,
40 πολλοὶ δ' οὐτάμενοι χαλκήρεσιν ἐγχείῃσιν,
ἄνδρες ἀρηίφατοι βεβροτωμένα τεύχε' ἔχοντες·
οἳ πολλοὶ περὶ βόθρον ἐφοίτων ἄλλοθεν ἄλλος
θεσπεσίῃ ἰαχῇ· ἐμὲ δὲ χλωρὸν δέος ᾕρει.[1]
δὴ τότ' ἔπειθ' ἑτάροισιν ἐποτρύνας ἐκέλευσα
45 μῆλα, τὰ δὴ κατέκειτ' ἐσφαγμένα νηλέι χαλκῷ,
δείραντας κατακῆαι, ἐπεύξασθαι δὲ θεοῖσιν,
ἰφθίμῳ τ' Ἀίδῃ καὶ ἐπαινῇ Περσεφονείῃ·
αὐτὸς δὲ ξίφος ὀξὺ ἐρυσσάμενος παρὰ μηροῦ
ἥμην, οὐδ' εἴων νεκύων ἀμενηνὰ κάρηνα
50 αἵματος ἆσσον ἴμεν, πρὶν Τειρεσίαο πυθέσθαι.

"Here Perimedes and Eurylochus held the victims, while I drew my sharp sword from beside my thigh, and dug a pit of a cubit's length this way and that, and around it poured a libation to all the dead, first with milk and honey, thereafter with sweet wine, and in the third place with water, and I sprinkled on it white barley meal and I earnestly entreated the strengthless heads of the dead, vowing that when I came to Ithaca I would sacrifice in my halls a barren heifer, the best I had, and load the altar with rich gifts, and to Teiresias alone would sacrifice a ram, wholly black, the finest of my flocks. But when with vows and prayers I had made supplication to the tribes of the dead, I took the sheep and cut their throats over the pit, and the dark blood flowed. Then there gathered from out of Erebus the ghosts of those that are dead, brides, and unwed youths, and toil-worn old men, and frisking girls with hearts still new to sorrow, and many, too, that had been wounded with bronze-tipped spears, men slain in battle, wearing their blood-stained armor. These came thronging in crowds about the pit from every side, with an astounding cry; and pale fear seized me. Then I called to my comrades and told them to skin and burn the sheep that lay there killed with pitiless bronze, and to make prayer to the gods, to mighty Hades and dread Persephone. And I myself, drawing my sharp sword from beside my thigh, sat there, and would not allow the strengthless heads of the dead to draw near to the blood till I had inquired of Teiresias.

---

[1] Lines 38–43 were rejected by Zenodotus, Aristophanes, Aristarchus.

"πρώτη δὲ ψυχὴ Ἐλπήνορος ἦλθεν ἑταίρου·
οὐ γάρ πω ἐτέθαπτο ὑπὸ χθονὸς εὐρυοδείης·
σῶμα γὰρ ἐν Κίρκης μεγάρῳ κατελείπομεν ἡμεῖς
ἄκλαυτον καὶ ἄθαπτον, ἐπεὶ πόνος ἄλλος ἔπειγε.
55 τὸν μὲν ἐγὼ δάκρυσα ἰδὼν ἐλέησά τε θυμῷ,
καί μιν φωνήσας ἔπεα πτερόεντα προσηύδων·
"'Ἐλπῆνορ, πῶς ἦλθες ὑπὸ ζόφον ἠερόεντα;
ἔφθης πεζὸς ἰὼν[1] ἢ ἐγὼ σὺν νηὶ μελαίνῃ.'
"ὣς ἐφάμην, ὁ δέ μ' οἰμώξας ἠμείβετο μύθῳ·
60 'διογενὲς Λαερτιάδη, πολυμήχαν' Ὀδυσσεῦ,[2]
ᾆσέ με δαίμονος αἶσα κακὴ καὶ ἀθέσφατος οἶνος.
Κίρκης δ' ἐν μεγάρῳ καταλέγμενος οὐκ ἐνόησα
ἄψορρον καταβῆναι ἰὼν ἐς κλίμακα μακρήν,
ἀλλὰ καταντικρὺ τέγεος πέσον· ἐκ δέ μοι αὐχὴν
65 ἀστραγάλων ἐάγη, ψυχὴ δ' Ἀϊδόσδε κατῆλθε.
νῦν δέ σε τῶν ὄπιθεν γουνάζομαι, οὐ παρεόντων,
πρός τ' ἀλόχου καὶ πατρός, ὅ σ' ἔτρεφε τυτθὸν ἐόντα,
Τηλεμάχου θ', ὃν μοῦνον ἐνὶ μεγάροισιν ἔλειπες·
οἶδα γὰρ ὡς ἐνθένδε κιὼν δόμου ἐξ Ἀίδαο
70 νῆσον ἐς Αἰαίην σχήσεις ἐυεργέα νῆα·
ἔνθα σ' ἔπειτα, ἄναξ, κέλομαι μνήσασθαι ἐμεῖο.
μή μ' ἄκλαυτον ἄθαπτον ἰὼν ὄπιθεν καταλείπειν
νοσφισθείς, μή τοί τι θεῶν μήνιμα γένωμαι,
ἀλλά με κακκῆαι σὺν τεύχεσιν, ἅσσα μοι ἔστιν,
75 σῆμά τέ μοι χεῦαι πολιῆς ἐπὶ θινὶ θαλάσσης,
ἀνδρὸς δυστήνοιο καὶ ἐσσομένοισι πυθέσθαι.
ταῦτά τέ μοι τελέσαι πῆξαί τ' ἐπὶ τύμβῳ ἐρετμόν,

---

[1] ἰὼν Aristarchus: ἐὼν

"The first to come was the ghost of my comrade
Elpenor. Not yet had he been buried beneath the broad-
wayed earth, for we had left his corpse behind us in the hall
of Circe, unwept and unburied, since another task was
then urging us on. When I saw him I wept, and my heart
had compassion on him; and I spoke, and addressed him
with winged words:

"'Elpenor, how did you come beneath the murky dark-
ness? You coming on foot have outstripped me in my black
ship.'

"So I spoke, and with a groan he answered me and said:
'Son of Laertes, sprung from Zeus, Odysseus of many dev-
ices, an evil doom of some god was my undoing, and meas-
ureless wine. Having lain down to sleep in the house of
Circe I did not think to come down again by the long
ladder, but fell headlong from the roof, and my neck was
broken away from the spine and my ghost went down to
the house of Hades. Now I beseech you by those whom we
left behind, who are not present with us, by your wife and
your father who reared you when a baby, and by
Telemachus whom you left an only son in your halls; for I
know that as you go from here, from the house of Hades,
you will touch at the island of Aeaea in your well-built ship.
There, then, my lord, I bid you remember me. Do not,
when you depart, leave me behind unwept and unburied
and turn away; I might become a cause of the gods' wrath
against you. No, burn me with my armor, such as it is, and
heap up a mound for me on the shore of the gray sea, in
memory of an unlucky man, that men yet to be may know
of me. Do this for me, and fix upon the mound my oar with

---

² Line 60 is omitted in most MSS.

τῷ καὶ ζωὸς ἔρεσσον ἐὼν μετ' ἐμοῖς ἑτάροισιν.'

"ὣς ἔφατ', αὐτὰρ ἐγώ μιν ἀμειβόμενος προσέειπον·

80 'ταῦτά τοι, ὦ δύστηνε, τελευτήσω τε καὶ ἔρξω.'

"νῶι μὲν ὣς ἐπέεσσιν ἀμειβομένω στυγεροῖσιν
ἥμεθ', ἐγὼ μὲν ἄνευθεν ἐφ' αἵματι φάσγανον ἴσχων,
εἴδωλον δ' ἑτέρωθεν ἑταίρου πόλλ' ἀγόρευεν·

"ἦλθε δ' ἐπὶ ψυχὴ μητρὸς κατατεθνηυίης,
85 Αὐτολύκου θυγάτηρ μεγαλήτορος Ἀντίκλεια,
τὴν ζωὴν κατέλειπον ἰὼν εἰς Ἴλιον ἱρήν.
τὴν μὲν ἐγὼ δάκρυσα ἰδὼν ἐλέησά τε θυμῷ·
ἀλλ' οὐδ' ὣς εἴων προτέρην, πυκινόν περ ἀχεύων,
αἵματος ἆσσον ἴμεν, πρὶν Τειρεσίαο πυθέσθαι.

90 "ἦλθε δ' ἐπὶ ψυχὴ Θηβαίου Τειρεσίαο
χρύσεον σκῆπτρον ἔχων, ἐμὲ δ' ἔγνω καὶ προσέειπεν·
'διογενὲς Λαερτιάδη, πολυμήχαν' Ὀδυσσεῦ,[1]
τίπτ' αὖτ', ὦ δύστηνε, λιπὼν φάος ἠελίοιο
ἤλυθες, ὄφρα ἴδῃ νέκυας καὶ ἀτερπέα χῶρον;
95 ἀλλ' ἀποχάζεο βόθρου, ἄπισχε δὲ φάσγανον ὀξύ,
αἵματος ὄφρα πίω καί τοι νημερτέα εἴπω.'

"ὣς φάτ', ἐγὼ δ' ἀναχασσάμενος ξίφος ἀργυρόηλον
κουλεῷ ἐγκατέπηξ'. ὁ δ' ἐπεὶ πίεν αἷμα κελαινόν,
καὶ τότε δή μ' ἐπέεσσι προσηύδα μάντις ἀμύμων·

100 "'νόστον δίζηαι μελιηδέα, φαίδιμ' Ὀδυσσεῦ·
τὸν δέ τοι ἀργαλέον θήσει θεός· οὐ γὰρ ὀίω
λήσειν ἐννοσίγαιον, ὅ τοι κότον ἔνθετο θυμῷ
χωόμενος ὅτι οἱ υἱὸν φίλον ἐξαλάωσας.
ἀλλ' ἔτι μέν κε καὶ ὧς κακά περ πάσχοντες ἵκοισθε,

which I rowed in life in the company of my comrades.'

"So he spoke, and I made answer and said: 'All this, unlucky man, will I perform and do.'

"Thus we two sat exchanging sad words one with the other, I on one side holding my sword over the blood, while on the other side the phantom of my comrade spoke at length.

"Then there came up the ghost of my dead mother, Anticleia, the daughter of great-hearted Autolycus, whom I had left alive when I departed for sacred Ilium. At sight of her I wept, and my heart had compassion on her, but even so I would not allow her to come near the blood, for all my great sorrow, until I had inquired of Teiresias.

"Then there came up the ghost of the Theban Teiresias, bearing his golden staff in his hand, and he knew me and spoke to me: 'Son of Laertes, sprung from Zeus, Odysseus of many devices, what now, unlucky man? Why have you left the light of the sun and come here to behold the dead and the place where there is no joy? Draw back from the pit and take away your sharp sword, so that I may drink of the blood and speak the truth to you.'

"So he spoke, and I drew back and thrust my silver-studded sword into its sheath, and when he had drunk the dark blood, then the flawless seer spoke to me and said:

"'You ask of your honey-sweet return, glorious Odysseus, but this shall the god make hard for you; for I do not think you shall elude the Earth-shaker, seeing that he has laid up wrath in his heart against you, angered because you blinded his own son. Yet even so you and your comrades may reach home, though suffering hardships, if you will

---

¹ Line 92 is omitted in most MSS.

105 αἴ κ' ἐθέλῃς σὸν θυμὸν ἐρυκακέειν καὶ ἑταίρων,
ὁππότε κε πρῶτον πελάσῃς ἐυεργέα νῆα
Θρινακίῃ νήσῳ, προφυγὼν ἰοειδέα πόντον,
βοσκομένας δ' εὕρητε βόας καὶ ἴφια μῆλα
Ἠελίου, ὃς πάντ' ἐφορᾷ καὶ πάντ' ἐπακούει.

110 τὰς εἰ μέν κ' ἀσινέας ἐάᾳς νόστου τε μέδηαι,
καί κεν ἔτ' εἰς Ἰθάκην κακά περ πάσχοντες ἵκοισθε·
εἰ δέ κε σίνηαι, τότε τοι τεκμαίρομ' ὄλεθρον,
νηΐ τε καὶ ἑτάροις. αὐτὸς δ' εἴ πέρ κεν ἀλύξῃς,
ὀψὲ κακῶς νεῖαι, ὀλέσας ἄπο πάντας ἑταίρους,

115 νηὸς ἐπ' ἀλλοτρίης· δήεις δ' ἐν πήματα οἴκῳ,
ἄνδρας ὑπερφιάλους, οἵ τοι βίοτον κατέδουσι
μνώμενοι ἀντιθέην ἄλοχον καὶ ἕδνα διδόντες.
ἀλλ' ἦ τοι κείνων γε βίας ἀποτίσεαι ἐλθών·
αὐτὰρ ἐπὴν μνηστῆρας ἐνὶ μεγάροισι τεοῖσι

120 κτείνῃς ἠὲ δόλῳ ἢ ἀμφαδὸν ὀξέι χαλκῷ,
ἔρχεσθαι δὴ ἔπειτα λαβὼν ἐυῆρες ἐρετμόν,
εἰς ὅ κε τοὺς ἀφίκηαι οἳ οὐκ ἴσασι θάλασσαν
ἀνέρες, οὐδέ θ' ἅλεσσι μεμιγμένον εἶδαρ ἔδουσιν·
οὐδ' ἄρα τοί γ' ἴσασι νέας φοινικοπαρῄους

125 οὐδ' ἐυήρε' ἐρετμά, τά τε πτερὰ νηυσὶ πέλονται.
σῆμα δέ τοι ἐρέω μάλ' ἀριφραδές, οὐδέ σε λήσει·
ὁππότε κεν δή τοι συμβλήμενος ἄλλος ὁδίτης
φήῃ ἀθηρηλοιγὸν ἔχειν ἀνὰ φαιδίμῳ ὤμῳ,
καὶ τότε δὴ γαίῃ πήξας ἐυῆρες ἐρετμόν,

130 ῥέξας ἱερὰ καλὰ Ποσειδάωνι ἄνακτι,
ἀρνειὸν ταῦρόν τε συῶν τ' ἐπιβήτορα κάπρον,
οἴκαδ' ἀποστείχειν ἔρδειν θ' ἱερὰς ἑκατόμβας

curb your own spirit and that of your comrades, once you have brought your well-built ship to the island of Thrinacia, escaping from the violet-blue sea, and you find grazing there the cattle and fat sheep of Helios, who sees and hears all things. If you leave these unharmed and are careful of your homeward way, you still may reach Ithaca, though suffering hardships. But if you harm them, then I foresee ruin for your ship and your comrades, and even if you shall yourself escape, late shall you come home and in distress, after losing all your comrades, in a ship that is another's, and you shall find troubles in your house—contemptuous men that devour your livelihood, wooing your godlike wife, and offering wooers' gifts. Yet in all truth, on their violent deeds shall you take vengeance when you come. But when you have slain the suitors in your halls, whether by guile or openly with the sharp sword, then go abroad, taking a shapely oar, until you come to men that know nothing of the sea and eat their food unmixed with salt, who in fact know nothing of ships with ruddy cheeks, or of shapely oars, which are a vessel's wings. And I will tell you a most certain sign, which will not escape you: when another wayfarer, on meeting you, shall say that you have a winnowing fan on your stout shoulder, then fix in the earth your shapely oar and make handsome offerings to the lord Poseidon—a ram, and a bull, and a boar that mates with sows—and depart for your home and offer sacred heca-

ἀθανάτοισι θεοῖσι, τοὶ οὐρανὸν εὐρὺν ἔχουσι,
πᾶσι μάλ' ἑξείης. θάνατος δέ τοι ἐξ ἁλὸς αὐτῷ
135 ἀβληχρὸς μάλα τοῖος ἐλεύσεται, ὅς κέ σε πέφνῃ
γήραι ὕπο λιπαρῷ ἀρημένον· ἀμφὶ δὲ λαοὶ
ὄλβιοι ἔσσονται. τὰ δέ τοι νημερτέα εἴρω.'

    "ὣς ἔφατ', αὐτὰρ ἐγώ μιν ἀμειβόμενος προσέειπον·
'Τειρεσίη, τὰ μὲν ἄρ που ἐπέκλωσαν θεοὶ αὐτοί.
140 ἀλλ' ἄγε μοι τόδε εἰπὲ καὶ ἀτρεκέως κατάλεξον·
μητρὸς τήνδ' ὁρόω ψυχὴν κατατεθνηυίης·
ἡ δ' ἀκέουσ' ἧσται σχεδὸν αἵματος, οὐδ' ἑὸν υἱὸν
ἔτλη ἐσάντα ἰδεῖν οὐδὲ προτιμυθήσασθαι.
εἰπέ, ἄναξ, πῶς κέν με ἀναγνοίη τὸν ἐόντα;'
145   "ὣς ἐφάμην, ὁ δέ μ' αὐτίκ' ἀμειβόμενος προσέειπεν·
'ῥηίδιόν τοι ἔπος ἐρέω καὶ ἐπὶ φρεσὶ θήσω.
ὅν τινα μέν κεν ἐᾷς νεκύων κατατεθνηώτων
αἵματος ἆσσον ἵμεν, ὁ δέ τοι νημερτὲς ἐνίψει·
ᾧ δέ κ' ἐπιφθονέῃς, ὁ δέ τοι πάλιν εἶσιν ὀπίσσω.'
150   "ὣς φαμένη ψυχὴ μὲν ἔβη δόμον Ἄιδος εἴσω
Τειρεσίαο ἄνακτος, ἐπεὶ κατὰ θέσφατ' ἔλεξεν·
αὐτὰρ ἐγὼν αὐτοῦ μένον ἔμπεδον, ὄφρ' ἐπὶ μήτηρ
ἤλυθε καὶ πίεν αἷμα κελαινεφές· αὐτίκα δ' ἔγνω,
καί μ' ὀλοφυρομένη ἔπεα πτερόεντα προσηύδα·
155   "'τέκνον ἐμόν, πῶς ἦλθες ὑπὸ ζόφον ἠερόεντα
ζωὸς ἐών; χαλεπὸν δὲ τάδε ζωοῖσιν ὁρᾶσθαι.
μέσσῳ γὰρ μεγάλοι ποταμοὶ καὶ δεινὰ ῥέεθρα,
Ὠκεανὸς μὲν πρῶτα, τὸν οὔ πως ἔστι περῆσαι
πεζὸν ἐόντ', ἢν μή τις ἔχῃ ἐυεργέα νῆα.[1]
160 ἦ νῦν δὴ Τροίηθεν ἀλώμενος ἐνθάδ' ἱκάνεις

tombs to the immortal gods who hold broad heaven, to each one in due order. And death shall come to you yourself away from the sea, the gentlest imaginable, that shall lay you low when you are overcome with sleek old age, and your people shall be dwelling in prosperity around you. This is the truth that I tell you.'

"So he spoke, and I made answer and said: 'Teiresias, of all this the gods themselves must have spun the thread. But come, tell me this and declare it truly. I see here the ghost of my dead mother; she sits in silence near the blood and cannot bring herself to look upon the face of her own son or to speak to him. Tell me, my lord, how she may recognize that I am he?'

"So I spoke, and at once he made answer and said: 'Easy is the word that I shall say and put in your mind. Whoever of those that are dead and gone you shall allow to approach the blood, he will speak truly to you; but whoever you refuse, he will go back again.'

"So saying, the ghost of the lord Teiresias went back into the house of Hades, when he had declared his prophecies; but I remained there steadfastly until my mother came up and drank the dark blood. At once then she knew me, and with wailing she spoke to me winged words:

"'My child, how did you come beneath the murky darkness, being still alive? Hard is it for those that live to behold these realms, for between are great rivers and appalling streams; Oceanus first, which one may in no way cross on foot, but only if one has a well-built ship. Have you only now come here from Troy after long wanderings

---

[1] Lines 157–59 were rejected by Aristarchus.

νηί τε καὶ ἑτάροισι πολὺν χρόνον; οὐδέ πω ἦλθες
εἰς Ἰθάκην, οὐδ' εἶδες ἐνὶ μεγάροισι γυναῖκα;'
    "ὣς ἔφατ', αὐτὰρ ἐγώ μιν ἀμειβόμενος προσέειπον·
'μῆτερ ἐμή, χρειώ με κατήγαγεν εἰς Ἀίδαο
165 ψυχῇ χρησόμενον Θηβαίου Τειρεσίαο·
οὐ γάρ πω σχεδὸν ἦλθον Ἀχαιίδος, οὐδέ πω ἁμῆς
γῆς ἐπέβην, ἀλλ' αἰὲν ἔχων ἀλάλημαι ὀιζύν,
ἐξ οὗ τὰ πρώτισθ' ἑπόμην Ἀγαμέμνονι δίῳ
Ἴλιον εἰς εὔπωλον, ἵνα Τρώεσσι μαχοίμην.
170 ἀλλ' ἄγε μοι τόδε εἰπὲ καὶ ἀτρεκέως κατάλεξον·
τίς νύ σε κὴρ ἐδάμασσε τανηλεγέος θανάτοιο;
ἦ δολιχὴ νοῦσος, ἦ Ἄρτεμις ἰοχέαιρα
οἷς ἀγανοῖς βελέεσσιν ἐποιχομένη κατέπεφνεν;
εἰπὲ δέ μοι πατρός τε καὶ υἱέος, ὃν κατέλειπον,
175 ἦ ἔτι πὰρ κείνοισιν ἐμὸν γέρας, ἦέ τις ἤδη
ἀνδρῶν ἄλλος ἔχει, ἐμὲ δ' οὐκέτι φασὶ νέεσθαι.
εἰπὲ δέ μοι μνηστῆς ἀλόχου βουλήν τε νόον τε,
ἠὲ μένει παρὰ παιδὶ καὶ ἔμπεδα πάντα φυλάσσει
ἦ ἤδη μιν ἔγημεν Ἀχαιῶν ὅς τις ἄριστος.'
180   "ὣς ἐφάμην, ἡ δ' αὐτίκ' ἀμείβετο πότνια μήτηρ·
'καὶ λίην κείνη γε μένει τετληότι θυμῷ
σοῖσιν ἐνὶ μεγάροισιν· ὀιζυραὶ δέ οἱ αἰεὶ
φθίνουσιν νύκτες τε καὶ ἤματα δάκρυ χεούσῃ.
σὸν δ' οὔ πώ τις ἔχει καλὸν γέρας, ἀλλὰ ἔκηλος
185 Τηλέμαχος τεμένεα νέμεται καὶ δαῖτας ἐίσας
δαίνυται, ἃς ἐπέοικε δικασπόλον ἄνδρ' ἀλεγύνειν·
πάντες γὰρ καλέουσι. πατὴρ δὲ σὸς αὐτόθι μίμνει
ἀγρῷ, οὐδὲ πόλινδε κατέρχεται. οὐδέ οἱ εὐναὶ

with your ship and your companions? And have you not yet reached Ithaca, nor seen your wife in your halls?'

"So she spoke, and I made answer and said: 'My mother, necessity brought me down to the house of Hades, to seek prophecy from the ghost of Theban Teiresias. For not yet have I come near to the shore of Achaea, nor have I as yet set foot on my own land, but have constantly been wandering, laden with woe, from the day when first I went with noble Agamemnon to Ilium, famed for its horses, to fight with the Trojans. But come, tell me this, and declare it truly. What fate of pitiless death overcame you? Was it long disease, or did the archer, Artemis, assail you with her gentle shafts, and slay you? And tell me of my father and my son, whom I left behind me. Does the honor that was mine still remain with them, or does some other man now possess it, and do they say that I shall no longer return? And tell me of my wedded wife, of her purpose and of her mind. Does she remain with her son, and keep all things safe? Or has one already married her, whoever is best of the Achaeans?'

"So I spoke, and my honored mother answered without delay: 'Only too truly she remains with steadfast heart in your halls, and ever sorrowfully for her do the nights and days wane, as she weeps. But the noble honor that was yours no man yet possesses, but Telemachus holds your lands unchallenged, and feasts at equal banquets, such as it is fitting that a lawgiving man should share, for all men invite him. But your father remains there in the tilled land, and does not come to the city, nor has he bed and cloaks

δέμνια καὶ χλαῖναι καὶ ῥήγεα σιγαλόεντα,
190　ἀλλ' ὅ γε χεῖμα μὲν εὕδει ὅθι δμῶες ἐνὶ οἴκῳ,
ἐν κόνι ἄγχι πυρός, κακὰ δὲ χροΐ εἵματα εἶται·
αὐτὰρ ἐπὴν ἔλθῃσι θέρος τεθαλυῖά τ' ὀπώρη,
πάντῃ οἱ κατὰ γουνὸν ἀλωῆς οἰνοπέδοιο
φύλλων κεκλιμένων χθαμαλαὶ βεβλήαται εὐναί.
195　ἔνθ' ὅ γε κεῖτ' ἀχέων, μέγα δὲ φρεσὶ πένθος ἀέξει
σὸν νόστον ποθέων,[1] χαλεπὸν δ' ἐπὶ γῆρας ἱκάνει.
οὕτω γὰρ καὶ ἐγὼν ὀλόμην καὶ πότμον ἐπέσπον·
οὔτ' ἐμέ γ' ἐν μεγάροισιν ἐύσκοπος ἰοχέαιρα
οἷς ἀγανοῖς βελέεσσιν ἐποιχομένη κατέπεφνεν,
200　οὔτε τις οὖν μοι νοῦσος ἐπήλυθεν, ἥ τε μάλιστα
τηκεδόνι στυγερῇ μελέων ἐξείλετο θυμόν·
ἀλλά με σός τε πόθος σά τε μήδεα, φαίδιμ' Ὀδυσσεῦ,
σή τ' ἀγανοφροσύνη μελιηδέα θυμὸν ἀπηύρα.'
"ὣς ἔφατ', αὐτὰρ ἐγώ γ' ἔθελον φρεσὶ μερμηρίξας
205　μητρὸς ἐμῆς ψυχὴν ἐλέειν κατατεθνηυίης.
τρὶς μὲν ἐφωρμήθην, ἐλέειν τέ με θυμὸς ἀνώγει,
τρὶς δέ μοι ἐκ χειρῶν σκιῇ εἴκελον ἢ καὶ ὀνείρῳ
ἔπτατ'. ἐμοὶ δ' ἄχος ὀξὺ γενέσκετο κηρόθι μᾶλλον,
καί μιν φωνήσας ἔπεα πτερόεντα προσηύδων·
210　"'μῆτερ ἐμή, τί νύ μ' οὐ μίμνεις ἐλέειν μεμαῶτα,
ὄφρα καὶ εἰν Ἀίδαο φίλας περὶ χεῖρε βαλόντε
ἀμφοτέρω κρυεροῖο τεταρπώμεσθα γόοιο;
ἦ τί μοι εἴδωλον τόδ' ἀγαυὴ Περσεφόνεια
ὤτρυν', ὄφρ' ἔτι μᾶλλον ὀδυρόμενος στεναχίζω;'

[1] νόστον ποθέων: πότμον γοόων

and bright coverlets for bedding, but through the winter he sleeps in the house, where the slaves sleep, in the ashes by the fire, and wears upon his body humble clothes. But when summer comes and rich autumn, then all about the slope of his vineyard plot are strewn his humble beds of fallen leaves. There he lies sorrowing, and nurses his great grief in his heart, in longing for your return, and heavy old age has come upon him. In the same way I too perished and met my fate. Neither did the keen-sighted archer goddess assail me in my halls with her gentle shafts, and slay me, nor did any disease come upon me, such as oftenest with loathsome wasting takes the spirit from the limbs; no, it was longing for you, and for your counsels, glorious Odysseus, and for your gentle-heartedness, that robbed me of honey-sweet life.'

"So she spoke, and I wondered in my heart how I might clasp the ghost of my dead mother. Three times I sprang toward her, and my will said, 'Clasp her,' and three times she flitted from my arms like a shadow or a dream. As for me, the pain grew ever sharper in my heart, and I spoke and addressed her with winged words:

"'My mother, why do you not stay for me when I wish to clasp you, so that even in the house of Hades we two may throw our arms about each other and take our fill of chill lamenting. Is this some phantom that august Persephone has sent me so that I may lament and groan still more?'

215   "ὣς ἐφάμην, ἡ δ' αὐτίκ' ἀμείβετο πότνια μήτηρ·
   'ὦ μοι, τέκνον ἐμόν, περὶ πάντων κάμμορε φωτῶν,
   οὔ τί σε Περσεφόνεια Διὸς θυγάτηρ ἀπαφίσκει,
   ἀλλ' αὕτη δίκη ἐστὶ βροτῶν, ὅτε τίς κε θάνῃσιν·
   οὐ γὰρ ἔτι σάρκας τε καὶ ὀστέα ἶνες ἔχουσιν,
220   ἀλλὰ τὰ μέν τε πυρὸς κρατερὸν μένος αἰθομένοιο
   δαμνᾷ, ἐπεί κε πρῶτα λίπῃ λεύκ' ὀστέα θυμός,
   ψυχὴ δ' ἠΰτ' ὄνειρος ἀποπταμένη πεπότηται.
   ἀλλὰ φόωσδε τάχιστα λιλαίεο· ταῦτα δὲ πάντα
   ἴσθ', ἵνα καὶ μετόπισθε τεῇ εἴπῃσθα γυναικί.'
225   "νῶι μὲν ὣς ἐπέεσσιν ἀμειβόμεθ', αἱ δὲ γυναῖκες
   ἤλυθον, ὤτρυνεν γὰρ ἀγαυὴ Περσεφόνεια,
   ὅσσαι ἀριστήων ἄλοχοι ἔσαν ἠδὲ θύγατρες.
   αἱ δ' ἀμφ' αἷμα κελαινὸν ἀολλέες ἠγερέθοντο,
   αὐτὰρ ἐγὼ βούλευον ὅπως ἐρέοιμι ἑκάστην.
230   ἥδε δέ μοι κατὰ θυμὸν ἀρίστη φαίνετο βουλή·
   σπασσάμενος τανύηκες ἄορ παχέος παρὰ μηροῦ
   οὐκ εἴων πίνειν ἅμα πάσας αἷμα κελαινόν.
   αἱ δὲ προμνηστῖναι ἐπήισαν, ἠδὲ ἑκάστη
   ὃν γόνον ἐξαγόρευεν· ἐγὼ δ' ἐρέεινον ἁπάσας.
235   "ἔνθ' ἦ τοι πρώτην Τυρὼ ἴδον εὐπατέρειαν,
   ἣ φάτο Σαλμωνῆος ἀμύμονος ἔκγονος εἶναι,
   φῆ δὲ Κρηθῆος γυνὴ ἔμμεναι Αἰολίδαο·
   ἣ ποταμοῦ ἠράσσατ' Ἐνιπῆος θείοιο,
   ὃς πολὺ κάλλιστος ποταμῶν ἐπὶ γαῖαν ἵησι,
240   καί ῥ' ἐπ' Ἐνιπῆος πωλέσκετο καλὰ ῥέεθρα.
   τῷ δ' ἄρα εἰσάμενος γαιήοχος ἐννοσίγαιος
   ἐν προχοῇς ποταμοῦ παρελέξατο δινήεντος·

"So I spoke, and my honored mother at once answered: 'Ah me, my child, ill-fated above all men, it is not that Persephone, daughter of Zeus, is deceiving you, but this is the appointed way with mortals, when one dies. For the sinews no longer hold the flesh and the bones together, but the strong force of blazing fire destroys these, as soon as the spirit leaves the white bones, and the ghost, like a dream, flutters off and is gone. But hurry to the light as fast as you can, and bear all these things in mind, so that hereafter you may tell them to your wife.'

"Thus we two talked with one another; and the women came, for august Persephone sent them, all those that had been the wives and the daughters of chieftains. These flocked in throngs about the dark blood, and I considered how I might question each; and this seemed to my mind the best plan. I drew my long sword from beside my stout thigh, and would not allow them to drink the dark blood all at one time. So they drew near, one after the other, and each declared her birth, and I questioned them all.

"Then, you must know, the first that I saw was highborn Tyro, who said that she was the daughter of flawless Salmoneus, and declared herself to be the wife of Cretheus, son of Aeolus. She fell in love with the river, divine Enipeus, who is far the most beautiful of rivers that send forth their streams upon the earth, and she used to haunt Enipeus' beautiful waters. But the Bearer and Shaker of the earth took his form, and lay with her at the mouths of the

πορφύρεον δ' ἄρα κῦμα περιστάθη, οὔρεϊ ἶσον,
κυρτωθέν, κρύψεν δὲ θεὸν θνητήν τε γυναῖκα.
245 λῦσε δὲ παρθενίην ζώνην, κατὰ δ' ὕπνον ἔχευεν.[1]
αὐτὰρ ἐπεί ῥ' ἐτέλεσσε θεὸς φιλοτήσια ἔργα,
ἔν τ' ἄρα οἱ φῦ χειρί, ἔπος τ' ἔφατ' ἔκ τ' ὀνόμαζε·

"'χαῖρε, γύναι, φιλότητι· περιπλομένου δ' ἐνιαυτοῦ
τέξεις ἀγλαὰ τέκνα, ἐπεὶ οὐκ ἀποφώλιοι εὐναὶ
250 ἀθανάτων· σὺ δὲ τοὺς κομέειν ἀτιταλλέμεναί τε.
νῦν δ' ἔρχευ πρὸς δῶμα, καὶ ἴσχεο μηδ' ὀνομήνῃς·
αὐτὰρ ἐγώ τοί εἰμι Ποσειδάων ἐνοσίχθων.'

"ὣς εἰπὼν ὑπὸ πόντον ἐδύσετο κυμαίνοντα.
ἡ δ' ὑποκυσαμένη Πελίην τέκε καὶ Νηλῆα,
255 τὼ κρατερὼ θεράποντε Διὸς μεγάλοιο γενέσθην
ἀμφοτέρω· Πελίης μὲν ἐν εὐρυχόρῳ Ἰαωλκῷ
ναῖε πολύρρηνος, ὁ δ' ἄρ' ἐν Πύλῳ ἠμαθόεντι.
τοὺς δ' ἑτέρους Κρηθῆι τέκεν βασίλεια γυναικῶν,
Αἴσονά τ' ἠδὲ Φέρητ' Ἀμυθάονά θ' ἱππιοχάρμην.

260 "τὴν δὲ μετ' Ἀντιόπην ἴδον, Ἀσωποῖο θύγατρα,
ἣ δὴ καὶ Διὸς εὔχετ' ἐν ἀγκοίνῃσιν ἰαῦσαι,
καί ῥ' ἔτεκεν δύο παῖδ', Ἀμφίονά τε Ζῆθόν τε,
οἳ πρῶτοι Θήβης ἕδος ἔκτισαν ἑπταπύλοιο,
πύργωσάν τ', ἐπεὶ οὐ μὲν ἀπύργωτόν γ' ἐδύναντο
265 ναιέμεν εὐρύχορον Θήβην, κρατερώ περ ἐόντε.

"τὴν δὲ μετ' Ἀλκμήνην ἴδον, Ἀμφιτρύωνος ἄκοιτιν,
ἥ ῥ' Ἡρακλῆα θρασυμέμνονα θυμολέοντα
γείνατ' ἐν ἀγκοίνῃσι Διὸς μεγάλοιο μιγεῖσα·

[1] Line 245, unknown to Zenodotus, was rejected by Aristarchus.

eddying river. And the dark wave stood about them like a mountain, arching over, and hid the god and the mortal woman. And he undid her maiden girdle, and shed sleep upon her. But when the god had finished his acts of love, he took her hand, and spoke, and addressed her:

"'Be happy, lady, in this love, and as the year comes round you shall bear glorious children, for not ineffectual are the embraces of a god. Tend and rear these children. But now go to your house and hold your peace and say nothing; but know that I am Poseidon, the shaker of the earth.'

"So saying, he plunged beneath the surging sea. But she conceived and bore Pelias and Neleus, who both became strong henchmen of great Zeus; and Pelias dwelt in spacious Iolcus, and was rich in flocks, and the other dwelt in sandy Pylos. But her other children, she, the queenly among women, bore to Cretheus: Aison, and Pheres, and Amythaon, full of the joy of chariot battle.

"And after her I saw Antiope, daughter of Asopus, who boasted that she had slept in the arms of Zeus himself, and she bore two sons, Amphion and Zethus, who first established the seat of seven-gated Thebes, and fenced it in with walls, since they could not dwell in spacious Thebes unfenced, mighty though they were.

"And after her I saw Alcmene, Amphitryon's wife, who conceived Heracles, staunch in fight, the lionhearted, when she lay in love in the embraces of great Zeus. And

καὶ Μεγάρην, Κρείοντος ὑπερθύμοιο θύγατρα,
270   τὴν ἔχεν Ἀμφιτρύωνος υἱὸς μένος αἰὲν ἀτειρής.
      "μητέρα τ᾽ Οἰδιπόδαο ἴδον, καλὴν Ἐπικάστην,
ἣ μέγα ἔργον ἔρεξεν ἀιδρείῃσι νόοιο
γημαμένη ᾧ υἷι· ὁ δ᾽ ὃν πατέρ᾽ ἐξεναρίξας
γῆμεν· ἄφαρ δ᾽ ἀνάπυστα θεοὶ θέσαν ἀνθρώποισιν.
275   ἀλλ᾽ ὁ μὲν ἐν Θήβῃ πολυηράτῳ ἄλγεα πάσχων
Καδμείων ἤνασσε θεῶν ὀλοὰς διὰ βουλάς·
ἡ δ᾽ ἔβη εἰς Ἀΐδαο πυλάρταο κρατεροῖο,
ἁψαμένη βρόχον αἰπὺν ἀφ᾽ ὑψηλοῖο μελάθρου,
ᾧ ἄχεϊ σχομένη· τῷ δ᾽ ἄλγεα κάλλιπ᾽ ὀπίσσω
280   πολλὰ μάλ᾽, ὅσσα τε μητρὸς Ἐρινύες ἐκτελέουσιν.
      "καὶ Χλῶριν εἶδον περικαλλέα, τήν ποτε Νηλεὺς
γῆμεν ἑὸν διὰ κάλλος, ἐπεὶ πόρε μυρία ἕδνα,
ὁπλοτάτην κούρην Ἀμφίονος Ἰασίδαο,
ὅς ποτ᾽ ἐν Ὀρχομενῷ Μινυείῳ ἶφι ἄνασσεν·
285   ἡ δὲ Πύλου βασίλευε, τέκεν δέ οἱ ἀγλαὰ τέκνα,
Νέστορά τε χρόνιον τε Περικλύμενόν τ᾽ ἀγέρωχον.
τοῖσι δ᾽ ἐπ᾽ ἰφθίμην Πηρὼ τέκε, θαῦμα βροτοῖσι,
τὴν πάντες μνώοντο περικτίται· οὐδ᾽ ἄρα Νηλεὺς
τῷ ἐδίδου ὃς μὴ ἕλικας βόας εὐρυμετώπους
290   ἐκ Φυλάκης ἐλάσειε βίης Ἰφικληείης
ἀργαλέας· τὰς δ᾽ οἶος ὑπέσχετο μάντις ἀμύμων
ἐξελάαν· χαλεπὴ δὲ θεοῦ κατὰ μοῖρα πέδησε,
δεσμοί τ᾽ ἀργαλέοι καὶ βουκόλοι ἀγροιῶται.
ἀλλ᾽ ὅτε δὴ μῆνές τε καὶ ἡμέραι ἐξετελεῦντο
295   ἂψ περιτελλομένου ἔτεος καὶ ἐπήλυθον ὧραι,
καὶ τότε δή μιν ἔλυσε βίη Ἰφικληείη,

Megara I saw, daughter of Creon, high of heart, whom Amphitryon's son, he whose strength never weakened, had to wife.

"And I saw the mother of Oedipodes, beautiful Epicaste, who did a monstrous thing in the ignorance of her mind, wedding her own son; and he, when he had slain his own father, wedded her; and soon the gods made these things known among men. Nevertheless, in lovely Thebes, suffering woes, he ruled over the Cadmeans by the dire designs of the gods; but she went down to the house of Hades, the strong warder, making fast a deadly noose from the high ceiling, caught by her own grief; but for him she left behind countless woes, all that a mother's Furies bring to pass.

"And I saw beauteous Chloris, whom once Neleus wedded because of her beauty, when he had brought countless gifts of wooing. Youngest daughter was she of Amphion, son of Iasus, who once ruled mightily in Orchomenus of the Minyae. And she was queen of Pylos, and bore to her husband glorious children, Nestor, and Chromius, and lordly Periclymenus, and besides these she bore noble Pero, a wonder to men. Her all who dwelt about sought in marriage, but Neleus would give her to no one except to him who should drive from Phylace the cattle of mighty Iphicles, spiral-horned and broad of brow, and hard they were to drive. These the flawless seer[a] alone undertook to drive off; but a harsh fate of the gods ensnared him, hard bonds and the country herdsmen. Nevertheless, when at length the months and the days were being brought to fulfillment, as the year rolled round, and the seasons came

[a] Melampus; see 15.225-42.

θέσφατα πάντ' εἰπόντα· Διὸς δ' ἐτελείετο βουλή.

"καὶ Λήδην εἶδον, τὴν Τυνδαρέου παράκοιτιν,
ἥ ῥ' ὑπὸ Τυνδαρέῳ κρατερόφρονε γείνατο παῖδε,
300 Κάστορά θ' ἱππόδαμον καὶ πὺξ ἀγαθὸν Πολυδεύκεα,
τοὺς ἄμφω ζωοὺς κατέχει φυσίζοος αἶα·
οἳ καὶ νέρθεν γῆς τιμὴν πρὸς Ζηνὸς ἔχοντες
ἄλλοτε μὲν ζώουσ' ἑτερήμεροι, ἄλλοτε δ' αὖτε
τεθνᾶσιν· τιμὴν δὲ λελόγχασιν ἶσα θεοῖσι.

305 "τὴν δὲ μετ' Ἰφιμέδειαν, Ἀλωῆος παράκοιτιν
εἴσιδον, ἣ δὴ φάσκε Ποσειδάωνι μιγῆναι,
καί ῥ' ἔτεκεν δύο παῖδε, μινυνθαδίω δ' ἐγενέσθην,
Ὦτόν τ' ἀντίθεον τηλεκλειτόν τ' Ἐφιάλτην,
οὓς δὴ μηκίστους θρέψε ζείδωρος ἄρουρα
310 καὶ πολὺ καλλίστους μετά γε κλυτὸν Ὠρίωνα·
ἐννέωροι γὰρ τοί γε καὶ ἐννεαπήχεες ἦσαν
εὖρος, ἀτὰρ μῆκός γε γενέσθην ἐννεόργυιοι.
οἵ ῥα καὶ ἀθανάτοισιν ἀπειλήτην ἐν Ὀλύμπῳ
φυλόπιδα στήσειν πολυάϊκος πολέμοιο.
315 Ὄσσαν ἐπ' Οὐλύμπῳ μέμασαν θέμεν, αὐτὰρ ἐπ' Ὄσσῃ
Πήλιον εἰνοσίφυλλον, ἵν' οὐρανὸς ἀμβατὸς εἴη.
καί νύ κεν ἐξετέλεσσαν, εἰ ἥβης μέτρον ἵκοντο·
ἀλλ' ὄλεσεν Διὸς υἱός, ὃν ἠύκομος τέκε Λητώ,
ἀμφοτέρω, πρίν σφωιν ὑπὸ κροτάφοισιν ἰούλους
320 ἀνθῆσαι πυκάσαι τε γένυς ἐυανθέι λάχνῃ.

"Φαίδρην τε Πρόκριν τε ἴδον καλήν τ' Ἀριάδνην,
κούρην Μίνωος ὀλοόφρονος, ἥν ποτε Θησεὺς
ἐκ Κρήτης ἐς γουνὸν Ἀθηνάων ἱεράων
ἦγε μέν, οὐδ' ἀπόνητο· πάρος δέ μιν Ἄρτεμις ἔκτα[1]

on, then at last mighty Iphicles released him, when he had told all the oracles; and the will of Zeus was fulfilled.

"And I saw Lede, the wife of Tyndareus, who bore to Tyndareus two sons, stout of heart, Castor the tamer of horses, and the boxer Polydeuces. These two the earth, the giver of life, covers, alive though they be, and even in the world below they have honor from Zeus. One day they live in turn, and one day they are dead; and they have won honor like that of the gods.

"And after her I saw Iphimedeia, wife of Aloeus, who declared that she had lain with Poseidon. She bore two sons, but they had short lives, godlike Otus, and far-famed Ephialtes—men whom the earth, the giver of grain, reared as the tallest, and far the most handsome, after famous Orion. For at nine years they were nine cubits in breadth and in height nine fathoms. They threatened to raise the din of furious war against even the immortals in Olympus. They yearned to pile Ossa on Olympus, and Pelion, with its waving forests, on Ossa, so that heaven might be scaled. And this they would have accomplished, if they had reached the measure of manhood; but the son of Zeus, whom lovely-haired Leto bore, slew them both before the down blossomed beneath their temples and covered their chins with a full growth of beard.

"And Phaedra and Procris I saw, and beautiful Ariadne, the daughter of Minos of baneful mind, whom once Theseus tried to bring from Crete to the hill of sacred Athens; but he had no joy of her. Before that, Artemis slew

---

[1] ἔκτα: ἔσχεν

325 Δίῃ ἐν ἀμφιρύτῃ Διονύσου μαρτυρίῃσιν.

"Μαῖράν τε Κλυμένην τε ἴδον στυγερήν τ'
Ἐριφύλην,

ἣ χρυσὸν φίλου ἀνδρὸς ἐδέξατο τιμήεντα.
πάσας δ' οὐκ ἂν ἐγὼ μυθήσομαι οὐδ' ὀνομήνω,
ὅσσας ἡρώων ἀλόχους ἴδον ἠδὲ θύγατρας·

330 πρὶν γάρ κεν καὶ νὺξ φθῖτ' ἄμβροτος. ἀλλὰ καὶ ὥρη
εὕδειν, ἢ ἐπὶ νῆα θοὴν ἐλθόντ' ἐς ἑταίρους
ἢ αὐτοῦ· πομπὴ δὲ θεοῖς ὑμῖν τε μελήσει."

ὣς ἔφαθ', οἱ δ' ἄρα πάντες ἀκὴν ἐγένοντο σιωπῇ,
κηληθμῷ δ' ἔσχοντο κατὰ μέγαρα σκιόεντα.

335 τοῖσιν δ' Ἀρήτη λευκώλενος ἤρχετο μύθων.

"Φαίηκες, πῶς ὕμμιν ἀνὴρ ὅδε φαίνεται εἶναι
εἶδός τε μέγεθός τε ἰδὲ φρένας ἔνδον ἐίσας;
ξεῖνος δ' αὖτ' ἐμός ἐστιν, ἕκαστος δ' ἔμμορε τιμῆς·
τῷ μὴ ἐπειγόμενοι ἀποπέμπετε, μηδὲ τὰ δῶρα

340 οὕτω χρηίζοντι κολούετε· πολλὰ γὰρ ὑμῖν
κτήματ' ἐνὶ μεγάροισι θεῶν ἰότητι κέονται."

τοῖσι δὲ καὶ μετέειπε γέρων ἥρως Ἐχένηος,
ὃς δὴ Φαιήκων ἀνδρῶν προγενέστερος ἦεν·[1]
"ὦ φίλοι, οὐ μὰν ἧμιν ἀπὸ σκοποῦ οὐδ' ἀπὸ δόξης

345 μυθεῖται βασίλεια περίφρων· ἀλλὰ πίθεσθε.
Ἀλκινόου δ' ἐκ τοῦδ' ἔχεται ἔργον τε ἔπος τε."

τὸν δ' αὖτ' Ἀλκίνοος ἀπαμείβετο φώνησέν τε·
"τοῦτο μὲν οὕτω δὴ ἔσται ἔπος, αἴ κεν ἐγώ γε
ζωὸς Φαιήκεσσι φιληρέτμοισιν ἀνάσσω·

350 ξεῖνος δὲ τλήτω μάλα περ νόστοιο χατίζων
ἔμπης οὖν ἐπιμεῖναι ἐς αὔριον, εἰς ὅ κε πᾶσαν

424

her in seagirt Dia because of the witness of Dionysus.

"And Maera and Clymene I saw, and hateful Eriphyle, who took precious gold as the price of the life of her own husband. But I cannot tell or name all the wives and daughters of heroes that I saw; before that immortal night would be gone. Now it is time to sleep, either when I have gone to the swift ship and the crew, or here. But my conveyance is in the hands of the gods, and of you."

So he spoke, and they were all hushed in silence, and were held spellbound throughout the shadowy halls. Then among them white-armed Arete was the first to speak:

"Phaeacians, how does this man seem to you for looks, and stature, and for the balanced mind within him? And moreover he is my guest, though each of you has a share in this honor. Therefore be in no haste to send him away, nor stint your gifts to one in such need; for many are the treasures which lie stored in your halls by the favor of the gods."

Then among them spoke also the old hero Echeneus, who was an elder among the Phaeacians: "Friends, certainly not wide of the mark or of our own thought are the words of our wise queen. Give heed to them. Yet it is on Alcinous here that word and deed depend."

Then in turn Alcinous answered him and said: "This word of hers shall certainly hold, as surely as I live and am lord over the Phaeacians, lovers of the oar. But let our guest, for all his great longing to return, nevertheless endure to remain until tomorrow, until I shall make all our

---

[1] Line 343 is omitted in many MSS.

δωτίνην τελέσω· πομπὴ δ' ἄνδρεσσι μελήσει
πᾶσι, μάλιστα δ' ἐμοί· τοῦ γὰρ κράτος ἔστ' ἐνὶ δήμῳ."
    τὸν δ' ἀπαμειβόμενος προσέφη πολύμητις Ὀδυσσεύς·

355 "'Αλκίνοε κρεῖον, πάντων ἀριδείκετε λαῶν,
εἴ με καὶ εἰς ἐνιαυτὸν ἀνώγοιτ' αὐτόθι μίμνειν,
πομπήν δ' ὀτρύνοιτε καὶ ἀγλαὰ δῶρα διδοῖτε,
καί κε τὸ βουλοίμην, καί κεν πολὺ κέρδιον εἴη,
πλειοτέρῃ σὺν χειρὶ φίλην ἐς πατρίδ' ἱκέσθαι·

360 καί κ' αἰδοιότερος καὶ φίλτερος ἀνδράσιν εἴην
πᾶσιν, ὅσοι μ' Ἰθάκηνδε ἰδοίατο νοστήσαντα."
    τὸν δ' αὖτ' 'Αλκίνοος ἀπαμείβετο φώνησέν τε·
"ὦ Ὀδυσεῦ, τὸ μὲν οὔ τί σ' ἐΐσκομεν εἰσορόωντες,
ἠπεροπῆά τ' ἔμεν καὶ ἐπίκλοπον, οἷά τε πολλοὺς

365 βόσκει γαῖα μέλαινα πολυσπερέας ἀνθρώπους,
ψεύδεά τ' ἀρτύνοντας ὅθεν κέ τις οὐδὲ ἴδοιτο·
σοὶ δ' ἔπι μὲν μορφὴ ἐπέων, ἔνι δὲ φρένες ἐσθλαί.
μῦθον δ' ὡς ὅτ' ἀοιδὸς ἐπισταμένως κατέλεξας,
πάντων τ' 'Αργείων σέο τ' αὐτοῦ κήδεα λυγρά.

370 ἀλλ' ἄγε μοι τόδε εἰπὲ καὶ ἀτρεκέως κατάλεξον,
εἴ τινας ἀντιθέων ἑτάρων ἴδες, οἵ τοι ἅμ' αὐτῷ
Ἴλιον εἰς ἅμ' ἕποντο καὶ αὐτοῦ πότμον ἐπέσπον.
νὺξ δ' ἥδε μάλα μακρή, ἀθέσφατος· οὐδέ πω ὥρη
εὕδειν ἐν μεγάρῳ, σὺ δέ μοι λέγε θέσκελα ἔργα.

375 καί κεν ἐς ἠῶ δῖαν ἀνασχοίμην, ὅτε μοι σὺ
τλαίης ἐν μεγάρῳ τὰ σὰ κήδεα μυθήσασθαι."
    τὸν δ' ἀπαμειβόμενος προσέφη πολύμητις Ὀδυσσεύς·
"'Αλκίνοε κρεῖον, πάντων ἀριδείκετε λαῶν,
ὥρη μὲν πολέων μύθων, ὥρη δὲ καὶ ὕπνου·

gift complete. His conveyance shall be the concern of the men, of them all, but most of all of me; for mine is the power in the land."

Then resourceful Odysseus answered him and said: "Lord Alcinous, renowned above all men, if you should bid me remain here even for a year, and should further my conveyance, and give glorious gifts, even that would I choose; and it would be better far to come with a fuller hand to my own native land; and I should win more respect and love from all men who should see that I had returned to Ithaca."

Then again Alcinous made answer and said: "Odysseus, in the first place we do not at all suppose, as we look at you, that you are the kind of dissembler and cheat which the dark earth breeds in such numbers among far-flung humankind, men that fashion lies out of what no man could ever see. But upon you is grace of words, and within you is a heart of wisdom, and your tale you have told with skill, as a minstrel does, the grievous woes of all the Argives and of your own self. But come, tell me this, and declare it truly, whether you saw any of your godlike comrades, who went to Ilium together with you, and there met their fate. The night before us is long, marvelously long, and it is not yet the time for sleep in the hall. Tell me these wondrous deeds. I could hold out until bright dawn, such time as you would be willing to tell in the hall of these woes of yours."

Then resourceful Odysseus answered him and said: "Lord Alcinous, renowned above all men, there is a time for many words, and there is a time also for sleep. But if

380　εἰ δ' ἔτ' ἀκουέμεναί γε λιλαίεαι, οὐκ ἂν ἐγώ γε[1]
　　τούτων σοι φθονέοιμι καὶ οἰκτρότερ' ἄλλ' ἀγορεύειν,
　　κήδε' ἐμῶν ἑτάρων, οἳ δὴ μετόπισθεν ὄλοντο,
　　οἳ Τρώων μὲν ὑπεξέφυγον στονόεσσαν ἀυτήν,
　　ἐν νόστῳ δ' ἀπόλοντο κακῆς ἰότητι γυναικός.

385　　"αὐτὰρ ἐπεὶ ψυχὰς μὲν ἀπεσκέδασ' ἄλλυδις ἄλλη
　　ἁγνὴ Περσεφόνεια γυναικῶν θηλυτεράων,
　　ἦλθε δ' ἐπὶ ψυχὴ Ἀγαμέμνονος Ἀτρεΐδαο
　　ἀχνυμένη· περὶ δ' ἄλλαι ἀγηγέραθ', ὅσσοι ἅμ' αὐτῷ
　　οἴκῳ ἐν Αἰγίσθοιο θάνον καὶ πότμον ἐπέσπον.

390　ἔγνω δ' αἶψ' ἔμ' ἐκεῖνος, ἐπεὶ πίεν αἷμα κελαινόν·
　　κλαῖε δ' ὅ γε λιγέως, θαλερὸν κατὰ δάκρυον εἴβων,
　　πιτνὰς εἰς ἐμὲ χεῖρας, ὀρέξασθαι μενεαίνων·
　　ἀλλ' οὐ γάρ οἱ ἔτ' ἦν ἲς ἔμπεδος οὐδέ τι κῖκυς,
　　οἵη περ πάρος ἔσκεν ἐνὶ γναμπτοῖσι μέλεσσι.

395　　"τὸν μὲν ἐγὼ δάκρυσα ἰδὼν ἐλέησά τε θυμῷ,
　　καί μιν φωνήσας ἔπεα πτερόεντα προσηύδων·
　　'Ἀτρεΐδη κύδιστε, ἄναξ ἀνδρῶν Ἀγάμεμνον,
　　τίς νύ σε κὴρ ἐδάμασσε τανηλεγέος θανάτοιο;
　　ἦε σέ γ' ἐν νήεσσι Ποσειδάων ἐδάμασσεν

400　ὄρσας ἀργαλέων ἀνέμων ἀμέγαρτον ἀυτμήν;
　　ἦέ σ' ἀνάρσιοι ἄνδρες ἐδηλήσαντ' ἐπὶ χέρσου
　　βοῦς περιταμνόμενον ἠδ' οἰῶν πώεα καλά,
　　ἦε περὶ πτόλιος μαχεούμενον ἠδὲ γυναικῶν;'
　　　"ὣς ἐφάμην, ὁ δέ μ' αὐτίκ' ἀμειβόμενος προσέειπε·

405　'διογενὲς Λαερτιάδη, πολυμήχαν' Ὀδυσσεῦ,
　　οὔτ' ἐμέ γ' ἐν νήεσσι Ποσειδάων ἐδάμασσεν
　　ὄρσας ἀργαλέων ἀνέμων ἀμέγαρτον ἀυτμήν,[2]

you still yearn to listen, I would not begrudge to tell you of other things more pitiful still than these, the woes of my comrades, who perished afterward, who escaped from the dread battle cry of the Trojans, but perished on their return through the will of an evil woman.

"When then holy Persephone had scattered this way and that the ghosts of the women, there came up the ghost of Agamemnon, son of Atreus, sorrowing, and round about him others were gathered, ghosts of all those who were slain with him in the house of Aegisthus, and met their fate. He knew me instantly, when he had drunk the dark blood, and he wept aloud, and shed big tears, and stretched out his hands toward me eager to reach me. But no longer had he anything of strength or might remaining, such as of old was in his supple limbs.

"When I saw him I wept, and my heart had compassion on him, and I spoke, and addressed him with winged words: 'Most glorious son of Atreus, king of men, Agamemnon, what fate of pitiless death overcame you? Did Poseidon overcome you on board your ships, when he had roused a furious blast of cruel winds? Or did hostile men do you harm on the land, while you were cutting off their cattle and fine flocks of sheep, or were fighting to win their city and their women?'

"So I spoke, and he at once made answer and said: 'Son of Laertes, sprung from Zeus, Odysseus of many devices, neither did Poseidon overcome me on board my ships, when he had roused a furious blast of cruel winds, nor did

---

[1] ἐγώ γε: ἔπειτα
[2] Line 407 is omitted in most MSS.

οὔτε μ' ἀνάρσιοι ἄνδρες ἐδηλήσαντ' ἐπὶ χέρσου,
ἀλλά μοι Αἴγισθος τεύξας θάνατόν τε μόρον τε
410 ἔκτα σὺν οὐλομένῃ ἀλόχῳ, οἶκόνδε καλέσσας,
δειπνίσσας, ὥς τίς τε κατέκτανε βοῦν ἐπὶ φάτνῃ.
ὣς θάνον οἰκτίστῳ θανάτῳ· περὶ δ' ἄλλοι ἑταῖροι
νωλεμέως κτείνοντο σύες ὣς ἀργιόδοντες,
οἵ ῥά τ' ἐν ἀφνειοῦ ἀνδρὸς μέγα δυναμένοιο
415 ἢ γάμῳ ἢ ἐράνῳ ἢ εἰλαπίνῃ τεθαλυίῃ.
ἤδη μὲν πολέων φόνῳ ἀνδρῶν ἀντεβόλησας,
μουνὰξ κτεινομένων καὶ ἐνὶ κρατερῇ ὑσμίνῃ·
ἀλλά κε κεῖνα μάλιστα ἰδὼν ὀλοφύραο θυμῷ,
ὡς ἀμφὶ κρητῆρα τραπέζας τε πληθούσας
420 κείμεθ' ἐνὶ μεγάρῳ, δάπεδον δ' ἅπαν αἵματι θῦεν.
οἰκτροτάτην δ' ἤκουσα ὄπα Πριάμοιο θυγατρός,
Κασσάνδρης, τὴν κτεῖνε Κλυταιμνήστρη δολόμητις
ἀμφ' ἐμοί, αὐτὰρ ἐγὼ ποτὶ γαίῃ χεῖρας ἀείρων
βάλλον ἀποθνήσκων περὶ φασγάνῳ· ἡ δὲ κυνῶπις
425 νοσφίσατ', οὐδέ μοι ἔτλη ἰόντι περ εἰς Ἀίδαο
χερσὶ κατ' ὀφθαλμοὺς ἑλέειν σύν τε στόμ' ἐρεῖσαι.
ὣς οὐκ αἰνότερον καὶ κύντερον ἄλλο γυναικός,
ἥ τις δὴ τοιαῦτα μετὰ φρεσὶν ἔργα βάληται·
οἷον δὴ καὶ κείνη ἐμήσατο ἔργον ἀεικές,
430 κουριδίῳ τεύξασα πόσει φόνον. ἦ τοι ἔφην γε
ἀσπάσιος παίδεσσιν ἰδὲ δμώεσσιν ἐμοῖσιν
οἴκαδ' ἐλεύσεσθαι· ἡ δ' ἔξοχα λυγρὰ ἰδυῖα
οἷ τε κατ' αἶσχος ἔχευε καὶ ἐσσομένῃσιν ὀπίσσω
θηλυτέρῃσι γυναιξί, καὶ ἥ κ' ἐυεργὸς ἔῃσιν.'
435 "ὣς ἔφατ', αὐτὰρ ἐγώ μιν ἀμειβόμενος προσέειπον·

430

hostile men do me harm on the land, but Aegisthus brought upon me death and fate, and slew me with the aid of my accursed wife, when he had bidden me to his house and made me a feast, just as one slays an ox at the crib. So I died by a most pitiful death, and round about me the rest of my comrades were slain relentlessly like white-tusked swine, which are slaughtered in the house of a rich and powerful man at a marriage feast, or a joint meal, or a gay drinking bout. Before now you have been present at the slaying of many men, killed in single combat or in the press of the fight, but in heart you would have felt most pity had you seen that sight, how about the mixing bowl and the laden tables we lay in the hall, and the floor all swam with blood. But the most piteous cry that I heard was that of the daughter of Priam, Cassandra, whom guileful Clytemnestra slew as she clung to me. And I, lying on the ground, trying to raise my arms, tossed dying upon Aegisthus' sword. But she, bitch that she was, turned away, and did not deign, though I was going to the house of Hades, either to draw down my eyelids with her fingers or to close my mouth. So true is it that there is nothing more frightful or more shameless than a woman who puts into her heart such deeds, like the ugly thing she plotted, contriving her wedded husband's murder. You may be sure that I thought that I should come home welcome to my children and my household; but she with her heart set on utter horror, has shed shame on herself and on women yet to be, even on her who does what is right.'

"So he spoke, and I made answer and said: 'Alas, how

'ὢ πόποι, ἦ μάλα δὴ γόνον Ἀτρέος εὐρύοπα Ζεὺς
ἐκπάγλως ἤχθηρε γυναικείας διὰ βουλὰς
ἐξ ἀρχῆς· Ἑλένης μὲν ἀπωλόμεθ' εἵνεκα πολλοί,
σοὶ δὲ Κλυταιμνήστρη δόλον ἤρτυε τηλόθ' ἐόντι.'

440   "ὣς ἐφάμην, ὁ δέ μ' αὐτίκ' ἀμειβόμενος προσέειπε·
'τῶ νῦν μή ποτε καὶ σὺ γυναικί περ ἤπιος εἶναι·
μή οἱ μῦθον ἅπαντα πιφαυσκέμεν, ὅν κ' ἐὺ εἰδῆς,
ἀλλὰ τὸ μὲν φάσθαι, τὸ δὲ καὶ κεκρυμμένον εἶναι.
ἀλλ' οὐ σοί γ', Ὀδυσεῦ, φόνος ἔσσεται ἔκ γε γυναικός·

445 λίην γὰρ πινυτή τε καὶ εὖ φρεσὶ μήδεα οἶδε
κούρη Ἰκαρίοιο, περίφρων Πηνελόπεια.
ἦ μέν μιν νύμφην γε νέην κατελείπομεν ἡμεῖς
ἐρχόμενοι πόλεμόνδε· πάις δέ οἱ ἦν ἐπὶ μαζῷ
νήπιος, ὅς που νῦν γε μετ' ἀνδρῶν ἵζει ἀριθμῷ,

450 ὄλβιος· ἦ γὰρ τόν γε πατὴρ φίλος ὄψεται ἐλθών,
καὶ κεῖνος πατέρα προσπτύξεται, ἣ θέμις ἐστίν.
ἡ δ' ἐμὴ οὐδέ περ υἷος ἐνιπλησθῆναι ἄκοιτις
ὀφθαλμοῖσιν ἔασε· πάρος δέ με πέφνε καὶ αὐτόν.
ἄλλο δέ τοι ἐρέω, σὺ δ' ἐνὶ φρεσὶ βάλλεο σῇσιν·

455 κρύβδην, μηδ' ἀναφανδά, φίλην ἐς πατρίδα γαῖαν
νῆα κατισχέμεναι· ἐπεὶ οὐκέτι πιστὰ γυναιξίν.[1]
ἀλλ' ἄγε μοι τόδε εἰπὲ καὶ ἀτρεκέως κατάλεξον,
εἴ που ἔτι ζώοντος ἀκούετε παιδὸς ἐμοῖο,
ἤ που ἐν Ὀρχομενῷ ἢ ἐν Πύλῳ ἠμαθόεντι,

460 ἤ που πὰρ Μενελάῳ ἐνὶ Σπάρτῃ εὐρείῃ·
οὐ γάρ πω τέθνηκεν ἐπὶ χθονὶ δῖος Ὀρέστης.'
    "ὣς ἔφατ', αὐτὰρ ἐγώ μιν ἀμειβόμενος προσέειπον·
' Ἀτρεΐδη, τί με ταῦτα διείρεαι; οὐδέ τι οἶδα,

terribly from the beginning thundering Zeus has per-
secuted Atreus' race through women's guile! For Helen's
sake many of us perished, and against you Clytemnestra
spread a snare while you were far away.'

"So I spoke, and he at once made answer and said,
'Therefore in your own case never be gentle even to your
wife. Do not declare to her every thought that you have in
mind, but tell her some things, and let others also be hid-
den. Yet not upon you, Odysseus, shall death come from
your wife, for very prudent and of an understanding heart
is the daughter of Icarius, wise Penelope. Leave her we
did, a bride newly wed when we went to the war, and a boy
was at her breast, a baby, who now doubtless sits in the
ranks of men, in prosperity. Behold him his dear father
will, when he comes, and he will embrace his father, as is
right and good. But my wife did not let me sate my eyes
even with the sight of my son. Before that it was I myself
whom she slew. And another thing will I tell you, and you
may lay it to heart: in secret, and not openly, bring your
ship to the shore of your own native land; for no longer is
there faith in women. But come, tell me this, and declare
it truly, whether perchance you hear of my son still alive in
Orchomenus it may be, or in sandy Pylos, or perhaps with
Menelaus in wide Sparta; for not yet has noble Orestes
perished on the earth.'

"So he spoke, and I made answer and said: 'Son of
Atreus, why do you question me of this? I know not at all

---

[1] Lines 454–56 were lacking in most ancient editions.

ζώει ὅ γ' ἢ τέθνηκε· κακὸν δ' ἀνεμώλια βάζειν.'
465 "νῶι μὲν ὣς ἐπέεσσιν ἀμειβομένω στυγεροῖσιν
ἕσταμεν ἀχνύμενοι θαλερὸν κατὰ δάκρυ χέοντες·
ἦλθε δ' ἐπὶ ψυχὴ Πηληϊάδεω Ἀχιλῆος
καὶ Πατροκλῆος καὶ ἀμύμονος Ἀντιλόχοιο
Αἴαντός θ', ὃς ἄριστος ἔην εἶδός τε δέμας τε
470 τῶν ἄλλων Δαναῶν μετ' ἀμύμονα Πηλεΐωνα.
ἔγνω δὲ ψυχή με ποδώκεος Αἰακίδαο
καί ῥ' ὀλοφυρομένη ἔπεα πτερόεντα προσηύδα·
"'διογενὲς Λαερτιάδη, πολυμήχαν' Ὀδυσσεῦ,
σχέτλιε, τίπτ' ἔτι μεῖζον ἐνὶ φρεσὶ μήσεαι ἔργον;
475 πῶς ἔτλης Ἄιδόσδε κατελθέμεν, ἔνθα τε νεκροὶ
ἀφραδέες ναίουσι, βροτῶν εἴδωλα καμόντων;'
"ὣς ἔφατ', αὐτὰρ ἐγώ μιν ἀμειβόμενος προσέειπον·
'ὦ Ἀχιλεῦ Πηλῆος υἱέ, μέγα φέρτατ' Ἀχαιῶν,
ἦλθον Τειρεσίαο κατὰ χρέος, εἴ τινα βουλὴν
480 εἴποι, ὅπως Ἰθάκην ἐς παιπαλόεσσαν ἱκοίμην·
οὐ γάρ πω σχεδὸν ἦλθον Ἀχαιΐδος, οὐδέ πω ἁμῆς
γῆς ἐπέβην, ἀλλ' αἰὲν ἔχω κακά. σεῖο δ', Ἀχιλλεῦ,
οὔ τις ἀνὴρ προπάροιθε μακάρτατος οὔτ' ἄρ' ὀπίσσω.
πρὶν μὲν γάρ σε ζωὸν ἐτίομεν ἶσα θεοῖσιν
485 Ἀργεῖοι, νῦν αὖτε μέγα κρατέεις νεκύεσσιν
ἐνθάδ' ἐών· τῷ μή τι θανὼν ἀκαχίζευ, Ἀχιλλεῦ.'
"ὣς ἐφάμην, ὁ δέ μ' αὐτίκ' ἀμειβόμενος προσέειπε·
'μὴ δή μοι θάνατόν γε παραύδα, φαίδιμ' Ὀδυσσεῦ.
βουλοίμην κ' ἐπάρουρος ἐὼν θητευέμεν ἄλλῳ,
490 ἀνδρὶ παρ' ἀκλήρῳ, ᾧ μὴ βίοτος πολὺς εἴη,
ἢ πᾶσιν νεκύεσσι καταφθιμένοισιν ἀνάσσειν.

434

whether he is alive or dead, and it is an ill thing to speak words vain as wind.'

"Thus we two stood and exchanged sad words with one another, sorrowing and shedding big tears; and there came up the ghost of Achilles, son of Peleus, and those of Patroclus and of peerless Antilochus and of Aias, who in beauty and form surpassed all the Danaans except the flawless son of Peleus. And the ghost of the swift-footed grandson of Aeacus recognized me, and weeping, spoke to me winged words:

"'Son of Laertes, sprung from Zeus, Odysseus of many devices, stubborn man, what deed yet greater than this will you devise in your heart? How did you dare to come down to Hades, where dwell the unheeding dead, the phantoms of men outworn?'

"So he spoke, and I made answer and said: 'Achilles, son of Peleus, far the mightiest of the Achaeans, I came through need of Teiresias, if perchance he would tell me some plan whereby I might reach rugged Ithaca. For not yet have I come near to the land of Achaea, nor have I as yet set foot on my own country, but am forever suffering woes; whereas no man before this was more blessed than you, Achilles, nor shall ever be hereafter. For before, when you were alive, we Argives honored you equally with the gods, and now that you are here, you rule mightily among the dead. Therefore, grieve not at all that you are dead, Achilles.'

"So I spoke, and he at once made answer, and said: 'Never try to reconcile me to death, glorious Odysseus. I should choose, so I might live on earth, to serve as the hireling of another, some landless man with hardly enough to live on, rather than to be lord over all the dead that have

ἀλλ' ἄγε μοι τοῦ παιδὸς ἀγαυοῦ μῦθον ἐνίσπες,
ἢ ἕπετ' ἐς πόλεμον πρόμος ἔμμεναι, ἦε καὶ οὐκί.
εἰπὲ δέ μοι Πηλῆος ἀμύμονος, εἴ τι πέπυσσαι,
495 ἢ ἔτ' ἔχει τιμὴν πολέσιν μετὰ Μυρμιδόνεσσιν,
ἦ μιν ἀτιμάζουσιν ἀν' Ἑλλάδα τε Φθίην τε,
οὕνεκά μιν κατὰ γῆρας ἔχει χεῖράς τε πόδας τε.
οὐ γὰρ¹ ἐγὼν ἐπαρωγὸς ὑπ' αὐγὰς ἠελίοιο,
τοῖος ἐών, οἷός ποτ' ἐνὶ Τροίῃ εὐρείῃ
500 πέφνον λαὸν ἄριστον, ἀμύνων Ἀργείοισιν·
εἰ τοιόσδ' ἔλθοιμι μίνυνθά περ ἐς πατέρος δῶ·
τῷ κέ τεῳ στύξαιμι μένος καὶ χεῖρας ἀάπτους,
οἳ κεῖνον βιόωνται ἐέργουσίν τ' ἀπὸ τιμῆς.'
    "ὣς ἔφατ', αὐτὰρ ἐγὼ μιν ἀμειβόμενος προσέειπον·
505 'ἦ τοι μὲν Πηλῆος ἀμύμονος οὔ τι πέπυσμαι,
αὐτάρ τοι παιδός γε Νεοπτολέμοιο φίλοιο
πᾶσαν ἀληθείην μυθήσομαι, ὥς με κελεύεις·
αὐτὸς γάρ μιν ἐγὼ κοίλης ἐπὶ νηὸς ἐίσης
ἤγαγον ἐκ Σκύρου μετ' ἐυκνήμιδας Ἀχαιούς.
510 ἦ τοι ὅτ' ἀμφὶ πόλιν Τροίην φραζοίμεθα βουλάς,
αἰεὶ πρῶτος ἔβαζε καὶ οὐχ ἡμάρτανε μύθων·
Νέστωρ ἀντίθεος καὶ ἐγὼ νικάσκομεν οἴω.
αὐτὰρ ὅτ' ἐν πεδίῳ Τρώων μαρναίμεθα χαλκῷ,²
οὔ ποτ' ἐνὶ πληθυῖ μένεν ἀνδρῶν οὐδ' ἐν ὁμίλῳ,
515 ἀλλὰ πολὺ προθέεσκε τὸ ὃν μένος οὐδενὶ εἴκων,
πολλοὺς δ' ἄνδρας ἔπεφνεν ἐν αἰνῇ δηιοτῆτι.
πάντας δ' οὐκ ἂν ἐγὼ μυθήσομαι οὐδ' ὀνομήνω,
ὅσσον λαὸν ἔπεφνεν ἀμύνων Ἀργείοισιν,
ἀλλ' οἷον τὸν Τηλεφίδην κατενήρατο χαλκῷ,

perished. But come, tell me tidings of my son, that lordly
youth, whether or not he followed to the war to be a leader.
And tell me of flawless Peleus, if you have heard anything,
whether he still has honor among the host of the Myrmi-
dons, or men do him dishonor throughout Hellas and
Phthia, because old age binds him hand and foot. For I am
not there to bear him aid beneath the rays of the sun in
such strength as once was mine in wide Troy, when I slew
the best of their army in defence of the Argives. If only in
such strength I could come, even only for an hour, to my
father's house, I would give many a one of those who do
him violence and keep him from his honor cause to rue my
strength and my invincible hands.'

"So he spoke, and I made answer and said: 'In fact of
flawless Peleus I have heard nothing, but as touching your
staunch son Neoptolemus I will tell you all the truth, as you
bid me. I it was, myself, who brought him from Scyros in
my shapely, hollow ship to join the army of the well-
greaved Achaeans. And in truth, as often as we took coun-
sel around the city of Troy, he was always the first to speak,
and never erred in his words; godlike Nestor and I alone
surpassed him. But as often as we fought with the bronze
on the Trojan plain, he would never remain behind in the
throng or press of men, but would run forward far to the
front, yielding to none in his prowess; and many men he
slew in dreadful combat. All of them I could not tell or
name, all the host that he slew in defence of the Argives;
but what a warrior was that son of Telephus whom he slew

---

[1] οὐ γὰρ: εἰ γὰρ Zenodotus
[2] μαρναίμεθα χαλκῷ: μαρναίμεθ᾽ Ἀχαιοί

520 ἥρω' Εὐρύπυλον, πολλοὶ δ' ἀμφ' αὐτὸν ἑταῖροι
Κήτειοι κτείνοντο γυναίων εἵνεκα δώρων.
κεῖνον δὴ κάλλιστον ἴδον μετὰ Μέμνονα δῖον.
αὐτὰρ ὅτ' εἰς ἵππον κατεβαίνομεν, ὃν κάμ' Ἐπειός,
Ἀργείων οἱ ἄριστοι, ἐμοὶ δ' ἐπὶ πάντα τέταλτο,
525 ἠμὲν ἀνακλῖναι πυκινὸν λόχον ἠδ' ἐπιθεῖναι,[1]
ἔνθ' ἄλλοι Δαναῶν ἡγήτορες ἠδὲ μέδοντες
δάκρυά τ' ὠμόργνυντο τρέμον θ' ὑπὸ γυῖα ἑκάστου·
κεῖνον δ' οὔ ποτε πάμπαν ἐγὼν ἴδον ὀφθαλμοῖσιν
οὔτ' ὠχρήσαντα χρόα κάλλιμον οὔτε παρειῶν
530 δάκρυ ὀμορξάμενον· ὁ δέ γε μάλα πόλλ' ἱκέτευεν
ἱππόθεν ἐξέμεναι, ξίφεος δ' ἐπεμαίετο κώπην
καὶ δόρυ χαλκοβαρές, κακὰ δὲ Τρώεσσι μενοίνα.
ἀλλ' ὅτε δὴ Πριάμοιο πόλιν διεπέρσαμεν αἰπήν,
μοῖραν καὶ γέρας ἐσθλὸν ἔχων ἐπὶ νηὸς ἔβαινεν
535 ἀσκηθής, οὔτ' ἄρ βεβλημένος ὀξέι χαλκῷ
οὔτ' αὐτοσχεδίην οὐτασμένος, οἷά τε πολλὰ
γίγνεται ἐν πολέμῳ· ἐπιμὶξ δέ τε μαίνεται Ἄρης.'
    "ὣς ἐφάμην, ψυχὴ δὲ ποδώκεος Αἰακίδαο
φοίτα μακρὰ βιβᾶσα κατ' ἀσφοδελὸν λειμῶνα,
540 γηθοσύνη ὅ οἱ υἱὸν ἔφην ἀριδείκετον εἶναι.
    "αἱ δ' ἄλλαι ψυχαὶ νεκύων κατατεθνηώτων
ἕστασαν ἀχνύμεναι, εἴροντο δὲ κήδε' ἑκάστη.
οἴη δ' Αἴαντος ψυχὴ Τελαμωνιάδαο
νόσφιν ἀφεστήκει, κεχολωμένη εἵνεκα νίκης,
545 τήν μιν ἐγὼ νίκησα δικαζόμενος παρὰ νηυσὶ

[1] Line 525 was unknown to Aristarchus.

with the sword, the hero Eurypylus!—and many of his comrades, the Ceteians, were slain about him, because of gifts a woman craved.[a] He in truth was the handsomest man I saw, next to noble Memnon. And again, when we, the best of the Argives, were about to go down into the horse which Epeus made, and the command of all was laid upon me, both to open and to close the door of our stout-built ambush, then the other leaders and counselors of the Danaans would wipe away tears from their eyes, and each man's limbs shook beneath him, but never did my eyes see his handsome face grow pale at all, nor see him wiping tears from his cheeks; but he earnestly besought me to let him go out from the horse, and kept handling his sword hilt and his spear heavy with bronze, and was eager to work harm to the Trojans. But after we had sacked the lofty city of Priam, he went on board his ship with his share of the spoil and a noble prize—all unscathed as he was, neither struck with the sharp spear nor stabbed in close combat, as often befalls in war; for Ares rages confusedly.'

"So I spoke, and the ghost of the grandson of Aeacus departed with long strides over the field of asphodel, joyful in that I said that his son was preeminent.

"And the other ghosts of those dead and gone stood sorrowing, and each asked about those dear to him. Alone of them all the spirit of Aias, son of Telamon, stood apart, still full of wrath for the victory that I had won over him in the contest by the ships for the arms of Achilles, whose

[a] The reference is to the golden vine given by Priam to Astyoche, wife of Telephus, which gift led her to send her son Eurypylus to the aid of the Trojans. M.

τεύχεσιν ἀμφ' Ἀχιλῆος· ἔθηκε δὲ πότνια μήτηρ.
παῖδες δὲ Τρώων δίκασαν καὶ Παλλὰς Ἀθήνη.
ὡς δὴ μὴ ὄφελον νικᾶν τοιῷδ' ἐπ' ἀέθλῳ·
τοίην γὰρ κεφαλὴν ἕνεκ' αὐτῶν γαῖα κατέσχεν,
550   Αἴανθ', ὃς πέρι μὲν εἶδος, πέρι δ' ἔργα τέτυκτο
τῶν ἄλλων Δαναῶν μετ' ἀμύμονα Πηλεΐωνα.
τὸν μὲν ἐγὼν ἐπέεσσι προσηύδων μειλιχίοισιν·

   "'Αἶαν, παῖ Τελαμῶνος ἀμύμονος, οὐκ ἄρ' ἔμελλες
οὐδὲ θανὼν λήσεσθαι ἐμοὶ χόλου εἵνεκα τευχέων
555   οὐλομένων; τὰ δὲ πῆμα θεοὶ θέσαν Ἀργείοισι,
τοῖος γάρ σφιν πύργος ἀπώλεο· σεῖο δ' Ἀχαιοὶ
ἶσον Ἀχιλλῆος κεφαλῇ Πηληϊάδαο
ἀχνύμεθα φθιμένοιο διαμπερές· οὐδέ τις ἄλλος
αἴτιος, ἀλλὰ Ζεὺς Δαναῶν στρατὸν αἰχμητάων
560   ἐκπάγλως ἤχθηρε, τεῒν δ' ἐπὶ μοῖραν ἔθηκεν.
ἀλλ' ἄγε δεῦρο, ἄναξ, ἵν' ἔπος καὶ μῦθον ἀκούσῃς
ἡμέτερον· δάμασον δὲ μένος καὶ ἀγήνορα θυμόν.'

   "ὣς ἐφάμην, ὁ δέ μ' οὐδὲν ἀμείβετο, βῆ δὲ μετ' ἄλλας
ψυχὰς εἰς Ἔρεβος νεκύων κατατεθνηώτων.
565   ἔνθα χ' ὅμως προσέφη κεχολωμένος, ἤ κεν ἐγὼ τόν·
ἀλλά μοι ἤθελε θυμὸς ἐνὶ στήθεσσι φίλοισι
τῶν ἄλλων ψυχὰς ἰδέειν κατατεθνηώτων.

   "ἔνθ' ἦ τοι Μίνωα ἴδον, Διὸς ἀγλαὸν υἱόν,
χρύσεον σκῆπτρον ἔχοντα, θεμιστεύοντα νέκυσσιν,
570   ἥμενον, οἱ δέ μιν ἀμφὶ δίκας εἴροντο ἄνακτα,
ἥμενοι ἑσταότες τε κατ' εὐρυπυλὲς Ἄϊδος δῶ.

   "τὸν δὲ μετ' Ὠρίωνα πελώριον εἰσενόησα
θῆρας ὁμοῦ εἰλεῦντα κατ' ἀσφοδελὸν λειμῶνα,

honored mother had set them for a prize; and the judges were the sons of the Trojans and Pallas Athene. I wish that I had never won in the contest for such a prize, over so noble a head did the earth close because of those arms, over Aias, who in beauty and in deeds of war was above all the other Danaans, next to the flawless son of Peleus. To him I spoke with winning words:

"'Aias, son of flawless Telamon, were you then not even in death to forget your wrath against me because of those accursed arms? Surely the gods set them to be a bane to the Argives: such a tower of strength was lost to them in you; and for you in death we Achaeans sorrow unceasingly, as much as we do for the life of Achilles, son of Peleus. Yet no other is to blame but Zeus, who bore terrible hatred against the army of Danaan spearmen, and brought on you your doom. No, come closer, my lord, that you may hear my word and what I have to say; curb your wrath and your proud spirit.'

"So I spoke, but he answered me not a word, but went his way to Erebus to join the other ghosts of those dead and gone. He might yet have spoken to me for all his wrath, or I to him, but the heart in my breast desired to see the ghosts of those others that are dead and gone.

"There, you must know, I saw Minos, the glorious son of Zeus, golden scepter in hand, giving judgment to the dead from his seat, while they sat and stood about the king in the wide-gated house of Hades and asked him for judgment.

"And after him I became aware of huge Orion herding together over the field of asphodel the wild beasts he him-

τοὺς αὐτὸς κατέπεφνεν ἐν οἰοπόλοισιν ὄρεσσι
575 χερσὶν ἔχων ῥόπαλον παγχάλκεον, αἰὲν ἀαγές.

"καὶ Τιτυὸν εἶδον, Γαίης ἐρικυδέος υἱόν,
κείμενον ἐν δαπέδῳ· ὁ δ' ἐπ' ἐννέα κεῖτο πέλεθρα,
γῦπε δέ μιν ἑκάτερθε παρημένω ἧπαρ ἔκειρον,
δέρτρον ἔσω δύνοντες, ὁ δ' οὐκ ἀπαμύνετο χερσί·
580 Λητὼ γὰρ ἕλκησε, Διὸς κυδρὴν παράκοιτιν,
Πυθώδ' ἐρχομένην διὰ καλλιχόρου Πανοπῆος.

"καὶ μὴν Τάνταλον εἰσεῖδον κρατέρ'[1] ἄλγε' ἔχοντα
ἑστεῶτ' ἐν λίμνῃ· ἡ δὲ προσέπλαζε γενείῳ·
στεῦτο δὲ διψάων, πιέειν δ' οὐκ εἶχεν ἑλέσθαι·
585 ὁσσάκι γὰρ κύψει' ὁ γέρων πιέειν μενεαίνων,
τοσσάχ' ὕδωρ ἀπολέσκετ' ἀναβροχέν, ἀμφὶ δὲ ποσσὶ
γαῖα μέλαινα φάνεσκε, καταζήνασκε δὲ δαίμων.
δένδρεα δ' ὑψιπέτηλα κατὰ κρῆθεν χέε καρπόν,
ὄγχναι καὶ ῥοιαὶ καὶ μηλέαι ἀγλαόκαρποι
590 συκέαι τε γλυκεραὶ καὶ ἐλαῖαι τηλεθόωσαι·
τῶν ὁπότ' ἰθύσει' ὁ γέρων ἐπὶ χερσὶ μάσασθαι,
τὰς δ' ἄνεμος ῥίπτασκε ποτὶ νέφεα σκιόεντα.

"καὶ μὴν Σίσυφον εἰσεῖδον κρατέρ'[1] ἄλγε' ἔχοντα
λᾶαν βαστάζοντα πελώριον ἀμφοτέρῃσιν.
595 ἦ τοι ὁ μὲν σκηριπτόμενος χερσίν τε ποσίν τε
λᾶαν ἄνω ὤθεσκε ποτὶ λόφον· ἀλλ' ὅτε μέλλοι
ἄκρον ὑπερβαλέειν, τότ' ἀποστρέψασκε κραταιΐς·
αὖτις ἔπειτα πέδονδε κυλίνδετο λᾶας ἀναιδής.

---

[1] κρατέρ': χαλέπ'

self had slain on the lonely hills, and in his hands he held a club all of bronze, forever unbroken.

"And I saw Tityos, son of glorious Gaea, lying on the ground. Over nine plethra[a] he stretched, and two vultures sat, one on either side, and tore his liver, plunging their beaks into his bowels, nor could he beat them off with his hands. For he had raped Leto, the honored consort of Zeus, as she went toward Pytho through lovely Panopeus.

"Yes, and I saw Tantalus in bitter torment, standing in a pool, and the water came close to his chin. He was wild with thirst, but had no way to drink; for as often as the old man stooped down, eager to drink, so often would the water be swallowed up and vanish away, and at his feet the black earth would appear, for some god would dry it all up. And trees, high and leafy, let hang their fruits from their tops, pears, and pomegranates, and apple trees with their bright fruit, and sweet figs, and luxuriant olives. But as often as the old man would reach out toward these, to clutch them with his hands, the wind would toss them to the shadowy clouds.

"Yes, and I saw Sisyphus in bitter torment, seeking to raise a monstrous stone with his two hands. In fact he would get a purchase with hands and feet and keep pushing the stone toward the crest of a hill, but as often as he was about to heave it over the top, the weight would turn it back, and then down again to the plain would come rolling the shameless stone.[b] But he would strain again and thrust

[a] The length of a plethron was later fixed at 100 feet. D.

[b] This is Murray's brilliant rendition of Homer's own onomatopoeia. D.

αὐτὰρ ὅ γ᾽ ἂψ ὤσασκε τιταινόμενος, κατὰ δ᾽ ἱδρὼς
600   ἔρρεεν ἐκ μελέων, κονίη δ᾽ ἐκ κρατὸς ὀρώρει.
      "τὸν δὲ μετ᾽ εἰσενόησα βίην Ἡρακληείην,
      εἴδωλον· αὐτὸς δὲ μετ᾽ ἀθανάτοισι θεοῖσι
      τέρπεται ἐν θαλίῃς καὶ ἔχει καλλίσφυρον Ἥβην,
      παῖδα Διὸς μεγάλοιο καὶ Ἥρης χρυσοπεδίλου.[1]
605   ἀμφὶ δέ μιν κλαγγὴ νεκύων ἦν οἰωνῶν ὥς,
      πάντοσ᾽ ἀτυζομένων· ὁ δ᾽ ἐρεμνῇ νυκτὶ ἐοικώς,
      γυμνὸν τόξον ἔχων καὶ ἐπὶ νευρῆφιν ὀιστόν,
      δεινὸν παπταίνων, αἰεὶ βαλέοντι ἐοικώς.
      σμερδαλέος δέ οἱ ἀμφὶ περὶ στήθεσσιν ἀορτὴρ
610   χρύσεος ἦν τελαμών, ἵνα θέσκελα ἔργα τέτυκτο,
      ἄρκτοι τ᾽ ἀγρότεροί τε σύες χαροποί τε λέοντες,
      ὑσμῖναί τε μάχαι τε φόνοι τ᾽ ἀνδροκτασίαι τε.
      μὴ τεχνησάμενος μηδ᾽ ἄλλο τι τεχνήσαιτο,
      ὃς κεῖνον τελαμῶνα ἑῇ ἐγκάτθετο τέχνῃ.
615   ἔγνω δ᾽ αὖτ᾽ ἔμ᾽ ἐκεῖνος, ἐπεὶ ἴδεν ὀφθαλμοῖσιν,
      καί μ᾽ ὀλοφυρόμενος ἔπεα πτερόεντα προσηύδα·
      "'διογενὲς Λαερτιάδη, πολυμήχαν᾽ Ὀδυσσεῦ,
      ἆ δείλ᾽, ἦ τινὰ καὶ σὺ κακὸν μόρον ἡγηλάζεις,
      ὅν περ ἐγὼν ὀχέεσκον ὑπ᾽ αὐγὰς ἠελίοιο.
620   Ζηνὸς μὲν πάις ἦα Κρονίονος, αὐτὰρ ὀιζὺν
      εἶχον ἀπειρεσίην· μάλα γὰρ πολὺ χείρονι φωτὶ
      δεδμήμην, ὁ δέ μοι χαλεποὺς ἐπετέλλετ᾽ ἀέθλους.
      καί ποτέ μ᾽ ἐνθάδ᾽ ἔπεμψε κύν᾽ ἄξοντ᾽· οὐ γὰρ ἔτ᾽ ἄλλον
      φράζετο τοῦδέ γέ μοι κρατερώτερον[2] εἶναι ἄεθλον·
625   τὸν μὲν ἐγὼν ἀνένεικα καὶ ἤγαγον ἐξ Ἀίδαο·
      Ἑρμείας δέ μ᾽ ἔπεμψεν ἰδὲ γλαυκῶπις Ἀθήνη.'

it back, and the sweat flowed down from his limbs, and dust rose up from his head.

"And after him I became aware of the mighty Heracles—his phantom; for he himself among the immortal gods takes his joy in the feast, and has for wife Hebe of the beautiful ankles, daughter of great Zeus and of Hera of the golden sandals. About him rose a clamor from the dead, as of birds flying everywhere in terror; and he like dark night, with his bow uncased and with arrow on the string, glared about him terribly, like one about to shoot. Terrifying was the belt about his breast, a baldric of gold, on which wondrous things were fashioned, bears and wild boars, and lions with flashing eyes, and conflicts, and battles, and murders, and slayings of men. May he never have designed, or hereafter design, such another, he who stored up in his craft the device of that belt. He in turn knew me when his eyes beheld me, and weeping spoke to me winged words:

"'Son of Laertes, sprung from Zeus, Odysseus of many devices, ah, wretched man, do you, too, drag out an evil lot such as I once bore beneath the rays of the sun? I was the son of Zeus, son of Cronos, but I suffered woe beyond measure; for I was made subject to a man far worse than I, and he laid on me hard labors. Once he sent me even here to fetch the hound of Hades, for he could devise for me no other task harder than this. The hound I carried off and led out from the house of Hades; and Hermes was my guide, and flashing-eyed Athene.'

---

[1] Lines 602–4 were rejected by some ancient critics as having been inserted in the text by Onomacritus.

[2] κρατερώτερον: χαλεπώτερον; cf. 582, 593

"ὣς εἰπὼν ὁ μὲν αὖτις ἔβη δόμον Ἄϊδος εἴσω,
αὐτὰρ ἐγὼν αὐτοῦ μένον ἔμπεδον, εἴ τις ἔτ' ἔλθοι
ἀνδρῶν ἡρώων, οἳ δὴ τὸ πρόσθεν ὄλοντο.

630 καί νύ κ' ἔτι προτέρους ἴδον ἀνέρας, οὓς ἔθελόν περ,
Θησέα Πειρίθοόν τε, θεῶν ἐρικυδέα τέκνα·[1]
ἀλλὰ πρὶν ἐπὶ ἔθνε' ἀγείρετο μυρία νεκρῶν
ἠχῇ θεσπεσίῃ· ἐμὲ δὲ χλωρὸν δέος ᾕρει,
μή μοι Γοργείην κεφαλὴν δεινοῖο πελώρου

635 ἐξ Ἀΐδεω πέμψειεν ἀγαυὴ Περσεφόνεια.

"αὐτίκ' ἔπειτ' ἐπὶ νῆα κιὼν ἐκέλευον ἑταίρους
αὐτούς τ' ἀμβαίνειν ἀνά τε πρυμνήσια λῦσαι.
οἱ δ' αἶψ' εἴσβαινον καὶ ἐπὶ κληῖσι καθῖζον.
τὴν δὲ κατ' Ὠκεανὸν ποταμὸν φέρε κῦμα ῥόοιο,

640 πρῶτα μὲν εἰρεσίῃ, μετέπειτα δὲ κάλλιμος οὖρος."

[1] Line 631 was attributed to Pisistratus by Hereas of Megara
(Plut. *Thes.* 20).

"So saying, he went his way again into the house of Hades, but I remained there steadfastly, in the hope that some other perchance might still come forth of the warrior heroes who died in the days of old. And I should have seen yet others of the men of former times, whom I was eager to behold, Theseus and Peirithous, glorious children of the gods, but before that the myriad tribes of the dead came thronging up with an eerie cry, and pale fear seized me, that august Persephone might send upon me out of the house of Hades the head of the Gorgon, that terrible monster.

"At once then I went to the ship and told my comrades themselves to embark, and to loose the stern cables. So they went on board quickly and sat down upon the benches. And the ship was borne down the river Oceanus by the swell of the current, first with our rowing, and afterwards the wind was fair."

Μ

"Αὐτὰρ ἐπεὶ ποταμοῖο λίπεν ῥόον Ὠκεανοῖο
νηῦς, ἀπὸ δ' ἵκετο κῦμα θαλάσσης εὐρυπόροιο
νῆσόν τ' Αἰαίην, ὅθι τ' Ἠοῦς ἠριγενείης
οἰκία καὶ χοροί εἰσι καὶ ἀντολαὶ Ἠελίοιο,
5 νῆα μὲν ἔνθ' ἐλθόντες ἐκέλσαμεν ἐν ψαμάθοισιν,
ἐκ δὲ καὶ αὐτοὶ βῆμεν ἐπὶ ῥηγμῖνι θαλάσσης·[1]
ἔνθα δ' ἀποβρίξαντες ἐμείναμεν Ἠῶ δῖαν.

"ἦμος δ' ἠριγένεια φάνη ῥοδοδάκτυλος Ἠώς,
δὴ τότ' ἐγὼν ἑτάρους προΐειν ἐς δώματα Κίρκης
10 οἰσέμεναι νεκρόν, Ἐλπήνορα τεθνηῶτα.
φιτροὺς δ' αἶψα ταμόντες, ὅθ' ἀκροτάτη πρόεχ' ἀκτή,
θάπτομεν ἀχνύμενοι θαλερὸν κατὰ δάκρυ χέοντες.
αὐτὰρ ἐπεὶ νεκρός τ' ἐκάη καὶ τεύχεα νεκροῦ,
τύμβον χεύαντες καὶ ἐπὶ στήλην ἐρύσαντες
15 πήξαμεν ἀκροτάτῳ τύμβῳ εὐῆρες ἐρετμόν.

"ἡμεῖς μὲν τὰ ἕκαστα διείπομεν· οὐδ' ἄρα Κίρκην
ἐξ Ἀΐδεω ἐλθόντες ἐλήθομεν, ἀλλὰ μάλ' ὦκα
ἦλθ' ἐντυναμένη· ἅμα δ' ἀμφίπολοι φέρον αὐτῇ
σῖτον καὶ κρέα πολλὰ καὶ αἴθοπα οἶνον ἐρυθρόν.
20 ἡ δ' ἐν μέσσῳ στᾶσα μετηύδα δῖα θεάων·

---

[1] Line 6 is omitted in many MSS.

448

BOOK 12

"Now after our ship had left the river Oceanus and had come to the swell of the broad sea, and the Aeaean island, where is the dwelling of early Dawn and her dancing places, and the risings of the Sun, there on our coming we beached our ship on the sands, and ourselves disembarked upon the shore of the sea; there we fell asleep, and waited for the bright Dawn.

"As soon as early Dawn appeared, the rosy-fingered, then I sent off my comrades to the house of Circe to fetch the body of the dead Elpenor. Quickly then we cut billets of wood and gave him burial where the headland runs farthest out to sea, sorrowing and shedding big tears. But when the dead man was burned, and the dead man's armor, we heaped up a mound and dragged on to it a pillar and on the very top of the tomb we fixed his shapely oar.

"We then were busied with these several tasks but neither was Circe unaware that we had returned out of the house of Hades, but speedily arrayed herself and came, and her handmaids brought with her bread and meat in abundance and sparkling red wine. And the beautiful goddess stood in our midst, and spoke among us, saying:

"'σχέτλιοι, οἳ ζώοντες ὑπήλθετε δῶμ' Ἀίδαο,
δισθανέες, ὅτε τ' ἄλλοι ἅπαξ θνήσκουσ' ἄνθρωποι.
ἀλλ' ἄγετ' ἐσθίετε βρώμην καὶ πίνετε οἶνον
αὖθι πανημέριοι· ἅμα δ' ἠοῖ φαινομένηφι
25 πλεύσεσθ'· αὐτὰρ ἐγὼ δείξω ὁδὸν ἠδὲ ἕκαστα
σημανέω, ἵνα μή τι κακορραφίῃ ἀλεγεινῇ
ἢ ἁλὸς ἢ ἐπὶ γῆς ἀλγήσετε πῆμα παθόντες.'

"ὣς ἔφαθ', ἡμῖν δ' αὖτ' ἐπεπείθετο θυμὸς ἀγήνωρ.
ὣς τότε μὲν πρόπαν ἦμαρ ἐς ἠέλιον καταδύντα
30 ἥμεθα δαινύμενοι κρέα τ' ἄσπετα καὶ μέθυ ἡδύ·
ἦμος δ' ἠέλιος κατέδυ καὶ ἐπὶ κνέφας ἦλθεν,
οἱ μὲν κοιμήσαντο παρὰ πρυμνήσια νηός,
ἡ δ' ἐμὲ χειρὸς ἑλοῦσα φίλων ἀπονόσφιν ἑταίρων
εἷσέ τε καὶ προσέλεκτο καὶ ἐξερέεινεν ἕκαστα·
35 αὐτὰρ ἐγὼ τῇ πάντα κατὰ μοῖραν κατέλεξα.
καὶ τότε δή μ' ἐπέεσσι προσηύδα πότνια Κίρκη·

"'ταῦτα μὲν οὕτω πάντα πεπείρανται, σὺ δ' ἄκουσον,
ὥς τοι ἐγὼν ἐρέω, μνήσει δέ σε καὶ θεὸς αὐτός.
Σειρῆνας μὲν πρῶτον ἀφίξεαι, αἵ ῥά τε πάντας
40 ἀνθρώπους θέλγουσιν, ὅτις σφεας εἰσαφίκηται.
ὅς τις ἀιδρείῃ πελάσῃ καὶ φθόγγον ἀκούσῃ
Σειρήνων, τῷ δ' οὔ τι γυνὴ καὶ νήπια τέκνα
οἴκαδε νοστήσαντι παρίσταται οὐδὲ γάνυνται,
ἀλλά τε Σειρῆνες λιγυρῇ θέλγουσιν ἀοιδῇ
45 ἥμεναι ἐν λειμῶνι, πολὺς δ' ἀμφ' ὀστεόφιν θὶς
ἀνδρῶν πυθομένων, περὶ δὲ ῥινοὶ μινύθουσι.
ἀλλὰ παρεξελάαν, ἐπὶ δ' οὔατ' ἀλεῖψαι ἑταίρων
κηρὸν δεψήσας μελιηδέα, μή τις ἀκούσῃ

450

"'Stubborn men, who have gone down alive to the house of Hades to meet death twice, while other men die but once. But come, eat food and drink wine here this whole day through; but at the coming of Dawn you shall set sail, and I will point out the way and declare to you each thing, in order that through wretched ill-contriving you may not suffer pain and woes either by sea or on land.'

"So she spoke, and our proud hearts consented. So then all day long till sunset we sat feasting on abundant meat and sweet wine. But when the sun set and darkness came on, they lay down to rest beside the stern cables of the ship; but Circe took me by the hand, and leading me apart from my staunch comrades, made me sit, and lay down beside me and asked me all the tale. And I told her all in due order. Then queenly Circe spoke to me and said:

"'So did all that come to pass; and now listen to what I shall tell you, and a god shall himself bring it to your mind. First you will come to the Sirens, who beguile all men who come to them. Whoever in ignorance draws near to them and hears the Sirens' voice, his wife and little children never stand beside him and rejoice at his homecoming; instead, the Sirens beguile him with their clear-toned song, as they sit in a meadow, and about them is a great heap of bones of moldering men, and round the bones the skin is shriveling. But row past them, and anoint the ears of your comrades with sweet wax, which you have kneaded, for

τῶν ἄλλων· ἀτὰρ αὐτὸς ἀκουέμεν αἴ κ᾽ ἐθέλῃσθα,
50 δησάντων σ᾽ ἐν νηὶ θοῇ χεῖράς τε πόδας τε
ὀρθὸν ἐν ἱστοπέδῃ, ἐκ δ᾽ αὐτοῦ πείρατ᾽ ἀνήφθω,
ὄφρα κε τερπόμενος ὄπ᾽ ἀκούσῃς Σειρήνοιιν.
εἰ δέ κε λίσσηαι ἑτάρους λῦσαί τε κελεύῃς,
οἱ δέ σ᾽ ἔτι πλεόνεσσι τότ᾽ ἐν δεσμοῖσι διδέντων.
55 αὐτὰρ ἐπὴν δὴ τάς γε παρὲξ ἐλάσωσιν ἑταῖροι,
ἔνθα τοι οὐκέτ᾽ ἔπειτα διηνεκέως ἀγορεύσω,
ὁπποτέρη δή τοι ὁδὸς ἔσσεται, ἀλλὰ καὶ αὐτὸς
θυμῷ βουλεύειν· ἐρέω δέ τοι ἀμφοτέρωθεν.
ἔνθεν μὲν γὰρ πέτραι ἐπηρεφέες, προτὶ δ᾽ αὐτὰς
60 κῦμα μέγα ῥοχθεῖ κυανώπιδος Ἀμφιτρίτης·
Πλαγκτὰς δή τοι τάς γε θεοὶ μάκαρες καλέουσι.
τῇ μέν τ᾽ οὐδὲ ποτητὰ παρέρχεται οὐδὲ πέλειαι
τρήρωνες, ταί τ᾽ ἀμβροσίην Διὶ πατρὶ φέρουσιν,
ἀλλά τε καὶ τῶν αἰὲν ἀφαιρεῖται λὶς πέτρη·
65 ἀλλ᾽ ἄλλην ἐνίησι πατὴρ ἐναρίθμιον εἶναι.
τῇ δ᾽ οὔ πώ τις νηῦς φύγεν ἀνδρῶν, ἥ τις ἵκηται,
ἀλλά θ᾽ ὁμοῦ πίνακάς τε νεῶν καὶ σώματα φωτῶν
κύμαθ᾽ ἁλὸς φορέουσι πυρός τ᾽ ὀλοοῖο θύελλαι.
οἴη δὴ κείνη γε παρέπλω ποντοπόρος νηῦς,
70 Ἀργὼ πᾶσι μέλουσα, παρ᾽ Αἰήταο πλέουσα.
καὶ νύ κε τὴν ἔνθ᾽ ὦκα βάλεν μεγάλας ποτὶ πέτρας,
ἀλλ᾽ Ἥρη παρέπεμψεν, ἐπεὶ φίλος ἦεν Ἰήσων.
    "'οἱ δὲ δύω σκόπελοι ὁ μὲν οὐρανὸν εὐρὺν ἱκάνει
ὀξείῃ κορυφῇ, νεφέλη δέ μιν ἀμφιβέβηκε
75 κυανέη· τὸ μὲν οὔ ποτ᾽ ἐρωεῖ, οὐδέ ποτ᾽ αἴθρη
κείνου ἔχει κορυφὴν οὔτ᾽ ἐν θέρει οὔτ᾽ ἐν ὀπώρῃ.

fear any of the rest may hear. But if you yourself have a will to listen, let them bind you in the swift ship hand and foot upright in the step of the mast, and let the ropes be made fast at the ends to the mast itself, that with delight you may listen to the voice of the two Sirens. And if you shall implore and command your comrades to free you, then let them bind you with yet more bonds. But when your comrades shall have rowed past these maidens, at that point I shall no longer tell you fully on which side your course should lie, but you must yourself decide in your own heart, and I will tell you of both ways. On the one side are beetling crags, and against them roars the great wave of dark-eyed Amphitrite; the Planctae the blessed gods call these. By that way not even winged creatures pass, not even the timorous doves that bear ambrosia to father Zeus, but the smooth rock always snatches away one even of these, but the father sends in another to make up the number. And by that way has no ship of men ever yet escaped that has come there, but the planks of ships and bodies of men are hurled confusedly by the waves of the sea and the blasts of dreadful fire. One seafaring ship alone has passed by those, that Argo famed of all, on her voyage from Aeetes, and even her the wave would speedily have dashed there against the great crags, had not Hera sent her through because Jason was dear to her.

"'Now on the other side are two cliffs, one of which reaches with its sharp peak to the broad heaven, and a dark cloud surrounds it. This never melts away, nor does clear sky ever surround the peak of this cliff in summer or in har-

οὐδέ κεν ἀμβαίη βροτὸς ἀνὴρ οὐδ' ἐπιβαίη,
οὐδ' εἴ οἱ χεῖρές τε ἐείκοσι καὶ πόδες εἶεν·
πέτρη γὰρ λίς ἐστι, περιξεστῇ ἐικυῖα.
80 μέσσῳ δ' ἐν σκοπέλῳ ἔστι σπέος ἠεροειδές,
πρὸς ζόφον εἰς Ἔρεβος τετραμμένον, ᾗ περ ἂν ὑμεῖς
νῆα παρὰ γλαφυρὴν ἰθύνετε, φαίδιμ' Ὀδυσσεῦ.
οὐδέ κεν ἐκ νηὸς γλαφυρῆς αἰζήιος ἀνὴρ
τόξῳ ὀιστεύσας κοῖλον σπέος εἰσαφίκοιτο.
85 ἔνθα δ' ἐνὶ Σκύλλη ναίει δεινὸν λελακυῖα.
τῆς ἦ τοι φωνὴ μὲν ὅση σκύλακος νεογιλῆς
γίγνεται, αὐτὴ δ' αὖτε πέλωρ κακόν· οὐδέ κέ τίς μιν
γηθήσειεν ἰδών, οὐδ' εἰ θεὸς ἀντιάσειεν.
τῆς ἦ τοι πόδες εἰσὶ δυώδεκα πάντες ἄωροι,
90 ἓξ δέ τέ οἱ δειραὶ περιμήκεες, ἐν δὲ ἑκάστῃ
σμερδαλέη κεφαλή, ἐν δὲ τρίστοιχοι ὀδόντες
πυκνοὶ καὶ θαμέες, πλεῖοι μέλανος θανάτοιο.
μέσση μέν τε κατὰ σπείους κοίλοιο δέδυκεν,
ἔξω δ' ἐξίσχει κεφαλὰς δεινοῖο βερέθρου,
95 αὐτοῦ δ' ἰχθυάᾳ, σκόπελον περιμαιμώωσα,
δελφῖνάς τε κύνας τε, καὶ εἴ ποθι μεῖζον ἕλῃσι
κῆτος, ἃ μυρία βόσκει ἀγάστονος Ἀμφιτρίτη.
τῇ δ' οὔ πώ ποτε ναῦται ἀκήριοι εὐχετόωνται
παρφυγέειν σὺν νηί· φέρει δέ τε κρατὶ ἑκάστῳ
100 φῶτ' ἐξαρπάξασα νεὸς κυανοπρώροιο.

"'τὸν δ' ἕτερον σκόπελον χθαμαλώτερον ὄψει, Ὀδυσσεῦ.
πλησίον ἀλλήλων· καί κεν διοϊστεύσειας.
τῷ δ' ἐν ἐρινεὸς ἔστι μέγας, φύλλοισι τεθηλώς·
τῷ δ' ὑπὸ δῖα Χάρυβδις ἀναρροιβδεῖ μέλαν ὕδωρ.

454

vest time. No mortal man could scale it or set foot upon the top, not though he had twenty hands and feet; for the rock is smooth, as if it were polished. And in the midst of the cliff is a dim cave, turned to the West, toward Erebus, the way by which indeed if you listen to me you shall steer your hollow ship, glorious Odysseus. Not even a man of great strength could shoot an arrow from the hollow ship so as to reach into that vaulted cave. In it dwells Scylla, yelping terribly. Her voice to be sure is only as loud as the voice of a newborn whelp, but she herself is an evil monster, nor would anyone be glad at the sight of her, not even though it should be a god that met her. She has, you must know, twelve legs, all flexible, and six necks, exceedingly long, and on each one a frightful head, and in it three rows of teeth, thick and close, full of black death. Up to her middle she is hidden in the hollow cave, but she holds her head out beyond the dread chasm, and fishes there, eagerly searching around the rock for dolphins and sea dogs and whatever greater beast she may happen to catch, such creatures as deep-moaning Amphitrite rears in multitudes past counting. By her no sailors yet may boast that they have fled unscathed in their ship, for with each head she carries off a man, snatching him from the dark-prowed ship.

"'But the other cliff, you will observe, Odysseus, is lower—they are close to each other; you could even shoot an arrow across—and on it is a large fig tree with rich foliage, but beneath this divine Charybdis sucks down the

105 τρὶς μὲν γάρ τ' ἀνίησιν ἐπ' ἤματι, τρὶς δ' ἀναροιβδεῖ
δεινόν· μὴ σύ γε κεῖθι τύχοις, ὅτε ῥοιβδήσειεν·
οὐ γάρ κεν ῥύσαιτό σ' ὑπὲκ κακοῦ οὐδ' ἐνοσίχθων.
ἀλλὰ μάλα Σκύλλης σκοπέλῳ πεπλημένος ὦκα
νῆα παρὲξ ἐλάαν, ἐπεὶ ἦ πολὺ φέρτερόν ἐστιν
110 ἓξ ἑτάρους ἐν νηὶ ποθήμεναι ἢ ἅμα πάντας.'

   "ὣς ἔφατ', αὐτὰρ ἐγώ μιν ἀμειβόμενος[1] προσέειπον·
'εἰ δ' ἄγε δή μοι τοῦτο, θεά, νημερτὲς ἐνίσπες,
εἴ πως τὴν ὀλοὴν μὲν ὑπεκπροφύγοιμι Χάρυβδιν,
τὴν δέ κ' ἀμυναίμην, ὅτε μοι σίνοιτό γ' ἑταίρους.'

115   "ὣς ἐφάμην, ἡ δ' αὐτίκ' ἀμείβετο δῖα θεάων·
'σχέτλιε, καὶ δὴ αὖ τοι πολεμήια ἔργα μέμηλε
καὶ πόνος· οὐδὲ θεοῖσιν ὑπείξεαι ἀθανάτοισιν;
ἡ δέ τοι οὐ θνητή, ἀλλ' ἀθάνατον κακόν ἐστι,
δεινόν τ' ἀργαλέον τε καὶ ἄγριον οὐδὲ μαχητόν·
120 οὐδέ τις ἔστ' ἀλκή· φυγέειν κάρτιστον ἀπ' αὐτῆς.
ἢν γὰρ δηθύνῃσθα κορυσσόμενος παρὰ πέτρῃ,
δείδω, μή σ' ἐξαῦτις ἐφορμηθεῖσα κίχῃσι
τόσσῃσιν κεφαλῇσι, τόσους δ' ἐκ φῶτας ἕληται.
ἀλλὰ μάλα σφοδρῶς ἐλάαν, βωστρεῖν δὲ Κράταιιν,
125 μητέρα τῆς Σκύλλης, ἥ μιν τέκε πῆμα βροτοῖσιν·
ἥ μιν ἔπειτ' ἀποπαύσει ἐς ὕστερον ὁρμηθῆναι.

   "'Θρινακίην δ' ἐς νῆσον ἀφίξεαι· ἔνθα δὲ πολλαὶ
βόσκοντ' Ἠελίοιο βόες καὶ ἴφια μῆλα,
ἑπτὰ βοῶν ἀγέλαι, τόσα δ' οἰῶν πώεα καλά,
130 πεντήκοντα δ' ἕκαστα. γόνος δ' οὐ γίγνεται αὐτῶν,

----

[1] ἀμειβόμενος: ἀτυζόμενος

black water. Three times a day she belches it forth, and three times she sucks it down terribly. May you not be there when she sucks it down, for no one could save you from ruin, no, not the Earth-shaker. Instead, draw very close to Scylla's cliff, and drive your ship past quickly; for it is far better to mourn six comrades in your ship than all together.'

"So she spoke, but I made answer and said: 'Come, I pray you, goddess, tell me this thing truly, if in any way I might escape from dread Charybdis, and ward off that other, when she tries to make prey of my comrades.'

"So I spoke, and the beautiful goddess answered and said: 'Stubborn man, now again is your heart set on deeds of war and on toil. Will you not yield even to the immortal gods? She is not mortal, but an immortal evil, dread, and dire, and fierce, and not to be fought with; there is no defence; the best course is to flee from her. For if you wait to arm yourself by the cliff, I fear that she may again dart forth to attack you with as many heads and seize as many men as before. Instead, row past with all your might, and call upon Crataiis, the mother of Scylla, who bore her for a plague to mortals. Then will she keep her from darting forth again.

"'And you will come to the island of Thrinacia. There in great numbers feed the cattle of Helios and his sturdy flocks, seven herds of cattle and as many fine flocks of sheep, and fifty in each. These bear no young, nor do they

457

οὐδέ ποτε φθινύθουσι. θεαὶ δ᾽ ἐπιποιμένες εἰσίν,
νύμφαι ἐυπλόκαμοι, Φαέθουσά τε Λαμπετίη τε,
ἃς τέκεν Ἠελίῳ Ὑπερίονι δῖα Νέαιρα.
τὰς μὲν ἄρα θρέψασα τεκοῦσά τε πότνια μήτηρ
135 Θρινακίην ἐς νῆσον ἀπώκισε τηλόθι ναίειν,
μῆλα φυλασσέμεναι πατρώια καὶ ἕλικας βοῦς.
τὰς εἰ μέν κ᾽ ἀσινέας ἐάᾳς νόστου τε μέδηαι,
ἦ τ᾽ ἂν ἔτ᾽ εἰς Ἰθάκην κακά περ πάσχοντες ἵκοισθε·
εἰ δέ κε σίνηαι, τότε τοι τεκμαίρομ᾽ ὄλεθρον,
140 νηί τε καὶ ἑτάροις· αὐτὸς δ᾽ εἴ πέρ κεν ἀλύξῃς,
ὀψὲ κακῶς νεῖαι, ὀλέσας ἄπο πάντας ἑταίρους.᾽
    "ὣς ἔφατ᾽, αὐτίκα δὲ χρυσόθρονος ἤλυθεν Ἠώς.
ἡ μὲν ἔπειτ᾽ ἀνὰ νῆσον ἀπέστιχε δῖα θεάων·
αὐτὰρ ἐγὼν ἐπὶ νῆα κιὼν ὤτρυνον ἑταίρους
145 αὐτούς τ᾽ ἀμβαίνειν ἀνά τε πρυμνήσια λῦσαι·
οἱ δ᾽ αἶψ᾽ εἴσβαινον καὶ ἐπὶ κληῖσι καθῖζον.
ἑξῆς δ᾽ ἑζόμενοι πολιὴν ἅλα τύπτον ἐρετμοῖς.[1]
ἡμῖν δ᾽ αὖ κατόπισθε νεὸς κυανοπρώροιο
ἴκμενον οὖρον ἵει πλησίστιον, ἐσθλὸν ἑταῖρον,
150 Κίρκη ἐυπλόκαμος, δεινὴ θεὸς αὐδήεσσα.
αὐτίκα δ᾽ ὅπλα ἕκαστα πονησάμενοι κατὰ νῆα
ἥμεθα· τὴν δ᾽ ἄνεμός τε κυβερνήτης τ᾽ ἴθυνε.
    "δὴ τότ᾽ ἐγὼν ἑτάροισι μετηύδων ἀχνύμενος κῆρ·
'ὦ φίλοι, οὐ γὰρ χρὴ ἕνα ἴδμεναι οὐδὲ δύ᾽ οἴους
155 θέσφαθ᾽ ἅ μοι Κίρκη μυθήσατο, δῖα θεάων·
ἀλλ᾽ ἐρέω μὲν ἐγών, ἵνα εἰδότες ἤ κε θάνωμεν
ἤ κεν ἀλευάμενοι θάνατον καὶ κῆρα φύγοιμεν.
Σειρήνων μὲν πρῶτον ἀνώγει θεσπεσιάων

ever die, and goddesses are their shepherds, fair-tressed
nymphs, Phaethusa and Lampetie, whom beautiful Neaera
bore to Helios Hyperion. These their honored mother,
when she had borne and reared them, sent to the island of
Thrinacia to dwell afar, and keep the flocks of their father
and his spiral-horned cattle. If you leave these unharmed
and are careful of your homeward way, indeed you may yet
reach Ithaca, though in distress. But if you harm them,
then I foretell ruin for your ship and for your comrades,
and even if you shall yourself escape, late shall you come
home, and in distress, after losing all your comrades.'

"So she spoke, and at once came golden-throned Dawn.
Then the beautiful goddess departed up the island, but I
went to the ship and roused my comrades themselves to
embark and to loose the stern cables. So they went on
board quickly and sat down upon the benches, and sitting
well in order struck the gray sea with their oars. And for
our aid in the wake of our dark-prowed ship a fair wind that
filled the sail, a good comrade, was sent by fair-tressed
Circe, dread goddess of human speech. So when we had
quickly made fast all the tackling throughout the ship we
sat down, and the wind and the helmsman guided the ship.

"Then at last I spoke among my comrades, grieved at
heart: 'Friends, since it is not right that one or two alone
should know the oracles that Circe, the beautiful goddess,
told me, instead I will tell them, in order that knowing
them we may either die, or, shunning death and fate,
escape. First she bade us avoid the voice of the wondrous

---

[1] Line 147 is omitted in most MSS.

φθόγγον ἀλεύασθαι καὶ λειμῶν' ἀνθεμόεντα.
160 οἶον ἔμ' ἠνώγει ὄπ' ἀκουέμεν· ἀλλά με δεσμῷ
δήσατ' ἐν ἀργαλέῳ, ὄφρ' ἔμπεδον αὐτόθι μίμνω,
ὀρθὸν ἐν ἱστοπέδῃ, ἐκ δ' αὐτοῦ πείρατ' ἀνήφθω.
εἰ δέ κε λίσσωμαι ὑμέας λῦσαί τε κελεύω,
ὑμεῖς δὲ πλεόνεσσι τότ' ἐν δεσμοῖσι πιέζειν.'
165   "ἦ τοι ἐγὼ τὰ ἕκαστα λέγων ἑτάροισι πίφαυσκον·
τόφρα δὲ καρπαλίμως ἐξίκετο νηῦς ἐυεργὴς
νῆσον Σειρήνοιιν· ἔπειγε γὰρ οὖρος ἀπήμων.
αὐτίκ' ἔπειτ' ἄνεμος μὲν ἐπαύσατο ἠδὲ γαλήνη
ἔπλετο νηνεμίη, κοίμησε δὲ κύματα δαίμων.
170 ἀνστάντες δ' ἕταροι νεὸς ἱστία μηρύσαντο
καὶ τὰ μὲν ἐν νηὶ γλαφυρῇ θέσαν,[1] οἱ δ' ἐπ' ἐρετμὰ
ἑζόμενοι λεύκαινον ὕδωρ ξεστῇς ἐλάτῃσιν.
αὐτὰρ ἐγὼ κηροῖο μέγαν τροχὸν ὀξέι χαλκῷ
τυτθὰ διατμήξας χερσὶ στιβαρῇσι πίεζον·
175 αἶψα δ' ἰαίνετο κηρός, ἐπεὶ κέλετο μεγάλη ἲς
Ἠελίου τ' αὐγὴ Ὑπεριονίδαο ἄνακτος·
ἑξείης δ' ἑτάροισιν ἐπ' οὔατα πᾶσιν ἄλειψα.
οἱ δ' ἐν νηί μ' ἔδησαν ὁμοῦ χεῖράς τε πόδας τε
ὀρθὸν ἐν ἱστοπέδῃ, ἐκ δ' αὐτοῦ πείρατ' ἀνῆπτον·
180 αὐτοὶ δ' ἑζόμενοι πολιὴν ἅλα τύπτον ἐρετμοῖς.
ἀλλ' ὅτε τόσσον ἀπῆμεν ὅσον[2] τε γέγωνε βοήσας,
ῥίμφα διώκοντες, τὰς δ' οὐ λάθεν ὠκύαλος νηῦς
ἐγγύθεν ὀρνυμένη, λιγυρὴν δ' ἔντυνον ἀοιδήν·
   "'δεῦρ' ἄγ' ἰών, πολύαιν' Ὀδυσεῦ, μέγα κῦδος Ἀχαιῶν,
185 νῆα κατάστησον, ἵνα νωιτέρην ὄπ' ἀκούσῃς.
οὐ γάρ πώ τις τῇδε παρήλασε νηὶ μελαίνῃ,

Sirens, and their flowery meadows. Me alone she bade
listen to their voice; instead, you must bind me with harsh
bonds, that I may remain fast where I am, upright in the
step of the mast, and let the ropes be made fast at the ends
to the mast itself; and if I implore and command you to
free me, then tie me fast with still more bonds.'

"I did, you must know, rehearse all these things and tell
them to my comrades. Meanwhile the well-built ship
speedily came to the island of the two Sirens, for a fair and
gentle wind bore her on. Then quickly the wind ceased
and there was a windless calm, and a god lulled the waves
to sleep. My comrades stood up and furled the sail and
stowed it in the hollow ship, whereupon, sitting at the oars,
they made the water white with their polished oars of pine.
But I with my sharp sword cut into small bits a great round
cake of wax, and kneaded it with my strong hands, and soon
the wax grew warm at the bidding of the strong pressure
and the rays of the lord Helios Hyperion. Then I anointed
with this the ears of all my comrades in turn; and they
bound me in the ship hand and foot, upright in the step of
the mast, and made the ropes fast at the ends to the mast
itself, and themselves sitting down struck the gray sea with
their oars. But when we were as far distant as a man can
make himself heard when he shouts, driving swiftly on our
way, the Sirens failed not to note the swift ship as it drew
near, and they raised their clear-toned song:

"'Come hither on your way, renowned Odysseus, great
glory of the Achaeans; stop your ship that you may listen to
the voice of us two. For never yet has any man rowed past

---

[1] θέσαν: βάλον
[2] ἀπῆμεν ὅσον: ἀπῆν ὅσσον

461

πρίν γ' ἡμέων μελίγηρυν ἀπὸ στομάτων ὄπ' ἀκοῦσαι,
ἀλλ' ὅ γε τερψάμενος νεῖται καὶ πλείονα εἰδώς.
ἴδμεν γάρ τοι πάνθ' ὅσ' ἐνὶ Τροίῃ εὐρείῃ

190　Ἀργεῖοι Τρῶές τε θεῶν ἰότητι μόγησαν,
ἴδμεν δ', ὅσσα γένηται ἐπὶ χθονὶ πουλυβοτείρῃ.'

"ὣς φάσαν ἱεῖσαι ὄπα κάλλιμον· αὐτὰρ ἐμὸν κῆρ
ἤθελ' ἀκουέμεναι, λῦσαί τ' ἐκέλευον ἑταίρους
ὀφρύσι νευστάζων· οἱ δὲ προπεσόντες ἔρεσσον.

195　αὐτίκα δ' ἀνστάντες Περιμήδης Εὐρύλοχός τε
πλείοσί μ' ἐν δεσμοῖσι δέον μᾶλλόν τε πίεζον.
αὐτὰρ ἐπεὶ δὴ τάς γε παρήλασαν, οὐδ' ἔτ' ἔπειτα
φθογγῆς Σειρήνων ἠκούομεν οὐδέ τ' ἀοιδῆς,
αἶψ' ἀπὸ κηρὸν ἕλοντο ἐμοὶ ἐρίηρες ἑταῖροι,

200　ὅν σφιν ἐπ' ὠσὶν ἄλειψ', ἐμέ τ' ἐκ δεσμῶν ἀνέλυσαν.

"ἀλλ' ὅτε δὴ τὴν νῆσον ἐλείπομεν, αὐτίκ' ἔπειτα
καπνὸν καὶ μέγα κῦμα ἴδον καὶ δοῦπον ἄκουσα.
τῶν δ' ἄρα δεισάντων ἐκ χειρῶν ἔπτατ' ἐρετμά,
βόμβησαν δ' ἄρα πάντα κατὰ ρόον· ἔσχετο δ' αὐτοῦ

205　νηῦς, ἐπεὶ οὐκέτ' ἐρετμὰ προήκεα χερσὶν ἔπειγον.
αὐτὰρ ἐγὼ διὰ νηὸς ἰὼν ὤτρυνον ἑταίρους
μειλιχίοις ἐπέεσσι παρασταδὸν ἄνδρα ἕκαστον·

"'ὦ φίλοι, οὐ γάρ πώ τι κακῶν ἀδαήμονές εἰμεν·
οὐ μὲν δὴ τόδε μεῖζον ἔπει[1] κακόν, ἢ ὅτε Κύκλωψ

210　εἴλει ἐνὶ σπῆι γλαφυρῷ κρατερῆφι βίηφιν·
ἀλλὰ καὶ ἔνθεν ἐμῇ ἀρετῇ, βουλῇ τε νόῳ τε,
ἐκφύγομεν, καί που τῶνδε μνήσεσθαι ὀίω.

[1] ἔπει: ἔπι: ἔχει Zenodotus

the island in his black ship until he has heard the sweet voice from our lips; instead, he has joy of it, and goes his way a wiser man. For we know all the toils that in wide Troy the Argives and Trojans endured through the will of the gods, and we know all things that come to pass upon the fruitful earth.'

"So they spoke, sending forth their beautiful voice, and my heart desired to listen, and I commanded my comrades to free me, nodding to them with my brows; but they fell to their oars and rowed on. At once Perimedes and Eurylochus arose and bound me with yet more bonds and drew them tighter. But when they had rowed past the Sirens, and we could no longer hear their voice or their song, then quickly my trusty comrades took away the wax with which I had anointed their ears and freed me from my bonds.

"But when we had left the island, I soon saw smoke and a great billow, and heard a booming. Then from the hands of my men in their terror the oars flew, and splashed one and all in the swirl, and the ship stood still where it was, when they no longer plied with their hands the tapering oars. But I went through the ship and cheered my men with winning words, coming up to each man in turn:

"'Friends, hitherto we have been not at all ignorant of sorrow; surely this evil that besets us now is no greater than when the Cyclops penned us in his hollow cave by brutal strength; yet even from there we made our escape through my valor and counsel and wit; these dangers, too, I think, we shall some day remember. But now come, as I bid, let

νῦν δ' ἄγεθ', ὡς ἂν ἐγὼ εἴπω, πειθώμεθα πάντες.
ὑμεῖς μὲν κώπῃσιν ἁλὸς ῥηγμῖνα βαθεῖαν
215 τύπτετε κληΐδεσσιν ἐφήμενοι, αἴ κέ ποθι Ζεὺς
δώῃ τόνδε γ' ὄλεθρον ὑπεκφυγέειν καὶ ἀλύξαι·
σοὶ δέ, κυβερνῆθ', ὧδ' ἐπιτέλλομαι· ἀλλ' ἐνὶ θυμῷ
βάλλευ, ἐπεὶ νηὸς γλαφυρῆς οἰήϊα νωμᾷς.
τούτου μὲν καπνοῦ καὶ κύματος ἐκτὸς ἔεργε
220 νῆα, σὺ δὲ σκοπέλου ἐπιμαίεο, μή σε λάθῃσι
κεῖσ' ἐξορμήσασα καὶ ἐς κακὸν ἄμμε βάλῃσθα.'
    "ὣς ἐφάμην, οἱ δ' ὦκα ἐμοῖς ἐπέεσσι πίθοντο.
Σκύλλην δ' οὐκέτ' ἐμυθεόμην, ἄπρηκτον ἀνίην,
μή πώς μοι δείσαντες ἀπολλήξειαν ἑταῖροι
225 εἰρεσίης, ἐντὸς δὲ πυκάζοιεν σφέας αὐτούς.
καὶ τότε δὴ Κίρκης μὲν ἐφημοσύνης ἀλεγεινῆς
λανθανόμην, ἐπεὶ οὔ τί μ' ἀνώγει θωρήσσεσθαι·
αὐτὰρ ἐγὼ καταδὺς κλυτὰ τεύχεα καὶ δύο δοῦρε
μάκρ' ἐν χερσὶν ἑλὼν εἰς ἴκρια νηὸς ἔβαινον
230 πρῴρης· ἔνθεν γάρ μιν ἐδέγμην πρῶτα φανεῖσθαι
Σκύλλην πετραίην, ἥ μοι φέρε πῆμ' ἑτάροισιν.
οὐδέ πῃ ἀθρῆσαι δυνάμην, ἔκαμον δέ μοι ὄσσε
πάντῃ παπταίνοντι πρὸς ἠεροειδέα πέτρην.
    "ἡμεῖς μὲν στεινωπὸν ἀνεπλέομεν γοόωντες·
235 ἔνθεν μὲν Σκύλλη, ἑτέρωθι δὲ δῖα Χάρυβδις
δεινὸν ἀνερροίβδησε θαλάσσης ἁλμυρὸν ὕδωρ.
ἦ τοι ὅτ' ἐξεμέσειε, λέβης ὣς ἐν πυρὶ πολλῷ
πᾶσ' ἀναμορμύρεσκε κυκωμένη, ὑψόσε δ' ἄχνη
ἄκροισι σκοπέλοισιν ἐπ' ἀμφοτέροισιν ἔπιπτεν·
240 ἀλλ' ὅτ' ἀναβρόξειε θαλάσσης ἁλμυρὸν ὕδωρ,

us all obey. Keep your seats on the benches and strike with your oars the deep surf of the sea, in the hope that Zeus may grant us to escape and avoid this death. And to you, steersman, I give this command, and be sure you lay it to heart, since you wield the steering oar of the hollow ship. From this smoke and surf keep the ship well away, and hug the cliff, for fear that before you know it, the ship swerve off to the other side and you throw us into destruction.'

"So I spoke, and they swiftly hearkened to my words. But of Scylla I did not go on to speak, an unpreventable disaster, for fear that my comrades, seized with terror, should cease from rowing and huddle together in the hold. Then it was that I forgot the hard command of Circe, who bade me under no circumstances to arm myself; but when I had put on my glorious armor and grasped in my hand two long spears, I went to the foredeck of the ship, from where I expected that Scylla of the rock would first be seen, who was to bring ruin to my comrades. But nowhere could I descry her, and my eyes grew weary as I gazed everywhere toward the misty rock.

"We then sailed on up the narrow strait with wailing. For on one side lay Scylla and on the other divine Charybdis terribly sucked down the salt water of the sea. Indeed whenever she belched it forth, like a cauldron on a great fire she would seethe and bubble in utter turmoil, and high over head the spray would fall on the tops of both the cliffs. But as often as she sucked down the salt water of

πᾶσ' ἔντοσθε φάνεσκε κυκωμένη, ἀμφὶ δὲ πέτρη
δεινὸν ἐβεβρύχει, ὑπένερθε δὲ γαῖα φάνεσκε
ψάμμῳ κυανέη· τοὺς δὲ χλωρὸν δέος ᾕρει.
ἡμεῖς μὲν πρὸς τὴν ἴδομεν δείσαντες ὄλεθρον·

245 τόφρα δέ μοι Σκύλλη γλαφυρῆς ἐκ νηὸς ἑταίρους
ἓξ ἕλεθ', οἳ χερσίν τε βίηφί τε φέρτατοι ἦσαν.
σκεψάμενος δ' ἐς νῆα θοὴν ἅμα καὶ μεθ' ἑταίρους
ἤδη τῶν ἐνόησα πόδας καὶ χεῖρας ὕπερθεν
ὑψόσ' ἀειρομένων· ἐμὲ δὲ φθέγγοντο καλεῦντες

250 ἐξονομακλήδην, τότε γ' ὕστατον, ἀχνύμενοι κῆρ.
ὡς δ' ὅτ' ἐπὶ προβόλῳ ἁλιεὺς περιμήκεϊ ῥάβδῳ
ἰχθύσι τοῖς ὀλίγοισι δόλον κατὰ εἴδατα βάλλων
ἐς πόντον προΐησι βοὸς κέρας ἀγραύλοιο,
ἀσπαίροντα δ' ἔπειτα λαβὼν ἔρριψε θύραζε,

255 ὣς οἵ γ' ἀσπαίροντες ἀείροντο προτὶ πέτρας·
αὐτοῦ δ' εἰνὶ θύρῃσι κατήσθιε κεκληγῶτας
χεῖρας ἐμοὶ ὀρέγοντας ἐν αἰνῇ δηϊοτῆτι·
οἴκτιστον δὴ κεῖνο ἐμοῖς ἴδον ὀφθαλμοῖσι
πάντων, ὅσσ' ἐμόγησα πόρους ἁλὸς ἐξερεείνων.

260 "αὐτὰρ ἐπεὶ πέτρας φύγομεν δεινήν τε Χάρυβδιν
Σκύλλην τ', αὐτίκ' ἔπειτα θεοῦ ἐς ἀμύμονα νῆσον
ἱκόμεθ'· ἔνθα δ' ἔσαν καλαὶ βόες εὐρυμέτωποι,
πολλὰ δὲ ἴφια μῆλ' Ὑπερίονος Ἠελίοιο.
δὴ τότ' ἐγὼν ἔτι πόντῳ ἐὼν ἐν νηῒ μελαίνῃ

265 μυκηθμοῦ τ' ἤκουσα βοῶν αὐλιζομενάων
οἰῶν τε βληχήν· καί μοι ἔπος ἔμπεσε θυμῷ
μάντηος ἀλαοῦ, Θηβαίου Τειρεσίαο,
Κίρκης τ' Αἰαίης, ἥ μοι μάλα πόλλ' ἐπέτελλε

the sea, within she could all be seen in utter turmoil, and round about, the rock roared terribly, while beneath, the earth appeared, black with sand; and pale fear seized my men. So we looked toward her and feared destruction; but meanwhile Scylla seized from out the hollow ship six of my comrades who were the best in strength and in might. Turning my eyes to the swift ship and to the company of my men, even then I noted above me their feet and hands as they were raised aloft. To me they cried aloud, calling upon me by name for that last time in anguish of heart. And as a fisherman on a jutting rock, when he casts in his bait as a snare to the little fishes, with his long pole lets down into the sea the horn of a field-dwelling ox, and then as he catches a fish flings it writhing ashore, even so were they drawn writhing up toward the cliffs. Then at her doors she devoured them shrieking and stretching out their hands toward me in their awful death struggle. Most piteous did my eyes behold that thing of all that I bore while I explored the paths of the sea.

"Now when we had escaped the rocks, and dread Charybdis and Scylla, soon then we came to the perfect island of the god, where were the fine cattle, broad of brow, and the many sturdy flocks of Helios Hyperion. Then while I was still out at sea in my black ship, I heard the lowing of the cattle that were being stalled and the bleating of the sheep, and upon my mind fell the words of the blind seer, Theban Teiresias, and of Aeaean Circe, who most strictly charged

νῆσον ἀλεύασθαι τερψιμβρότου Ἠελίοιο.
270　δὴ τότ' ἐγὼν ἑτάροισι μετηύδων ἀχνύμενος κῆρ·
　　"'κέκλυτέ μευ μύθων κακά περ πάσχοντες ἑταῖροι,
ὄφρ' ὑμῖν εἴπω μαντήια Τειρεσίαο
Κίρκης τ' Αἰαίης, ἥ μοι μάλα πόλλ' ἐπέτελλε
νῆσον ἀλεύασθαι τερψιμβρότου Ἠελίοιο·
275　ἔνθα γὰρ αἰνότατον κακὸν ἔμμεναι ἄμμιν ἔφασκεν.
ἀλλὰ παρὲξ τὴν νῆσον ἐλαύνετε νῆα μέλαιναν.'
　　"ὣς ἐφάμην, τοῖσιν δὲ κατεκλάσθη φίλον ἦτορ.
αὐτίκα δ' Εὐρύλοχος στυγερῷ μ' ἠμείβετο μύθῳ·
　　"'σχέτλιός εἰς, Ὀδυσεῦ· περί τοι μένος, οὐδέ τι γυῖα
280　κάμνεις· ἦ ῥά νυ σοί γε σιδήρεα πάντα τέτυκται,
ὅς ῥ' ἑτάρους καμάτῳ ἀδηκότας ἠδὲ καὶ ὕπνῳ
οὐκ ἐάᾳς γαίης ἐπιβήμεναι, ἔνθα κεν αὖτε
νήσῳ ἐν ἀμφιρύτῃ λαρὸν τετυκοίμεθα δόρπον,
ἀλλ' αὔτως διὰ νύκτα θοὴν ἀλάλησθαι ἄνωγας
285　νήσου ἀποπλαγχθέντας ἐν ἠεροειδέι πόντῳ.
ἐκ νυκτῶν δ' ἄνεμοι χαλεποί, δηλήματα νηῶν,
γίγνονται· πῇ κέν τις ὑπεκφύγοι αἰπὺν ὄλεθρον,
ἤν πως ἐξαπίνης ἔλθῃ ἀνέμοιο θύελλα,
ἢ Νότου ἢ Ζεφύροιο δυσαέος, οἵ τε μάλιστα
290　νῆα διαρραίουσι θεῶν ἀέκητι ἀνάκτων.
ἀλλ' ἦ τοι νῦν μὲν πειθώμεθα νυκτὶ μελαίνῃ
δόρπον θ' ὁπλισόμεσθα θοῇ παρὰ νηὶ μένοντες,
ἠῶθεν δ' ἀναβάντες ἐνήσομεν εὐρέι πόντῳ.'
　　"ὣς ἔφατ' Εὐρύλοχος, ἐπὶ δ' ᾔνεον ἄλλοι ἑταῖροι.
295　καὶ τότε δὴ γίγνωσκον ὃ δὴ κακὰ μήδετο δαίμων,
καί μιν φωνήσας ἔπεα πτερόεντα προσηύδων·

me to shun the island of Helios, who gives joy to mortals.
Then indeed I spoke among my comrades, grieved at
heart:

"'Hear my words, comrades, for all your distress, that I
may tell you of the oracles of Teiresias and of Aeaean
Circe, who most strictly charged me to shun the island of
Helios, who gives joy to mortals; for there, she said, was
our most terrible danger. No, row the black ship out past
the island.'

"So I spoke, and their spirit was broken within them,
and at once Eurylochus answered me with words of doom:

"'You are stubborn, Odysseus; you have strength
beyond that of other men and your limbs never grow
weary. Indeed you are wholly made of iron, seeing that
you do not allow your comrades, worn out with toil and lack
of sleep, to set foot on shore, where on this seagirt island
we might once more make ready a savory supper; instead
you bid us even as we are to wander on through the swift
night, driven away from the island over the misty deep. It
is from the night that fierce winds are born, wreckers of
ships. How could one escape utter destruction, if per-
chance there should suddenly come a blast of the South
Wind or the blustering West Wind, which oftenest wreck
ships in despite of the sovereign gods? No, by all means.
For the present let us yield to black night and make ready
our supper, remaining by the swift ship, and in the morn-
ing we will go aboard, and put out into the broad sea.'

"So spoke Eurylochus, and the rest of my comrades
gave assent. Then it was that I realized that some god was
assuredly devising ill, and I spoke and addressed him with
winged words:

"'Εὐρύλοχ', ἦ μάλα δή με βιάζετε μοῦνον ἐόντα.
ἀλλ' ἄγε νῦν μοι πάντες ὀμόσσατε καρτερὸν ὅρκον·
εἴ κέ τιν' ἠὲ βοῶν ἀγέλην ἢ πῶυ μέγ' οἰῶν
300   εὕρωμεν, μή πού τις ἀτασθαλίῃσι κακῇσιν
ἢ βοῦν ἠέ τι μῆλον ἀποκτάνῃ· ἀλλὰ ἕκηλοι
ἐσθίετε βρώμην, τὴν ἀθανάτη πόρε Κίρκη.'
"ὣς ἐφάμην, οἱ δ' αὐτίκ' ἀπώμνυον, ὡς ἐκέλευον.
αὐτὰρ ἐπεί ῥ' ὄμοσάν τε τελεύτησάν τε τὸν ὅρκον,
305   στήσαμεν ἐν λιμένι γλαφυρῷ ἐυεργέα νῆα
ἄγχ' ὕδατος γλυκεροῖο, καὶ ἐξαπέβησαν ἑταῖροι
νηός, ἔπειτα δὲ δόρπον ἐπισταμένως τετύκοντο.
αὐτὰρ ἐπεὶ πόσιος καὶ ἐδητύος ἐξ ἔρον ἕντο,
μνησάμενοι δὴ ἔπειτα φίλους ἔκλαιον ἑταίρους,
310   οὓς ἔφαγε Σκύλλη γλαφυρῆς ἐκ νηὸς ἑλοῦσα·
κλαιόντεσσι δὲ τοῖσιν ἐπήλυθε νήδυμος ὕπνος.
ἦμος δὲ τρίχα νυκτὸς ἔην, μετὰ δ' ἄστρα βεβήκει,
ὦρσεν ἔπι ζαῆν ἄνεμον νεφεληγερέτα Ζεὺς
λαίλαπι θεσπεσίῃ, σὺν δὲ νεφέεσσι κάλυψε
315   γαῖαν ὁμοῦ καὶ πόντον· ὀρώρει δ' οὐρανόθεν νύξ.
ἦμος δ' ἠριγένεια φάνη ῥοδοδάκτυλος Ἠώς,
νῆα μὲν ὡρμίσαμεν κοῖλον σπέος εἰσερύσαντες.
ἔνθα δ' ἔσαν νυμφέων καλοὶ χοροὶ ἠδὲ θόωκοι·
καὶ τότ' ἐγὼν ἀγορὴν θέμενος μετὰ μῦθον[1] ἔειπον·
320   "'ὦ φίλοι, ἐν γὰρ νηὶ θοῇ βρῶσίς τε πόσις τε
ἔστιν, τῶν δὲ βοῶν ἀπεχώμεθα, μή τι πάθωμεν·
δεινοῦ γὰρ θεοῦ αἵδε βόες καὶ ἴφια μῆλα,
Ἠελίου, ὃς πάντ' ἐφορᾷ καὶ πάντ' ἐπακούει.'

470

"'Eurylochus, certainly you all constrain me, who stand alone. But come now, all of you swear me a mighty oath: that if perchance we find a herd of cattle or a great flock of sheep, no man will slay either cow or sheep in the blind folly of his mind; instead, be content to eat the food which immortal Circe gave.'

"So I spoke, and they at once swore that they would not, as I ordered them.[1] But when they had sworn and made an end of the oath, we moored our well-built ship in the hollow harbor near a spring of sweet water, and my comrades disembarked from the ship and skillfully made ready their supper. But when they had put from them the desire of food and drink, then they fell to weeping, as they remembered their dear comrades whom Scylla had snatched out of the hollow ship and devoured; and sweet sleep came upon them as they wept. But when it was the third watch of the night, and the stars had turned their course, Zeus, the cloud-gatherer, roused against us a fierce wind with a wondrous tempest, and hid with clouds the land and sea alike, and night rushed down from heaven. And as soon as Dawn appeared, the rosy-fingered, we dragged our ship, and made her fast in a hollow cave, where were the lovely dancing places and seats of the nymphs. Then I called my men together and spoke among them:

"'Friends, in our swift ship is meat and drink; let us therefore keep our hands from those cattle for fear we come to harm, for these are the cows and sturdy sheep of a dread god, of Helios, who sees all things and hears all things.'

---

[1] μῦθον: πᾶσιν

"ὣς ἐφάμην, τοῖσιν δ' ἐπεπείθετο θυμὸς ἀγήνωρ.

325 μῆνα δὲ πάντ' ἄλληκτος ἄη Νότος, οὐδέ τις ἄλλος
γίγνετ' ἔπειτ' ἀνέμων εἰ μὴ Εὖρός τε Νότος τε.

"οἱ δ' ἧος μὲν σῖτον ἔχον καὶ οἶνον ἐρυθρόν,
τόφρα βοῶν ἀπέχοντο λιλαιόμενοι βιότοιο.
ἀλλ' ὅτε δὴ νηὸς ἐξέφθιτο ἤια πάντα,

330 καὶ δὴ ἄγρην ἐφέπεσκον ἀλητεύοντες ἀνάγκῃ,
ἰχθῦς ὄρνιθάς τε, φίλας ὅ τι χεῖρας ἵκοιτο,
γναμπτοῖς ἀγκίστροισιν, ἔτειρε δὲ γαστέρα λιμός·
δὴ τότ' ἐγὼν ἀνὰ νῆσον ἀπέστιχον, ὄφρα θεοῖσιν
εὐξαίμην, εἴ τίς μοι ὁδὸν φήνειε νέεσθαι.

335 ἀλλ' ὅτε δὴ διὰ νήσου ἰὼν ἤλυξα ἑταίρους,
χεῖρας νιψάμενος, ὅθ' ἐπὶ σκέπας ἦν ἀνέμοιο,
ἠρώμην πάντεσσι θεοῖς οἳ Ὄλυμπον ἔχουσιν·
οἱ δ' ἄρα μοι γλυκὺν ὕπνον ἐπὶ βλεφάροισιν ἔχευαν.
Εὐρύλοχος δ' ἑτάροισι κακῆς ἐξήρχετο βουλῆς·

340 "'κέκλυτέ μευ μύθων κακά περ πάσχοντες ἑταῖροι.
πάντες μὲν στυγεροὶ θάνατοι δειλοῖσι βροτοῖσι,
λιμῷ δ' οἴκτιστον θανέειν καὶ πότμον ἐπισπεῖν.
ἀλλ' ἄγετ', Ἠελίοιο βοῶν ἐλάσαντες ἀρίστας
ῥέξομεν ἀθανάτοισι, τοὶ οὐρανὸν εὐρὺν ἔχουσιν.

345 εἰ δέ κεν εἰς Ἰθάκην ἀφικοίμεθα, πατρίδα γαῖαν,
αἶψά κεν Ἠελίῳ Ὑπερίονι πίονα νηὸν
τεύξομεν, ἐν δέ κε θεῖμεν ἀγάλματα πολλὰ καὶ ἐσθλά.
εἰ δὲ χολωσάμενός τι βοῶν ὀρθοκραιράων
νῆ' ἐθέλῃ ὀλέσαι, ἐπὶ δ' ἕσπωνται θεοὶ ἄλλοι,

350 βούλομ' ἅπαξ πρὸς κῦμα χανὼν ἀπὸ θυμὸν ὀλέσσαι,
ἢ δηθὰ στρεύγεσθαι ἐὼν ἐν νήσῳ ἐρήμῃ.'

"So I spoke, and their proud hearts consented. Then for a full month the South Wind blew unceasingly, nor did any other wind arise except the East and the South.

"Now so long as my men had grain and red wine they kept their hands from the cattle, for they were anxious to save their lives. But when all the stores had been consumed out of the ship, and now they must roam about in search of game, fishes, and fowl, and whatever might come to their hands—fishing with bent hooks, for hunger pinched their bellies—then I went apart up the island that I might pray to the gods in the hope that one of them might show me a way to go. And when, as I went through the island, I had got away from my comrades, I washed my hands in a place where there was shelter from the wind, and prayed to all the gods that hold Olympus; but all they did was to shed sweet sleep upon my eyelids. And meanwhile Eurylochus began to give evil counsel to my comrades:

"'Hear my words, comrades, for all your distress. All forms of death are hateful to wretched mortals, but to die of hunger, and so meet one's doom, is the most pitiful. Instead, come, let us drive off the best of the cattle of Helios and offer sacrifice to the immortals who hold broad heaven. And if we ever reach Ithaca, our native land, we will at once build a rich temple to Helios Hyperion and put in it many choice offerings. And if perchance he be at all angry because of his straight-horned cattle, and wish to destroy our ship, and the other gods consent, I would rather lose my life once for all with a gulp at the wave, than pine slowly away in a desert island.'

“ὣς ἔφατ' Εὐρύλοχος, ἐπὶ δ' ᾔνεον ἄλλοι ἑταῖροι.
αὐτίκα δ' Ἠελίοιο βοῶν ἐλάσαντες ἀρίστας
ἐγγύθεν, οὐ γὰρ τῆλε νεὸς κυανοπρώροιο
355 βοσκέσκονθ' ἕλικες καλαὶ βόες εὐρυμέτωποι·
τὰς δὲ περίστησάν τε[1] καὶ εὐχετόωντο θεοῖσιν,
φύλλα δρεψάμενοι τέρενα δρυὸς ὑψικόμοιο·
οὐ γὰρ ἔχον κρῖ λευκὸν ἐϋσσέλμου ἐπὶ νηός.
αὐτὰρ ἐπεί ῥ' εὔξαντο καὶ ἔσφαξαν καὶ ἔδειραν,
360 μηρούς τ' ἐξέταμον κατά τε κνίσῃ ἐκάλυψαν
δίπτυχα ποιήσαντες, ἐπ' αὐτῶν δ' ὠμοθέτησαν.
οὐδ' εἶχον μέθυ λεῖψαι ἐπ' αἰθομένοις ἱεροῖσιν,
ἀλλ' ὕδατι σπένδοντες ἐπώπτων ἔγκατα πάντα.
αὐτὰρ ἐπεὶ κατὰ μῆρ' ἐκάη καὶ σπλάγχνα πάσαντο,
365 μίστυλλόν τ' ἄρα τἆλλα καὶ ἀμφ' ὀβελοῖσιν ἔπειραν.
καὶ τότε μοι βλεφάρων ἐξέσσυτο νήδυμος ὕπνος,
βῆν δ' ἰέναι ἐπὶ νῆα θοὴν καὶ θῖνα θαλάσσης.
ἀλλ' ὅτε δὴ σχεδὸν ἦα κιὼν νεὸς ἀμφιελίσσης,
καὶ τότε με κνίσης ἀμφήλυθεν ἡδὺς ἀϋτμή.
370 οἰμώξας δὲ θεοῖσι μέγ'[2] ἀθανάτοισι γεγώνευν·

“'Ζεῦ πάτερ ἠδ' ἄλλοι μάκαρες θεοὶ αἰὲν ἐόντες,
ἦ με μάλ' εἰς ἄτην κοιμήσατε νηλέϊ ὕπνῳ.
οἱ δ' ἕταροι μέγα ἔργον ἐμητίσαντο μένοντες.'

“ὠκέα δ' Ἠελίῳ “Υπερίονι ἄγγελος ἦλθε
375 Λαμπετίη τανύπεπλος, ὅ οἱ βόας ἔκταμεν ἡμεῖς.
αὐτίκα δ' ἀθανάτοισι μετηύδα χωόμενος κῆρ·

---

[1] περίστησάν τε Bekker: περιστήσαντο MSS
[2] μέγ' Bekker: μετ' MSS

"So spoke Eurylochus, and the rest of my comrades gave assent. At once they drove off the best of the cattle of Helios from near at hand, for not far from the dark-prowed ship were grazing the pretty, spiral-horned cattle, broad of brow. Around these, then, they stood and made prayer to the gods, plucking the tender leaves from off a high-crested oak; for they had no white barley[a] on board the well-benched ship. Now when they had prayed and had cut the throats of the cattle and flayed them, they cut out the thigh pieces and covered them with a double layer of fat and laid the raw bits[b] upon them. They had no wine to pour over the blazing sacrifice, but they made libations with water, and roasted all the entrails over the fire. Now when the thighs were wholly burned and they had tasted the inner parts, they cut up the rest and spitted it. Then it was that sweet sleep fled from my eyelids, and I went my way to the swift ship and the shore of the sea. But when, as I went, I drew near to the curved ship, then it was that the sweet savor of the hot fat was wafted about me, and I groaned and cried aloud to the immortal gods:

"'Father Zeus and you other blessed gods that are for-ever, certainly it was for my ruin that you lulled me in piti-less sleep, while my comrades remaining behind contrived this monstrous deed.'

"Swiftly then to Helios Hyperion came Lampetie of the long robes, bearing tidings that we had slain his cattle; and at once he spoke among the immortals, angry at heart:

[a] Cf. 3.445. D.
[b] See note on 3.458. D.

"'Ζεῦ πάτερ ἠδ' ἄλλοι μάκαρες θεοὶ αἰὲν ἐόντες,
τῖσαι δὴ ἑτάρους Λαερτιάδεω Ὀδυσῆος,
οἵ μευ βοῦς ἔκτειναν ὑπέρβιον, ἧσιν ἐγώ γε
380 χαίρεσκον μὲν ἰὼν εἰς οὐρανὸν ἀστερόεντα,
ἠδ' ὁπότ' ἂψ ἐπὶ γαῖαν ἀπ' οὐρανόθεν προτραποίμην.
εἰ δέ μοι οὐ τίσουσι βοῶν ἐπιεικέ' ἀμοιβήν,
δύσομαι εἰς Ἀίδαο καὶ ἐν νεκύεσσι φαείνω.'

"τὸν δ' ἀπαμειβόμενος προσέφη νεφεληγερέτα Ζεύς·
385 'Ἠέλι', ἦ τοι μὲν σὺ μετ' ἀθανάτοισι φάεινε
καὶ θνητοῖσι βροτοῖσιν ἐπὶ ζείδωρον ἄρουραν·
τῶν δέ κ' ἐγὼ τάχα νῆα θοὴν ἀργῆτι κεραυνῷ
τυτθὰ βαλὼν κεάσαιμι μέσῳ ἐνὶ οἴνοπι πόντῳ.'

"ταῦτα δ' ἐγὼν ἤκουσα Καλυψοῦς ἠυκόμοιο·
390 ἡ δ' ἔφη Ἑρμείαο διακτόρου αὐτὴ ἀκοῦσαι.[1]

"αὐτὰρ ἐπεί ῥ' ἐπὶ νῆα κατήλυθον ἠδὲ θάλασσαν,
νείκεον ἄλλοθεν ἄλλον ἐπισταδόν, οὐδέ τι μῆχος
εὑρέμεναι δυνάμεσθα, βόες δ' ἀποτέθνασαν ἤδη.
τοῖσιν δ' αὐτίκ' ἔπειτα θεοὶ τέραα προύφαινον·
395 εἷρπον μὲν ῥινοί, κρέα δ' ἀμφ' ὀβελοῖσι μεμύκει,
ὀπταλέα τε καὶ ὠμά, βοῶν δ' ὣς γίγνετο φωνή.

"ἑξῆμαρ μὲν ἔπειτα ἐμοὶ ἐρίηρες ἑταῖροι
δαίνυντ' Ἠελίοιο βοῶν ἐλάσαντες ἀρίστας·
ἀλλ' ὅτε δὴ ἕβδομον ἦμαρ ἐπὶ Ζεὺς θῆκε Κρονίων,
400 καὶ τότ' ἔπειτ' ἄνεμος μὲν ἐπαύσατο λαίλαπι θύων,
ἡμεῖς δ' αἶψ' ἀναβάντες ἐνήκαμεν εὐρέι πόντῳ,
ἱστὸν στησάμενοι ἀνά θ' ἱστία λεύκ' ἐρύσαντες.

"ἀλλ' ὅτε δὴ τὴν νῆσον ἐλείπομεν, οὐδέ τις ἄλλη
φαίνετο γαιάων, ἀλλ' οὐρανὸς ἠδὲ θάλασσα,

"'Father Zeus and you other blessed gods that are for-ever, take vengeance now on the comrades of Odysseus, son of Laertes, who have insolently slain my cattle, in which I took delight whenever I mounted to the starry heaven, and when I turned back again to the earth from heaven. If they do not pay me fit atonement for the cattle I will go down to Hades and shine among the dead.'

"Then Zeus, the cloud-gatherer, answered him and said: 'Helios, for your part do not fail to go on shining among the immortals and among mortal men upon the earth, the giver of grain. As for these men I will soon strike their swift ship with my bright thunderbolt, and shatter it to pieces in the midst of the wine-dark sea.'

"This I heard from lovely-haired Calypso, and she said that she herself had heard it from the guide Hermes.

"But when I had come down to the ship and to the sea I upbraided my men, coming up to each in turn, but we could find no remedy—the cattle were already dead. For my men the gods then at once showed forth portents. The hides crawled, the meat, both roast and raw, bellowed upon the spits, and there was a lowing as though of cattle.

"For six days then my trusty comrades feasted on the best of the cattle of Helios which they had driven off. But when Zeus, the son of Cronos, brought upon us the seventh day, then the wind ceased to blow tempestuously, and we at once went on board, and put out into the broad sea when we had set up the mast and hoisted the white sail.

"But when we had left that island and no other land appeared, but only sky and sea, then the son of Cronos set

---

[1] Lines 374–90 were rejected by Aristarchus.

405　δὴ τότε κυανέην νεφέλην ἔστησε Κρονίων
　　　νηὸς ὕπερ γλαφυρῆς, ἤχλυσε δὲ πόντος ὑπ' αὐτῆς.
　　　ἡ δ' ἔθει οὐ μάλα πολλὸν ἐπὶ χρόνον· αἶψα γὰρ ἦλθε
　　　κεκληγὼς Ζέφυρος μεγάλῃ σὺν λαίλαπι θύων,
　　　ἱστοῦ δὲ προτόνους ἔρρηξ' ἀνέμοιο θύελλα
410　ἀμφοτέρους· ἱστὸς δ' ὀπίσω πέσεν, ὅπλα τε πάντα
　　　εἰς ἄντλον κατέχυνθ'. ὁ δ' ἄρα πρυμνῇ ἐνὶ νηὶ
　　　πλῆξε κυβερνήτεω κεφαλήν, σὺν δ' ὀστέ' ἄραξε
　　　πάντ' ἄμυδις κεφαλῆς· ὁ δ' ἄρ' ἀρνευτῆρι ἐοικὼς
　　　κάππεσ' ἀπ' ἰκριόφιν, λίπε δ' ὀστέα θυμὸς ἀγήνωρ.
415　Ζεὺς δ' ἄμυδις βρόντησε καὶ ἔμβαλε νηὶ κεραυνόν·
　　　ἡ δ' ἐλελίχθη πᾶσα Διὸς πληγεῖσα κεραυνῷ,
　　　ἐν δὲ θεείου πλῆτο, πέσον δ' ἐκ νηὸς ἑταῖροι.
　　　οἱ δὲ κορώνῃσιν ἴκελοι περὶ νῆα μέλαιναν
　　　κύμασιν ἐμφορέοντο, θεὸς δ' ἀποαίνυτο νόστον.
420　αὐτὰρ ἐγὼ διὰ νηὸς ἐφοίτων, ὄφρ' ἀπὸ τοίχους
　　　λῦσε κλύδων τρόπιος, τὴν δὲ ψιλὴν φέρε κῦμα,
　　　ἐκ δέ οἱ ἱστὸν ἄραξε ποτὶ τρόπιν. αὐτὰρ ἐπ' αὐτῷ
　　　ἐπίτονος βέβλητο, βοὸς ῥινοῖο τετευχώς·
　　　τῷ ῥ' ἄμφω συνέεργον, ὁμοῦ τρόπιν ἠδὲ καὶ ἱστόν,
425　ἑζόμενος δ' ἐπὶ τοῖς φερόμην ὀλοοῖς ἀνέμοισιν.
　　　　　"ἔνθ' ἦ τοι Ζέφυρος μὲν ἐπαύσατο λαίλαπι θύων,
　　　ἦλθε δ' ἐπὶ Νότος ὦκα, φέρων ἐμῷ ἄλγεα θυμῷ,
　　　ὄφρ' ἔτι τὴν ὀλοὴν ἀναμετρήσαιμι Χάρυβδιν.
　　　παννύχιος φερόμην, ἅμα δ' ἠελίῳ ἀνιόντι
430　ἦλθον ἐπὶ Σκύλλης σκόπελον δεινήν τε Χάρυβδιν.
　　　ἡ μὲν ἀνερροίβδησε θαλάσσης ἁλμυρὸν ὕδωρ·
　　　αὐτὰρ ἐγὼ ποτὶ μακρὸν ἐρινεὸν ὑψόσ' ἀερθείς,

a black cloud above the hollow ship, and the sea grew dark beneath it. She ran on for no long time, for then at once came the shrieking West Wind, blowing with a furious tempest, and the blast of the wind snapped both forestays of the mast, so that the mast fell backward and all its tackling was strewn in the bilge. On the stern of the ship the mast struck the head of the steersman and crushed all the bones of his skull together, and like a diver he fell from the deck and his proud spirit left his bones. At the same time Zeus thundered and hurled his bolt upon the ship, and she quivered from stem to stern struck by the bolt of Zeus, and was filled with sulphurous smoke, and my comrades fell out of the ship. Like sea crows they were borne on the waves about the black ship, and the god took from them their returning. But I kept pacing up and down the ship till the surge tore the sides from the keel, and the wave bore her on dismantled and snapped the mast off at the keel; but over the mast had been flung the backstay fashioned of oxhide; with this I lashed the two together, both keel and mast, and sitting on these was borne by the terrible winds.

"Then, let me tell you, the West Wind ceased to blow tempestuously, and swiftly the South Wind came, bringing sorrow to my heart, that I might traverse again the way to terrible Charybdis. All night long was I borne, and at the rising of the sun I came to the cliff of Scylla and to dread Charybdis. She for her part sucked down the water of the sea, but I, springing up to the tall fig tree, laid hold of it,

τῷ προσφὺς ἐχόμην ὡς νυκτερίς. οὐδέ πη εἶχον
οὔτε στηρίξαι ποσὶν ἔμπεδον οὔτ' ἐπιβῆναι·
435   ῥίζαι γὰρ ἑκὰς εἶχον,[1] ἀπήωροι δ' ἔσαν ὄζοι,
μακροί τε μεγάλοι τε, κατεσκίαον δὲ Χάρυβδιν.
νωλεμέως δ' ἐχόμην, ὄφρ' ἐξεμέσειεν ὀπίσσω
ἱστὸν καὶ τρόπιν αὖτις· ἐελδομένῳ δέ μοι ἦλθον
ὄψ'· ἦμος δ' ἐπὶ δόρπον ἀνὴρ ἀγορῆθεν ἀνέστη
440   κρίνων νείκεα πολλὰ δικαζομένων αἰζηῶν,
τῆμος δὴ τά γε δοῦρα Χαρύβδιος ἐξεφαάνθη.
ἧκα δ' ἐγὼ καθύπερθε πόδας καὶ χεῖρε φέρεσθαι,
μέσσῳ δ' ἐνδούπησα παρὲξ περιμήκεα δοῦρα,
ἑζόμενος δ' ἐπὶ τοῖσι διήρεσα χερσὶν ἐμῇσι.
445   Σκύλλην δ' οὐκέτ' ἔασε πατὴρ ἀνδρῶν τε θεῶν τε
εἰσιδέειν· οὐ γάρ κεν ὑπέκφυγον αἰπὺν ὄλεθρον.[2]

     "ἔνθεν δ' ἐννῆμαρ φερόμην, δεκάτῃ δέ με νυκτὶ
νῆσον ἐς Ὠγυγίην πέλασαν θεοί, ἔνθα Καλυψὼ
ναίει ἐυπλόκαμος, δεινὴ θεὸς αὐδήεσσα,
450   ἥ μ' ἐφίλει τ' ἐκόμει τε. τί τοι τάδε μυθολογεύω;
ἤδη γάρ τοι χθιζὸς ἐμυθεόμην ἐνὶ οἴκῳ
σοί τε καὶ ἰφθίμῃ ἀλόχῳ· ἐχθρὸν δέ μοί ἐστιν
αὖτις ἀριζήλως εἰρημένα μυθολογεύειν."

---

[1] εἶχον: ἦσαν
[2] Lines 445–6 were rejected in antiquity.

and clung to it like a bat. Yet I could in no way plant my feet firmly or set myself upon the tree, for its roots spread far below, and its branches hung out of reach above, long and massive, and overshadowed Charybdis. There I clung relentlessly until she should spew out mast and keel again, and to my joy they came, though late. At the hour when a man rises from the assembly for his supper, one that decides the many quarrels of young men that seek judgment, just at that hour those spars appeared out of Charybdis. And I let go hands and feet from above and plunged down into the waters out beyond the long spars, and sitting on these I rowed onward with my hands. But as for Scylla, the father of gods and men did not allow her again to catch sight of me; never otherwise should I have escaped utter destruction.

"From there for nine days was I borne, and on the tenth night the gods brought me to Ogygia, where the lovely-haired Calypso dwells, dread goddess of human speech, who loved and took care of me. But why should I tell you this tale? For it was only yesterday that I told it in your hall to yourself and to your stalwart wife. It is a tiresome thing, I think, to tell again a plain-told tale."